Praise for Claire Lorrimer's novels:

Ortolans

'A sweeping saga of powerful passions, mystery and a house full of secrets'   *Woman's Realm*

'A story of three women's passion and turmoil within the house they love'   *Bookseller*

'A hefty romantic saga of love, mystery and romance'
                                                                                Bookworld

Frost in the Sun   WITHDRAWN

'Passion in the bloody battlefields of the Spanish Civil War . . . a huge and powerful novel' *Evening Standard*

'A magnificent international historical saga' *Bookseller*

'A sizzling read . . . exciting to the end' *Woman's Realm*

'[The] setting is sheer glamour'   *Evening Telegraph*

The Silver Link

'Lovers of romantic fiction will love this book'
                                                                                Bookseller

'Yet another successful historical family saga – perfect holiday read'   *Yorkshire Post*

Claire Lorrimer wrote her first book at the age of twelve, encouraged by her mother, the bestselling author Denise Robins. After the Second World War, during which Claire served in the WAAF on secret duties, she started her career as a romantic novelist under her maiden name, Patricia Robins. In 1970 she began writing her magnificent family sagas and thrillers under the name Claire Lorrimer. She is currently at work on her seventy-first book. Claire lives in Kent.

Find out more about Claire: www.clairelorrimer.co.uk

Also by Claire Lorrimer and available from Hodder

CLAIRE LORRIMER

LAST YEAR'S NIGHTINGALE

HODDER

First published in Great Britain in 1984
by Century
a division of Transworld Publishers Ltd.

This paperback edition published in 2015
by Hodder & Stoughton
An Hachette UK company

2

A CIP catalogue record for this title is available from the British Library

Paperback ISBN 978 1 473 61302 7
eBook ISBN 978 1 444 75047 8

Typeset in Sabon LT Std by Palimpsest Book Production Ltd,
Falkirk, Stirlingshire

Printed and bound by Clays Ltd, St Ives plc

Hodder & Stoughton policy is to use papers that are natural, renewable
and recyclable products and made from wood grown in sustainable
forests. The logging and manufacturing processes are expected to conform to
the environmental regulations of the country of origin.

Hodder & Stoughton Ltd
338 Euston Road
London NW1 3BH

www.hodder.co.uk

In gratitude to my secretary, Pennie Scott, whose patience, hard work and skilful research have contributed so much to this book.

CAST OF CHARACTERS

Viscount CHARLES BURNBURY	
DEVERIL GRAYSHOTT	Lord Burnbury's elder grandson
Admiral, the Hon Sir WILLIAM GRAYSHOTT	Deveril's father
PERCY GRAYSHOTT	Deveril's brother
SELINA and GRACE	Two of Deveril's four sisters
Lady MARGARET McDOONE	Deveril's great-aunt
CLEMENTINE FOSTER	
The Rev GODFREY FOSTER and MRS WINIFRED FOSTER	Clementine's uncle and aunt
CLEMENT FOSTER Lady ENID FOSTER	Clementine's parents
The Earl and Countess WHYTAKKER	Clementine's grandparents
ADAM	Clementine's son
The Hon MURIEL LAWRENCE	Deveril's fiancée
Lord and Lady LAWRENCE WALTER GRIMSHAW	Muriel's parents Grayshott family lawyer
Doctor BENJAMIN BROOK	Country physician

Professor ALGERNON BROOK	Benjamin's father
FREDERICK and EDITH BROOK	Benjamin's brother and sister-in-law
ANTHEA WILCOX	American widow
Miss EMILY FOTHERGILL	Elderly spinster
Miss ELIZABETH GRANTLY	Miss Fothergill's friend
Mr and Mrs MATHESON	Colonists in Upper Canada
JANE and KATHERINE	The Mathesons' daughters
Sir JOHN MELTON	London physician
DOMINIC WADE	Friend of Deveril Grayshott
ROBERT MCUIST	Highlander
Mr BRYANT	Brighton lawyer
MARY	The Rev and Mrs Foster's maid
JENNIE	Miss Fothergill's maid
CELESTE	Muriel's French maid
SUSAN	Professor Brook's maid
JOSEPH CROWLEY	Tutor

Servants of the Burnbury Family

Mrs JACOBS	Housekeeper
JOHNSEN	Butler
HOPKINS	Valet

PEARCE	Groom
DAWKINS	Butler
OLIVE	Scullery maid

Servants at Castle Clunes

HUTCHINS	Gamekeeper
Mrs DEWAR	Maid
Mrs CAMPBELL	Housekeeper
ROBBIE	Gillie's son

PART ONE

1830–1834

LAST YEAR'S NIGHTINGALE

From the brake the Nightingale
  Sings exulting to the Rose;
Though he sees her waxing pale
In her passionate repose,
While she triumphs waxing frail,
Fading even while she glows;
  Though he knows
  How it goes—
Knows of last year's Nightingale
Dead with last year's Rose . . .

W. E. Henley

CHAPTER ONE

June–August 1830

With a haste that was totally at variance with his befuddled
state of mind, Deveril Grayshott pulled his white breeches up
over his buttocks and tried ineffectually to fasten the buttons.
The discovery that the girl was a virgin had momentarily
sobered him, if far from completely, at least sufficiently to
know that he had been damnably stupid to deflower her, no
matter how willing she had seemed to be.

He was tempted to take a closer look at her face, until now
only a white hazy blur in the night-shadowed cornfield; but
a deep-rooted, innate sense of shame forbade a closer study
of her features. He'd not been too drunk to know that she
was very young and he did not want to see the tears, the look
of reproach, the horror he supposed she must be feeling. He
bent down to pick up his horse's loosely trailing reins and
staggered dizzily as the brandy fumes swirled in his head.
What he wanted more than anything now was sleep, he
reflected, but he still had six miles to ride. It was as well his
horse knew the way home, he thought with a flash of drunken
humour.

His back to the girl who was lying motionless on the ground,
he drew out a sovereign from his waistcoat pocket. But once
again, instinct prevented him from committing himself in any
respect to his victim. If he gave her so valuable a coin, her
parents would undoubtedly want to know how she came by
it. If she kept her mouth shut, it might save them both a parcel
of bother.

'Go home!' he said, his voice as blurred as his vision. He

wanted to add that if she kept her own counsel, there'd be no harm done. But he had despoiled her and sooner or later, some man was going to know of it. The damage could not now be undone. Nevertheless he muttered:

'The leasht you shay about this night, the better for us both. D'you undershtand?'

He managed with difficulty to scramble on to his horse. Clouds had long since obscured the bright orange harvest moon and his backward glance at the girl revealed no more than a slender heap of clothing in a nest of crushed corn. For a second, he was shocked by the terrible thought that she might be dead. But that, he knew, was nonsense. It was but a few minutes at most since she had cried out as he forced his way into her and he had felt her nails digging into his back through the thin silk of his shirt.

Damnation to all women! he thought as he kicked his horse into movement. It had been a thoroughly bad night from start to finish – his last night at home, too, before going up to Scotland for the grouse shooting. It was all Peggy's fault – the buxom, comely landlord's daughter at the Pig and Whistle. Throughout the summer vacation, he and his four university friends had been vying with one another for Peggy's favours, and he had wagered no small sum that this very night she would prove she fancied him above his friends – prove it by permitting him a lot more than a kiss or two by the stables. How his friends had taunted him on the ride home because Peggy had had her head turned by a dashing dragoon and been too busy flirting with the handsome officer to pay her customary attention to any of the young 'genulmen', as she called them, from the manor.

'Not long enough out of the schoolroom to satisfy our Peggy!' one friend jeered as they left the inn.

'Our Peggy reckons that dragoon knows a thing or two more about women than a lad of your age, Deveril!' teased another.

'She never did take you seriously, old boy. Stood out a mile she was not going to let you have more than a bite of the old cake!'

So it was not just the frustration of wanting her plump, tempting body and finding himself refused when he had been so certain she would agree that had upset him. It was his pride that was damaged. He'd known for a long time now that he was considered to have more than his share of good looks. In his youthful experience, he'd been aware that women of all ages noticed him. Eventual heir to his grandfather's viscountcy, he accepted as his due that he would be one of the most eligible young men in Society once he was finished with schooling and was old enough to marry. He had looks, money, position, he told himself bitterly on that ride home, yet a common slut like Peggy McGregor had turned up her pert little nose at him as if he were a farm lad! No wonder he'd been so shamed.

He and his friends were but a mile out of the village when they'd come upon the girl. She'd appeared from the depths of the corn like some wraith from the sea. At first, they had formed a circle about her, their mounts shying nervously from the slim white ghost. The scurrying clouds were casting shadows over the girl's face and they noticed little other than that she was blonde, young and slender. Then the questioning had begun. What was she doing out here alone? Was she from the village? Was she lost? Was she in distress? Or was she, perhaps, just out looking for male company?

His friends had begun to dispute amongst themselves as to who had seen her first; who, of the five of them, might offer the mysterious damsel his companionship. Surely she could not wish to spend this hot August night all alone? they enquired.

Only then had the girl spoken, lifting her arm and pointing at him – Deveril Grayshott.

'I came to say goodbye to him!'

Perhaps, when he was once more sober, he could make sense of it all, he thought now, as indeed he had thought then.

But at that moment, he had neither questioned nor cared about the extraordinary turn of events. His friends' taunts had turned to envious leers as they asked him if this was a secret assignation he had kept quiet from them; if all along he'd been trying to throw them off the scent by pretending an interest in Peggy McGregor. They all accepted that indisputably the girl had chosen *him*, and they had no wish to spoil his fun.

'Make the most of what the gods give you, Deveril, old fellow!' they had shouted as they rode off laughing. 'And if you are not sober enough to make the most of your good fortune, then you have but to ride after us and one of us will take your place!'

He had dismounted his horse, his legs nearly giving way beneath him as he faced the silent shadow before him. He could not discern the colour of the girl's eyes nor even her features; but he could make out the womanly shape of her.

'Since you say you came to bid me farewell, then 'tis a farewell kiss I can claim from you,' he said boldly, taking a step towards her.

Half asleep as his horse jogged along the familiar cart road towards the Grayshott estate, Deveril could not remember how he and the girl had come to be lying in the corn. Maybe he had fallen. But the night's frustrated desire for Peggy was not as dulled as his other senses and the girl's moist lips were as welcoming as the soft murmur of her voice. She had made no attempt to remove his hands when they had uncovered her breasts. She had wanted him – he was sure of it. Yet when he had taken her, fiercely, hungrily, she had cried out and dug her nails into his back and only then, suddenly sobered, had he known beyond doubt that she was a virgin – had been a virgin.

His horse stumbled and he jerked into momentary wakefulness. He had no idea who the girl was. Nor, since he had certainly not raped her against her will, should he care, he told himself. The best thing he could do would be to forget about her. He and his friends would be off to Scotland tomorrow and the night's episode forgotten. As for the girl – she must have known the risks she was taking, out alone, not far off midnight. No decent girl would dare such a thing. Despite her voice she must have been a farm girl who had slipped out for a taste of nature's delights, fancying the idea of giving her favours to a gentleman instead of an uncouth farmer's boy.

Deveril Grayshott, eldest son of Admiral Sir William Grayshott, and grandson of Viscount Burnbury, slouched across the saddle of his horse as it ambled slowly up the mile-long drive to the family mansion, Chiswell Hill House. He was nineteen years of age, he thought incoherently; he had imbibed a little too much wine at dinner and then he had drunk far too much of the landlord's best French brandy. He had also had a woman. When he reached home, his valet would be waiting up to undress him and put him to bed, so he had nothing in the world to worry about. His eyes closed and he slept peacefully, unaware of the wheels of Fate this night's behaviour had set in motion for the future, as his horse plodded forward, instinct directing the animal home.

It seemed to Clementine as if the whole summer of 1830 had been one long stream of golden days – sunny days when her youthful body craved the soft sweet scents of gardens and woods; of fields and hedgerows; of haymaking and fruit harvesting. For hour upon hour, imprisoned in her bedroom, she had knelt at the open window, her soft breasts pressed against the wooden sill, imagining herself in the shining golden countryside which surrounded her present home on the outskirts of the little village of Lower Chiswell.

Without doubt, she thought each morning on waking, it had been the unhappiest of the fifteen summers of her life. In the first place, when she had arrived at The Rectory with her father, it was intended to be but a brief farewell visit to her hitherto unknown uncle and aunt before she emigrated to British North America to begin a new life with her parents.

Poor Papa had lost all his money and hoped to remake his fortunes in Upper Canada. A great many people were emigrating now that the war was over, and Papa had a friend who was busy making his fortune out there with the Hudson's Bay Company. Clementine had been enormously excited at the prospect, despite her mother's misgivings. Mama was delicate and did not have her papa's blustering good health – due to her sheltered aristocratic upbringing, Papa said. Nevertheless, he would not be parted from his wife and bravely she had agreed to accompany him to this wild, desolate land, taking their only child, Clementine, with them.

But a cruel Fate had determined that Clementine was not to go with her parents. The day following their arrival at The Rectory she had succumbed to the scarlatina and been so ill with the complaint that the doctor had ruled out any chance of her travelling on such a long arduous journey this year. Papa had already paid for their passages and her tearful mama had explained that they could not afford to delay their going. There were other reasons why her parents could not wait for her recovery. Clementine only vaguely understood that it had something to do with people called creditors waiting to send poor darling Papa to prison despite the fact that he had committed no crime but was the butt of misfortune – or so Mama said.

Reluctantly, the Rev and Mrs Foster had agreed to take care of Clementine until such time next year as a suitable travelling companion could be found to escort her safely to her parents in North America. By then, they would have a new home ready to receive her.

Ill though she was, Clementine had been miserably aware of her parents' departure and her feeling of isolation and abandonment greatly added to her general malaise. Her Aunt Winifred, she soon discovered, was quite unlike dear Mama. She was an austere, childless woman whose word was law in the household. The servants were terrified of her since even the smallest fault resulted in severe reprimand, if not a harsh punishment or a fine of wages. Her aunt's religious fervour did not, Clementine soon realized, include the virtues of kindness, forgiveness or tolerance. A thin, angular, rod-backed woman, Winifred Foster was always dressed in black – probably in deference to the death in June of King George, Papa had joked. She reminded Clementine of a crow, and was the very opposite of her gentle adoring mother, whose rare reproofs were issued in a quiet loving voice.

The Rev Godfrey Foster, in the brief moments Clementine had seen him before she was confined to her bedroom, was a round, red-faced, portly little man who had seemed to Clementine to be as frightened as herself of his wife's tongue. He was her father's brother, five years older and, according to Papa, a weak, not very intelligent man who would never have survived outside the protection of the Cloth. As he kissed his daughter goodbye, Papa had looked both worried and uncertain, and he had said with a lack of confidence quite foreign to him:

'I hope you will not be too unhappy, my darling. Your aunt and uncle mean well and in any case, what alternative have I but to leave you here? You will be safe from harm. 'Tis only for a year, Clemmie.'

Her uncle, as gently as he could, had tried to comfort her.

'If there is anything you want, child . . . anything I can do . . .'

As soon as she was over the worst of her illness, she reminded her uncle of his promise.

'Please, Uncle, if you really desire to make me happier, try to persuade Aunt Winifred to allow me downstairs. I have been confined to my room now for over two months and the physician has said I am well enough to leave my sickroom. I am so . . . so lonely up there . . . and . . .'

But they had both known there was little chance of his changing her aunt's relentless decision that following upon her illness, a long period of convalescence was essential if her future health was not to be undermined. Aunt Winifred stated that this meant continued confinement to her room.

The Fosters' little maid, Mary, now Clementine's only companion, was shrewd enough to hit on the truth of the situation.

'You be a sight too pretty for *her* liking, Miss Clementine!' she said, her cheerful rounded face creasing into a smile as she brushed her young mistress's long golden hair. ''Taint so much Parson having a soft spot for you she be minding, as young Doctor Brook taking a fancy to you. Only time as I ever do see her smile is when he comes a-visiting.'

As always, Mary had turned Clementine's sighs to laughter, for it was quite true that the stern, scowling Aunt Winifred positively simpered with coy smiles when the physician called. He was a good-looking, pleasant-spoken man in his late twenties – an age Clementine thought of as old.

Clementine had been intrigued by the idea that any man should 'fancy' her. Until this summer, she had given little thought to adult life, content to remain in the carefree world of a child without concern for the future. When Papa was away at sea, Mama had taught her to play the spinet, to sing, to dance, to curtsey, to speak French and to master the rudiments of Latin. But when Papa was home, Mama had little time to spare for her daughter's education. Then she gave Clementine books to read – dozens upon dozens of books. There were the classics, which Clementine was too young to appreciate fully; but there were also books of poetry and, equally pleasing to Clementine, novels from which she extracted her first romantic impressions of love. She had grown up in an atmosphere of love, for there was little doubting the closeness of her mother and father, and if she had given thought at all to the future, it was with no higher aspiration than to marry for love as Mama had done.

Here in this gaunt, loveless rectory, Clementine had turned more and more often to her books and her dreams. Mary, who had been courted by a local farmer's son for the past two years, fed her imagination still further with her vague, blushing allusions to her feelings for her sweetheart.

'Furst moment I set eyes on my Jack, I just about knew for sure there beant no other chap as I'd want for to marry. When my Jack do steal a kiss, my knees goes all a-tremble . . .'

It was Mary who had first drawn Clementine's attention to the young men from Chiswell Hill House riding past the rectory one hot summer's night.

'They do be the genulmen friends of the young milord from Chiswell Hill House,' Mary informed her as night after night they watched the finely dressed figures galloping down the dirt road that led to Upper Chiswell village. The lane divided the rectory orchard from old Farmer White's ten-acre cornfield and was the most direct route from the big manor house into the village.

'They be making for the Pig and Whistle!' Mary informed her young mistress. 'Go there every night, Peggy McGregor says. She be landlord's daughter and mighty purty, too. Beant much else to amuse them young'uns at the manor, I duresay. She told me as how the young genulmen is all on holiday from that there university Lunnon way.'

It was the first Clementine had heard of the family who owned the big house that lay between Upper and Lower Chiswell. Mary was happy enough to satisfy her curiosity. The old Viscount Burnbury was in his seventies, a widower, whose eldest son was an admiral in the Royal Navy. He also had four granddaughters, all married, and two grandsons, the eldest being Deveril Grayshott. Mary was vague about the younger grandson, Percy, who it seemed led the secluded life of an invalid and never left Chiswell Hill House.

Young Mr Deveril, Mary told her wide-eyed audience, was said to be as handsome as he was wild.

His friends were a wild lot, too. They'd been up to all sorts of mischief this summer, so Peggy had told her; they'd set six of Farmer Bastable's piglets 'a-running races, like that there Derby, wagering guineas – on pigs, of all things!' Mary exclaimed. 'And they nearly drownded theirselves trying to balance on miller's water wheel and broke two of the paddles.'

Clementine's vivid imagination was fired by these tales of Deveril Grayshott's escapades. The young men had ridden up the valley to the old Stone Age graveyard known as Chiswell Barrow and with white sheets draped over their heads, had shrieked and groaned as if they were ghosts risen from the ancient graves. Old Tom, the shepherd, had been scared out of his wits – as, indeed, were his flock, which raced in panic down into the valley and had woken half the village bleating and baaing on the green at midnight.

Boredom that plagued her imprisonment prompted Clementine to an adventure of her own. Overruling Mary's apprehension, she had climbed out of her bedroom window one evening onto the branches of the walnut tree and from thence descended into the garden. Barefoot on the dew-wet grass, she had stolen down to the orchard and hidden there until the young men came by on their horses, riding in the direction of the village. For the first time, she was able to see Deveril Grayshott closely enough to discern his features. He had struck her as even more handsome than Mary had described – deep shining brown eyes burning with youthful excitement; a wide laughing mouth and aquiline nose set in a nobly shaped face. His lips were parted in a delightful smile, and his voice, as he addressed one of his companions, was deep-toned and exciting to the young girl.

It was the beginning of a love that was to grow and dominate Clementine's thoughts throughout the summer. Her diary was filled with tiny remembered facets of his appearance. Her books of poetry were thick with paper markers highlighting those verses which seemed best to express her torment and her longing to meet this attractive stranger who haunted her dreams. Now at last, she thought, she understood the poet's meaning of love and why Mary had said that the mere sight of her Jack set her knees a-tremble. Not only Clementine's knees but her whole body trembled with excitement those evenings she saw Deveril ride by.

Mary's initial fear that these sorties might be discovered

was gradually allayed as July gave way to August without detection. They gave meaning to the otherwise tedious days spent cooped up in Clementine's large bedroom with only occasional visits from the unloving Aunt Winifred and Sunday prayers in the parson's study to break the monotony; but they also increased Clementine's restlessness. She was no longer ill and her young body craved activity. Only her mind was fully engaged as she created her imaginary encounters with her 'beloved'.

This harmless pastime was brought to a rude halt when the inevitable happened, and Mary announced that 'the young genulmen wus a-going away'.

Clementine was overwhelmed with dismay. Brought down to earth by the reality of the situation, she realized that often as she had seen her secret love from afar, she had never spoken to him, and the chance to do so was slipping away. He might not return to Chiswell Hill House before next summer, by which time she would have joined her parents in North America. No matter what the consequences, she told Mary, she was going to speak to him – to bid him farewell. At least he could then take away with him a memory of her which might burgeon into love. Perhaps he would find a way to write to her, telling her he could not forget his one brief encounter; begging her to reply and send him some small token of her affection.

Mary was a great deal more realistic. A young girl alone approaching a group of strange young gentlemen was unheard of, improper, against every convention. Were they discovered, it would mean instant dismissal without a reference for her and goodness only knew what dire punishment for Miss Clementine. It was too dangerous, too risky.

But Clementine would not be deterred from her plan. There was no risk worth mentioning, she assured Mary. No one had discovered them thus far. Why should this be the one night Aunt Winifred made an unannounced, unprecedented visit to Clementine's room after retiring to bed? And who was there to betray them since no one but themselves knew of her plan? Mary could watch from the orchard and warn her if anyone approached.

Mary's mother had been in service and had brought up her children to know the ways of the gentry. The maid therefore was far less naïve than Clementine when it came to correct standards of behaviour. To Clementine's dismay, she refused to condone her young mistress's plan.

'If'n you go, Miss Clementine, you goes on your ownsome!' she said firmly. Nor, when the church clock struck ten and Clementine donned her shawl with set mouth and a stubborn tilt to her chin, would Mary relent. Alone, Clementine climbed down the walnut tree and tiptoed past her uncle's study windows. A faint glow came from a chink in the velvet curtains but was dimmed by the brilliance of an orange harvest moon, shining on purpose, she decided, to guide her steps to the apple orchard.

Within minutes, she was in her usual hiding place – a dark corner behind the potting shed from which she could see the lane through the hawthorn hedge without fear of being seen. She paused there, wishing suddenly that she had not been quite so adamant when she had told the white-faced Mary that nothing but death would stop her crossing the lane and going to the cornfield. Now she was regretting that proud boast. Suppose Mary was right, and far from being the pleasurable encounter she had dreamed of, her meeting with the young man she loved turned out to be awkward, embarrassing, or even, as Mary suggested, humiliating for herself.

She drew a deep breath as she brushed the thought quickly from her mind. She would not forgo this one moment of pleasure in her life – she would see Deveril once more as he rode home. If she were to cross the road and hide in the cornfield, she would be even closer to him than she was here in the orchard.

Slowly, her heart beating nervously, Clementine crawled through a gap in the hedge into the lane. It had not rained for the past four weeks and the dust lay inches deep in the ruts the carts had made earlier in the year. On the far verge of the lane there was no hedgerow – only a ditch separating it from the great sea of ripe corn awaiting the coming harvest.

Quietly, although there was no one to hear her, Clementine slipped across the dusty cart track and slid down amongst the corn. It rustled as the stalks bent beneath her weight and tiny grains fell into the folds of her lavender muslin skirt.

For a little while, Clementine was reassured by the total seclusion of her new hiding place. But clouds were gathering now in the sky and once in a while, dark shadows obscured the comforting light of the moon and then she longed to be back in the safety of her bedroom at the rectory. But pride forbade such a reversal of her plans. She would remain here until Deveril and his friends returned from the village – no matter how long that might be.

Almost in the same instant as the clock chimed eleven, Clementine heard voices. She sat up, her heart thudding as she recognized the customary singing of the young men as they made their way homeward.

In the stillness of the night air, the sound of their laughter and voices above the thudding of their horses' hooves sent a sudden chill of apprehension through Clementine. There was little doubting that they were very drunk.

In sudden panic, she stood up, intending to dart back across the road to the safety of the orchard. But she had delayed her escape too long and as her white figure rose out from the corn, the leading horse shied, rearing up in alarm. Within seconds, she was surrounded.

Although the voices calling to her were slurred, their questions were clear enough to overcome her first feelings of fear. Was she lost? What was she doing so far from the village? Why was she there, alone? Who was she?

Clementine found the courage to raise her face. Her cheeks were burning with blushes as she pointed shyly to Deveril

Grayshott. He was grinning down at her with amused curiosity. Somehow, she found her voice and her courage.

'I came to say goodbye to him!' she replied with simple honesty.

The look of surprise mingled with pleasure on the young man's face restored her courage. Now that the meeting was accomplished, it seemed quite pointless to flee. His companions were laughing, teasing him in none too kind a fashion. But within minutes, they were riding away, leaving her alone with Deveril.

Now reality gave place to the dream-world in which she had lived for so many weeks. It seemed not the least strange when Deveril dismounted and put his arms around her, claiming that he deserved a farewell kiss since on her own admission she had come to bid him goodbye. He, like herself, had fallen in love at first sight, she thought happily as she melted into his arms. He must indeed love her if he wanted so ardently to kiss her, for kisses preceded proposals as well she knew from the romances she had read.

How handsome he was! How brightly his eyes shone as his face came down to hers! How swiftly her heart was beating at the touch of his hands on her arms! She could not suppress a little cry of pleasure as they moved upwards over her shoulders and then down to her breasts.

What happened next was too sudden, too swift, for Clementine to voice any protest. Afterwards, she was to tell Mary that she was not even certain if she wished to protest. His hands were moving rapidly all over her body, tearing open her bodice, lifting her skirt with a violent passion. His hurried breaths, his gasps, were drowned by her own as they fell to the ground and he lay atop her, his breeches about his ankles. Involuntarily, her hands closed over his back as he forced her legs apart with his knees. She could feel the bent corn stalks digging into her back, the pain only momentary as another pain wracked her body. Now she realized that something was happening that was both right and wrong. Such intimacy could only be wrong and yet – yet she wanted him to go on moving inside her. She wanted him never to stop kissing her. She wanted . . .

He lay suddenly still, his breathing slowing, his eyes closed. He seemed now quite unaware of her, his weight heavy and burdensome. Now she could smell the brandy fumes on his breath and she felt a sudden chill where the night breeze was blowing over her bared thighs. Instinctively, she pulled down her skirt in a belated need for modesty.

'Dear God, what have I done!' he murmured as he fumbled ineffectually with his own clothing. 'Who are you? Forgive me. I thought . . . Peggy McGregor . . . I don't understand . . .' His voice trailed into silence.

Clementine remained where she lay. The dream was turning into a nightmare. Why was Deveril not telling her that he loved her? Why was he turning his head away as if he had no wish to look at her?

'I love you!' she whispered. But the only coherent answer she received was a curt 'Go home', followed by a series of loud hiccoughs as he turned his back on her and awkwardly mounted his waiting horse. She could not believe that he was riding off, leaving her – without even a promise that he would write to her; without even knowing her name.

She would have called out to him but for the fact that her voice was strangled in her throat by tears of disappointment. Mutely, she watched her dream-lover ride away into the darkness. Only then did she become more fully aware of the soreness between her thighs. But the pain was as nothing beside the pain in her heart. Gathering her torn clothing about her, she ran blindly back to the house. Somehow, she scaled the walnut tree and scrambling through the window, fell into Mary's waiting arms. Then only did she give way to the sobs that wrenched her shivering body.

'He did not want me. He does not love me,' she wept.

Mary rocked her, stroking the dishevelled hair, tears streaming down her round, chalk-white cheeks.

'I was there – all the time – in the orchard!' she whispered. 'Oh, Miss Clementine, I ought to've rescued you but I was too scared . . . that I was. O, dearie, dearie me! I should've stopped it, surely, but . . .'

She broke off, her eyes moving involuntarily down Clementine's clothes until she saw the specks of blood on the edge of the skirt. There could be no denying that she had witnessed her mistress's seduction. The very worst had happened and Miss Clementine had allowed it – never once put up a fight. But then why should she? Mary had not spent the whole summer in proximity to her young mistress without coming to know her total innocence. A country girl herself, she knew nature's ways – and the ways of men. Miss Clementine knew nothing – not even that men were fashioned differently from women.

'You b'aint no virgin no more, Miss Clementine!' she said through her tears. 'And 'tis my fault, surely. If Parson found out . . . or the mistress . . . and your poor mama would break her heart. Oh, Miss Clementine, doan't you unnerstand nuffing? You be spoiled.'

Clementine regarded Mary through tear-washed eyes.

'Everything is spoiled!' she said. 'He does not love me. He did not want me. I would have done anything in the world for him; given him anything he wanted . . .'

With an unconscious sarcasm, Mary regarded the innocent face with despair.

'He done got what he wanted, Miss Clementine. You done given him the most precious thing in the world you got. Now you and me must pray to God for forgiveness lest He thinks fit to punish us more for what's happened this night.'

She had neither the courage nor the heart to tell the unhappy girl confronting her that this night's calamity might have terrible consequences for them both.

'Pray – that's all us can do now!' she muttered as she poured water from the china jug into the washbowl and began to flannel Clementine from head to toe.

'Pray for what?' Clementine asked miserably as she shivered at the touch of the cold water against her burning skin. 'That he will come back? That he will find out who I am and write to me? Oh, Mary, do you think he will? He cannot have intended to leave me so, without a word. He . . . he kissed me . . . I know he loved me . . . and then . . . then . . .'

'Doan't think about it no more, Miss Clementine,' Mary whispered, horrified. 'Best forget it ever happened. Young genulman like that should've known better than to . . .'

Words failed her as she towelled Clementine's shivering body, wiping away the bloodstains before the girl noticed them. She was not up to answering any more questions. All she wanted now was to tuck Clementine into bed and go to her own small attic room where she could kneel on the hard carpetless floor and pray nothing worse came of this night.

CHAPTER TWO

October 1830

'His Lordship will be with your directly, sir!' the butler said as he ushered the Rev Godfrey Foster into the library of Chiswell Hill House. As the servant closed the door behind him, the parson stared nervously around the big room. The walls were adorned with huge, gilt-framed oil paintings – all of them portraits of the Grayshott family. The parson recognized the likeness of the man he had come to see – Charles, Viscount Burnbury – despite the unfamiliar regalia of ermine-trimmed cloak, coronet and white breeches. He was accustomed to seeing him in hunting pink or reading the lesson in church, wearing the garb of a country squire. The old aristocrat was an imperious-looking man, with the high forehead and aquiline nose so often to be seen in the Grayshott males. The parson, already nervous, began to tremble at the prospect of the coming interview.

In an effort to distract his thoughts, he studied the other portraits. There was one of the Viscount's son, Admiral Sir William Grayshott, in his blue, gold and white naval uniform. The Admiral was, as usual, away at sea and his two sons were under the guardianship of their grandfather. There was a delightful painting by Lawrence of the two little boys in velvet suits with lace collars standing beside their mother, Lady Ursula Grayshott, a beautiful but delicate woman who had died from consumption several years ago.

The parson leant forward, staring short-sightedly at the two children. The elder boy, Deveril, already showed promise of the dark good looks he now possessed at the age of nineteen.

The younger child, Percy, was fair and delicate like his mother and rumour had it that the boy was sickly and not altogether quite normal.

The parson's thoughts were interrupted by the arrival of the Viscount – a tall, thin man now in his mid-seventies.

'Apologies for keeping you waiting, Parson!' he said, as he walked stiffly towards his guest. 'Been out riding, y'see, and had to change me clothes!'

'It's kind of you to spare me your time, Milord!' the parson stammered, as his host bade him be seated.

'Your note said the matter was of some importance?' Lord Burnbury prompted, eyeing the shabby little man with impatience. Parsons were never much to his liking and the Rev Foster less than most. A man of God should have more presence, he thought, noting the way the man's brow was glistening with perspiration and his whole body was trembling inside the worn full-skirted coat and breeches. He was twisting his flat, broad-brimmed hat round and round in his reddened hands and his eyes were centred on his silver-buckled shoes.

'Well, Sir, what have you on your mind?' he enquired, an edge of pity softening his contempt for his visitor.

The Rev Foster drew a deep breath. Given his own way, he would have terminated this interview before ever the truth were spoken. But he dared not go home to the rectory and face his wife's outrage were he to lack the courage to speak. His Lordship's reaction was, in the last resort, less to be feared than Winifred's bitter tongue.

Haltingly, he stammered out the unsavoury facts of his niece's seduction by young Deveril Grayshott. So nervous and disjointed was his speech that the Viscount was hard put at first to understand the circumstances. When at last he was forced to appreciate that his eldest grandson had got the parson's niece with child, he gave a deep sigh of resignation. He was not in the least surprised. His favourite grandchild was very much to his liking – a bold, handsome, wild young blood in line with all the Grayshott men who had for generations past left their mark on the world one way or another. Deveril's father was one of the youngest naval officers ever to be promoted to admiral – and that entirely due to his courage and enterprise in battle. He himself had made his mark in politics, and was still a prominent member of the Whig party. The Grayshott males were never insignificant, and young Deveril showed promise of following suit. As for getting a girl into trouble – well, that was unfortunate and tiresome but only to be expected at his age when the hot young blood was flowing so swiftly through his veins. The girl would have to be paid off, of course, and some kind of compensation paid to the parson. A bigger stipend, no doubt, would ease the poor fellow's discomfiture . . .

His thoughts were brought to an abrupt halt as the parson's stammering voice broke through his consciousness.

'. . . my niece is very well connected, Milord, on her mother's side. My sister-in-law was Lady Enid Whytakker before her marriage . . .'

For the first time Lord Burnbury felt a moment of genuine alarm. Lord Whytakker was not only a fellow member of the House of Lords but of Brooks's, his club, and was a close friend of William's, too. Whytakker's eldest son was serving under William . . . It would not do for Deveril's seduction of one of the earl's granddaughters to reach Whytakker's ears – or anyone else's.

The Viscount did not doubt the truth of the parson's accusation, for he knew the miserable fellow would never have approached him on so delicate a matter had he not been certain of his facts. But he could not make any decision until he had spoken to his grandson and to his London lawyer, Walter Grimshaw. The fellow knew his way round his law books, but the Viscount had felt an instinctive dislike for the man on the few occasions he had met him. He wished the uncle, old Robert Grimshaw, was still alive. He had been a fine man with whom Lord Burnbury had dealt for most of his lifetime. He preferred old Grimshaw's straightforward approach and mistrusted the nephew's shifty way of getting around problems.

Nevertheless, he thought now, Young Grimshaw was probably the best chap to deal with this present difficulty. The fellow was nothing if not discreet, and this kind of thing must be kept quiet at all costs. Deveril was as yet unaware of his grandfather's and father's plan to marry him to Lord Lawrence's eldest girl, Muriel, as soon as he came of age in two years' time. The Lawrences' house in London adjoined Burnbury House and the girl would make an excellent match for his grandson.

It would certainly scotch all the plans for Deveril's future marriage were Lord Lawrence to get wind of this little peccadillo. He too, was a Whig and a close friend of the Whytakkers. Walter Grimshaw would have to hush it all up as quickly as possible. Sighing, the Viscount instructed his visitor to return in ten days' time.

The Viscount decided he would say nothing to Deveril for the time being. The boy was up in Scotland and the distance was too far to consider sending for him to return to Dorset merely to give an account of his behaviour during the summer vacation. Deveril was impulsive and filled with a youthful idealism. He was quite capable of considering it the honourable thing to do to marry the girl – and that must be avoided at all costs.

The costs, however, were not at all to his liking when finally Walter Grimshaw travelled to Chiswell Hill House to present his solution to the problem. It was now two weeks since the parson had approached Lord Burnbury and the Viscount had grown somewhat anxious when the days went by without a reply to his letter to Grimshaw. He had ascertained from the Admiralty that there was no chance of Sir William returning from the Baltic Sea within the next few months, so the Viscount could not delegate either the problem or the responsibility to Deveril's father. He was, therefore, ready to accede to any reasonable suggestion – but not to the plan Grimshaw was now putting before him.

'Totally immoral – dishonest!' he spluttered, his face scarlet.

'There is no dishonour to any of the parties named in my proposal, Milord,' the small, bespectacled lawyer replied smoothly. 'On closer reflection, you will see that it is a matter of expediency . . .'

He was well aware that the old man needed time to come round to what he himself considered a stroke of genius in solving a very ticklish matter. He had expected that the Viscount would react in exactly this way – rejecting the idea out of hand. But equally, he had the utmost confidence in his own powers of persuasion. The clear, cold processes of his brain enabled him to reach to the core of a problem and then use the law to prevent a client becoming its victim.

Lord Burnbury was already growing calmer as he said awkwardly:

'Your Uncle Robert must have advised you of all our family affairs. You must know, therefore, that my younger grandson, Percy, is . . . is an invalid?'

Walter Grimshaw concealed a smile. Did the old man think him a fool? Of course he knew the boy was mentally retarded. How else could his plan be successful? Its brilliance lay in the fact that the seventeen-year-old Percy was in no position to argue against it. His mental powers were, so far as Grimshaw knew, those of a child of seven or eight. It was a closely guarded family secret, of course. Percy was thought by most people to be an invalid of such physical delicacy that he could not go to school as his brother Deveril had done, or ever appear in public. Deveril and the four married daughters were perfectly normal children, but the unfortunate Percy had suffered severe convulsions as an infant and whilst his looks were in no way afflicted, his mental processes had been damaged. It was by no means an unknown occurrence. Augustus, the only child of the Home Secretary, Viscount Melbourne, was similarly afflicted. Grimshaw had been reliably informed that such children might be expected to die long before they reached middle age.

The Viscount's outraged voice interrupted the lawyer's thoughts.

'Then if you are aware of my younger grandson's state of health, Grimshaw, how can you possibly propose his marriage to anyone?'

'It would be a marriage in name only, Milord. The young lady, as I understand, is due to depart to North America next year to be reunited with her parents. By then the child will have been born *in wedlock* and they will have no cause to censure the Rev Foster or indeed, to appeal to Lord Whytakker to raise objections to the way your family, Milord, has treated their daughter.'

He glanced at the Viscount and noted that this last point had not fallen on deaf ears.

'Whytakker always was a damnably ill-tempered fellow,' the old man muttered. 'Cut off his nose to spite his face rather than budge an inch from his own pig-headed ideas of right and wrong. Known him for years and he was no different even in his younger days.'

'Quite so!' Grimshaw murmured. 'But with the girl married to your grandson – legally married, I must emphasize – the Earl would have to agree that your family was behaving most honourably.'

He ignored the Viscount's doubting expression and continued calmly:

'I think we may safely discount any repercussions from the Fosters or the Whytakkers, Milord. As for your grandson, Mr Percy will be unaffected by the transaction. Mr Deveril's reputation will remain unsullied and his eventual marriage to a suitable young lady will not be in jeopardy. The parson's niece, of course, can be financially recompensed. I would suggest that if a live child is born, her uncle be paid the more than generous annual sum of £50 until such time as she may be free to remarry.'

Grimshaw made only the lightest of references to the possibility that Mr Percy would almost certainly die before

Clementine Foster ceased to be of a marriageable age. The girl was, after all, only just sixteen.

Lord Burnbury gave a tetchy cough.

'Yes, yes, I understand all that, Grimshaw. But I fail to see how you intend to keep this whole unfortunate business hushed up. Someone is bound to notice the girl is with child and start asking questions. Far too many people round here are aware of poor young Percy's afflictions and I will not have it spread about that he . . .'

'If I may interrupt you, Milord,' Grimshaw broke in, 'these are small technicalities which need not concern you. I shall ensure that no one but ourselves and the Fosters know of the girl's condition *or of her marriage*. It will be in the Fosters' interest as well as ours to maintain the utmost secrecy. I sincerely believe, Milord, that my plan covers every contingency.'

The Viscount gave an uneasy sigh.

'I am not denying that it would solve a good many problems. Nevertheless, I do not like it – not one bit. Is there no alternative?'

The question was rhetorical, for he had searched his mind these past two weeks for a solution and found none at all. He was not surprised, therefore, when the lawyer shook his head.

'None that would obviate the risk to your grandson, Milord,' he said pointedly.

'I cannot bring myself to approve,' Lord Burnbury muttered. 'I cannot quite put my finger on the reason but it strikes me as immoral . . .' His voice trailed away into silence.

'Milord, what we must consider is the possible consequences to your eventual heir if we do not protect him from future scandal. Mr Deveril *cannot* be expected to marry a girl whose paternal side of her family is, I must warn you, most disreputable; and if he does not marry her and the Rev Foster sees fit to appeal to the maternal side – well, frankly Milord, I do not care to think of our position if Lord Whytakker chose to champion his granddaughter. The Earl may have severed his ties with his daughter, Lady Enid, when she married against his wishes, but blood is all too often thicker than water . . .'

He broke off as he saw the old Viscount's rigidity replaced by a drooping weariness. The initial antipathy to his plan was giving way to an appreciation of its merits – as Walter Grimshaw had rightly guessed it would. In a quiet voice, seeming to suggest rather than dictate, the lawyer continued softly:

'The ceremony must take place at once, of course. Perhaps it could be arranged whilst I am down here in Dorset?'

Lord Burnbury stood up, conscious of the gout which now plagued him in his old age as he hobbled over to the window. From here there was a magnificent view of the driveway, lined by giant chestnut trees. To the south, beyond the drive, he could see the blue of the sea and westward, the rolling sweep of the Purbeck hills.

Like his son and his grandson he had lived here as a small boy and there was nowhere in the world he loved more. The family had had this estate encompassing both Upper and Lower Chiswell villages for five hundred years, when a grateful King Edward II donated the land to one of the Grayshott ancestors for services rendered in the Battle of Bannockburn, and Lord Burnbury was fiercely proud of the name and the title. That his only son had chosen the Navy as a way of life was a bitter disappointment to him at the time, but the birth of his grandsons had reconciled him to this break away from the family tradition of land-owner. Now young Deveril was showing every sign of loving this house as much as he himself loved it.

His thoughts turned to Percy – the pale, sickly boy who lived the life of a child in the west wing of the house. He had a kindly nurse to mother him and a male attendant who looked to his physical needs. Occasionally his nurse read stories to him and he could repeat simple nursery rhymes. It was just possible, therefore, that he might be persuaded to repeat the

lines required of him for his marriage. Yet he would know
nothing of the intent, nor understand the meaning of his vows.
Did it matter if this parody were executed before God, all
those present but poor Percy himself knowing there would
never be a true marriage?

As if in answer to Lord Burnbury's thoughts, the lawyer
reached inside the pocket of his tailcoat and withdrew a three-
page document which he presented to the Viscount.

'I have prepared a preliminary draft of a contract of
marriage, Milord. If you would care to glance through it, I
can present it later to the Rev Foster with your approval.'

Reluctantly, Lord Burnbury took the document and allowed
his eyes to travel down the neatly written pages.

The first five clauses dealt with the wedding ceremony to
be held in Chiswell Hill House chapel. Clause 5 was concerned
with quarterly payments to be made to the parson on his
niece's behalf. The remaining clauses were restrictions placed
upon the Rev Foster's behaviour and the Viscount studied
them with growing concern.

> Clause 6. Miss Foster's condition is to be kept a closely
> guarded secret and should word of it reach the ears of
> anyone in Upper or Lower Chiswell, the allowance
> mentioned in Clause 5 will immediately be forfeit.

Lord Burnbury felt a fleeting moment of pity for the
unfortunate girl, but he appreciated the necessity for her
banishment from the neighbourhood.

> Clause 7. Miss Foster shall not adopt the name Mrs Percy
> Grayshott until after she has arrived in North America. She
> may be given the courtesy title of Mrs Foster or any other
> name of her choice to protect her reputation in the meanwhile.

> Clause 8. Miss Foster shall not be given her marriage lines,
> these to be retained by the Rev Foster until such time as

his niece embarks for North America, when he will transmit them to her parents.

Clause 9. It is clearly understood and agreed by the Rev Foster that:
(a) the ex gratia payments made to him on his niece's behalf will be discontinued if this agreement is not strictly adhered to in all respects; and that:
(b) he, his wife and his niece, shall swear upon oath to maintain total secrecy regarding Miss Foster's marriage to Mr Percy Grayshott, it being understood that they are released from this pledge solely in regard to Miss Foster's parents, and then not until after Miss Foster has left the country.

With an uneasy sigh Lord Burnbury handed the document back to Grimshaw, offering no word of congratulation on its astuteness.

'I suppose a written contract *is* necessary?' he enquired stiffly. 'I cannot say I care to have this sort of thing in writing.'

'It is my intention to have one copy only, Milord,' Grimshaw replied smoothly, 'and this, of course, will remain in *your* possession.'

'Oh, very well then,' the Viscount said irritably. 'Parson must know that I will honour my word and that he needs no signed pledge from me. I trust he will not raise any objections to your plans.'

Grimshaw's slight smile was complacent.

'I hardly think that likely, Milord. One has only to consider his position and that of his niece to appreciate the immense advantage this marriage offers them.'

Lord Burnbury frowned.

'How will the girl explain to her parents why she is not living with her husband?' he queried sharply.

Grimshaw gave an imperceptible shrug of his shoulders.

'She will tell the truth, Milord – that Mr Percy Grayshott is an invalid. It is up to the Parson to instruct her how much of the truth it is advisable for her to reveal. The most important point is that she cannot prove Mr Deveril is her child's true father, any more than she can produce proof of the fact that Mr Percy Grayshott is not.'

'Yes, yes. I take your point, Grimshaw. You had better proceed on the lines you suggest. As for the . . . er . . . ceremony itself . . . it can be arranged as soon as Parson sees fit. I leave it all to you. Johnson, my butler, will arrange suitable quarters for you. You may see the Rev Foster in your rooms. I have little wish to talk to him myself unless it is unavoidable. You may leave now.'

Walter Grimshaw smiled as he rose swiftly, made a slight bow to his illustrious client and slid unobtrusively out of the room, well satisfied to have had his plan so quickly approved.

Lord Burnbury was far from satisfied. Having given Grimshaw his authority to go ahead, he was immediately regretting it. He had always felt a deep pity for the sickly boy upstairs, and this plan of Grimshaw's left a nasty taste in the mouth.

He pulled the bellcord to summon his butler. A glass of port might settle the anxious rumblings of his stomach. He was too old and tired, he thought, to argue the rights and wrongs of the matter and Grimshaw must now settle the affair as best he could.

CHAPTER THREE

October 1830

Clementine looked at the physician's serious face, her own expressing her bewilderment. Despite the long explanation he had just given her, she still did not understand how she could possibly be with child. Children, so Mama had told her, came *after* marriage.

Following the incident in the cornfield, she had lived in blissful ignorance of the horror that might lie in store for her, and her unhappy memories of that night were compensated by the arrival of a letter from her mother. Mama had written from New York to say that she and Papa had arrived safely and were having a brief rest in comfortable lodgings before undertaking the next stage of the journey in company with a Mr and Mrs Matheson. She and Papa had met this friendly and hospitable couple on board ship and were invited to spend a week or two at their home in Hamilton on Lake Ontario before proceeding to their proposed destination, Fort William, on the far shores of Lake Superior.

'Papa has assured me that you will be able to join us there just as soon as the harsh winter climate permits you to travel in safety. I comfort myself with the thought that it will not be many months longer before I shall hold you in my arms again . . .'

Now, with a sinking heart, Clementine realized that there could be no question of her travelling in the spring. Greatly though she longed to disbelieve the physician's prediction, deep down within her, she feared he could be right. In recent weeks, along with the unusual cessation of her monthly course, had come bouts of nausea and occasional attacks of giddiness quite at variance with the natural good health she had enjoyed since her recovery from the scarlatina. Her aunt, fearful lest Clementine had contracted some other contagious disease, had finally summoned Doctor Brook to examine her.

Clementine's face paled as she glanced anxiously at the physician.

'I beg you, Sir, please do not tell my aunt of your suspicions,' she pleaded.

'Miss Foster,' he said quickly, 'you must know that I am forced to inform Mrs Foster of my findings. You are a minor and she and your uncle are your guardians. Even if I were not so obliged, it would not be long before your condition revealed itself . . .' He glanced with a mixture of anxiety and pity at the girl's terrified face. 'Come now,' he said gently, 'your aunt is a Christian lady, and in the light of your youth, I am sure we can persuade her that the responsibility for this lies with the young man who seduced you.'

But his voice lacked conviction. None knew better than he how sorry was Mrs Foster's reputation throughout the neighbourhood. Her ministrations to the sick, troubled or dying were performed as an unwelcome duty and were accompanied by harsh criticisms and the belittlement of such pride as these humble people possessed. Nor was she better liked by those of higher rank. The two spinster ladies who ran the school and orphanage had long since ceased to call, as had the lawyer's wife from Poole with whom Mrs Foster had once been so friendly. It seemed that the unfortunate woman could not guard her bitter tongue.

A little of Clementine's desperation communicated itself to the physician as he stared down into her stricken face. He was momentarily confused by the unexpected strength of his emotions; pity was uppermost, but almost as overwhelming was his astonishment. How could this child – for such she was – have landed herself in this shocking state?

'There is no need for you to be present, Miss Foster, when I break the news to your uncle and aunt,' he said in a reassuring tone. 'I give you my word that I shall do everything within my power to persuade them to take a lenient view. But first I want you to explain to me when and how this happened. You may trust me to respect your confidence.'

Strangely, Clementine thought, she *did* trust the quietly spoken Doctor Brook. She grew calmer as she listened to his questions and attempted to give him the replies he awaited with such patience. But she felt too shy to tell him the details of what had happened the night she had met Deveril in the cornfield, and it was Mary who found the courage to do so. Haltingly, the physician attempted to explain the ways of nature to his young patient.

But it was a task he had found almost impossible, he thought as he went downstairs to the parlour where the parson and his wife were awaiting him. The diagnosis that Clementine was with child had been simple, but explaining the reasons for it to the unhappy confused girl was not. There was little doubt in his mind that she had been cruelly taken advantage of, and it was this point he stressed when finally he faced Mrs Foster's horrified gaze.

Ignoring the physician's pleas for understanding, forgetting even his presence, she turned to her husband and said with bitter contempt:

'What else might we have expected from the offspring of that low-minded, degenerate, ungodly brother of yours! And your father was no better. I always told you bad blood will out, and now the girl has brought disgrace upon *us*. I *told* you we should never have taken her in.'

The unhappy little parson was trembling so much that even the jowls of his cheeks shook as he stammered:

'Let us not be too hasty, my dear. The girl is very young and . . .'

'But not too young to be tempted by the lusts of the flesh,' his wife interrupted, her voice shrill. 'I will not permit her to stay a day longer beneath this roof.'

Sensing that any appeal must be made to the parson, Doctor Brook addressed the Rev Foster.

'You, Sir, are Miss Foster's guardian and the responsibility for her lies in *your* hands.' He emphasized the pronoun. 'You cannot turn so young and innocent a girl onto the streets, for it is a certainty that she could not care for herself. She is greatly in need of your protection, Parson.'

'She shall not remain here to bring shame on us,' Mrs Foster began, but her husband found sufficient courage to request her to stay silent.

'You have not told us when the . . . er . . . child . . . will be born, Doctor Brook,' he said nervously. 'My niece is to rejoin her parents in the colonies next spring. Perhaps we could despatch her immediately . . .'

Before Doctor Brook could reply Mrs Foster said scornfully:

'If you had given it a moment's thought, you would realize how ridiculous is such a notion. We have no address as yet to which we could send the girl.'

Ignoring her, Doctor Brook addressed himself once more to the Rev Foster.

'Do you not consider it your Christian duty, Sir, to maintain your niece beneath your roof until her child is safely delivered?' he said in a firm voice. 'Since she is to leave the country shortly after, it would require your tolerance and compassion but a few months longer. I would expect the infant's birth to be towards the end of May, and by the end of July your responsibilities would be at an end.'

The parson shifted uneasily from one foot to the other and rivulets of sweat gathered in the wrinkles of his forehead.

'I do not see how we could possibly keep my niece here without the entire village being aware of her condition,' he said unhappily. 'Think of my reputation, Sir, and what of my brother's feelings towards me were I to return his daughter to him in company with an illegitimate child? No! Whoever is responsible for her seduction must be made to marry her and make her an honest woman. Who *was* the blackguard?'

Briefly Brook recounted the little he knew of Clementine's single tragic encounter with Deveril Grayshott. It did not escape his notice that Mrs Foster's expression changed greatly at the sound of the Grayshott name. She turned to her husband and said eagerly:

'Then all is by no means so dreadful a disaster as I feared. That young man shall be made to redress the wrong he has done. You must go at once to the Viscount, and demand that his grandson makes an honest woman of your niece.'

The Rev Foster looked far from happy at this proposition.

'Lord Burnbury would never allow his grandson to marry so far beneath him. It would be a gross presumption on my part to suggest it and . . .'

'What nonsense. You are forgetting that Clementine's mother is Earl Whytakker's daughter and *she* is a Lady in her own right. The scoundrel should be forced to marry the girl. He took advantage of her and should be made to answer for his wrongdoing.' Without waiting for his assent, she added forcibly, 'Moreover, you should leave for Chiswell Hill House at once. It still lacks two hours before Evensong, so you will have time to make your call. Time,' she added pointedly, 'is not on our side, with the girl already two months gone!'

'I too, must be on my way,' Brook said, suddenly aware that there would be a queue of patients awaiting him at his house.

'I will visit Miss Foster again in a fortnight's time. But do not hesitate to call on my services should you require me before then.'

Once the physician had departed, Winifred Foster gave her husband not a moment's peace until she had despatched him, too, upon his way. Immediately his pony and trap disappeared down the drive, she sent for Clementine.

Mary's expression betrayed her anxiety when she informed

Clementine that she was to see her aunt in the parlour, and that her uncle had left the house. The maid's obvious fear increased Clementine's own. Hurriedly straightening her hair and clothes, she clung to Mary's hand until she reached the parlour door, not releasing it until she heard her aunt's voice instructing her to enter.

Winifred Foster was standing in front of the mantelpiece. The room was cold since the fire was unlit and Clementine shivered as she curtseyed and waited for her aunt to speak. The stream of invectives which then issued from the woman's thin lips had far less meaning for Clementine than the tone in which they were spoken. Used as she had been throughout her childhood to an environment of love, she was torn now between disbelief and fear as her aunt's meaning became clear. She, Clementine, was no longer welcome beneath her uncle's roof and because of her behaviour she must expect to be turned out of the rectory, penniless and friendless, to fend for herself.

'Your uncle is even now considering the matter,' Aunt Winifred said her voice dropping to a low, threatening tone. 'Meanwhile you will remain in your room until he sends for you, and tell Mary to report here to me immediately.'

For the first time, Clementine found her voice.

'I beg of you, Aunt Winifred, do not punish Mary. She did her very best to discourage me from going out that night . . .' Her words trailed into silence as she saw that her aunt was quite unmoved by her appeal. But after dismissing her niece, Mrs Foster's enraged mind cooled and allowed a return to a more logical way of thought.

Perhaps, she pondered, it was not after all such a good idea to give the maid her notice. Mary could – and almost certainly *would* – give way to gossip were she so summarily dismissed. And until she herself and the parson were more certain of what was to be done with Clementine, it was best to take no risk.

It was an hour later when Mary returned to her young

mistress. Her eyes were red with weeping and as Clementine ran across the room to put an arm about her shoulders, the little maid broke into tears once more.

'Oh, Miss!' she sobbed. 'She done said some awful things to me and but for knowing as how you need me, I'd not stay a moment longer in this house, surely.'

'Oh Mary, she did not beat you, did she?' The little maid shook her head.

'Though I doesn't understand why not, seeing as how I deserve it. I shouldn't never have let you go that night, not nohow.'

Clementine's eyes flashed with indignation.

'You must not say that, Mary. You know you tried and I would not listen.'

She sat down wearily in the chair by the unlit fire. Twilight was creeping across the garden and the room was full of shadows. She drew a long shuddering sigh.

'Mary, why is it so terrible for me to be with child? I know I am very young to be a mother, but I am quite old enough to look after a baby and Mama and Papa will take care of us, I know they will.'

Mary's tears dried on her cheeks as she regarded her young mistress with pity . . .

'Oh, Miss Clementine, don't you understand nuffin'? Your babe will be born out of wedlock, and not even your mam and da would think it aught but a disgrace, and all its life your child will have the evil mark on it and know it's a bastard. 'Twouldn't be so bad if you was a village girl, Miss Clementine – but you being a lady . . . We must pray, Miss Clementine, that the young genulman will do right by you and marry you!'

Clementine's spirits lifted momentarily. If marriage to Deveril Grayshott could put an end to this nightmare, she would welcome it with open arms. She had not stopped loving him because of what had happened.

'Oh, Mary, do you think he *will* marry me? Or will he think too badly of me to want me for his wife?'

Mary looked at Clementine's pale worried face and decided this was not the moment to tell her that if Mr Grayshott did not make an honest woman of her, her aunt would ensure that her disgrace was absolute. Mary had been forced to kneel on the floor with her hand on the Bible and swear on oath that she would speak of Miss Clementine's condition to no one, neither to her family, nor even to Cook. Moreover, Mrs Foster had informed her that Miss Clementine's door was to be kept locked from now on, and that she would not be permitted to leave her room without her aunt's authorization. Mary could well imagine that Clementine's spirit, as well as her health, might be broken were she forced to remain incarcerated for the next seven months.

Clementine's next words revealed how greatly she needed the maid's support.

'You are the only friend I have, Mary,' she said forlornly.

'And that's a load of fiddle-faddle, Miss Clementine,' Mary said brusquely, as she went to draw the curtains across the darkened windows. 'That there Doctor Brook is as good a friend to you as what I am.' She gave an unexpected giggle. 'I were listening at parlour door and I heered him tell Parson it were his Christian duty to tek care of you till you was safe away to your parents.'

But the brief comfort that Mary's revelations gave Clementine was little enough to sustain her during the next ten days when she remained locked in her bedroom in an agony of uncertainty. It was almost with a feeling of relief therefore that at last she learned she had been summoned to the study to see her uncle.

She felt a moment's giddiness as she knocked on the study door and it was several minutes before she could steel herself to answer the summons and go in. With a sigh of relief, she saw that her uncle was alone. He was seated in front of the oak desk at which he wrote his sermons. He glanced at her briefly and looked quickly back at some papers before him.

'Sit down, sit down, child!' He waved a hand vaguely in the

direction of the window seat. 'I have something of importance to tell you.'

As she obeyed his command, she sensed instinctively that something was very wrong. 'An honest man will always look you straight in the eye,' her father had remarked on many occasions.

Shuffling the papers meaninglessly, the Rev Foster said: 'You are a very fortunate young lady. I have reached agreement with Viscount Burnbury. You are to be married next week.'

'Married? Next week?' Clementine whispered. 'So soon?'

Her uncle still did not look at her and tapped his quill repeatedly on the desktop.

'Surely you understand, my dear, that it is a matter of the sooner the better. As it is, your . . . er . . . offspring will be a seven-months child.'

His eyes travelled briefly down Clementine's small frame and centred on her grey cambric dress as if already her figure might betray the child's existence. He looked up quickly and encountered her white, shocked face. The pathos of her situation did not escape him, and he coughed uneasily.

Not for the first time, he told himself that Clementine was exactly the kind of daughter he would have liked to soften his old age with her pretty smile and gentle voice. If Winifred had not been so painfully averse to performing her marital duties, maybe they would have had children. Her barrenness was hardly surprising when he thought how quickly he had learned in his marriage never to expect Winifred to welcome him to her bed.

His charming little niece, the parson thought, would never be like the cold, spiteful woman he had married. Clementine's nature was loving and giving.

With an effort of will, the Rev Foster brought his attention back to the task in hand – to advise his niece of his agreement with Viscount Burnbury.

'The wedding will take place at Chiswell Hill House chapel,' he told her, his voice, as always when he addressed her, gentle and kindly. 'The Grayshotts' chaplain will perform the rites. It will not take long and we should be back within the hour.'

The door opened suddenly and his wife stormed into the room. She looked at her husband accusingly, ignoring Clementine's curtsey.

'You should have told me you were going to see the girl before tea. You know very well that I wished to be present at the interview.'

Perspiration broke out on the parson's bald pate. He drew out a handkerchief and mopped his forehead before ushering his wife into a chair.

'We have only just begun our little discussion, my dear,' he said nervously. 'I was just explaining to Clementine that the wedding will take place in the Grayshotts' private chapel, where there is no chance of our being observed.'

With difficulty, Clementine found her voice.

'It is to be a secret wedding, then?' she whispered, her thoughts whirling in confusion.

'What else did you expect, you ignorant girl, when you have been carrying for over two months!' her aunt said fiercely. 'Even now there will be gossip when you give birth. You will have to go away for the confinement. I will not have that child of the Devil born under *this* roof!'

'Let us not worry about that for the moment, my dear,' the parson broke in quickly. 'Let us get the wedding over first. Then we will consider the future.'

Clementine stood up and moved closer to her uncle's chair. She gazed at him pleadingly.

'I still do not understand, Uncle,' she murmured. 'Am I not then to live with my husband?'

Winifred Foster's small black eyes blazed as she rose to her feet and stood towering over Clementine's small frame.

'It is not just Percy Grayshott who is out of his mind, but you too, you stupid girl. Do you think Viscount Burnbury wants you or your brat under his roof any more than I do?

He will be happy enough if he *never* has to see you, and I cannot say I blame him. You . . .'

'Clementine is not yet aware of . . . er . . . of all the facts.' The parson interrupted his wife's tirade with his usual stammering nervousness. 'I should explain to you, Clementine, that the dear Lord did not see fit to give Percy Grayshott full possession of his faculties – and it is not our business to question His reasons,' he added sanctimoniously. 'The Viscount has kindly agreed that the young man shall give your child a name. But of course, there can be no real marriage as such since the poor young man is an invalid and cannot lead a normal life . . .'

He broke off, aware that Clementine was not listening.

'I do not understand,' she was saying. 'What has Percy Grayshott to do with me – or – the baby? It is Deveril Grayshott who . . .'

'Yes, yes, I know all that,' the parson interrupted. 'But you must understand, child, that Deveril Grayshott will one day be Viscount Burnbury. When his grandfather and his father, the Admiral, die, *he* will inherit. Naturally he cannot be saddled with an unsuitable wife and child. He must marry well.'

Clementine's eyes were wide with disbelief.

'But I do not know this Percy you speak of. Even if I am not to live with him, I cannot marry a man I neither know nor love. Please, Uncle . . .'

'I have heard enough of this twaddle!' Aunt Winifred's voice cut across Clementine's whisper. 'You appear to have no shame nor appreciation of your position. Your uncle and I would not be condemned were we to turn you out onto the streets to fend for yourself. Yet here is your uncle charitably allowing you to remain under his protection and now arranging for your sin to be hidden beneath the respectability of marriage – and *you* talk of *love*!'

'I am sure Clementine understands very well that we are trying to do our best for her in these . . . er . . . unfortunate circumstances,' the parson said in an attempt to halt his wife's scathing torrent of words. He turned away from her implacable face to look at his niece. His voice held a note of pity as he observed the confusion in her eyes.

'Now, child, let us get down to practicalities. When you have given this marriage some careful thought, you will better appreciate its advantages. I will not go into the financial arrangements, since these will not concern you until after you have gone to live with your parents. I am satisfied that the terms are generous and I do not consider that the Grayshotts' demands upon us are unreasonable. I have this afternoon on your behalf signed a document guaranteeing that this marriage to Mr Percy Grayshott shall be kept secret from everyone but those of us directly involved.'

For one of the few times that Clementine could remember, her uncle looked directly into her eyes.

'Make no mistake about this mandate, Clementine. Everything rests upon our adherence to it. We can be assured that the Grayshotts will not speak of the marriage, and if word of it were to get out, the fault would be attributable to us. I am therefore going to ask you to place your hand upon this Bible and to swear before God that you will speak of your marriage to no one – and by that I include the physician, the maid, Mary, and for the time being, your parents.'

He heard his niece's small gasp of dismay and added quickly:

'For the present we have no address to which we can send word to your father. The time will come when they have finally settled upon a new life and it will be appropriate for me to enlighten them as to your circumstances. Now, child, place your hand here and make your solemn oath to the Almighty.'

Obediently, Clementine put her hand upon the Bible her uncle placed before her, but the words he wished to hear remained unspoken as she looked into his eyes, pleading for understanding.

'I am sure Papa and Mama would take care of me and my baby even although I am disgraced. Can we not wait until a letter may be got to them to ask their opinion upon this marriage? Surely it will not be long now before we hear from them again?'

But her Aunt Winifred could remain silent no longer. She reached out and gripped Clementine by the shoulders. In a shrill voice she exclaimed:

'You will do what your uncle tells you – this minute – and without further argument, do you understand? One word of complaint from you and you will forfeit your uncle's leniency and be out of this house before nightfall. I will hear no more from you.' She gripped Clementine's wrist, pressing her hand more firmly on the hard leather cover of the Bible. 'Now repeat after me: "I swear by Almighty God . . ."'

Too terrified to disobey, Clementine repeated her aunt's words with a feeling of unreality. She was only half aware of her promise as for the first time in her life, hatred surged through her. She was frightened – not just by her aunt's demeanour but by the implied threats. Yet at the same moment, she longed to cry out:

'You would not dare to speak to me so if Papa were here . . .'

When at last Clementine was dismissed and could escape to the comparative solace of her own room, the little maid was awaiting her. With the words of the oath still ringing in her ears, Clementine could not give way to her longing to reveal the facts to Mary – that in a week's time she was to be married. All she could do was confess her fear of and loathing for the woman downstairs.

'She hates me, I know she does!' she wept, as she knelt on the floor with her head buried in Mary's apron. 'One day I shall tell her that she is cruel, horrible.'

Anxiously, Mary cautioned the young girl against voicing her true feelings.

'You got to think on your baby, Miss Clementine. It got to have a roof over its head, surely, till you can tek it to Americky. You'm no choice but to do as she says and submit.'

Clementine's fists clenched against her sides. Mary was

right. There was nothing she could do – a girl just sixteen with no money, no parents within call, and an aunt and uncle who were her legal guardians. She did not want to get married – to a stranger who, so her uncle said, had lost his wits. But it seemed she had no alternative if her child was to be born without the stigma of illegitimacy.

Because this boy, Percy, was an invalid, she would not share his bed or his home. She would be his wife but only as a name on a piece of paper. Her marriage vows – and she had read them often in the prayer book – would be meaningless, for she could never love, honour or obey this man she was to wed. Nor would they be marrying to 'procreate children' – that was already done without God's blessing. Was that why her aunt called her baby 'a child of the Devil'? she wondered. Would it be born with some terrible deformity – horns, perhaps? A hunchback? For once Clementine did not resent her uncle's admonitions to pray for salvation. But it was for the baby's salvation she prayed those long hours on her knees by her bed. She was determined it would be perfect despite her sin.

The Parson too, was spending long hours in prayer, but his pleas to the Almighty were for patience and for the strength of will to withstand his wife's unceasing demands that his niece should be turned out of the house before it was too late and their reputations were ruined. He tried to silence his wife's nagging tongue by conceding that the girl should be kept in the strictest confinement. He would make it his responsibility, he said, to ensure that no word reached the parish as to Clementine's condition and that no caller at The Rectory would be permitted to see her. Furthermore, he stated, since there would inevitably be enquiries from his parishioners about his niece, he would let it be known that she had had a relapse following upon her summer indisposition and that she was once again confined to her bed.

'You will never conceal the truth in a place like this,' Winifred Foster declared harshly. 'What makes you think you can keep the servants from gossiping – or the physician come to that? And suppose the post carrier or the baker's boy catches sight of her? It will not be long now before her sin is obvious for all to see. You must be out of your mind even to consider it.'

The parson felt a tiny surge of elation as with unaccustomed sarcasm he said flatly:

'We are not blessed with many friends, my dear, and of those who used to call, remarkably few still do, aware no doubt that they are unwelcome. Which now proves to our advantage. I do not intend to discuss this question further with you, my dear,' he added, taking what advantage he could of his wife's momentary silence. 'Clementine is *my* niece and I shall decide what is best for her.'

Upstairs, Clementine was unaware of the debt of gratitude she now owed her uncle, or how hard put he had been to summon the courage to defy his wife on her behalf.

It was Mary's afternoon off when after luncheon the following day Mrs Foster appeared without warning at Clementine's bedroom door. Her face expressionless, she handed her niece a small box.

'You will find in there one of the Confirmation veils put by for the village girls,' she announced. 'Now wash your hands and face, tidy your hair and put on your Sunday dress – the blue jaconet. You are to be downstairs with your cloak in exactly ten minutes.' Her lips curled into the parody of a smile. 'We cannot have you late for your wedding, can we,' she remarked, adding pointedly, 'seeing that we are nearly three months late already.'

Despite the turmoil into which this sudden news flung her, Clementine was still young enough to be happy at the thought of leaving her room for whatever purpose. She longed for the fresh country air as much as for the sight of fields and hedgerows and even for a glimpse of the bare wintry trees.

But her excitement subsided, leaving her strangely calm when twenty minutes later she was seated in the dogcart, the old white mare pulling them slowly along the lane leading to Chiswell Hill House.

Far away across the fields she heard the church clock in the village strike the half hour, the sound muffled by the thick bank of white fog rolling in from the sea. As it gradually enveloped them, the trees and hedgerows lost their shapes and her uncle and aunt became shadowy silhouettes.

The muffled clip-clop of the mare's hooves on the stony lane was accompanied by the creaking of the shafts in the tugs and the occasional squeak of the traces as they rubbed against the metal harness. The oppressive silence of the countryside was broken only by the flutter of a pigeon's wings as it flew into a nearby tree to roost and the ghostly shriek of a dog fox from some distant spinney.

Clementine shivered, uncertain whether she should try to convince herself that this truly was her wedding day; that within the next hour she was to make her marriage vows. The eerie silence was more appropriate to a funeral, she decided, her spirits falling still further. But as they turned suddenly into the drive of Chiswell Hill House, a natural youthful curiosity set her leaning forward to obtain her first view of the big Elizabethan manor. By its dark shape Clementine saw that its size was impressive, like a castle in a storybook.

They drew up outside a small door leading from the house to the stables. Mr Grimshaw had made all the arrangements and discretion was foremost in his thoughts when he did so. The servants were downstairs preparing the evening meal. He was standing ready, by the side door, so that Johnson, the butler, would not be aware of the visitors. Percy was already in the chapel, conducted there by his attendant who would depart on a signal from Mr Grimshaw before the ceremony began. He himself would lead Percy through the ritual which, since the boy seemed amenable if he were proffered sweetmeats at intervals, should not prove too difficult. The chaplain was to keep the ceremony as brief as he could.

Walter Grimshaw was seldom out of countenance. He had

trained himself to control his emotions, especially those that might betray his thoughts to those he wished to manipulate. He had planned this event meticulously, and was even looking forward to its execution. Nevertheless, as he watched the shabby little parson assist Percy's future bride down from the dogcart, he could not refrain from a small gasp of surprise. This was no scheming young woman, no daring hussy, no precocious village girl. This was a child, looking far younger than her sixteen years, her eyes as they regarded him wide apart and enquiring, with an innocent curiosity. She radiated a genuine innocence that he recognized instantly.

It was not often nowadays that Walter Grimshaw felt any qualms about his own actions. Having made a decision, he never looked back or doubted its wisdom. But now, as he held out his arm to Clementine and felt her small fingers encircle his sleeve, he wondered if they were justified in binding her legally to a mental defective. This child would be tied to Percy until his death – and no one seemed certain when *that* would be.

They were in the chapel now and as he conducted Clementine to the chair where Percy sat, the boy smiled up at them disarmingly. He was dressed in a brown coat and lavender moleskin trousers, his fair hair curling softly about his thin shoulders, his blue eyes fastened on the white veil covering Clementine's hair.

'Pretty!' he said. And without warning, he broke into a song. '. . . *Hey, Ho, to the Greenwood*,' he sang in a sweet tenor.

'Hush now, Percy,' his attendant said. 'You be a good boy and do what Mr Grimshaw tells you.'

'Can we now proceed?' Winifred's sharp voice broke the silence that followed the attendant's departure. She prodded the parson sharply with her elbow. He gave a despairing look, first at Clementine, then at Percy and finally at Mr Grimshaw for guidance. The lawyer nodded and placed himself behind Clementine at the side of Percy's chair.

'There is nothing to be afraid of,' he said in an undertone, as he felt Clementine's sudden trembling. 'You will leave here with your marriage lines and that is what you want, is it not?'

But it was not what Clementine wanted. She wanted to be in a beautiful white wedding gown – not in her Sunday best – marrying the man she loved just as Mama had done. She wanted it to be Deveril here beside her – not the smiling young man in the chair for whom she could feel only pity. She wanted to run away – far, far away. She wanted her mama, her papa. She wanted to wake up from this terrible nightmare and discover it was all just a horrid dream.

Percy had begun to hum softly beneath his breath, '*Green grow the Rushes, oh!*' The lawyer gave him a sweetmeat and he stopped singing and smiled happily around him. Clementine found herself following his gaze which was now centred on the gilded arches of the chapel. There were blue angels painted on the domed ceiling and a statue of the Virgin Mary on the white-and-gold-clothed altar before which the chaplain stood. She strained to hear his voice. A few feet from her stood her aunt, her back ramrod stiff in her black velvet pelisse and dress; her grey hair covered by her best black-ribboned bonnet.

She might be attending my funeral! Clementine thought with a sudden hysterical desire to giggle with Mary at this irrelevance. Then the chaplain's words became audible and she no longer felt like laughing. '. . . that if either of you know any impediment why ye may not be lawfully joined together in Matrimony, ye do now confess it . . .'

Why did nobody speak, Clementine thought. Surely one of these adults would explain that she could not marry the poor, sick young man at her side. Surely the lawyer must know that this could not be legal matrimony when she and Percy were no more than strangers to each other and might never see one another again. Surely . . .

But the chaplain had now moved over to Percy's chair and was asking him if he would take her, Clementine, to be his wedded wife.

'Say, "*I will!*" Percy,' instructed Mr Grimshaw firmly. 'Be a good boy now and say "*I will!*"'

Obediently, Percy repeated the words and would have continued to do so had he not been hushed. Now the chaplain was addressing her. '. . . wilt thou love, honour, and keep him in sickness and in health; and forsaking all other, keep thee only unto him, so long as you both shall live?'

The awaited reply lodged in Clementine's throat. She could not make that vow, knowing it to be false. A terrible silence gripped the room as Clementine fought to still her rising panic. She could feel her aunt's eyes boring into her. She felt too, the slight pressure of her uncle's hand on her arm. Frantically her eyes sought his, but he was staring down at his hands. Despairingly, she looked at the statue of the Virgin Mary. Would not even the Mother of God help her? But the Virgin held the baby Jesus in her arms – a pretty, golden-haired baby like the one she herself might give birth to. She must think of that child, not of herself. It needed a name – a father's name. Otherwise it would be branded for life – Mary had told her so.

'You must answer, Miss Foster!' the lawyer prompted at her elbow. 'Just say "*I will!*"'

I must answer, Clementine thought dully as she tried to whisper the words. I have no choice. I will be turned out of the house and my baby will starve and I will never see my parents again!

This time, her whisper was audible and the three witnesses let out their breath. The chaplain's voice, in contrast, was quite loud.

'Who giveth this woman to be married to this man?'

Behind her, the parson moved forward, muttering his willingness to give her away as if she belonged to him and not to dear Papa, Clementine thought wildly. But the chaplain had no such misgivings, and taking her right hand, placed it in Percy's. Now there remained only the hurdle of prompting Percy through his declaration.

It took a long time, for Percy's attention frequently wandered and he could remember only one or two words at a time. He became bored and had to be coaxed with more sweetmeats; and when finally he was given the small gold band to put on Clementine's finger, he wanted to keep it and wear it himself. Clementine saw her aunt move towards the boy, her mouth a thin hard line, her eyes narrowed with purposefulness. She was going to make him give the ring up – even perhaps slap him as she had often slapped her, Clementine thought.

'No!' she cried out. 'I will do it. Leave him alone!'

Without waiting to see her aunt's reaction, she bent down and held out her hand, palm uppermost.

'Please, Percy, give it to me,' she said softly, her eyes gentle as they looked into the boy's questioning face. 'You would like to give it to me, would you not? See, you shall put it on for me.'

Responsive to her gentleness, the boy allowed her to help him slip the ring on her finger. Clementine stood up and with a hardness that had not been in her before, she stared into the chaplain's eyes.

'You may proceed, Sir!' she said firmly, her voice sounding loud and challenging as if she were daring him to do so against his wishes.

Mr Grimshaw barely awaited the ceremony's completion before he called for Percy's attendant to come back into the chapel. The boy seemed to have lost all interest in the strangers and he welcomed his nurse as a familiar face. Within minutes he had gone and the lawyer addressed the parson.

'You understand, Parson, that you and I will sign as witnesses. The financial settlement will be arranged as soon as I return to London, and you may draw on it as from the first of next month. You do understand, I trust, that everything that has just happened must be kept absolutely confidential. Should word of this marriage be leaked, I would know at once from which source.'

The threat in his words was beyond doubt. But in his heart, Grimshaw did not really believe it necessary. The parson would never reveal his part in this conspiracy. Nor indeed would that sanctimonious old crow, his wife, who had made no secret of the fact that she would go to any lengths to avoid a scandal. The girl was the only weak link – yet she, too, needed secrecy to protect her child. As the law stood, any child she bore now was presumed to be her husband's unless it could be proved otherwise – and no one could prove young Deveril had fathered the brat.

Well satisfied with his night's achievement, Walter Grimshaw saw his visitors into their dogcart and went back indoors to report to Lord Burnbury that all was well. The old man would be distinctly relieved that everything had been resolved so quickly and simply, he thought. He might worry for a day or two longer about the ethics of the matter but then he would forget. Wealthy, titled people like the Viscount had better things to think about than their families' by-blows, unless they posed a threat to the entailment of the estates. That unhappy young girl's child could never do that, boy or girl. It was Deveril who mattered; who eventually would have the title; the money; the power. And although Mr Deveril Grayshott did not know it, he was already satisfactorily in Walter Grimshaw's debt.

CHAPTER FOUR

February 1831

It was a bitterly cold February day. Outside the frosted window, the rectory garden was transformed by a white carpet of snow blanketing the rhododendron and laurel bushes with foot-thick humped quilts. Every few minutes a gust of wind blew a white spray from their summits and little icy lumps would fall from the trees dimpling the white lawn beneath.

For once Clementine was not sorry to be incarcerated in her room. Aunt Winifred had finally relented and permitted Mary to light a small coal fire in the grate, and although it gave only an illusion of heat, its faint glow was comforting.

Beside her lay her work and on her lap one of the many tiny garments she had been embroidering for her baby's layette. Aunt Winifred had refused to waste money on new materials, but had given Clementine an old flannel petticoat and a torn pair of lace curtains with which to make something for 'that miserable unhappy child you bear'. The garments Clementine had made from these cast-off remnants were small works of art which had drawn admiring praise from the ever-loyal Mary.

But for the comfort of the little maid, Clementine would have been even more unhappy these past three months. Having spent the entire summer imprisoned in her bedroom, she had been aghast when her aunt had informed her that after her marriage she must now return there where no one could see her shame. Doctor Brook had pleaded that she be permitted at least an hour a day of exercise in the open air. But whilst the parson was prepared to agree, Aunt Winifred refused adamantly to consider it. Her uncle had won one concession for her however – that for an hour every evening after supper she could go down to the parlour where, with her aunt's eye upon her, she could be given instruction in Latin and Greek.

'The devil makes mischief for idle hands,' the parson had told his wife, 'and it will improve her mind.' For once, Aunt Winifred had had no answer. Once or twice of late, she had fallen asleep over her tapestry work, and then the parson's voice would soften and he patted his niece's hand surreptitiously.

Clementine always felt oddly guilty at such moments, wishing she could like her uncle better since he was at least trying to be kind to her. But whereas she had loved to sit upon her papa's knee and feel his bristly beard tickle her cheek with kisses and his strong sailor's hands stroke her hair, she shrank from her uncle's touch. His hands were small and white and pudgy, and made her think of big fat maggots creeping over her skin.

Were it not for the promise her uncle had given her that by July at the very latest she would be on her way out to be reunited with her parents, Clementine could not have endured the long lonely days of winter. She tried hard not to think about Deveril, although she could not prevent herself wondering if he knew about the child she carried – his child. Did he know about her marriage to Percy? Was he sorry for his part in their shared wickedness?

Most difficult of all the promises her aunt and uncle had forced from her, Clementine thought, was her vow not to tell nice Doctor Brook of her marriage. He alone seemed to understand that she had intended no wrong. He was really interested in her baby and spoke of it as if it were a tiny human being rather than a scourge she should wish to be rid of. He understood, too, how desperately she needed her beloved mama at such a time as this. It still lacked six months before she could set sail. The baby was not due until the end of May, and it would need two more months before she would be strong enough to withstand so long a sea journey. But at least it could be no later than August, her uncle comforted her, for the winters in Upper Canada were very severe and she must be safely in her parents' charge before the rigours of winter travel became a danger to her and the child.

Clementine's reverie was interrupted as the door burst open and Mary, her carroty hair straggling beneath her white frilled mob-cap, hurried into the room.

'Miss Clementine!' she gasped. 'You'll not believe as who is downstairs. The mistress wouldn't see him but Parson's taken him into the study and left the door open, and if'n you was to creep on to the landing, you could see him, surely, just as clear as clear and . . .'

'Mary, whatever are you talking about? *Who* is downstairs with my uncle?'

Mary giggled and blushed simultaneously.

'Mebbe as how I didn't ought to be tellin' you, Miss Clementine, but he's ever so handsome – just like a prince and . . .'

'*Who!*' Clementine said, exasperation and curiosity vying with one another as she laid down her sewing and stood up.

'Why, Mr Deveril, your Mr Deveril . . .'

The colour drained from Clementine's face and then her cheeks reddened. Deveril Grayshott – here in The Rectory! But why? What could have brought him here? What was being said? Could he have come to see her?

Mary was tugging at her arm, her finger to her lips.

'The mistress is in the kitchen with Cook,' she said. 'If'n we're quiet as mouses, she won't hear us up on the landing nohow.'

Taking Clementine's acquiescence for granted, she opened the bedroom door and crept out on to the landing. Her heart thudding, Clementine followed her. They were in shadow, for Mary had left the oil lamp in the bedroom. Both girls leaned cautiously over the wooden balustrade. Down below, an orange glow came from the open parlour door. The silhouettes of the two men were clearly visible.

'I know as how it's *him*,' Mary said as if in answer to Clementine's unspoken question. ''Twas me what opened the front door to him!'

Clementine was now trembling, partly from the fear of discovery by her aunt but even more from nervous excitement. She must go further down the stairs where she could see Deveril properly. No matter if reason bade her remain where she was, her heart demanded that she did not waste this miraculous chance to see her lover again. She still loved him . . . no matter how often she had told herself that she did not, must not do so. Only love could set her legs trembling so much that she feared she might fall down the ill-lit stairway.

A few steps short of the dark hall, Clementine stopped, crouching down with Mary behind her. She could now see clearly into the room. Her uncle's back was towards her and Deveril Grayshott stood facing him. Clementine felt her heart jolt. As Mary had said, he was handsome – far more handsome even than she remembered. A picture she had once seen of the poet, Lord Byron, came into her head. Deveril was every bit as romantic with his dark curly hair and fine disdainful profile.

Now she could hear his voice – a pleasant low tenor with a hint of authority to it – as he replied to some remark her uncle had made.

'My grandfather says our chaplain will, of course, be present to assist with the funeral. He will call upon you tomorrow. Will you please make the necessary arrangements for the family vault to be opened.'

'Of course, I shall carry out the Viscount's instructions to the letter, Mr Grayshott . . .' her uncle stammered.

'I must be going,' Deveril said abruptly. 'I have much to do at the house, but I felt the matter was urgent since we are obliged to expedite the funeral in light of the fact that the weather may worsen.'

'Yes, yes, I quite understand. You need have no worry, Sir . . . but may I offer you a glass of Madeira before you leave?'

'Thank you, but no. I must be on my way.'

Mary was tugging at Clementine's dress.

'We best go, Miss, quickly, afore he comes out,' she pleaded. 'Come along, Miss Clementine, quick, do now, make haste.'

Mary's urgent voice penetrated the vortex of emotions into which Clementine had been flung. Automatically, she followed the maid's stout little back as she scuttled up the stairs to the safety of the bedroom. Clementine's feet dragged reluctantly, for she could hear her uncle and his visitor going into the hall. In a minute, Deveril would be gone and she would be alone again. The thought was unbearable. He did not even know she was alive, carrying his child and needing him to come to her rescue.

Mary hurried back downstairs to give the visitor his hat and greatcoat. Tears rolled slowly down Clementine's cheeks. Maybe, she thought wearily, it would have been better had she not seen Deveril. Since her marriage, she had almost resigned herself to the fact that she was unlikely to set eyes on him again before she left England. She picked up her sewing, the tears clouding her vision so that she pricked her finger.

'Oh, Miss, you mustn't cry!' Mary said, as she came back into the room and saw the forlorn figure of her young mistress by the embers of the fire. She knelt down and held a sheet of paper over the grate until the ashes sparked into life again. 'There now, that's a bit more cheerful like!' she exclaimed. 'And Cook's made kedgeree for your supper – and you like that, don't you now! You must look on the bright side of things, Miss Clementine – that's what my mam says, and my aunty says it do not do to be miserable when you'm carrying, else you'll get a wailing baby and you do not want that now, surely.'

'I do not want a baby at all!' Clementine wept as Mary's arms went round her. 'And I do not want any kedgeree either, and I wish . . . I wish I was dead!'

Mary tut-tutted as she stroked Clementine's long gold curls.

'You'm be sixteen year old Miss Clementine!' she told her

comfortingly. 'Things'll look a mite different in a while, you see if they doesn't. You'm got to get that baby born, Miss Clementine, and then tek it out to Americky for your mam to look after.'

Clementine smiled tremulously at the faithful little servant. Whether or not she was married to the wrong Grayshott son, she was at least married. Papa would fuss over his grandchild and Mama would love it and she could be happy again. Quite suddenly her healthy young appetite returned.

'All right, Mary,' she said. 'Perhaps after all I will have a little of Cook's kedgeree.'

Benjamin Brook was twenty-eight years old and a bachelor. His mother had died of typhoid before he had finished his studies at medical school, and his elder brother had long since disappeared into the African continent where he lived the life of a dedicated missionary. Benjamin's only other relative was his elderly father, a retired professor whose passion in life was the study of entomology. The old man lived alone in a small house in the fashionable Sussex seaside resort of Brighton. When Benjamin's grandparents had purchased the house in their youth, Brighthelmstone, as the town was then called, had been very quiet and secluded; but then the Prince of Wales had taken a fancy to the place, built the impressive Pavilion, and Society had quickly followed suit and built houses for themselves. The young physician had been unable to afford a practice there and had finally taken over the small country practice which included the two villages of Upper and Lower Chiswell.

He was as dedicated to his medical profession as his father was to his studies of butterflies and insects and his brother to his missionary work. Here in Dorset, he treated only the sick – for the village population were far too poor to be able to employ the service of a physician for minor ailments.

There were times when Benjamin felt very deeply the injustice of a world where the poor fought a daily fight for survival and the rich – like the Grayshotts up at Chiswell Hill House – had more money than they knew what to do with. Not for the Grayshotts a stone cottage with a leaking roof, outside privy, and perhaps only two rooms to house a family of ten. They owned not only the huge Elizabethan mansion and a vast estate which covered the valley of Bourne Brook almost as far south as the little village of Bournemouth, but two London houses where they spent the Season, and a castle in Scotland where they went for the shooting.

Yet for all Benjamin's conscience smote him when he went up to Chiswell Hill House, he could not dislike any of the Grayshotts whom he attended professionally. The old Viscount was a charming, unassuming man with a deep pride in his family and his country. The poor old fellow suffered a great deal from gout. Benjamin had known Sir William less well, for the Admiral spent months on end at sea. The daughters were unknown to him for they had all been married off before he had arrived in Dorset. But he had met Deveril on several occasions and thought the boy was a bit of a madcap, always damaging himself in some wild escapade. He had taken his misfortunes with a laugh and a shrug for his own stupidity and until Benjamin had learned the story of Deveril's seduction of the parson's innocent little niece, he had approved of the young man.

For Percy Grayshott, Benjamin felt only pity and a helpless wish for medical science to increase its knowledge so that physicians like himself could understand what went on in the human brain. From all accounts, the boy had been normal enough at birth, his mental development ceasing after an attack of croup which had brought on serious convulsions. Although, understandably, Percy was confined to his quarters where his condition would not be an embarrassment to the family, he was never ill-treated, and his father, grandfather and brother all seemed fond of him. Deveril in particular treated him with a gentleness that had surprised Benjamin, for he seemed better able even than the attendant to quieten his brother when he was disturbed.

Benjamin sat now in his customary chair in Clementine's room and looked anxiously at his patient. She seemed quieter than usual and he observed that she had been crying. His heart filled with pity for this young girl whose life had been ruined barely before it had begun.

During these monthly visits – there had been six so far – his professional interest and his pity had deepened and changed as his need to protect and help her stirred all that was chivalrous in his nature. He could think of no one who required his protection more. Had it not been for Clementine's unalterable determination to travel out to her parents as soon as was possible, he would have permitted himself to dwell more often on his growing desire to offer her the protection of his name in marriage. As her pregnancy developed, she seemed to him to grow even prettier. The rounded sweetness of childhood had fined down to a more delicate, sculptured beauty, revealing a mature loveliness that was not just in her features but in her character.

In short, Benjamin Brook was fighting a growing love for a girl soon to give birth to another man's child and who would eventually be leaving England for ever. He tried therefore, to deny the emotions that beset him and retain only a professional interest in her.

'You are not apprehensive about the coming confinement?' he asked gently. 'I promise you that I shall do whatever is possible to make it easy for you.'

Clementine looked at him gratefully. Other than Mary, she thought, this man was her only friend.

'Mary said I might be attended by the midwife!' she said anxiously. 'She told me Mrs Higgins was quite rough with her mama when she had her last two babies and that she would not have the midwife near if there was another one.'

Benjamin glanced at the maid who was sitting by the window and concealed a sigh of exasperation. He had not wanted Clementine frightened.

'Do not worry about the midwife,' he said gently. 'I shall deliver your baby myself.'

Clearly, he thought, her aunt had still not informed her that she was not, after all, to be permitted to have her child at The Rectory. Mrs Foster had finally overruled her husband's wishes to keep his niece beneath his roof and but for Benjamin's intervention, Clementine would now be far away in some nameless refuge for 'fallen women' where even he would be unable to befriend her. He had made himself responsible for finding somewhere for her to go before she birthed her child and where she and the infant could remain until she left to join her parents.

With such little time as Benjamin had at his disposal, he had been trying to contact a former patient of his – a certain Miss Emily Fothergill – who resided in the nearby seaport of Poole. A respectable lady in her sixties, she was much involved with the Poor Hospital there. When he had last seen her, Miss Fothergill had been on the committee of the Friendly Society, and aware that the aim of this society was for local citizens to help each other in time of trouble, it was Benjamin's hope that she would be willing to offer Clementine a refuge. But it was now over a year since he had last visited her and for all he knew, the good lady could have other commitments. He did not think it right, therefore, to raise Clementine's hopes of exchanging the deprivations of her life at The Rectory for so agreeable an alternative, until he was certain of Miss Fothergill's welcome. The bleakness and solitude she was enduring meanwhile distressed him sufficiently to keep him awake at night.

Now it seemed as if even her extraordinary courage was deserting her. There was a dejected droop to her shoulders which touched his heart and filled him with an unbearable longing to put his strong arms around her to protect and comfort her. Restraining the impulse with difficulty, he confined himself to taking her small hand and holding it reassuringly in his own as he regarded her anxiously.

'Are you going to tell me why you have been crying, for I know that you have?' he said.

Clementine attempted a smile.

'Only for a little while,' she admitted, and on impulse, confessed that Deveril's visit last evening had disturbed her.

Abruptly, Benjamin released her hand and walked across to the window. The sky had darkened ominously and the cold break room was even gloomier and more oppressive than usual. But for the absence of bars on the window, it might indeed be a prison, he thought. He was shocked yet again by the idea of so young and vital a creature buried away in this tomb as if to deny her very existence.

Now, to add to her present tribulations, she had had the emotional impact of seeing once more the man responsible for her unhappiness. What could have possessed Grayshott to call at the rectory, he muttered, as he turned from the window with a look of deep concern in his eyes.

'The young genulman was a-talking to Parson about ringing the knell for Admiral's burying,' Mary volunteered helpfully.

Benjamin nodded. He knew that the Viscount intended a hasty funeral lest the weather deteriorated still further and it became impossible for the funeral cortège to reach the village graveyard through the snowdrifts. But he had not known of Deveril's ride down to The Rectory to discuss the matter with the parson.

He felt a surge of anger which he quickly controlled. The boy was eventual heir to the family title, and even had he wished to marry the young girl he had dishonoured, the old Viscount would never have permitted it.

Benjamin looked once more into the wistful little face regarding him now so trustingly.

'I am trying to keep cheerful, Doctor Brook,' she said earnestly. 'But I wish this waiting were over and my baby was born.'

'It will not be long now!' Benjamin replied, his voice a little husky but determinedly professional. 'These next few weeks will soon pass. Now I really must be going, Miss Foster. I shall see you next month and hopefully it will be better weather by then and the garden will be filled with the first daffodils.'

He stood up and turned to Mary, who was hovering nearby with his black physician's bag.

'Take good care of her, Mary!' he said, and unobserved by Clementine, he slipped a sovereign into the girl's hand. 'Buy your young mistress some little treat with it,' he said in an undertone. 'I dare say she does not get much spoiling.'

Mary was still smiling roundly as she returned from showing the physician out of the rectory.

'He be a real nice genulman do Doctor, surely,' she commented as she put another coal on the meagre fire. 'And I tell 'ee, Miss Clementine, as sure as ducks is ducks, he be sweet on you.'

Clementine frowned and then laughed.

'You are just being romantic and silly, Mary,' she chided affectionately.

Mary's mouth set in a stubborn line.

'I know what I sees – and it ain't no mistake, Miss Clementine. And he be the marryin' age and needin' a wife and there bain't many young ladies round these parts for him to choose from. Just you wait, Miss Clementine. He'll be proposing for you after that little 'un of yourn is come, mark my words.'

'Well, I am paying no attention to them, Mary,' Clementine said laughing. 'Even if you were right and he did propose, how could I marry him when . . .' She caught her breath, realizing with horror how very nearly she had broken her vow never to speak of her marriage to Percy to a living soul this side of the Atlantic Ocean. Hastily, she searched her mind for a completion of her remark to Mary: '. . . when you know that nothing in the world will stop me going to join Papa and Mama,' she improvised.

Mary sighed as she tucked the ever-errant wisps of red hair back beneath her mob-cap.

''Tis a pity, all the same. I reckon as how Doctor Brook 'ud be a right good husband – and handsome, too!'

'I shall tell your Jack you have eyes for another man!' Clementine teased.

Mary blushed and giggled and, still tut-tutting, left her young mistress alone whilst she went downstairs to help Cook prepare tea.

CHAPTER FIVE

May 1831

Dawn had still not broken when at four o'clock on a Friday morning in mid-May, Clementine sat waiting in the dark hall of the rectory for the sound of the physician's pony and trap. A tearful Mary stood beside her.

'Master and Mistress will be down directly,' she remarked, sniffing as the tears dropped down her cheeks. 'Oh, Miss Clementine, I'm not 'alf a-goin' to miss you.'

'I will write to you, Mary, I promise – as often as I can,' Clementine said huskily.

The maid's tears ran even faster.

'You be forgettin' as 'ow I can't read,' she muttered reproachfully.

Clementine stood up and put her arm around the girl's shoulders.

'I know, Mary, but I will send the letters to Doctor Brook and he will read them to you and write to tell me your news, too. I shall be wanting to hear all about it when you marry your Jack.'

Mary's tears ceased and she smiled.

'Now you is a-goin' away, Miss Clementine, Jack and me decided as 'ow we wouldn't wait no longer to get wed. 'Appen we'll 'ave the banns called next Sunday. Then after we be wed, I'll give in my notice.'

Clementine nodded, well aware that the maid had only stayed on so long at The Rectory because of her.

Both girls looked up as the parson came down the stairs carrying his candle, his wife a dark shadow behind him.

'Ah, my dear, you are all ready to go!' he remarked, his eyes glancing uneasily from the small figure in the shabby over-long mantle her aunt had given her, to the pitifully small box by her side containing her belongings. Any further remarks were cut short by the arrival of the physician. As Mary went to open the door, Clementine crossed to the foot of the stairs, looking up unhappily at her aunt's rigidly averted face. A week ago, her uncle had informed her that she was to be sent away now that the birth of her child was imminent. His embarrassment was all too obvious, and she had not needed to be told that it was on her Aunt Winifred's insistence that she must leave. Her first feelings of shock and dismay were quickly allayed when she heard that the physician and not her aunt had made the arrangements. Doctor Brook had called on her next day and assured her that she would receive an uncritical welcome from a certain Miss Fothergill in whose house she would be living.

But although in one way Clementine was thankful beyond measure to be leaving the rectory, this unhappy household was her one link with her papa's relations, and now her heart filled with bitterness at the thought that at this moment of parting, almost a year to the day since her arrival at The Rectory, her aunt's dislike of her had not abated.

As Doctor Brook greeted her uncle, Clementine realized that in but a few minutes, she would be on her way and she would never see this house again. With an effort, she found her voice:

'I want to thank you for looking after me this past year, Aunt Winifred,' she said with difficulty. 'I am sorry that I have been such a trouble to you and I am grateful to you for allowing me to remain here until now.'

There was no softening of Winifred Foster's stern visage as she said coldly:

'No thanks to me, my girl! Had I had my way, you would not have spent one single night under my roof after your downfall . . .' She looked pointedly at Clementine's bulky figure and added: 'That child of the Devil will be your punishment, mark my words – and that bastard child will be the cross you will bear. Get out of my house and take your sin with you.'

Neither the parson's muttered protest nor the physician's shocked face halted Aunt Winifred's diatribe. Hurriedly, Doctor Brook took Clementine's arm and hastened her out of the house. In silence he helped her into the trap, and climbing up beside her, he took up the reins.

Clementine did not turn her head to see if her uncle and aunt had come to the door to watch her departure. She kept her eyes on Mary's dumpy figure as the maid stood in the driveway wiping her eyes with her apron until the trap turned out into the lane.

A heavy dew covered the fields on either side of the road. They glimmered a ghostly white in the half-darkness that preceded the dawn. This early departure was due to the fact that her uncle was determined no one should see and recognize her. Too many questions might be asked, he had attempted to explain a few days earlier, were she to be seen travelling on the Poole road with the physician.

Benjamin glanced at the face of the girl beside him and was relieved to see that her aunt's cruel words of parting had not reduced her to tears. Clementine's small bonneted head was held high as she looked towards the east where the first delicate streaks of pink heralded the rising sun.

Noting his eyes upon her, Clementine smiled.

'I can scarcely believe I shall never have to set eyes on that horrible house again,' she said, her face clouding momentarily as she added: 'Nor ever again speak to my aunt.'

'You must try to forget her!' Benjamin said quietly, although he knew it would be a very long time before he himself would do so. 'Why, in ten or twelve weeks' time, you will be sailing across the sea to your parents.'

The trap lurched suddenly as the pony swerved, startled by a badger making its way home to its sett.

'In the meanwhile,' he added, as he steadied the pony, 'I have little doubt that you will like Miss Fothergill and be happy lodging with her.'

To pass the time, he told her about his former patient.

'She is the very soul of kindness, as of course might be expected of an active member of the Friendly Society. The sect are dedicated to providing relief and sustenance for the poor, and the number of lives Miss Fothergill and those like her have saved is beyond my reckoning. She is now in her late sixties, but despite her age, she is busy from dawn to dusk and seems quite tireless.'

He promised her that she would find the old lady as different from her aunt as it was possible to imagine.

This indeed proved to be the case, Clementine thought, when the moment came for Miss Fothergill to welcome her guests into her neat, cheerful front parlour. She was chirruping and smiling as she chattered and fussed around them. Tiny, round, rosy-cheeked and plump, she reminded Clementine of a robin redbreast.

'Any friend of dear Doctor Brook is welcome in my house,' she said, as she sent her maidservant off to the kitchen to make tea. Clementine's heart warmed to the old lady and the welcome raised her spirits instantly.

'And how have you been keeping, Doctor dear?' Miss Fothergill asked, as she assisted Benjamin out of his cloak and moved a footstool near to his chair so that he could stretch out in comfort. 'I have so often hoped that your affairs might bring you to Poole, and now I have had the pleasure of two visits from you in as many weeks! I shall never forget how kind you were to me and my sister that terrible winter when we were both smitten with chills and fever. No one could have been more attentive,' she added, turning back to Clementine.

Clementine smiled.

'I have no difficulty in believing you, Miss Fothergill. Doctor Brook has been caring for me this past eight months and before, when I was ill with the scarlatina.'

'So . . . we will have breakfast shortly,' the old lady said. 'I am sure you must be hungry. But first I want to say how pleased I am that Doctor Brook has brought you here, my dear, to keep an old maid company. I have arranged for you to have the guest room which used to be my sister's before she passed away, poor soul; and in due course the baby shall have the dressing-room adjoining, unless of course, you prefer to have it with you? Now I will go and tell my maid, Jennie, to prepare a good hot meal for you both.'

She hurried out of the room before Clementine or Benjamin could protest. Benjamin looked at Clementine and smiled.

'I told you you would take to Miss Fothergill,' he said.

He did not add that, unlike Winifred Foster, Miss Fothergill was prepared to welcome Clementine even although – like Benjamin himself – she supposed her to be unmarried and the coming child illegitimate. It had been agreed between them that they would give her the courtesy title of Mrs Foster, lest she should feel at a disadvantage.

Any fears Clementine had secretly nursed were swept aside as the three of them sat down to a hearty breakfast. The meal proved a surprisingly jolly occasion, and Benjamin was delighted to see the look of strain leave Clementine's face as she realized that the warmth of Miss Fothergill's welcome was unfeigned.

Nevertheless when the time came for Benjamin to leave, Clementine's smile vanished and she felt a moment of sadness which bordered on panic. For almost a year, Doctor Brook had proved himself in every way to be the best friend that anyone could wish for in times of trouble. She had found it all too easy to lean upon his strength, take his advice, allow him to manage everything for her without fear that the outcome might fail. Now she wanted very much to be able to show her gratitude. But suitable words would not come, and impulsively she crossed the room and, standing on tiptoe, kissed his cheek. It was a kiss she might have given her dear papa on receipt of a gift from him, a child's embrace. But as she heard the quick intake of his breath, she was suddenly overcome by the forwardness of her behaviour and her cheeks flamed. Miss Fothergill, pretending not to notice the tension between the two young people, tactfully covered their mutual embarrassment with more of her chatter.

'You need have no worries concerning this dear girl,' she said to Benjamin, putting an arm around Clementine's shoulders. 'I shall send Jennie to advise you the first moment your patient shows signs that she is about to bring her little treasure into the world.'

As the maid conducted him to the front door, Miss Fothergill turned to Clementine:

'He is one of the dearest, kindest men I know!' she said. 'And I owe him a great deal more than I may have led you to believe. My poor sister was very ill and in great pain for some while before she passed away. Doctor Brook called *every* day, busy though he always is, and gave her opium to ease her suffering. So you see, child, even had I not taken a fancy to you, I would welcome this opportunity to repay him. Now off you go and Jennie shall help you unpack. When you are refreshed, we shall set about getting to know each other better.'

After the privations, loneliness and boredom at The Rectory, the next two weeks passed so happily for Clementine that she felt she must be living in a dream. But although Doctor Brook had told her that it might be another week before her baby arrived, on the night of the last day of the month, she went into labour. In the early hours of the first of June she gave birth to Deveril Grayshott's son.

Her delight and joy in the advent of her little son was too intense to allow of any other deep emotion. She no longer believed God intended to punish her, for the baby was not only beautiful but perfectly formed and, so Doctor Brook told her, as healthy and bonny an infant as any he had brought into the world.

Miss Fothergill doted upon it. She had arranged for one of the girls from the orphanage to see to Clementine's and the baby's needs until such time as Clementine was allowed out of bed. For two whole weeks, she lay in the warmth and comfort of her room with no more arduous task than to nurse her infant. Doctor Brook called to see her every other day. On one such visit, he told her that he had advised her uncle and aunt of the birth. There was no word of congratulation from Winifred Foster, but somewhat to Clementine's surprise, her uncle drove into Poole to visit her. He brought with him a letter from her mother and a longer one from her papa telling her that she could now begin the journey out to them. She read it in a fever of excitement.

'You are to travel to New York with a suitable companion which your Uncle must arrange,' Papa had written. 'You will be met on your arrival by Mr and Mrs Gordon Matheson, the friends your mother and I encountered on board ship. With astonishing generosity they took your mother and me into their home here in Hamilton on Lake Ontario where we have wintered, as your dear Mama suffered a severe attack of the ague before we could depart to Fort William.

'Happily she is now fully recovered and we are on the point of leaving Hamilton. Mr Matheson is employed by the Hudson's Bay Company, and he has assured me that we may hope to prosper in this developing territory.

'I have today despatched a letter to your Uncle requesting him to advise Mr Matheson in advance of your sailing date. He has business to do in New York which will coincide with your arrival.

'Your Mama and Mrs Matheson have become devoted friends and Mama asks me to tell you that they have two charming daughters only a little older than you. You will therefore be quite at home in their house whilst they find a reliable person with whom you can travel to us at Fort William.'

'It is my intention to go to the shipping office when I leave here,' her uncle told her as she put down the letter. 'I shall I trust be able to arrange a passage for you by the first week of August. Doctor Brook tells me that you will be strong enough to travel by then.'

To her added surprise and delight, he drew out from his pocket a gold hunter watch which he handed to her.

'It is for the boy,' he murmured. 'Keep it safe until he is old enough to have it – a little present from his old uncle, eh?'

Clementine was touched, knowing that the timepiece was a particular treasure. Clearly Aunt Winifred knew nothing of the gift, for her uncle added hurriedly:

'I fear your aunt would not approve. But there, she will not know anything about it. You must take care it is not stolen on the journey, my dear child.'

Clementine's feelings were confused. She had never really liked her uncle, although he was her papa's only brother. No two men could have been less alike, she decided, as dutifully she kissed the proffered cheek. Nevertheless, she was profoundly touched by the gesture, more especially as he had shown kindness not just to her but towards her little son.

But the primary purpose of his visit, he now told her, was to baptize the child. With Miss Fothergill and Jennie witnessing the occasion, he donned his surplice and stole and christened the infant Adam, with the second name of Clement, which Clementine hoped would please her father.

The parson did not stop for tea, but left with the promise that he would visit his niece again shortly.

'And I shall certainly come to Poole to see you safely on board,' he promised. 'In the meanwhile, I am happy to know that you are in such good hands.'

It was, however, Doctor Brook and not her uncle who brought her the news that the parson had been unable to arrange a suitable sailing date from Poole and that it would be necessary for her to embark at Bristol. Furthermore, Doctor

Brook informed Clementine, her uncle had slipped on the path leading from the vestry and fractured his ankle. It would therefore be he who would escort her to Bristol in place of the Rev Foster. Her uncle had written a letter for the physician to give her, enclosing a sum of money which, he said, would pay for her fare and provide for her expenses during the journey.

'There are other monies due to you,' he wrote, 'but I shall remit these directly to your father, together with your marriage lines. I cannot be sure how reliable these new friends of your father's are and I prefer not to entrust such valuables and personal items to your care upon so long and hazardous a journey.'

The physician visited her twice a week and never failed to make encouraging comments. Clementine was a natural mother, he told her when she took over the care of the baby herself. The little boy was gaining weight most satisfactorily and he could see no reason why they should not keep to their planned date of departure for Bristol on the first of the month.

Although Clementine had imagined that this longed-for moment would never come, so great was her impatience, the eight weeks following upon little Adam's birth passed astonishingly quickly.

'Without doubt that is because I have been so very happy during my stay with you, Miss Fothergill,' she said. Both she and the old lady were close to tears when the moment of parting finally came.

Doctor Brook arrived soon after daybreak in his pony and trap, in which, he told her, they would accomplish the first leg of the journey to Wimborne Minster.

The moment of sadness which Clementine felt on leaving the kindly Miss Fothergill was quickly supplanted by excitement when she climbed into the trap and they started upon their way. She felt doubly blessed by the fact that it was

Doctor Brook and not her uncle who was taking her to Bristol. The baby, wrapped warmly in his shawl, slept peacefully in her arms, and was undisturbed by the change on to the coach at the staging inn. It was a beautiful morning, the dew still wet upon the ground as Clementine watched the passing countryside with a feeling of exhilaration.

'How long before we reach Wimborne Minster?' she asked as they slowed to climb a steep hill.

'We should be there within the hour,' Benjamin replied, smiling at her impatience. After a moment's silence, he cleared his throat and said awkwardly: 'Do you not think that having known each other so long, we are now able to look upon one another as friends? It would make me very happy if you would call me Benjamin. Doctor Brook sounds excessively formal, do you not agree?'

'I will try to remember,' she said shyly.

I am twelve years older than this girl, Benjamin thought, suddenly deeply miserable. I have my life to lead and most important of all, my work. I should not allow my heart to be so moved by a mere child!

Yet she no longer looked a child as she sat poised and beautiful beside him, the coach swaying along the rutted road at a fairly fast pace. It was only a small consolation that for the next three days, she was his responsibility; that she must depend upon him until he could place her and the baby in the care of a respectable female travelling companion on board.

It was a comfort of sorts to know that physically Clementine was in perfect health. She had made a remarkably quick recovery from a confinement that had been lengthy but not too difficult, and perhaps because of her youth, she seemed even to have benefited from the experience. She had quite literally blossomed in the two months since the baby's arrival.

Benjamin had been almost as delighted as she by the birth of so pretty and healthy a baby. Not that the boy bore any resemblance to her. He had a smattering of dark hair, and eyes that were nearer grey than the blue of his mother's. They would almost certainly turn brown as he grew older, and the boy would favour his father. Would that please Clementine, he wondered? Did she still secretly harbour a girlish sentimental love for her seducer? If so, the quicker it was dispelled, the better.

'I cannot recall if I have already mentioned the fact,' he said, in as casual a tone as he could achieve, 'but before he died, the Admiral told me that he had agreed a betrothal between Deveril Grayshott and a certain Miss Muriel Lawrence. Of course, with Sir William's death, there can be no marriage until the year of mourning is over, but Lord Burnbury is anxious for his grandson to settle down as soon as he reaches his majority.'

Clementine was totally unprepared for any mention of Deveril, and she was quite unable to withhold a tiny gasp of surprise. In all the many hours she had spent thinking about him, she had never once imagined his marriage to someone else. Despite all logic, the news shocked and wounded her.

'How – how old is he now?' she asked, trying to keep her voice steady.

Not looking at her unhappy face and hating himself for making it so, Benjamin informed her that Deveril lacked but a year to his majority.

'He is a little young for matrimony, I suppose,' he said, more to give his companion time to recover her composure than because he wished to prolong the conversation. 'But I gather Miss Lawrence is older by two or three years. The old Viscount described her as beautiful and accomplished.' He could no longer restrain himself as he turned to look at Clementine and added: 'She cannot be more beautiful than you, Miss Foster, if you will permit me to say so.'

He heard the bitter note in her voice as she attempted a smile.

'Even if you are right, it serves me no purpose, does it?' She glanced down at the sleeping child in her arms. 'Adam may be Deveril Grayshott's child, but if Deveril knows of the fact, he does not nor ever will care. The *beautiful* and *accomplished* Miss Lawrence will doubtless give him many more sons and he will have no interest in my little Adam's existence.'

'Perhaps that is for the best!' Benjamin said gently. 'It will not be long before you will meet some young man out there in Upper Canada and fall in love and marry. I have no doubt of it.'

Clementine sighed.

'I do not think I want to fall in love – ever again,' she said, more to herself than to her companion. 'The condition causes more suffering than joy – or such has been my experience of it.'

Mine too, thought Benjamin, wishing he could find the courage to beg this young girl to marry him. But he knew the futility of doing so. He must try to forget her – as he had advised her to forget young Deveril. He had been foolhardy ever to make mention of Deveril's betrothal.

They had by now reached the outskirts of Wimborne Minster. It was half-past nine in the morning and the sun was climbing upwards into a cloudless blue sky. It was the start of a perfect summer day, and Clementine gazed excitedly at the bustle of traffic making its way towards the pretty little market town. As they crossed over the River Stour, the towers of the beautiful old minster were already visible above the roofs of the houses.

'Believe it or not,' Benjamin said with a smile, 'the minster was once a nunnery, founded in the year 705, I think.' But Clementine had been starved of the sights and sounds of people and she was more interested in the vehicles now sharing the road with them than in the historic old church. It was market day and the narrow street was crowded with wagons, some laden with fruit and vegetables, others with crates of livestock. Tinkers' carts, dogcarts and drays jostled with panniered donkeys and mules, all laden with produce. Farmers' wives and their children herded geese or goats or carried baskets of cheeses or fruit on their shoulders. Dogs of all breeds and sizes barked, fought or ran beside the wagons. Everywhere the simple weather-beaten faces were smiling as people called friendly greetings to one another and exchanged gossip as they walked the last half-mile into town. Their coach slowed to a walking pace behind a farmer who was herding two milk cows with their calves towards the marketplace.

The baby, disturbed by the noises, woke suddenly, and his plaintive hungry cry demanded attention.

'Only a few minutes more, young man, and we shall be at the Crown Inn where you, your mama and I shall breakfast,' Benjamin said with a reassuring smile at Clementine. Thoughtful as always, he paid for her to have the use of a small room in the coaching inn where she could nurse the infant in privacy. The task accomplished, she joined him in the taproom, where other travellers were awaiting the arrival of the stagecoach.

With the baby lying contentedly on the bench beside her, Clementine's youthful hunger made light of the huge platters of food being brought to the tables by the waiters and a serving wench. She had lost a great deal of weight, confined as she had been for nearly a year to the bare minimum of food her Aunt Winifred had allowed her. Benjamin had suspected that his patient, if not exactly on a bread and water diet, had not been adequately fed at The Rectory, and his bitter dislike of Winifred Foster momentarily overwhelmed him.

But now he realized that his compassion for the girl's unhappy past was not necessary. Clementine's face radiated excitement as she watched the stage roll into the yard, enjoying the bustle and activity as the ostlers put fresh horses into the traces. Despite the growing heat of the day, Benjamin decided to book a seat for them inside the coach so that he could enjoy Clementine's company. Her small portmanteau was put on the roof with his own and the other passengers' luggage. Four middle-aged gentlemen, who Benjamin took to be merchants, climbed onto the seats at the back of the coach whilst their wives settled themselves inside with a great deal of chatter and fussing.

As the coach set off northwards towards Blandford Forum, the ladies became bored with their gossip and turned their attention to Clementine's baby. Not unnaturally they assumed as a matter of course that Benjamin was the infant's father. This assumption both pleased and hurt him. He realized that it protected Clementine from the awkward questions that might have been voiced had she denied their supposition, but it grieved him to realize that he did not have the right to give her the protection of his name; to be able to boast proudly that she was his wife.

Benjamin remained preoccupied by such thoughts until they reached Blandford. After a change of horses, they set off once more on the road to Shaftesbury. The heat inside the coach rose alarmingly and the stout merchants' wives began mopping their scarlet faces as the temperature climbed towards the eighties. Only a little air wafted in through the small windows, and they were all delighted to have the chance to disembark for ten minutes whilst the dragsman and the guard manoeuvred the coach past an overturned ox-cart which was blocking the road.

By mid-morning they were climbing the steep hill into Shaftesbury, where they halted briefly for a cup of coffee at the Grosvenor Arms. They were soon upon their way again, passing through the villages of Gillingham and Mere without mishap, but the intensity of the heat, now nearing ninety degrees, was affecting the infant. Clementine was greatly relieved when the coach drew into the yard of the Angel Inn at Warminster. There she was able to relax as she fed the child. He was sleeping peacefully when at three o'clock she went down to the crowded Travellers' Room. Benjamin was sitting in a chair by the window where the barber was shaving him. Whilst waiting for the task to be completed, Clementine sat down at one of the luncheon tables, where finally he joined her.

They began their meal with jellied eels, followed by mutton cutlets with caper sauce. The last vestige of their hunger was satisfied by a liberal helping of trifle and custard and a slice of cheese. Clementine drank only tea, but Benjamin enjoyed a glass of the landlord's best wine. When the coachman's horn sounded, there was a general scramble by the passengers to find coats, cloaks and shawls, pay bills and tip waiters.

The road between Warminster and Bath had been newly macadamed, which multiplied the speed of the coach that was now taking them towards Bath. But the number of passengers had multiplied, and there were now six travellers wedged inside and twice as many on top. As a consequence, the low-slung coach was top-heavy and it tipped alarmingly each time they rounded a corner. Clementine's fears for her child increased as one of the ladies recounted in great detail how her husband had suffered a broken leg not a week since on this very stretch of road, and that the coachman, poor fellow, had broken his neck when the stage had overturned. Benjamin put a protective arm around Clementine's shoulders and assured her that there was no real cause for fear unless a horse bolted or a wheel came loose from its axle.

Clementine was growing very tired as they covered the last of the nineteen miles into Bath. There was no breath of air and the atmosphere was suffocatingly oppressive. By the time they drove up to the Lamb Inn, the first heavy drops of rain had begun to fall.

'How long shall we remain here?' she asked Benjamin, adding ruefully: 'I had not thought this journey would be so tiring. When Mama and Papa took me from Bristol to The Rectory, we travelled in our own carriage and seemed to go much faster.'

Benjamin noted the girl's pale face with some concern. After the birth of her child, it was only natural that she should tire quickly.

'We will make better time to Bristol,' he told her. 'It is but thirteen miles and I have booked seats for us on one of the

London mails. They can travel at fourteen miles an hour on these roads, so we should make good speed.'

Clementine smiled, reflecting yet again on how lucky she was to be travelling with someone who always seemed able to reassure her. She looked with interest at the Bristol mail with its gleaming black-and-maroon coachwork and mud-bespattered scarlet wheels. Benjamin drew her attention to the royal arms painted on the doors and the chivalric orders – Bath, Garter, Thistle and St Patrick – painted on the panels flanking the windows. The guards wore top hats and frogged scarlet coats. One of them was pushing a live goose into the boot beneath his seat.

Seeing Clementine's astonished face, Benjamin laughed.

'I do not doubt there is a lot else in there beside that fowl,' he whispered. 'The guards receive very low wages and doubt-less the goose will be sold at a profit when we reach Bristol. The last time I travelled on the mail to Brighton to see my father, one of the guards stopped the coach, shot a pheasant and later picked off a hare as we crossed the South Downs. All the guards carry blunderbusses, cutlasses and pistols to repel highwaymen, but I fancy the weapons are more often required for bagging game.'

The coachman was now urging the passengers to hurry, explaining that the mails must arrive on time and delays now would have to be made up if they dallied.

Although the severity of the rain lessened as they left Bath behind them, it was by now nearing sunset and by the time they drew into the courtyard of the Talbot, darkness had fallen and only a few people were wandering about the cobbled streets of Bristol.

Clementine had fallen asleep against Benjamin's shoulder, and he had to wake her before she could alight from the coach and follow him sleepily into the bustling inn. Yet again it was assumed they were husband and wife, and the innkeeper looked at him oddly when Benjamin demanded two separate bedrooms in which to spend the night.

Clementine was too exhausted to notice or to care, and she declined to take dinner with Benjamin. The baby was stirring in her arms and she was grateful when a sleepy-eyed chambermaid led her to a bedroom where she could feed her little son undisturbed. Undressing quickly, she climbed between the sheets, taking the small replete infant with her, and fell into a deep slumber.

The following day when she awoke, clouds had swept in from the sea; the cobbled streets were shining and the gutters were awash with dirt and refuse as the rainwater swept them downwards towards the harbour. From her window, she could see the top masts of the sailing ships moored there, and a smile lit up her face. Bristol was home – the harbour dear and familiar; and the ships were her future, for on one of them she would sail to her new life and her beloved parents.

Hastily seeing to the baby's needs, she dressed and hurried downstairs to find Benjamin already at breakfast. He smiled a greeting.

'You look well refreshed!' he told her, astonished at how quickly she had recovered from the long journey, 'and impatient, no doubt, for me to go out and arrange your passage. I shall go down to the shipping offices as soon as I have eaten.'

'Perhaps I shall embark today,' she said eagerly.

'It is possible,' Benjamin said doubtfully. 'But I will go now and ascertain the facts of the matter.'

Clementine would have accompanied him but for his insistence that she must enjoy a good breakfast – if not for her own sake, then for the child's. He left her tucking into cold mutton, kidneys, ham, the landlady's best eel pie and hot muffins straight from the ovens.

The morning passed pleasantly enough as Clementine sat at the window of her room staring down into the busy street below. The whole world seemed to be passing by beneath her – ladies in fine clothes and bonnets, gentlemen in top hats and gaiters, sailors, washerwomen with laundry baskets on their arms, pedlars with trays of trinkets, Romanies in bright skirts and shawls with clusters of children around them. There were milk and bakers' carts and a big dray bringing ale to the inn with four huge horses pulling the heavy wagon into the courtyard. There were carriages, too – coaches, carts, phaetons, gigs – all seeming in an excessive hurry as if there were not a moment to lose.

Not far distant she could see the beautiful fifteenth-century tower of the church of St Stephen. As it chimed out the midday hour she was reminded of the many times her mama had taken her there. It also reminded her that Doctor Brook – Benjamin – was not yet back. What difficulties was he encountering to take him so long?

Impatiently, she made the baby comfortable upon the big feather bed and went downstairs to the Travellers' Room to make certain that the physician was not awaiting her there.

Benjamin came in from the street as she appeared. As he opened the door, the sunshine streamed in behind him. Clementine ran over to him with more eagerness than propriety in so public a place.

'What news have you? You have been so long. Is all well?' she demanded urgently.

Smiling, Benjamin removed his top hat and gloves and drew Clementine into the comparative seclusion of the parlour.

As soon as they were both seated, he said:

'It is all arranged! You will sail tomorrow on a passenger packet-ship to Halifax. Moreover, I have found you an escort.'

He subdued the longing to cover Clementine's hands with his as she clasped them together in excitement, her eyes dancing with pleasure.

'And who is this lady I am to travel with?' she enquired. 'Did you meet her? Will I like her? Does she object that I have a baby?'

The questions poured from her, making it impossible for him to ignore the fact that she cared not one whit about the impending parting from *him*.

'She is a delightful lady with two small children of her own.

She suggested very kindly that I should place you in her care immediately – they are staying at the White Hart. If you would care to take advantage of her offer, I will settle your account and conduct you to her this afternoon.'

Clementine regarded him with sudden anxiety.

'Oh, but I thought you would remain with me until I sailed . . .' she faltered, breaking off abruptly and then adding, 'but of course I'm being very selfish. You have a long journey back and your practice to think of.'

Benjamin grinned – a smile of boyish pleasure that suddenly made him seem far younger than his twenty-eight years.

'It is quite a novelty for me to play truant,' he said sincerely. 'One more day will scarcely matter – at least, I trust not. As far as I am aware, none of my patients is at death's door! I shall be happy to remain here until you sail!'

Clementine's face revealed her pleasure.

'Now I will have time to take you to see my old home,' she said happily. 'You have said you are not familiar with this lovely city and there is so much to show you . . .'

She prattled on contentedly, charming and delighting him until she recalled her child and the need to satisfy his hunger.

'For a little while, I had almost forgot I was a mother!' she confessed. 'Perhaps being back here in Bristol, I have reverted to being a child again. Oh, if you only knew how deeply I long to see Mama and Papa!'

Clementine's devotion to her parents became more apparent to him as they toured the city together, walking like any married couple with their child along the sunny streets, looking in the shop windows where Clementine stopped to admire the latest fashions.

As they walked back to the inn, Clementine was deep in thought. It had been a happy afternoon and even the memory of Deveril could not lessen her high spirits. Sighing to herself, she wished that she could have fallen in love with her delightful companion instead of the heir to the Grayshott estate.

But the practical, honest side of Clementine's nature allowed such imaginings to go no further. She did not love Benjamin, nice as he was. Her legs did not tremble when he smiled at her or spoke to her. She felt no stirring of her heart when he looked into her eyes.

Her thoughts turned to Adam. Since his birth, his hair had thickened and darkened and his eyes were now brown. He was going to be just like his father, thus making the man she loved even harder to forget. But she was about to leave England and Deveril for ever, she reminded herself. Soon she would begin a new life in a new country and hopefully, the thought of Deveril would fade from her mind.

She awoke the following morning to yet another sunny day and forgot everything but the fact that she must make haste to feed her baby and pack her few belongings. Immediately after breakfast, Benjamin was to take her in a hackney cab down to the shipping office to collect her ticket and proceed to the dock. They were to meet her escort on board the *Endurance* at eleven o'clock. An hour later they would sail on the noonday tide.

In contrast to Clementine's radiant spirits, Benjamin's were never lower as the cab drew to a halt outside the shipping office. In less than three hours' time he would be bidding Clementine farewell for ever, and it was unlikely they would ever meet again.

The same clerk who had attended him the previous day recognized him immediately. Regarding Benjamin over his spectacles, he said:

'I have been awaiting your return, Sir. Unfortunately I did not know where you and the young lady were lodging, or I would have forwarded this to you.' He retrieved a letter from the shelf beneath the counter. 'This was brought here yesterday by a country lad. He had been travelling post-haste from Dorset, I think he said. I understood it was most urgent and quite imperative that you should receive it before the young lady embarked.'

He handed the letter to Benjamin who looked at it anxiously.

He recognized the painstakingly formed script as being the hand of the parson. He felt his heartbeat quicken. Whatever the contents of this letter, he was certain that they were ill tidings for Clementine.

Relieved to see that she was still sitting quietly in a chair by the window with her baby and unaware of anything untoward, he tore open the letter and began to read:

'Dear Sir,

I pray to God this letter reaches you in time to forestall my Niece's departure to North America. With a measure of Good Fortune, the messenger I am despatching immediately on the next stage will reach Bristol before my Niece sets sail . . .

. . . It cannot have been more than an hour after your departure from Poole that a letter arrived here from the London offices of the Hudson's Bay Company, advising me of the deaths of my Brother and his Wife.'

Benjamin paused and glanced anxiously at Clementine. Then hurriedly, his eyes scanned the next paragraph of the parson's letter.

'. . . I will not go into the sad details here since Time is of the utmost importance if this letter is to be delivered before it is too late.

I shall rely on you to break this tragic news to my Niece as gently as possible. Of course, she can no longer travel to North America.'

The letter concluded with a desperate plea to Benjamin to use his influence with Miss Fothergill to allow his niece to return there, at least until sufficient time had elapsed to permit her to go back to The Rectory as a respectably married woman.

Benjamin's heart sank. That Clementine's parents had died so tragically was a terrible enough blow. But her eventual return to The Rectory where she had been so unhappy, so reviled by her aunt, was an unbearable thought.

She looked up as he approached her, her eyes bright with anticipation.

'You have my ticket, Doctor Brook? We may leave now for the quay?'

There had been many occasions in the past when Benjamin had had to impart dreadful news to a patient, but never before had be been at a loss for words.

Clementine stared at his anguished face and her own paled.

'What is it, Doctor Brook? Can not I go today after all? Do not be afraid to tell me. I can find strength to bear a short delay.'

Benjamin sat down beside her and took one of her hands in his.

'Oh, my dear!' he whispered. 'If it were only the short delay you imagine! Clementine, you will have to be very brave, very brave indeed. I can think of no kind way to soften the blow this news will be to you. No one knows better than I how greatly you have counted upon this reunion with your parents. But I have to tell you – it is not to be.'

CHAPTER SIX

July 1831

Deveril Grayshott sat watching the rise and fall of his fiancée's bosom as she stood by the rosewood piano singing the Scottish air, 'Bonnie Mary of Argyll'. It was a haunting melody, but his attention was wandering nonetheless as he studied his future bride.

Muriel Lawrence's figure was statuesque, he decided, noting the elegant lift of her head, her proud stance. Her hazel eyes were fastened on some unseen object at the far end of the room. Her chestnut hair was drawn back from the high forehead and coiled into a knot on top of her head. Tight ringlets covered her ears and reached down to a chin that was sharply pointed. Her evening gown of flowered green silk revealed white, smooth, unusually broad shoulders and the long column of her neck. Cream lace bordered the hem of the full skirt and a posy of cream flowers was fastened between her breasts. She was singing effortlessly, perfectly in tune but without emotion.

There was little doubting that she presented a striking figure. If fault there was in her appearance, it was her height. She was unusually tall, head and shoulders taller than Deveril's sister, Selina, who was their hostess this evening. But this did not particularly disturb Deveril, who was six foot three and therefore untroubled by the feelings of inferiority shorter men might suffer when partnering Muriel in a dance.

Deveril had known Muriel since childhood. Living as they both did in Grosvenor Square, the two families were frequent visitors to one another's houses, with Muriel a welcome friend of his four sisters. He himself had not much cared for the tall, thin, angular girl who had struck him as far too dictatorial, especially since all but his youngest sister, Grace, were Muriel's superior in age. Provided her companions fell in with her wishes, she was sweet-tempered and agreeable, but left no one in doubt of her displeasure if she was thwarted. Deveril's sisters, easy-going and used to sharing, put up with this side of Muriel's character for the sake of having someone new in their circle. Moreover, Muriel was far better able to sway their governess and obtain privileges not granted in her absence.

An only child, it was hardly surprising that Muriel was spoiled by her parents. Lord and Lady Lawrence welcomed the companionship offered to their beloved daughter and frequently permitted her to go on holiday with the Grayshott children to Castle Clunes, Viscount Burnbury's Scottish estate in Perthshire.

Deveril had tended not to join in his sisters' pursuits when Muriel was there, preferring the company of the gillie who took him salmon fishing or the keeper who would put up some game for an hour or two's rough shooting over the moors. If the weather were inclement, he would visit his beloved and eccentric Aunt Meg in her suite of rooms. His great-aunt had been married at seventeen to Lord Alastair McDoone, a Highland army officer who was killed within the year during the American War of Independence. When her home in the Highlands passed to her late husband's brother, Lady McDoone had moved south to take up residence in Castle Clunes. She had never remarried and her thwarted maternal instincts were redirected to her four great-nieces and Deveril; and when they were absent in London or Dorset, to her extraordinary menagerie of animals. Not only did she keep half a dozen deerhounds and a Manx cat, but a multitude of exotic birds which she had had imported from overseas. She kept, too, a marmoset and a pair of red squirrels, which were always getting loose from their cages and running amok in her apartments to the servants' horror.

Deveril smiled, remembering the ceremonies his great-aunt had performed when any of her pets had died, burying them herself with great formality in the animal graveyard she had begun fifty years earlier in the castle grounds.

Muriel's song had come to its conclusion and Deveril joined in the applause. When she began again with a sentimental rendering of 'The Blue Bells of Scotland', his thoughts wandered once more to his childhood. Muriel had never quite understood Aunt Meg, whose lack of conventionality had confused her. The old lady refused to wear fashionable attire. She appeared in clothes more befitting an ancient Highland crone, a plaid shawl over a voluminous woollen skirt which more often than not was covered with dog and cat hairs.

Deveril had seen the little girl wrinkling up her nose in ill-disguised disgust. She seemed quite unable to understand the family's affection for the old lady, whom clearly she found repulsive.

But since she had been presented and come out in Society, Muriel had changed beyond recognition, Deveril told himself, shrugging off the unwelcome memory of their childhood. The lanky, uncoordinated girl had emerged as a singularly beautiful woman and, so Deveril understood from his grandfather, had been proposed for by several most eligible suitors. He had been astonished and mildly flattered to hear that for some reason he did not yet understand, the handsome Muriel had set her heart upon *him*. As far as he was aware, she had never taken the slightest interest in him during their childhood, and it was only since he himself had reached manhood that Muriel had shown any pleasure in his company. He had met her on several occasions in recent years at parties and balls, where he had dutifully danced with her and had been surprised by her friendly, even coquettish manner.

Muriel, so he now learned from his grandfather, had fallen in very readily – even enthusiastically – with the two families' desire to unite themselves by her marriage to him. It was a plan which had been kept from him, although Muriel seemed to have been informed of it several years previously. Deveril was at first very far from happy about it. It was not so much marriage to Muriel which appalled him, as marriage to anyone. Not yet twenty-one, he had looked forward to a good many carefree bachelor years, enjoying himself with his many male friends. Now he realized uneasily that whilst he could continue to enjoy many of his pursuits after marriage, he would no longer have the freedom to depart on the whim of the moment to wherever pleasure beckoned. Nor, he suspected, would Muriel approve of his gambling until sunrise or enjoying a week in the company of a paramour at Brighton.

It was not unusual for married ladies to have lovers, albeit discreetly, but even his sister Selina had complained to him that Muriel was a little too narrow-minded for her taste – and always looked immensely disapproving when her friends told bawdy stories or related some gossip about a lusty love affair. Deveril did not harbour the slightest wish to have his 'fun' curtailed by a puritanical wife, but he understood his grandfather's anxieties.

'I am only four years short of eighty, my boy,' the old man had said. 'And you are my sole heir. I cannot die happily without being assured of the next generation . . .'

Deveril's initial dismay was tempered by the realization that the succession of the title was indeed precariously poised. It was not as if poor Percy could ever produce an heir. And if he himself were to die, then the Grayshott name would lapse with his grandfather.

Deveril's thoughts had brought him full circle back to the figure of his future bride. Perhaps, he decided, there were compensations for the loss of his freedom. Muriel was undoubtedly beautiful and would grace his house and his table. She was young, strong, healthy, and would give him children. Her upbringing was such that she would take her future place as Lady Burnbury with ease. His friends would admire her and even envy him his choice of wife. Not least, of course, were the huge financial benefits that would ultimately derive from the marriage. Muriel was Lord Lawrence's only surviving child, and everything the old peer owned would one day be hers. The generous dowry Muriel was to bring with her meant that Deveril could indulge to the full his desire to improve the Dorset estate.

Chiswell Hill House was in excellent order, but the condition of some of the farm cottages was a disgrace. Even Deveril, whose thoughts were more often than not concerned with his amusements, had been unable to ignore the dilapidation of one of the labourer's homes when he had taken refuge there in a storm one day last summer. He had been made sufficiently uneasy by the state of the leaking hovel to ride out next day with the bailiff to inspect the other cottages. But Deveril's father, whose thoughts seemed always confined to naval matters, had declared himself uninterested in the rioting of the farm labourers in nearby villages who were living in similar conditions.

Since Sir William's death, Deveril had persuaded his grandfather to increase the wages of their farm workers from six shillings a week to eight, but the Viscount had adamantly refused to better their working and living conditions. Although the old man had been horrified to hear of the burning of hayricks and the destruction of machinery by men so close to Chiswell, he insisted that *their* tenants would never behave like ruffians and hooligans. Deveril himself could see no reason why they should not do so.

'The unrest is widespread,' he had said. 'I think it is foolhardy to ignore these uprisings. Surely we do not want to find ourselves forced to follow their example and be obliged to call in special constables and the yeomanry to keep our ricks from burning.'

''Twas naught but a storm in a teacup, m'boy!' said his grandfather, dismissing the topic.

In fact, last summer's riots had for the most part died down by December, but Deveril believed that his grandfather and their unenlightened neighbours would very soon have to adopt his own belief that reforms were long overdue.

'Why so thoughtful, my dear?'

Muriel's voice broke in on his reflections and he sprang quickly to his feet, embarrassed by the fact that he had not joined in the applause when her song ended, nor even been aware of her approach.

'I was quite carried away by the tune you sang so sweetly,' he improvised quickly. 'My spirit was roaming the Scottish moors, where you and I holidayed in our childhood!'

Mollified as much by his words as by his charming smile, Muriel Lawrence allowed him to lead her to a sofa where they could speak more privately. She herself had engineered this evening's little dinner party, persuading Deveril's sister, Lady Selina Allendale, to invite them both to what served as a small, unofficial engagement party. Owing to the death of the Admiral, there could be no public engagement, and Deveril was not appearing at the Season's social functions in deference to his parent's demise. Muriel's opportunities for seeing him had therefore been greatly curtailed.

Very much aware of his admiring gaze, she smiled at him with genuine affection. He was looking very distinguished, she thought, in a black dress-coat and tight black kerseymere trousers which accentuated his tall, slim figure. His violet satin waistcoat was his only deviation from these mourning clothes – a weakness Muriel could understand, since Deveril was known to be somewhat of a dandy and was usually attired in the very height of fashion. It excited her to see him in this unaccustomed formal dress, so different from the way she remembered him best, striding bareheaded across the moors in a kilt or seated on his big chestnut gelding, his green hunting coat bespattered with mud, his top hat at a rakish angle, his young, laughing face aglow with the excitement of the chase.

Did Deveril return her interest? she wondered, as she replied to his polite enquiries about her family. She was reasonably certain that he did not as yet return her love. For she did love him – of that she was in no doubt. There was something challenging in his wild, adventurous nature which appealed to her. So used to obtaining her own way, spoiled by an adoring father and dominant over her weak-willed mother, Muriel respected only those she believed to be stronger than herself. Deveril, she sensed, could not be moulded, bent to her will, or ever become a supplicant. Young though he was, he showed the self-confidence of a man many years his senior, and she had never yet known him at a loss in any situation.

She would have felt happier this evening had he shown signs of falling prey to her beauty. She had sat beside him at dinner and set out to charm him. But he had not yet referred in any way to their betrothal, although her father had assured her that it was definite. She would not feel entirely secure until they were actually married, she thought, as she fanned her hot cheeks and listened to Deveril's voice telling her about his father. He made only passing reference to his younger brother, Percy, whom he clearly adored. She knew that the boy was an invalid and never left the Dorset estate.

Sensing her lack of interest, he talked instead of horses, a subject in which he knew Muriel to be as absorbed as himself. It was an interest they would have in common in their marriage, he thought with some relief, for he could see little by way of others. Her enthusiasms lay mainly in Society, he decided, as she told him with shining eyes:

'I have recently made the acquaintance of the Russian Ambassador's wife, Princess Lieven. She, as you may know, Deveril, is one of the patronesses who rule Almack's.'

Only by invitation of one of the five patronesses could any member of Society attend these weekly balls at the Assembly Rooms in St James's. Deveril was aware that such invitations were greatly sought after, since they established the social standing of the recipient.

He himself had several times received vouchers and put in an appearance at these Wednesday gatherings, principally because they afforded a young man the opportunity to meet the current season's debutantes. But he found the rigid rules governing these balls excessively tiresome, for it was forbidden to arrive after half past eleven (after which time only Members of Parliament were allowed in) and since he and his friends were frequently still at the gaming tables or in their clubs till this hour, they often left it too late and were refused admittance.

Deveril shrugged.

'I confess I consider the food and drink served at Almack's to be of an indifferent standard,' he said, adding frankly, 'and the rigid formality observed is not exactly to my taste.'

Muriel, however, was clearly overcome with pleasure at the thought of being allowed to help the Princess on Mondays, when the vouchers for hundreds of applicants who craved the honour of selection were sorted and either allocated or refused. Muriel was always invited, being on the Princess's visiting list – a necessary prerequisite for any aspirant of the *haut ton*. Despite this, Deveril thought, she sounded surprisingly concerned with matters concerning her prestige, and inordinately proud of the fact that the Princess considered her to be one of the beauties of the day.

Deveril gave no such importance to *his* popularity. He had no need, for his good looks, his charm and his laughing good humour made him a welcome guest in any household. If his reputation was slightly that of a 'rake', in no way did it debar him from Society.

His mind had wandered once again from Muriel's bright chatter. But now she was tugging gently at his sleeve and her voice had a pleading note.

'You will be in London for the King's coronation in September, will you not, Deveril?' she was saying persuasively. 'Papa has promised we may delay our departure to our house in Buckinghamshire until after the event.'

Deveril tried hard to conceal his lack of enthusiasm for such a proposal. He had little desire to forgo his sporting activities in order to sit for hours watching the pomp and ceremony of a coronation.

'It may not be possible for me to attend, Muriel. I have already invited a number of friends to join me for a month at Castle Clunes for the start of the grouse shooting.'

Muriel's smooth white forehead was creased momentarily by a slight frown. Her mouth looked sulky. She hated Scotland, disliking the cold climate almost as much as she disliked Castle Clunes, situated as it was miles from anywhere civilized in the wilds of Perthshire. She always recalled with distaste the seemingly endless week-long journeys to and from the north, and the even more distasteful, eccentric old great-aunt whose animals frightened her and offended her with their dirty feet and unpleasant odours. Only the companionship of Deveril's sisters had enticed her to holiday with them, and as she grew older and her circle of friends in London increased, she quickly ceased her sojourns at Castle Clunes.

She had no desire, therefore, to hint now to Deveril that she might be included in his shooting party. She glanced at him prettily – a look which seldom failed to move her papa to comply with her wishes.

'But surely there is yet time to alter such arrangements? Won't your grandfather be taking his place in the Abbey? Papa has said he can certainly arrange for us to see the procession from the stands in Parliament Square . . .'

'I fear my grandfather may not be well enough to attend, Muriel,' Deveril broke in gently. 'He has been far from well of late. My father's death in February was a great shock to him. He was his only son, you see, and although Father was so often away at sea, Grandfather was deeply attached to him.'

Muriel's frown quickly softened to a compassionate smile.

'Oh, I do understand, and I am so very sorry, Deveril. I trust you received my letter of condolence at the time?' Her voice was warm with sympathy. 'We would have attended your papa's funeral but for the terrible weather which precluded our travelling so long a journey. Nevertheless, my thoughts were entirely with you that day. It made me miserable just to think of *your* unhappiness.'

Deveril preferred not to recall the bitterly cold morning in Chiswell Church graveyard when his father's coffin had been carried to the family vault, the few mourners huddled in black cloaks against the biting north wind. The Rev Foster and their own chaplain had hurried through the service, eyes streaming and faces pinched with cold. Knowing as Deveril did how anxious his father had always been to be buried at sea, the whole ceremony had struck him as horrifying, its only redeeming feature being that the Admiral was at last rejoining his beloved wife, whose body had lain in the vault for the past ten years.

The ordeal had proved almost too much for his grand-father, and Deveril had had to send for the physician on the following day to give the old man a physic to restore him. Brook had always struck him as being a pleasant, competent fellow but on this occasion he was strangely reserved. He had politely but firmly refused Deveril's offer of hospitality which had puzzled him, seeing that it was not every day a country physician could expect to be invited to partake of a drink at Chiswell Hill House.

'It was most kind of your sister to arrange this small dinner party for us, Deveril,' Muriel said beside him. 'Selina, of course, is very devoted to you. But then so are all your dear sisters. They spoiled you dreadfully when we were children!'

Deveril smiled, relieved to have his thoughts diverted from his father's funeral.

Poor Muriel, he thought affectionately, wondering suddenly whether that affection might deepen into love. Romance did not normally attend the kind of fleeting relationships he and his companions enjoyed with women.

Now he found himself wondering how sweet a bedfellow his future wife would make. It was difficult to imagine the stately Muriel *en déshabillé*. Her hips were wide and rounded, but her bosom was somewhat lacking in comparison. Devoid of the excessive width of the shoulders of her dress, her breasts and hips might almost seem disproportioned.

Deveril concealed an inward chuckle as he realized he had been assessing his fiancée's physical attributes much as he might have judged a filly's. How scandalized she would be if she knew! He wondered how innocent she was of men's bodies. He supposed that like his own sisters prior to matrimony, Muriel was completely ignorant as to what the marriage bed would mean. Some women, he knew, enjoyed this very pleasurable side of nature. But others did not. Deveril could only assume it was entirely a matter of chance whether one's chosen wife was responsive or not. He hoped Muriel would be, since he knew his own nature to be lusty and, at the same time, romantic. There were always women to be had outside marriage, but he had thought many times how pleasant it must be for a man not to have to leave his own roof to enjoy the pleasures of a woman's body.

Tentatively, he essayed a test of Muriel's feelings, taking her hand and holding it surreptitiously in his own. Muriel's response was immediate as a faint blush stained her cheeks and she gently squeezed his fingers. So Muriel was not indifferent, Deveril thought with amusement, wondering at the same time why his own heart was not fluttering as the poets would have had it do. Perhaps, given time, he would learn to love Muriel. For the moment, he was a trifle overwhelmed by her, believing quite rightly that it was Muriel who had sought him out in marriage rather than he who had pursued her.

I dare say I am still too young for matrimony! he told himself ruefully, as he rose to make his adieux. His sister managed to enquire in a soft aside whether he was very smitten with his fiancée.

'Is she not the most beautiful girl we know, dearest Deveril?' she said excitedly. 'George and I are so thrilled about your engagement. So too, are the other girls. Muriel has always seemed like a sister to us, and now she will be our sister-in-law.'

'But not quite yet!' Deveril whispered back, his good spirits suddenly deserting him. He shook his brother-in-law's hand, bowed smilingly at Muriel and made his way downstairs where the butler was waiting with his hat and gloves.

As he let himself out into the lamplit street of Piccadilly, he felt unusually dejected. Declining the use of his waiting curricle, he told his groom he would walk home. Perhaps the soft warm air of this summer night would cheer him once again, he thought, as he set off in the direction of Mayfair, keeping a weather eye open for pickpockets as he did so. A hackney cab passed him, the horse clip-clopping tiredly as the coachman urged it on towards Hyde Park.

Most of the houses were in darkness, though here and there a soirée was in progress and the sound of a piano or a voice would float into the street. Two prostitutes in gaudy clothes with painted faces and smiling lips sidled up to him and away again when they realized he was not after all a potential customer. From nearby, an owl hooted from the trees in Green Park. The noise added to Deveril's malaise. He thought longingly of the owls in the chestnut trees lining the drive to Chiswell Hill House and wished he were walking there instead of to his London home. He was never really content away from country sounds and smells. Big cities were not to his liking, despite the amusements they offered. The gaming tables, the parties, the balls were no match for a day out on the Purbeck Hills riding to hounds, or an early morning canter through the green fields of the estate.

Nowhere in the world could bring him the same sense of completeness as Chiswell Hill House. It was not just *his* home, but the home of his ancestors. One day his sons would grow up there, discovering every pasture and stream, every meadow and farmstead as he had done; exulting in the beauty of the Dorset landscape in all the changing seasons. Like himself, they would delight in the mellowed bricks of the Elizabethan house and the eldest would know, as he did, that one day it would be all his.

By the time Deveril's feet had taken him to Grosvenor
Square, he had recovered his good spirits; for tomorrow, he
had decided, he would leave London and drive down to the
country. His grandfather would be happy to see him and he
to see the old man.

He loved his grandfather – and it was entirely to please
him that Deveril had come to London last week. The old man
had wanted him to confirm his betrothal to Muriel by putting
in a personal appearance at her side. That deed was now done
– the duty performed, Deveril told himself, as a sleepy-eyed
servant let him into the hall. Now he could return to the
country and enjoy all the pursuits he loved best.

With a feeling that all was now well with his world, Deveril
allowed his valet to put him to bed and almost instantly, he
fell into a healthy, dreamless sleep.

CHAPTER SEVEN

August 1831

For one brief moment, Clementine thought that she could not have heard Benjamin correctly. Her mind refused to accept that she was not after all to set out upon the journey that would reunite her with her parents. But the look on Benjamin's face was so full of pity that she was no longer able to reject the truth. Her body began to tremble so fiercely that Benjamin took the child from her. She grasped his arm.

'Tell me!' she said in a hard cold voice. 'Whatever has happened, I want to know the worst.'

But he still could not speak the words he feared would break her heart. Silently, he handed her her uncle's letter.

She had read but a few lines before he heard her cry out. He longed to put his arms around her, but the little boy was stirring in his embrace and he feared to wake him lest his cries added to Clementine's distress.

Miserably, he watched the changing expressions on her face as her eyes scanned the remainder of the letter. After what seemed to him an eternity, she laid it down on her lap. Although she had turned white, no tears spilled from her eyes, and but for the tight clenching of her fists, she gave no other outward sign of the horror she must be feeling. Her voice was hardly above a whisper as she said: 'I will not go back to The Rectory, Doctor Brook,' and then she added in a hard, tight voice: '*I would rather die than ever again live under the same roof as my aunt.* I will find work, lodgings, live anywhere but there.'

Benjamin's pity and concern were so great that he forgot

the child and put one arm around Clementine in an attempt
at comfort.

'Let us go back to the inn,' he said gently. 'We will discuss
the future there in greater privacy.'

He led her unresisting out of the offices and was glad to
see that the hackney was still patiently awaiting them. Five
minutes later, they were back in the front parlour of the Talbot
and Benjamin was insisting that Clementine drink a little of
the brandy he had poured for her. She was shaking now, and
her eyes were full of tears as she began to appreciate for the
first time that she would never see her beloved parents again.

'I cannot bear to think of it,' she murmured brokenly. 'Now
I am quite alone in the world – for I shall never accept my
uncle and aunt as true relatives.'

'You must try not to be too distressed,' Benjamin broke in
softly. 'Your parents would not wish it, and you have little
Adam to think of. A shock such as this could affect your
ability to nurse him.' He saw that he had her attention and
added: 'And please, never ever think of yourself as alone in
the world whilst I am alive. I had believed that you considered
me your friend!'

'Oh, I do, I do!' Clementine said quickly. 'But I realize that
you will have to go back to Upper Chiswell and I can never
go back. You, of all people, must understand that. You heard
those terrible words my aunt spoke that day I left her house.
She called my little Adam "a child of the Devil". I would
rather die than return to The Rectory and be beholden to her
for her so-called charity.'

Benjamin remained silent. He understood her sentiments
but he could see no alternative . . . unless . . . unless she would
agree to marry him. His heart leaped as the idea took hold.
She could remain here in Bristol, in lodgings perhaps, during
the three weeks whilst the banns were called. Then they could
be married quietly and she could go to live with his father in
Brighton until he could find a new practice. Perhaps his father
might be able to help him find a place in Sussex, far away

from the Chiswell villages with all their unhappy memories for Clementine. She would be loved – greatly loved – her child accepted by him as his own . . .

Slowly, haltingly, he put the proposition to her. Mistaking the look of dismay on her pale little face, he added fervently:

'Clementine, I am aware you do not love me as I do most earnestly assure you I love you, but . . .'

'Please say no more!'

Clementine's cry halted his speech. He had no way of knowing that his proposal could never be accepted since she was already married. Nor, thought Clementine, could she confess this to Benjamin, for her oath to keep the secret was sacred and could never be broken. Had that clandestine marriage never taken place, perhaps she might have considered Benjamin Brook's solution to her predicament. But now she must invent some other reason to refuse him, and none seemed to her better than the truth – that she did not love him.

'I could not agree to such an arrangement,' she said quietly, her hand on his in a strange reversal of their roles as she sought to comfort him. His sincerity was beyond doubt, and she could not fail to recognize the deep disappointment in his eyes as she spoke. 'It would not be fair in any way to you, and I should feel unworthy, indebted and untrue to myself. I cannot tell you how grateful I am for the honour you bestow upon me even by thinking of marriage to me, the greater because, as I know full well, I have been disgraced and I have a child. Please do not think I am unmindful of this. But it is not the only solution. I am young, in good health, and I can work. I know I am not trained for domestic service but . . .'

'My dear child,' Benjamin broke in aghast, 'how can you suggest such a thing! Imagine the life led by that poor little skivvy of your aunt's at The Rectory – scrubbing floors, washing, ironing, cleaning pots. The very idea of you engaged in Mary's work horrifies me. Besides, how could you care for

Adam in that kind of employment? I beg you, Clementine, reconsider your rejection of my proposal.'

But she could not, even though the vulnerability of her present situation was only now fully impressing itself upon her. Of one thing only was she certain – she would never return to the rectory.

Clementine's silence had answered Benjamin's question. Her anxious face revealed that she was not unaware of her predicament.

'Perhaps it would be possible for you to obtain work of a more delicate nature,' he said, and with an attempt to sound optimistic, he added: 'I noted many times how beautifully you embroidered your child's clothes. There is a chance that Miss Fothergill might agreed to your lodging with her on a permanent basis. You could look for employment in Poole and there at least I would be near enough at hand to ensure that you were not entirely friendless. I am certain I can recover the money for your passage. That will enable you to survive for a little while. Miss Fothergill might be pleased to further augment her income in these hard times.'

For the first time since he had imparted to her the terrible news about her parents, the colour returned to Clementine's cheeks.

'Oh, if only such a thing were possible!' she cried. 'But surely Miss Fothergill only agreed to give me a refuge on the understanding that it was to be for but a few months? Do you really believe she will consider it on a more permanent basis?'

Benjamin nodded, but his eyes were uneasy. He was by no means certain that the old lady would be willing to harbour Clementine and the baby indefinitely. But he wanted desperately to offer Clementine some hope.

'We will return to Poole and see what she has to say,' he told her.

She made a brave attempt to smile.

'It seems I am forever saying "thank you",' she said.

Her companion sighed but forbore from remarking that it was not her gratitude he required but her willingness to marry him. But perhaps now, if he was not going to lose touch with her after all, she would in time reconsider his proposal. He must not forget that at the age of sixteen, despite her motherhood, she was still little more than a child herself and not yet ready for marriage.

As she stood up, settling the baby in her arms, he smiled down at her.

'I ask only one thing of you,' he said earnestly. 'And that is that you should honour the promise you gave me and call me Benjamin. "Doctor Brook" reminds me that I have been your physician, whereas I wish you now to think of me only as your friend.'

Tears sprang to Clementine's eyes as she attempted to return his smile.

'You are already my friend, Benjamin,' she said huskily. And before the threatening tears could fall, she hurried away to the privacy of her bedroom where at last she could weep, not for herself, but for the beloved parents she would never see again.

On the following day's journey to Poole, she continued to grieve. Her heartbreak over the loss of her parents did not lessen with the miles, and such was her exhaustion that when the astonished Miss Fothergill opened the door, she burst into tears. One glance at Benjamin's face was sufficient to warn the old lady that disaster of some kind had befallen them, and she sent Clementine upstairs to feed the baby with no more ado than if she had been expecting her. As soon as they were gone, she sat Benjamin down, saying:

'Now, Doctor dear, you shall tell me what has happened!'

Without preamble he did so, ending his sad tale with the simple statement that he had come to ask a very great favour of her.

'You must tell me at once if the idea is in the slightest degree unfavourable to you,' he said, having outlined

Clementine's tragic circumstances. 'I feel she is greatly in need of a motherly eye to watch over her. I wondered if you . . .'

'Say not one word more!' Miss Fothergill interrupted. 'I shall be happy to have them back. I have grown very fond of the dear girl, and to tell you the truth, I have found these past few days quite unbearably lonely.'

When Clementine came back into the room, there could be no doubt as to the genuine warmth of the old lady's embrace when she announced that the decision was made – Clementine would live with her.

Benjamin gave Clementine a reassuring smile.

'There is our first and most important hurdle behind us,' he said, as if the problem were as much his concern as hers, she thought gratefully. 'And I have little doubt that dear Miss Fothergill will do what she can to help you find suitable employment.'

'I will do my best,' Miss Fothergill said, 'but I would be less than honest if I did not admit that the prospects are not very good. These are days of unparalleled poverty, degradation and misery in our little county of Dorsetshire. Did you know, Doctor dear, that over thirteen per cent of the population are receiving poor relief? It is small wonder that they have been rioting.'

For once Benjamin allowed himself to be drawn into discussion about such matters. He understood very well his own patients' resentment at the intensity of their poverty whilst their landlords lived in extravagant luxury.

'I fear the landowners are untouched by the recession that has so blighted the state of the country's agriculture, Miss Fothergill,' he said quietly. 'They seem quite unaware of their tenant farmers' misery.'

When he had been treating the Admiral the previous year, the old Viscount had read out to him in a shocked voice the contents of a letter received by an acquaintance of his. This landowner, a Mr Castleman, had been openly threatened:

'Sunday night your house shall come down to the ground for you are an inhuman monster and we will dash out your brains . . .'

There had been further threats in the same vein. The elderly Viscount had been appalled by the effrontery, and only last week he had been further angered by Benjamin's defence of the thirteen rebels who had been recently sentenced to transportation for life.

'To me, Milord, that punishment is a miscarriage of justice. The men were only trying to gain a living wage – and surely all men should have that as a right.'

The Viscount had turned purple as he spluttered angrily:

'You sound like my grandson, Deveril! I do not know what the younger generation are coming to with all this talk of reform. What was good enough for the working classes in my day is good enough for them now. Raise their standard of living and next thing they will be thinking themselves equal to us. If Russell brings that disgraceful Reform Bill before the House, I shall vote it thrown out. A lot of balderdash, I say.'

'Men are not beasts of burden,' Benjamin said now, as he had thought then. 'They should not have to eat and sleep and live like animals – if, indeed, half as well as Viscount Burnbury's dogs and horses. *They* are always well fed, their kennels and loose boxes rainproof, their every need attended to by a posse of grooms. I can think of several of my patients who would gladly exchange their leaking hovels for one of the Chiswell Hill House stables!' He broke off, his face losing its expression of anger as he said quickly: 'But it is not my job to play the politician and try to win the old aristocrat round to a more liberal view. I have quite enough to do trying to keep the undernourished, struggling, work-worn bodies of his labourers alive.'

'And talking of nourishment, you must both be hungry,' Miss Fothergill said. 'So let us go and enjoy the meal Jennie has prepared for us.'

Benjamin was delighted to see the look of happiness and relief on Clementine's face as the old lady led her into the dining-room with an arm around her shoulders. Clementine was still so young that grief could not overwhelm her for long, he thought. Her eyes regained their sparkle, her mouth that familiar pretty smile, as she responded to Miss Fothergill's chatter about her baby.

'I fear I may spoil him with too much affection!' Clementine said, sighing. 'He is so tiny and helpless and so dependent upon me, I cannot help but love him. I never thought when I was carrying him that I could feel as I do about a baby. It is hard to believe sometimes that he is mine – entirely my own. It is quite a responsibility!'

As Clementine continued to talk happily about her child, Miss Fothergill glanced at Benjamin's face. She noted the expression of tender concern in his eyes each time he looked at Clementine. No wonder he was worried about the poor girl, she thought – alone in the world without husband or parents. His voice, too, was full of concern when he rose to go.

'I shall be obliged to give an account of your whereabouts to your uncle, Clementine,' he said. 'He placed you in my charge and I cannot tell him that I have abandoned you in Bristol!'

Clementine's face was a mask of dismay.

'Oh please, Doctor Brook, I mean Benjamin, *must* you tell them where I am? My uncle might insist I return to The Rectory and . . .'

'I do not think he will, Clementine, not if he is assured of your welfare,' Benjamin broke in, aware that the parson would be only too happy to be relieved of his responsibility.

'If it will help in any way, my dear,' Miss Fothergill said, 'I shall be happy to pen a quick note to your uncle offering myself as your guardian.'

Clementine's eyes filled with tears of gratitude.

'Oh, if you would, Miss Fothergill. How good you are! I promise I will not be a burden to you.'

'You and I will be very happy together – just as we were before,' Miss Fothergill replied easily. 'Now, Doctor dear, it is growing late, and you should not risk travelling alone in darkness on so isolated a road. If you will just wait but a moment longer, I will see to the letter for the Rev Foster. And do, I beg you, beware of highwaymen.'

The tension eased as Benjamin and Clementine expressed their doubts that a highwayman would consider it worth his while holding a poor country physician to ransom. True to her word, Miss Fothergill took no more than a few minutes to write to Clementine's uncle, and Benjamin made a hurried departure.

When Jennie had shown him out, Miss Fothergill turned to Clementine and put her arms around her.

'Now off to bed with you, my dear,' she said, 'and you are not to lie awake worrying. As soon as you are recovered from your journeying, you and I will go out together and set about finding you some work.'

But despite Miss Fothergill's cheerful optimism, the kind of work that Clementine could do was limited. As she told the old lady next day, her mama had not thought to train her to earn a living. Her only accomplishment was her ability to sew. Although they trudged tirelessly from one shop to another for two whole days, the employers they approached already had seamstresses, nearly all of whom were living in attic rooms above the shops. The one modiste who might have had a vacancy for her would not even consider employing her once she knew that Clementine had a babe in arms.

By the third day, even Miss Fothergill was beginning to lose hope.

'I know of only one more possibility,' she told Clementine. 'A French dressmaker by the name of Madame Tamara has a small premises not far from here. But I must warn you that it is unlikely she will be lacking employees.'

Nevertheless, they trailed down to the tiny shop near the harbour and went inside. As the doorbell jangled, a tightly corseted lady in a black dress came forward to greet them. Miss Fothergill began her request that Madame Tamara should spare a moment to look at the samples she had brought of Clementine's tiny stitching. But before she could complete her appeal, a customer came into the shop. Immediately, the modiste hurried to her side and by the effusiveness of the greeting that followed, Clementine and Miss Fothergill realized that this was a much valued patroness of the establishment. They therefore remained quietly in the background as Madame Tamara called to one of the girls in the upstairs workshop:

'Suzanne, bring down madame the Lady Mayoress's dress, *toute suite! Depéchons-vous!*'

Clementine subdued a sudden desire to laugh as she whispered to Miss Fothergill that she did not think Madame Tamara was genuinely of French nationality, as she was pretending.

'Her accent is quite English!' she murmured, 'and her grammar is incorrect.'

The Lady Mayoress was a stout, portly woman in her forties. The dress Madame Tamara had been making for her was an elaborate creation in pale yellow silk. Its bodice '*en coeur*' was covered with a profusion of lace ruffles which also decorated the huge puffed 'beret' sleeves. A big posy of violets adorned the waist and smaller posies were stitched around the low neck and hem.

'I trust it ees now *exactement* to your measurements,' Madame Tamara was saying as her customer eyed the dress doubtfully. 'You weesh to try it on 'ere, Madame, or do you prefer the privacee of your 'ome?'

'I will try it on here,' the stout lady replied firmly. 'I do not want the trouble of having to return it a *second* time if it is wrong,' she added pointedly. Madame Tamara hurried to the shop door and locked it, drawing down the blind as she did so.

'You will be quite private 'ere, I do assure you,' she gushed, as she assisted her customer in removing her hat, gloves and gown. Clementine and Miss Fothergill might not have existed as they pretended an interest in the bolts of cloth on the far side of the room.

Presently Madame Tamara lifted the yellow silk ball gown over the Lady Mayoress's head and began with deft fingers to button the back. All the while she bombarded her customer with compliments: 'So tiny, zee waist! So noble, *la poitrine!*'

'I would describe the Lady Mayoress as more fat than noble!' whispered Miss Fothergill mischievously. 'As for "zee waist", it does not exist!'

The woman they were regarding surreptitiously from the shadowed interior of the shop was surveying her reflection in the cheval mirror, her expression very far from satisfied.

'Madame ees not pleased? But she looks so charming and *distinguée* . . .' Madame Tamara gushed, as she straightened the skirt and pulled ineffectually at a ruffle on the sleeve.

'No, I cannot say I am at all pleased, Madame Tamara. In fact, I am more than a little disappointed. The dress makes me look – well, to be quite frank, it is not at all enhancing to my . . . my figure. In your sketch, the waist looked very much smaller and I am now of the opinion that your design is much more befitting a young girl than a lady of my years.'

And I am not in the least surprised, thought Clementine, for it was quite obvious that however pretty the dress might have looked on a slim figure, it merely exaggerated the Lady Mayoress's sizable hips and bosom.

Without stopping to think that she was here to request employment by the modiste, and that her interference was totally unwarranted if not actually rude, Clementine stepped forward and touched the big bunch of violets attached to the waistline of the offending gown. Miss Fothergill's restraining hand reached out too late to deter her as, impulsively, Clementine murmured in her quiet cultured voice:

'If Madame would permit, I would like to suggest that these flowers would look very much prettier at the hem of the gown.' She picked up a pair of scissors and ignoring Madame Tamara's protest, she quickly snipped the stitches holding the posy and held it at the base of the gown.

'Is that not better – and so much kinder to your waistline, Madame?' she enquired with a smile. Madame Tamara's face was now red with anger at this strange girl's impertinence, but the scowl had left the mayoress's face and she was nodding approvingly at her reflection.

Clementine had by now become aware of her own audacity. She had certainly ruined her chances of endearing herself to Madame Tamara, by whom she could no longer expect to be offered employment. But since it was obviously too late to put matters right, and feeling that she might as well be hung for a sheep as a lamb, she gave voice to her genuine feelings regarding the unfortunate gown. How often she had heard her beautiful mama point out that simplicity was the essence of chic!

'The neckline would be softer if these ruffles were to be a little lower,' she said defiantly. 'See, Madame, how much smarter it looks this way! Then, if we were to gather the skirt here at the side, I think the whole effect would be far more to your liking.'

'The girl is absolutely right!' the plump matron cried, turning to Madame Tamara. 'I could not put my finger on what was wrong, but she has done so. As it was before, the dress lacked those little touches which make all the difference. Please make all the alterations your assistant has suggested.' She turned back to Clementine, eyeing her now and approving the simple lines of her grey dress, the only suitably coloured mourning garment Clementine had found to wear out of respect for her parents.

'You are new here, are you not?' she enquired. 'I can see you have good taste. You shall advise me on the design of my new gown. I require a day costume for autumn wear, Madame Tamara – in a grey merino, I think.'

It was several more minutes before she had decided upon the new garment and Madame Tamara had made arrangements to deliver the yellow ball gown at the end of the week. Finally, in a flurry of flattering comments from Madame Tamara, she left the shop smiling contentedly.

Madame Tamara beckoned to Clementine. Her eyes were not exactly kindly but speculative.

'Did I understand you to say you are looking for work?'

Clementine nodded. Miss Fothergill stepped forward and handed the modiste the samples of Clementine's stitching. Madame Tamara examined them closely and nodded appreciatively.

'It is clear you stitch a neat hand,' she said approvingly. 'It also seems that you have a certain flair for fashion . . .' Her French accent had now quite disappeared and she spoke with a marked Dorsetshire burr. 'Have you been previously employed in such work? You do not look like a working girl!'

Miss Fothergill spoke up.

'Mrs Foster has had a sheltered upbringing. She married very young and sadly has been widowed and needs to earn a living for herself and her child.'

'Child? I cannot have children living here . . .' Madame Tamara broke in. 'It is a pity – I could have found work for your protégée. I was impressed, I admit it, by the Lady Mayoress's approval of the girl's suggestions. Nevertheless . . .'

Now it was Miss Fothergill's turn to protest.

'If you would permit Mrs Foster to take the dress home with her, I have no doubt she would be very happy to make the alterations there. I can assure you, you need have no fears for the safety of the gown, or any other work you may wish to give her. My home is a most respectable one which you are welcome to inspect at any time . . .'

Clementine felt a thrill of excitement as the two women began to discuss the very real possibility of her employment. The wage Madame Tamara was offering did not seem very high, but at least it would pay for her food and something towards her lodging. It seemed an eternity before Madame agreed to employ her on a trial basis.

On the way home, Miss Fothergill sounded quite satisfied by the proposed rate of pay and more than content with Clementine's suggestion that at least half her wages should be handed over for her board and lodging.

'The sum will greatly ease my budget,' she admitted, 'for I fear I have only a very small income left me by my father. Otherwise I would be more than happy to have you as a guest, dear child. Now let us go home and have a little glass of Madeira to celebrate, shall we? And you shall sit down and write a letter to dear Doctor Brook to tell him of your good news.'

During the first three weeks of Clementine's employment, Madame Tamara placed more and more work upon her shoulders. She was therefore up at six in the morning feeding, washing and settling the little boy in his crib before walking the two miles to the shop to deliver the previous day's sewing and collect a further bundle of garments. Miss Fothergill was out of the house a large part of the day, busy about her own charitable affairs, and with only the little orphan girl, Jennie, to cook and clean, Clementine's moments of idleness were few and far between. At such moments, she would sit in the rocking chair nursing the baby and crooning lullabies to him, sometimes sending them both to sleep so tired was she by the end of the day.

The baby thrived despite his mother's ignorance of looking after so small an infant. Nevertheless Clementine worried unduly over every hiccough or sneeze, terrified lest she was doing something wrong and that she was harming him.

Miss Fothergill teased her gently about the devotion she lavished on Adam. 'So much love for one so small!' she commented, smiling. They laughed together at this gentle criticism, agreeing that Clementine had very little time to 'lavish so much love'.

Happily, Madame Tamara seemed pleased with her work and admitted that she was finding Clementine a great asset, particularly with her better class customers. She had made enquiries about Miss Fothergill and been reassured by the good lady's excellent reputation and standing in the community. She had no fear therefore, for the safety of the expensive garments she allowed Clementine to take home.

But Clementine's relative contentment with her new life was not to be left undisturbed. Late in August, she received a letter from her uncle:

'My dear Niece,' he had written, 'Despite Doctor Brook's assurances that you are settled with both home and employment you are still much upon my mind. Your poor dear Father left you in my guardianship and my conscience will not permit me to disregard this responsibility. I must therefore ascertain your welfare with my own eyes and now that my ankle is restored to use, it is my intention to pay you a visit in the following week.

'I am sure the death of your parents must have come as a very great shock to you, dear child, as indeed, the news shocked me. We must remember them always in our prayers and pray for the peace of your poor Father's soul. The scriptures tell us the Good Shepherd forgives all those who repent and it comforts me to remember that your Father's intention was to begin a new life.

'I fear that your Aunt's attitude towards you cannot be altered and it would therefore be useless to suggest that you should visit us here. However, I shall make the journey to Poole as soon as my duties allow and trust that in the meanwhile, you are keeping well.

'With kindest regards from

Your affectionate Uncle Godfrey.'

'Post Script: I shall bring with me the Hudson's Bay letter giving the news of your poor dear parents, as I expect you will wish to learn the sad facts at first hand.'

Miss Fothergill saw Clementine's anxious face and said quickly:

'Not bad news, my dear?'

Clementine attempted a smile.

'Not really, Miss Fothergill. The letter is from my uncle who will be paying me a visit in the near future. I . . . I suppose I must see him. He is bringing me a letter concerning my mama and papa. I believe Doctor Brook told you they had both been drowned somewhere in Upper Canada.' Her voice shook and tears filled her eyes.

Miss Fothergill rose from the breakfast table and went round to Clementine's chair. Stroking the girl's fair shining hair, she offered a silent sympathy which did much to comfort Clementine.

'You are very good to me,' she said simply. 'I wish *you* had been my aunt. At least I must be thankful that *she* is not coming to see me.'

Another week passed before the Rev Foster arrived in his dogcart to visit his niece. It was five o'clock on a mild September evening when he rang the front door bell.

Clementine laid down the gown she was embroidering and rose from her chair by the parlour window. She liked to work there since not only was the light good but with the windows open, the baby lying in the crib beside her obtained the benefit of the fresh summer air and sunlight.

When Jennie ushered her uncle into the room, he did not at first notice the infant. His eyes focused upon his niece, who had risen to her feet and was gazing at him expressionlessly. There was no smile of welcome in her eyes as she stepped forward dutifully to receive his kiss.

The Rev Foster was struck by the change in Clementine. She stood neatly gowned in a charming flowered chintz dress, a rosy glow in her cheeks. Her small delicate figure had filled out to a womanly roundness. The pity he had once felt for his pretty little niece was now replaced by a very different emotion – one he tried quickly to subdue. He could think of no more shocking a sin than that of a man lusting after his own niece. Yet there was no denying his reactions as he sat down in the chair she drew up for him beside her own.

Embarrassed by her uncle's stare, Clementine bent down over the baby's crib and drew the blanket away from his face.

The parson barely looked at the infant. His eyes were drawn to the low neck of Clementine's bodice, her posture revealing the soft white swell of her breasts and the delicate smoothness of her shoulders. He felt an almost irresistible urge to reach out his hand and touch her warm skin.

God forgive me! he thought, horrified and shamed by his emotions. To cover his embarrassment, he stuttered random questions about the baby.

Her uncle's unexpected interest in little Adam warmed Clementine's heart and she smiled as she answered him. She forgot momentarily her intention to be coolly remote with him and barely noticed when in a seemingly unconscious gesture, he put a hand on her arm. When he gave her the Hudson's Bay Company letter to read, she was unaware that he had taken one of her hands and was holding it tightly in his own.

The letter itself gave few details. It seemed that her mama and papa had set sail in April to make the journey to Lake Superior. But disaster had struck before even they had crossed Lake Huron. A violent storm had swept their packet-boat onto a rocky shore off the island of Manitoulin. The crew, together with other passengers, had managed to scramble to safety, but Mrs Foster had been carried back into the straits. Mr Foster had drowned in a brave attempt to save his wife.

It was only with the greatest effort that Clementine could read on. Tears were coursing down her cheeks as she learned that her mama's body had eventually been retrieved and given a Christian burial, but that no trace had been found of her poor papa.

Word of the tragedy had reached the Mathesons in Hamilton. They in turn, notified the Hudsons' Bay Company offices in London, asking them to trace the Rev Foster in Dorset, of whose address they were ignorant.

'I wrote immediately to the Mathesons to request any further details,' the Rev Foster said. 'But I fear there will be little else they can tell us, other than your poor mother's burial place, perhaps. It is very sad – very sad indeed, but at least we must be thankful that we learned of these terrible events before you crossed the ocean.' He gave a deep sigh. 'My poor little Clementine bereaved so young!'

Clementine, suddenly conscious of the dampness of her uncle's pudgy palm, quickly withdrew her hand from his. Deep within her she felt a growing desire to be above this man's pity. Without understanding the cause, it belittled her to know he felt sorry for her. Her mouth tightened and her head lifted proudly as she said:

'As it has all worked out, Uncle Godfrey, I am no longer alone and unbefriended. Doctor Brook has been very kind and helpful, and Miss Fothergill takes almost as great an interest in my well-being as Mama once did. She is very kind and affectionate, not just towards me but towards my child, too.'

The Rev Foster's face flushed as he registered the implied rebuke to his wife. Since Clementine's departure he had taken care never to mention the girl's name to Winifred, but the subject of his niece and her profligacy was seldom far from his wife's conversation. It was difficult to ignore her sharp, bitter tongue, and in the light of her attitude, he had not had the courage or inclination to discuss with her the problem uppermost in his mind. At the time he and the Viscount's lawyer had discussed Clementine's marriage to Percy Grayshott, it had been firmly established that his niece would be departing to British North America as soon as possible after the birth of her child. The Rev Foster was uncomfortably aware that it was now his duty to advise Lord Burnbury that through no fault of his, or indeed of Clementine's, she was still in England. Her presence in Poole – only five miles distant from Chiswell

Hill House – might not be at all agreeable either to the Grayshotts or their lawyer.

So far he had taken the easy way out by not confronting the Viscount with the facts. He hoped that by keeping silent, Clementine's departure abroad would be assumed, since he had notified Lord Burnbury that his niece would be sailing in July. It was most unlikely that Winifred would meet any member of the Grayshott family, and that left only the physician who knew of Clementine's present circumstances. The Rev Foster was convinced that he could count upon Brook's discretion, since he believed the young man did genuinely have his niece's welfare at heart – a probability which did not surprise him. What man, the parson now asked himself bitterly, could remain unaffected by Clementine's beautiful expressive eyes, in which the confusion of vulnerability and passion was so exciting and inviting a challenge.

Conscious of her uncle's eyes fastened upon her in an unwavering stare, Clementine said awkwardly:

'You will forgive me, Uncle, if I continue with my work whilst we converse. I must have this gown finished by nightfall so that it is ready to deliver first thing in the morning.'

'Of course, of course!' the parson agreed hurriedly. 'It was a great relief to me to learn from Doctor Brook that you had found suitable employment . . .' It had been an added relief, he thought, that the physician had been tactful enough to impart this information out of his wife's hearing. He had had no wish to listen to yet another torrent of abuse about his niece. Mrs Foster knew nothing of this afternoon's visit to Clementine. Too frightened of her reactions to admit the truth, he had muttered something about seeing an old parishioner who was ill, and he had escaped from The Rectory like a schoolboy playing truant from the classroom. The harmless little lie gave an added piquancy to the occasion, he realized, as he had set off to drive into Poole.

'You have seen Doctor Brook recently, Uncle?' Clementine

asked, feeling the need to make conversation as she sat beneath his watchful eyes. She did wish he would not stare so!

'On one occasion only, when he called to tell me you had written to him to say you had found employment. A charming man, but it would perhaps be appropriate at this moment for me to remind you that not even *he* is to be trusted.' Seeing the frown of puzzlement in Clementine's eyes, he added quickly: 'In relation to your . . . er . . . marriage to Percy Grayshott, I mean.' He looked deep into her eyes with genuine anxiety.

'You have not told him anything?'

Clementine sighed.

'But of course I haven't, Uncle. I gave my solemn oath I would not speak of it to anyone other than Mama and Papa. You need be in no fear that I will break my word, although I am certain that Doctor Brook could be trusted.'

'Yes, yes, I agree – but nevertheless, we cannot be too guarded. You must never lose sight of the interests of your child, my dear. At the moment the Grayshotts are being most generous – but were there any mishap, any hint of our not keeping our side of the agreement . . .'

Clementine sighed again. She needed no reminder that she must keep Adam's welfare foremost in her thoughts and heart. But on hearing her uncle's words, she felt an intense resentment that the Grayshotts were paying him money in return for his silence.

Were the Grayshotts so ashamed of her background that they felt it necessary to hide her away as if she were a leper? Or were they only concerned at their own guilt in forcing that poor, sick young man, Percy, into a marriage he had wanted no more than she? Was there really such need for secrecy and deceit? She must suppose that since her uncle and the Viscount were in accord about it, they must know what was best. At the same time, she disliked the position she found herself in now – of being someone who must be hidden away.

Her uncle was mopping his brow with a white handkerchief – something Clementine had often seen him do when he was nervous or embarrassed.

'I . . . er wish to have a little talk with you, my dear,' he stammered, 'that is to say, a little discussion about the . . . er . . . payments the Grayshotts are making to me . . . er, on your behalf, of course.' He was now fiddling with his watch-chain. 'I have quite a tidy sum set aside for you which I had . . . er, intended to remit to your father. As it is . . . well, it is as well I have been a trifle dilatory in this respect. Now, my dear, if you are in need, I could . . .'

'No, Uncle!' Clementine's voice was sharper than she had intended as she halted him in mid-sentence. 'I will not take their money. I can manage quite well without it, and I will not be bribed to keep my oath.'

The Rev Foster forgot his embarrassment and regarded his niece anxiously.

'You must not think of it as a bribe, dear child. It is after all your due. You are the wife of Percy Grayshott and as such, are entitled to his support – and to support for your child.'

Clementine's face was white but her expression was proudly determined as she said quietly:

'I have never considered myself Percy Grayshott's wife nor ever will, despite that terrible ceremony and the vows I made. They were as false as Percy's – only *he* could be excused the deceit since he understood nothing of it. But I will not take their money, Uncle Godfrey, and you cannot force me to do so. If you insist upon it, I shall give it to Miss Fothergill for her charities.'

The parson decided to let the matter drop for the time being. The girl was very young and did not realize the penalties and degradation attendant upon the poor. In the meanwhile, he could continue to take care of the money for her.

The arrival of the little maid, Jennie, with a tray of tea, brought their conversation to a natural conclusion.

Clementine smiled at Jennie who bobbed a curtsey and said:

'Little 'un's wakened up, Ma'am. Will I tek him into the kitchen whilst you's entertaining like?'

Clementine nodded gratefully and bent down to lift the baby

from his crib. At the same time her uncle leant over to assist
her and his arm brushed against her breasts. He stammered an
apology, his face scarlet. Clementine, innocent of the ways of
all men other than Benjamin and her father, and in particular
of the perverse thoughts that could assail lonely, thwarted old
men like her uncle, would have paid little attention to the
contact had it not been for *his* reactions. As Jennie left the room
carrying the baby in her arms, her uncle continued to excuse
his 'clumsiness'. His hand holding the teacup was trembling so
much the china rattled in the saucer. To turn the conversation,
she told him how Miss Fothergill had rescued Jennie from the
workhouse where her mother had died, leaving her an orphan.
Her uncle seemed uninterested however, and rose to make his
departure soon after declining a second cup of tea.

'Your aunt will be wondering what has become of me,' he
excused himself. 'But do not fear, dear child, I shall visit you
again – yes, indeed, as often as I can.' As he gathered up his
hat and gloves, he began at once to stutter. '. . . my poor
brother's only child . . . naturally very fond of you . . . only
surviving relatives, of course . . . we must not lose touch . . .'

Clementine was greatly relieved when finally he drove
off. As far as she was concerned, she wished he did not feel
it his duty to visit her regularly. But she quickly chided
herself for so ungrateful an attitude. He was doing his best
to be kind – as he always had done – and she pitied him
for the life he had to lead under Aunt Winifred's domin-
ation. She must try harder to make him feel welcome when
next he came to see her, she told herself.

Clementine might have taken a very different attitude had
she known that for most of the drive back to The Rectory,
the parson was making solemn vows to his Saviour not to
permit his keen interest in his niece to go beyond the bounds
of decency. He had never understood why the Good Lord
should have seen fit to burden him with such ungovernable
lustful urges . . . he who had chosen to be the the Good Lord's
servant and dedicate his life to the Church!

It was less than two years since he had had to fight one of the hardest battles of his life over his terrible desire for Miss Thomas, the organist. A spinster lady who had come to live in the village as housekeeper to her unmarried brother, the schoolmaster, she had developed a romantic interest in him which she had been unable to conceal. Silly, fluttering, plain little woman though she was, her coquettish manner and coy smiles had quickly turned his thoughts to ungodly possibilities. The woman needed love – as much as he did, he tormented himself at night as he lay beside Winifred's rigid body. Miss Thomas's figure was by no means shapeless beneath her shapeless gowns, and when she leant over his arm on the pretext of selecting a hymn or psalm, he had felt the pressure of soft breasts bursting from the confines of her corset.

One dark winter's night, he recalled with bitter shame, when they had been alone in the church after evensong, he had lost control of himself and kissed her. Shortly afterwards, Miss Thomas had left her brother's house, and for months after, he lived in dread of a vengeful visit from the schoolmaster. Fortunately, so it transpired, Miss Thomas had not given her brother the real reason for her sudden departure, but *he* knew he was responsible and his guilt lay heavy on his conscience. He thought often of that stolen kiss, of the unhappy woman's tears as she admitted that she loved him, a married man, and that for both their sakes, she must go. But even whilst he had been relieved to be rid of future temptation, he had suffered untold regrets for the pleasures they had had to forgo.

Now, once again, the Evil Spirit was upon him . . . only this time he was being even more severely tested by his God, the parson thought bitterly, since the object of his lustful thoughts was his own niece. His depravity shocked him deeply – yet his shame did nothing to halt his imagination as he recalled Clementine's soft young body. He knew that it would only add to his discomfort and agony were he to see her again and yet, he argued with himself, it would be a means of testing himself; of proving that he *could* deny himself the pleasure of

kissing her cheek or touching her hand or allowing his eyes
to rest on the gentle curves of her bosom. No, he thought, a
man should not run away from temptation. He should face
up to it and win the battle for Good.

By the time the parson reached The Rectory, he had
overcome his resolve to stay away from Clementine. As he
went indoors, he told his unsuspecting wife that 'the poor
parishioner' in Poole was terminally ill and that he would
shortly have to visit her again.

CHAPTER EIGHT

September–October 1831

Although the memory of her parents and their terrible deaths was never very far from Clementine's thoughts, she was not unhappy living with Miss Fothergill. Often she was very tired and her back and eyes ached as she plied her needle hour after hour in order to earn the pittance Madame Tamara paid her. And her baby son, now three months old, required constant feeding, which, Miss Fothergill warned her, was causing her fatigue and was a great draw upon her energies.

Benjamin had been to see her twice. She had finally lost her shyness with him and was able to call him by his Christian name without having to remind herself to do so. Knowing how happy it would make Clementine, he carried a letter from her to read to Mary and brought back an account of the little maid's pleasure in hearing that all was well with her and the baby.

Clementine had no desire to question Benjamin for news of her uncle and aunt and he made no mention of them. Nor did he mention the Grayshotts, although she learned from her uncle on his second visit that Deveril was back in Dorset.

Her uncle's second visit was no more welcome to Clementine than the first and had given her cause to lie awake worrying about his manner towards her. She hated the feel of his wet lips against her cheek and even more, his habit of holding her hand in his own, which was cold and clammy. To avoid such contact, she had taken up her sewing as quickly as possible after his arrival. She had difficulty in making conversation and she found his remarks too personal and probing for her liking. He was overenthusiastic in complimenting her upon her appearance, and he invited confidences about her relationship with Benjamin, the nature of his questioning leading her to suspect that he imagined they might be behaving improperly.

She tried to convince herself that his interest in Benjamin was intended to protect her and could never have been prompted by so mean and unnatural a vice as jealousy.

But when next he called to see her, he left her in no doubt as to his meaning. He sat in his usual chair in Miss Fothergill's little sitting room, and after having reassured himself as to her health and that of the baby, he enquired if she had received a further visit from the physician.

'Benjamin was here two days ago,' Clementine replied openly, for she had nothing to hide. Made uneasy by his stare, she quickly resumed her sewing. Since his niece's hands were now occupied, the Rev Godfrey Foster laid his own on her shoulders.

'I feel it is my duty to caution you, my dear!' he said, his tone both unctuous and portentous. 'Doctor Brook is unaware of your marriage and his . . . er, pity for your circumstances – well, it might lead him to offer his protection in a manner which is perhaps not entirely honourable. He is a comparatively young man and you . . . well, you are a very pretty young woman even if you are . . . er, encumbered with a child. You must discourage him, my dear, in *every* way.'

Clementine regarded her uncle in wide-eyed disbelief.

'You cannot mean to suggest that Benjamin – Doctor Brook – would take advantage in any way!' she cried aghast. 'He is my very good friend . . .'

'If you were older and wiser in the ways of men, you would know that no man is to be trusted,' the Rev Foster broke in, and then, as if regretting his words, he added hastily: 'Unless, of course, he should be a man of the cloth or a relative such as myself!'

Clementine flushed with indignation. No friend could have

proved himself more trustworthy and honourable than Benjamin. If anyone took advantage, it was her Uncle Godfrey! She felt her cheeks burn an even deeper red at the indecency of such a thought. But it was not easily dispersed when she considered how despite her discouragement he always imposed his greeting and farewell kisses upon her. His small white hands were always touching her, and when she looked up from her sewing, she had all too often caught him staring at her bodice or ankle.

Despite the heat of the September afternoon, Clementine shivered as she stitched furiously at the ruffle on the Lady Mayoress's new gown.

'Benjamin Brook is a good man!' she said hotly. 'It may interest you, Uncle, to know that he has already proposed a most honourable relationship between us – *marriage*. I would prefer it therefore, if you would not belittle his character to me.'

The Rev Foster managed with difficulty to bite back the further questions which rose in his mind. He feared by the defensive tone of Clementine's voice that her affection for the young physician had deepened since his last visit. But for the moment, he let the matter drop and enquired instead about the baby.

'You are . . . er, still nursing him, my dear?' he asked, watching with mixed emotions the hot colour deepen in the girl's cheeks. Even as the sight of her blush excited him, he was appalled by his own sinfulness. His question was most improper, and he had known it even before the words slipped out. Despite all his promises to himself and his God, the Devil was once again gaining the upper hand, he thought wretchedly. Hurriedly, he rose to go.

'Do please give my kindest regards to Miss Fothergill,' he stammered hastily as Clementine put down her sewing and rose to her feet. So great was his fear of losing all control of himself, that for once he made no attempt to kiss that soft pink cheek. But he could not resist patting Clementine's arm as he said:

'I have been considering the possibility of renewing your Latin and Greek lessons, dear child. It is a pity to forget all I have taught you. I will see if I can rearrange my duties in the parish so that we can spend more time together.'

Clementine's expression of dismay did not escape him and as he drove away from Miss Fothergill's little house, he warned himself to be more careful. It would never do for his niece to guess the extent of the feelings she aroused in him. These visits were only in the smallest degree pleasurable for they left him afterwards with a hopeless, despairing frustration from which there was no relief. In the dead of night, the word 'incest' caused him to cry out in horror – and Winifred to shake him impatiently by the shoulder, supposing him to be having a nightmare. Indeed, it *was* a nightmare – one from which he knew he could only awake were he to cease his visits to Poole. As dawn broke he would resolve to write to Clementine, offering a suitable excuse for not calling upon her again. But within a day or two at most, that resolve was destroyed by the intensity of his longing to see her again; to be within touching distance of that sweet young body, those tempting red lips. And no amount of prayer lessened his desire. If there was a God – and he was beginning to doubt it – He was deaf to his pleas for strength to resist the lustful demands of the Devil.

Benjamin, too, was drawn inevitably back to Miss Fothergill's house. But his growing love for Clementine sprang from the heart rather than the body. It was not just her beauty which fascinated him – but her courage and tenacity. Despite her long arduous hours of painstaking work, she never once complained.

'At seventeen,' he told her, 'you should be free from responsibilities. You should be attending parties and balls, with no more to worry about than a new gown or a new suitor!'

But Clementine denied any longing for such simple things and talked happily of her baby son and the plans she had to save enough money to send him to a good school when he was old enough. On such occasions, Benjamin consoled himself with the thought that if the future turned out as he planned, Clementine would be Mrs Brook long before Adam was of school age, and it would be his concern then to look after the little boy's education.

Their conversations were never lacking in topics. Clementine was interested in his work and by now knew many of his patients by name. She, in turn, described the dreadful working conditions of the apprentices in Madame Tamara's shop. The girls toiled in airless rooms above the salon, and they had to sleep, all eighteen of them, in a dark damp room in the basement. They were country girls from the villages between Poole and Dorchester, all bound to a three-year apprenticeship and expected to work for twelve hours every day except Sundays.

Such tales always ended in Clementine's grateful thanks for her own good fortune in being permitted to take work home. She laughed with Benjamin when he argued that it was not her good fortune but her good sewing that had brought about this special privilege.

Both Clementine and Benjamin were aware that Miss Fothergill was romantically engaged in forwarding a match between them. When she praised Benjamin, pointing out his eligibility, it distressed Clementine that she could not openly confess that she was already married and that for this reason alone Miss Fothergill's hopes were without foundation. It was something of a relief that Benjamin himself made no further proposal and appeared to be content with their ripening friendship.

It was Miss Fothergill's practice always to attend church on Sunday mornings, and occasionally Clementine left Adam with Jennie and accompanied the old lady. On the third Sunday of the month it was Clementine's birthday, and to please Miss Fothergill she attended the service with her, although nowadays she derived little comfort from prayer, it being too reminiscent of her year at The Rectory.

But her spirits lifted immediately when, on arriving home, she recognized Benjamin's pony and trap outside Miss Fothergill's front door.

'Did you tell him it was my birthday?' she chided the old lady, who was beaming cheerfully.

'I did, my dear, and why not? If Jennie has carried out my orders, she will have a birthday cake packed in a picnic hamper and Doctor Brook will drive us to the seaside.'

Clementine's excitement was all the reward Benjamin needed for this small treat he had secretly planned with Miss Fothergill. She was like a little girl again, he thought tenderly, clapping her hands and avowing her intention to search for crabs amongst the rock pools as she used to do with her mama when she was a child.

'Oh, I do wish Adam was old enough to run about on the sand!' she said happily when after a short drive, Benjamin halted the trap on the edge of a large deserted beach. There was not a cloud in the sky and the seagulls were wheeling and screaming above their heads as the little party made its way down to the water's edge, Clementine carrying the infant and Benjamin the hamper. Settling Miss Fothergill comfortably upon a carriage rug with the baby in his basket beside her, Clementine and Benjamin took off their shoes and stockings and, since there was no one to see them and disapprove, paddled in the warm water.

'You should have your parasol to protect you from the sun,' Benjamin said solicitously for it was hotter than he had at first supposed. But Clementine laughed, her hair falling from its pins about her shoulders.

'What do I care if I become freckled!' she said happily. 'Is this not fun, Benjamin? Are you not happy too?'

He smiled down at her.

'How could I be otherwise when I see you so carefree,' he replied simply. 'And I have a surprise for you, Clementine. Let us go and retrieve the package from my coat pocket.'

Clementine was deeply touched by his remembrance of her

birthday and by his gift – a Spode candlestick decorated with tiny red rosebuds.

'I shall keep it for ever,' Clementine vowed, 'in memory of one of the happiest days I can remember. Look, Adam, look! Is it not pretty?'

She bent over the baby who was staring up at her from eyes which were now almost completely brown and fringed with thick dark lashes. Although he was far too young to identify the object his mother was holding out to him, the sound of her happy loving voice was sufficient to make him smile.

Clementine lifted him up and hugged him.

'See, he approves, Benjamin, do you not, my darling.' She swayed to and fro, rocking him as a little girl might rock a doll. 'Next year he will be walking,' she said. 'And we shall come down to the seaside again and . . .'

But for once Benjamin was not listening. His eyes, shaded by one hand, were focused on a yacht not very far out to sea.

'It is not becalmed,' he said, more to himself than to his two companions. 'But I fear the occupants are not too skilled in seamanship judging by the way they are trying to beat against the wind.'

Miss Fothergill was unpacking Jennie's picnic and the yacht was momentarily forgotten while they enjoyed the repast. Jennie had placed a single candle on the cake and Clementine was as pleased as if it had been her first ever birthday party.

'You are both so very, very good to me!' she said huskily. 'When I recall how unhappy I was this time last year . . .'

But Benjamin would not permit her to dwell on those memories and drew her attention to the yacht which was now less than five hundred yards offshore.

'I think they must have been trying to get her into Poole harbour,' he said, 'but if they do not alter course quickly, she will be beached here.'

It soon became evident that the occupants of the yacht were very inexperienced. The watchers could hear the sound of their voices calling instructions to one another and, as they neared the surf, shouting warnings of impending disaster. Benjamin and Clementine could now see quite clearly the white trousers and colourful waistcoats of the crew, all of whom were unbearded and looked very young.

As the impending tide took hold of the boat, the surf built up behind it and, gathering speed, it came rushing inwards and keeled over as the bows hit the sand. Two of the three occupants were thrown on to the beach and the third fell into the water. Benjamin raced forward to lend assistance, but Clementine stood rooted to the spot. She had recognized one of the young men – how could she ever forget him? It was Deveril Grayshott. He was smiling at Benjamin.

'Why, Brook, how fortuitous your being here. Give me a hand, old fellow. Not our boat, do y'see. Dare not let it sink. Come on, you chaps, let us see if we can pull her up a bit higher.'

If Deveril was surprised and delighted to see the physician, Benjamin was shocked beyond measure to see him. As far as he was aware, Clementine had never met the man who had seduced her since that fateful night a year ago. This meeting would be a dreadful embarrassment to all of them. But he had no time to note how this unfortunate encounter was affecting Clementine as he hurried to the crew's assistance.

Miss Fothergill came to stand beside Clementine.

'Dearie me!' she exclaimed excitedly, 'who would have expected to see a real shipwreck!'

Deveril and his two friends, together with Benjamin, were by now proving successful in their attempts to drag the small yacht up the beach. They were all drenched to the thighs by the surf and seemed not the least put out by the experience. Deveril was laughing, albeit ruefully, as he walked towards the two women.

'I daresay we deserve our comeuppance, Brook. Had a wager, don't y'know. Bet our friends we would race them from Poole Harbour to the Needles and back . . . Easy enough going out this morning, but our group have only been sailing a couple of times and we had a bit of trouble beating back against the wind.'

He looked away from Benjamin towards the two ladies and with a charming smile, bowed gracefully and bid them good afternoon.

Clementine's heart was thudding so fiercely she wondered for a moment if she were going to faint. It was immediately obvious that Deveril did not recognize her, for he was glancing at her enquiringly and his voice was merry and teasing as he said to Benjamin:

'I had no idea you were married, Brook. Pray introduce me to your charming wife!'

Benjamin was at a loss for words. Was it really possible that this feckless young man did not *remember* Clementine? Totally perplexed, he searched his memory and suddenly recalled the words of the untidy little rectory maid: "E were that befuddled, Doctor Brook, Sir, I do reckon 'e didn't know what 'e was about, not nohow. 'Twere all over in a minute, surely, afore I did mek up me mind what was a-going on like . . .'

Now, apparently, Deveril seemed unaware of his silence and was busily introducing himself first to Miss Fothergill and then to Clementine, who was as tongue-tied as Benjamin.

'You must forgive me for intruding on your delightful picnic,' he was saying, his eyes returning mischievously to Clementine's face, his expression openly admiring and not a little curious about Benjamin's pretty wife. Why on earth had his valet not told him about the marriage when he had related all the other village gossip on their arrival last week at Chiswell Hill House? Come to that, how on earth had Brook kept his betrothal a secret from his grandfather? The Viscount expected to be appraised of all the births, marriages and deaths of his employees and tenants, and Brook was a frequent visitor to the house these days what with his father's illness last winter and his grandfather's health deteriorating so much this year.

But it was a trivial matter and Deveril had little interest in the physician's personal affairs. Besides, he could not blame Brook for keeping so attractive a young wife to himself. She would certainly cause a few hearts to flutter amongst *his* friends, he thought with amusement, as he eyed Clementine's shapely figure and watched the blushes come and go in her cheeks. However, this was hardly the moment to pursue a flirtation; his three friends were waiting patiently by the side of the yacht.

He inclined his head in Miss Fothergill's direction.

'With your permission, dear lady, we may need to borrow your pony and trap to go into town for assistance. With the tide coming in, the confounded boat will be afloat again in a short while . . .'

Miss Fothergill was clearly charmed by the young man. She smiled at him in her usual friendly way and explained that they themselves would shortly be returning to Poole, since the baby must be fed and put to bed before long.

'We can send someone back to lend you assistance, can we not, Doctor Brook? Then Mr Grayshott and his friends can remain here and guard the vessel!'

Deveril nodded approvingly.

'But that is a splendid idea – if it does not put you to too much trouble, Ma'am. I would hate to feel responsible for curtailing what I see is a most pleasant occasion. I must confess, it would seem to be a far better way to enjoy oneself than battling with the elements off shore!' He turned to look at Clementine. 'Have you ever been sailing, Ma'am? Do you like the sea?'

Words failed her and Benjamin stepped forward, linking his arm firmly in Clementine's.

'I think if we are to obtain help for Mr Grayshott, we should leave immediately,' he said firmly. 'Good day, Sir. I trust you will not have to wait too long for help.'

One of Deveril's companions bent to assist Clementine as she stopped to pack the picnic hamper. Deveril's dark eyes held a wicked smile as she stood up.

'It has been a very great pleasure meeting you, Ma'am. May I hope that one day I may persuade your husband to bring you sailing with me? I promise I will take the greatest of care and not allow you to be beached!'

Clementine felt her cheeks burning and she quickly turned her head as she muttered some incomprehensible reply. But she was not to escape so easily. Deveril, with a polite 'May I?', took the hamper from her and, tucking his arm beneath hers, followed Benjamin and Miss Fothergill, who was carrying Adam. Through the light muslin sleeve of her dress, Clementine could feel the warmth of Deveril's arm and her skin burned at the contact. Inexperienced as she was, she knew very well that he was flirting with her for his voice held a laughing, challenging tone that she could not ignore. Her thoughts were in chaos, the uppermost being astonishment that he seemed to have no prior recollection of her at all – whilst she . . . she could think of little else but the shocking intimacy of their last encounter.

They had almost reached Miss Fothergill and Benjamin when she heard Deveril's voice:

'I must confess you to be the most silent lady I have ever had the pleasure of meeting,' he said. 'Will you at least bid me goodbye, Ma'am?'

But she could not. Her baby's cries saved her the necessity as she quickly detached her arm from Deveril's and hurried towards the trap. Benjamin, glancing at her face, realized something of her perturbation and made the necessary adieux to Deveril. Within minutes they were bumping over the sandy track on their way back to Poole.

Only Miss Fothergill was unaffected by this little adventure as she chattered excitedly from her seat beside Benjamin. The baby was quietened now that Clementine held him in her arms, soothed by her proximity and the movement of the carriage.

'What a very charming young man,' the old lady was remarking to Benjamin. 'Is he one of your patients, Doctor dear? I have not noticed him before in Poole. Perhaps he does not live round these parts?'

Reluctantly, Benjamin satisfied her curiosity as to Deveril's background, but he would have preferred not to talk of him. Knowing Clementine's every expression, he was painfully aware of the effect seeing Deveril had had upon her. No less than he, she must have been astonished that the young man had failed utterly to recognize her. Grayshott must indeed have been very drunk that fateful night, he thought bitterly, resenting the humiliation Clementine must be suffering now.

His bitterness and frustration mounted as he considered that through no fault of his own, his planned treat for Clementine for her birthday had turned out to be a disaster. How could he ever have imagined that Fate would choose this very day to cast young Deveril Grayshott up on the beach where Clementine, until that moment, had been so carefree and happy! If it had been possible to behave so churlishly, he would not now be going for assistance but would have left the young blackguard to make the best of his stupid mishap. But Miss Fothergill had proffered their help and there was little he could do about it. His trousers were soaked to the knees and as every minute passed, he felt more and more angry. He managed at last to silence Miss Fothergill by informing her that Deveril Grayshott was an irresponsible young rake and that even were he to call upon her at some future date to render his thanks, she would be ill-advised to receive him since his reputation was questionable.

If Miss Fothergill was surprised, she did not argue or question the point and neither did Clementine, whose thoughts were with her uncle. If he were to learn of this encounter, he would be even angrier than Benjamin! He had never ceased reiterating that she must never, *never*, have any contact with the Grayshotts and that this was part of his agreement with the Viscount.

Well, the meeting had not been of her devising, she thought with a flash of spirit, as she envisaged her uncle's words of condemnation. In any event, since he seemed always to visit her in Miss Fothergill's absence, it was unlikely he would hear of it. She felt certain Benjamin would not make mention of the encounter, which hopefully would soon be forgotten by them all.

But even as the thought went through her mind, she knew that *she* would not forget it. She had so many times tried to turn her heart against Deveril and had almost succeeded in convincing herself that he was not nearly as handsome as she had once thought and certainly unworthy of her affection. But it was impossible now that she had seen him again, not to know that the very reverse was true. The memory of his laughing dark eyes boldly appraising her was imprinted for ever on her mind, as was his voice, intimate and mischievous at the same time, chiding her for her silence. Yet there had been so much she *could* have said to him!

She glanced down at the baby she was holding and saw that he was wide awake. Her heart jolted as she realized for the first time the astonishing likeness of her child to his father. Had Deveril troubled to look at Adam, would he, too, have noticed it? Would Miss Fothergill? Clementine hugged the baby closer. At least she had him to comfort her – a living proof of the love she could no longer deny despite all logical reasons for hating the man who had ruined her young life.

But she would not allow it to be ruined, she thought, as she felt the hot tears stinging the back of her eyes. No matter how long and hard the battle, the day would come when Adam should take his rightful place in the world as his father's equal. She would bring him up to be good and strong, like her own papa; to be kind and gracious and understanding, like Mama; to be dedicated to the good of his fellow men, like Benjamin . . . oh, and to have his father's easy, natural charm, she thought finally. She *wanted* him to be like Deveril in so many ways . . . wrong though it might be for her to wish it so.

It took but a short detour to the harbour to arrange for

help for the stranded yachtsmen, and by six o'clock they were back in Miss Fothergill's house. Benjamin declined the old lady's invitation to remain for supper and muttered some excuse for returning home at so early an hour.

When Clementine showed him to the door and he was certain they were out of Miss Fothergill's earshot, he said stiffly:

'Perhaps I should apologize, Clementine, for not having corrected Mr Grayshott's mistaken supposition that you were my wife. I thought really . . . well, it seemed best not to belabour the point at that moment.'

Clementine felt her cheeks burning. She realized now how embarrassed Benjamin must have felt, but at the time she herself had been too shocked by the sudden appearance of Deveril to feel more than relief that he had not recognized her. She had humiliated herself beyond forgetting that night last summer by throwing herself into Deveril Grayshott's arms.

'Please do not give the matter another thought, Benjamin,' she pleaded. 'It was of no consequence and in any event, it is far better that he should not know who I really am. It is most unlikely we shall ever meet again.'

But Benjamin was only partially mollified by Clementine's dismissal of the whole unfortunate encounter. As he rode slowly home, he knew that *he* minded, even if Clementine did not. Deveril Grayshott was a useless irresponsible bounder who should not be allowed to escape his responsibilities so easily. Why should he go unscathed whilst poor sweet Clementine had to toil such long weary hours to keep herself and her child? Bitterly, Benjamin reflected that it was by her own choice she did so, rather than become his wife as Grayshott had supposed her to be.

For a long time after she had put the baby to bed, Clementine sat by her bedroom window gazing at the Spode candlestick. She was torn by feelings of guilt, for although she had been quite delighted with the thoughtful gift at the time Benjamin had presented it to her, all she could think of now was how much, much more it would have meant to her had it come from Deveril. Her ingratitude to her dear friend appalled her.

If only she could love Benjamin, she thought. But that too, would have made him as well as herself miserable since she was not free to love or marry anyone. Perhaps on her uncle's next visit, she should enquire whether there was any way of terminating her marriage to Percy Grayshott.

However, when her uncle called a week later, he was unwilling to discuss the matter. He took a long hard look at her, his eyes probing into hers as if he hoped to detect some inner secret.

'That young physician has not been filling your head with a lot of nonsense, has he? I warned you not to do anything to encourage him, Clementine. I hope you have not disobeyed me. Has he been here lately?'

For the first time in her life, Clementine told a deliberate lie. She did so knowingly, caring more for the avoidance of any suggestive talk about Benjamin's behaviour towards her than she did for the sin she was committing.

'No, Uncle, I have not seen him lately.'

'I am glad to hear it,' he said, patting her hand. 'Now, my dear, have you thought more about those lessons I intend to resume if you can find time?'

Clementine bent her head over her sewing.

'I fear I am too busy, Uncle Godfrey. Madame Tamara keeps me fully occupied . . .' she murmured.

'Yes, well . . . I suppose I should not seek to deter you from your work, dear child. It is not of any consequence. We can continue to enjoy our little talks whilst you do your sewing. I think it important that you feel there is one person in the world in whom you can confide . . . even those little matters you might in different circumstances have confided in your poor mama.'

Clementine looked at her uncle in genuine bewilderment.

'What sort of things do you refer to?' she asked.

Faced with so bold a demand for clarification, the parson hummed and stuttered as he said:

'You may sometimes find yourself thinking . . . well, imagining things . . . of a sinful nature. If such is the case, you must not be too greatly shocked, for it is part of our misfortune to be born with sinful desires. With God's help, these lusts of the flesh can . . . er, may be overcome.'

He saw the colour rush into Clementine's cheeks and mistook her embarrassment for guilt. Reaching once more for her hand, he clasped it earnestly and said:

'There, there, child, do not distress yourself. It is only to be expected that once having tasted the carnal pleasures of the body, you should feel the need, although indeed not all women do so . . . but be that as it may, you are young and healthy and it is only natural that you should thirst for . . . well, let us call it "a man's loving attentions" . . . his . . . er, touch . . . kisses perhaps and . . . you appreciate my meaning, dear girl?'

Throughout this preamble he did not release her hand, and now Clementine felt his other hand close over it, imprisoning it. She felt a moment of panic. Jennie had taken the baby out for an airing and Miss Fothergill was attending a committee meeting. She and her uncle were alone in the house. He was stroking her hand as if . . . as if he derived pleasure from doing so. His breathing was hurried and noisy and she could not avoid noticing how his body trembled.

Horrified, she tried to prise her hand free.

'You must not be afraid of me, my dear,' he gasped. 'You are my niece and I would never . . . do not take your hand away . . . such a tiny, pretty little hand.' He paused, as if trying to regain control of himself, and with an obvious effort said sternly: 'It is my duty to warn you, Clementine, that innocent though you may be of evil intent, nevertheless it is sinful to encourage a man's baser instincts. You must be on your guard for you have a most . . . er, most inviting smile and it seems even to . . . to an old man like myself . . . as if you are perhaps

intentionally inviting a man to . . . by the very posture of your
body. You may be unaware how you might give quite the
wrong impression. You must try to be . . . well, circumspect
in your manner, your attire . . .'

He broke off, at last removing his hand and releasing hers,
but only to lift it to touch the lace edge of her gown where
it curved above her bosom.

'. . . so smooth and white and inviting . . .' he muttered.

Clementine was no longer in any doubt whatsoever that
her uncle had momentarily forgotten who he was – who *she*
was. More shocked and revolted than frightened, she stood
up, brushing his hand from her bodice, and said sharply:

'It is not Doctor Brook with whom I need to be on my
guard, Uncle. I suspect that you have been attributing to him
your feelings. I will try to put such a fearful supposition from
my mind, but I would prefer it if you would never touch me
again . . . in fact I would prefer that I should not have to see
you again.'

The parson was on his feet, his face perspiring, his small
watery eyes fastened upon Clementine's face in frightened
appeal.

'You must not make so hasty and terrible a judgement upon
me, my dear. It is clear I have expressed myself very badly . . .
most misleading . . . and I do assure you that your imagination has entirely run away with your senses. I am your uncle
. . . and indeed, a man of God. It shocks and hurts me . . .
yes, hurts me very, very deeply, to hear you voice such terrible
suspicions as to my . . . my character. You are like my own
daughter to me – the daughter I so much wanted to comfort
me in my old age. Your mind has become twisted, my dear,
by all your misfortunes, I daresay, but in no respect must you
ever again think such terrible thoughts . . .'

He saw the confusion in Clementine's face, noted her hesitation as she struggled with renewed uncertainty.

'Come now, my dear, I think you owe me an apology, do
you not? You have done me a great wrong – I who helped

to extricate you from the unfortunate . . . er . . . situation in which you landed yourself. I think I am entitled to something a great deal kinder, am I not? I had hoped that I had both your respect and affection.'

Clementine bit her lip as her gaze dropped. *Had she been mistaken?* If so, how unforgivable the accusation she had made!

'I am sorry if I . . . I misunderstood you, Uncle,' she said. 'Perhaps you are right and I am overtired, overimaginative. But if you will forgive me now, I think I will retire to my room.'

'Of course, of course. Let us think no more about this . . . this unfortunate little misunderstanding. We are both sensible enough to realize that you intended no . . . no insult to your loving old uncle. You go and lie down, my dear, and I shall see myself out. And do not worry your pretty little head about this . . . this contretemps. I give you my word I shall not speak of it to anyone and I know you will not, either.'

He is going to kiss me goodbye, Clementine thought in sudden panic. But the parson was too frightened lest his madness overcame him once more and he betrayed himself beyond redemption.

'I will see you again very soon, dear child. In the meanwhile, do not forget your prayers. God is very understanding.'

God may understand, Clementine thought bitterly, as she went to her room to wash her burning face with cold water. She herself did not. Her every instinct warned her that she had not misjudged her uncle's lascivious attentions and yet to attach such a disgraceful label to him, a parson, her own uncle, seemed an outrageous affront.

Miss Fothergill noticed Clementine's unusual pensiveness as later that night they sat enjoying a cup of hot milk as was their custom before retiring to bed. The girl looked pale and worried. Quite wrongly, Miss Fothergill attributed this to the fact that she had been disappointed that Doctor Brook was not her afternoon visitor. The physician had not called on them since the day of their picnic, and the romantic Miss Fothergill now jumped to the conclusion that Clementine was pining to see him.

'I am not one for prying into people's private affairs, as well you know, my dear,' she said in her sweet, clear voice. 'But you are far too young to remain a widow, and it has become quite obvious to me in recent weeks that dear Doctor Brook is very smitten with you. You do not mind me speaking so directly?'

Clementine drew a deep sigh.

'Dear Miss Fothergill!' she said. 'How could I take offence at anything you might say to me. But it is not my relationship with Benjamin which causes me anxiety. It is . . . it is my uncle. I am not comfortable in his presence. I . . . I may be doing my Uncle Godfrey the greatest wrong, but he leaves me with the fear that his . . . his feelings toward me are not entirely . . . well, avuncular!'

'Oh dear, oh dear!' exclaimed the old lady. 'Oh dearie me! I had no idea of this else I would not have left you alone with him. My poor child! But are you *quite* certain? It is not in your imagination? Sometimes . . . well, it is not unnatural for an old man to like to make a fuss of a pretty young niece, to pet her a little as one might a child.'

'I know, Miss Fothergill. Papa would often stroke my hair and kiss my cheek when he cuddled me but . . . well, I cannot describe my feelings when my uncle comes near me. I feel guilty even speaking of it, and I pray I have misjudged the situation. I am not very experienced in such matters!'

Miss Fothergill tried to conceal her worry from the young girl. She had not worked for so many years amongst the poor and the deprived not to know that terrible things could and did happen in families. There was even one poor child, younger than Clementine, who had been raped by her drunken father! Unmarried she herself might be, but her duties to those in trouble had left her with very few illusions.

'Next time your uncle calls, I will tell Jennie to say that you are indisposed – or that you are out!' she suggested.

Clementine sighed.

'But even if we tell a lie on the next occasion, there will be further visits from my uncle in the future,' she said unhappily. 'Perhaps it was wrong of me to talk of my fears. I could easily have been mistaken.'

'Let us hope so,' the old lady said soothingly, wishing for the time being to drop the conversation. On Doctor Brook's next visit, she would enquire from him what kind of man the Rev Foster was. Perhaps he could enlighten her as to his character.

When next he called early in October, Benjamin Brook was deeply shocked when finally he extricated from Miss Fothergill the reason behind her flustered enquiries. Unhappily he could find no reason to belittle Clementine's fears. The parson had never been a man to his own liking, although he had pitied him, married as he was to such a cold, bitter woman. A man unhappy in his marriage, nearing the end of his active life, unloved and lonely, might very well lose his head over a pretty young girl, Benjamin reflected. Yet the parson was a man of the Cloth – and Clementine his niece!

'Let us wait until after the gentleman's next visit,' he suggested to Miss Fothergill. 'Now that the subject has been discussed between you, I am sure that Clementine will inform you if anything . . . well, untoward takes place. I shall rely on you to tell me, Miss Fothergill. If Clementine's fears are justified, we shall have to protect her.'

It was late October before the Rev Foster dared trust himself to drive once more to Poole. Night after night he had prayed for long hours at a time for God to give him the strength to deny the lusts of his flesh. Now he believed he had at last succeeded in casting out the devil that was in him. Furthermore, he convinced himself that it was his duty as her only relative to reassure himself that his niece was well and happy. Armed with this spurious confidence, he took the dogcart to Poole.

Jennie showed him into the sitting-room where, as the parson had pictured so often in his thoughts, Clementine was seated by the window busily engaged in her stitching. Her fair head was bent over her work and a shaft of autumn sunlight lit up her hair so that it shone like molten gold. His hand ached to touch it, but as he moved towards her, Clementine rose quickly from her chair and turned to face him.

'I was not expecting you, Uncle,' she said, her voice cool and far from welcoming. He forced a beaming smile to his mouth and in as jolly a voice as he could muster, he said:

'My dear child, how very well you look. Do pray be seated and do not allow me to interfere with your work. How is your little one?'

Briefly, Clementine's eyes shone as she spoke of the baby. He was continuing to thrive and was growing so fast she vowed it would not be long before he was walking.

Her uncle moved his chair a little closer to hers – he was growing a trifle deaf in his old age, he explained, as he leant across the small gap between them to admire her work. His balding, perspiring scalp was now level with and far too close to her bosom, Clementine thought in sudden panic. Was she really only being stupid to imagine it was intentional? Her body tautened and she saw him draw back as if he had been stung. He stuttered badly as he murmured:

'Yes, yes, my dear, your stitching is excellent . . . excellent!' Suddenly his eyes lifted and slowly covered her body. 'The dress you are wearing – did you make it yourself? How cleverly you have stitched the ruffle, if such it is, around the neck . . .'

His white wet hand was moving upward towards her – his fingers like fat crawling maggots, Clementine thought, as she shrank back, her face burning, her eyes narrowed in horror.

'Do not touch me!' No sound seemed to come from her throat and his hand crept nearer. 'Please . . . please do not touch me, Uncle!'

This time she must have spoken aloud, for his hand moved

quickly back to his lap and, drawing a handkerchief from his pocket, he mopped at his face and forehead.

'It is still quite warm despite the onset of autumn,' he said in a hard, tight voice. 'We shall be having fires to attend to soon.'

Clementine's eyes were dark with distress.

'I will ring for Jennie to bring us some tea,' she said, rising quickly to her feet and moving away from him.

He made no reply, but she sensed that his eyes were boring into her back as she crossed to the fireplace to pull the bell rope. Her skin prickled and her voice trembled as the little maid came into the room and she gave orders for tea to be brought in immediately.

The parson was once again battling with his unnatural desires, which had returned in full force. His prayers for assistance from above remained unanswered, and try though he might, he could not take his eyes from Clementine's beautiful young body. Unbidden, his imagination stripped her of her clothing and he was racked with longing.

Appalled by his incestuous thoughts, he both feared Clementine's awareness of them and at the same time *wanted* her to be aware of him. Her nervous fear of him was an added excitement even whilst he appreciated the dreadful precariousness of his position. He could not bear it were she to forbid him these visits around which his whole mental existence centred. To be so close to her and to know she was forever barred to him was one kind of torment, but the thought of never seeing her again was even greater.

The Rev Foster was unaware that he had already sealed his fate. When Miss Fothergill returned from her committee meeting that evening, one look at Clementine's pale, unhappy face was sufficient for her to hazard a guess that the parson had been to visit his niece again. When Clementine confirmed this and admitted that her fears had increased rather than diminished, Miss Fothergill waited only until the girl had retired to bed before she composed a long, frankly explicit letter to Doctor Brook.

Benjamin arrived three days later. After a quick conversation with Miss Fothergill, he asked Clementine to join him in the sitting-room for a private talk.

'I have been speaking to Miss Fothergill,' he said without preamble, 'and we are both of the opinion that you should leave Poole and go to live much further afield.'

Clementine's eyes widened.

'Leave Poole? Leave Miss Fothergill? But why, Benjamin? I am happy here. Were it not for . . .'

She broke off, embarrassed to mention her uncle's unseemly behaviour to her companion. It had been difficult enough to speak of her fears to Miss Fothergill, a member of her own sex.

'I do not think we need discuss in any detail the reason for your going, Clementine,' Benjamin said gently. 'I need only say that I believe you should not live so near to your uncle.'

Her eyes were downcast and he could see the colour burning her cheeks, but he knew he must warn her of the danger she was in.

'A man of your uncle's age is often very vulnerable – more especially if his relationship with his wife is incomplete. He would need to have a great deal of willpower to quell those forces that prompt him to do wrong. If your uncle is thus tempted, it would be kinder to him for you to be beyond his reach, Clementine, and a good deal safer for you.'

Clementine looked up at last, her embarrassment tempered by relief as she realized that Benjamin was aware of her fears and was bringing a measure of understanding to the problem. But her thoughts were far from happy.

'Where could I go? Suppose that I could not again find work such as Madame Tamara allows me to bring home?'

'I have given much thought to the matter, Clementine,' Benjamin replied. Only with difficulty did he keep any emotion from his voice, for the suggestion he was about to make was to his own detriment and he did not wish her to take his feelings into consideration. 'I have written to my father in

Brighton – a seaside town in Sussex. In his last letter to me, he spoke of his concern that his elderly housekeeper was upon the point of retirement. He himself is long since retired, and his mind being still very active despite his advanced years, he is fully occupied writing a book on entomology. There are two capacities, therefore, in which you could be of great assistance to him – as his housekeeper and, when time permitted, in making a legible copy of his manuscript. I noted that you have beautiful, neat handwriting, and if my father agrees with my plan, which I feel certain he will, then you would have both work and lodging.'

The enthusiasm which had lit up Clementine's face as Benjamin outlined his proposal gave way to a look of dismay.

'But Brighton is very far away from here, Benjamin. I should never see you . . . or dear Miss Fothergill . . .'

Benjamin turned away so that she was unaware of the pain in his eyes as he replied with forced casualness:

'You could correspond with Miss Fothergill, could you not? As for me . . . well, I do not see nearly enough of my dear father and now that he is nearing the end of his life, it behoves me to undertake the journey a good deal more frequently than has been my wont. I think you could expect me to visit at least every three months and in the summer, when travelling conditions are more favourable, perhaps more often.'

Clementine's face brightened.

'Please tell me more about your father – and about Brighton, too. Is that where the late King George built a beautiful pavilion? Do you really think your father would accept someone so young to act as his housekeeper? And what of Adam? If your father is advanced in years, perhaps he will not care to have a small child in his house . . .'

Benjamin laughed.

'So many questions! All of which I will answer in due course. But first, Clementine, we should consider what is to be done about your uncle. He will almost certainly question me, and Miss Fothergill too, as to your whereabouts.'

Clementine bit her lip. Without breaking her oath, she could not explain to Benjamin that since her marriage to Percy Grayshott, *he* was responsible for her, not her uncle.

'I will write to Uncle Godfrey,' she said persuasively. 'I will tell him that I have found employment elsewhere and that I shall not give anyone an address where I can be found, as I wish to make my own way in the world and have no desire to see him again in the meanwhile. I will inform him that I shall change my name also, so that no one can trace me.'

Benjamin still looked doubtful. Nevertheless, he replied quietly:

'In other circumstances, I would feel I had no justification for encouraging you to lie to your uncle. But in the light of your fears regarding him, perhaps it is best for him too if he does not know where to look for you. There would be little point in your removing from here were he to follow you to Sussex and bring you back.'

Which he had not the right to do now that he was no longer her legal guardian, Clementine thought. She would make a point of reminding him in her letter that Percy Grayshott and not he was now responsible for her. The thought held an ironic satisfaction since it was her uncle who had arranged the marriage.

'Now we must consider the question of adopting a new name for you,' Benjamin said. 'Not too different a one, I think, for I have noticed the initials you have embroidered on your handkerchiefs – CF.'

'Mama often said that she thought the name Clemency prettier even than Clementine,' she suggested tentatively.

Benjamin nodded approvingly.

'Then it is agreed. As for your surname, suppose we take an anagram of Foster – Forest, for example. Clemency Forest! How does that appeal to you?'

Forgetting the proprieties, as she so often did with Benjamin, Clementine jumped to her feet and hugged him childishly.

'I am so grateful, Benjamin!' she said. 'Each time I have been in trouble, you have been there to help me out of it.'

Benjamin patted her hand with a paternalism he certainly did not feel. He loved these moments when Clementine was so openly and impulsively affectionate – yet he could wish it otherwise, for he knew that had she felt any emotions of romantic love towards him, she would have been too shy and modest to fling herself into his arms!

He released her gently and after a quick professional examination of the baby, whom he pronounced in perfect health, he made his adieux, answering Clementine's protestations at so early a departure with the explanation that he wished to send a letter to his father by the next mail coach.

After he was gone, Clementine went to find Miss Fothergill, her eyes shining as she outlined Benjamin's plan.

'If it comes about, it will mean a new start in life for me,' she enthused, 'although I shall miss you very *very* much, dear Miss Fothergill. Oh, you do believe Benjamin's father will agree to this proposal, do you not? Benjamin sounded so certain – but suppose the Professor is not . . .'

Miss Fothergill smiled.

'I am sure Doctor Brook will be most persuasive . . . and I shall write an excellent reference for you. Now curb your impatience, child. If it is the Good Lord's will, it will come to pass.'

Clementine sighed.

'I do not wish to belittle your faith in any way, Miss Fothergill, but it has sometimes struck me quite forcibly that it is not quite fair to God to attribute everything that happens to us as being His will. Is it not sometimes through our own fault or our own efforts that we fail or achieve in our lives?'

But Miss Fothergill was not prepared to be drawn into a philosophical argument before supper. With a sigh she handed back the baby she was rocking to Clementine.

'There is a pattern to our lives, each one of us,' she said. 'And we must submit to God's will.'

But as Clementine carried her hungry little son up to her bedroom to feed him, she found herself in disagreement with the old lady. Right or wrong, she was discovering that it was not in her nature to submit. True enough her failure to submit to Mary's admonitions had resulted in her disgrace! But if she had not lain with Deveril that night, defying all proper behaviour for young ladies, she would not now have her darling Adam.

'And I would not be without you for all the riches in the world, my sweetheart!' she crooned, as with a deep surge of love she nursed the hungry infant at her breast.

CHAPTER NINE

March 1832

Deveril stood outside his wife's bedroom, his hand poised as he hesitated, wondering whether after all he would knock on the door. It was the fifth night of their honeymoon and if the last four nights were anything to go by, he could not exactly expect a rapturous welcome. His wife, he was discovering, possessed an almost fanatical concern for orderliness, and when Deveril climbed into bed beside her, she would not lie back upon her pillow until she had straightened the covers he had disturbed and rearranged the sheet to her satisfaction. As if this was not sufficiently disquieting, she requested him politely not to untie the ribbons on her nightgown as they had only just been ironed by her maid and she did not wish them creased.

Once the candle had been extinguished, Deveril was permitted to lift the hem of her gown and 'do as he pleased' so long as he did not rumple her hair or the bed. She gave no sign that she wished to participate in the act of love and as soon as it was accomplished, she hurried to her boudoir from whence came the vigorous splashing of water, indicating her desire to be cleansed of all evidence of his passion. On her return, she made no reference to the subject and such conversation as ensued covered her plans for the following day. Intentionally or otherwise, she managed in this manner to make Deveril feel there had been no union at all.

Perhaps the fault is mine, Deveril thought, as finally he brought himself to rap gently on the door. A virgin, so he had been told, needed time to become accustomed to sharing her body with a man. He must try to be more patient, to initiate Muriel slowly and gently into the pleasures that could be theirs.

His wife was in bed. The big room looked warm and inviting in the soft candlelight, and the heavy brocade drapes muffled the sounds of the carriages still bowling down the Champs Élysée. Deveril was pleased to see that Muriel had dismissed her *femme de chambre* and that like himself, she was already in her night attire. She was sitting in the centre of the large double bed, her hands grasping the coverlet which she had drawn up to her shoulders when he came into the room. He walked over and sat down beside her.

'You enjoyed the opera, my dear?' he asked conversationally, hoping that his casual enquiry would help to wipe the look of apprehension from her face. For a moment, a feeling of bitterness swept over him as he realized that her expression would shortly become one of revulsion when he climbed in beside her.

'You must not be afraid of me, Muriel,' he said softly, removing his robe. 'We are man and wife, and you have nothing to fear from me,' he added, as he blew out the candles. As he slipped into bed and put his hands gently on her shoulders, he felt her body stiffen.

'You are lying on my arm, Deveril,' he heard her whisper in the darkness. Ignoring her protest, he undid the ribbons of her nightgown. As his hand covered her breast, he was aware that although he could see nothing, she was gritting her teeth in horror.

'Would you rather that I did not stay with you tonight? Perhaps you are tired?' he suggested in a hard tight voice. There was a moment's hesitation before Muriel said:

'No, you can stay if you want to. I really do not mind, Deveril . . .' Nevertheless she edged away, and the lack of welcome in her tone successfully quelled any last vestige of desire he might have felt.

Dammit, he thought, what in heaven's name am I doing

here in bed with a woman I do not want and who most certainly does not want me! The sensible thing to do now, he decided, was to extricate himself from a thoroughly uncomfortable situation.

He pretended a deep yawn.

'Nevertheless, my dear, on reflection we do have quite a heavy schedule tomorrow, do we not? Perhaps it would do us both good to have an early night.'

At once Muriel's body relaxed and she actually turned her head and kissed his cheek.

'Of course, if you say so, Deveril, I *am* a little tired, but . . . well, naturally, dearest, I did not want to disappoint you . . .'

Knowing that he had no right to be angry since the suggestion that he should leave had been his, Deveril nevertheless returned to his adjoining room in an unsettled frame of mind. He would be a fool to go on pretending that this side of his marriage might ever prove satisfactory. There were many women who were cold and frigid like Muriel – a fact he had learned from other females who had welcomed him to their bed. It was far from uncommon, he remembered one young actress telling him, and was one of the main reasons why married men were so frequently unfaithful to their wives.

But he did not want his marriage to be lacking in this respect, he told himself, as he walked over to the window and stared down into the street below. He had been looking forward to this fortnight in the romantic city of Paris, supposing that he and Muriel would set the foundations for a happy life together. Now he could only hope that when they were back in England and Muriel had had time to become more accustomed to her married status, matters would improve.

But three weeks later, seated on the sofa in the drawing-room at Grayshott House, regarding Muriel's straight back with a sense of unreality, he recalled that moment of tentative optimism and realized that it was unfounded. There, he thought, seated at her escritoire writing out invitations, sat his wife, twenty-two years old, poised, beautiful in her pale blue foulard evening dress, her black hair knotted on the crown of her head, which was slightly inclined as she applied herself to her task.

Was it really possible that he was married to this woman, he thought uneasily, as he listened to the scratch of her pen and the faint regular tapping as she dipped the quill into the silver inkwell. The words of the marriage ceremony crossed his mind – 'love', 'cherish', 'worship'. Somehow they did not seem to apply to his feelings for Muriel.

His thoughts slipped further back to the memory of his bride as she walked up the aisle of St George's in a cloud of virginal white satin on the arm of a proud, smiling Lord Lawrence. The church had been crowded. The colourful attire of their hundreds of fashionable friends added to the festivity of the occasion and momentarily dispelled the depression that had inevitably followed the carousing at his stag party the night before. His friends had ribbed him unmercifully, calling him a halfwit and an imbecile to be tying himself up in matrimony at so young an age. At twenty-one he should be making the most of his youth and freedom, they had pointed out; *they* would be adventuring abroad, sowing their wild oats where their fancy took them, free to do exactly as they pleased, whilst poor Deveril would be forced to trim his sails according to his wife's wishes . . .

Ordinarily, Deveril took his friends' teasing in good humour, laughing and countering their jibes with his own. But on that occasion, however unintentionally, they had endorsed his own doubts as to the wisdom of so early – and hasty – a marriage. Those doubts had become more akin to certainties, he reflected, remembering that his wife's attitude had been no different during the last ten days of their honeymoon from at the start.

Unaware of her young husband's feelings, Muriel was in the best of moods. That afternoon she had given her first 'At

Home' since her honeymoon, and she had received a gratifying
number of callers, amongst whom was Princess Lieven.

'The Princess was accompanied by her new friend, Caroline
Norton,' she said brightly to Deveril over her shoulder. 'You
may have heard of her, Dearest. She is quite a well-known
writer and I have to admit she is something of a beauty too
– in a rather flamboyant way, of course. I thought her flame-
coloured velvet gown a trifle *outré*, but it was quite striking.'

Unaware that Deveril's thoughts were elsewhere, she
continued volubly:

'The Princess told me that Mrs Norton has managed to
gain the interest of the Home Secretary, Lord Melbourne, and
his sister, Lady Cowper, and that they are frequently guests in
the Nortons' little home at Storey's Gate. We must definitely
cultivate Caroline, Deveril, for she seems to know a great
many interesting and famous people.'

With an effort, Deveril tried to match his wife's preoccupation with her social acquaintances.

'You say this Mrs Norton is a writer?'

Muriel turned towards him, her face almost beautiful as
she regarded him with a look of excited animation.

'Oh yes, indeed! Caroline is quite talented. But that is not
to be wondered at since she is the granddaughter of the
playwright Richard Sheridan, from whom, I imagine, she has
inherited her gift. She has written two poems which have
been widely read, and now, Princess Lieven tells me, she has
been made editor of *La Belle Assemblée*.'

'And is there a Mr Norton?' Deveril enquired.

'Very much so, although the Princess told me that the young
couple are not well-matched. It would seem George Norton
greatly resents his wife's popularity, especially since she seems
so often to attract the opposite sex. But the Princess liked her.
She thought her very amusing.' The brightness left her face as
she recalled the Princess's further remark – that Caroline was
a devoted mother and had just produced a second son. Muriel's
mouth tightened. Motherhood was not something she cared

to think about, and it was already proving a slight bone of contention between her and her beloved Deveril. Even during their honeymoon he had harped on the subject – delicately, of course, but nevertheless making it clear he wanted children and before too long. It was partly because that old grandfather of his was badgering him for an heir, she thought resentfully. She certainly had no wish to be with child and to have to withdraw from all the social activities she had planned for their first year of marriage.

Deveril yawned and shifted uneasily on the sofa as he wondered whether he could possibly escape to his club. Since their return to England he had once or twice suggested tentatively that he pay a quick visit there, but Muriel had clung to him in a most possessive manner, indicating quite clearly that she felt it his duty to remain with her at least until she had had time to formulate her own social calendar. She was clearly in the mood to talk, and she launched now into further gossip about her latest acquaintance.

'The Princess told me that Caroline's temperament may not be as well suited to marriage as mine. She has a very strong will and a keen intelligence which she is either unwilling or unable to hide. Men do not care for it – at least, husbands do not. It would seem, Deveril, that Mr Norton is not finding it easy to bend his wife to his will, nor is she finding it easy to submit. I gather she is much cleverer than her husband.'

Muriel's thoughts turned once more to her own relationship with Deveril. He was not proving as easy to twist around her little finger as was her dear papa. Deveril, like herself, had been used to having his own way, and she felt it just a little irksome that he expected total submission from her now that she was his wife.

Muriel sighed, recalling suddenly her mama's counselling that a man wanted a peaceful atmosphere in his home above all, and since he was The Provider, he had every right to expect it. Not that every husband received it, Muriel thought, as she repeated more of Princess Lieven's comments about the Nortons' marriage.

'Despite George's jealousy of his wife's success, he is not above making use of it. Apparently he persuaded Caroline to approach the Home Secretary to obtain a position for him and seemed glad enough when Lord Melbourne secured him a judgeship in the Metropolitan Police Court. Caroline told the Princess that the Nortons rely heavily upon her literary earnings. I imagine her husband does not care for the situation, but I suppose it does account in part for Caroline's independent spirit, do you not agree, Deveril? I understand she is very self-willed. Rumour has it that the couple quarrel quite violently. However, they seem to be reconciled since the birth of their second son earlier this year.'

Nevertheless, Muriel mused, Caroline Norton seemed to illustrate by her immense social success that it was far from necessary to be weak, retiring and selfless in order to be so popular. According to the Princess, men both famous and acclaimed in their field were among her admirers and friends.

'Of course, she is immensely charming and witty,' she told Deveril. 'She told me herself that Mr William Wordsworth dined with her recently, and she knows Charles Lamb and Thomas Moore as well as Samuel Rogers, not to mention Edwin Landseer *and* John Hayter, who is painting her portrait. I shall definitely put her on my calling list.'

'By all means, my dear,' Deveril replied indifferently as he put down his brandy glass and stood up to walk over to the fireplace. Muriel had returned momentarily to writing out the invitations for the ball they were to give at Easter. But it was only a minute or two before her clear high voice invaded his thoughts once more.

'I am uncertain whether to send an invitation to Sir Paul and Lady Kingston. What is your opinion, Deveril, my dear? Sir Paul is quite an interesting man but his wife . . . well, Princess Lieven has not sent her an invitation for some time . . .'

Deveril drew a deep sigh as he stifled a yawn of acute boredom.

'I would have thought your invitation would depend upon your own opinion of the poor woman rather than upon someone else's,' he murmured.

Muriel turned to look at him, her brows drawn together as she frowned.

'I cannot agree with you, Deveril. I wish our first big party to be a success, and *who* we invite to it is of the utmost importance.'

'Is the lady in question of attractive appearance?' Deveril enquired, with a glint of mischief in his dark eyes. 'After all, if my friends are to be invited, they will want a few pretty women to flirt with.'

By the tightening of Muriel's mouth, he knew that his quip had not been appreciated. Fortunately, she chose to ignore his remark and returned to her work. Deveril reached for the decanter old Dawkins had left on the sofa table, hoping that a second glass of brandy would cheer his flagging spirits. He was feeling not only restless but restricted. With a little luck, he thought, Muriel would shortly decide to retire for the night and he could slip away unnoticed to Brooks's, where he would be certain to encounter one or more of his friends. It should not be too difficult, since Muriel would be most unlikely to demand that he should retire to bed with her.

On their return to London, she had toured Grayshott House from attics to cellar, fussing interminably about even a speck of dust. She spent each morning exhorting the servants to clean and polish more assiduously and even to plump up the cushions each time they had been flattened, so that at no time ever did a single object in their home look out of place or used.

Muriel was quite unaware how foreign her attitude was to him, Deveril thought, for he had grown up for the most part in the bachelor atmosphere of Chiswell Hill House where he, his grandfather and father had been content to allow

their housekeeper to maintain her own standards. The dogs'
hairs upon the carpet, the muddy boot prints on the polished
floors were part of their way of life in the country. As for
life at Castle Clunes in Scotland, his beloved Great-Aunt Meg
lived in total disregard for the domestic side of life. Her
animals and other pets roamed freely in the ninety-roomed
mansion, and guests were never surprised to find a parrot's
feather on their counterpane or a jackdaw's hoard in a clothes
closet! The servants did their best but fought a losing battle,
and the castle was a glorious shambles, resembling more a
zoological garden than the home of one of the country's
leading families.

It was true that their London home, Burnbury House, was
of necessity more formal, but neither he nor his grandfather
had really lived in it and used it only as a convenience.

Deveril's thoughts turned inevitably at this point to his
grandfather, who was far from well and very lame now that
his gout had worsened. Deveril doubted very much whether
he would ever undertake the long journey to Scotland again.
Because the old man's heart was so set upon Deveril's
marriage, he had driven to London for the wedding, and
despite his obvious fatigue, he had clearly been happy and
delighted to see his grandson married to the woman he had
selected for him. In fact, Deveril thought now, had it not
been for his grandfather's obsessive wish to see him married,
he would no more have contemplated settling down than
did his contemporaries, especially with a woman he scarcely
knew. Yet the Muriel who now shared his life and home
was not so different, he thought uneasily, from the bossy
little girl he had disliked in his childhood. He would have
to take a firm hand with her in future. He had probably
been too lax during their honeymoon in his attempt to
soften her heart a little. Not that Muriel was altogether
unloving. She responded with affectionate kisses and loving
smiles when he paid her a compliment or gave her some
little present. If she seemed to want to avoid his company

at night in the bedroom, she made up for it during the day, requiring him to be constantly by her side. She was not happy unless he was dancing attendance upon her, he thought, his restiveness increasing.

Despite the warmth of the room, he shivered. There seemed to have been a chill around his heart ever since he had returned to England. His home – the Grayshotts' second London house which his grandfather had given him as a wedding present – no longer seemed the same familiar establishment, and he did not feel at ease in it. Muriel had had it redecorated and refurbished during the month preceding their wedding, and although he approved of much of the beautiful new furniture she had selected, he missed the familiar antiques that long ago, his mother had chosen for Grayshott House. The plain fact was that he was always pleased to be out of the place!

With an impulsiveness that was typical of him, he suddenly stood up and said in a firm voice that brooked no argument:

'I am going to my club after all, Muriel, so do not wait up for me. I am really not of any use to you here, and I am sure you will be able to select our guests more than adequately without my assistance.'

The astonished expression on her face revealed her shock – and dismay.

'But Deveril, dearest . . .'

Her protest died on her lips as she saw the flash of anger in his eyes – the first time he had ever shown this emotion. Quickly, she altered her tone as she rose from her escritoire to go to him.

'Of course you are longing to see your friends after so long,' she said tenderly. 'How selfish of me to want to keep you at my side. But do not be too long away, my darling, as I shall miss you sorely!'

Her murmur was softly seductive and for a moment, Deveril hesitated. Was it possible that suddenly, when he had all but given up hope, Muriel had had a change of heart – or at least a surge of emotion? If he were to return from his club early, would Muriel be awaiting him in her bedroom with a look of welcome on her face?

His eyes travelled swiftly over her figure. It was not voluptuous, and the swell of her breasts which he had observed before their marriage had been assisted by padding, he now knew. But her skin was young and smooth and fresh, silky to his touch, and despite everything he was not without desire for her.

She was brushing her lips against his cheek – the first approach she had ever made of her own accord. But as Deveril put his hand beneath her chin and turned her face so that he could kiss her lips, he discovered them cold and firmly closed against his tongue.

With a sigh, he drew back from her embrace and said lightly:

'Do not wait up for me, my dear. I will see you at breakfast!'

There were three of Deveril's close friends at his club, he discovered to his delight and relief. They greeted him warmly.

'Missed you, old fellow.'

'How's married life, eh?'

'What say we drive down to Vauxhall Bridge?' another suggested. 'There's a jolly inn down by the river where the ale is excellent and I have heard that the female performers from the Coburg Theatre quite often amuse themselves there.'

'Cannot have young Grayshott blotting his copybook so soon after his marriage!' quipped another. 'He can enjoy the ale and we will enjoy the girls!'

Once more Deveril's spirits fell, but only momentarily. He was not going to allow his marriage to change his life all that much. And after the disaster of his honeymoon with Muriel, he would enjoy a romp with a female who really appreciated what he had to offer.

'My carriage is outside,' he said shortly. 'I'll race you there. We each put two guineas in the pot, making eight for he who arrives first – agreed? No coachman allowed; we drive ourselves!'

In the end, Deveril's faithfulness to Muriel was not put to the test. One of the curricles overturned in Horseferry Road, and by the time they had extricated their friend, they were all too thirsty to be bothered to make their way to the river. Stopping at the nearest inn, they sat down to toast first Deveril's marriage, then Muriel, followed by themselves, their university, their school, the girls whose favours they had enjoyed on past occasions, and finally sobriety. By then there was little of it in evidence, and thanks to a kindly landlord, men were found to drive Deveril and his friends to their homes, not one of them being in a fit state to drive himself.

Muriel woke from a light sleep to the sound of Deveril's raised voice and that of his valet trying to quieten him. She sat upright, her head on one side, listening. There was little doubt that her young husband was drunk, she thought furiously. At least this would be one night when she had every possible excuse to refuse his presence in her bed. Not that he had given her reason to suppose he might come to her room when he returned from his club. On the contrary, he had expressly told her not to wait up for him. Nevertheless, she would have to upbraid him in the morning – gently and sweetly, of course, so that he did not begin to think of her as a tyrant.

'It is the only way to achieve what you want, my dear,' her mama had said during those last few weeks prior to her wedding, when she had thought Muriel should be warned of the less obvious facets of married life. 'You do not want to give him grounds for taking a mistress . . .'

A mistress, according to Lady Lawrence, was an almost unavoidable evil if a wife refused her husband his marital rights. Although the good lady did not actually say so in as many words, Muriel gathered that her mother had done just this and thrown Papa into the arms of a more willing female. And, of course, there was nothing a wife could do if such a thing happened, other than pretend to her women friends (who

would certainly gossip about it) either that she did not know
or she did not care. A mistress was to be avoided at all costs,
since it was not unknown for a husband to end up preferring
such a woman's company to that of his wife, who could then
risk the terrible consequence of being turned out of her own
home to make room for her rival.

'It is really quite unfair,' Lady Lawrence had admitted to
the round-eyed Muriel, 'but such is life, my dear. You must
never forget that a man is the superior of a woman, born with
more intelligence and a greater understanding of life. God has
created them so, and those strange women one hears about
of late who profess themselves the equal of men are to be
abhorred.' Moreover, her mother had added, they courted
disaster for themselves, since were they to pursue their beliefs,
they would very soon find themselves at serious loggerheads
not only with Society but with their husbands. Which was as
maybe, Muriel thought, but Caroline Norton's social success
did seem to disprove Mama's belief that a woman who revealed
her intelligence and opinions was necessarily unpopular with
the opposite sex.

When at last Muriel dozed off to sleep again, it was without
resolving the conflict of opinions that had disturbed her equilibrium. She had yet to make up her mind how she would
'manage' Deveril – since 'managing' him was the most important
thing in her life now that at long last she was his wife. There
had not been one morning since her wedding when she had
not woken to a feeling of intense satisfaction that he was hers
at last. Not one of her friends had a husband as devastatingly
attractive, as charming, amusing or as popular as Deveril.

She genuinely loved him. His four sisters declared that he was
'wild' and 'irresponsible'; that he liked women, hunting them,
flirting with them, even seducing them, and causing his family
not a little concern lest he should involve them all in some
dreadful scandal, young though he was. But there had never
been anyone else Muriel wished to marry and she had been
steadfast in her determination to wait for him.

'I dare say he will grow out of his unruliness,' his sister Selina had said comfortingly. 'You will just have to be firm with him when you marry him, Muriel!'

When Muriel awoke next morning, she was no longer in doubt about it. Gently, persuasively, so that he barely noticed it, Deveril Grayshott must be broken in like an unruly colt and made to toe her line.

CHAPTER TEN

March–December 1832

'That is most welcome, my dear!' Professor Brook said, setting aside his paintbrush and leaning back in his chair as Clemency Forest put a tray of tea things on his work table. He took off his spectacles and rubbed his eyes, sighing. 'How much easier I would find it were I painting large elephants rather than little butterflies.'

Clemency sat down opposite him and smiled at her employer's sally.

'Benjamin says it is quite remarkable that you can still manage to paint at all,' she said, cutting into the freshly baked cherry cake she knew he loved.

'That is mainly because I now have you to do all my writing, Clemency,' the old man replied with a twinkle. 'It saves my eyes from becoming too strained.'

It was surprising how quickly she had become used to her new name, Clemency thought, as she and the elderly professor sat momentarily in a companionable silence. She seldom thought of herself as Clementine now and had even begun to prefer her alias.

A coal fire burned merrily in the little grate, for the March winds were cold and the Professor, being old, complained that he could not work if his hands were inflamed by chilblains. Clemency had become remarkably fond of the old man in the five months she had been his housekeeper and copyist. A tiny, frail gentleman with faded, periwinkle-blue eyes and wispy grey hair, he made up in intellect what he lacked in stature. A former don teaching mathematics at Oxford University, he had lost none of his clear, precise thinking since his retirement ten years previously. Now in his seventies, the only sign of age lay in his increasing physical disabilities, about which he complained only when they diminished his ability to work.

It was his custom, since her arrival, to devote half his day to the dictation of his book on butterflies and other insects, and an hour or two, following his afternoon rest, to painting the beautiful watercolour illustrations for it. Clemency had become fascinated by the whole subject of entomology, and was captivated by some of the beautiful colours of the butterflies he painted. To please him, she had secretly copied one in tapestry wools on a cushion she made for his birthday.

Benjamin had paid them one visit since he had first escorted Clemency to Brighton. He had returned home after this second visit with a quiet mind, delighted by the fact that she and his father had become such firm friends.

Although Clemency worked very hard in the neat little house, the Professor never treated her as a servant and insisted she partook of her meals in company with him. Of late, he had permitted her to bring Adam down to the drawing-room in the early evening and had begun to take an interest in the little boy, who was now ten months old.

'I was far too busy at college to observe my own sons at this tender age,' he told her, 'and now I realize that I have missed one of life's most absorbing conundrums – to wit, whether an infant's character is inherited or moulded by the adult influences that surround him. Perhaps your next task will be to help me to compile a book about human behaviour. It could be almost as fascinating as insect behaviour . . .'

The Professor never reproved Clemency for her curiosity but applauded it.

'You have a lively mind, young lady, and should use it. Not all God's creatures are blessed with a natural intelligence, and although too much may not be advisable for a pretty young female to exhibit in the presence of her male counterparts, nevertheless all knowledge is an asset if it is correctly used.'

He had explained to her that their present Prime Minister, Lord Grey, was a Whig whose government was greatly in favour of reform. Until the King, on his succession, had invited Grey to form a government, the Tories had held power for ten years. This change of ministry was to be welcomed, the Professor told her. The Whigs were pledged to rectify the injustices of the present Parliamentary representation, and he believed Lord Russell's bill for reforms would be approved before many months were out.

'Fortunately our new King William is basically in favour of all kinds of reforms,' he told Clemency, 'unlike the late King George, who was concerned in the main with his own self-indulgence. However, it would be wrong to denigrate our former monarch entirely, since by his interest in the arts, he has left England a great architectural heritage. When the weather is warmer and we can enjoy some walks further afield, I shall show you some of the beautiful crescents built here in Brighton as a result of his influence. In London too, you will find many magnificent new buildings – Regent Street, of course, has been named after him. His architect, John Nash, designed the royal Buckingham Palace and the Marble Arch of which you will have heard.'

Clemency was learning without realizing it. The Professor's explanations more often than not led to further questions, and he was happy to enlighten her about the other reforms the Whig government wished to effect, not the least important of these being the bettering of the working conditions of the poor. For far too long, he maintained, the rich had continued to prosper, whilst those who laboured to provide that wealth were living close to starvation.

The Professor pointed to a copy of *The Times*, which he read every morning whilst he breakfasted.

'Only the other day, I was considering the cost of one of those big fashionable weddings that Society favours for the élite,' he commented. 'To tell you the truth, my dear, weddings do not customarily hold any interest for me, but I took note of this one as the young bridegroom – I forget his name – is Viscount Burnbury's heir, and the family seat is in Dorset in Benjamin's neighbourhood. Ben has treated the family from time to time and speaks well of them. However, I am digressing from my point, which is that the money spent on that one wedding would have kept a whole village in food for the best part of a year and would amount to more than a common labourer might hope to earn in his whole lifetime. Now from this viewpoint, one cannot deny that there is an injustice which should be rectified.'

For once, Clemency welcomed the fact that Professor Brook's eyesight was failing, for he was unaware that her face had flushed a deep pink when she realized that the wedding to which he referred was Deveril's. At one and the same time, she both longed and dreaded to hear more about his marriage.

'According to the report,' the Professor continued, 'the wedding took place at St George's, Hanover Square, with a big ball afterwards for close on eight hundred guests, including the King and Queen. But I daresay that pompous old peer, Lord Lawrence, will not even have skimmed the surface of the family coffers to meet the bills. He is one of the wealthiest men in England, I believe.'

By now Clemency had regained her outward composure, although her heart was beating furiously as he continued:

'Not that I have anything against our aristocracy.' He wagged a thin forefinger as if to emphasize his point. 'They are a necessary part of our social structure. But men born to wealth and title have a responsibility to those who do the work to keep their estates financially viable.'

Clemency cleared her throat and asked:

'Is . . . is Viscount Burnbury's heir as indifferent as his grandfather to the plight of their workers?'

The Professor shrugged his shoulders.

'That I cannot say, my dear. You will have to ask Benjamin. I would suspect, however, that young Grayshott is little different from most youths of his age and rank. There is no real purpose to their lives other than to enjoy themselves. Now Benjamin, as you know, is dedicated to the care of the sick – always was, even as a young lad – and my elder son, Frederick – he is just as dedicated to the care of men's souls. I cannot say I would much like the life of a missionary myself, but it is a worthy calling. We shall have to wait and see what that young son of yours does with his life, will we not?'

He helped himself to another slice of cake and smiled vaguely at Clemency.

'Remember this, my dear, there are only two really important things you must give your little son. One is knowledge, and the second is love. Money certainly does not buy love or affection, and a child is rich beyond measure if he has the kind of love you give him, my dear.'

How very different the old Professor was from her uncle, Clemency thought, as she sat down to write out the week's menus for the cook. No matter how depressed her mood, he could always cheer her with his kindly remarks and advice. She was very fond of him and she loved her work. Her baby was growing fast into a healthy, happy child in a home where he was welcome. Each day of his development, she found something new to fascinate her, and she loved him passionately and selflessly. Even the work required to cater to his needs was pleasure of a kind.

Sometimes she asked herself if the true reason she loved Adam so much was that daily he seemed to resemble more closely the man who had fathered him. Reason, logic, commonsense all told her that she should hate Deveril – but she could not, and she felt a guilty delight when the little boy's face broke into an impish grin, bringing back the memory of Deveril on the seashore at Poole when he had invited her to go sailing with him. Adam's dark hair seemed to curl in the same unruly fashion over his forehead, his eyebrows to have darkened and to turn up slightly at the outer edge in the same devilish manner as his father's.

He was a well-behaved baby, content to be left for long

periods on his own – if his cradle was not too far from the sound of his mother's voice. Already he could sit up alone, and Clemency was convinced he would soon begin to crawl. She longed for him to be able to talk, so that she could have conversations with him: learn what he was thinking; listen to his hopes and wishes and dreams.

For the present, there were solitary hours in the late evening when, despite her tiredness, she could not sleep but lay awake, conscious of her loneliness. Her imagination conjured up a life whereby she was happily married and now lying in the arms of the man she loved, their child asleep in the cradle by the bed. How perfect life would be then, she thought! She could understand now how her mama and papa had been so happily content with their lives and each other.

Never, if Clemency could help it, did she think of The Rectory and her uncle and aunt. But true to her word, she wrote every week to Miss Fothergill and received a regular letter in reply. Benjamin wrote, too – giving news of Mary and of his patients. He came to stay for a few days over Easter. The weather had turned springlike and as a result, he took Clemency and his father out on little trips; one westward to Shoreham and one eastward to the pretty little seaside village of Rottingdean. After church on Easter Sunday, they took a stroll among the crowds on the Chain Pier, Benjamin carrying Adam pick-a-back and Clemency trying hard to walk sedately and not run from side to side to look at the waves bowling past them towards the shore. The Professor took off his broad-brimmed hat and allowed the sea breeze to ruffle his hair, smiling benignly as he took them to see the steam packets newly arrived from France and now tied up at the end of the pier.

It was a happy day at the conclusion of which Benjamin sealed Clemency's contentment by informing her that she need no longer worry that her uncle might yet trace her to Brighton.

'I encountered him by chance in the village last week,' he told her, when they were alone for a short while after the old Professor had retired early to bed. 'I feared his further questioning, but he wished only to inform me that he had now resigned himself to your sudden disappearance. I thought you would be the happier for knowing that he has abandoned any idea of searching for you, my dear.'

For the most part, Benjamin's visit held nothing but pleasure for Clemency. But on his last evening, he enquired if there was any possibility, however remote, that she might reconsider marriage to him in the future. She did not have the heart to deny him all hope.

'Perhaps, dearest Benjamin, I shall feel differently in a few years' time,' she said uneasily. 'For the present, I am very happy here with your father, and he assures me he too is well content. I would not want to alter my way of life just now. Besides, we are only one third of the way through the writing of his book. Who would finish it for him were I not here to help?'

They both knew this was but an excuse, since a promise of betrothal would not necessarily have entailed an immediate marriage. But the excuse sufficed for the occasion and their parting was friendly, if a trifle sad. The Professor seemed fully appraised of the situation. Alone once more with Clemency as they sat down to their evening repast, he said:

'I warned the boy not to press his suit with you, my dear! Ben wears his heart on his sleeve, and I have known ever since he brought you here to live with me that he had lost his heart to you. And I do not blame him. One day, perhaps, you will make a perfect wife for him – and he would make you a good husband. But not yet! You remind me of one of my pupae – your character and beauty only half-formed. One day, you will emerge as a fully fledged butterfly and like all God's creatures, you will want a mate. In the meanwhile, you have your child to fuss over and give you an outlet for your maternal instincts. Now am I not right?'

Clemency longed to be able to tell the old man that she did already know what it meant to love – to see one man's face in her dreams, to long for his kisses, his touch; to feel her heart race at no more than his smile. But Deveril was her secret and one she must bury for ever deep inside her. Fortunately she had her work to distract her, and the baby, whom she could no longer confine to his cradle. He was now crawling and trying to pull himself upright. He had begun to talk, although neither she nor the Professor could understand his baby language.

Throughout the spring and into the month of June, when Adam celebrated his first birthday, the three of them took little expeditions whenever the afternoons were fine. The Professor seemed to take great delight in including Clemency in his outings.

His favourite sortie was to the site where the foundations were being laid for a huge iron and glass conservatory. It was to have a dome some 160 feet wide and sixty-four feet in height, where tropical trees, plants and birds were to be housed. Here they frequently encountered Henry Phillips, the botanist and chief projector of the scheme, whose enthusiasm for this edifice, which he called the 'Antheum', was echoed by the Professor. Mr Phillips was consulting the elderly don with regard to the introduction of some of the world's most beautiful tropical butterflies and moths.

'Just think, my dear,' the Professor enthused, 'what an education this will be to the thousands of inhabitants and visitors to Brighton, who are presently quite ignorant of the beauties of nature to be found in tropical countries. What joys and pleasures are in store for them!' he exulted, wringing his hands in excitement. Clemency became almost as anxious as he for the completion of the Antheum by the end of the year.

By now Brighton was thronged with summer visitors, and she envied the many bathers dipping into the cool sea water from their bathing machines. When the Professor was too tired or too busy to go out, Clemency took the little boy down past the Esplanade on to the pebbly beach and allowed him to dabble his feet in the water when it was not too rough. By August he was walking firmly on his plump, sturdy little legs and talking incessantly. He was twenty-two pounds in weight and stood a fraction over two and a half feet in height.

'He is going to be a tall young man, Clemency,' the Professor forecast. 'Takes after your father, I daresay,' he added, not seeing the blush that coloured Clemency's cheeks as she remembered how tall Deveril was.

But for the Professor's generosity, Clemency thought, she would not have been able to look after her growing child and carry out her duties efficiently. The kindly old man, seeing how much of her time the little boy now needed, altered her hours for transcribing his book until after Adam had been put to bed.

'It makes very little difference to me when you work, my dear,' he told her, 'and we are progressing far more quickly than I had dared to hope. My publisher has given me until the end of 1834 to complete the book, but at this rate we may well be finished much sooner!'

Despite her determination to forget Deveril Grayshott's very existence, Clemency could not refrain from reading the Court Circular in *The Times*. When she read that the Court might come down to Brighton in October, she found herself wondering whether she might one day by chance see Deveril and his wife driving along Marine Parade or along New Road on their way to the theatre. She had seen their names mentioned as guests of the Devonshires at a performance of *The Rivals* at Drury Lane. Muriel was described as 'The Hon Deveril Grayshott's beautiful young wife', and Clemency could imagine her, poised, regal, and smiling proudly as she entered a room on Deveril's arm. She could not help but envy her.

In September she celebrated her eighteenth birthday, which occasion, Benjamin wrote regretfully, he was too busy to attend. But in late October he was home once more on a short visit. As always, Clemency was delighted to see him, and dinner on his first night was made a festive occasion when the Professor brought out a bottle of his best claret which he knew his son enjoyed. Conversation flowed easily as Benjamin talked of his patients and the Professor of his book. But when Susan, the maid, had cleared away the meal and they had repaired to the little drawing-room for a glass of port, the talk turned to politics.

Would the passing of the Reform Bill make any change in people's attitudes, the Professor asked Benjamin.

'D'you see any sign of improvement down your part of the world, my boy?' he enquired innocently. 'Are the Grayshotts showing a greater willingness to improve the conditions in the villages and farmsteads?'

Neither man noticed Clemency's hand as it poised in mid-air over her sewing at mention of the Grayshotts' name. Benjamin seemed to have forgotten that the subject held any special interest for her.

'I have certainly not noticed any changes,' he replied wryly. 'The old Viscount is physically unable to get out and about these days. As for Deveril Grayshott, he has not been near the estate all summer. I understand his wife miscarried their first child – in June I think it was. According to Lord Burnbury, who I now attend quite regularly, Mrs Grayshott insisted her husband should remain with her in London for the Season "to cheer her spirits". I fancy we shall not see much of the young man in Dorset if the Honourable Mrs Grayshott has her way!'

Clemency digested this news with mixed feelings. She felt pity for the woman for losing her baby, but envy too, that she had Deveril at her side to love and comfort her.

'I have little other news to impart,' Benjamin said, oblivious to her private thoughts. 'Mary and Jack have had their first baby – a little girl with Mary's ginger curls. Miss Fothergill is as busy as ever with her impoverished dependants, and I myself have been coping with a scourge of whooping cough which sadly has taken its toll of the less healthy infants in the villages.'

The following day he complimented Clemency upon the obvious health and vigour of her little son, and spent a large part of his visit playing with the boy. When he departed, it was with the promise that he would try to join them for Christmas. Much depended upon the weather.

'In the meanwhile, Clemency,' he said wistfully, 'try to make time to write to me as often as you can.'

He himself never failed to write long affectionate letters every week. Several times, he mentioned the possibility of removing from Dorsetshire to Brighton '*to be nearer to the three people who mean most to me in the world – Father, you and Adam.*' Clemency was touched by his unerring devotion, and although she was far too busy ever to be lonely, nevertheless she found herself wondering more and more frequently whether, were she ever free, she would marry Benjamin. Adam would soon need a father's firm hand – and Benjamin really loved the little boy. Was it possible, she asked herself, that she could grow to love Benjamin in the way that marriage required of her? And if that were so, if there was not some way by which her marriage to Percy could be dissolved. It had been forced upon her, a minor, by her uncle under threat of her disgrace and surely could not have true legality?

She was careful not to allow any sentiment other than affection to show in her letters. But there was a new pleasure in awaiting his Christmas visit, and she was quite as excited as the Professor when Benjamin's letter arrived two days beforehand to announce his arrival on Christmas Eve.

Her last two Christmases had been far from happy, Clemency reflected as she decorated the Professor's house with red-berried holly and wrapped the presents she had bought for the little family. She had missed her papa and mama unbearably, and it was only now after two long years that she was reconciled to the fact that she would never see them again.

For the first time that she could remember, Clemency felt shy and awkward when finally Benjamin arrived, armoured against the cold by a big, handsome, caped overcoat and muffler, his face smiling and happy as first he kissed his father's cheek and then Clemency's.

'You look so pretty standing there in front of the fire,' he said, his eyes fastened on her admiringly. 'I suppose your young ragamuffin is asleep and I shall have to wait till morning before I can see him.'

I *am* pleased to see him, Clemency thought, as she took his coat and pulled an armchair nearer to the blazing fire. He is all we need to complete the family circle!

The feeling persisted throughout Christmas Day. Presents were exchanged after luncheon and then, while the Professor and Adam had their afternoon naps, Benjamin and Clemency went for a brisk walk along the Esplanade, his arm supporting her as they watched the incoming waves race over the pebbles and pound against the wooden piles of the Chain Pier. They seemed to be the only people abroad, apart from an occasional landau or curricle bowling down the street.

Susan and Cook had been given the afternoon off, and whilst Clemency made the tea in the kitchen, Benjamin sat at the scrubbed wooden table watching her.

'I have a small surprise for you,' he said. 'Father told me that you had never yet been to the theatre, so as soon as I was certain that I would be here for Christmas, I wrote and obtained tickets for *The School for Scandal*. It is being performed at the New Theatre on the 29th of the month. As it is an evening performance, I thought it only fair to advise you in good time since Father informed me that he did not think you had suitable attire.'

Clemency stood poised with the big copper kettle in one hand, the teapot in the other, as she regarded Benjamin with shining eyes.

'So that is why you gave me the length of organdie for my Christmas present!' she exclaimed, 'and why Miss Fothergill sent me that recent copy of *La Belle Assemblée*.'

She was speechless with pleasure. 'You shall help me to select a gown to copy,' she said, as Benjamin carried the heavy tea-tray up to the drawing-room. 'That is if Adam will allow us to study its pages in peace!'

'He will be content to play with the box of wooden bricks Father gave him,' Benjamin said, laughing. 'I never saw a child less willing to be parted from a toy when you carried him off for his nap.'

For the next two days, while Benjamin and the Professor amused themselves with long, complicated games of chess, Clemency stitched away at her dress, pricking her finger with pins as she hurried to have it finished in time for the theatre. Not only did she wish to look grown-up and beautiful on this very special occasion, but she wanted Benjamin to be proud to have her on his arm. He deserved some reward after all the trouble he had taken to prepare this surprise.

She completed the pink organdie gown on the afternoon of the performance. Cook – the only one permitted to see it – was satisfactorily impressed with its beauty when Clemency tried it on.

'Ooh, Ma'am, you do look like a princess, surely,' she said in her Sussex burr. 'Mayhap the King and Queen theirselves will be there at the theatre. Mr Benjamin is a-goin' to be that proud to have you on his arm!'

Benjamin was wearing his one and only dress coat, a trifle dated now with its velvet collar and sleeves gathered at the shoulders, but nonetheless giving him an unusual air of elegance. He looked almost as self-conscious as Clemency when they presented themselves to the Professor prior to their departure. The old man regarded them approvingly.

'You make a fine pair,' he said, causing Clemency to blush and Benjamin to look both happy and embarrassed.

They travelled to the New Theatre in a hackney cab and discovered the road outside crowded with people. Members of the Royal family were expected, and a vast number of Brighton's populace had turned out to see them. One by one the elegant carriages of the aristocracy drew up and footmen alighted to help their passengers down. A murmur went through the crowd each time they recognized the identity of the occupants. A loud cheer accompanied the arrival of the

King's sister, Princess Augusta, who was closely followed by his youngest daughter, Lady Amelia, and her husband, Lord Falkland. A moment later, there were gasps of admiration for the magnificence of the sable cloak worn by the Princess of Madagascar.

'There is Lady Holland,' Benjamin told Clemency, 'and behind her I recognize Count Giuseppi Pecchio and his English wife. They live in Brighton.'

The biggest cheer of all went up for the soldierly figure of the Duke of Wellington. Clemency sat in a confusion of excitement and impatience as they awaited their turn to alight. But her excitement turned suddenly to dismay as she heard a voice near their cab call out:

'That be Viscount Burnbury's grandson. He were the one wot scored a century last summer in that there cricket match on Ireland's gardens, remember? He were playing against our Gentleman of the Sea-coast team, and 'twas his century wot lost us the match – more's the pity.'

Clemency closed her eyes. She was not certain if Benjamin had heard the voice but above all, she did not want him to know how desperately she longed to lean out of their cab and search for Deveril's tall figure. Was his wife with him, she wondered in an agony of curiosity? Would she be able to see either or both of them once they were in their seats?

The press of carriages thinned suddenly and their cabbie drew forward, permitting them to alight. Clemency felt Benjamin's arm at her elbow and took a long deep breath as she tried to steady her heartbeat. He could not have known Deveril would be here tonight, she thought, else he would never have brought her. Or did he believe she had long since recovered from her girlish romantic dreams? Was it possible for her to sit through the play without turning her head to look for the one man in the world she most longed to see?

So lost was she in the confusion of her thoughts, she nearly missed Benjamin in the crush of people in the foyer as she emerged from the cloakroom where she had deposited her pelisse. But he had been watching out for her, and at the same moment as he stepped forward to claim her, another man moved away from the group of people surrounding him and approached them. There was no mistaking the immaculate figure of Deveril Grayshott.

The colour flooded Clemency's cheeks as her eyes took in the cut of his black evening coat, the brilliance of his peacock blue silk waistcoat. The face above the frilled shirt and white satin cravat wore an amused smile. Unbidden, the thought flashed across Clemency's mind that this man's elegance was entirely in keeping with the occasion, and she felt a moment's sympathy for poor Benjamin.

'If I am not mistaken, it is my grandfather's most excellent physician and the beautiful young lady who helped rescue my friends and me on the beach at Poole.'

Deveril bowed to Clemency as he spoke. She heard Benjamin mutter a stiff, 'Good evening, Sir,' as she dipped in a curtsey. Deveril raised her gloved hand and kissed it politely.

'Memory forbids that I should recall to mind my inadequate seamanship that merry afternoon when last we met,' he said. 'Yet how could I forget so beautiful a rescuer!' His dark eyes were dancing, whether in amusement or devilment Clemency was not sure. 'And still, I note, speechless? You are one of the few females I have ever encountered, if you will forgive me for saying so, who has nothing to say for herself. But perhaps that is because you have no need – your beauty speaks for you!'

Clemency felt Benjamin's hand tighten on her arm and knew that he resented Deveril's outrageous compliment.

'Is your wife not with you, Sir?' he asked pointedly.

'Regrettably, no!' Deveril said easily. 'Her condition – you will appreciate my meaning, Brook – does not permit her to appear in company!'

Clemency felt her cheeks burn. Deveril was implying obliquely that his wife was again with child. Were congratulations in order, or should she or Benjamin commiserate with

Deveril on the loss of their last baby? She was so ignorant of the social niceties! But Deveril saved her the necessity of a decision. Placing a friendly hand on Benjamin's arm, he said pleasantly:

'You must bring your lovely wife up to Chiswell Hill House one evening to dine, Doctor Brook.'

Clemency felt a small thrill of fear. She was certain Deveril was deliberately provoking Benjamin's jealousy.

'You appear to be unaware, Sir, that although Mrs Forest and I are distantly related, she is *not* my wife,' she heard Benjamin say in a curt unfriendly tone. 'You made the same wrong assumption when I came to your aid at Poole. Mrs Forest resides here in Brighton, and was only sojourning in Dorset.'

Clemency stole a glance at Deveril's face and saw that he was quite unabashed.

'Well, damme for a fool!' he exclaimed, and with a distinct sparkle of amusement in his brown eyes, he added for Clemency's benefit: 'If you will forgive my bad language, Ma'am!'

But Benjamin was in no mood for further conversation.

'If you will excuse us, Sir, I think we should go in,' he said angrily. 'The performance is due to begin very shortly. Come along, my dear!'

Deveril's mouth twitched as he smiled at Clemency regretfully.

'My pleasure!' he murmured. He bowed, kissed Clemency's hand once again, and added softly: 'Do, I beg you, bid me goodbye, so that I can be certain you do really possess the power of speech.'

Despite herself, despite the knowledge that Benjamin was stiff with anger at her side, Clemency smiled.

'I hope you enjoy the performance, Sir!' she said, and fearing an outburst from Benjamin, she dipped another curtsey and turned away. But even as she walked beside her escort, she knew, without turning her head to see, that Deveril Grayshott was staring after her.

'Impudent, conceited young pup!' Benjamin muttered furiously. 'My apologies, Clemency. It never occurred to me *he* might be here.'

'Please think no more about it,' Clemency said with difficulty. 'It would be the greatest shame were we to let so unimportant an incident spoil our evening.'

'You are quite right, of course,' Benjamin agreed, his frown easing into a smile as he stopped to buy a programme. 'I want this to be a perfect evening for you. I do so hope you will enjoy the performance.'

But Clemency barely heard his words. Her heart had not stilled its hurried beat and she could not prevent her gaze from wandering. High above her, only just beneath the roof, was the gallery where the masses who could not afford better seating were gathered. Beneath it were the red plush circle seats, whose occupants were more elaborately dressed, but all those of real importance were grouped in the boxes curving towards the stage in three tiers.

Most eyes were centred on the Royal Box, where the royal party was ensconced, but Clemency's eyes were searching for the lesser personage of Deveril Grayshott. She could see no sign of him, but she knew he must be somewhere there, perhaps even quizzing her through his opera glasses! Was his wife jealous when he smiled at or flirted with other women? He *had* been flirting with her, Clemency, teasing her gently, somehow managing to imply that her silence that day at Poole was a little private secret between them, excluding poor Benjamin.

Benjamin! Clemency thought with a deep sense of distress as he took her arm at the conclusion of the play and looked at her with such anxious concern to see that she had really enjoyed it. How dear and kind and thoughtful he was! But how strangely he seemed to pale into insignificance beside the colourful figure of Deveril Grayshott. There could no longer be any doubt in her mind – she did not love Benjamin as she *should* love him if ever she were free to marry him. Never once in the two years she had known him had he caused her heart to beat fiercely, her legs to tremble and her whole body to be alive with awareness of him.

Sitting silent and thoughtful at Benjamin's side as they drove home, Clemency abandoned the effort to convince herself that she no longer loved Deveril. It made no difference that he was married to Muriel Grayshott and she to his brother, Percy. It was *his* arms she needed around her, *his* voice whispering endearments, *his* mouth on hers.

Sadly, with a deep sense of loss, Clemency turned her head away as Benjamin's lips softly brushed her cheek, and her eyes were too full of tears to see the look of disappointment on his face as he paid off the cab driver and led her into the darkened house.

She might have felt elated but a great deal more perturbed had she been able to guess Deveril Grayshott's thoughts as he drove away from the theatre.

'Why so silent, Deveril?' his sister Selina was enquiring as their carriage carried them along Western Road towards the big house she and her husband had rented in Brunswick Terrace.

Deveril sighed.

'Did you ever meet Brook – our physician in Dorset, Selina? I ran into him in the foyer with a remarkably pretty young woman who I once before mistook for his wife. He admitted this evening that she was no such thing.'

His sister shrugged.

'And why should that cause you concern, little brother?'

It was Deveril's turn to shrug.

'Deuced if I know! I suppose I am annoyed with myself for misjudging the fellow. I had always thought him rather a dull old stick, and now it turns out he is squiring one of the prettiest girls I have seen in a long time.'

'Why, I do believe you are envious of his good fortune!' Selina teased affectionately. She tapped his hand with her fan. 'Do not put the cat among the pigeons, my boy,' she added. 'Doctor Brook is quite possibly hoping to marry the girl and . . .'

'She is already married!' Deveril broke in. 'Or so it seems, since he introduced her as *Mrs* Forest, which leads me to wonder where Mr Forest is.'

George, his brother-in-law, gave a friendly laugh.

'Dead, quite probably! Nothing like a merry widow to lighten a dark night, what, Grayshott?'

Deveril grinned.

'Or maybe it is a courtesy title and the girl is some little Brighton doxy Brook has found to amuse him.'

'If I were not your sister, Deveril, I would not permit this indecent conversation to continue in my presence,' Selina interrupted. 'Do you men think of nothing else but bedding females? Perhaps your physician enjoys the *company* of this young woman, Deveril, and their relationship is a perfectly proper one.'

'That I doubt,' Deveril sighed. 'For one thing, Brook dragged her away from me as speedily as decency allowed. I had the impression he wanted to prevent me questioning him about her. I must confess regretfully that I suspect she is his mistress.'

'There you are, I said you were jealous!' Selina cried. 'Yet I cannot believe that you of all people, Deveril, lack for female company. What is so special about Doctor Brook's girl? Is that who you were quizzing during the play?'

'I do not deny it, but "Doctor Brook's" girl, as you call her, warrants my curiosity. She is not so much pretty as . . . as interesting. It is difficult to define the exact reason for her charm. It lingers in the mind long after she herself has vanished.'

'Bless my soul!' George muttered. 'I never thought to hear you wax the poet, Grayshott.'

'Nor I!' said Selina, her face unsmiling as she added softly: 'If it is your intention to pursue her, Deveril, I would hazard the suggestion that you choose some other prey. It would be taking an unfair advantage of the physician for one thing, and for another, Muriel would not turn the usual blind eye she casts upon your peccadillos. So long as she knows you are merely amusing yourself, she disregards your unfaithfulness. But if she suspected you were seriously interested in another woman – then you would forfeit the freedom she allows you.'

Deveril scowled.

'You speak as if my wife is master in our household,' he said sharply.

'I know that is not the case, Deveril, but I also know Muriel. Do not push her too far.'

She sighed. None knew better than she how skilfully Muriel managed to manipulate Deveril without ever appearing to do so. She took advantage of the innate good nature and kindliness which she, his sister, was aware lay hidden beneath the shallow exterior he chose to present to the world. Most people mistook Deveril for a profligate rakehell, but Selina knew better. He was easy prey for someone like Muriel, who played upon his soft heart and compassion for anyone who suffered or was less fortunate than himself.

Deveril made light of his thoughtful good deeds, his sensitivity, but Selina had noted how readily and instinctively her young children trusted him; how the tenants of Chiswell Hill House revered him. He was spending a large amount of his inheritance from his father effecting vast improvements to the estate – more than he need have done, so George had told her. The ill-health of their grandfather had enabled him to sack the old bailiff who was opposed to the renovations Deveril was demanding, and he had employed a young man who was as enthusiastically in favour of reforms as Deveril himself.

Looking at her brother's handsome young face, serious and unhappy now that she had raised the subject of his wife, Selina wished she had not reminded him of Muriel. The marriage was far from proving the success she herself had hoped it might be, and the miscarriage of their first child had merely exacerbated the disunity between the couple. Deveril could not be blamed for seeking diversion elsewhere, she thought, more especially since Muriel had confided in her quite openly that she disliked children only a little less than she disliked the intimacies of married life. Poor Deveril, who adored his nieces and nephews and whose very nature was loving and giving!

One of the things Selina most admired in him was that he voiced no criticism of his wife – although Muriel complained about him to anyone who would listen to her. But there was little she herself could do to improve Deveril's marriage, other than to hope that the coming child would bring them into closer harmony and meanwhile, to offer her own happy home as a refuge. Invariably he left her house after such visits fully recovered of his good spirits. It was seldom that he brooded for long, and now his scowls turned once more to laughter as he said:

'What nonsense we are talking, Selina. I have not the slightest intention of pursuing the pretty little Mrs Forest, nor ever suggested it. By tomorrow, I shall have quite forgot her!'

For on the morrow he would be on his way to Chiswell Hill House, there to enjoy the pleasures of the chase and to host the annual Hunt Ball.

CHAPTER ELEVEN

May 1833

'I am extremely sorry, Mr Grayshott. We did everything we possibly could to save the child. I am afraid Mrs Grayshott had an unusually prolonged labour. When finally the infant came into the world, it was too late, and it never drew breath. Your wife, I am glad to say, should make a good recovery in due course.'

Deveril looked away from the sympathetic gaze of the physician who had attended the birth. Sir John had an excellent reputation, and Deveril assumed that if he had been unable to save the baby, no one else could have done so. He must try now to follow Sir John's advice and be grateful that Muriel had survived.

He walked over to the table and poured two glasses of the champagne which had been awaiting very different news. Muriel had gone into labour the previous morning, and twenty-four hours later the physician had arrived on the supposition that the birth was imminent. But it had taken the whole afternoon before Muriel had finally stopped screaming and the attendant midwife had informed him that it was all over.

'Was it a boy or girl?' he asked Sir John as he handed him his glass.

'A boy – a fine looking baby. I really am very sorry, Sir.'

Deveril drew a deep sigh. It would have been better had he not asked his last question. He had counted so much upon his firstborn being a son. It was not just for his own satisfaction, but for his grandfather's sake. The old fellow was very ill. Brook had written to say he was really only clinging on to life by force of will, waiting to hear of the birth of an heir. More than anything he wanted for himself, Deveril had wished to give his grandfather the news that he could die reassured as to the continuance of the Grayshott line. By the time Muriel produced another child, it would be too late . . .

As if aware of the trend of Deveril's thoughts, Sir John said unhappily:

'I do understand what a disappointment this must be – and I wish it was not my duty to add to your sorrow at this time, Mr Grayshott; nevertheless I would be very remiss if I did not advise you that . . . that Mrs Grayshott must not be allowed to conceive another child. It is doubtful if she could do so, but in any event, the birth of another baby would certainly kill her. I shall leave it to you to break the news to her when you feel she is strong enough to support it. You . . .'

But Deveril was not listening.

'You mean no more children – *ever?* You are *sure* of this?' he asked harshly.

Sir John nodded, his head bowed. He coughed uneasily.

'You have a younger brother, I believe? No doubt in due course he will marry and you will have nephews and nieces to comfort your childlessness. Your sisters . . .'

Once again Deveril interrupted.

'Dammit, man, I want a son! Do you not understand? I want an heir. As for my brother, Percy, he is an invalid. He can never marry.'

Sir John bit his lip. He had heard rumours that the younger boy was sickly. Or was it that he was an epileptic? Despite his exhaustion, Sir John's professional mind wandered momentarily to treatment – opium, arsenic, zinc, digitalis and, most commonly used, potassium and belladonna. Incurable. Cause unknown.

With an effort, he brought his thoughts back to the present. If it was true the younger son could never marry, then the loss of the male infant upstairs must indeed be a severe blow to the family. Deuced bad luck! But, as he now told Deveril, he would be failing in his duty to pretend otherwise – Mrs Grayshott must not have any more children.

He put down his glass and, with a final glance at Deveril's bowed head, he excused himself with a further murmur of sympathy.

It was only with the greatest effort of will that Deveril managed to force himself to go up the wide curving staircase and make his way along the landing to Muriel's room. In the twenty-two years of his life he had never felt more unhappy, more devastated. Bitterly he reflected that the stillborn infant, had it lived, would have obviated the necessity for Muriel to have more children. He had wanted a son – one son; that would have been sufficient, provided he was strong and healthy.

Deveril paused outside his wife's door. In common decency he must try to hide his disappointment and lessen Muriel's, he told himself. Judging by the commotion of the last twenty-four hours, she had suffered a great deal – and it was not even as if *she* had wanted the baby in the first place. She had hidden the signs as long as she decently could, wearing flowing, concealing dresses until she was within two months of the birth. She had made Deveril promise on his oath not to tell anyone until the secret could no longer be kept.

Was it possible that her insistence on carrying out all her normal occupations had contributed to this difficult and fatal birth, he asked himself? Yet Sir John had attributed the tragedy to the prolonged labour. He must not think of it as poor Muriel's fault. He owed it to her to try now to be sympathetic, kindly, loving. But it would not be easy. He did not love her – and that was the whole unfortunate truth. After fourteen months of marriage, they were still strangers to one another. It seemed to him that they had very little in common, and daily the bonds of marriage became more irksome to him. Muriel was both demanding and possessive. She did not nag or attempt to dominate him, but she had the damnedest way of making him feel guilty whenever he did not accede to her wishes. There was always so much she wanted to do that could not be done without him – or so it seemed. It was not 'right' for her to appear at this or that function without her husband. People would think it very 'odd', if he went off for weeks at a time to Dorset; or spent too many nights at his club. His behaviour, Muriel frequently informed him, reflected upon her social success. She could not bear it if people thought they were not a happy and united couple.

We have never been united, except by the Church, Deveril thought bitterly, neither in bed nor out of it. The fact was, he was always a good deal happier away from his wife than with her.

With a feeling close to despair, Deveril went into his wife's room. She was lying in the vast double bed, propped up by a small mountain of pillows. Her dark hair was tied back from her white, exhausted face with a pale blue ribbon, matching the ribbons on her lawn nightgown. Her eyes were closed. The midwife, sitting in a chair beside the bed, vacated it immediately when she saw Deveril. She put a finger to her lips.

'Madam is sleeping!' she mouthed.

With a sense of relief he was hard put to conceal, Deveril backed out of the room. He really did not feel up to consoling Muriel at the moment when he himself felt so inconsolable – if indeed she required comforting, he told himself bitterly, as he went back to the empty library. Now that he came to think upon the matter, Muriel would doubtless be *pleased* there could be no more children.

But he knew that he was being unfair to her. She had said over and over again these past months: 'I mean to give you a son, Deveril, because I know that is what you most want of me. It is entirely for your sake and because I love you so dearly. I myself do not much care for infants, and I shall not want a *large* family . . .'

There was only one way to avoid that, Deveril had thought at the time, and maybe Muriel's reluctance to share her bed with him was in part due to her wish to avoid the resultant pregnancies. But Muriel must have known they were unavoidable when she agreed to marry him! Naturally, they had not discussed so intimate a subject before marriage. It was only afterwards that he had learned of her attitude to motherhood. It was not one that would have endeared her to him had he known of it earlier, he thought wryly.

He poured himself another drink and sat down in the high winged chair, stretching out his long legs as he became aware of his tiredness. Like everyone else in the house, he had had very little sleep the previous night. Perhaps his present fatigue was in part responsible for his depression, he told himself. Or was it this big, empty room? His home was more like a museum – everything perfectly in place, beautiful, but soulless; and he felt like a prisoner in it – always anxious, as he was now, to escape.

There was a discreet knock on the door and one of the footmen came in carrying a silver salver.

'The letter-carrier just delivered this for you, Sir,' he said. 'It is marked "Urgent".'

With a sigh, Deveril sat up and took the letter, while the footman first lit the candles and then crossed the room to draw the heavy damask curtains. The soft glow of the flickering lights cheered the room but not Deveril's spirits. It seemed as if everything was conspiring to distress him today. The letter he held was from his grandfather's physician, Doctor Brook. It was dated the twenty-fifth of May.

'. . . think I should warn you that Viscount Burnbury has taken a turn for the worse and might well not last out the month. Should you wish to see him before . . .'

'Tell Pearce to bring the post-chaise round to the door at once,' he told the startled footman as he jumped to his feet. 'And send Hopkins to me on the double. You can also tell Cook I shall not be in to dinner tonight or at all tomorrow. I am leaving at once for Chiswell Hill House.'

As the footman hurried away to do his bidding, Deveril went over to the leather-topped desk and picked up a quill. Hurriedly he penned a note for Muriel.

'My dear wife,' he wrote,
    'Nothing but a matter of life and death would take me from your side at such a time but Grandfather is dying and you will understand that I must go to him. I pray I shall be in time.
    'Sir John tells me you suffered a great deal and I cannot adequately express my sorrow for us both that your suffering has proved for nothing. At least you are well and for that blessing I am thankful.
    'Believe me, you will be continually in my thoughts.
                                    'Your devoted husband
                                            Deveril.'

Within half an hour, Deveril and his valet Hopkins were upon their way through London, with Pearce riding postillion, heading the four greys south-westward over Chelsea Bridge towards Kingston. Deveril's and the servants' boxes were securely strapped on the luggage rack at the back.

Seated opposite his master inside the leather-upholstered travelling carriage, Hopkins eyed Deveril's tense face anxiously. He knew, of course, as did all the household servants, that the baby had been stillborn. Equally, he knew the importance to his master of having a son. Big families like the Grayshotts were a dynasty, and it was the reason Mr Deveril had got married in the first place. Hopkins, his personal servant, was fully aware how little his master had desired to settle down when the Viscount first suggested the marriage. But for all his wild ways, young Mr Deveril was always one to do his duty, and the Viscount had been very determined.

A great pity, thought Hopkins, that it had had to be Mrs Muriel Grayshott. Downstairs in the servants' hall, there was not one of them really liked her. The mistress's standards were too high for comfort. But provided the servants did their work properly, she was fair in her dealings. Mr Dawkins, the butler, called her 'uppity', and complained about the way she gave him orders – not like the old days when the Admiral's wife was alive.

'Lady Ursula,' he said all too often, 'never spoke to me in that tone, God rest her soul!' Hopkins himself was not bothered by his young mistress, since he took his orders direct from Mr Deveril, or from Mr Dawkins. He had been with Mr Deveril since he was twelve years old, and although he, Hopkins, would never dream of taking advantage, his master treated him more like a friend than a servant. There was not much Hopkins did not know about him and his 'goings-on', but his loyalty to Deveril was total, and both knew it.

'It is not just losing my son,' Deveril said suddenly, as if speaking his thoughts aloud. 'The damnable part of it all, Hopkins, is that Sir John tells me my wife cannot have other children in the future. God knows what went wrong this time, but if there *were* any more, he says it would kill her.'

'That *is* bad news, Sir,' Hopkins said. 'Perhaps the physician is mistaken and . . .'

'I doubt a man of Sir John's eminence would make a mistake about a matter of such importance, Hopkins. It was a direct warning.'

Hopkins cleared his throat.

'Will you tell his lordship, sir?' he enquired.

Deveril sighed.

'I suppose I will have to. My grandfather is bound to ask. I really hate the thought of *his* disappointment. It is not as if there is a chance of him living to see a great-grandson – at least not a Grayshott. My sisters' boys cannot inherit.' He drew another deep sigh.

'Mebbe it would be kinder not to tell him the truth,' Hopkins suggested tentatively. 'Don't see much point to it myself. It's not as if his lordship knew that the babe was about to arrive – I mean, the mistress might not have gone into labour for another week . . .'

Deveril looked at his valet's sympathetic face, his own taking on a happier expression.

'I suppose I *could* just let him think the child has yet to be born. I have never told him a lie in the whole of my life but . . .'

He pondered the matter uneasily while the chaise swayed and bumped along the Kingston road, passing all but the mail coach as Pearce whipped the four greys to greater speed now that they were out on the open road. They would have to stop before long for a change of horses. Deveril fretted at the thought of the delay. He did not want his beloved old grandfather to die alone. He wanted to be on hand to ease his passing as best he could.

He felt a deep misery at the thought of losing this particular relative. He had been more like a father than grandfather, and he himself had been the old man's favourite. Stubborn he might be, but at heart he was a good man with simple straightforward codes of behaviour carried on from his youth in George III's days. Right was right and wrong was wrong and what mattered in life was the family. Families such as theirs, he had so often told Deveril, had one overriding duty – to leave their estates in a better condition for the next generation. If a tree was cut down, then another or two more must be planted in its place. A Grayshott did not own anything – he held it in trust for those to come.

I *cannot* tell him that there will be no more generations of Grayshotts to follow me, Deveril thought. Hopkins is right – I must keep it from him. At least no one else would reach Chiswell Hill House before him with the truth, he consoled himself. Once there, he could intercept any letter from London – supposing his grandfather were still well enough to read a communication.

It was four in the morning when finally the carriage turned into the drive to Chiswell Hill House. Dawn had not yet broken, but the big house was aglow with light, upstairs, belowstairs and on the ground floor. The butler informed him that both Brook and the chaplain were in attendance. The servant's eyes were red-rimmed, and Deveril put a hand on his shoulder, realizing that this faithful old retainer would be almost as grieved as he himself at his grandfather's passing.

He took the stairs two at a time, sensing the need for urgency. The room was in semi-darkness. A white-aproned nurse sat at one side of the bed. Doctor Brook stood at the other side, his hand round the Viscount's wrist. He shook his head and moved away from the bedside to make room for Deveril.

There was a lump in Deveril's throat as he gazed down at the gaunt, white-haired old man lying propped against the pillows. Swallowing hard, he bent over and said:

'It is Deveril, Grandfather.'

Slowly, with an obvious effort, the dying man's eyelids lifted, and his eyes focused on his grandson. A faint smile lifted the corners of his mouth. His breathing was very shallow and seemed to Deveril to be intermittent. He grasped the frail hand and carried it to his lips, tears stinging his eyes as he realized how very deeply he loved this old man. He longed to cry out: 'Do not die, Grandfather. You must not die. I need you . . .'

There was a question in the Viscount's eyes which, without a word spoken, Deveril understood.

'Yes, it is good news – just what you are waiting to hear, Grandfather. Muriel gave birth to a son yesterday evening – a fine boy weighing eight pounds. I came straightaway to tell you . . .'

His voice faltered and stopped as he saw his grandfather's eyes close. The face was peaceful as he drew a long shuddering breath and then was still.

Deveril, his face white and strained, stooped to kiss the gaunt white cheek. Then, without a word, he walked out of the room.

The last words I ever spoke to him were tantamount to a

lie, he thought despairingly. But what alternative was there? I wanted him to be happy.

Tormented by his thoughts, his feet took him automatically into the library – the room where his grandfather had spent so many of his last months of life. One of the servants came to enquire if he wanted breakfast, but he shook his head. Alone once more, he walked slowly around the big room, drawing back the heavy curtains and standing for a moment by the tall windows looking out over the lawns. Dawn was breaking, and the sky in the east was a pale duck-egg green which, as he stood watching, turned slowly to a soft orange glow. The dew sparkled like frost as the rising sunlight reflected from it, and Deveril caught his breath at the beauty of the panorama before him.

How well he understood his grandfather's love for this place! It was part of England, part of himself and his ancestors, and it should have been part of all the future generations of Grayshotts. Now, when *he* died, it would pass into other hands, strangers' hands. Would some uncaring fool a hundred years from now cut down the beautiful avenue of chestnut trees just breaking into leaf? Would some ignorant prospector, anxious to pour money into his coffers, plough up the soft green lawns or sell his land to their neighbours? He could, of course, leave the house and estate to one of Selina's boys – but it would not be a Grayshott . . .

Deveril turned away from the window and walked slowly around the room, studying each of the family portraits as if he were seeing them for the first time. His father, mother, grandfather – the latter looking so young and vigorous and proud. He would try to remember him like that and forget the sight of the frail pathetic old man in the bed upstairs – death written so clearly on his face. Deveril's face softened as he came to the picture of his mother, her two little boys grouped on either side of her skirts. How pretty little Percy looked in his blue velvet suit! If only his brother had been strong and healthy like himself, he thought! Then he could have married and produced the Grayshott heirs that he could not.

There was a discreet knock on the door and one of the footmen came into the room to say that the family lawyer, Mr Grimshaw, presented his compliments and wished to see Lord Burnbury as soon as possible.

'Ask him what it is about,' Deveril said, frowning. 'I really do not wish to be bothered for the moment.'

The footman departed, only to return a moment later with a note from Grimshaw stating that there were certain matters regarding the birth of milord's son which required discussion insofar as they affected the late Viscount's will.

Deveril felt a brief moment of surprise as he realized that he had now succeeded his grandfather to the title. The King is dead, long live the King, he thought wryly! From now on Deveril Grayshott was Viscount Lord Burnbury, a fact which gave him no pleasure when he thought of his beloved grandfather lying dead upstairs.

'Show Mr Grimshaw in,' he instructed the footman, suddenly aware that any company at this moment of depression was better than his own.

It was the first time Deveril had met old Sir Robert's nephew, Walter Grimshaw. He eyed the small, sharp-featured young man with much the same instinctive aversion as had his grandfather before him. He listened impatiently while the lawyer offered his condolences, and then in a sharper tone than he had intended, Deveril said:

'Your business must be urgent, Grimshaw, since you felt it necessary to see me at so early an hour in the morning, and my grandfather's body not yet cold.'

Walter Grimshaw nodded, his emotions too well controlled to betray his irritation at the implied rebuke. He resented Deveril's proud, haughty tone, and he resented the expensive clothes he was wearing. His sharp eyes had noted the heavy gold seal-ring on Deveril's finger, the diamond pin in his cravat. The new Viscount towered above him by at least a foot, and

Walter felt the inferiority of his height as much as his position. But his face was expressionless as he said:

'Your grandfather, apart from a few minor bequests, has left everything to you, Lord Burnbury. There are, however, two trust funds set up – one for your brother Percy, and another for the eldest son born to you. Doctor Brook told me that Lady Burnbury has just presented you with a fine healthy boy, so the Trust . . .'

Biting his lower lip, Deveril broke in harshly:

'You have been misinformed, Sir. My wife gave birth to a male infant yesterday, but it was stillborn. I omitted this fact when I informed my grandfather, since I wished to make his last moments on this earth happy ones. So, since you seem to consider this Trust important at such a time, it is best you know the facts – all the facts. My wife and I will have no further children. Any Trust set up for my heir, therefore, is invalidated. I hope I have made myself clear, Grimshaw? My wife's physician has forbidden further offspring this year, next year or at any time in the future.'

Walter Grimshaw only just succeeded in concealing his surprise at this bland statement. Beneath Deveril's harsh tone there was bitterness and pain.

'My most sincere sympathies, your lordship,' he murmured. He looked at the hard set of Deveril's mouth and added tentatively: 'Forgive me, Milord, but may I suggest that another medical opinion might be sought? This is a very delicate area and opinions are not always facts.'

Deveril shook his head.

'My wife's physician is a most eminent man of great repute. He was adamant and I have no reason to doubt his prognosis. I have resigned myself to the situation, Grimshaw, and have no wish to discuss it further.'

Resigned you are not, milord Burnbury, Grimshaw thought. Aloud he said, choosing his words with care:

'But it is imperative in your family's interests that there should be an heir, is it not? It would be a tragedy were the title to become obsolete . . .'

'There *is* no alternative, Grimshaw. *I* faced up to the unpalatable truth last night,' Deveril said flatly.

Grimshaw's mind was working furiously.

'There is, perhaps, an alternative, Lord Burnbury. It is just possible in the circumstances that . . . that an annulment of your marriage might be arranged!'

At that precise moment, Walter Grimshaw knew his instinct was right – an heir was more important to Deveril than his wife. There was an expression of sudden hope in the younger man's eyes, as if he actually welcomed the chance of ridding himself of his spouse. But a moment later, his taut, unhappy expression was resumed.

'You must know as well, if not better than I, Grimshaw, that is out of the question. My wife's family are quite as influential as mine and would resist any such suggestions with the greatest objections. Lord Lawrence has the King's ear, for a start. No, no, my good fellow – put any such thought from your mind. To pursue that line of action would be dishonourable, to say the least, and not even for the sake of an heir will I permit the Grayshott name to be brought into disrepute.'

'Naturally, I quite understand and applaud your sentiments, Lord Burnbury,' Walter Grimshaw said quickly. Behind his bland façade, his brain was scheming. The old Viscount was dead. He himself had nothing to fear from that quarter were he to break his promise of silence regarding Deveril's bastard. It could prove advantageous to him, personally, if he chose to do so. Deveril Grayshott would at this moment give his right arm to know that he did, in fact, have an heir. Legally of course, the child born to Miss Foster was Percy's. But that altered nothing – it was a boy, and on Percy's and Deveril's deaths, he would be next in line. In fact, the hitherto unwanted brat was the *only* heir! Heaven alone knew where the child was now. Somewhere in the North American colonies, he assumed. That old fool of a parson would doubtless know where he could be found. It would cost money to bring the child back to England . . . but the Grayshotts were hardly short of that commodity! He, Grimshaw, could charge what he pleased to bring the boy back, and pocket the difference between his charges and the true ones.

He looked at the dejected droop of Deveril's shoulders and calculated swiftly how the young aristocrat would react to the truth were he to tell it. There was no knowing whether he would take a moral stand against the trick which had been perpetrated upon his helpless younger brother. The old Viscount had jibbed at first. On the other hand, if Deveril was pleased with the knowledge that he had an heir, Grimshaw would certainly benefit from his gratitude. It would involve Deveril in a shared conspiracy with him, since the true state of Percy's mental disability must never become public knowledge. Such a conspiracy would put Deveril in his power, just as the original contract had put the old Viscount in his power. He, Grimshaw, had doubled his fees since that day two years ago when the old man had signed his name to the contract, and the increase had never been questioned.

Only a few minutes had passed in silence, but already Grimshaw knew that he was going to speak out. But it would not be the entire truth.

'This might be the appropriate moment, Lord Burnbury, to confess that, unwilling party though I was, your grandfather took certain actions to safeguard you from . . . shall we say an unfortunate little incident in your life that could have resulted in your undoing . . .'

Slowly, relentlessly, he unfolded the summer of 1830 and its consequences. There was disbelief at first on Deveril's face as he listened in silence, but gradually, Grimshaw noted, there dawned an acceptance of his own culpability.

'Your grandfather called me down from London to discuss with me the possibility of marriage between your brother and the parson's niece,' Grimshaw continued. 'I must confess that I was deeply shocked when first he put forward his proposal. It struck me as – as most unethical. However, your grandfather's mind was made up – and although I resisted it to the last moment, I could not disobey his direct orders to draw up a contract. Of course, his lordship believed he was acting in everyone's best interests, yours especially, Milord. Naturally, all the parties involved were sworn to secrecy, but . . . well, in the present circumstances, I feel myself obliged to speak out, since you have assured me you cannot produce an heir yourself. One exists, Lord Burnbury. Moreover, your son is not illegitimate – he is legally your brother's child.'

Deveril ceased his pacing and sat down heavily in one of the armchairs. His thoughts were racing as he tried to think clearly. He did not doubt Grimshaw's assurance that he, Deveril, had despoiled the girl that summer night in the cornfield. He still had a hazy recollection of the incident. It followed that a child might well have been the result. But that his grandfather had pressured poor Percy into a *marriage* with the unfortunate girl seemed harder to believe. As Grimshaw had pointed out, it was a totally immoral act perpetrated by his grandfather, a man so punctilious about honour.

Deveril bit hard on his lip. None knew better than he how deeply concerned the old man had always been about the future. It was upon Deveril all his hopes had centred – Deveril who must marry suitably and produce an heir! But right or wrong, the simple truth remained – he, Deveril, had a son, a living son, albeit he knew neither the child's name nor the girl who was his mother.

What must *she* have thought of it all? he asked himself. But that scarcely mattered. She cannot have been worth much if she had been prepared to throw herself into the arms of a stranger. However, as Grimshaw had informed him, the girl was a distant relative of the Whytakkers – and he could well understand his grandfather's concern for giving offence to that old Whig!

'But why did my grandfather not tell me all this at the time?' he asked Grimshaw. 'Surely I, of all people, should have been informed – consulted?'

'Lord Burnbury was afraid you might feel you were honourably obliged to marry the girl yourself,' Grimshaw said, truthful at last. 'Besides, he had set his heart upon your marriage to Lord Lawrence's daughter.'

There was a bitter twist to the corners of Deveril's mouth as he nodded. Of all the 'eligible' young women he might have taken to wife, Muriel had turned out to be the least suitable – or so it seemed. Her social and domestic attributes might be faultless, but as a companion . . . as a mother . . .

'You do not feel I have been remiss in breaking my vow of silence?' the lawyer broke in on his thoughts.

'No, no, of course not. Perhaps had my grandfather lived long enough to hear that I could have no children, he would have told me the facts himself. I am finding it hard to believe – that I do already have a son. He must be two years old! Confound it, Grimshaw, I wonder now how many other little bastards I have fathered!'

'This one has the advantage of being your brother's *legal* child,' Grimshaw repeated softly. 'If you are in agreement, Milord, I will begin enquiries as to his whereabouts. It could take time . . . and of course, money . . .'

'As if I care about that!' Deveril broke in, his dark eyes glowing with sudden excitement. 'I do not give a rap what it costs, Grimshaw. *I want my child.* But suppose the girl – the mother – is not prepared to relinquish it?'

Grimshaw's mouth twisted into a small sneer.

'It is my experience that no one is without his price, and if the inducement to hand the boy over is not sufficient, then we shall have to fall back on the law. As you may know, Milord, a mother may not keep a child against the father's wishes. In fact, she has no claim upon it at all!'

Deveril's eyebrows lifted in surprise.

'I did not know of it – but no matter; however harsh this law may seem, it acts in this instance in my favour. But try to induce the mother to allow the boy to go voluntarily, Grimshaw. Point out the advantages he will have. I shall rear him as my own child, with all the privileges of his class and position. He will one day have the title as well as everything in the world I possess. No mother, however loving, will deny her child these benefits.'

'Very well, Milord, I shall call upon the Rev Foster later today. Whilst doing so, do you desire me to make arrangements for the funeral? Your grandfather made clear his wishes to be buried in Chiswell church in the family vault.'

'Of course – and thank you, Grimshaw. I . . . I am grateful to you. And can you arrange at the same time for the infant to be brought down here from London. It too, will have to be buried, and I would prefer that it lay in the family vault. I am sure you can find a way round any difficulties that may arise.'

'You may leave the matter in my hands,' Grimshaw said reassuringly.

Deveril sighed.

'You cannot know what a load you have taken off my mind. Last night, as I drove down here, my spirits had never been lower. My child had been stillborn and my grandfather was dying. There seemed so little hope for the future. Now . . . well, my only regret is that my grandfather is not here for me to discuss this with him. It is at least a comfort to me to know that, after all, I did not tell him a lie – *I do have a child, a son!* Now I can look forward to the day I set eyes upon him!'

Grimshaw concealed his smirk of satisfaction. It had all gone far, far better than he had hoped when he had asked to see Deveril. He had not known then about the stillborn baby. Yet his quick thinking had enabled him to turn matters to his own advantage, and he congratulated himself. The new Lord Burnbury was delighted – a happy man, and most important of all to Grimshaw, a very grateful one. In little less than an hour, he had given new hope to his client and acquired a considerable degree of hope for his own future aggrandisement.

'There is one last thing, Milord,' he said, as he turned to go. 'Six months ago your grandfather instructed me to take the necessary legal steps to make you your brother's guardian. He knew that his own health was failing and wished to protect your brother's future. I do not have the papers with me, but I will have them sent round to Grayshott House if that is in accordance with your wishes.'

Sensing Deveril's lack of interest as he nodded, Grimshaw bowed twice and backed out of the room. Deveril looked up once more at the portrait of his grandfather, a puzzled frown creasing his forehead. Clearly the old man had done everything within his power to protect Percy, indicating his lifelong concern for his invalid grandson. Somehow this expression of his thoughtfulness made the marriage contract seem all the more out of character. But all this was in the past now, and it was up to him – not only as Percy's guardian but as guardian of the Grayshott heritage – to safeguard the future.

His head lifted and his shoulders straightened as he turned to glance out of the window. With surprise he noted that despite all that had transpired these past few hours, the new day had only just begun.

CHAPTER TWELVE

June 1833

'I would suggest, Parson, that it is high time your evasiveness ceased!'

Grimshaw's voice was as sharp as his eyes as he leant forward in his chair and stared into the Rev Foster's perspiring face.

'I do not see how you can be in any doubt whatever whether your niece left England or not. You say you are uncertain if a passage was booked immediately, but heavens above, man, that was two years ago. Are you trying to say you have had no word of the girl since the physician took her to Bristol? No word from her *parents* to say she had arrived? If so, Parson, you take me for a fool. I suspect that you know very well where your niece is and that she never left this country. I want the truth, and I will not be put off by garbled tales such as you have been giving me!'

The parson shrank visibly as he slumped back in his chair. He was far from well, and his body was now thin and bony where once he had been plump with excess weight. As often as not these days he was racked with pain, and not without good cause, he believed he had not long to live.

At least he should have been allowed to die in peace, he thought bitterly, as he tried unconsciously to edge further away from his unwelcome visitor. He had hoped that he would never again be involved in the unsavoury affairs of his niece. Having no word from her these past two years, he had begun to hope that he could forget her existence. But for the letters in his bureau . . .

Drawing a deep breath, he resigned himself to the fact that

the Burnburys' lawyer would be certain to get at the truth eventually. He might as well tell him the little he knew and face his anger.

In a thin, reedy voice he told his inquisitor of Clementine's ill-fated journey to Bristol and of the Hudson's Bay letter informing him of her parents' deaths. He gave Grimshaw Miss Fothergill's address in Poole, and giving no reason for Clementine's sudden disappearance, told the lawyer that three months later she had quite simply vanished.

'You may enquire from Miss Fothergill and the physician,' he said wearily. 'The girl just upped and left without a word of explanation to any of us.'

Grimshaw's mouth tightened.

'It was your duty to tell this immediately to Lord Burnbury,' he said harshly. 'Am I to believe that the allowance paid to your niece has not been given to her these past months? Could it be that you have been quietly pocketing it for yourself?'

The parson nodded unhappily, a flush stealing over his pale cheeks as he admitted Grimshaw's implications were justified. To divert him from further enquiries as to the whereabouts of the money, he said:

'We must not disallow the possibility that my niece went to British North America after all. She may have heard from some other source that despite the letter from the Hudson's Bay Company, her father was not in fact drowned in the accident which befell her parents.'

Grimshaw's eyes narrowed.

'You have heard from your brother?' he asked sharply.

The Rev Foster bit his lip.

'Yes, I have had several communications from him. As you know, he and his wife never reached their destination. After their steamer was wrecked, my brother was found uncon- scious on the northern shore of Lake Huron by a solitary trapper. This man, together with a half-caste Indian he employed, carried my brother to his cabin up in the hills.

There he nursed him back to health during the winter months. It seems he nearly died of pneumonia prior to his recovery. Owing to the severity of the winter, it was not until April that he could make his way back to Lake Huron and from thence by boat to Hamilton, to the house of a Mr and Mrs Matheson. He wrote immediately upon his arrival to inform me of his survival and to request that Clementine be sent to him at once.'

Grimshaw, who had listened to this astonishing tale in silence, now commented shrewdly:

'And by the time his letter reached you, your niece had vanished, of which fact you immediately appraised your brother?'

The parson twisted uncomfortably in his chair, his eyes shifting nervously as he stammered:

'In point of fact, I did not do so. I suppose I was hoping that the girl would notify me of her whereabouts. My brother had left her in my charge you see, and . . . well, to be frank, I was ashamed to write and say she had run away lest he thought me responsible in some way for her disappearance.' He looked at Grimshaw's scornful face and hurried on with his story.

'My brother wrote a second time, supposing his earlier letter to have gone astray and urging me to send Clementine to him before the winter weather set in again. I did write finally in March of this year, admitting that my niece had vanished from our lives. I . . . I informed him that . . . that the girl had married, but rest assured, Mr Grimshaw, *I made no mention of Mr Percy Grayshott*. I give you my word on it. I said that it was an elopement – a little lie, I know, but I felt it would protect the Grayshotts from further enquiries.'

'And you, too,' Grimshaw said bitingly, 'since your story neatly explained your niece's disappearance and excused your irresponsibility. Well, I have urgent reasons for wishing to get in touch with the girl, although they need not concern you,' he added, looking contemptuously at the shabby old man. The less the parson or anyone else knew of the truth the better, when there was so much at stake. 'Let me have the address in Hamilton of these friends of Mr Clement Foster,' he said firmly. 'I will make further enquiries from them – and if need be, from your brother.'

'You *will* let me know if you find my niece,' the parson said anxiously as Grimshaw rose to leave. 'I have . . . naturally . . . I have often wondered . . . worried . . .'

But not enough to write to me about it, Grimshaw thought, as the maid showed him to the door. Driving back to Chiswell Hill House, he reflected that the girl could scarcely be blamed for leaving so unprepossessing a household. He felt reasonably certain that she had left the country, perhaps having learned through the Hudson's Bay Company that her father was alive after all. If she had travelled to the colonies, it would explain why she had not approached her uncle or indeed the Grayshotts for money to support herself and her brat.

No, Grimshaw told himself, he must not think of the child in such derogatory terms! The infant was now the Grayshotts' only hope for the future. He would be heir eventually to the viscountcy too! Unless, of course, Deveril Grayshott could be persuaded to forget his scruples and seek to have his marriage annulled.

Grimshaw sighed as he turned into the long drive up to the house. He was glad for once that he himself was no gentleman. These confounded aristocrats were frequently far too concerned with ethics and honour for their own good. Not all of them, as he well knew, but the Grayshotts unfortunately were imbued with such nonsense. Their family motto was *Honour Before All*, and with young Deveril now head of the family, he would be certain to take his new role to heart.

Not that it really mattered. Deveril's son would be found in good time. There was no real haste, except to make sure of the child's well-being. It would not do for the future Lord Burnbury to be dying of starvation in a workhouse! Perhaps haste *was* a necessary precaution. The boy was undoubtedly a very important person now, and at all costs he *must* be found.

'At all costs!' Deveril used the same words when Grimshaw related the information he had obtained from the parson. 'We can only pray that the boy is still alive. The mother cannot simply disappear into thin air, Grimshaw.'

'Have no fear, Milord,' Grimshaw said with confidence. 'I shall return immediately to London where I have at my disposal a number of reliable investigators. One shall be despatched forthwith to Hamilton by the fastest ship. He will be more dependable than the mail. If the boy is there, I shall go myself to retrieve him.'

Deveril regarded the lawyer uneasily.

'Will that not take several months? Perhaps you yourself should go to Upper Canada in the first instance.'

Grimshaw said soothingly:

'I do understand your impatience, Milord, but we must remember that the girl may have no knowledge of her father's survival. The parson could not inform her of it, since she disappeared *before* he heard from his brother, although it is possible that Miss Foster approached the Hudson's Bay Company, who may also be in possession of the facts. It is my intention to make enquiries from them. If they do not know of her father's survival, then the girl cannot know of it, and I doubt very much if she would have left England to go so far afield without friends to receive her. If such is the case, my services will be better employed making enquiries in this country.'

Deveril nodded.

'That sounds logical, Grimshaw. But I insist you spare no expense. *I want my son*, Grimshaw, and I want him quickly, before harm can befall him.'

When Grimshaw had departed, Deveril went up to the west wing to see his brother. Percy was having one of his bad days, and the attendant was only managing to control him with difficulty. Deveril looked at his brother's thin body, arms and legs restrained with broad white tapes, a slight foam coming from his lips. He seemed quite unaware of Deveril's presence. Pity stirred Deveril's heart as it so often did when he visited his brother.

'No one has told him of my grandfather's death?' he enquired. 'I gave orders that he should not be informed.'

The attendant shook his head.

'No, Milord, no one has been up here other than the servants, and I was present at the time they were in the room with Mr Percy. He may, of course, have sensed that something was amiss. One of the maids was crying, and people in his condition can be very sensitive to the moods of those around them.'

'Yes, I suppose so,' Deveril agreed unhappily. 'Let me know if he is calmer later on today. I will visit him again then.'

Nevertheless he stood for a moment longer looking down at his brother's thin tormented body and wondered how his grandfather could possibly have countenanced his marriage. Even on one of his good days, Percy understood very little of what the adults around him said or did.

Deveril turned away, perplexed once more by his grandfather's part in arranging Percy's marriage. It seemed so unlike the old man to have thought up such a wily scheme which, however practical, could scarcely be called honourable, bearing in mind his brother's mental state.

Confused and disturbed, Deveril went back downstairs. The house was in semi-darkness. The curtains had been drawn across all the windows and black mourning drapes had been placed over portraits and fireplace mantles. Many of the female servants were openly in tears. There was little doubt that his grandfather had been much loved by all those who served him, Deveril thought, as he wandered uneasily into the library.

He must try not to think of the old man lying upstairs awaiting burial, he told himself. He concentrated his mind instead upon the future. Poor Muriel would be wondering what was happening. He must send a man to London to inform her of the sad tidings and to advise her that he would not be returning until after the funeral.

Deveril walked over to the window and held back the curtains so that he could look out onto the sunlit lawns. His spirits lifted immediately. It did not now matter so much that the infant had been stillborn. He had a son – a boy over two years old.

He let the curtain fall again as he walked back to the fireplace, frowning. His grandfather was dead and could never be questioned about the past. However unethical his deed, as things had turned out it was proving Heaven-sent that the unwanted child he, Deveril had fathered was legally Percy's offspring. It did not matter that he himself could never claim the boy as his own. He could claim him as a nephew, and there would be a Grayshott to inherit when he and Percy died.

A footman came into the room, interrupting Deveril's thoughts as he said:

'The physician is outside, Milord. He wishes to know if it would be convenient for your lordship to see him now.'

Brook! Deveril thought. The very man he wished to see.

'Tell him to come in,' he said and, glancing at his pocket watch, added: 'And tell Johnson to bring in some Madeira. I had no idea it was so late in the afternoon.'

He regarded his visitor speculatively as the footman showed him into the library. As he indicated to Brook to be seated, he was conscious of his twofold reaction to the family physician. His grandfather had thought highly of him, and he himself had no reason to do otherwise. But he found Brook's off-hand manner towards him disconcerting. He would like to have established a more friendly relationship than that which at present existed. But whenever he had run into the fellow, Brook had regarded him coldly and kept his conversation strictly professional, as if he were deliberately rejecting a lessening of formality between them. Never having given Brook cause to dislike him, Deveril could not understand his frigidity.

There was an uneasy silence before Deveril opened the conversation.

'You have something you wish to discuss, Brook?'

Benjamin nodded.

'Yes, Milord. I wanted to tell you that your grandfather took the somewhat unusual step of asking me to write down his last wishes. He . . . he seemed to have taken a dislike to his lawyer and did not want me to send for him until the very end. But I thought you should hear from me how they came to be in my penmanship. Doubtless Mr Grimshaw will advise you of the details when the Will is read. In the main, such alterations as he requested concern your heirs.'

Deveril nodded. Grimshaw had already told him of his grandfather's intent to leave a large bequest to Muriel's first child, if it proved to be the great-grandson he longed for. But he had no wish to discuss this unhappy topic at the moment.

'I would like to express my gratitude to you, Brook, for your attentions to my grandfather, and also for advising me in sufficient time for me to speak to him before he died.'

Benjamin nodded, conscious of the younger man's warmth of tone. There was no disputing his charm, he thought bitterly, but never as long as he lived could he forgive Deveril Grayshott the harm he had done Clemency.

With an effort, he forced himself to concentrate on Deveril's voice, stating his wishes for his grandfather's burial in five days' time. He himself would attend the ceremony, of course, since he had had a great admiration and respect for the old Viscount. But he wished he had no need to encounter Deveril again – then or ever.

'I have another matter I wish to talk to you about, Brook,' Deveril was saying. 'It concerns the Rev Foster's niece, who I believe you attended in a professional capacity when she was living at The Rectory two years ago.'

Brook looked up sharply.

'She was my patient,' he acknowledged briefly.

'Well, I want to find her,' Deveril said in a low, urgent tone.

'My lawyer went down to The Rectory this morning and learned from the parson that the girl disappeared not long after she had birthed a child. Somewhat strangely, her uncle has no knowledge of her whereabouts. He indicated that you befriended her so I am very much hoping that you can enlighten me as to her present address. The Rev Foster informed Grimshaw that it was originally intended she should go to the colonies.'

Benjamin's mind was working furiously. He sensed danger to Clemency and could see no possible reason why young Grayshott should wish to get in touch with her.

'Miss Foster was unhappy living with her uncle and aunt,' he said evasively, 'and spoke to me on a number of occasions of making a complete break from them. If she carried out this intention and her uncle has had no word from her since, I would suppose that she has found employment elsewhere and desires to remain independent of her relatives.'

Deveril's face revealed his disappointment.

'Then it would seem the parson has misled my lawyer into believing you might have assisted his niece *after* she had run away,' he said, sighing.

Benjamin felt a surge of anxiety and said quietly:

'I took a professional interest in the girl, Lord Burnbury. She was very young and had no one else to confide in. It does not surprise me that she wished to distance herself from her relatives. They took great exception to her condition and the arrival of her child exacerbated the situation. It does not surprise me,' he repeated, 'that she wished to make a new life for herself elsewhere. When she learned of her parents' deaths in the colonies, she indicated that this was her intention.'

Deveril nodded. Grimshaw had told him the girl had been sworn on oath not to reveal her marriage to anyone. It was understandable that Brook, knowing nothing of it, would have felt pity for her, assuming her to be disgraced, unwed and with an illegitimate child.

'I am aware that people can simply vanish – that young girls very often do so, especially if they are alone and unprotected,' he persisted. 'Nevertheless there must be some way by which she can be traced. There are considerable financial benefits for her if she can be found. In fact I could safely say that all her troubles would be resolved.'

Benjamin frowned as he tried to digest this information.

'Financial benefits?' he repeated. 'A legacy – from her late parents, perhaps?' he enquired awkwardly, well aware that Deveril might consider the matter to be none of his business since he had denied any close association with Clemency. But Deveril did not notice the strangeness of his unseemly curiosity. He was too intent upon his own train of thought.

'No, no, it has nothing to do with her family. As a matter of fact, it has to do with mine,' he added vaguely. He rose to his feet and held out his hand to Benjamin. 'But thank you anyway for your attentions to my grandfather. I regret you cannot help me with this further matter, Brook. I will see you at the funeral, I trust?'

Realizing he was being politely dismissed, Benjamin bowed stiffly and left the room, his thoughts and emotions in considerable turmoil. Did the circumstances oblige him to notify Deveril of Clemency's whereabouts, he pondered? He had no desire whatever to reunite them. Loving Clemency as he did, he wanted above all that she should forget Deveril's very existence. But at the same time, milord Burnbury had spoken of 'considerable financial benefits'.

As he turned his pony's head in a homeward direction, Benjamin wondered suddenly if these 'benefits' were conscience money; if on nearing death, the old Viscount had instructed his lawyer to make sure the girl and her child were well provided for. If such was the case, then he, Benjamin, was morally bound to advise Clemency of the fact, although he hoped desperately (and, he was well aware, selfishly), that she would be too proud to accept this 'pay-off'. He still believed that one day soon she would agree to marry him, and if she did become his wife, he did not want her to be in possession of Grayshott money.

He could never accept that his future wife had been paid off like some wretched servant girl, he told himself, as he rode past the rectory. Let the Grayshotts find her if they can! I'm damned if I'll help them! He would wait until after the funeral and the Will was read. If Clemency were named, then he might have to think again. In the meanwhile, he wanted to put the whole of his conversation with Deveril out of his mind.

His conscience troubled him less when three days later he paid a call on Miss Fothergill. She too had been approached by the lawyer for Clemency's address. The Rev Foster, it seemed, had informed Grimshaw that Clemency had resided with her for a short while before and after the birth of her child.

'I thought the lawyer a thoroughly uncouth little man!' the old lady said disparagingly as she served tea to Benjamin in her best porcelain teacups. 'I denied any knowledge of Clemency's whereabouts and indicated that she had left me without fair warning. Following upon such ingratitude, I told him, I had no further interest in her.'

Her blue eyes twinkled suddenly as she smiled at Benjamin.

'I trust the Good Lord will forgive me the little white lie,' she chuckled, adding, 'I was not convinced by the lawyer's story of "financial rewards" due to her. What possible reason could there be for the Grayshott family's wish to get in touch with her *personally*? They must – until they learned differently a few days ago – have supposed that the odious parson would know his niece's whereabouts and that he would forward any monies due to her. Why therefore, did they not pass these benefits directly to him? I can see no need for their enquiries.'

Benjamin relaxed in his chair, the tension leaving his face.

'I am very relieved that you told your "little white lie",' Miss Fothergill,' he said. 'I met the lawyer twice up at Chiswell Hill House and I also mistrusted him upon sight.'

Miss Fothergill nodded in agreement.

'Whether you or I like and trust him is not, I suppose, our

concern, Clemency's happiness is all that matters, and although it is unquestionable that financial security is to be welcomed, money is of secondary importance to peace of mind. In all the circumstances, I do not believe it to be in her best interests to become re-involved with the Grayshott family.'

Following their encounter with Deveril at Poole, Benjamin had told Miss Fothergill in the strictest confidence and certainty of the safety of the secret, that it was one of the Grayshott family who had fathered Clemency's child. Not unexpectedly, she had been entirely sympathetic. Patting Benjamin's arm, she said now:

'Speaking of Clemency's happiness, Doctor dear, I am sure you will not take it amiss if I say that I hope she will end up marrying you. You have not been able to hide your feelings from me, young man.'

Benjamin took considerable comfort from Miss Fothergill's encouragement and, believing her to be a woman of great commonsense, he appreciated her support regarding his decision to remain silent as to Clemency's present abode.

'If we discover there is money legally due to her,' Miss Fothergill said as he rose to go, 'we will advise her of it. If the unlikeable Mr Grimshaw turns up at my house again, as he told me he might well do when he is next in Dorset, I shall request a more detailed explanation of these promised benefits. As an old woman, I can be excused much unseemly curiosity.'

Benjamin drove back to Upper Chiswell in a far happier frame of mind. As if to compound his mood, he discovered a letter awaiting him from Clemency:

'I had to write at once to tell you. Dearest Benjamin,' she had written in her neat hand. 'Today Adam actually spoke a whole sentence – quite clearly. He said: 'Mama give Adam kiss!' He is quite adorable and growing so fast. I do so hope you will be able to come and see him soon. Your dear father and I both missed you very much at Easter.

The weather is quite perfect, and yesterday we took a drive in the trap up to the South Downs to show Adam the windmill. Your father, of course, told me all the details of its workings . . .

She went on to say that the Professor's book was progressing well. So, too, was the Antheum, whose big iron girders were now being erected. But most pleasing of all to Benjamin was her final remark:

'Do, I beg of you, come to visit very soon. It seems such a very long while since Christmas and we all long to see you . . .'

As soon as he could safely leave his patients, Benjamin thought, he would go to see her. Now that he was certain that Clemency wanted him with her, nothing in the whole world was going to keep him away. He sat down a happy man to write his eager reply.

CHAPTER THIRTEEN

August–November 1833

For the second year running, it seemed as if Deveril would miss the grouse shooting in Scotland. Muriel, although fully recovered, declared herself quite unfit to make the long journey north and play hostess to his guests.

'You know what a bad traveller I am, Deveril, and you also know how averse I am to the Scottish climate. I am sure you have no real need of me to play hostess to your shooting friends; nor do I enjoy any rapport with their wives.'

'I really do not think you would be overtaxed, my dear Muriel,' Deveril said wearily. 'Aunt Meg has an excellent housekeeper who deals with all the domestic arrangements.'

Muriel pouted as she went over to Deveril's chair and laid a conciliatory arm around his shoulders.

'If you wish so much to go, Dearest, then of course you must go without me.' She gave a long sigh and added wistfully: 'I shall miss you most terribly – as I did when you were away those two weeks in Dorset and I was left all alone in this big empty house. There is very little for me to do here in London when you are absent and – naturally after our great disappointment over the baby – I am inclined to feel very melancholic. I need you sorely to cheer me, Deveril.'

Deveril bit his lip, only with an effort curbing his impatience. It seemed as if Muriel was *always* needing him and now, if he were to abandon her to go to Scotland as he greatly desired to do, he would go with an ill conscience. She did look pale and wan, and it *was* only eight weeks since she had lost the baby. Too soon for him to tell her of the plans he had devised with Walter Grimshaw for the recovery of Percy's child – *his* son.

He did not expect Muriel to welcome the news, and it was going to require a great deal of tact to put the position to her in a way that she would find acceptable. It might be better not to tell her that the boy was actually his illegitimate child. She might be more willing to accept a legitimate nephew; and she was unaware that Percy could never have fathered the boy himself. Not that he, Deveril, wanted to lie to his wife. But Muriel was so strait-laced. Life would be easier for them all, including the boy, if she did not know the truth.

He stood up, his expression resigned.

'I will go to Castle Clunes alone,' he said, 'but only for a few weeks. Perhaps during that time, you should go away to a seaside resort to benefit your health. Did I not understand that your new friend Caroline Norton was taking her children to Worthing for a holiday? Perhaps you could accompany her.'

Muriel's face was averted so he could not see her angry expression as she retorted sharply:

'Caroline is not going until next month, Deveril. And in any event, I should not find it a holiday with a houseful of children to aggravate me. I cannot understand Caroline's obsession with her two offspring – and a third about to arrive at any minute. She has so many interesting and amusing friends and is herself so lively and active, one would imagine she had better ways to spend her time than in the nursery!'

Deveril shrugged, not really interested in the subject.

'The whole Sheridan family is very close knit,' he said vaguely. 'Some families are like that – as indeed are we Grayshotts. Perhaps it is less easy for you to understand, Muriel, being an only child.' No, he thought, as he made his way casually towards the drawing-room door, anxious as always to leave Muriel's company, this is not the moment to tell her about the parson's niece.

With a muttered explanation that he was going off for a ride along Rotten Row before luncheon, he made his escape.

His spirits lifted as he left the house in company with his groom. It was a beautiful morning and there would be plenty of people he knew in Hyde Park, not to mention the scores of pretty women riding out in their carriages, with whom he could stop and flirt as they smiled from beneath their parasols.

Deveril was sorely in need of diversion. As he had anticipated, he met with a number of friends out riding in the Row. As a matter of habit, they slowed their horses whenever they espied a pretty female in one of the open landaus, doffing their top hats and complimenting the ladies upon their delightful bonnets and dresses. The ladies coquetted, exchanged pleasantries and smiled up at the handsome young viscount from beneath their lashes, hearts fluttering at his attentions.

But one such female neither smiled nor flirted with Deveril when they were introduced by one of his companions.

'Mrs Wilcox, may I present Lord Burnbury.'

Devilish pretty, was Deveril's first thought, as he bowed and stared boldly into the woman's eyes. They were large and grey-green, with an expression of disdain which changed suddenly to amusement as a surprise gust of wind whipped Deveril's hat from his hand and sent it bowling down the Row, his groom in hot pursuit.

'Never mind, Lord Burnbury,' she said consolingly. 'If I may say so, you look every bit as handsome without your hat as with it!'

Why, she is mocking me! Deveril thought, as he pondered upon her strange accent.

'Mrs Wilcox is newly arrived from America,' his companion was commenting.

'I trust you are enjoying London in an English summer, Mrs Wilcox?'

The neat head in its high-crowned bonnet turned away from Deveril as she replied:

'It is all very quaint and I am finding your ancient city quite fascinating after our modern buildings in New York.'

'Perhaps I might call upon you and your husband and offer my services as escort,' Deveril suggested with impulsive boldness.

Anthea Wilcox turned to face him, the faintest of smiles uptilting the corners of her small red mouth as she said:

'I have no husband, Lord Burnbury. But I do happen to have many English friends who are showing me around London. However, do please call upon me if you have nothing better to do. I am staying at the Porchester Hotel.'

As Deveril rode home, he was deep in thought. Had he made a conquest as his companions had suggested? Or was the disdainful American making fun of him? She had rebuffed him with her reprovals and yet she had invited him to call. Had she really meant that she thought him handsome or had that, too, been her teasing? He knew nothing of American females. She must be quite a lot older than himself, he surmised, for there was a maturity about her figure and bearing that differed markedly from the young unmarried girls he knew. He judged her to be in her mid-thirties – but beautiful despite her age. She was very poised, very self-assured, and somehow she had succeeded in making him feel gauche and even a little absurd.

As he dismounted before his front door and handed his horse's reins to his groom to take round to the stables behind the house, he told himself that the American stranger had succeeded in that short while in both fascinating and irritating him. As he went upstairs to change into more suitable attire for luncheon, he knew that he would pursue this challenge further.

Looking across the table at his wife's calm, unsmiling face, Deveril felt an acute sense of isolation. He knew only too well how Muriel would react if he told her about the interesting Mrs Wilcox – with instant suspicion and wariness. It was almost as if she had made up her mind months ago that he intended to be unfaithful to her and was determined at all costs to prevent him associating with any pretty girls. Her attitude merely provoked him to a childish desire to outwit her.

As the saddle of lamb followed the fish course, Deveril's

mood changed yet again. He was leaving next week for Scotland, and since he would not be in London, he might as well set aside any idea of establishing a friendship with the beautiful American. Doubtless by the time he returned in a few weeks, she would have removed elsewhere.

The lovely Mrs Anthea Wilcox is not worth bothering my head about, he told himself, as hungrily he devoured the piece of cherry pie the footman had put before him. He would send flowers – just in case he changed his mind. But now he would concentrate upon his shooting trip.

'Your sister Selina is calling on us this afternoon.' Muriel's voice interrupted his thoughts. 'You *will* be here to see her, will you not, my dear?'

Deveril spooned a large portion of Stilton from the cheeseboard a footman was holding and shook his head.

'I regret I have to go and see about my shotgun,' he replied truthfully. 'Mr James Purdey has had it nearly a month and I want to be certain it is satisfactorily repaired.'

Muriel's mouth pursed in its familiar pout.

'But Selina particularly asked that you should be here,' she murmured.

'Then I fear my dear sister will be disappointed,' Deveril replied calmly. 'In any event, you two females will be able to gossip far more freely if I am not around, and that is all Selina will wish to do. You can regale her with every detail as to who was present at last Wednesday's ball at Almack's!'

He did not notice the flash of anger in Muriel's dark eyes as she pretended not to notice his jibe. It irritated her beyond measure that Deveril despised Almack's, calling some of her dearest friends 'a bunch of cackling old hens fighting over the pecking order'!

'We are dining tonight with Prince and Princess Lieven,' she said coldly. 'You will be sure to be dressed in time, won't you, my dear. I have asked for the carriage to be ready at five o'clock.'

'Confound it if I had not forgotten all about it!' Deveril

said, as he pushed back his chair. 'Oh well, I suppose there is no getting out of it now. Stop fussing, Muriel, I assure you I will be ready on time.'

As he called for his curricle to take him down to Purdey's, his thoughts turned once more to the mysterious Mrs Wilcox. She was undoubtedly a very interesting person, he reflected. He was not used to being overlooked by females when he took the trouble to notice them! He was both piqued and intrigued.

Nevertheless, as he guided his curricle through the mass of carriages in Oxford Street, he decided that he would not, after all, send flowers or call upon her. She was years older than himself and why *should* he be interested in a woman of her advanced age when there were unlimited pretty girls vying with one another for his attentions!

But it irritated him that he could not put her entirely from his thoughts, and although he did not alter his mind and send her flowers, he did ride out in the Park every day until he left for Scotland, in the hope of a by-chance meeting with her. But he was disappointed in his hopes.

With his easygoing nature, Deveril did not allow this disappointment to mar his shooting holiday. Aunt Meg, as always, took the influx of visitors with complete equanimity, wandering vaguely amongst her guests with a welcoming smile, mistaking their names with delightful inconsequence and, if they had them, their titles, too. Everyone loved her, and the house was filled with quarrelling gun-dogs, muddy sportsmen discussing the day's shoot, and servants hurrying with bowls of hot punch or decanters of good Scotch whisky.

Despite his promise to Muriel, Deveril delayed his return to London for a further week, sending word to her of his intention by one of his servants, knowing that there was little Muriel could do in the time to hasten his home-going. He would suffer her reproaches in due course, he thought, and promptly forgot London and his waiting wife.

Muriel only barely succeeded, with a great effort of will, in tempering her anger, and the atmosphere in Grayshott House on the night of Deveril's return was far from welcoming.

Deveril felt obliged during the next few days to escort his wife to every function entered in her diary, sitting through long tedious musical soirées at which their hostess naturally invited Muriel to play and sing; enduring even the Wednesday ball at Almack's and dutifully dancing the quadrille and the polka with his determined spouse. By the end of the week, Deveril's patience was deserting him, and only because he feared an outburst from Muriel did he refrain from refusing to dine at the weekend with her parents.

But Deveril's mood changed instantly when the Lawrences' butler showed them into the drawing-room of the Grosvenor Street house. Standing by the fireplace, obviously attempting to remain close to the warmth of the coal fire, stood Mrs Wilcox. Her head was turned towards Lady Lawrence, with whom she was conversing, and she did not look in Deveril's direction until Lady Lawrence cried:

'Deveril, dear – and Muriel, my darling! How lovely to see you both.'

Deveril bowed over his mother-in-law's hand and Lady Lawrence, in her usual fluttering manner, introduced them to her guest of honour.

'Mrs Wilcox has come all the way from America . . . is that not brave of her? And alone, too. You must tell my daughter and her husband all about your adventures on the ocean, my dear . . .'

She moved off to greet other guests who were arriving, and Deveril had time to appraise Mrs Wilcox's appearance as Muriel launched into conversation with her . . . which was to say, she quizzed the newcomer as she tried to establish her importance. With whom was Mrs Wilcox staying? Did she know so-and-so? Had she yet been invited to Almack's?

Mrs Wilcox seemed not in the least put out by so many questions. She was obviously well used to this kind of probing into her connections, Deveril thought with a furious glance at

Muriel, who was continuing her inquisition unabated. He stared unobtrusively at her victim. The green eyes were smiling, half in mockery, he decided, as she gave brief replies in her strange American accent. Her crimson coloured silk gown was unusual – and very becoming, he thought, its tight-fitting bodice revealing much of her figure. It had few embellishments and was sophisticated in its simplicity.

He quizzed her with unobtrusive interest as she stood slowly fanning herself with a beautiful ivory and lace fan. The general impression lent both by the colour of her dress and by her composure was faintly regal, he decided, despite the fact that she lacked height. Standing beside Muriel, she looked quite tiny. With an effort, he could lift her off the ground quite easily and . . .

'. . . do you not agree, Deveril?'

Muriel's voice, sharp in his ear, made him start guiltily.

'But of course!' he murmured, unaware of what he was agreeing to. He felt oddly nervous as he saw that the American was openly laughing at him. What could he possibly have agreed to, he wondered desperately.

Muriel, it seemed, was clearly very taken with this new acquaintance, and somewhat to Deveril's surprise, she now insisted that Anthea Wilcox should dine with them at the earliest opportunity.

Although Deveril was not seated next to the American at dinner that night, he was placed opposite her. While he listened politely to the somewhat boring conversation of two elderly friends of his mother-in-law chattering on either side of him, his eyes encountered those of the smiling Anthea. A small thrill of excitement swept through him each time this happened, and he knew without doubt that a private link was being forged between them.

As was customary at the Lawrences', recitals in the music room followed the meal. When the men had finished their brandy and cigars and rejoined the ladies, Deveril was not surprised to find Muriel already seated at the piano. Taking a quick glance around him, he crossed the room and settled himself in a vacant chair beside the American. As Muriel's high soprano drew all eyes to her, he turned a little so that his leg pressed against Anthea's. She made no move away, although he was certain she was aware of him. Her eyes remained fixed on Muriel's upright figure as if she was rapt in the music, but her eyelashes were fluttering and there was a faint blush on her cheeks.

Thus encouraged, when Muriel's song ended, Deveril whispered under cover of the applause:

'As the weather is so beautiful at the moment, would it interest you to take a drive down to Hampton Court tomorrow? I should be happy to show you the Maze if you have not already seen it?'

Anthea turned her head and looked steadily into his eyes, as if pondering the true meaning behind his invitation. After only a slight pause, she said softly:

'That sounds delightful, Lord Burnbury, but I do already have a luncheon engagement.'

'Then perhaps you could postpone it?' Deveril suggested boldly.

Anthea's brows lifted momentarily.

'I dare say I *could* extricate myself – but at the cost of being thought very ill-mannered.'

'I promise you it will be well worth the sacrifice,' he said eagerly. 'May I call for you – at the Porchester Hotel, I think you said you were staying? – at ten o'clock?'

'I am no longer there. I have rented a house overlooking Regent's Park,' Anthea informed him. Her glance returned to Muriel, who had now begun her second piece.

'Would it not bore your wife, Lord Burnbury? I imagine she must have visited this Hampton Court on many occasions!'

'Muriel will almost certainly have other engagements to fulfil,' he replied easily. 'My wife is a very involved socialite. But rest assured, Mrs Wilcox, you need have no fears for your complete safety in my hands.'

'Of that there is little doubt, but should I not fear for my reputation?' Anthea whispered. 'After all, I shall be unchaperoned, will I not? Or had you in mind to invite other ladies to join us?'

Deveril only just managed not to laugh out loud.

'You know very well that I had no such idea!' he whispered.

'Then I shall be delighted to accompany you, Lord Burnbury,' his companion replied.

'I shall call for you at ten o'clock,' he answered firmly.

There was no further exchange of conversation between them, for at that moment Muriel completed her repertoire. Anthea moved to another chair and began an animated discussion with one of the other guests. Deveril did not care. The assignation was made, and he was reasonably certain that she would not change her mind. Behind their polite exchange of words, they both knew that he was inviting her to far more than a day in the country; that he was hoping their relationship would develop into a deeper friendship.

Muriel had enjoyed her evening and was in good spirits as they drove home. She was particularly pleased with Deveril, who had behaved with great charm and even seemed to be enjoying himself – unlike at other dinner parties at her parents' house. She was therefore only mildly annoyed when he told her that he could not after all accompany her next day to luncheon at his sister's.

'I wonder sometimes how poor dear Selina tolerates your ill manners, Deveril,' she reproved him mildly, and having suffered Deveril to kiss her cheek, she departed to bed, forgetting to enquire why he had called off the luncheon.

When the valet drew back the curtains next morning, Deveril woke to blue skies and a balmy September sun. Hopkins bade him a cheerful good morning as he began the task of laying out his master's clothes for the day.

'My yellow silk waistcoat, I think, Hopkins, and that new frock-coat Westons delivered last week. They will suit my mood!'

Feeling like a schoolboy on the first day of the holidays,

he sprang out of bed. Pulling on a dressing-gown, he sat down in front of the china wash set and waited impatiently for Hopkins to shave him. Not since before his marriage had he woken in such good spirits. There was only one small point of aggravation niggling at the back of his mind, and that was Grimshaw's note, awaiting him on his return from Scotland, telling him that he had no good news as yet but he had put in hand all the methods of enquiry they had agreed.

Tactful fellow! Deveril thought grudgingly, as he realized that Grimshaw had put nothing in his note that would reveal the object of the 'enquiries'. He, Deveril, had still not mentioned his son to Muriel, and for the time being he was not intending to do so. That could be faced *when* the boy was found.

But his happy mood of anticipation quickly outweighed such a sombre reflection, and by the time Hopkins had finished dressing him, he was humming cheerfully as he joined his wife at the breakfast table. Helping himself from the sideboard to devilled kidneys and scrambled egg, he sat down opposite her. The morning's letters lay by his plate and Muriel was waiting impatiently for him to open them. There were the usual crop of invitations, which he dutifully passed over to her as he tucked into his meal with a healthy hunger.

'I do not desire to dine with the Cartfords. They are really low *ton*, Deveril, and we would only have to invite them back. Ah, just the *very* one I was hoping for – an invitation to Lord and Lady Trevelyan's masquerade on the tenth. We will go, of course . . .'

Her voice wandered in and out of his thoughts as he tried to decide whether he was justified in expecting that the day at Hampton Court would not end there. He had never before been in quite this same state of uncertainty as to the outcome of his pursuit of a female. *Would* he be able to entice the beautiful Anthea to bed? How conventional *were* American women? Had she really been interested in him, or was she toying with him for her momentary amusement?

It would not be long before he discovered the answer to

such questions, he told himself, as he kissed Muriel's cheek and left the room. His landau was waiting in the street, the groom standing by the greys' heads, his green livery as immaculate as the shining bodywork of the carriage. The Burnbury crest glittered in the morning sunlight.

'Regent's Park, Pearce – and stop by the first flower girl you see.'

Pearce's face was impassive as he climbed into the driving seat. But there was a contented look in his eyes as he touched his whip to the horses' flanks. Driving his master to the park would be a lot more entertaining than driving the mistress on one of her shopping expeditions, especially since Lord Burnbury wanted flowers. In Pearce's experience, that meant a female, which would be bound to add a little excitement to the day.

His face was still as impassive when, an hour later, Anthea emerged from her house on Deveril's arm. She looked younger than her true age in a rose pink and white carriage costume. Her face was framed by a high-brimmed bonnet lavishly trimmed with pink ribbon.

'Hampton Court, Pearce – and there is no great hurry!' Deveril said as he handed his companion into the landau.

Grinning broadly, Pearce turned the horses' heads and kept them at a gentle trot as he guided them down York Terrace.

'I am so very pleased you could come with me today,' Deveril said. 'I believe you will not feel your time has been wasted, Mrs Wilcox. Hampton Court is steeped in English history and if it would interest you, I will be pleased to tell you a little of its past on the way there.'

'I would be enormously interested,' the American replied. 'But I really do not think we can continue all day calling each other by such formal address. Will you please call me Anthea and I shall be a lot happier with Deveril rather than Lord Burnbury.' She smiled as she added: 'I suppose you have been told many times that your name suits you. There is a "devilish" mischief in your nature, I believe, that must have elicited such a comment before now.'

Deveril laughed.

'To tell you the truth, no one has ever remarked upon it to my knowledge. As a matter of fact, it is really a surname – from my mother's family.'

'Please tell me about your family before you begin on the history of Hampton Court,' she said. 'I did learn from Lady Lawrence that your grandfather died recently and that you were very devoted to him. I am sorry, and now may I be very impertinent and ask why you are not in mourning?'

'For the simple fact that my grandfather expressed a wish that the family should observe no more than a month's mourning for him,' he explained. 'It was one of the few conventions of which he disapproved if it was someone aged who died. He told me on one occasion that he believed such deaths should be looked upon as happy releases and a cause for celebration rather than sadness!'

'What a delightful old man he must have been – and how sensible!' Anthea said.

Throughout the remainder of the long day, Deveril found the American woman a delightful companion.

She was both restful and yet exciting to be with, Deveril reflected, realizing as they drove back to Regent's Park that he still knew remarkably little about her, whereas she knew almost all there was to know about him!

'You have encouraged me to talk too much about myself,' he said, as Pearce drew up once more outside her house. 'I fear you may have found my company exceedingly boring!'

Anthea smiled.

'Indeed not. I am most grateful for the interesting experience. Will you now take tea with me by way of a small thank-you? Or a glass of sherry?'

Deveril felt his heart leap. He had been afraid that he had not been successful after all in attracting his fascinating companion.

'I should be delighted!' he said, and with a quick word to Pearce not to wait beyond half an hour for him, he followed Anthea inside.

'It is not quite my choice of décor!' she said as she led him unhurriedly into the drawing-room overlooking the Park. She instructed her butler to bring in a tray of drinks and, drawing off her gloves, she sat down on the sofa and patted the cushions beside her. Her eyes were openly laughing and her small red mouth was twitching at the corners as she remarked:

'Are you aware that you are an exceedingly good-looking young man, Deveril? But of course you know it. You must be well accustomed to women's admiring glances.'

'I have not thought much about it,' Deveril said honestly. 'I only consider my appearance when I particularly wish to attract a particular female – such as you. You too, must be well accustomed to admiring glances from the opposite sex!'

Anthea sighed.

'Perhaps! I think I was probably a very beautiful girl. But those years are past, Deveril. I am almost old enough now for you to be my son!' The words were spoken lightly, but her gaze was searching as she awaited his reply.

'I refuse to believe such an absurd notion!' Deveril said truthfully. Indeed the thought had never crossed his mind. He reached for Anthea's hand and carrying it to his lips, he added: 'As far as I am concerned, you are very beautiful whatever your age and far more so than a dozen pretty young girls I could name. They lack your . . . your poise, your serenity!'

She did not try to withdraw her hand but lifted her other one and touched Deveril's hair.

'I am not always as serene inwardly as I may appear,' she said softly. 'I am a very emotional person at times. My nature is in fact quite a passionate one, and I warn you, I do have an exceedingly nasty temper!'

'I shall endeavour not to give you cause to be angry with me!' Deveril replied, releasing Anthea's hand as the servant reappeared with the drinks.

When they had been served and the butler dismissed, Deveril asked:

'Will you dine with me this evening, Anthea? Please?'

Anthea's green eyes were narrowed in a smile as she replied:

'You look just like a little boy asking for a sweetmeat,' she teased, her tone amused but not unkind. 'You are making it hard for me to refuse you, Deveril, but I think for a number of reasons, I *must* decline – not the least being that I am sure your wife is anxiously awaiting your return. It would be a little silly, would it not, to upset her?'

Deveril scowled.

'I am not tied to my wife's apron strings, despite what you may have supposed from her conversation,' he said angrily.

Anthea's smile deepened as she said:

'I never supposed so unlikely a thing, Deveril, my dear. I doubt if you could ever be ruled by a mere woman. But you *have* been absent from the house all day, and instinct tells me that it is very likely you have a dinner engagement. To break two appointments in one day is asking a little too much of any wife, is it not? But if you are free to do so, I will be happy to invite you to dine here with me tomorrow evening,' she added, softening her reproach.

Deveril's mood cheered immediately, as she must have known it would, he thought as he rose to make his adieux. He was relieved that she had thought of Muriel – for he himself had quite forgotten her! They were going to the theatre, and even now he would be late for dinner by the time he had reached home and changed his attire. He must stop thinking about Anthea and concentrate upon a reason for his tardiness.

Muriel, however, was unconcerned about Deveril's whereabouts that day. When he appeared only just in time for dinner, she began at once to talk of what did interest her.

'A most unpleasant little man called this afternoon, Deveril – a Mr Walter Grimshaw. Really, Deveril, I am hard put to believe that such an unsavoury character is your family lawyer, yet he insisted that he was.'

Deveril tried to hide both immediate reactions to his wife's announcement as they sat down to dine – relief that Muriel was not about to cross question him or complain about his lateness, and excitement at knowing that if Grimshaw had called, he must have news.

'He refused point blank to tell me why he wanted to see you so urgently,' Muriel was saying resentfully. "Just tell his lordship that it has to do with Upper Canada,' was all I could get out of him. What on earth concern is Upper Canada to you, Deveril? It is a positive wilderness there, is it not?'

'I know little about the place,' Deveril admitted, 'other than that it is attracting a great many immigrants nowadays.'

'That hardly enlightens me as to *your* interest in the place,' Muriel said stubbornly.

Deveril's mouth tightened.

'It really need not concern you, my dear – at least, not for the present. It is a family matter,' he added vaguely.

Muriel's dark eyes flashed warningly.

'You seem to forget, Deveril, that *I* am now part of "the family".' Her soft tone only barely concealed her anger. 'I sometimes wonder if you forget you have a wife, or that the purpose of a wife is to share her husband's worries.'

With difficulty, Deveril controlled his temper.

'I will consult you as soon as I am certain that it is necessary,' he said coldly. 'In the meantime, Muriel, you might care to remember that there are many matters which concern only a husband – such as money, business affairs, politics, and . . .'

'Politics!' Muriel interrupted rudely. 'You cannot really believe that women do not meddle in politics, Deveril – behind the scenes, I know, but nonetheless they do involve themselves. Take Caroline Norton as an example. Do you believe that the Home Secretary does not discuss affairs of State with her? What else do the two of them talk about when he is at her house nearly every day. Rumour has it that he spends more time at Storey's Gate than in his own home!'

Happy to have the conversation diverted from Grimshaw, the remainder of the meal was spent discussing Mrs Norton – which was to say, Muriel discussed her. She had had a third son, whom she had named William, and Muriel was convinced this name had been chosen as a sop to please the Home Secretary. But of still greater interest to Muriel was Caroline's confession – told her in *greatest* confidence – that she heartily disliked Miss Vaughan, an elderly relative of her husband's from whom George Norton had expectations.

'Muriel, if Caroline told you these things in *confidence*,' Deveril broke in sharply, 'you should not now be regaling me with the gossip.'

'There is no point in keeping Caroline's affairs confidential since, as you should well know, Deveril, she is indiscreet enough to regale everyone with details of her private life,' Muriel replied. 'You know, my dear, the trouble with you is that you are never interested in anything but your own affairs,' she added with ill-concealed bitterness.

'And you are only interested in other people's,' it was on the tip of Deveril's tongue to retort, but he remained silent, unwilling as always to arouse his wife's antagonism. Soon – he hoped *very* soon – Grimshaw would be informing him he had found his son. Then he would need Muriel's cooperation, her understanding and good will – characteristics which in no way matched her good looks.

Escorting his wife to the theatre, he was very well aware of the admiring glances she received. As she swept regally into the foyer, they were soon surrounded by a circle of friends who were quick to compliment her upon her appearance.

There was no denying that she was a remarkably handsome woman, Deveril thought dispassionately; that he possessed a strikingly beautiful wife. Undeniably, everyone *admired* Muriel, but how many really *liked* her? If the truth be told, he thought, *his* honest answer to that question was that he, for one, did not. Beneath the affectation of sweetness and gentleness, he knew her to be a cold, passionless female with a hardness of heart that did not bode well for the child he hoped soon to bring into his home.

CHAPTER FOURTEEN

September 1833

On the first of September Grimshaw and Coles, solicitors of King's Bench Walk in the Temple, put an advertisement in *The Times* requesting that Miss Clementine Foster, formerly of Poole, Dorset, should get in touch with them. From then on it reappeared daily, until finally nearly two weeks later, Clemency's eye fell upon it when she was handing Susan a copy of the newspaper with which to light the fire.

Hurriedly, she tore off the relevant page and took it to her bedroom.

'. . . when she will learn something greatly to her advantage . . .'

What could that mean, she wondered anxiously? Was her uncle still trying to discover her whereabouts after all this time? Nervously, she read it again, trying to calm her anxiety. Since the advertisement referred to her as 'Clementine Foster' and not as Clemency Forest, it must concern her past. She could not seek advice from the Professor, who knew nothing of her involvement with the Grayshotts. Instinct warned her not to make any hasty decision, and she decided her best solution was to write to Benjamin and let him advise her whether or not to go to the solicitors.

It was almost a week before she received his reply, the contents of which made her even more uneasy.

'It is quite possible – even probable – that the late Viscount Burnbury wished you to be given a sum of money to assure your future welfare,' he wrote. 'Enquiries as to your address were made by the Grayshotts' lawyer of both Miss Fothergill and myself.

'I have given the matter a great deal of thought, my dear, and I have reached the conclusion that it can do no harm for you to go to the lawyer's office as requested but keeping to your real name, Clementine Foster, and under no circumstances revealing your present address. You will then be in a position to hear why they are searching for you whilst maintaining your incognito. I wish I could accompany you, but three of the village children are down with diphtheria and I fear there will soon be many more.

'Do, I beg you, proceed with extreme caution. Do not sign any document without first consulting me.

'Perhaps you should now consider telling my father of the facts. I know how very fond of you he is, and he is the soul of discretion. He might prove a far better person than I to offer you advice . . .'

Later that evening, when Adam had been put to bed, Clemency read Benjamin's letter for a second time. At intervals throughout the day she had been distracted by the thought of his suggestion that she should confess the truth to his father. It disturbed her immeasurably that Benjamin himself knew only a part of the truth. The night she had given her oath of silence in her uncle's presence was etched deeply on her mind, and as so often in the past, she wished desperately she had never made it. It had necessitated so much deceit, forcing her into untruths and pretence not only to Benjamin but to his father, to Miss Fothergill and even to poor Mary.

Surely, she thought now, God would forgive her if she told the Professor the whole unhappy story. She knew she could trust him as absolutely as she would her own father, and somehow she did not believe that he would condemn her. The very depths of her affection for him and her conviction that it was returned urged her now to take Benjamin's advice and deceive him no longer.

Her indecision resolved, she gave herself no time to change her mind, and hurried downstairs to the drawing-room, where the Professor greeted her with his usual kindly smile as he put away the book he was reading and gave her his attention. By the tone of her voice and the hesitation of her speech, he realized at once that her confession was being made reluctantly. He understood the reason when she explained that she was breaking her promise of silence. He had believed himself too old to be shocked by any of life's vicissitudes, but as he listened to Clemency's story, it was only with difficulty that he kept his face impassive. He loved her like a daughter and, having heard how sorely life had so far treated her, his responses were as protective as Benjamin's.

'The boy is quite right, of course,' he said, when finally Clemency showed him Benjamin's letter. 'Nothing is to be lost by finding out the reason for this advertisement.'

Clemency, sitting on a stool at his feet, looked up at him gratefully.

'It is kind of you not to speak any word of reproach,' she said softly. 'But I was in part responsible for what happened, Professor, and I am not at all sure that I want any money from the Grayshotts – if such is to be offered me . . .' Her voice trailed away into an uneasy silence.

The Professor reached out and laid a hand on her shining hair.

'My dear child, pride has its place, but do you not think you should put your little boy first and foremost? You will need money to educate him as you have so often expressed a desire to do. He will need money when he decides upon a career for himself. Even if you were one day to marry Benjamin, you might still prefer not to place too heavy a financial burden on his back . . .'

'Yes, of course, you are quite right!' Clemency cried. And

pressing the gnarled old hand against her cheek in an impulsive show of affection, she added shyly: 'You speak of my marriage to Benjamin, but would you really want your son to marry a girl who . . .'

'The past is past!' the old man broke in firmly, 'and you could make him very happy, Clemency. He loves you dearly, as I am sure you know. I do, too!' he added affectionately. 'But let us leave that subject for the moment, since you are presently married to that unhappy invalid at Chiswell Hill House and no one can foresee how many more years he will live. I consider it most unethical of your uncle and the Grayshotts to bind you by such an oath of silence. It could be years yet before you are free to remarry, and Benjamin has a right to know the truth.'

Clemency smiled with relief.

'I am so very pleased to hear you say that, Professor Brook. I hated having to deceive you and Benjamin. As to my marriage to Percy Grayshott,' she added thoughtfully, 'I should never have agreed to it.'

The Professor sighed.

'Your agreement was never invited, my dear, and I suppose it *was* a means of protecting your reputation,' he said. 'But let us not bother our heads at this moment with the past. Let us turn our attention back to this advertisement. I suggest you take a holiday and go up to London tomorrow. Young Adam will be quite safe in Cook's care, and since it would be improper for you to travel alone, Susan shall go with you. You shall stay the night, as even if you travelled on the "Red Rover" coach and reached London before luncheon, I could not permit you and Susan to return unescorted after dark. Besides, we cannot be sure that an afternoon will suffice for you to conduct whatever business is afoot.'

He took off his spectacles and polished them absent-mindedly.

'If I am not mistaken, the coach will take you to Laurence Lane in the City, where you can reserve simple and clean accommodation at Blossoms Inn for the night.' With a kindly smile at Clemency, he added: 'Now, my dear, it was your birthday last week and I had still not decided upon a birthday present for you, so I shall finance this little adventure in lieu of a gift.'

Her eyes bright with excitement, Clemency kissed the old man's cheek.

'I am one of the most fortunate girls in the world in having Benjamin befriend me and bring me here to your house,' she told him. 'You are like my own family.'

'As indeed I hope we shall one day be,' the Professor said. 'Now be off with you, child. It is high time you settled down to some work or we will never get my book to the publishers on time!'

She knew he was only teasing her, for she had already transcribed three-quarters of the manuscript. Nevertheless, she was pleased to put her mind to something other than the curious advertisement and what it might portend.

At half past six the following morning, Clemency donned her bonnet, and with the newspaper cutting tucked safely into her reticule, she and her young companion caught the mail coach to London. The Professor had been a trifle worried that two such young females were travelling to the Metropolis unescorted, but Clemency assured him she would take the greatest care. She would not travel the streets except in a hackney cab, and under no circumstances would she leave the inn after dark, she promised. She had the lawyers' address written on two separate pieces of paper lest she should lose one! She and the little maid could come to no harm, she had insisted.

Clemency had never before been to London, and she felt pleasantly excited as the large fast coach bowled along at the great speed of twelve miles an hour, passing over the South Downs to Lewes and on through Uckfield, East Grinstead and Godestone to Croydon. They outpaced all the slower coaches which left Brighton for London every two minutes, and despite the frequent stops for changes of horses, crossed over the new London Bridge and reached the big city just before one o'clock.

Clemency was all but overcome by the bustle of the town. The streets were even more crowded than those of Brighton in the middle of the season. Butchers' and bakers' handcarts drawn by delivery boys vied with the costers' barrows; farm carts returning from a day selling their produce in Smithfield Market fought for room to pass the massive drays and wagons. And threading a way through this conglomeration of traffic were the smart coaches and carriages of the wealthy and the hackney cabs with their fares.

Susan's mouth was agape, partly with excitement, partly with apprehension, as they drew into the yard of the coaching inn. She had been brought up to believe that London was a place alive with cut-throats, pickpockets and evil foreigners, and despite her natural curiosity, she was quite relieved when Clemency told her that she was not to accompany her young mistress to the lawyers that afternoon.

Clemency was not entirely without her own misgivings when after luncheon the landlady despatched her young son to obtain a hackney for her. She was aware that all the respectable-looking ladies she had seen were accompanied by gentlemen or servants, and that she herself would be quite at the mercy of the cab driver if he chose not to deliver her to her desired destination. He however, proved to be a cheerful, middle-aged cockney, who informed her reassuringly that not only did he know where to find the lawyers' offices in King's Bench Walk, but that there was not a single street in the City with which he was unfamiliar.

'Don't you fret none, Miss,' he said, as he helped her into his cab. 'I'll see you doesn't come to no 'arm.'

Clemency relaxed as she sat back against the padded seat and gazed out of the little window above the door. The cobbled streets seemed so much narrower and more crowded than in Brighton – and a great deal noisier too! Somewhere in the distance she could hear the sound of bells. Her driver called down in his cheerful cockney voice:

'They be the bells of St Clement's, Miss! Now 'ows about me taiking a short diversion like and showing you St Paul's Cathedral?'

'Thank you kindly, but no,' Clemency said regretfully, remembering that she had not come on a sightseeing trip but to see the lawyers.

It was but a short drive past Ludgate Circus and up Fleet Street before the cab turned into King's Bench Walk and halted outside the office of Grimshaw and Coles, Solicitors. Clemency climbed down and paid the driver, tipping him generously in return for his kindness. Now that the moment had arrived when she would come face to face with the Grayshotts' lawyer, her excitement gave way to a nervous apprehension. She did not look forward to the encounter, despite the advertisement's promise of news to her advantage.

But refusing to give way to her nameless fears, she mounted the steps and lifted the knocker. The pimply-faced clerk who answered the door seemed surprised to see her.

'Sorry, Miss, but Mr Grimshaw is in court today and will not be back in the office until tomorrow morning. If you care to leave a message, I could . . .'

'No, but thank you,' Clemency broke in quickly. 'I will call again tomorrow morning – at about ten o'clock, if Mr Grimshaw will be here then?'

'Yes, indeed, most certainly, Miss. I will advise Mr Grimshaw to expect you. May I have your name, please?'

The clerk was unaware that his employer had been trying for some time to locate this young woman, else he might have tried to detain her. Innocently he hastened to recall Clemency's hackney cab which had stopped nearby while the driver fed his horse. He saw her off with a sigh of regret that Grimshaw and Coles did not more often have such pretty young ladies for clients.

On her return journey to Blossoms Inn, Clemency permitted

her friendly driver to take a detour first to Westminster, so that she could see the Houses of Parliament, and then along the side of the River Thames, so that she could glimpse the Tower of London. She might have permitted him to take her further afield had she not been concerned about little Susan alone in their room.

As it transpired, the girl was perfectly happy leaning out of the bedroom window watching the arrival and departure of the coaches in the courtyard below. Nevertheless she brought a smile to Clemency's face when she greeted her return with a cry of: 'Lawks-a-mercy, M'um, I just about thought you was not never coming back,' as she helped Clemency remove her pelisse and bonnet.

'I have come to no harm, Susan,' Clemency reassured her. 'So tidy your hair and we will go downstairs and have something to eat.'

Both girls were tired after all the excitement of the day, and despite the noise from the courtyard down below which continued far into the night, they slept until cockcrow. Susan chattered brightly as with youthful appetites they ate a hearty breakfast, but Clemency's thoughts were troubled as she tried to recall in more detail her last meeting with the Grayshotts' lawyer on her wedding day. She remembered a small, dark, sharp-featured man with a sallow complexion and a piercing gaze which she had found strangely unnerving. She remembered, too, the harsh tone of his voice when he had addressed her uncomprehending invalid bridegroom. The lawyer had appeared to be in charge of the proceedings, and had shown very little deference to the chaplain and still less to her uncle and aunt. But Clemency refused to allow such memories to intimidate her. He was a paid servant of the Grayshott family, she told herself, and she had nothing to fear from such a man.

Shortly before ten o'clock she was on her way to King's Bench Walk, and precisely on the hour the same pimply-faced clerk opened the door and ushered her inside. Before she could announce herself, Mr Grimshaw came scurrying down the dark passage towards her.

'Miss Foster!' He greeted her with surprising warmth. 'My name is Grimshaw, Walter Grimshaw. I am very pleased indeed to see you. We have of course met before. Come this way, please!' Without waiting for her reply, he led her into a small dingy room where only a faint glimmer of sunlight filtered through the sooty window-panes. Grimshaw drew up a chair for Clemency before seating himself behind the big mahogany desk which filled most of the room.

'We have been searching for you for quite a time, Miss Foster – yes, quite a time!' he said, his eyes fastened upon her face with such a rude, unblinking stare that Clemency's gaze fell. She reached in her reticule and drew out the piece of paper she had torn from *The Times*.

'You have certain matters to discuss with me?' she asked in a cold voice.

'Yes, indeed! May I ask where you have come from, Miss Foster?'

'I travelled to London by the mail yesterday,' Clemency said obliquely. 'And as it is my intention to return home today, Mr Grimshaw, can we please complete whatever business it is you have with me?'

Grimshaw's mind was working furiously. The girl was more poised, much prettier, and far more mature than he remembered. The dress she had worn that evening in the chapel at Chiswell Hill House was shabby and ill-fitting. He had had the impression of an orphanage child with that air of poverty and hunger which epitomized such children of charity. On this occasion, however, although her general appearance was modest, it was nevertheless that of a young lady of quality, and he would do well not to forget that she was the grand-daughter of Earl Whytakker. The settlement would have to be a lot higher than the sum he had intended.

Hurriedly, he put such speculation out of his mind. It was not the girl who was important – it was her child.

His voice hardening imperceptibly, he said:

'As you know, Miss Foster, I am the Grayshotts' lawyer. I have been instructed by Lord Burnbury to make certain enquiries regarding the child you bore – over two years ago, I believe.'

Clemency was prepared for Adam to be brought into the discussion. Benjamin had suspected that the Grayshotts might intend to secure his future. She waited silently for Grimshaw to continue.

'The child lives with you?'

'Naturally – although he is not here in London, of course. He is much too young to make so long a journey.'

Grimshaw shuffled some papers on his desk.

'You have come a long way then?' he enquired with assumed casualness. 'Are you still living in Dorset, Miss Foster? Your uncle, the Rev Foster, was unable to give me your address – which is why I had to resort to the advertisement.'

'My association with my uncle was not a happy one,' Clemency said, choosing her words with care. 'It is my hope never to have to renew the relationship.'

Grimshaw's eyes narrowed. He guessed that she was being deliberately evasive and tried once again to elicit her address.

'Your uncle told me he wished to get in touch with you because he had some excellent news for you,' he said. 'Would you allow me to act as an intermediary for you . . .'

He broke off suddenly as it occurred to him that it would be a great mistake to put the girl in touch with her uncle. She would learn that her father was alive, and with this knowledge might all too easily decide to embark on the next ship to the colonies and *take the boy with her*.

'I could enquire from your uncle the reason he desires to see you,' he continued glibly. 'If you will tell me where you are living, Miss Foster, I can write and advise you of his reply.'

No, thought Clemency, she must follow the Professor's advice and not reveal her whereabouts.

'You were enquiring about my son, Mr Grimshaw,' she

reminded him. 'Should we not keep to the matter in hand? I have no interest whatever in my uncle nor any curiosity to hear his news.'

She was either very clever or else single-minded, Grimshaw thought uneasily. He feared the former.

'Yes, yes, I see,' he said vaguely. 'Well now, Miss Foster, I myself have some very good news for you – very good indeed. Perhaps I should begin by saying that I am aware that your financial position cannot be entirely a satisfactory one. Your uncle told me you have no money of your own and this must be a great handicap to a pretty young woman such as yourself, if you will forgive me for being so blunt. Young ladies like pretty clothes and pretty jewels and, indeed, very often need a dowry in order to make a good marriage, do they not?'

He saw the tightening of Clemency's mouth and wished the last remark unspoken.

'Of course, I do know that you are er . . . already married to Mr Percy Grayshott, but his health being as it is, I imagine it may not be so very long before you are free to remarry. Then a young lady as charming and attractive as your good self would be even more likely to find another husband were she also wealthy. Now the happy news I have for you is that we are in a position to make you a handsome settlement – a *very* handsome settlement, if I may say so!'

The girl gave no indication that she was either surprised or pleased by his announcement as she waited silently for him to continue.

'Shall we say six thousand pounds? Properly invested that should earn you an annual income approximating to two hundred pounds,' he said tentatively, as he watched Clemency's young face with narrowed eyes, trying to gauge her reaction. She was no longer able to conceal her astonishment.

'Six thousand pounds!' she exclaimed. 'But that is a vast amount of money, Mr Grimshaw. I realize, of course, that my son's education and upbringing will be very costly, but . . .'

'No, no, Miss Foster, it is entirely for *your* benefit,' Grimshaw broke in quickly. 'You will not have to bother that pretty little head of yours about the boy. He will be Lord Burnbury's responsibility. That is as it should be, eh?'

Clemency frowned.

'I do not see why, Mr Grimshaw. Adam lives with me.'

'But my dear Miss Foster, you and I need not be less than frank with one another. We both know that Lord Burnbury is the boy's natural father.'

Clemency blushed, but she did not drop her eyes.

'I am not denying it,' she said. 'But I see no reason why Lord Burnbury should concern himself *now* with my child. Adam is well cared for and a healthy, happy boy. If Lord Burnbury's conscience is troubling him on that account, then please reassure him.'

This is not going to be quite so easy after all, Grimshaw thought ruefully. Small and frail and young the girl might look, but she was strong-minded and intelligent, too.

'Lord Burnbury has asked me to be quite blunt with you, Miss Foster,' he said slowly, rubbing his chin with a snuff-stained forefinger. 'He is unable to produce an heir – that is to say, his wife has been forbidden more children after the unfortunate stillbirth of the last. Lord Burnbury, therefore, is in the position of needing an heir and, quite naturally, he now wishes to claim his own son.'

'Claim Adam!' Clemency cried, sufficiently shocked to forget her poise. 'But he cannot do that, Mr Grimshaw. Adam is *my* child!'

'Yes, but he is also Lord Burnbury's – on your own admission,' Grimshaw said, his tone of voice hardening. 'You must see, my dear Miss Foster, that his need is a great deal more urgent than your own. You, I do not doubt, will have further children when you are free to re-marry, whereas Lord Burnbury . . .'

'I cannot believe my ears!' Clemency broke in. 'You are actually suggesting that I relinquish my child because Lord Burnbury *needs an heir*?'

'Oh, he *wants* a son very much,' Grimshaw hastened to add. 'You must calm yourself, Miss Foster, and think very carefully on what I am saying. As it seems you are genuinely devoted to the child, you will naturally have his best interests at heart. It would be selfish of you to do otherwise, would it not? So I ask you to envisage the alternative futures for him – as *your* son, or as the only child Lord Burnbury will ever have. The boy would be brought up by his father in the very lap of luxury. He would lack for nothing. The best education is assured him in due course, as would be his place in Society. On the deaths of Mr Percy Grayshott and Lord Burnbury, the boy will become the Viscount Burnbury.'

Clemency thought carefully.

'Since Adam is legally Mr Percy's child and if it is true Lord Burnbury can have no more children, then my son would be entitled to the viscountcy in any event. It makes no difference who raises him to manhood,' she said logically.

Grimshaw was not pleased to have his best card so easily trumped, but he concealed his irritation.

'But the boy must have the right and proper training for the future,' he argued persuasively. 'You will appreciate that point, I am sure. You would not want him in years to come to feel at a disadvantage in Society.'

Clemency's face revealed the terrible turmoil of her emotions. The mere thought of parting with Adam was inconceivable – and quite intolerable. Of course she was sorry for Deveril Grayshott, and she could appreciate that it was a dreadful thing for him to be without children – without an heir. Nevertheless, he could not have *her* child. Adam was hers.

'I could not let him go,' she said in a low intense voice. 'I love him very dearly. He is my whole life, Mr Grimshaw. He is really all that matters to me.'

Grimshaw was unaffected by her simple statement.

'It is a very hard decision for you to make, I do realize that,' he murmured with false sympathy. 'But loving the child as much as you do, Miss Foster, you must know in your heart that he

would have a far, far better life with his father than *you* could
ever give him. You will eventually have the compensation of a
happy marriage and a whole new family, perhaps, and . . .'

'I do not want "a happy marriage" or "a whole new family",'
Clemency cried, knowing with sudden clarity that marriage
to Benjamin, even children by him, could never, ever make up
for the loss of Adam. She looked into Grimshaw's cold, pale
grey eyes. 'When does Lord Burnbury suggest he might take
my son into his care? At what age? Perhaps when Adam is a
great deal older, I might agree to him visiting his father. He
could spend a few days with him now and again and . . .'

Grimshaw allowed her to go no further.

'Miss Foster, I do not think you quite understand what I
have been trying to explain.' His voice hardened slightly. 'Lord
Burnbury wants the child to live with him – *immediately*.'

Clemency's eyes widened in sudden apprehension.

'You mean, that *I* should only see Adam occasionally? But
he would be heartbroken if I were not there at all times. He
will not sleep at night unless I am there to kiss and cuddle him.
He loves me, Mr Grimshaw, and he is only a very little boy. It
would be cruel to uproot him.'

'Now I wonder if you are quite right in that supposition,
Miss Foster. Of course the child loves you – you are the only
parent he knows. But as you yourself say, he is very young.
At so tender an age, children quickly forget those who have
catered to their needs in infancy. They cry for a day or so and
then quickly readjust to someone new, so long as that person
is equally kind and affectionate.'

Grimshaw had prepared himself well for the possibility that
the subject of uprooting so young a child might arise. He saw
the flicker of doubt in Clemency's eyes and said swiftly:

'From everything Lord Burnbury has told me, Miss Foster,
I would not be misleading you if I promised that your child
would have all the loving care he needs.' Sensing that
Clemency was still shocked and deeply affected by the thought
of separation from the boy, he told a deliberate lie.

'His lordship appreciates that you, the boy's mother, will wish to see for yourself that the child is content and happy in his new environment. You could visit the boy whenever you wanted. You will not find his lordship unreasonable in this regard.'

For the first time since the subject of her surrendering Adam to his father had been introduced, Clemency wavered. Deveril Grayshott could give Adam so very much more than ever she could hope to give him. It would not be long before Adam needed a father, and deep in her heart she wanted Adam to be like him. Perhaps – if she were to be permitted to see Adam whenever she wished, have him to stay for short periods – *perhaps* she ought to set aside her own heartbreak and let him go, she thought unhappily.

Suddenly Benjamin's words sprang into her mind. *Do not agree any contract without first speaking to me or to my father.* Well, she would neither sign any agreement nor make any promises until she had done so.

'You will appreciate that I need time to consider this . . . this proposal,' she said stiffly. 'I will think about it and let you know what I decide, Mr Grimshaw.'

Grimshaw hesitated. This was not the moment to push her too far. Easy does it! he told himself. But at the same time, he could not afford to lose track of the girl now that finally, after so long, he had found her.

'Naturally you need a little time, Miss Foster. May I suggest that you go away and think it over – during luncheon, perhaps? Then later this afternoon you could come and see me again?'

'No!' Clemency said sharply. 'I am returning to . . . home this afternoon.' She only just prevented herself from mentioning Brighton. 'I will write to you, Mr Grimshaw.'

Grimshaw bit his lip. He truly did not dare to let her out of his sight. He searched his mind for reasons to detain her.

'I know it must be difficult for you to sympathize with Lord Burnbury, especially in view of the er . . . past,' he said persuasively, 'but you must see how *very* anxious he is to have this matter settled as soon as possible. I am sure that *if you were to talk it over with him in person*, you would feel greatly reassured about the boy's future. Could I persuade you to return to my office at around three o'clock? I would try to arrange for Lord Burnbury to attend a meeting between you. After all, Miss Foster, *his* attitude to this whole matter must be of importance to you and have considerable bearing on whatever decision you make. Indeed, it would assist you in reaching that decision.'

That was true, Clemency thought reluctantly, her heart thudding painfully at the thought of seeing Deveril again. She wished it were not in these circumstances. Was it possible, she wondered, that together they could work out some compromise whereby they shared the boy between them? If she could make Deveril understand just how much Adam meant in her life, he would not have the heart to . . .

'May I invite Lord Burnbury here for three o'clock?' Grimshaw's voice, quietly insistent, interrupted her thoughts.

She hesitated. She need agree nothing this afternoon if she did not wish it, and a meeting with Deveril need not commit her to a final decision.

'Very well, Mr Grimshaw. I will return this afternoon,' she said slowly.

She did not see the gleam of relief in Grimshaw's eyes as she rose to go.

'May I call a hackney cab to take you back to your hotel?' he asked politely, aware that his relief would be the greater were he to know where the girl was staying. That sixth sense which had so often proved of value in the past was warning him that Clemency had been deliberately reticent about herself, giving him no clue as to her address in London, let alone as to her permanent abode.

'I am staying at the staging post – Blossoms Inn,' Clemency acknowledged, as the lawyer sent his young clerk off to find a hackney for her. Later that afternoon, Grimshaw thought, if the girl had still not told him or Lord Burnbury where she was living with the boy, he would send a man round to question the landlord of Blossoms Inn to whom he felt hopeful she must have given her address.

Clemency's thoughts as she settled back in the cab were no longer on Grimshaw or the sights to be seen in the Metropolis. She felt only an agonizing ache in her heart as she contemplated the possibility of surrendering her beloved Adam to Deveril.

'I cannot let him go!' she told herself, close to tears. 'Just to see him once in a while can never be enough. I would worry whether he was receiving proper care; if he was forbidden the little night-light he hates to be without; if he was pining for me . . .'

Her fears slowly multiplied as her mind raced with misgivings. She knew nothing about Lady Burnbury, she thought unhappily. Despite Adam's sunny nature which endeared him to everyone, he was not Lady Burnbury's child, and she could not be expected to feel the same love for him as his mother. The lawyer had stressed only that Deveril wanted his son. Suppose Lady Burnbury did not?

Quite suddenly, Clemency knew what she must do – and quickly, before any further discussions took place. She would go to Deveril's house and talk over the whole situation openly and honestly with him *and his wife*. She would learn far more about the kind of future they could offer Adam if she saw them privately without the horrid lawyer intervening with his suggested bribes. Did Mr Grimshaw really believe that *money* could ever compensate for the loss of her baby?

She leant forward, her cheeks flushed, and called to the cab driver:

'Do you know where Lord Burnbury lives?'

The man grinned.

'Course I does, miss. 'E and his lady live by 'anover Square.'

'Take me there!' Clemency ordered quickly before she could change her mind. Her heart was beating furiously and the palms of her hands were sweating as the driver turned his horse's head down George Street. She wished beyond anything that Benjamin were here beside her to support her during this nightmare. Oh, if only she had never answered that advertisement, she would not now be forced to make such a terrible choice! The Grayshotts' lawyer had made certain she understood the alternatives – her own selfish need for Adam and the best interests of her child.

"Ere we are, miss, Grayshott 'ouse!'

Clemency glanced up at the big porticoed building as she paid off the driver. It looked very imposing, and her courage almost failed her as she mounted the steps and pulled hard on the iron bell handle.

Almost immediately, the big double doors swung open and the butler was staring down at her, his face impassive as his eyes travelled over her, as if gauging whether this might be some young 'person' to be sent round to the servants' entrance. Her genteel voice, however, changed his opinion.

'I wish to see Lord and Lady Burnbury,' she was saying. 'It is on a matter of great importance.'

'I am sorry, Miss, but Milord is not at home and Milady is taking luncheon,' he replied.

Clemency looked momentarily uncertain. But squaring her shoulders, she said:

'Nevertheless, would you inform Lady Burnbury that Miss Foster wishes to see her. I believe she will wish to receive me,' she added, for surely Lady Burnbury would want to meet the mother of the child she might be inviting into her home!

Still leaving her on the doorstep, the butler departed, to return a few moments later with a request from his mistress that Miss Foster should kindly state the nature of her business.

Clemency's cheeks flushed. The 'nature of her business' was scarcely fitting for a doorstep conversation with the butler. Her fear left her, to be replaced by determination. She would see Lady Burnbury, even if she had to wait all day.

'Please tell your mistress that the matter, as she must be

well aware, is a private one. Please tell her that I am in London only for the day.'

When the butler next returned, it was to invite Clemency into the house.

'If you will wait in the morning-room, Milady will see you as soon as she has finished luncheon,' he said, his face still impassive despite the curiosity that was consuming him.

In the ten minutes Clemency was kept waiting in the morning-room, her mood changed once again. Miserably, she noted the many beautiful ornaments and pieces of furniture that decorated the salon. She was unfamiliar with such luxurious surroundings, but with her innate good taste, she guessed that these were either priceless heirlooms or objects purchased for their beauty without regard to price. No matter how hard I work, she thought, I could never provide a background such as this for Adam!

In a corner of the room stood a spinet, and this, more than any other *objet d'art*, struck at Clemency's heart. She had not forgotten her mother's most treasured possession and how passionately she had clung to it. Mama had even determined upon taking it to the colonies with her! 'It is the one relic I have of my own beautiful home,' Clemency had heard her say to Papa in a voice so full of emotion, Clemency had been quite impressed by its pathos. Only now, as Clemency looked around her, did she fully understand what it meant to belong to an historic aristocratic family. And this was Adam's birthright!

She jumped to her feet as the doors were opened by a liveried footman and Lady Burnbury approached her. There was no welcome on her cold, frowning face. Taller than Clemency by at least six inches, she looked down on her visitor disdainfully.

'Miss Foster? I understand you have urgent business with me? I can allow you but five minutes of my time. I have another engagement . . .'

Clemency's eyes met those of Lady Muriel and her brief

grudging admiration of the woman's elegance was swept aside by the impression she received of haughty disdain.

'I am sorry if the time is inconvenient, Lady Burnbury, but I think our business will take longer than five minutes,' she said, surprised at her own spirit. She was not going to permit this woman to intimidate her. After all, she thought, it is Lady Burnbury who wants something from me. It is not I who have come here to beg!

Muriel did not invite Clemency to be seated and she herself remained standing as she said:

'*Our business*, Miss Foster? I am afraid I do not understand.'

'Perhaps your husband has referred to me by my married name,' Clemency suggested uneasily. 'I am Adam's mother. I am married to your brother-in-law, Percy Grayshott!'

The whitening of Muriel's face and the audible gasp she gave were the first indications Clemency had that Deveril's wife might be ignorant of past events; that clearly she did not know of Percy's marriage, if indeed she knew of Adam's existence. Embarrassed that she had not previously thought of such a possibility, she stammered.

'Perhaps I should wait until your husband . . . Lord Burnbury, is here. He . . .'

'Sit down!' Muriel interrupted rudely, too shocked for once to be in full command of the situation. 'You will please tell me everything there is to tell. There is no need whatever to await my husband's return!'

Clemency hesitated. She realized that if Deveril had made no mention of her to Lady Burnbury, her story would come as a dreadful shock to his wife.

But Clemency could not believe that Deveril had withheld all the facts. How else but by taking his wife into his confidence could he be contemplating rearing Adam beneath his own roof? Lady Burnbury's compliance was a vital factor in any arrangement they might come to. If she did not already know the truth, then it was high time she did so. But it was

Deveril's task and not hers to confess that he had had a child by another woman before his marriage; that Adam was his son.

Muriel's first reaction of shock had by now given way to one of total disbelief. In a cold, hard voice, she said:

'I should warn you, Miss Foster, that if you have come here with a pack of lies in the hope of receiving money then you have approached the wrong person. I am not open to blackmail and nor is my husband. Unless you can substantiate everything you say, I shall be obliged to hand you over to the constabulary!'

Clemency's mouth dropped open. Her cheeks flamed at the insult and she half rose in her chair but sat down again, knowing that matters could not be left at this point. If Deveril wanted to take Adam into his home, he would be obliged sooner or later to tell his wife of his plans. Having come this far, she herself might as well enlighten Lady Burnbury now. She did not consider her oath of silence regarding her marriage applied where a member of the Grayshott family was concerned.

'Your husband will substantiate what I am going to tell you,' she said firmly; 'and it may surprise you, Lady Burnbury, to hear that I am not in the least interested in your money. I am interested only in my child.'

Leaving Deveril to confess his part in the circumstances leading up to her marriage, Clemency continued quietly:

'I am Percy Grayshott's wife. Our wedding, which took place almost three years ago, was arranged very privately at Chiswell Hill House. The reason for this secrecy was that I was already with child and my guardians and the Grayshott family wished to avoid any scandal or gossip. Your husband, Lord Burnbury, knows of my little boy's existence and wishes to adopt Adam, he now being the only likely heir.'

She glanced briefly at the older woman's cold implacable face and continued:

'I have not been living at Chiswell Hill House since my

marriage, which, as you will appreciate, was one of convenience only. Recently Lord Burnbury instructed his lawyer to contact me, which is why I am in London today. It was not until my meeting with Mr Grimshaw this morning that I learned of your husband's desire to rear my little boy as his own son, and I came here today to discuss the matter with you both. Mistakenly, I assumed you knew of Lord Burnbury's intentions.'

To Muriel's credit, she had not once interrupted Clemency, only the tightening of her mouth giving any indication of her feelings. But now, as Clemency stopped talking, Muriel's dark eyes flashed venomously and she could retain her self-control no longer.

'And you are further mistaken in assuming those are my husband's intentions,' she cried in a low angry voice. 'There are no circumstances whatever – and understand that I mean what I say, Miss Foster – or should I call you Mrs Grayshott? – that will oblige me to have your little bastard under my roof. And do not try to tell me he is *not* a bastard, whatever steps were taken to legitimize the child. Personally, I find your story impossible to credit. For one thing, I doubt my idiot brother-in-law *could* father a child! So you had best forget whatever aspirations you have for your ill-gotten son. He will never set foot in my house – and that is final!'

Clemency knew then that Adam would have to forgo the material and social advantages his father could give him. Lady Burnbury had swept away her indecision and she no longer felt morally compelled to part with her son. No mother, she thought, who loves her child as I love Adam, would hand him voluntarily to a woman who is as deeply opposed to the proposal as was Lady Burnbury! Adam had grown up in an atmosphere of love, and that was how he would continue, she determined as she stood up and faced Deveril's wife.

'Do not concern yourself, Lady Burnbury,' she said coldly. 'Having ascertained your feelings in the matter, there are no circumstances which would persuade me to let you and your husband have my son. You may tell Lord Burnbury so! Perhaps you will also be good enough to inform him of my visit and that I wish him to desist from any further attempts to contact me, since I shall not change my mind. Good day to you, Lady Burnbury.'

If Muriel was surprised by Clemency's statement, she concealed it well. She reached for the bell rope to summon the footman to show her visitor out, but Clemency did not wait for the servant's appearance. With as much dignity as she could achieve, she turned on her heel and left the room. As the butler came hurrying towards her, she felt a sudden fear that Lady Burnbury's sharp angry voice would call out demanding her return. But only the butler spoke, wishing to know if she required a hackney cab.

Clemency shook her head. Reaction was setting in, and despite her promise to the Professor not to go about unescorted she felt the need to walk, if only for a little way.

As the front door of Grayshott House closed behind her, she became aware of the trembling of her hands and legs. An organ grinder was situated on the corner of Hanover Square, a group of street urchins around him as he turned the creaking handle of his instrument. A tiny wizened monkey in a red and yellow coat held out a cloth cap to Clemency as she passed by. Ordinarily, she would have stopped to put in a coin, unable to resist these small creatures' sad little faces. But she walked by unseeing, her one thought now being to find a hackney, collect her belongings as quickly as possible from Blossoms Inn, pay her bill and board the next coach leaving for Brighton.

Irrationally, she feared that the unpleasant little lawyer was following behind her; that he might trace her back to the Professor's house in Adelaide Crescent and that she would have to explain her actions to him. How fortuitous, she thought as a hackney halted at the kerb for her, that she had followed the Professor's advice and never once mentioned where she was living. She could return now to Brighton and hopefully never have to see the lawyer or the Burnburys, again.

Half an hour later, she and Susan were on one of the many

stagecoaches leaving London for the south coast. Gradually
her hurried breathing slowed and her anxiety and dismay
lessened. She was now able to think of Deveril not without
pity – married to such a cold-hearted, unsympathetic woman!
His wife had never once considered that *he* might be desperate
to have a child; that she owed it to him to consider his happiness, his wishes. She had pretended to disbelieve the fact that
Percy had a wife and son, but she must have known Clemency
would never have dared to fabricate such a story when it
could so easily be disproved if untrue. If the woman could
feel such a degree of antipathy towards the idea of adopting
her husband's nephew, how much more condemnatory she
would have been had Clemency revealed that *Deveril was
Adam's father*!

Now as the stage clattered over London Bridge and headed
towards open country, Clemency's heart hardened as she
recalled how harshly and disparagingly Lady Burnbury had
spoken of 'Percy's bastard', making no concession to the fact
that Clemency's marriage to Percy legitimized Adam. Her
outrage had not been feigned, and Clemency had sensed a
deep-rooted antipathy to the welfare of any child, not just
that of her son.

She felt a swift surge of protective love for Adam and a
great impatience to see him, to hold him safely in her arms.
She wished she had booked her return fare to Brighton on
the mail. The stage would prolong the journey by one and a
half hours, and with every minute that passed she was aware
of a growing fatigue. When at last she reached Adelaide
Crescent, it was nine o'clock, and she was close to tears of
exhaustion.

The Professor asked no questions immediately, but sent
Susan for a cup of hot milk into which he poured a measure
of brandy. Only when Clemency had drunk it did he allow
her to recount the day's events. His face gave no sign of his
emotions although the story she told worried him deeply.

'You are quite certain that you made no mention of this

address to the lawyer?' he asked gently. Clemency shook her head vehemently. 'And that you gave none at Blossoms Inn?'

'I was very careful to avoid doing so – just as you told me,' she assured him.

'Nevertheless it *is* possible that you were followed,' the old man muttered, as much to himself as to Clemency.

'What of it, Professor?' she asked with a sudden return of spirit. 'I will not surrender Adam – never, never, *never*!'

The old man sighed.

'I understand how you feel, my dear, but unfortunately it may not be simply a question of whether or not you are *willing* to surrender him. Deveril Grayshott is Adam's father, and you and he both know it even if Lady Burnbury does not.'

'Percy Grayshott is the *legal* father,' Clemency said uneasily.

'But the lawyer as well as Lord Burnbury knows whose child Adam really is. Did this Mr Grimshaw question you on the point?'

Clemency nodded.

'I . . . I did not deny it,' she whispered. 'I saw no danger in it and . . .' She broke off as the implications of her admission occurred to her. Her face whitened. 'You think Deveril may try to claim Adam as *his* son?' she whispered.

'The situation could be very precarious indeed,' the Professor acknowledged. 'In this country, Clemency, a father "owns" his child, just as he "owns" his wife. You may have no legal right to debar Lord Burnbury from claiming his son if he so desires, if not on his own behalf then on Percy's.'

It was a minute or two before her fear would allow Clemency to speak. When she did so, her voice trembled.

'How can I guard against it happening?' she begged.

The Professor attempted a reassuring smile.

'Well, for a start, I think you should leave this house as quickly as possible – tomorrow, in fact. It is quite probable that you have been followed. The lawyer would not want to lose sight of you having found you after so difficult a search. Yes, you must go tomorrow – to Benjamin. He will find somewhere for you – at Miss Fothergill's perhaps. You would enjoy seeing her again, would you not?'

'Yes, but . . . but what about you, Professor? What about the book?' Clemency enquired anxiously.

'My dear girl, I shall do perfectly well with Cook and Susan to look after me. As for the book, you know we are way ahead of schedule. Besides, if there have been no enquiries made for you here in the meanwhile, you may return in a few weeks.'

Clemency jumped up and flung her arms around the Professor.

'Where would I be without you to advise me?' she cried, her eyes filling with tears that were in part due to exhaustion. The old man patted her hand and extricated himself gently from her embrace.

'There, there, child, you must keep calm,' he said, smiling. 'It is a fact of human nature that we think best and act most wisely when we are not overcome by emotions. Now off you go to bed and try to get a good night's sleep. You have a long journey before you tomorrow and you will have to be up early to pack your own and Adam's belongings.'

For the most part of the following day, Clemency was kept from thinking too deeply about the reasons for her journey in her attempts to keep her small son from mischief. Now nearly two-and-a-half years old, Adam's curiosity and desire to experiment were paramount. He was very excited by the novelty of travelling on the big coach with so many horses to pull it and so many other passengers aboard. Any child as pretty as he was bound to attract attention, and he was greatly spoiled by the other females on the coach and tolerated benignly by the gentlemen.

But on the last leg of the route between Christchurch and Poole, the countryside became suddenly familiar to Clemency and she found herself recalling in detail the loneliness and deprivations of that dreadful year at the rectory. She shivered at the memories, hugging Adam's warm little body closer to her own. He was sleeping now, his long dark lashes lying softly on his rosy cheeks, his body relaxed and his little fat arms and legs dangling and swinging in time with the coach's movement. She consoled herself with the thought that on the morrow she would see both Miss Fothergill and Benjamin, and that she was exceedingly fortunate to have two such loving friends upon whom she could count for a welcome.

Since it was so late in the evening when Clemency arrived in Poole, she determined to stay overnight at the Angel rather than disturb poor Miss Fothergill. She knew if she arose early enough next morning, she could walk to the little house before Miss Fothergill departed to one of her meetings.

When Clemency finally settled down to sleep in the comfortable big feather bed, Adam tucked safely in beside her, her fears diminished and she felt more confident about the future. The Professor, she told herself, was probably one of the wisest men in England. She had complete faith in him and in the advice he had given her to protect Adam.

The Professor's advice, however, had for once been given too precipitately. Grimshaw, having failed to arrange for an investigator to follow Clemency when she had left his office, never thought to search for her in the unlikely town of Brighton. Since he now knew she had not gone to the colonies, the only place he could imagine she might be was somewhere in Dorset where her surroundings were familiar. He had never trusted Miss Fothergill, whose professed outrage at the girl's sudden departure from her house had struck him as feigned. For the past four months he had made certain that one of his men called regularly to spy upon her and by now he had determined upon a further enquiry there himself.

Clemency might have slept a deal less soundly had she realized that for once the old Professor had been sorely mistaken in his judgment and that Brighton, not Poole, was a far safer place for her and the child to have been.

CHAPTER FIFTEEN

September–October 1833

It was not until Deveril returned home after a night away, ostensibly paying a visit to Dorset but in truth, enjoying himself enormously in Anthea's house near Regent's Park, that he learned of Clemency's visit to his wife.

The plan Muriel had made to be coldly angry with her husband went by the board when he presented himself in the drawing-room in excellent good spirits. Deveril was hard put to make sense of her furious outcry which she had had, perforce, to bottle up until his return.

His first thought as she launched into her tirade was that she had learned of his now frequent assignations with Anthea. His relationship with the American woman had quickly become an exciting and, as far as Deveril was concerned, thoroughly novel experience. Somewhat shamefacedly, he discovered that he, who had thought himself so grand and competent a lover, knew practically nothing about females. Anthea was proving a willing and magnificent teacher, and he had returned home that evening congratulating himself upon finding so perfect a mistress. He was in no mood, therefore, for his wife's outbursts, although caution kept him silent until at last he understood that the mother of his son had actually come to the house the previous day and been sent packing by Muriel. He was beside himself with anger and disappointment.

'I have been months and months searching for her!' he said furiously. 'I want that boy, Muriel, and I intend to have him. You had no right to interfere.'

'And you had no right to keep me in ignorance of your

intentions,' she flared back, still too angry to be frightened by Deveril's uncustomary fury. 'I will not be humiliated in this way. It is outrageous of you even to imagine that I might take in your brother's by-blow – and do not pretend to me that Percy was not obliged to marry the girl. When I tell my father . . .'

She got no further, for Deveril caught her arm and held it in a vice-like grip.

'You can tittle-tattle to your father as much as you please, but it will make no difference to me, Muriel. Let that be clearly understood. It is up to you whether you wish this private matter to become public, as it soon will if you start complaining outside this house. As far as the boy is concerned, I shall have him here with me, and if you do not like it, you can go back to live with your parents. I hope that is understood.'

Muriel twisted free and turned away so that Deveril could not see the fear and fury in her eyes. She knew he did not love her – that he never had done so. But she had not expected him to feel so passionately about a mere child. In quieter tones, she told him:

'It is quite unfair of you, Deveril, not to see my point of view.' Her voice was now cajoling. 'You know I have never liked children – or wanted my own. The boy would only be a matter for discord between us. I know that you have not been entirely happy in our marriage, but I believed that of late matters had begun to improve. You seemed so much more content and . . .'

Deveril ceased to listen as he thought wryly that indeed, his relationship with Muriel had improved since Anthea had come into his life. In fact, he had been enjoying the best of both worlds. He had attended with Muriel those social functions that pleased him, and escaped when he wished to the arms of the delectable American. There was no doubt that it would cause an unholy scandal if Muriel were to walk out of his house in high dudgeon when the boy arrived. And knowing as much as she now knew about poor Percy's wedding, she could make matters very unpleasant for him and the family name. Perhaps, after all, he should make some concessions.

Of a sudden, it occurred to him that after his mother's death, he had spent a very large part of his childhood with his Great-Aunt Meg in Scotland. The old lady loved children quite as much as she loved her animals – and quite as much as Muriel disliked them! The boy could live with her until he was old enough to go to school. By then he would be more of an adult age and to Muriel's liking. But first his son had to be found.

'Of course, Grimshaw can tell me where he is!' he said aloud. 'Only Grimshaw can have told the girl of my plans to adopt the boy. He will know where she can be found.' He glanced at his wife's stony face and added placatingly: 'We will talk about it when I get back from the lawyer's, Muriel. I am sure we can arrange matters somehow to our mutual satisfaction. I suppose this has been a shock and I am prepared to admit that I ought to have forewarned you.'

The reason he had not, he thought, as he drove his curricle at breakneck speed towards the Temple, was that he feared exactly the outburst to which Muriel had subjected him.

It was as well the girl had not revealed that he, rather than Percy, was the natural father. If Muriel could feel such antipathy to the prospect of adopting his nephew, what greater objections might she have voiced had she been faced with his bastard! Sooner or later, Muriel would have to come to terms with the fact that the boy would live with them. But there was no hurry, and in the meanwhile, she could become adjusted to the idea.

It was by now seven of the clock and all the clerks had gone home. Grimshaw, too, was on the point of leaving the office when he saw Deveril's curricle pull up at the front door. He had actually prayed – something he seldom if ever did – that he would be able to trace the girl again before Deveril returned home. His heart sank as the young Viscount strode into the room.

As he listened to Deveril's angry account of the girl's visit to Grayshott House, Grimshaw understood two things which had been puzzling him – the first, why the girl had never returned as she had promised for the three o'clock appointment; the second, why milord Burnbury should have come hot foot to his office instead of summoning him to Grayshott House. His heart sank still further as he realized that he would now have to reveal his own incompetence.

'You damned fool!' Deveril raged. 'You should have foreseen her disappearing without warning. I do not care if she did promise to return at three o'clock. You should have had her followed.'

'Which I did, Milord, I assure you,' Grimshaw said, curbing with difficulty his hatred of the man who was berating him in so autocratic a manner. He was not a servant, he thought viciously; he was a fully trained lawyer. Aloud he said:

'At half past the hour, when Miss Foster had still not reappeared, I sent a man at once to the inn where we knew she was staying. But she had already left some two hours previously. My clerk did his utmost to discover if anyone had seen her board one of the coaches but no one appeared to have noticed her. The landlord said that there were at least eight stages and three mails either arriving or leaving around that time, and with luncheon required by many of the passengers, there was far too much confusion to bother himself about any one of them.'

He stole a brief glance at Deveril's furious face and added quickly: 'I could not possibly have suspected that Miss Foster would act so precipitately, not knowing of her visit to . . . to er, your lady wife.'

'Well, you had damned well better find her – and quickly,' Deveril said furiously. 'And I am warning you here and now, Grimshaw, if you fail, you can be certain I shall dispense with your services, and I do not give a farthing how long, or faithfully, your uncle acted for the family.'

Grimshaw felt a brief moment of apprehension.

'We will find her, Milord, have no fear. We already know two important things about her – her appearance and that she does not live in London. I am certain she is still in Dorset.' As much to boost his own morale as Deveril's, he expressed his doubts as to Miss Fothergill's reliability. 'I am convinced she is still in touch with the girl,' he added forcibly.

'It is a straw in the wind!' Deveril said scornfully. 'Why should an old woman try to protect the wretched girl from a lawyer, of all people, especially when you tell me you made it clear that there were benefits awaiting her. You did offer the girl money, I hope?'

'Of course, Milord – six thousand pounds.'

'Then next time you see her, double it,' Deveril said. 'It was you who told me every man has his price. You pitched hers too low, Grimshaw.'

It was not the moment for Grimshaw to argue that he did not think Clemency's reaction was due to an inadequate bribe but to a genuine love for her child. There was no advantage in adding to his client's concern at this time.

'Give me a week or two, Lord Burnbury. I am sure I shall have some good news for you by then.'

'I do not want "good news",' Deveril said as he made for the door. 'What I want, Grimshaw, is my son – and you had better hurry up and get hold of him before you find you have lost my patronage.'

Grimshaw, however, was unable to leave immediately for Dorset, as he would have wished. He was due in court next day and expected the case to last a further two days. He had no alternative therefore other than to instruct his best man to go down to Poole, giving him a detailed description of Clementine Foster's appearance.

'Try to discover if she was seen yesterday at any of the staging posts on the way down,' he instructed his investigator. 'Someone must have noticed her – a pretty young girl, probably travelling alone. She may or may not have had a child with her, male, about two years old. Follow up *any* lead at all. Then go to this address and watch the house. I do not want the owner, a certain Miss Fothergill, prewarned of our presence. You can call at Lower Chiswell Rectory too, just in case Miss Foster has gone to her uncle and aunt – though I doubt it. The parson would have told me if she was there, I am certain of it. Question the modiste Madame Tamara again. The girl may go to her for work. I understand her uncle never gave her any money after she disappeared, so she must be having to earn her living. She certainly did not look expensively dressed; her gloves were darned and her reticule was a cheap one.'

'Ain't goin' to do all that in five minutes, sir,' his employee mumbled.

'I am well aware of that, you fool!' Grimshaw retorted, pleased to be able to vent his own anger on someone else. 'You are getting well enough paid for your time, and there will be a nice big bonus for you if you find the girl.'

The man's face brightened as he heard this last remark, and having paid a quick visit home to inform his wife that he might be away for some weeks, he collected a few scanty belongings and set off for Dorset.

Clemency, meanwhile, was being given a royal welcome by a beaming Miss Fothergill, although her kindly face fell when Clemency related the reason for her unexpected visit.

'Much as I would really enjoy having you to stay with me,' she said, 'I cannot advise it, my dear. That horrible lawyer has been here several times and I fear that I did not after all convince him of my ignorance of your place of abode. Nor would it be proper for you to go to dear Doctor Brook. In any event, his house is too close to your uncle's and to Chiswell Hill House. No, Clementine, you and the dear boy shall go to a friend of mine, Miss Elizabeth Grantly. Like myself, she is a spinster, and one of our most trusted Friends of Society. I will take you there now and my committee will just have to do without me for once!'

Despite being physically Miss Fothergill's opposite, Miss

Grantly proved just as sweet-natured and welcoming both to Clemency and to little Adam. The two elderly ladies cooed over the child, who had fully recovered from the previous day's journey and was his usual smiling, happy self. Like Miss Fothergill, Clemency's new hostess refused even to discuss terms for her board and lodging.

'When and if you can afford to pay a little something, then you shall,' Miss Grantly said. 'But, meanwhile, I will not hear of it.'

'Then I shall go to Madame Tamara's tomorrow,' Clemency announced. 'Perhaps she will have work for me since it lacks but a month or two to Christmas!'

That afternoon when she had settled into the comfortable room Miss Grantly had offered her overlooking the busy harbour, Clemency sat down to write two letters, one to the Professor to say that she was happily settled; the other to Benjamin asking him to visit her as soon as he could.

Two days later he arrived with a bouquet of flowers and a broad smile of welcome. It quickly faded when he learned the reason for her unexpected appearance in Poole.

'Let us hope my father is right and that the lawyer will not think to find you here,' he said, frowning. He bounced the excited child on his knee absent-mindedly as he added: 'Like Miss Fothergill, I am concerned at the number of times Mr Grimshaw has called upon her and that he suspects you and Miss Fothergill did not part in anger.'

Clemency drew a deep sigh of anxiety.

'I seem to be causing so much trouble to everyone,' she murmured.

'Perhaps Father is right in believing you to be safe here,' Benjamin said reassuringly, 'and if no enquiries are made in Brighton, you can shortly resume your life with him. You were happy there, were you not?'

'Yes, indeed I was. I love your father, Benjamin, and I truly believe he loves me – and Adam, although . . .' She paused, as if unhappy with what she was about to say: '. . . although he did say that I should think very carefully about Adam's future. Benjamin, I believe in his heart your father feels I ought to surrender Adam to Deveril . . . Lord Burnbury. I tried to tell him how horrible a person Lady Burnbury is, but he pointed out to me that her reactions were only natural for a wife suddenly hearing about her husband's plans for their future – from me, of all people. I suppose she did have every right to be angry, hurt, disapproving. It was never my intention to shock her. I assumed her to be aware of the facts! But even then, I could never like her, Benjamin. I do not believe she is a warmhearted person like Miss Fothergill. I do not think she would *ever* love Adam.'

Benjamin remained silent for a moment or two before he said gently:

'Perhaps it would be unfair to expect her to *love* another woman's child, Clemency. Would it not be enough that she accepted him? I cannot believe she would ill-treat a little boy of Adam's age. In any event, his father would not allow it. I daresay she herself would have little to do with Adam's care or his upbringing.'

'You do not know her as I do!' Clemency cried, her cheeks pink. 'I have tried to do as your father suggested and make every possible allowance for her, but nothing will ever convince me that she would make Adam's childhood a happy one. Is it not a fact that love is the most important thing of all for him? Are wealth and position *more* important?' she asked bitterly.

'No, of course not, my dear,' Benjamin said. 'And I am sure Father would not want you to act against your instincts. He, like myself, merely wants you to see every point of view. He would not have sent you here to Poole if he genuinely disapproved of your hiding the boy from his father.'

'I know! But he frightened me!' Clemency admitted. 'He is always so knowledgeable about everything, and I value his opinion most highly.'

Benjamin smiled.

'No one is always right,' he said gently, 'and Father, bless his heart, is only a man. For all his wisdom, he cannot fully be expected to understand how a mother feels about her child.'

That the Professor was not always right was to be proved a week later. Grimshaw's investigator finally reached Poole and having so far discovered no clue whatever on the journey down, and with nothing better to do, he decided to follow Miss Fothergill on one of her visits to the harbour. Unsuspecting of this surveillance, she led him directly to the house of her friend Miss Grantly. Within the half hour, she reappeared with a young girl and a child. Keeping at a safe distance, the man followed them as they took the boy for a short walk to the nearby jetty to permit the child to look at the sailing ships.

As soon as they were back indoors, he hastily scribbled a note for Grimshaw and, hailing an idle lad lounging by the harbour wall, he told the astonished boy:

'A sixpenny piece if you make the London mail!' As the boy ran off, mouth agape at the promise of so large a sum, the man grinned, certain that Grimshaw would be more than happy to reimburse him on this occasion.

Despite the chill of the blustering October day, he settled down in the lee of a nearby wall to keep watch on Miss Grantly's house. When Miss Fothergill eventually departed, he remained where he was. It was worth a night without sleep, in the cold, to make sure that the girl did not leave, he told himself. Grimshaw had promised a big bonus for him if he traced her – and he was in no doubt whatever that he had found the female Grimshaw wanted. He had heard the parlour-maid say 'Good afternoon, Mrs Foster,' when she returned with the Fothergill woman from their walk.

When the lad returned to collect his sixpence, having caught the evening mail to London, Grimshaw's man sent him on another strange errand. This time it was to buy some grain sacks to wrap around himself that night. It would not be the first night he had spent in the open, he thought wryly, but it would be the first which had earned him so much money.

The next morning he followed Clemency to Madame Tamara's establishment, remaining outside until she retraced her steps, her arms filled with a large white cotton sack which he presumed held gowns. For the rest of the day the young woman did not leave the house, and since he was now dropping with fatigue, he put the same lad to keep watch while he departed for a meal and a few hours' sleep. By such methods he maintained his watch until Grimshaw arrived in person twenty-four hours later.

'You are certain?' were Grimshaw's first words as he joined his shabby employee by the wall. The man had not shaved for three days and his clothes looked filthy, but Grimshaw actually put an arm about his shoulders so great was his excitement. 'You have done well. I will send a man to relieve you in a half hour – I brought one with me. But do not go back to London yet; I may need you again. Here . . .' He handed the man a gold sovereign. '. . . go presently and buy yourself a drink and a good meal. You have earned it.'

He himself returned to the coaching inn where he had installed another of his investigators and a woman he had expressly employed for his purpose. She had advertised herself as a fully experienced nurse accustomed to the care of gentlefolks' children. Grimshaw had interviewed her and decided that she would make an excellent choice for the task he had in mind. Telling her no more than that there was a child to be collected from Dorset to be taken to London to his uncle – and then possibly to Scotland, where her responsibilities ended – he engaged her immediately to travel to Dorset together with him and a second sleuth. His man's dirty little note was definite enough to allow him to act so decisively, he had decided.

Grimshaw did not intend to take any further chances of losing the girl – or the child. There would be no more trying to bribe her as Lord Burnbury had suggested. He would get hold of the boy first and let them argue out a settlement later. Personally, Grimshaw saw no requirement to pay the girl anything at all. He would point out to milord Burnbury that if she had money, she would be better able to afford the expense of litigation – not that the law would do anything to assist her in reclaiming her child. The boy was his father's, and in any event, possession was always nine-tenths of the law. No, he would make his client see that it would be best if the girl were not paid at all. He had now but to kidnap the child to reinstate himself instantly in his lordship's good books.

At precisely eight o'clock the following morning, Clemency left Miss Grantly's house to go to Madame Tamara to return the gowns she had embroidered for her. Her mood was happy, the unpleasantness of meeting Grimshaw far from her thoughts as she waved goodbye to Adam, who was held up to the window by a doting Miss Grantly.

As she walked briskly along the sunny cobbled street, she hummed beneath her breath the nursery rhyme she had been teaching Adam before breakfast.

'Little Tommy Tucker,
Sings for his supper . . .'

Adam had been unable to pronounce the words properly, but he had tried to copy his mother's voice as she sang to him, his chubby arms beating in time to the rhythm. He is going to be musical like dearest Mama, she thought.

Her mood as she returned from the modiste was a lot less happy, for Madame Tamara had told her that someone had been making enquiries about her recently.

'I only recalled it yesterday after you had left,' the woman had said curiously.

Walking back to the harbour, Clemency's footsteps quickened. The pale October sun had disappeared behind scurrying clouds and she was feeling chilled as well as anxious. Perhaps she had been mistaken in going back to Madame Tamara, she thought uneasily. If Miss Fothergill's house was under suspicion, so too might be the modiste's.

It was only when Clemency was met at the door by a tearful, almost hysterical Miss Grantly that she realized her fears had overtaken her too late.

'He has gone – your little boy has gone, Mrs Foster. A horrible man forced his way in here – he pushed my poor maid so hard she fell over and bruised her back. He did not speak to me. He just went across the room to little Adam and picked him up and carried him out of the house.' The poor lady burst into a renewed shower of tears as Clemency grabbed her arms.

'Where did he go? Did you follow, Miss Grantly? Oh, do try to calm yourself, I beg of you, *Miss Grantly* . . .'

Something of Clemency's terrible fear penetrated the older woman's panic-stricken mind. She gulped and clung to Clemency's arms.

'He went so fast. I knew I would never catch up with him – and even if I did, how could I, a frail old woman, have stopped him?'

Clemency wrenched free from the woman's clasp and ran to the front door. Apart from two sailors, the street was empty. Realizing the stupidity of her hopes that she might catch sight of Adam, she went back inside. Miss Grantly had collapsed into a chair and was sobbing quietly.

'It was not your fault, Miss Grantly,' she said to the weeping woman, handing her her smelling salts. 'I know who has Adam. I shall go now and find him. I think I know where they have taken him.' For as sanity returned and she could think more calmly, she was certain that by now Adam would be on his way to Chiswell Hill House.

For the first time since she had set eyes upon Deveril, Clemency felt a raw, painful hate for the man she had secretly loved for so long. What he had now done was cruel, base, unforgivable. Man he might be, but even a man must be able to imagine what it would do to a mother to have her child kidnapped without warning, she told herself. Her hatred was equal to her fear, a fear not so much for her child's well-being

– for she was certain Deveril would not allow him to come to harm – but that she might not be able to retrieve him.

I will go first to Benjamin's house, she thought. He will come with me to Chiswell Hill House. He will make Deveril give Adam back!

'Miss Grantly,' she said quietly. 'I shall hire a hackney now to take me to Doctor Brook's house in Upper Chiswell. Try not to worry. I shall return as soon as I can.'

She must not allow her rising hysteria to overwhelm her, she told herself firmly, when at last she was upon her way. Provided she found Benjamin at home, he would not fail to help her get Adam back.

But although Benjamin came hurrying out to greet her with a surprised welcome, after he had paid off the cab driver and learned the reason for her visit, he was unable to offer her the reassurance she craved. Her heart filled with dread as she listened to his warning that she could not count upon the boy being at Chiswell Hill House. Aghast, she felt the first moment of terrifying alarm that Adam might not be back with her by nightfall.

Despite his misgivings, Benjamin went at once to harness his pony and trap. A few minutes later they were driving at what seemed to Clemency to be an agonizingly slow speed towards Chiswell Hill House. In reply to his questions she gave him the few details that she could about Adam's abduction. He did his best to be reassuring, but privately he was far from optimistic as he urged the pony on.

'The nearest place to hide Adam is at the manor,' he said thoughtfully. 'But equally they must know that you would follow them there, Clemency. When you did not return for the afternoon meeting with Grayshott, the lawyer must have guessed that you had no intention of handing over your son voluntarily. So he has had to resort to abduction. In my heart I do not think it likely that Adam will be kept in this neighbourhood.'

They were now driving past the rectory, and to divert her

thoughts from her child, he told her that both her uncle and aunt had been very ill, her uncle quite seriously.

'He is unlikely to live to the end of the year,' he said. 'So perhaps if the opportunity arises, you may wish to make your peace with him.'

'I suppose I should see him,' she murmured unhappily. 'But if I thought he had any part in this plot to take Adam from me . . .' She broke off, realizing that her uncle must be innocent of this particular crime since he had never known where she was after she left Dorset.

But not even her uncle's approaching death seemed of any consequence at this moment, she thought bitterly, as she waited impatiently for the driveway to come into view. She had never before seen the big house in broad daylight, but now, as she stared at it for the first time, its beauty escaped her as she looked desperately for signs of life – a carriage outside the big front door; open windows; even a servant going about his business. But the curtains were drawn and the house and gardens looked deserted.

Benjamin climbed down from the trap and told Clemency to remain where she was, since he thought it more likely he would elicit the facts if she were not beside him.

He pulled hard on the wrought-iron bell handle and, when no answer came, he rapped several times upon the big door knocker. It was a full four minutes before Johnson, the butler, opened the door. He had clearly only just donned his blue coat and his shirt frill was awry. He recognized Benjamin at once.

'I am sorry to have kept you waiting, Sir! I was not expecting visitors what with the family being away.'

Benjamin's face fell.

'There is no one here then, Johnson? No one at all?'

'No one barring Mr Percy and his attendant, Sir, other than the servants, of course. His lordship sent word to say he did not expect to be down again until after Christmas.'

'Thank you, Johnson!' Benjamin paused, and then added:

'If by chance you learn of a change of plan and Lord Burnbury or any of the family are to arrive after all, would you be so good as to send word to me?'

'Very good, Sir.'

The butler waited politely by the open door as Benjamin climbed back into the trap and took up the reins.

'I am afraid Adam is not there, Clemency,' he said, as he turned the trap in the big gravel approach. 'We must assume, I think, that Grimshaw has taken the boy to London.'

Clemency was close to tears of disappointment. But she refused to give way to them.

'Can we not return to Poole and ask at the staging posts if anyone saw them?'

Even as she spoke, she realized how much time this would take, and she immediately countermanded her own suggestion.

'No, I shall go straight to London,' she announced. 'Even if I cannot find Adam at Grayshott House, I know where I can find Mr Grimshaw.'

'But you cannot travel that long distance now, Clemency,' Benjamin protested. 'It will be night time long before you reach London, and I cannot accompany you. I am expecting a difficult breech birth tomorrow and the poor woman will certainly die if I do not attend her . . .'

'I am not in the least afraid to go alone,' Clemency interrupted. 'There will be others on the coach to see I come to no harm and you need not worry about me. If we should be held up by highwaymen, I shall cling to the nearest female and suffer no harm.' She attempted to smile, but it was only fleeting as she continued: 'Could you send a boy to Miss Grantly to advise her that I am quite safe – and to Miss Fothergill?'

They were by now almost abreast of the rectory and Benjamin slowed the tired pony.

'Do you think we should call in – just in case your uncle knows anything?' he said. 'We are fairly certain Grimshaw has been in this part of the country, and although it is only a very slight chance, he may have given your uncle some idea of what is afoot.'

Clemency hesitated. She dreaded the thought of confronting her uncle, but at the same time she could not afford to leave any stone unturned. Any lead, however small, would be better than this total ignorance, and Benjamin would be with her.

'Very well!' she murmured. 'But I will not stay beyond a few minutes, Benjamin, and you must promise not to leave me alone with him.'

Despite the terrible shock she had received from which she had far from recovered, the sight of her uncle put all other thoughts momentarily from Clemency's mind. It was Aunt Winifred's shopping day in the village, and he was alone, he told them, as he directed them into the gloomy parlour.

Had Clemency encountered her uncle somewhere in Poole, she thought, she would not have known him. The portly, ruddy-faced little man had shrunk to a mere skeleton of his former self. His skin was yellow, and he shuffled across the room and sank into his chair with the painful stiffness of an invalid. His voice was reed-like and quavering as he said:

'An unexpected pleasure, Doctor Brook.' He peered through his spectacles at Clemency and said doubtfully: 'I do not think I have had the pleasure . . . or have we met, young lady?'

'This is your niece, Clementine, Parson,' Benjamin said in the gentle voice he always used to little children and elderly patients. 'It must be two years now since you last saw her and of course, she has grown up in that time.'

'Clementine!' the sick man echoed. 'My niece? Clement's girl? I . . . I must be getting very silly in my old age. I did not remember . . . very silly . . . not been well, y'know. Apt to forget things these days.'

Clemency forced herself to move forward and touch his thin, blue-veined hand. She could not bring herself to kiss his cheek.

'Do not worry about it, Uncle Godfrey. I was passing by

with Benjamin – Doctor Brook – and thought I would call to pay my respects. Uncle, I do not want to press you, but do you by any chance know of a plot by the Grayshott family to take my child away? Please tell me the truth. It is very important, very urgent!'

He drew a long sigh and shook his head in confusion.

'The Grayshotts? Not seen any of them since I buried the Viscount. Or was that before the wedding? There was a wedding up at the chapel, y'know – that invalid boy, Percy. But we must not talk about that – gave my oath to the Viscount, do y'see. But that was a long while ago – before I got ill, I think.'

Clemency bit her lip as she realized that her uncle's mind was wandering and confused. Pity stirred her, but Adam was still uppermost in her thoughts as she persisted:

'Try to remember, Uncle. Have you seen Lord Burnbury's lawyer – a Mr Grimshaw – in the past week or two? Did he come to see you – to tell you about my son Adam? Please try to remember!'

She was now kneeling by his chair, her eyes fastened upon his as she spoke. For a moment, a faint smile seemed to creep over his parchment-like face as he said:

'What a pretty girl you are, my dear, if you will forgive an old man saying so. You remind me of . . . why yes, of my brother's little girl, Clementine. I want so very much to find her. She went away, y'know, and I have not been able to tell her that her father is alive. He has written to me – and to her – but I cannot send on the letters because I do not know where she is.'

Clemency's face whitened and then filled with colour as she looked from Benjamin to her uncle and back again.

Benjamin stepped forward.

'Perhaps I could do you a service, Sir, and forward the letters for you. Have you them to hand?'

'Yes, I think so, Brook. I seem to recall I put them in my desk – after that lawyer fellow asked to see them. Should be

in the pigeon-hole next to the one with my Sunday sermon
– unless Winifred's burned 'em!'

'Oh no!' Clemency whispered. 'Pray God not that!'

Benjamin had already crossed to the desk and was searching
there amongst the untidy collection of papers. They were in
total confusion but after a few minutes he found what he was
looking for.

He showed them to the parson, who did no more than
glance at them.

'Glad you have found what you wanted, Brook!' he said,
leaning back against the cushion. 'Tiresome things, papers.
Glad to be rid of 'em. I never did like Clement. Brought disaster
on us all – every one of us. How that Whytakker girl ever
stuck by him, I will never know. Good family, too. Could have
married anyone. And I had to marry Winifred!'

In other circumstances, Clemency might have tried to question her uncle as to what Papa had done to bring disgrace on
his family. But now all she could think of was that her father
had written to her uncle; that he could not be dead.

But when finally she and Benjamin bade the pathetic old
man goodbye and climbed back into the trap, Benjamin said
anxiously:

'He is so confused, Clemency. Those letters could have been
written before . . . before your poor parents . . .'

But Clemency was already opening the first and with a glad
cry of relief and joy, she cried out:

'This one is dated April 1832, Benjamin. Papa is alive! Oh,
if only Mama . . .'

But her eyes, quickly scanning the page, told her that this
was too much to hope for. Her sight was blurred by tears,
but she brushed them aside in order to read further. Even
Adam was forgotten for a brief spell while she read aloud to
Benjamin her father's letter begging her to go out to join him
as soon as she could.

'Do you see, Benjamin, now when I have Adam back, I can
go to the North Americas, where I shall be a whole ocean

away from the Burnbury family. They will never find him so far away. He will be out of danger and . . .'

She broke off as she realized that at this precise moment she was very far from finding her son. She could make no other plans until she had him safely in her arms once more, she thought, never doubting the possibility. If Deveril refused to give him up, she would simply abduct Adam as *they* had abducted him from Miss Grantly's. But Deveril would not keep Adam from her – he could not be so cruel; not when she explained to him how dearly and passionately she loved her son. He was not a cruel man at heart, she was convinced of it. No man would keep so small and young an infant from his mother.

'How far are we from Poole?' she asked, a renewed sense of urgency now overtaking her. 'How long will it take from there to London? Do you think my Adam is even now crying for me? Who will be putting him to bed – and where?'

'Try to calm yourself,' Benjamin said, understanding in part her agony and yet at the same time undergoing an agony of his own. Without thought of the pain it would cause him – and clearly with no regret – Clemency had spoken of taking her child to the colonies, to her father, where he himself would have no hope of ever seeing her again.

CHAPTER SIXTEEN

October 1833

Deveril's carriage drawn by his own four matching greys bowled swiftly up the Great North Road. Highgate Archway lay far behind them, the toll paid. The once gleaming coach-work was already bespattered by the ankle-deep mud they had encountered as they drove across Finchley Common.

It was still very early on a cold October morning, and Deveril's coachman sounded his horn to forewarn the ostler as they approached the next staging post where they would be changing horses. This advance warning enabled the change-over to take place speedily, the fresh steeds being already harnessed and awaiting them as they drove up.

Deveril looked at his son as the small boy clapped his hands delightedly at the sound of the bugle.

'I will buy you one of your own,' he said with a warm rush of pleasure. 'Would you like one, Adam?'

The child nodded, but the laughter left his face as he looked from Deveril to Hopkins and finally at the woman on whose lap he was sitting. Only momentarily diverted by the bugle, he suddenly realized they were all strangers.

'Mama?' he said in a small querulous voice. 'Adam see Mama?'

'Presently, my pretty!' said the woman comfortingly. She was a kindly soul who had been told by Mr Grimshaw that the little boy's mother had died suddenly, and she had set herself the task of consoling him on the long tiring journey from Dorset to London. The child had settled to sleep quickly enough when they reached the hotel where they were staying the night, for he had been too exhausted to cry for long. Now it would be five days or more of travel up to milord's Scottish home, and she had warned his lordship that so young a child might easily become tired and fretful.

So far he had been extremely good, only demanding occasionally to see his mother. A good night's sleep and a warming breakfast had restored his energy and his natural good spirits. Deveril was enchanted by the child and inordinately gratified when the nurse commented on the unusual likeness between them.

'Spitting image of you, Milord, if I may say so!' she had remarked. Suddenly curious, Deveril tried to recall the description Grimshaw had given of the boy's mother. He seemed to remember Grimshaw telling him that she was fair-haired and blue-eyed. But the boy had the dark eyes of most of the Grayshotts, Deveril thought with pleasure, and he was in the very best of moods as they sped northwards.

His thoughts returned to the previous evening when Grimshaw had called at his house to tell him the boy was safely installed in a hotel in London. He had immediately cancelled his proposed dinner with Anthea and hastened round to see the child, Grimshaw accompanying him with a smirk of self-satisfaction on his ugly face. Deveril recalled how gratified the man had been when he had taken him into the hotel and sat drinking with him as if he were an equal. Like him or not, Deveril thought, the fellow deserved some praise.

'You have done a splendid job, Grimshaw,' he had acknowledged, patting him on the back. He had supposed that the child's mother would make difficulties, but Grimshaw told him she had surrendered the boy without any fuss.

'It always surprises me what money will do if there is enough of it to offer,' Deveril had said then.

Grimshaw had long since decided to make no mention of the fact that he had abducted the child without the mother's knowledge and that no money had changed hands. Changing the subject, he congratulated Deveril on having thought of so excellent a solution to the problem of keeping the boy out of Lady Burnbury's way for the next few years.

Castle Clunes was a perfect place to hide his son for the time being, Deveril explained. Lady Burnbury refused to go to Scotland, and if any friend of hers returning from a visit to the neighbourhood reported the presence of a child at his great-aunt's house, it could be explained away as one of his sisters' children. His wife would have no more interest in the matter than she had in Lady Allendale's children when they were in London.

As for his great-aunt – she would ask no questions and accept the infant with the same tolerance as she adopted stray animals.

'The boy will be at a most satisfactory distance if by any chance Miss Foster changed her mind and sought to regain possession of her child,' the lawyer had remarked, warning Deveril that for this reason they must maintain the utmost secrecy as to the child's whereabouts.

Well, Perthshire was far enough from London to hide Adam, Deveril thought, as the coach lumbered more slowly through Welwyn and headed on towards Baldock. They were covering a steady ten miles an hour, and passed the mail coach on the open road after they had left the town behind them. He was not altogether happy at the idea of having to secrete Adam in Scotland perhaps for as long as four or five years. He was such a handsome child! He would have preferred to keep him in London, where he could show him off to all his friends. But that pleasure was for the future. In the meanwhile, Great-Aunt Meg would love and spoil the child and hopefully, before too long, he could talk Muriel round to a willing acceptance of his son.

By now it was midday, and with over fifty miles behind them, Deveril ordered his coachmen to halt in Huntingdon at the George Inn. It amused him to watch the nurse spoon-feeding the boy, whose appetite nearly matched his own. He allowed Adam to sip from his glass of wine, ignoring the frown of disapproval on the nurse's face. But he could not ignore her insistence that her small charge was growing tired, and they were not long back on the road before the boy fell asleep, his dark curly head resting on the nurse's ample bosom. He still clutched in one chubby hand a wooden horse Deveril had purchased for him from a pedlar early that morning. Deveril gave a sudden sigh. It could not have been easy for the mother to part with so pretty an infant, he thought, but quickly put such imaginings from his mind. A woman prepared to sell her child was not worth his sympathy, he told himself. She could have no more by way of true maternal feelings than had Muriel.

Muriel, he thought, would by now be paying her morning calls, little knowing that he was on his way to Scotland. He had told her that he was going down to Dorset again to see to affairs on the estate. As usual, she had complained bitterly at this proposed absence.

'You are more often away from home than in it!' she had remarked in that gentle voice which never quite succeeded in disguising its reproach. But she accepted his excuse quite readily, for she knew that following upon his grandfather's death, he was intending to make considerable changes at Chiswell Hill House. He was determined to improve many of the farm cottages and had already instructed his bailiff to draw up a detailed list of the repairs that were most urgent. Muriel herself took no interest in such matters and did not question Deveril's excuse that his bailiff could not act competently without him.

Although cold, it was a bright, crisp October afternoon, and Deveril decided to ride up alongside his coachman until shortly after four o'clock when the sun was low in the sky. He realized that they were not far distant from Burleigh House where he sometimes halted his journeys to Castle Clunes to call upon his friend, the Marquis of Exeter. But encumbered as he now was with the child, he decided to make as much distance as he could before nightfall.

Inside the coach, the nurse informed him that the boy had just woken. Adam was interested in Deveril's reappearance and was amused for some while when his father gave him his silver-cased, quarter-repeating watch and chain to play with. Only once did he enquire for his mama and was easily distracted when his nurse allowed him to kneel on the seat and gaze out of the window at the approaching lights of Grantham.

An hour later, with the child safely despatched to bed with his nurse, Deveril settled down to a pleasant evening playing cards with two gentlemen from Edinburgh who were also passing the night at the Angel. His run of good fortune was holding, he thought as, fifty guineas the richer, he set off the following morning soon after an early breakfast. The weather remained fine and they made good time, reaching Doncaster by one o'clock where they stopped at the Red Lion for a meal.

The child was now becoming restless and fretful and Deveril was glad to be able to leave the confines of the coach and the company of the nurse and the little boy. He took himself off to the dining-room. While the nurse was preoccupied in feeding Adam, he made the acquaintance of an attractive young lady travelling with her parents to Wetherby. Formal introductions were made, and Deveril spent a pleasant half hour flirting with the pretty daughter, who was finally bold enough to suggest to her father that Deveril should travel with them in their coach for this next leg of the journey.

'It must be very tedious for you with no one but the child and his nurse for company,' she said, looking hopefully at Deveril from beneath her lashes.

By no means displeased with the idea of furthering the acquaintance of so important a personage as Lord Burnbury, the girl's parents welcomed him, and the two carriages set off in the early afternoon one behind the other.

It helped to pass the time agreeably, Deveril thought with amusement, as occasionally he allowed his knee to touch that of the girl, under pretext that such contact was unavoidable with the lurching of the coach. The girl was pretty enough, but did not stir his senses as did Anthea. His affair with his American mistress was progressing splendidly. They spent long exciting hours together dallying in Anthea's large comfortable bed, where she abandoned herself unashamedly to the pleasures they derived from each other's bodies. It still surprised Deveril how passionate and eager Anthea was proving to be. He was nevertheless piqued that she was not a little more possessive.

'Are you not even a little bit in love with me?' he had asked her recently as they lay naked in one another's arms.

Anthea's green eyes had been gently teasing as she replied:

'But of course, my dearest. I am always in love with the man who is currently pleasuring me. I would not permit him to share my bed if I were not. You are a very sweet boy – and a very good pupil, too. Soon you will have learned everything I can teach you, and then you will become bored with me or I with you and we shall have to part.'

He would never become bored with her, Deveril thought, as he smiled into the eyes of the girl beside him. Part of Anthea's fascination for him was her elusiveness. He was her slave – but she refused to be his!

He allowed his hand to wander along the girl's arm while he distracted her parents' attention by pointing out the River Aire as they passed through Ferrybridge. It would serve Anthea right, he thought, if he were unfaithful to her . . . with a pretty little thing like this one sitting so demurely beside him. But the girl could not be much above seventeen and an innocent, he told himself, and he forgot her entirely as the two carriages halted at the Swan and Talbot staging post, for he could see the little boy struggling to get down from the nurse's arms to run to him. With a hurried farewell to his travelling companions, he went across to the nurse and took the boy from her arms.

'Did you miss me then?' he enquired gravely, and as Adam's arms went round his neck, he felt a totally new emotion. He had *wanted* the child mainly because he wanted an heir; he had not expected to *love* him – and yet now he was intensely pleasured by the boy's desire to be with him.

'Come, then,' he said, lifting the delighted Adam onto his shoulders. 'You and I shall take tea together since you did not appear to enjoy the landlord's best claret at the George!' He dismissed the nurse to do as she pleased and enjoyed the novelty of a thorough spoiling by the landlady, who had never before seen a gentleman spoon-feeding his own child.

But it was not long before the warmth of the fire and the late hour caused the boy's eyelids to droop. Deveril settled the bill and, summoning his servants, he carried Adam back to the coach where he allowed him to sit upon his lap.

'He is a sturdy little lad and will be quite heavy on your arm, Milord,' the nurse cautioned him, but Deveril shrugged indifferently.

'Let him be. I will hand him back when I have had enough of him,' he said. But although his arm was aching intolerably by the time they reached Boroughbridge, he refused to give way to the need to stretch himself, for fear of waking the boy. He sensed his weariness as if it were his own, but they had only another fourteen miles to travel to Northallerton, and he had already sent his footman ahead on horseback to arrange accommodation for them at the Golden Lion in the market place.

But by the end of their third day of travel, Deveril's un-accustomed patience was wearing thin when at six o'clock, sixty hours after leaving London, the carriage drew into the courtyard of the Queen's Head in Morpeth. Despite the distance already covered, they were still over ninety miles south of Edinburgh and, after consultation with his coachman, Deveril decided that on the morrow they would not take the same road to the north as the mails, but would save time by travelling through Elsdon and Jedburgh.

Although they pursued the faster route and met with no mishaps, it was nevertheless quite late at night before they reached the outskirts of Edinburgh. During the journey Adam had become restless and, from time to time, tearful. He cried more frequently for his mother, and Deveril, made uneasy by that plaintive little voice, had ridden most of the way with his coachman or on horseback. As the huge castle came into sight, he decided that in fairness to so young a child, he must forgo further travel on the morrow and remain in the city an extra night.

After a leisurely breakfast next morning, he left the boy with his nurse and set about shopping for a present for his great-aunt. He finally selected two fantail doves which she had long coveted. They proved an excellent choice, keeping the boy amused when they set off for Perth the next day, for Adam begged to be permitted to have the birds' cage inside the carriage with him. Despite the obvious disapproval on the nurse's face, Deveril was pleased that he had indulged his son, since the birds distracted him and there were no more tears before they reached Perth at midday on their sixth day of travel. Deveril allowed only a short halt for luncheon, aware that they would be leaving the main road at Dunkeld and that they would be travelling a great deal more slowly across the moors to Castle Clunes.

It was growing dark as at the conclusion of their long journey the carriage finally drew up outside the huge stone portico of the castle. Adam was wailing fretfully as he realized that he had not seen his mother for a very long while, and that everything around him appeared strange and hostile. It was with a great feeling of relief that Deveril saw his great-aunt come hurrying into the hallway followed by two female servants.

'Why, Deveril, my dear boy! How very pleased I am to see you,' she cried. 'Your servant arrived on horseback two hours since and advised me of your arrival. Everything is prepared for you and the boy . . .'

The child's soft sobbing trailed into silence as this new stranger bent over him. Her face was as wrinkled as a walnut shell, her white hair as disorderly as that of a witch. She smelt strangely too, and Adam was on the edge of a scream when she spoke to him.

'Now guess what I have upstairs to show you,' she said. 'It is a real live little monkey in a bright red coat! I will wager you have only seen a monkey before in your picture books!'

She turned back to Deveril and, noting his exhaustion, instructed him to go into the drawing-room where the butler would bring him some whisky.

'You come with me,' she said to Adam. 'We will go and see Jacko together, shall we? Then you can have a nice glass of hot milk and a good sleep and when you wake up, we will go and see all the other animals.'

Two big deerhounds came ambling over to the small group, their tails wagging, their noses pushing into the old lady's hands.

'There, Deveril!' she said beaming. 'The boy is not the least bit frightened of Sean and Moira, are you, my darling. Goodness me, he does not take after poor Percy. He is the very spitting image of you when you were his age, Deveril. You must tell me all about him later. Come, dear, we will go with Nurse to see Jacko!'

As fascinated by the marmoset as Aunt Meg had expected, Adam once more forgot his mother and was willing finally to be put in the big four-poster without further tears. Too young to assess the old lady's age or character, nevertheless he was instinctively aware that he had found a friend. His wooden horse safely tucked into bed with him, he settled down to sleep with no more than a fleeting whimper for Mama to come and kiss him goodnight.

At approximately the same time as Deveril's carriage was passing through Huntingdon, Clemency stood outside the front door of Grayshott House, trembling with anxious excitement. It was now two whole days since she had held Adam in her arms and it was beginning to feel more like a year, she thought, as the butler opened the door to her and she once again demanded to see Lord Burnbury.

'I am afraid his lordship is not at home, Miss,' he said.

Clemency had been expecting this answer.

'Kindly tell his lordship that Miss Foster wishes to see him and will not be put off by stories that he "is not at home". I know he is here and I intend to see him.'

As shocked by this unconventional retort as by the violent tone in which it was delivered, Dawkins drew himself up to his full height and said haughtily:

'I assure you, Miss, that his lordship is *not* in residence. He left early this morning and will not be back for some time.'

'Then is Lady Burnbury at home?'

'No, Miss, her ladyship is also away,' Dawkins replied, and seeing her crestfallen face, he added more kindly: 'Lady Burnbury is visiting her parents in Buckinghamshire, so I believe.'

Clemency's mouth fell open, her mind racing. Was the butler telling the truth, or was he merely repeating what he had been instructed to say?

'But . . . but I *must* see Lord Burnbury!' she said, her tone now so despairing that Dawkins took pity on her.

'I think I did overhear his lordship mention to Milady that he might be going to Dorset.'

'Dorset!' Clemency echoed. 'But I have just come from there!'

Dawkins was already regretting his indiscretion.

'Is there anything else, Miss?' he enquired.

Clemency stood staring at the man's implacable face. The thought that Deveril was on his way to Dorset whilst she had been travelling to London, and that they might actually have passed one another en route, was a shattering one. Now she must make the long journey back to Chiswell Hill House and confront Deveril there. But first she would go to see Mr Grimshaw. If he admitted to Adam's abduction, she could at least be certain no one other than Deveril was involved.

Suddenly aware that the butler was waiting for her to leave, she murmured a brief 'thank you' as the door was closed firmly behind her.

For the second time in her life, Clemency walked down George Street in search of a hackney cab. On this occasion, there was no organ grinder at the corner, only an old tramp, huddled in rags against the cold October wind. He held out his hand as she passed, and despite her own sense of urgency and her very limited means, Clemency withdrew a three-penny piece from her reticule and put it in the outstretched palm.

'God bless you, lady!' the old man said as he touched his cap. As Clemency moved on past him, she hoped that this benediction would be heard by a God who seemed to have deserted her.

Twenty minutes later she arrived at Grimshaw's offices in King's Bench Walk. The same pimply-faced clerk opened the door to her. This time she did not request to see the lawyer but pushed past the boy and walked into Grimshaw's office, startling him where he sat at his desk.

'Where is my son?' Clemency demanded, her fear for Adam causing her to forget her manners. 'Where has Lord Burnbury taken my son? I demand to know!'

Grimshaw got up, closed the door and tried to urge Clemency into a chair. She remained standing, her eyes boring into his, her breath coming swiftly.

'I shall find out sooner or later, Mr Grimshaw. I want my son back, and I intend to have him. He is my child – mine! Tell me where he is.'

Grimshaw took his time as he walked back behind his desk and sat down. He realized the young woman was near to hysterics, and he did not want a noisy scene in the office where the clerks outside might overhear what was said.

'You have nothing whatever to worry about, Miss Foster,' he murmured soothingly. 'If you will only be seated, I will tell you what you want to know.'

Lulled into a false sense of security, Clemency did as she was bid.

'Well now,' Grimshaw began. 'I should tell you first of all that the boy has come to no harm. I guarantee that. He is well and being looked after by a trained nurse especially employed for the purpose. She has excellent references and . . .'

'I want to know where he is!' Clemency broke in. 'I insist that you tell me.'

'Yes, of course, Miss Foster. I do understand your anxiety. The boy is with his father, which, when you are calmer, you will have to admit is where he should be . . .'

'I want to see Adam – now, as soon as possible,' Clemency cried. 'You have still not told me where he is, Mr Grimshaw.'

A determined young woman, Grimshaw told himself warningly.

'I am afraid I cannot divulge his exact whereabouts,' he said slowly. 'Lord Burnbury has ordered me to remain silent on that point for the time being. But I do assure you, Miss Foster, when you and his lordship have had a little time to discuss matters, he will allow you to . . .'

Clemency jumped to her feet, her eyes blazing, partly in anger but mostly in fear.

'Are you telling me that Lord Burnbury has hidden my son from me? That he has no intention of giving him back?'

Grimshaw's silence was all the answer necessary. Clemency fought to calm her rising panic. The Professor's words shot through her brain: *'a person's reasoning is best when it is not clouded by emotions.'* She *must* keep calm.

'As it happens, I know Lord Burnbury left this morning for his home in Dorset. I do not need you to tell me where Adam is,' she said coldly.

'But . . .' Grimshaw broke off before he had voiced his denial. Why not let the girl go back to Dorset if that was where she thought her son was. It would allow time for Deveril Burnbury to reach Scotland and for the trail to grow cold. If this persistent young woman were ever to start making enquiries at the staging posts, no one would remember Deveril and the child after a week with so many hundreds of passengers passing through each day.

'Do not deny that Lord Burnbury has gone to Dorset,' Clemency cried. 'His butler told me so.'

Grimshaw looked genuinely surprised. Then he smiled inwardly. Clearly Deveril had taken his advice and kept his true destination secret.

'Do not think that you can prevent me from recovering Adam!' Clemency said, as she turned towards the door. 'If need be, I shall take the matter to law. I no longer consider myself bound by an oath of secrecy and, if it is necessary, I shall announce that I am Mrs Percy Grayshott and that Adam is legally *his* son and not Lord Burnbury's.'

Grimshaw decided that this was not the moment to discuss her legal rights with her. It was enough that *he* knew she had none. Any lawyer she might approach now or in the future, if it came to that, would advise her that she had no cause. He felt a fleeting moment of pity for the girl. He had seen the boy and grudgingly admitted that he was a handsome, healthy-looking child. Doubtless the girl was fond of him. But Grimshaw's rare moment of pity did not last long and had disappeared completely as he conducted Clemency to the door.

Riding in the hackney cab towards the Bell and Crown, where she knew she could board a coach for Poole, Clemency realized how terribly tired she was. She had barely slept the previous night, tormented as she was by fears for Adam. Now at least she knew he was safe and, according to the revolting Grimshaw, being cared for by a qualified nurse. This small measure of relief almost moved her to the tears which had threatened all day. Had she not felt compelled to go back immediately to Dorset, she would have wanted to return to Brighton, to the calm, sensible and affectionate Professor. She was beginning to feel as if she was living in a terrible nightmare from which she could not wake up.

But there was to be no relief for Clemency. When she called at Chiswell Hill House with Benjamin the second time, it was as deserted as it had been three days earlier. They both realized that Clemency had to sleep somewhere that night, and a tearful Miss Fothergill did her best to be kind and comforting when they arrived upon her doorstep. But there was no real comfort for Clemency until she had her child back in her arms.

Benjamin called to see her the following morning and was deeply concerned by the pallor of her face and the dark shadows beneath her eyes.

'I am convinced we shall not find Adam in Dorset,' he said. 'I think you should return now to Brighton. Father will know what steps you should take next, Clemency, my dear. For my part, I can do so little to help. But if it is any consolation whatever, try to remember that we know Deveril Grayshott wanted Adam; therefore he will not ill-treat him.' He attempted a smile as he added: 'I dare say that at this very moment Adam is being quite hopelessly indulged, and although it must distress you beyond measure to be without him, *he* is still so young he will not be as aware of the separation as you. He is doubtless quite happy!'

Clemency's tear-filled eyes regarded him accusingly.

'You think I should leave him with his father, do you not, Benjamin? You think Adam will have a better life with Deveril than with me.'

'Clemency, I said no such thing!' Benjamin protested. 'I wished only to point out to you that even if the worst comes to the very worst and you cannot reclaim Adam, he . . .'

'I will never accept that – *never!*' Clemency broke in. 'I can never be at peace without him, Benjamin. He is my child – part of me. Oh, why do you not understand!'

Despite Benjamin's efforts to assure her of his understanding, Clemency left Poole with a feeling of alienation from him. The emotion only added to her unhappiness, for until now she had taken for granted his unqualified support.

By the time she reached Brighton and the safe haven of Adelaide Crescent, she was on the point of collapse. Nevertheless, she refused to retire to bed until she had recounted the whole story to the Professor. Although he was shocked and deeply distressed by her account of her misfortunes, he refused to offer false hopes.

'I would be failing in my duty to you were I to do so,' he told her gently. 'You see, Clemency, men in Lord Burnbury's position wield a great deal of power – a lot of it behind the scenes. And he is enormously wealthy, my dear. He can employ the very best legal brains in the country should it be necessary. Whilst you were away, I have been studying some law books I obtained from a friend and unhappily, it appears that as the law now stands, a wife does not even have the rights of a mistress where her children are concerned. Paradoxically, an unmarried mother may claim access to her child but a married woman may not. In retrospect, therefore, your marriage to Percy Grayshott, made to protect you, may now prove to be to your disadvantage where Adam is concerned.'

Clemency listened appalled and her heart twisted with bitterness. She had entered into that strange unnatural union entirely to protect her unborn child. Her uncle's suggestion that it would ensure that the infant would not be born with the stigma of illegitimacy had impressed her far more deeply than did her escape from her own disgrace. Now it seemed as if it was going to prove an effective barrier between her and the child she loved.

'Of course,' the Professor continued, 'we must not forget that Adam is legally Percy's and not Deveril's son. There is always the possibility that we might be able to go to court and prove that Percy is incapable of carrying out his paternal duties to the boy. But I know very little about the law and we shall require expert advice. Fortunately, I do have the name of an excellent lawyer here in Brighton. He was recommended to me by the architect Mr Wilds, that friend of mine who was building the Antheum. You have been away, of course, so you will not perhaps know of the tragedy that befell last month.'

Hoping that he might divert her attention for a little while from her unhappy situation, he related how the ill-fated

Antheum, the beloved brainchild of his botanist friend Henry Phillips, had disintegrated that summer. The building contractor had taken away the supporting scaffolding without reference to Mr Wilds, and the entire edifice had disintegrated, decimating the tropical gardens beneath. Now nothing remained but broken girders, and the tangled wreckage was there for all to see, an amazing claw-like silhouette against the sky.

But not even this disaster could deflect Clemency's thoughts from her own personal tragedy.

'You think I should leave matters be, do you not, Professor?' she said, unable to keep the bitterness from her voice. 'Like Benjamin, you believe I should allow Deveril to keep Adam.'

'My dear child, I have said no such thing, although Benjamin could very well be right. But one thing is certain, you must be granted access to Adam. It would be quite outrageous if you were not, an outrage against nature. Any child as young as Adam needs a mother – and you have assured me that Lady Burnbury cannot and will not fulfil that rôle. To be practical, Clemency, I think we might consider the possibility of obtaining an agreement from Lord Burnbury whereby you should have care and control of the boy until he is at least six or seven years old. After that, you should perhaps allow his father to have him and for the boy to spend his holidays with you.'

But Clemency was in no mood for compromise. She had had her child stolen from her, and it was now one whole week since she had set eyes on him. Moreover, she was still without any inkling of his whereabouts. All she knew was that Deveril Grayshott had taken him from her in total disregard for her feelings or Adam's. She hated him now as deeply as she had once loved him, and the idea of sharing Adam with him was abhorrent. She looked at the Professor despairingly.

'You are suggesting that I shall never have him back entirely,' she cried. 'And I had intended to take him to the colonies, Professor. I have not yet had time to tell you that by a miracle my father's life was saved and that he has been trying to get in touch with me. I have a letter from him, begging me to go out there and keep him company. When I find Adam, I can begin a new life with him and . . .'

She broke off suddenly as she saw the expression on the Professor's face.

'Maybe you *should* go to your father, Clemency,' he said gently, 'but without the boy. Unless you could get the court to agree that you and you alone have custody of Adam, then you could never take him out of England. But let us not ponder that question at the moment. It is late and you are very tired, and perhaps this is not the time to be discussing the future. Tomorrow we will go to Mr Bryant, the lawyer I have in mind, and discover what he has to say.'

The Professor was aware that Clemency's endurance was at breaking point and he forbore to add that he believed her case already lost. He sent her off to bed, sadly conscious of the fact that she first visited Adam's little room and spent an hour there weeping quietly before finally she retired. Her distress upset him far more than she could have supposed, for although earlier in the evening she had entirely vindicated him from any blame, he knew himself partly responsible for what had transpired. It had been on *his* advice that Clemency had answered the advertisement in *The Times*; on *his* advice that she had returned to Dorset rather than remaining in Brighton, where Grimshaw might never have found her and the boy.

But even as he admitted to himself the extent of his responsibility, he knew that once Lord Burnbury had decided he wanted his son, it was only a matter of time before he would have found him. It was not only nature, he thought, which could sometimes be inexplicably cruel. It was life itself, and the rules Society made for its so-called benefit. England was proud of her legal system, and yet not even in the least civilized of tribes was a child torn from its mother's arms unless by an enemy.

Ironically, the Professor thought wearily, Clemency had chosen for her enemy Deveril, Viscount Burnbury – one of the leading peers in the land.

CHAPTER SEVENTEEN

November 1833–March 1834

While Deveril was escorting his son to Scotland, Grimshaw enjoyed a brief period of smug self-satisfaction as he contemplated the success of his planned operation. It had been accomplished with admirable speed and efficiency, he thought, and he had every reason to congratulate himself. Having seen his lordship, the boy and the hired nurse depart in their carriage that morning, Lord Burnbury grinning cheerfully as he waved a grateful farewell, Grimshaw returned to his office in the pleasantest of moods. He sat at his desk, enjoying a brief respite from more mundane duties whilst he reviewed the past few months.

But his complacency was short-lived. Only the day after Lord Burnbury had departed to Scotland, he, Grimshaw, was obliged to face the fact that he had mistaken the strength of will which lay behind the girl's extreme youth. Her second visit to him proved all too clearly that she was neither simple nor pliable and had no intention of accepting the *status quo*. By allowing her to suppose that Deveril had returned to Dorset, he had merely gained a little time. As soon as she discovered Lord Burnbury and the boy were not at Chiswell Hill House, he, Grimshaw, would have her back on his doorstep; or worse still, back on the doorstep of Grayshott House. It brought a chill to Grimshaw's spine to imagine his client's anger if he learned on his return from Scotland that Miss Clementine Foster had been badgering his wife.

Somehow, he thought, he must endeavour to persuade his lordship to leave England for a while. It would not be easy in midwinter, and even less easily engineered at short notice. Nor was Grimshaw in the least aware of what private engagements the Burnburys might have planned for the next few months. Time was not on his side, since his client could be back in London in two weeks, three at the most if he dallied in Perthshire to settle the boy in his new surroundings.

Perhaps, Grimshaw thought, he could send the girl off on another wild goose chase to Dorset, or if he could find the courage to do so, he might persuade Lord Burnbury to leave London for a month or two. He could then negotiate with the girl – perhaps even arrange for her to be reunited with her father in the colonies. It was a stroke of good fortune that one of her parents had after all survived the boating tragedy, and that he had learned of the fact from the Rev Foster. He had now but to convince the girl she had no chance of discovering her son's whereabouts – leaving her own lawyer to advise her that she had no rights to the boy – to put a satisfactory end to the whole affair. But first lay the tricky problem of how to persuade his client to go away – and quickly.

Luck favoured Grimshaw, for on Deveril's return from Scotland, Anthea Wilcox announced that she had received an invitation to spend the Christmas festivities in Paris, after which she had resolved to complete the 'Grand Tour', visiting Italy, Greece and the Near East, before returning to New York. Instead of the warm welcome Deveril had anticipated on his return to London, she greeted him without passion. There was no hasty departure to the bedroom, and she made no prevarication as she outlined her intentions.

'My dearest boy,' she said, smiling as she smoothed the frown from his forehead, 'the essence of a romantic liaison such as ours lies in its timing. We should bring it to a conclusion before either of us begins to take the other for granted. The excitement is in the novelty, and I realized whilst you were away that our meetings were becoming a habit for us both. If they were to continue, you would soon become bored, as, indeed, might I.'

'But Anthea, I love you and . . .'

His protest was silenced by her finger on his lips.

'You do no such thing, my dear,' she said gently. 'You may know my body as intimately as I know yours, but you do not know *me* at all. Love, as I understand it, is a communion of two spirits, and that hardly describes our very earthy encounters, however unromantic that may sound. Let us not delude ourselves, Deveril dear. My mind is made up.'

Thoroughly put out by his mistress's independence, Deveril reacted like any spoilt child. He scowled and sulked by turns.

'I cannot see why you should want to go to Paris. Have you a lover there? Were you unfaithful to me whilst I was in Scotland? What has changed you so suddenly?'

Anthea Wilcox resisted the urge to bring back the carefree smile she so loved to see on his handsome face. The very last thing she could tell him was the truth – namely that she knew herself to be falling in love with him, just as surely as she knew he was not in love with her. It was not until Deveril had suddenly absented himself for three weeks that she had appreciated how hopelessly dependent she had become, despite her determination to keep their affair lighthearted. More and more frequently, she had found herself cancelling engagements and invitations she would otherwise have accepted with alacrity, simply in order to be at home when he called, whereas *he* came to see *her* only when it suited him. Deveril's absence at the very moment the invitation from Paris arrived gave her the strength of will to make the first move.

'I am not going to visit a new lover. I am going to stay with some delightful French friends,' she told him. 'So you have no cause for jealousy, my dear!'

Slightly mollified, Deveril changed his tactics.

'If you will not stay here with me, then I shall come with you!' he volunteered. 'I will follow you to Paris!'

Despite the seriousness of his expression, Anthea smiled.

'Dearest boy, you appear to find it the easiest thing in the world to forget that you are a married man. For that very reason, I could not ask my friends the Comte and Comtesse de Maurois to invite you to their house. They are very conventional people and would not approve!'

'Then I shall reside in a hotel nearby!' Deveril declared. 'You cannot deny me that privilege. And if it is respectability which concerns you, I will bring my wife as a chaperone!'

'Deveril, you are sometimes so immoral, my sympathies lie entirely with poor Muriel. I am thankful that I am not in her shoes!'

The first hint of a smile curved Deveril's mouth.

'If you were in her shoes, they would fit a deal more comfortably,' he said, 'for you would also be in her bed and I should be with you!'

Anthea allowed him to draw her into his arms, but her face remained unsmiling as she said:

'Can she really not want you there, Deveril? I do not understand it! I have seen for myself that she is both possessive and very jealous of your attentions to other women. I would have taken an oath on the fact that she loves you.'

Deveril shrugged indifferently.

'Muriel's way of loving is not mine!' he said. 'Let us not talk about her, Anthea. We have never done so before, and I have no wish to do so now when there are so many more important matters for us to discuss.'

Muriel was the very last person he wanted to remember. She had given him an exceedingly chilly welcome on his return from Scotland the previous day. Unaware of the true reasons why he had been absent for so long, she had complained endlessly of the length of time he had been away.

'If I had known you intended to remain so long in Dorset, I would have come with you,' she told him. 'You told me "a few days". It is really most unfair of you to leave me alone for weeks on end! Whatever happened to delay you? You know very well I was only going to stay with Papa and Mama for ten days.'

There had been 'a very desperate young lady' on his

doorstep while he had been away, Dawkins had told him, demanding to see his lordship 'on a matter of great urgency'. Deveril assumed that this had been Adam's mother, and the thought made him uneasy. Now, even in Anthea's company, he could not ignore the feeling of discomfiture. It was Grimshaw's task to keep the girl away from him, he thought, and he, Deveril, would be better employed charging the man with his inefficiency than dallying longer with his mistress.

He was in no happy mood, therefore, when he left Anthea's house and drove to Grimshaw's offices in the Temple. It did not improve when the lawyer attempted to make light of the girl's visit to Grayshott House.

'You told me she had given the boy up without fuss!' Deveril said accusingly. 'And *I* told *you*, Grimshaw, that I will *not* have my wife brought into this for the time being.'

'Of course, of course, Milord!' Grimshaw stammered as he urged Deveril into a chair and sent one of his clerks scurrying for a glass and a bottle of brandy. 'But you know what females are like . . . always changing their minds without rhyme or reason. Believe me, I am doing all I can to bring Miss Foster to her senses. It is simply a matter of time, Milord, I do assure you. And doubtless a little more money . . .' He broke off and decided this might be the best moment to take the bull by the horns. 'I was thinking, Milord, that as it is a matter of the utmost concern to you that Lady Burnbury should not be troubled, perhaps if it were at all possible for you to take your wife away . . . that is to say, away from London . . . a little holiday abroad, for example . . .?'

He broke off once more as Deveril's face flushed with anger.

'Damnation, Grimshaw, what gives you the idea that I might be willing to go into hiding like some miserable servant who has stolen his mistress's purse and dare not face the consequences! Confound it, it is an infernal insult! *You* set all this in motion. You should have warned me if we were doing anything illegal. Yet you have insisted all along that the boy is rightfully mine!'

'Indeed he is, Milord, make no mistake about it. The girl can do nothing – nothing at all to reclaim him. But . . . but until she has had time to appreciate this, she *could* cause you or your wife further inconvenience. I could always arrange for a member of the constabulary to protect Grayshott House, but I know you wish to avoid any undue publicity and the *girl is your brother's wife* – a fact we cannot entirely overlook.'

Deveril felt his anger subsiding. Grimshaw was no fool, and it was true that he did not want to be drawn into any public controversy. Moreover, although Grimshaw was unaware of it, his suggestion that he should 'disappear' from London for a while exactly coincided with his intentions. He would not allow the delectable Anthea to put an end to their relationship without his approval, and he certainly did not approve of her going to Paris without him.

To Grimshaw's astonishment – and relief – he said:

'Very well, since it is my intention anyway to go to France within the next week, and in all probability from there to Italy and Greece, I am quite agreeable to leaving London for the time being. When I do return, I shall expect you to have all these tiresome details cleared up once and for all. As I have said many times before, I do not give a tinker's damn what it costs, but send the girl away. As to the boy, you can tell her he is in excellent hands and, barring an occasional tear from time to time, is far too engrossed with his new life to be pining for his mother. That is God's truth, and if that is what is bothering her, it should put her mind at rest.'

As he left Grimshaw's dingy offices, he dismissed the girl from his thoughts and turned his mind to his wife. Doubtless Muriel would be aghast at the idea of going away for several months at a mere fortnight's notice. He could anticipate her objections – she would need clothes; and the house must be shut up; there were invitations outstanding of the utmost importance.

Deveril was prepared with answers when he broached the

subject after dinner that evening. He promised his wife that she could buy what clothes she wished in Paris. As for closing up the house, the servants were there to carry out such tasks, he assured her. Moreover, if she did not wish to accompany him, he was fully prepared to go alone. At that juncture, Muriel changed her objections to minor complaints. She would almost certainly be ill during the Channel crossings. The long carriage drive from Calais to Paris would be exhausting. Paris was scarcely at its most fashionable in wintertime! They would know no one of importance with whom to associate.

'What nonsense, my dear,' Deveril argued amiably. 'That charming American friend of yours – Mrs Anthea Wilcox – was saying at dinner recently that she thought Paris the most amusing of places. She is to be the guest of the Comte and Comtesse de Maurois, I understand. I have no doubt she will introduce you if you so desire, and they, as I am sure you are aware, are very close indeed to the French Royals.'

Muriel's objections ceased. She had encountered Mrs Wilcox at several luncheons whilst Deveril had been away and been impressed by the American woman's effortless success in making the most influential of friends. She was invited everywhere that mattered. Of course, she was too old to be of any real interest to Deveril, Muriel supposed, but possibly his impulsive decision to go to Paris had been influenced by the fact that Mrs Wilcox considered it amusing. If nothing else, it would keep Deveril from 'disappearing' – something her young husband had been doing far too often of late.

Deveril's independence both irritated and worried her. She had no reason to suspect a mistress, but she deeply resented the fact that he preferred the male company of his irresponsible young friends to her own. As far as she could see, he had altered his bachelor habits very little since his marriage. By no means was she able to exert the influence over him that she had intended when she became his wife. Her women friends all envied her so dashing and handsome a husband, but privately Muriel would have preferred a more homely man who would have interested himself in *her* affairs; or a politician, perhaps, who depended upon her to entertain and encourage those people who were influential in his career. As far as Muriel could see, her role in Deveril's house was little more than that of a housekeeper. At least if she accompanied him to France, she could be certain to have an attentive husband at her side.

Exactly two weeks later, the Burnburys left England, travelling to Paris in company with Anthea Wilcox – a ruse Deveril had easily engineered, not altogether with his mistress's approval.

'You are quite wicked to invite me to your carriage,' she had remonstrated in a private moment together, 'and in front of poor Muriel so that I could not refuse. Have you no sense of propriety?'

'None at all!' Deveril replied. 'Having my wife as a chaperone lends our affair a certain piquancy, do you not agree? Besides, Muriel is delighted!'

With a feeling that all was very well with his life, Deveril contemplated the start of the new year with the utmost satisfaction, his mood entirely in keeping with the festive season.

In contrast, meanwhile, the house in Adelaide Crescent was very far from festive when Benjamin arrived for a three-day visit at the beginning of the year. 1833 had drawn to its close, Clemency realized, with less and less hope of her recovering her child.

Regarding her pale thin face anxiously, Benjamin gently chided her for the loss of so much weight, although he was well aware of the reasons for it. She was close to despair as she recounted her visit with his father to the Brighton lawyer.

'Mr Bryant could not have been more patient or sympathetic to my cause,' she told him as they sat by the fire. The room seemed strangely over-quiet without the little boy's chatter, Benjamin noted, and there were no toys to be seen. It was as if there had been a death in the family, he thought uneasily.

'Yet there was nothing at all the lawyer could suggest to your benefit?' he asked.

Clemency shook her head.

'Only that I should appeal again to Deveril – Lord Burnbury – to take pity on me and permit me to see Adam from time to time . . .'

Benjamin's mouth tightened as he heard the note of bitterness in Clemency's voice. He looked across the room to his father.

'Surely Clemency has some rights!' he insisted. 'You were present at the lawyer's, Father. Was there no point you could raise in Clemency's favour?'

The old man drew a long sigh as he met Benjamin's eyes.

'I fear that no point I raised was of any avail, my boy. As I had already warned Clemency, a wife has no legal claim to her child if her husband chooses to deny her access.'

Benjamin's face darkened.

'But Lord Burnbury is not Clemency's husband. Percy Grayshott is Adam's legal father!'

'Which point, of course, I raised with Bryant,' the Professor replied patiently. 'But it appears that Burnbury became Percy's legal guardian on the death of the old Viscount, and can therefore take any action he pleases on his brother's behalf. Clemency cannot therefore question whether Percy wished Adam to be removed from her care. Besides, she admitted to Grimshaw that Deveril, not Percy, was Adam's true father. We must face these facts, however unpalatable. Moreover, as Bryant pointed out, Burnbury can afford the best legal brains in the country to fight his case. Judgement would almost certainly be in his favour, since the Burnburys can offer the boy every advantage and, moreover, have an obligation to rear Adam in the kind of circumstances that will prepare him for his ultimate position as heir to both title and estate.'

His father's words confirmed Benjamin's private beliefs. But he could not bear the look of distress on Clemency's face, and he said desperately:

'Can we not threaten the Burnburys in some way with the exposure of that clandestine marriage to Percy Grayshott? Surely Lord Burnbury would not want to face the scandal and gossip that would inevitably result . . .'

'There is no inevitability about it, Ben,' the Professor interrupted. 'As Bryant pointed out, both Clemency's uncle and the late Viscount approved the marriage. It was performed quite legally, even though both parties to the marriage were minors at the time. Who is there to prove that Percy was incapable of understanding his vows? His attendant, who is in Lord Burnbury's employ? You, Benjamin, who have attended him professionally but will be proved to have been Clemency's friend? Moreover, it is almost certain that should the Burnburys wish it, they could produce medical evidence from far more eminent men than yourself to disprove anything you might say. Besides, you yourself told me that there are days when Percy appears almost normal, just as there are days when he is totally irrational. If a physician were to examine him now, who is to prove that the young man's condition has not deteriorated since the marriage three years ago?'

He shook his head sadly.

'No, Benjamin, I do not think we can achieve anything by blackmailing Lord Burnbury with threats of exposure. At best it would inconvenience him; but he would not be held responsible, even were the marriage contract condemned. The late Viscount is dead, and Lord Burnbury himself knew nothing of the arrangements made by his grandfather. The court and the public would be sympathetic to him.'

Benjamin jumped to his feet and paced the room with an angry impatience quite foreign to his nature.

'He cannot be permitted to prevail!' he cried. 'It is not fair on Clemency. Even if she cannot have possession of Adam, at least she should be allowed access to him. How can any human being deny a mother the right to see a little boy of Adam's age? It is intolerable!'

Clemency's voice when she spoke was filled with bitterness.

'Deveril does not share your views, Benjamin. He has not answered one of my letters, although Mr Grimshaw assures me he has forwarded them all. Milord Burnbury, you see, has gone abroad, and will be out of the country for at least six months. He may even have taken Adam with him to be sure I cannot find him. I went twice in person to Grayshott House, but there is no one there other than a few servants who confirmed Mr Grimshaw's statement that both Lord and Lady Burnbury were abroad. He – Mr Grimshaw – says he can do nothing more until they return. Although I could never like the man, he did appear sympathetic and promised me he would appeal to Lord Burnbury on my behalf as soon as he next sees him.'

'You cannot trust Grimshaw, Clemency,' Benjamin said abruptly. 'The fellow is in Burnbury's pay and will say anything that suits his client. Besides, he *must* know where Adam is. If he were truly sympathetic, he would tell you.'

'Come now, Benjamin, you are being irrational,' the Professor chided gently. 'As you yourself admit, Grimshaw is paid by the Viscount and therefore *obliged* to observe *his* wishes, not Clemency's.'

'He assured me Adam was in excellent hands and in good health,' Clemency added. 'I suppose in my heart of hearts, I do not believe Deveril would allow him to come to any harm. But I do miss Adam so terribly, Benjamin. There is not a minute in the day when I am not wondering and worrying about him. It is twelve weeks now since he was taken from me, yet it seems like twelve years!'

Her voice broke, and Benjamin went immediately to her side and put his arm comfortingly around her shoulders. She smiled up at him wanly.

'It is strange, is it not, Benjamin, but I cannot cry. It is as if my grief is too great for tears. I know it is madness to think so, but everywhere I go, even here in Brighton, I look at children of Adam's age and wonder for a second if the little boy I am seeing is my own son. If I only knew where he was! It is as if he has disappeared off the face of the earth.'

'He is too important to Lord Burnbury for him not to be in the best of hands,' the Professor said firmly. 'I doubt very much that he has taken so young a child upon his travels.'

'Then why could he not have left Adam with me?' Clemency cried, two spots of colour flaming in her cheeks. 'Who is there to love him? Not even his father!'

'The boy is very young,' Benjamin said softly. 'At his age, he will be easily comforted. I will wager your suffering is a hundred times greater than Adam's, my dear.'

'I hope so!' Clemency whispered. 'I cannot bear to think of him crying for me. Oh, Benjamin, is it possible for Deveril to be so heartless? I know you believe him worthless and irresponsible, but he has never given you cause to think him cruel!'

'How can he be less than cruel to allow the boy to be stolen from you in so heartless a manner!' Benjamin protested violently.

'I know. I have told myself so many times,' Clemency whispered. 'But I do not want to believe it, Benjamin, because if it is true, it leaves me no hope for the future. I have nothing to count upon now but my appeal to Deveril when he returns to England. If he ignores my letters . . .'

Her voice broke and she was unable to continue. The Professor stood up, his voice firm as he said:

'Let us not discuss it further for the moment. We will take a walk down to the seafront. I wish to show Benjamin the sad effects of the terrible storm we had in October. Our magnificent Chain Pier was struck by lightning, Ben, and fire demolished the second bridge; the third disappeared and the fourth was left hanging down to the water. It is thought to require well over a thousand pounds to repair it, and the populace are trying to raise the money by private subscription.'

Well aware that his father was attempting to distract Clemency's thoughts elsewhere, Benjamin agreed to walk down to East Cliff to see the damage. But his thoughts remained with Clemency long after he had returned to Upper Chiswell, and realizing the near hopelessness of her position, his pity for her was almost as consuming an emotion as his love.

While Deveril was enjoying life in Paris and Italy with his wife and mistress, Clemency grew more and more impatient for his return. The continued separation from Adam tormented her, as did her inability to take any action for his recovery. During the month of February, Benjamin several times found excuses to go to Chiswell Hill House lest Adam had been taken there, but his weekly letters could offer no solace.

In March, he wrote to inform her that her uncle was dying, and had asked to see her. Although Clemency dreaded the prospect of going once more to The Rectory, she departed at once for Dorset. A stony-faced, bitter-voiced Aunt Winifred greeted her with the announcement that she had arrived too late to make her last farewell to her uncle.

'I came as soon as I could,' Clemency replied, steeling herself to go up to the bedroom where her uncle's wasted body was laid out ready for burial. She tried to feel sad as she stood by the waxen-faced corpse, but her only emotion was of pity as she returned to the parlour to sit opposite her newly bereaved aunt. At once it became clear to Clemency that her Aunt Winifred was far from overcome by grief at her husband's passing.

'Your uncle has left me the merest pittance,' she said in a high complaining voice. 'Were it not for the charity of my sister in Yorkshire, I would be ending my days in the poor-house. Thankfully, my sister has offered me a home with her, but your uncle made no provision for me . . . none at all . . . and after all those years I sacrificed to his comfort and well-being.'

Clemency tried to hide her own feeling of revulsion for the

thin, sharp-featured woman regarding her from beneath her black mourning veil.

'I do not suppose a parson's stipend amounts to very much, Aunt Winifred,' she said quietly. 'And he may not have been able to save enough to provide for you . . .'

'He received little over two hundred and fifty pounds a year!' her aunt broke in sharply. 'But what of all that money he got from the Grayshotts – for *you*!' she added, her eyes boring into Clemency's as if she were accusing her once more for her past misdeeds. 'Your uncle was not too proud to take it. Oh, no, he welcomed that hush money – for that is what it was, for all he refused to admit it.' Ignoring Clemency's horrified expression, she continued remorselessly: 'He welcomed every penny, but instead of putting something aside for his poor wife, it was nearly all dissipated on the orphanage. I told him he had lost his wit . . . and he had too, insisting that it eased his conscience regarding *you*. You had no right to disappear the way you did. He was never the same after you left, muttering for hours on end that it was all *his* fault and that we should have done better for you. But you showed no gratitude and it did not matter to you the disgrace you brought upon us. You are no better than your father!'

Partly out of respect for her uncle's body lying upstairs and partly from curiosity, Clemency bit back her longing to defend herself, and in a voice carefully devoid of emotion, she said:

'You and my uncle have often inferred that Papa was not a good man. I think you owe it to me to tell me the truth about him, Aunt Winifred, since I may not see you again after the funeral.'

Her aunt's mouth tightened and, briefly, a look of eager satisfaction brightened her small black eyes as she replied bitingly:

'Oh, I will tell you, my girl. It is no secret, and I wonder your uncle did not tell you when you were living here. It might have brought you to your senses, knowing you came of bad blood. Your father, I will have you know, was a slave trader

like his father before him. That is how they made their money
– only your father lost his fortune when slaving became illegal
in 1807. Not that *that* stopped him. He went on with the
business until the law caught up with him, and he spent a
year in prison for it.' Her thin lips twisted with bitterness.
'Imagine what that did to us, his relations! As for your mother
– well, it served her right for marrying out of her class, and
I do not wonder her family refused to have anything to do
with her. Clement . . . your father, that is, always swore your
mother knew nothing about his trading, but she *must* have
known and condoned it, or she would have left him and taken
you back to live with her family. But she would never hear a
word against your father and he ended up killing her, or as
good as, God rest her soul.'

Clemency closed her eyes as her aunt's words beat about
her head like angry wasps. Uppermost in her thoughts was a
deep well of pity for her mother, who had suffered most terribly
when she, Clemency, was still too young to realize it. But try
as she might, she could not think of her big, bearded, laughing,
affectionate father as a renegade – a man who made his living
by the sale of other human beings' lives! There were still some
who thought little harm in the shipment of black slaves across
the seas. It was only in August of the previous year that the
practice had been abolished in the Dominions, and in many
parts of the world it still continued. But Papa, Clemency
thought now, was always a man of action rather than thought,
and had doubtless followed his own father into trading in
slaves without consideration for the ethics.

'There is another letter from your father since you were
last here,' she heard her aunt say as if from a distance. 'You
left no address so we could not forward it.'

'I wrote to Papa at once,' Clemency replied. 'He cannot
have received it, for I did give him my address. May I have
the letter now, Aunt Winifred?'

The several untidily written pages of her father's letter did
little to alleviate the unhappiness that day of Clemency's last

visit to The Rectory. His words were outpourings of regret for the untimely death of his beloved wife – for which he seemed to hold himself entirely responsible. He begged Clemency to join him in the colonies as soon as ever she could.

'A grandson would be a great consolation to me,' he wrote, 'and I shall not condemn you for I am singularly lonely here and when you and the boy arrive we shall be a family once more . . .'

As she read the words to Benjamin after the funeral and before she left once more for Brighton, Clemency could not withhold her tears.

'I cannot go to Papa!' she wept. 'I know he needs me, but I could not abandon Adam. Oh, Benjamin, can you have any idea how tormented I am; how I long to see my little boy; how I worry about him! *I must find him.* I must know where he is! Adam is my baby, a part of me. I know he is somewhere in this country, perhaps wanting me, crying for me. I want him back!'

Benjamin looked at Clemency's white despairing face with misgiving. He longed to be able to offer her hope and yet had none to offer. He could not bear to see her so unhappy, and yet he was powerless to alleviate her suffering.

'I am thinking now of what could be best for you, Clemency,' he said uneasily. 'What you *want* most in the world is not necessarily what will bring you happiness. Do you understand that even if you find where Adam is hidden, Burnbury may *never* return him to you; and even if he did, it would be only to remove the boy once more when he was older. A second parting would be even more tragic for you, and meanwhile you would live every day of your life in fear of losing Adam again. You are now still so young. At nineteen years of age, you have time to create an entirely new life for yourself.'

Clemency's chin lifted and her mouth set in a tight, stubborn line.

'I do not want a new life, Benjamin. I do not need a new life to make me happy. I only need Adam. If I may not have him to live with me all the time, then I will make the best of it and be happy with what part of each year Deveril may allow me. I will never give him up entirely. *Never!*'

Benjamin was silenced, for he dared not destroy her last deluded notion that the decisions regarding Adam's future were still to be made. Either she did not or would not accept that Adam had been removed from her not just for the time being, but for the remainder of his childhood; that logically his father was bound to do his utmost to ensure that Clemency never saw the boy again.

CHAPTER EIGHTEEN

February–April 1834

By the end of February, Clemency's powers of endurance were stretched to breaking point. She paid a further visit to the sympathetic Mr Bryant, begging him to take some kind of action on her behalf. Her aunt was now forwarding to her the Grayshott annual payment agreed under the marriage contract, and although Clemency's instinct was to reject it, the Professor advised her to take it in order to meet any further legal costs she might incur. As usual, he was proving to be right, for she could not otherwise have afforded to pay Mr Bryant for his services.

Although the lawyer repeated that there were no legal steps he could advise Clemency to take to recover her child, he did agree to write to Mr Grimshaw regarding Deveril's return to England. Grimshaw's reply to Mr Bryant did nothing to pacify Clemency.

'Lord Burnbury is somewhere in the Near East, and we do not expect his return to this country until April at the earliest. Meanwhile, he has instructed me to deal with all matters relating to the child, Adam Grayshott. You should therefore write directly to me if your client requires to communicate with His Lordship regarding the infant.'

'I am beginning to lose hope that Deveril will respond to any appeal I may make to him,' Clemency said bitterly, as she walked slowly home with the Professor. 'But he shall not ignore me in so heartless a fashion. I shall devise some way to make him listen to my demands.'

After sleepless nights pondering the situation, Clemency suddenly realized that she had not after all explored every possibility. Somewhere in England, perhaps even now in London, were her maternal grandparents, the Earl and Countess Whytakker. Adam was their great-grandchild, she thought, and surely now that her poor mama had passed away, they would not reject a plea for help from their dead daughter's child? Her eyes were alight with renewed hope, and for the first time in months, there was a pink glow of excitement in her cheeks as she put the idea to the Professor.

'My grandparents must be people of influence,' she told him excitedly. 'They will see the injustice of my situation, and if Lord Burnbury is made aware that they are supporting my cause, he may be more amenable. He almost certainly cannot be less so!'

The Professor sighed. Even if the Whytakkers were agreeable to forgetting past family dissent, he doubted whether there was much they could do. But he could not bring himself to wipe the look of elation from Clemency's face. He patted her hand and told her she could most certainly take a day or two off from her work on his book – now nearing completion – to go to London to see her grandparents.

She was too afraid of a refusal to risk a written request to see them and, as a consequence, she realized that her journey to London could prove fruitless were the Earl and Countess at their country house in Hertfordshire. Her hands were trembling therefore, and her heart was beating suffocatingly, as an immaculately attired servant opened the front door of the Whytakkers' imposing mansion in Curzon Street.

'Please tell them that I am a relation,' Clemency said as he enquired her name, 'and that I am here on an urgent family matter.'

The butler's face gave no indication of his curiosity as he departed into the interior of the house. He had been with the

Whytakkers for many years and thought he knew everyone in the family. The Earl was as mystified as his servant.

'Mrs Grayshott? Never heard of her. Have you, m'dear?' he asked his wife. He had been enjoying his after-luncheon nap and was irritated by the disturbance. A red-faced, portly man, Lord Whytakker suffered from high blood pressure, which did nothing to improve his natural propensity for irascibility. His wife spent most of her time either attempting to soothe her short-tempered husband or else trying to conceal from him matters which might irritate him. A thin, nervous, fluttering woman, she nevertheless still showed signs of the beauty which had marked her out as a young girl. Her once golden hair was now grey, and the cornflower blue of her eyes had faded, but the fine bone structure of her face lent her an air of delicate beauty most apparent when she smiled.

She looked now at the butler, a gentle frown creasing her forehead.

'You say the young lady is fair-haired, Dalby? It cannot therefore be Mrs Muriel Grayshott. In any event, she would have announced herself now as Lady Burnbury.'

Dalby gave a slight cough.

'The young lady was very insistent, Milady. I was asked to inform you that it was a family matter.'

'Confound it!' the Earl said. 'Why cannot people pay their calls at the proper hours. Tell her to leave her card, and if my wife chooses, she will return the call some other time.'

His wife put down her tapestry and stood up, her movements deliberately unhurried.

'Do not worry, my dear. You enjoy your nap and I will see the visitor in the library. I have nothing else to do. You may show the young lady in there, Dalby.'

Despite the self-control Lady Whytakker had acquired during the many years of her difficult marriage to her dictatorial and demanding husband, the sight of Clemency was too overwhelming for her to prevent a little cry as Dalby showed the girl into the room.

'Enid!' she gasped. 'But it cannot be . . .'

Clemency dipped into a curtsey and regarded her grand-mother with curiosity. Her first impression was of a gentle, colourless but elegant woman with a marked resemblance to her beloved mama. Her flowing challis dress was the identical amber tone that had been Mama's favourite colour. The Countess had the same petite figure as Mama, and her slender form would have given the illusion of youth but for the criss-cross of fine lines on her face, momentarily exaggerated by the shock Clemency had inadvertently caused her. But the Countess quickly recovered her composure and indicated a chair for Clemency to be seated.

'There is no need to introduce yourself, child,' she said gently. 'You must be Enid's girl.'

When Clemency nodded, Lady Whytakker's face softened and she smiled.

'You are so very like her. How old are you, my dear? Not much older I think, than my little Enid when last I saw her.'

The wistful tone of her voice brought a lump to Clemency's throat. There was no doubting that love had once existed between her mother and grandmother. Hesitantly, she said:

'You know Mama died in a tragic accident two years ago?'

The Countess's mouth trembled.

'The Earl . . . that is to say, your grandfather, heard of the sad news and told me. It was the only time he has ever mentioned Enid's name since she left our house.' She drew a long shuddering sigh. 'You are Clementine, of course. Your mother used to write and tell me about you. I was not permitted to reply, but I kept all her letters – every one . . .'

Clemency leant forward in her chair, her hopes steadily rising as she realized that her grandmother held no ill feeling towards Mama but, on the contrary, was still grieving at their separation. This woman, perhaps more than any other, would understand how terrible it was to be parted from a beloved child.

'Will you tell me about her?' she prompted.

Her grandmother looked nervously at the door as if afraid that her husband might come striding in to reprimand her. But remembering he would by now be sleeping, she relaxed in her chair and in a rush of words, began talking.

'She was so pretty – the prettiest of girls! The others favoured your grandfather. Enid's disposition was angelic, too. Your grandfather idolized her, and it broke his heart the day she ran away . . . with your father.'

Clemency's head lifted.

'Papa loved her as no other man could,' she said defensively. 'He and Mama were devoted and perfectly happy together. He would have given her the sun and moon and stars had he been able!'

Lady Whytakker drew another deep sigh.

'But that was the whole trouble, my dear child. Your father had nothing whatever to offer Enid except love – neither money nor standing. Of course your grandfather could never condone a marriage between his daughter and a man whose business was trading in slaves!'

'How did Papa and Mama meet,' Clemency asked, 'if their worlds were so far apart?'

Lady Whytakker looked surprised.

'Did your mother never tell you? Your grandfather, Enid and I were returning from a visit to Bath, having taken the waters there. Enid was sixteen years old. We had stopped at the Pelican at Speenhamland for luncheon and to change the horses. Your father was seated at a nearby table in the dining-room. He fell instantly in love with Enid – so overwhelmingly that he set aside his plans for continuing to Bristol and followed our coach to London. Having discovered Enid's residence, he remained in London and tricked his way into houses where my daughters were invited to balls and masquerades. It was a romantic courtship – sufficiently so to turn any young girl's head.'

Lady Whytakker's eyes filled suddenly with tears.

'I always hoped that in time the Earl would become

reconciled to the marriage, although I see now that it could never have happened. Your grandfather, you see, is a man of principle, and to give way on such a matter would have seemed a weakness to him.' She dabbed at her eyes with a lace-edged cambric handkerchief. 'Now we shall never see our beloved daughter again!'

Clemency drew a breath.

'Do you think Mama's passing might have softened his attitude, and that perhaps he will receive *me*?' she said tentatively.

Lady Whytakker shook her head vehemently.

'Oh, no, my dear, I am afraid not. Had he known you were Enid's child, he would not have allowed Dalby to bring you into the house. But you have not told me what does bring you here? Dalby said your name is Mrs Grayshott. You look very young to be married.'

'I am nineteen,' Clemency said, 'older than I appear. I have a child, too – a little boy called Adam. It is on his account that I need your help, Lady Whytakker.'

The elderly woman facing her looked at her granddaughter unhappily.

'I will do anything within my power, my dear child,' she said, adding with a sigh: 'but my husband . . . your grandfather . . .' She broke off, as if she were ashamed of her submissiveness to her husband's will.

Clemency's heart sank. If Lord Whytakker would not even see her, what hope had she of eliciting his help? Nevertheless, she had to try.

'Three years ago, my uncle arranged my marriage to Mr Percy Grayshott, Lord Burnbury's brother,' she said carefully. 'Lord Burnbury's wife cannot have children and, against my wishes, he has taken my son from me. I have not been permitted to see Adam or even to know where he is. Lady Whytakker, my little boy is still only two years old and he needs his mother. It is not even as if Lady Burnbury wanted Adam – she was violently opposed to the idea of having him to live with her.

I cannot bear the separation, and I must find him. Lord Burnbury must be persuaded to allow me to see my own baby – but he will not listen to my appeals and . . .'

Even as her voice trailed into silence, she knew that this appeal, too, would be as useless. Her grandmother was twisting her handkerchief between her small white hands, her eyes avoiding Clemency's as she whispered:

'But what could *I* do? I could not approach Lord Burnbury without my husband's knowledge. I would help you if I could, my poor child,' she added with genuine regret. 'But your grandfather would forbid me absolutely to become involved, and I cannot disobey him. I see no way in which I could be of help. Those men of importance amongst our friends are all of Whig persuasion and therefore well disposed towards the Burnbury family. The late Viscount was much admired and respected by his fellow members in the House of Lords, and there would be few willing to support you against his grandson, however sympathetic they might be towards you, the unfortunate mother.'

She saw the tears of disappointment trembling on Clemency's cheeks, and rising from her chair, went to put her arm around the girl's shoulders.

'Believe me, dearest child, I do understand how terrible this must be for you,' she said gently, 'but in the light of all the circumstances, do you not think your little boy may be well content with his uncle? Had the child been a girl, the situation could have been otherwise. But a boy – well, his place *is* with his family, is it not?'

'He is not yet three years old!' Clemency cried. 'His place is with me!'

'I do realize that he is still very young. But that too, can be a blessing, for he is young enough to forget the past and settle into a new life. Perhaps you will be blessed in time with other children?' she added, hopefully.

'I do not want other children!' Clemency cried. Did no one realize that another child could never replace Adam in her heart?

'Are you not happy with your husband?' Lady Whytakker enquired. 'Has he no say in this affair? After all, he too has lost a son and . . .'

'My husband is an invalid,' Clemency broke in. 'Our marriage was one of convenience and not of love. It is Adam who is – or was – my whole life. I want him back, or if that cannot be, I want the right to see him . . .'

Lady Whytakker regarded her unhappy granddaughter with pity.

'I only wish there were some way I could help you,' she said. 'We may not meet again, and I would so much like to be able to give you something.'

She broke off, lifting one hand suddenly to touch the emerald brooch in the pelerine collar around her neck. For the first time, she smiled as she unfastened it and handed it to Clemency.

'I shall tell my husband a little white lie and say I mislaid it,' she said, delighted at her own ingenuity. 'It is of some value, my dear, so do not sell it unless circumstances force you. I would like you to have it as a memento of your grandmother.'

Clemency stood up, comforted just a little by her grandmother's warmth of heart. But as she left the house, she knew that she would be unlikely ever to go there again. The Countess would not act against her husband's wishes and she, Clemency, had not the right to beg her to do so.

The now familiar coach ride back to Brighton seemed to her to be longer and more tiring than ever before. All but her very last hope had vanished, and that could not be put to the test until Deveril returned from Europe in two months' time. She would have somehow to live through another eight weeks without sight or word of Adam, and she was not sure she could endure it.

'Work is one of the best antidotes to worry,' the Professor announced wisely, when she related her adventures to him. 'We will make a joint effort these next few weeks to finish the book. That will keep our minds occupied!'

Clemency hugged him. He had become as dear to her as any grandfather could have been. Her past, her parentage, her troubles never changed the old man's affection and solicitude for her. She both loved and respected him even while she feared his sagacity and realism. From the time of Adam's abduction, he had cautioned her that she might have lost her child for ever. Unbiased, logical, unaffected by emotion, he had assessed how limited were her chances of reclaiming Adam and so far he had been proved unhappily right.

With a resolve bordering on despair, Clemency took the Professor's advice and settled back to work on his book, sometimes remaining at her task so late that the candles were guttering in their holders and her eyelids were drooping with fatigue when she put away the papers and climbed the stairs to bed. No longer did she permit herself the bitter-sweet consolation of a halt at Adam's room. His bed lay untouched, his toys still lying on the counterpane where he had left them on the morning they had made their hurried departure to Poole. The door of his room remained closed, and sometimes she dreamt that she would find him in there, his dark eyes bright with laughter, his chubby arms held out to her in happy welcome.

There were moments when Clemency's despondency lifted for a little while. She was now receiving letters from her father, albeit irregularly, the mail from the North Americas being often delayed by the severe winter weather. She always hastened to answer them immediately. In May, he wrote to say that his labours were beginning to show a small profit.

'If you cannot come to me this year, then perhaps I shall be able to afford a passage to England in '35 to see you!' he advised her.

Clemency knew he must be very lonely, but she delayed her reply, believing that since Deveril's return to England was overdue, it would be only a matter of days before she had news of Adam to relate to her father. But these expectations, like all the others before, were quickly dashed when a week later she was invited to go to see her lawyer, Mr Bryant, at his office near the Steyne. He did not have good news to impart, he warned her.

The information he gave her was of the very worst. Grimshaw had advised him that Lord and Lady Burnbury were back in London; that he had personally pleaded Clemency's case with his lordship and begged him to read her many letters of appeal. Unfortunately, Grimshaw had written, Lord Burnbury saw no reason to complicate his life or that of the boy by allowing his mother access.

'The child has settled very happily in his new life and Lord Burnbury considers it inadvisable to disturb him with reminders of the past. He is quite adamant that he will not receive Miss Foster if she calls at Grayshott House and will not hesitate to summon the Metropolitan Police to remove her if she does so . . .'

Mr Bryant's voice sounded almost apologetic as he read the final part of Grimshaw's letter. It contained threats of legal action against Miss Foster if '*she subsequently proves herself a nuisance either to Lord Burnbury or still more objectionably, to her Ladyship.*'

'You must be advised by me, Miss Foster,' the lawyer told Clemency quietly but firmly. 'Your appearance at Lord Burnbury's house can only serve to provoke him if you ignore this warning. You cannot force your way in and the servants will have orders to deny you admittance. It would be most undignified were you to be removed by the Peelers, and it would gain you no sympathy nor enable you to achieve your objective. At best, we must hope that given a little time, Lord Burnbury will relent and permit you to visit the boy. Once he is assured that you have relinquished all idea of recovering him, he may well soften his attitude. Allow me, I beg you, to write to his lawyer on these lines.'

Clemency's hesitation was only momentary. White-faced, her hands gripped tightly about her reticule, she said:

'You may write to Mr Grimshaw on my behalf, Mr Bryant, but only to say that I will never give up Adam voluntarily; that I shall never stop looking for my son. And when I do find him, I shall remove him with as little warning, as little consideration for Lord Burnbury's feelings as he has shown for mine.'

'And I meant every single word I said,' she vowed to the Professor when she returned home, her cheeks flaming, her eyes blazing. 'Why should Deveril be permitted to sleep at night when I lie awake in unhappy concern for my son's whereabouts? Why should he be allowed to push me out of his life as if . . . as if I were dead! I am as much Adam's mother as he is the boy's father, and he shall not deny me. I hate him so much that were I to see him now, I think I might kill him if I could!'

'Come now, my dear,' the Professor said soothingly. 'You know you do not really mean that. And you know without my telling you that Bryant's advice is sound. We should allow Lord Burnbury to be lulled into a false sense of security. It would appear he is afraid that you will find some way to upset his plans. It is not unreasonable of him to wish the boy to adapt to his new life without the emotional disturbance your reappearance would cause. You must try to keep your mind clear, my dear girl, and knowing you as I do, it is Adam you care most about, not yourself. Be comforted by the fact that the boy has settled happily in his new environment.'

He sighed, adding more to himself than to Clemency: 'Ah, the young! They are always so impatient. What matter a few more weeks or months measured against life's span. Be patient, child, and if fortune favours you, you will hold your little boy in your arms again before too long.'

But even one more day was 'too long', Clemency thought, as her emotions cooled and she was forced to accept that the confrontation with Deveril was not to take place. She had imagined it so often, Deveril listening to her heartbreak, telling her that he had had no true idea of the extent of her suffering! How often had she daydreamed those words he would speak to her: 'You shall never be parted from the boy again, I promise you. From now on, we will share him!'

How naïve of her ever to suppose milord Burnbury might behave in so generous and sympathetic a manner! He was egotistical, selfish, cruel beyond words, and for the remainder of her life he would be her enemy.

Barely four weeks later, Clemency was summoned once again to Mr Bryant's office. On this occasion, it was to be informed that Percy Grayshott had died quite suddenly following upon an epileptic fit and that she was now a widow.

For a fleeting moment, Clemency was reminded of the thin, golden-haired boy gazing at her so wistfully as she helped him place the ring upon her finger. He was her husband, yet she had seen him for little more than ten minutes in the whole of their three-and-a-half-year marriage! Poor, unhappy boy, she thought. But perhaps life had no real meaning for him shut away as he had been in Chiswell Hill House. He had no need of her sympathy – yet she was saddened by the news of his death.

Bryant noted her changing expressions with uncertainty. On her last visit, the girl had shown herself capable of a passionate violence which had astonished him. He could understand then her hatred of the aristocratic family with whom she had been coerced into union, yet now she seemed genuinely distressed by the news he had imparted.

'Mr Grimshaw informs me that Lord Burnbury intends that your annual allowance should cease,' he said, 'but that in fairness to your good self, you should receive six thousand pounds by way of a legacy. Mr Percy Grayshott died intestate. There were certain assets in his name left to him by his father and grandfather, and Lord Burnbury desires that these should be assigned to his er . . . son . . . as his rightful heir. It is presumed you will have no objections to this and will be content with the legacy, which I think we are all agreed is a generous one.'

Clemency's mouth tightened.

'Lord Burnbury appears always to be generous with his money,' she said bitterly. 'He is not so generous in spirit unfortunately! He can keep the Grayshott money if he will return my son!'

'Come now, Miss Foster, or should I be calling you Mrs Grayshott? You have not come here today to discuss those matters. May I take it that you will be happy to accept the legacy offered to you in lieu of the annual payments guaranteed by your contract? As your legal adviser, I must point out that it is statistically probable that you will remarry within the next five years. The annual payments, which would cease on your remarriage, would not amount to half this sum. You would be wise to accept it.'

'Then I will do so!' Clemency said, with a bright, hard smile. 'It will be useful when I decide to employ the best legal brains in the country to fight Lord Burnbury's lawyers for access to my son. And do not tell me that I cannot do so, Mr Bryant, for it will be my money and I shall spend it as I choose.'

'Of course, of course!' Mr Bryant said placatingly. 'But first we must make sure you receive it. I will write to Mr Grimshaw immediately!'

Clemency's mood changed yet again as she walked back to Adelaide Crescent. Her defiance had given way once more to depression.

'Is it not ironic,' she said to the Professor, as she poured his tea and handed it to him, 'that I am now a comparatively rich young widow and yet I cannot buy the only thing in the world I want – the right to be with my son! Was any woman as poor as I!'

'Where there is life there is hope,' the Professor said with a gentle smile, as he patted her hand. 'You will be reunited with Adam one day, Clemency, I am sure of it, if for no better reason than that you are determined upon it. Now write and tell Benjamin all the news. He will be wondering why he has not heard from us for so long.'

Instinct warned Clemency that immediately Benjamin learned she was now a widow, he would propose marriage to her. So deep was her depression that she was almost tempted to accept such a simple solution to her life. The Professor would be delighted. Benjamin would rejoice.

She would have his company and the distraction of helping him with his work. Now that the Professor's book was so nearly finished, she would soon be without a task to fill her lonely days. Why then could she not bring herself to put pen to paper and let Benjamin know that she would welcome him with open arms?

But her quill remained poised above the writing paper and she leant back in her chair, allowing her thoughts to roam at will. Marriage to Benjamin would be one of affection and respect, but without love – without the kind of love which had sent Papa post-haste after Mama's coach; given him the courage to pursue her in disguise until he had wooed and won her; the kind of love which had given Mama the courage to leave everything behind her to begin a new unknown life full of restrictions.

But with all the deprivations, the unrelenting attitude of her family, Mama had been happy – Clemency was certain of it, remembering how she had sung as she went about her work, happy little songs that spoke always of love. Even now, four years after she had last seen her, her mother's words still rang in her ears: '*Never marry lest it be for love, my darling!*'

No, Clemency thought, she would not marry Benjamin – not for his sake nor her own. Until she found Adam, she had no right to take on wifely duties, for she would abandon them on the instant if they conflicted with a need to journey off to see her son. Perhaps when she had found him, she might think again about marriage to Benjamin – if he was still waiting for her.

Poor Benjamin, she thought. He must be almost as lonely as she.

PART TWO

1834–1839

LAST YEAR'S ROSE

. . . Wise the enamoured Nightingale,
   Wise the well-beloved Rose!
Love and life shall still prevail,
   Nor the silence at the close
   Break the magic of the tale
In the telling, though it shows—
   Who but knows
   How it goes!—
Life a last year's Nightingale,
   Love a last year's Rose.

W. E. Henley

CHAPTER NINETEEN

April 1834–September 1836

In the spring, the Professor took Clemency to London to deliver his book to his publishers, Saunders and Otley. By coincidence, the young novelist Mrs Norton was also delivering the manuscript of her first book, *The Wife and Woman's Reward*. The publisher introduced his two authors to one another, and the Professor generously acknowledged Clemency's contribution to his finished work.

Clearly charmed by the attractive young author, the Professor said:

'If ever you should be in need of assistance, pray allow me to recommend Mrs Forest. She is the most able and conscientious of workers.'

Caroline Norton had there and then made note of the Professor's address, but Clemency did not expect to meet the novelist again. Early in the spring of 1835 however, Caroline wrote to the Professor asking him if by any chance he could spare his scribe for a few weeks. She was engaged in the writing of an opera and required immediate assistance. Although Clemency had no great desire to leave Brighton, where she nursed a secret but forlorn hope that she might one day run into Deveril, the Professor persuaded her that a change would be beneficial to her and that the work might prove interesting.

'I know that you try very hard to conceal your unhappiness from me,' he said gently, 'but nobody is more aware than I of your growing despondency this past year.'

'If it were not for my conviction that sooner or later I shall learn of Adam's whereabouts, I would have lost all hope,' Clemency sighed.

She was unable to raise any enthusiasm for the prospect of going to Caroline Norton's house in London. But surprisingly she found the next two months absorbing, and a firm friendship developed between her and the fascinating young writer. It was born partly because of their closeness in age, Caroline being only six years Clemency's senior and the first young female friend Clemency had ever had; but it was also due in part to their feminine sympathies towards each other. Caroline understood, as no one else appeared to do, just how devastated Clemency was by the continued disappearance of her child. Herself the mother of three boys and with the strongest maternal instincts, she pledged herself to help Clemency in any way that presented itself.

'Do not count too much upon her promise,' the Professor cautioned, when Clemency returned to Brighton in June. 'Doubtless her intention to help you was made on impulse.'

But Clemency clung to the hope, however slight, that her new friend would not forget her, since although Caroline had professed an acute dislike of Lady Burnbury, they met infrequently on social occasions. But by the end of the year, when she had still received no word from Caroline, Clemency was forced to accept that the Professor had been right, and that the novelist had undoubtedly forgotten her insignificant summer scribe.

She knew that Benjamin was very concerned about her. Each time he visited them, he chided her gently for her loss of weight, and he detected from the deep violet shadows beneath her eyes that she was not sleeping well. He ceased urging her to relinquish her hopes of finding her son, realizing that however forlorn, she needed this dream to cling to.

'Adam must be somewhere!' she told Benjamin during his Christmas visit. 'Deveril cannot conceal him for ever. After all,' she added bitterly, 'Adam is the Burnbury heir, which fact they must eventually acknowledge.' She could see the doubt in Benjamin's eyes, and as the months went by, she herself began to doubt that she would ever see her son again.

Suddenly, in the August of 1836, she received a letter from Caroline Norton.

'I beg you not to raise your hopes too high,' Caroline wrote, 'but I myself think there is no doubt that *your little boy is in Scotland!*'

She invited Clemency to go to Green Street, where she was living with her Uncle Sheridan, to discuss the situation.

In a fever of excitement, Clemency went up to London. She was shocked to see the vivacious Caroline so quiet and subdued. Nevertheless, she was welcomed by her friend who, with typical impulsiveness, hugged Clemency with tears in her eyes. Without giving her time to remove her bonnet, she drew Clemency down beside her on the sofa.

'It would not surprise me if you supposed I had quite forgotten you,' she said, with a sad smile, 'although I do not doubt that you have read in the papers of the many misfortunes which have befallen me since we were last together. I have been so vilified by the Press, it would not have surprised me if you, too had taken against me! I have learned to my cost how few real friends I possess.'

Briefly she spoke of the increasing quarrels she had had with her husband George, which had culminated in his unwarranted attack upon the Prime Minister.

'You, Clemency, who lived with me for two whole months, know very well that my friendship with Lord Melbourne was perfectly innocent; and indeed when he was brought to trial in June on a charge of adultery, this was proved to be the case.' Her eyes filled suddenly with bitterness. 'But now, my dear friend, my situation is like to your own. George has taken the children from me. I have not seen my boys since he put them in the care of his sister Lady Menzies, in Scotland. Is it not ironic that I, totally innocent of any wrongdoing, should be denied by my husband the right to see my own babies?'

Clemency felt Caroline's pain as if it was her own, and for a moment or two, they embraced one another tearfully. Then Caroline's face brightened.

'At least,' she said, 'some good has come from all this horror in my life. Whilst making desperate enquiries concerning the welfare of my own sons, I have discovered the whereabouts of your little boy. It seems that Lord Burnbury placed him in the care of his great-aunt Lady McDoone, in Perthshire. In any event, there is a five-year-old boy living at Castle Clunes with the old lady . . .' She looked at Clemency's radiant face and smiled.

'Fearing for your disappointment should the child not have proved to be yours, I thought it best to speak to Lady Springfield before writing to you. Not only is she on intimate terms with Lady Burnbury, but she must be Society's biggest gossip.' Forgetful of her own concerns, she laughed. 'I had no difficulty in persuading her to talk. She told me that Lady Burnbury knew about the boy, but believed him to be Percy Grayshott's child. Obviously your Deveril has not told his wife the whole truth – which does not surprise me, knowing how puritanical she is. However, Lady Burnbury was ill-advised enough to confess to Lady Springfield that she feared the boy could have inherited his late father's mental weakness, and that she has refused to adopt him despite Lord Burnbury's desire to do so. I think there can be no doubt that Lord Burnbury is keeping the boy in Perthshire.'

Clemency burst into tears of joy.

'I shall go there at once . . . immediately . . . tomorrow,' she cried in a fever of excitement. 'I am convinced by your story, and yet I hardly dare believe that after all this time Adam has been found. I am so grateful – so very grateful. To think that in a few days time I might actually hold him in my arms . . .'

Caroline laid a restraining hand on Clemency's shoulder.

'You must calm yourself, Clemency,' she said gently, 'and I beg you, do not act too impulsively – although I am scarcely the person to be preaching this to you,' she added wryly, 'since I so seldom think first myself!' Seeing the look of anxiety in Clemency's face, she said with renewed bitterness:

'Believe me, I have learned to my cost that mothers have no rights, however innocent they may be. You cannot expect Deveril Burnbury to permit you to remove Adam merely because you wish it. Besides, I have further news for you which might prove far safer than an impromptu attempt to reclaim your child.'

She went on to tell Clemency that Deveril's great-aunt, now in her mid-seventies, had suffered a nasty fall during the summer. She had fractured her leg and was confined to an invalid chair. Deveril had asked his wife to find her a suitable companion to assist her during her convalescence.

'Perhaps you will reproach me for acting too precipitately, but I have recommended you for the position and promised that you would write *immediately* to Lady McDoone. You may, of course, not wish to do so. But if Lady McDoone were to offer you the post, it would at least afford you the opportunity to see your son without revealing your true interest. I understand that Lady Burnbury *never* goes to Scotland, so you would not be recognized.'

It was with a feeling of exultation that Clemency boarded the coach to Brighton. Wisely the Professor attempted to curb her excitement, although clearly he too was affected by her radiant happiness. He helped her compose a letter to Lady McDoone and wrote a magnificent reference for her which, he said with a twinkle, he hoped would not strike the old lady as 'too good to be true'.

Somehow Clemency managed to live through the ten days which passed before she received Lady McDoone's reply.

'You may come as soon as you wish, Mrs Forest,' she wrote in a thin spidery hand. 'But be sure to preadvise me of the day and time of your arrival at Perth, so that I can send a carriage to meet the London Mail.'

Once again the Professor tried to curb Clemency's excitement.

'You must keep very calm,' he cautioned. 'So long as your true identity remains unknown to the Grayshotts, there is no reason for any of them to object to your presence at Castle Clunes. Once there, you must take time to assess your position very carefully, and only then reach a decision as to whether you intend to remove the boy, as you have so often threatened to do were you ever to locate him. Remember, my dear, that you do not have the law on your side, and every effort would be made to arrest you if you attempted to set sail with your child to the colonies. Now that you will be reunited with Adam, there is no urgency to remove him. Therefore, I beg you, be cautious.'

Clemency despatched her answer to Lady McDoone that afternoon, together with a letter to Caroline promising to do anything within her power whilst she was in Scotland to obtain news of her three little boys. She hoped fervently that an opportunity would arise when she could repay Caroline's altruism, her friend's kindness seeming all the greater coming in the midst of the dreadful tribulations that had beset her this past year.

But even Caroline was forgotten when on the fifteenth of September, by coincidence her twenty-second birthday, she found herself in Lady McDoone's two-horse phaeton, bumping over the rutted road leading to Strath Clunes. Having already travelled non-stop for two days and nights on the fast mail from London to Perth, Clemency's impatience was increasing with every passing minute. She was trembling as she clasped her hands together inside her muff. It was not going to be easy, she thought, pretending she was a complete stranger to her own child.

'Can we not go a little faster?' she begged the burly Scot seated beside her.

'Whist the noo! We're going as fast as the puir wee horses can manage, Mistress,' he replied with a pleasant smile, albeit a reproachful one. 'We'll be there in nae mair than a quarter 'oor.'

Clemency sighed. Her driver could not know the reason for her urgency, and even if he did, he would be justified in remarking that another hour or two on top of a lifetime of waiting, or so it seemed, could make little difference.

She turned her attention to the great sweep of purple heather moorland lying to the south. The distant hills visible on the horizon looked alien and forbidding, she decided, accustomed as she was to the rolling Purbeck Hills of Dorset and the gentle sweep of the Sussex Downs. There were no trees to be seen, no sign of cultivation or habitation, and it seemed to Clemency that she and the driver were the only two people left alive in this wild, desolate world.

But the rough track had now begun to rise, and as the phaeton breasted the summit, she could see before her in the misty gleam of afternoon light a green valley leading to a hamlet.

''Tis Clunes yonder, Mistress,' the driver informed her. 'We're aye passing by Strath Clunes the noo!'

Clemency felt a fresh surge of excitement which swept away her growing fatigue. They were finally nearing her destination, and unless the Fates were about to strike some terrible blow at this eleventh hour, it could not be long now before she saw her child.

The horses were moving at a slow walking pace as they descended the hill into the narrow glen before them. On either side of her, there were steep rocky crags. A brook ran noisily in parallel with the road. They crossed a bridge where the ground levelled out, and now she could see an occasional farmhouse with here and there slate- or thatch-roofed cottages surrounded by small pastures. Smoke from the peat fires rose from every chimney, and now and again Clemency saw a man or woman busy about their work. The village of Clunes was small, comprised for the most part of simple crofts with only one stone house which was the inn. A boy came out to throw rubbish into the roadway and touched his forelock to Lady McDoone's driver, staring at Clemency with undisguised curiosity.

For a mile beyond the village, the countryside was open, without hedgerows, sometimes arable land, but edged by a large expanse of moor. Suddenly the terrain changed yet again, and Clemency could see areas of woodland, oaks and birches amongst the Scots pines. These grew thinner until they became a single avenue of lime trees, and the groom informed her that they were now in Castle Clunes' driveway.

Clemency shivered, partly with the cold of which she was unaware, but mostly because a breathless excitement had now taken hold of her. The long, seemingly endless journey was nearly over, and she was on the point of being reunited with her baby. Deveril might have tried to hide Adam here – in what seemed like the very end of the world, so far away was this desolate castle from Brighton – but thanks to her good friend Caroline Norton, she had found Adam – or was about to do so.

As the driver guided his horses at a walking pace towards the castle, Clemency was trembling, and she clasped her hands together inside her muff. It was not going to be easy pretending she was a complete stranger to her own child. How was she going to find the strength not to gather him into her arms when she saw him? The emotion of the approaching moments for once robbed her of clear thought as she envisaged her beloved baby in her mind. But even Adam was momentarily forgotten as Castle Clunes came into view. The huge house did not strike her as at all beautiful and, indeed, the original building, erected in 1650, had been so built upon in a hotch-potch of varying styles of architecture that it was impressive now only on account of its size. Four little peak-hatted turrets bulged out at the corners of the roof, and wings had been added to the east and west sides of the house, giving it most ungainly proportions.

The groom halted the phaeton at the foot of an imposing double flight of stone steps curving upwards to the entrance on the first floor. The front door swung open and two small boys clad in tartan kilts and jackets came racing down the steps towards her. Clemency's eyes alighted first upon the bright copper-coloured head of the larger of the two boys. She knew that this was not her son, and her head turned swiftly to the other child. Her heart lurched as she realized that the sturdy, laughing five-year-old with his unruly mop of dark curls could be no other than Adam. Not even in her imagination had she appreciated that he would have left baby-hood so far behind him. She felt as if her legs were giving way beneath her, and she clung to the side of the phaeton as the child approached.

'Aunt Meg has allowed us to come and greet you, Ma'am,' he said in a clear high-pitched voice with a marked Scottish lilt to it. 'You are Mrs Forest, are you not? I am Adam Grayshott and this is Robbie, my friend. He is the gillie's son, and he is two years older than me.'

Clemency nodded and attempted a smile, but she was too overcome by emotion, and tears of joy were threatening.

'One of the servants will bring in your luggage,' the little boy said. 'If you would care to take my hand, Ma'am, I will help you up the steps.'

Clemency's heart melted with love. It was clear to her that Adam was attempting to appear very grown-up. She longed to sweep him into her arms and hug him, but he had placed one hand gently beneath her arm and, totally unaware of his true relationship to her, he was guiding her up the steps.

'We will be having high tea in a minute,' he confided. 'Aunt Meg has instructed Cook to make fresh baps and a treacle cake in your honour, and I am to be allowed to take tea with you. I am not usually permitted if there are guests – unless, of course, it is my uncle who is visiting. Otherwise I always have tea with my aunt. She is really my great-*great*-aunt and she is very old!'

Clemency did not find her voice until the little boy had conducted her into the house where Lady McDoone was seated in an invalid chair in the big stone-walled entrance hall. Clemency's first impression was of an old witch, similar to the ones pictured in her childhood fairy story books. Wisps of white hair floated around a wrinkled, peaked little face from which two dark eyes scrutinized her keenly.

'Come here, girl, closer, so that I may take a good look at you!'

The voice was unexpectedly youthful, the tone sharp but kindly. As Clemency stepped forward, the old lady's face was suddenly transformed by a delighted smile.

'You look younger than I expected – but prettier too,' she said. 'Welcome to Castle Clunes.' She handed the Manx cat that had been curled up on her plaid skirt to the little boy. 'I hope you will be very happy with us, Mrs Forest.'

Now at last Clemency found her voice. As she dipped a curtsey, she said fervently:

'Oh, I will, I know I will!' For how could she be otherwise now that she was at last beneath the same roof as her child, she thought, her eyes radiant as she regarded him.

'This is Pandora!' Adam was saying. 'We have hundreds and hundreds of other animals, don't we, Aunt Meg? I will introduce them to you after tea.'

'Not quite hundreds!' the old lady corrected gently, but her eyes were smiling as she looked fondly at the boy. 'Now off you go, young man, and wash your hands. We shall be having tea shortly. And tell Mrs Dewar to come at once and conduct Mrs Forest to her rooms.'

As the boy ran off obediently, Clemency's eyes followed him from the room. She was loath to see him disappear, even for a few minutes. Observing the direction of her visitor's glance, Lady McDoone said:

'I hope you like children, Mrs Forest, for I fear that young man occupies a great deal of my time. I know it is the proper thing for children to be seen and not heard, but frankly I find the boy's conversation most entertaining. He has a delightful disposition – not that he has cause to complain, since he has most things that he needs to keep him happy and a great deal more freedom than he would enjoy if he lived with his uncle in London.'

Clemency would have liked the conversation to continue, but an elderly female retainer arrived to conduct her to the suite of rooms she had been allotted in the west wing. The large bedroom included the base of one of the four circular turrets she had noted from outside the castle, and not even the huge four-poster bed could dwarf the immense proportions of the room. Adjoining it was a smaller sitting-room with two chairs and a sofa, a pretty black and gold lacquer bureau and a tallboy. Against one wall stood a large ivory inlaid table cabinet. A fire was burning cheerfully in the open grate.

'Will I be helping you with your unpacking, Mistress?' the servant enquired, in a voice so heavily accented Clemency was hard put to understand the question. She shook her head, wishing to be alone to recover her equilibrium. The emotional drain of the last quarter of an hour had left her limp and physically exhausted, while her mind still raced with excitement.

Would she be able to retain her incognito? she asked herself, as she drew off her travelling costume and searched in her trunk for a gown suitable for wear in this huge castle. Did Lady McDoone observe the formalities of Society which Clemency had learned whilst living with Caroline Norton? After a brief moment of indecision, she selected a warm dress of French challis. It was a deep sea-green colour, and she hoped it would be an appropriate choice of apparel for a lady's companion.

Thoughts continued to whirl around in her head as she dressed. Somehow these past weeks she had formed quite the wrong opinion of Lady McDoone, supposing her to be of similar ilk to the snobbish, cold-hearted Lady Burnbury. Yet her first impression was quite the opposite, and Clemency had been moved by Lady McDoone's obvious affection for Adam.

Standing in front of the black japanned toilet mirror, Clemency brushed her thick gold hair with automatic strokes. Her mind was recalling the day she had last seen her child – three unbelievably long years ago. He had been no more than a baby, not yet old enough to walk properly or converse with her. His chubby face had fined down now, revealing the same clear-cut, recognizable features as his father. His eyes, too, were Deveril's, full of brightness and laughter. Once, long ago, she had wanted Adam to be like his father, but that was before she had discovered that beneath the charming façade Deveril showed to the world lay a hard, unrelenting cruelty. She could but pray now that although his son had inherited his good looks, Adam would not possess his selfish, unfeeling nature.

Suddenly Clemency felt the need to hurry, to be back in the same room with Adam, able to watch and observe all the minute details that in the emotion of their reunion she had failed to notice. But so vast was the house, and so many the rooms leading off corridors which seemed to stretch in every direction, that it was nearly ten minutes before she discovered a servant to direct her to Lady McDoone's quarters.

As the footman opened the door into Lady McDoone's drawing-room, Clemency had a brief impression of a menagerie as two huge deerhounds bounded over to her, their shaggy grey tails waving a welcome at the same moment as a large grey-capped jackdaw flew down from the curtain rail and landed on her shoulder. A small red squirrel was simultaneously attempting to climb the skirt of her gown.

The boy ran to her side.

'You must not be frightened!' he said solicitously. 'The animals are all quite tame and will not harm you, will they, Aunt Meg?'

'Of course not, Adam. Bring Mrs Forest over here. She shall sit in this chair beside mine. Be seated, my dear. You must be tired after so long a journey. Adam, ring the bell, child. Campden can bring in the tea.'

The old lady leaned over and pushed a small furry animal from the faded brocade chair in which Clemency had been instructed to sit.

'That is Mr Peel, a baby fox-cub we discovered last week and which is still too young to look after itself,' Adam informed her, as he went towards the bell rope. 'We called him Mr Peel after the last Prime Minister. Aunt Meg says that Lord Melbourne is back in power God-be-thanked!'

Both Lady McDoone and Clemency smiled at the obvious repetition of grown-up opinion.

'I daresay, Mrs Forest, that you will be asking yourself what a child of Adam's age is doing alone up here in Perthshire with no one but an ancient great-great-aunt for company!' Lady McDoone remarked unexpectedly. But before Clemency could think of a suitable reply, Adam had returned to stand beside his aunt's chair.

'Begging your pardon, Ma'am,' he said in his clear piping voice, 'but you know very well that I am *not* alone. I have Robbie to play with when I wish, and when I do not, I enjoy very much playing games with you.' He turned his bright eyes to the visitor. 'We play backgammon together, Aunt and I. I am learning quite fast, am I not, Aunt Meg? And we play draughts and chess. And Aunt Meg reads to me. And when we can be out of doors, we tend all the animals and hunt for butterflies. Aunt Meg says you wrote a book about butterflies. Did you bring it with you, Ma'am?'

'Hush now, chatterbox!' Lady McDoone said, laughing. 'I did not tell you that Mrs Forest *wrote* the book – only that she helped the author prepare it. Now run and find out what is keeping Campden!'

As the boy left the room obediently, she turned back to Clemency.

'Adam is of an age when he desires to know and explore everything,' she said, adding with a sigh: 'Sometimes I regret very much that I am so old and cannot keep up with the child. He has a tutor, of course, and an old nurse who once looked

after his uncle and aunts. But neither is young, and I fear the
boy lacks suitable companionship of his own age. The gillie's
son Robbie is a nice enough lad but, understandably, he has
neither the education nor the background one would really
desire for Adam. However, he is still of an age where it cannot
hurt him to run wild for a little longer. Soon he will be off
to school and freedom will be a thing of the past. He is happy
enough, as you can see. Now that you are here, and since Mrs
Norton wrote that you were not only fond of children but
very good with them, I hope you will spend a little time each
day with the boy. He lacks a younger woman's influence,
having no mother of his own.'

The arrival of Adam followed by two servants carrying
heavily laden tea-trays precluded Clemency's chance to learn
more about Adam's 'mother'. With difficulty she curbed her
impatience. She needed to know what Deveril had told their
son; that his mother was dead? Did the boy really have no
recollection of her? The Professor had thought it unlikely that
since he had been only two years old at the time of his abduction, Adam would now recall even the sound of his voice, let
alone her face. Caroline Norton had shared his doubts.

It had hurt Clemency unbearably to think that those hours
she had cuddled and nursed and sung to her baby had vanished
from his memory as if they had never existed. Now she was
faced with the proven fact that she was no more than a total
stranger to him, she told herself with a bitterness she could
not subdue. But the pain vanished as Adam came to her side
and asked politely if she liked milk or lemon in her tea.

It was only with a conscious effort that Clemency turned
her full attention from the boy to Lady McDoone, who was
quizzing her about her period of employment with Caroline
Norton.

'You must forgive an old lady's curiosity,' she was saying
with a twinkle in her dark eyes. 'Personally, I enjoy her work,
although not as much as I once admired the plays of her
grandfather, Mr Richard Sheridan. I have never met Mrs

Norton, as I have not been to London since before she was born. I am aware she herself comes north from time to time to visit her husband's sister in Perthshire, but the Menzies and our family are not well acquainted. I believe Lady Menzies is a dour, ill-tempered female, who I doubt will make her unfortunate sister-in-law welcome again now that Mrs Norton has left her husband – presumably for good this time.'

'Mrs Norton is a charming and kindly person,' Clemency said defensively. 'I truly believe her innocent of any wrongdoing.' She glanced at Adam, who had moved away to sit on the window seat and was engrossed in feeding titbits to the two deerhounds who were sitting at his feet, their shaggy heads laid expectantly on his lap. In an undertone, she continued: 'I was living in her house for over two months last year and had many occasions to meet Lord Melbourne. He and Mrs Norton took a great but entirely *innocent* pleasure in each other's company, and I consider it most unjust of her husband and her enemies to continue to make more of it, despite the jury declaring them guiltless.'

'It pleases me to hear you speak so forcibly in defence of your previous employer,' Lady McDoone replied. 'I like loyalty. I followed the accounts of the trial with very great interest, yet still I cannot understand how Mrs Norton's husband can have accused the Prime Minister of adultery with his wife on no more than servants' gossip. Obviously it was a trumped-up charge. You and I shall discuss the subject at greater length, as I am sure I shall find your views enlightening. Frankly, I was somewhat astonished to receive Mrs Norton's long letter concerning *you* when she must have had so many worries of her own to contend with. She spoke very highly of you, my dear, and mentioned that you were previously employed by Professor Brook. I understand that you assisted him with his magnificent encyclopaedia on entomology, and I have requested my nephew to bring me a copy when he comes up from London at the end of the month.'

Clemency's heart jolted. So Deveril would be at Castle

Clunes before long. Was he aware that Lady McDoone had engaged a companion, she wondered? She recalled the Professor's warnings that she must guard her incognito at all costs. She must take great care not to betray herself by revealing her interest in Adam. There was no need to fear that anyone would guess her real reason for coming to Castle Clunes. As for Deveril, he knew her only as a friend of Benjamin's, if indeed he remembered her at all.

Once again Lady McDoone's voice broke in on her thoughts.

'I may not have made clear in my letter to you, Mrs Forest, exactly what your duties will be. The reason for this omission is that I have not yet decided how to make best use of your services. I do not require nursing, and my maid attends to my dressing and personal needs. But I have been finding it most irritating that I have always to ring for a servant to push my invalid chair if I wish to leave my rooms.' She smiled disarmingly. 'I am unused to depending upon someone else for help and I find it quite exasperating! You will have to be very tolerant, my dear, and put up with my ill-temper!'

Often as Clemency's thoughts had dwelt recently on the varying emotions she might feel when she arrived at Castle Clunes, a spontaneous liking for Deveril's great-aunt was not amongst them. In the past few years, her heart had hardened against the Grayshott family as one after another, her appeals to Deveril through her lawyer had been ignored.

There was a discreet knock on the door and an old woman wearing a dark serge dress covered by a crisp bibbed apron came hobbling into the room. She bobbed a stiff-kneed curtsey to Lady McDoone, her white mob-cap none too securely fastened beneath her chin.

''Tis time young Maister Adam was awa' to his bed,' she announced in a strong Scottish accent. 'Will I take him the noo, Milady?'

Adam ran to his great-aunt's side.

'May I not stay up a little longer, Ma'am?' he begged, his dark eyes beseeching, his voice full of persuasion. He glanced at Clemency as if for support and added craftily: "'Tis a special occasion, is it not, with Mistress Forest but newly arrived from England?'

'Which happens to be no concern of yours, young man!' Lady McDoone said, but her eyes softened as the little boy wound his arm about her neck. 'A half hour and not a minute more,' she added. 'Bring me your storybook and I will read you a chapter. No, Mrs Forest shall read to you. It will be good for you to hear a pure English voice for a change.' She smiled at Clemency. 'He hears nothing but Scottish accents here, and no one will understand him when he gets to school if he does not soon learn to pronounce the King's English. You are not too tired, Mrs Forest?' she added solicitously.

'No, indeed I am not!' Clemency cried with ill-concealed enthusiasm. The thought of reading a bedtime story to her own child was like a dream come true.

Without any sign of shyness, Adam brought the book to her and leant against her knees. Unable to stop herself, Clemency put one arm around him so that he nestled against her. His soft rosy cheek lay close to hers and she could see the tiny mole beneath his right cheekbone. Her heart melted with tenderness, as he said confidentially:

'The book is called *The Life and Strange Surprising Adventures of Robinson Crusoe*, Ma'am. It is by an author called Daniel Defoe, and it is very exciting. Sometimes Robbie and I play at being on a desert island and I am Robinson Crusoe and he is Man Friday, but Robbie is not very good at pretending, although he does know absolutely everything about nature, does he not, Aunt Meg?' he asked loyally.

'If you go on chattering, there will be no time left for reading,' Lady McDoone said tartly.

As Clemency read, the boy leant closer and closer against her. She could see by the occasional droop of his eyelashes that he was growing sleepy but was determined to learn what happened next in the story. Once in a while he would interrupt her to question the meaning of a word he did not understand, and patiently, she explained it to him. When his nurse reappeared, Clemency was no less disappointed than her child at how quickly the half hour had sped past.

'Never mind!' she comforted him. 'There will be time to read again tomorrow – that is if Lady McDoone will permit,' she added quickly.

'My dear girl, I shall be delighted to be freed from the task,' the old lady commented, smiling. 'Reading aloud is not my favourite pastime, I assure you. Mercifully the boy can now read quite well, and once he can keep pace with his own impatience, he can read to himself!'

Adam withdrew reluctantly from the curve of Clemency's shoulder and went dutifully to his great-aunt's chair to kiss her hand. He bowed politely to Clemency, and without argument went off with his nurse.

Lady McDoone sighed.

'I can well understand why my nephew is so taken with the boy,' she said. 'He looks upon him as his own, but Adam is his brother's child. Poor Percy died two years ago and Deveril was heartbroken. I suspect that is another reason why he dotes upon young Adam.'

Attempting to keep her voice casual, Clemency said very quietly:

'Has the boy no mother, Ma'am?'

Her employer's hesitation was only momentary.

'I suppose there is no harm in your knowing, Mrs Forest. The fact is Lord Burnbury's brother made a hasty and unfortunate marriage to a young girl beneath his rank – a parson's daughter, I believe. In any event, the girl deserted both her husband and her infant son after the baby's birth and disappeared. My nephew believes that she emigrated to the colonies. I wonder sometimes how the girl could have borne to part with her own flesh and blood. But there! There is no understanding human nature, and Deveril tells me I should not be surprised since she was little more than a child herself and far too young for motherhood.'

Bitterness welled in Clemency's heart so forcefully that she was prevented from making any reply. But since Lady McDoone seemed inclined to talk, she could not resist asking:

'Lord Burnbury, so you said, is devoted to Adam. Why therefore does he not have Adam to live with him in London? He has a very long way to travel to visit the child here.'

Lady McDoone gave a deep sigh.

'I daresay my nephew *will* take Adam to live with him once the boy is older. But Lady Burnbury does not care for small children and has none of her own. In the meanwhile, Adam is happy enough here at Castle Clunes so there has been no requirement to remove him. I personally would be heartbroken to lose him.'

The old servant Campden came in to remove the tea things, and Lady McDoone turned to Clemency with a kindly smile.

'I shall not require your services this evening, Mrs Forest,' she said. 'You must be quite exhausted and longing for your bed. You are to ring for one of the servants – we have so many I am always forgetting their names – if you lack for anything you need. Finally, my dear, you must be wondering about your position in the household, so I wish you to know that it is not my intention that you should be treated as a servant. I can see that you are well-born and I appreciate that circumstances have forced you into taking employment. You will therefore be treated in this house as a member of the family. When we have time, you must tell me about your life, which I suspect has been a sad one since you were widowed so young. But away you go now, child, and I shall see you in the morning.'

Clemency stood up and acknowledged her gentle dismissal with a curtsey before leaving the room. Finding herself once again in the labyrinth of corridors, tired though she was, she longed to go in search of the nursery quarters where presumably the old nurse was tucking Adam into bed. She was not sure if she could wait until morning to see him again. Yet she had lived three years without him, she reminded herself, and should be able to face a few more hours separation with equanimity.

When at last she discovered her own rooms, she did not go at once to bed but sat down at the bureau and began a long letter to the Professor. Her joy in being at last reunited with her son spilled from every page as she wrote in minutest detail of his character, appearance and surroundings. Nearing the end of this epistle, she paused, her hand remaining poised above the paper as she turned her head to stare into the dying embers of the fire. Her candle had burned low and was guttering in its holder. Somewhere outside in the castle grounds an owl hooted, and further away, another replied. She drew a long sigh as she returned to her task.

'I understand from Lady McDoone that it is only a matter of a week or two before Deveril will arrive on a visit to Adam. It seems he, too, is devoted to the boy, but I have only his great-aunt's word for that. I shall make no decisions about the future until after he has been here. Lady McDoone believes Percy to be Adam's father, but Adam is so like Deveril, I am surprised she has not suspected the truth. Perhaps she has – but naturally she would not tell me!'

It had been her intention to write also to Benjamin and to Caroline, but suddenly her eyes would not remain open any longer. Obedient to Lady McDoone's instructions, she pulled on the bell rope to summon a servant to bring her hot water in which to wash. After what seemed a very long time, a girl arrived bringing with her a big copper jug of hot water. Clemency only half understood the girl's chatter as she made up the fire, turned down the bed and ascertained that the warming-pan was still hot.

'Will there be anything else, Mistress?' she enquired as Clemency climbed into bed with a sigh of pleasure. The sheets were of pure linen, and a thick quilted cover filled with feathers added to her feeling of comfort and luxury.

When the girl had departed with a cheery goodnight, Clemency extinguished her candle and lay back on the soft pillows. Her last waking thought was not of the future but of the past, as she pondered how much heartbreak and torment she might have been spared had she known three years ago that one day she would again be sleeping under the same roof as her son. Tonight it did not matter that Adam was unaware she was his mother; she could bear the pain of knowing that she must not gather him into her arms and kiss him. She could still feel the pressure of his small body against her breast; still hear that sweet treble voice bidding her goodnight. Now, she thought drowsily, were she to see him in the street, she would recognize the boy her baby had become. Never again need she fear that she might pass him by, not knowing that he was her son.

Her last thought before sleep overtook her was that nothing and no one in the world would ever separate her from her child again.

CHAPTER TWENTY

October 1836

Deveril Grayshott stood with his back to the window of the grand drawing-room at Castle Clunes and tapped his highly polished Hessian boots with his ebony cane. His valet and two of the servants had been despatched to discover the whereabouts of his great-aunt and the boy, and so far not one of them had reappeared. It was almost ten minutes since he had arrived after a long and tiring journey from London, and he was in no mood to be kept waiting.

His eyes wandered to the blue watered-silk papered walls of the big room upon which hung several portraits. One which he especially liked was of his great-grandfather in the cere- monial robes he had worn at the coronation of George III. Before too long he must arrange to have Adam's portrait painted, he thought. It could go on the wall in place of the Van Dyck, which he had never much cared for. His great-aunt would not object to the exchange, for she seldom came into this room nowadays. For many years there had been no large family gatherings or social functions at Castle Clunes and the drawing-room, like the long dining-room, was only opened up when he was in residence. The dining-room was a particular favourite of Deveril's. It, too, had a decorated ceiling and frieze, smoke grey in colour, with shades of pale green, cinnamon and apricot giving it both warmth and charm. The walls there were prepared in apple-green silk, and he wished that Muriel would choose such delightful colours for Grayshott House.

Where was everybody, he thought with renewed impatience. He was eager to see the boy, who he had not visited these past three months. But for the confounded golden wedding celebrations of his parents-in-law, he would have come up on the twelfth for the grouse shooting. He could hardly blame Muriel this time for setting the date at so inconvenient a time for himself, he reflected wryly. Nevertheless he would gladly have forgone the limited pleasure of the Lawrences' party to be up here in Scotland with his son. A footman came hurrying into the room.

'One of the maids just told me that young Maister Adam is with Milady's companion in her rooms,' he announced breathlessly. 'Will I go and advise them of your arrival, Milord?'

Deveril was on the point of giving his consent when he changed his mind.

'No, I will go to them, and where shall I find Milady's companion?'

'She is in the west wing, Milord,' the footman said. 'Her name, Milord, is Mistress Forest! She arrived from England two weeks ago.'

Deveril had not the slightest interest in his aunt's new employee; and the name struck no chord of recognition in his memory. His restless energy had been aggravated by the long hours of travel. He had had to remain seated in his coach, the bad weather having precluded the relief of horse-riding. With growing impatience he strode down the corridor and turned into the west wing. This suite of rooms was normally reserved for the more important of their guests, and he was briefly surprised that a mere lady's companion should have been allocated such good quarters.

His hand raised to knock upon the door, he paused as his ears caught the faint sound of a musical instrument. A moment later, he heard a woman's voice, gentle and sweet-toned, singing:

'Oh, do you know the muffin man, the muffin man, the muffin man? Oh, do you know the muffin man who lives in Drury Lane?'

This was followed by a clear high treble which Deveril recognized immediately as that of his son.

'Oh, yes I know the muffin man, the muffin man . . .'

An amused smile lighting up his face, Deveril opened the door very softly and when it came to the next verse, he joined in heartily:

'Then three of us know the muffin man . . .'

The woman at the spinet ceased playing and Adam ran across the room and threw himself into Deveril's open arms.

'Uncle 'Vril!' he cried. 'We did not know you were here. We did not know you had arrived!'

Deveril swept the child high off the floor and hugged him.

'And I did not know you were hiding from me!' he said. Setting the boy down, two small chubby arms left clinging about his legs, he looked over the top of Adam's head and, for the first time, he noticed Clemency. A broad grin spread slowly over his face as he said:

'Damme for a fool, if it is not Mrs Forest! But when I was told your name, I never thought it could be *you* – my silent lady from the past.' He made a leg and continued: 'Let me see now, it was in Brighton, was it not? Why, yes, at the New Theatre, and you were accompanied by poor old Brook. But what on earth brings you here to Castle Clunes, Ma'am?'

The unexpected sight of Deveril had unnerved Clemency sufficiently for her to forget that he was her bitter enemy, the cause of all her unhappiness these past three years. Her heart leapt into her throat as she saw the half-remembered quizzical smile light up those brilliant dark eyes. She recalled his immense good looks and his unusual height, as he stood towering over his little son.

But the attraction lasted only while he spoke and she had

time to regain her composure. Her hands clenched at her sides and her chin lifted as she said in a cold, clear voice:

'You seem to forget, Sir, that Doctor Brook is both a very dear friend and . . .'

'. . . and a "distant relation", if my memory serves me right,' Deveril broke in, his eyes still full of laughter. 'My apologies, Ma'am, if I have spoken out of turn, but in all honesty you cannot persuade me that the worthy physician is a Don Juan and likely to turn a maiden's head, now can you? Ergo, he *is* a poor fellow and one who has my pity.'

'Your remark is uncalled for, Sir!' Clemency protested. But Adam could contain his impatience no longer. He was tugging at Deveril's hand, saying:

'Uncle 'Vril, Aunt Meg has permitted Mrs Forest to bring the spinet up here to her sitting-room so that we can sing together. I am learning to play it. No one that I can remember has ever played the spinet before and it was dreadfully out of tune, Mrs Forest said. But Aunt Meg called in a funny old man from Perth and he has made it quite perfect. Can we now sing together, all three of us? Please Uncle 'Vril?'

Clemency laid a restraining hand upon Adam's arm.

'No, not now,' she said in a sharper tone than she had intended. 'As your uncle has only just arrived, he will be tired.'

'I have been more bored than tired during the journey,' Deveril replied, 'but now I am neither. You have not replied to my question, Mrs Forest. What brings you to Castle Clunes? Am I to understand that *you* are my great-aunt's new companion?'

'But how clever of you to guess it, Uncle 'Vril,' Adam broke in, saving Clemency the need for a reply. 'Mrs Forest has been with us nearly two weeks, and I cannot now think how ever I amused myself before she came. We do all sorts of exciting things together. We . . .'

'Adam, you must learn not to be such a nuisance with your chatter,' Clemency reproved him, again more sharply than she had intended; but Deveril's amused, unwavering stare was unnerving her. She saw the look of hurt reproach in the boy's eyes and weakening, she added: 'Tomorrow, perhaps, I will tell you the story of the little girl who talked so much she was put in a box so that no one could hear her chatter . . .'

Adam's mouth curved upwards in a delighted smile.

'Why, a chatterbox,' he cried. 'Tell me the story now, Ma'am, I beg you.'

'Yes, indeed, tell us both,' Deveril said, and to Clemency's acute discomfiture he sat down in one of the armchairs and pulled Adam on to his lap. 'Now tell us both, Mrs Forest, what became of little Miss Chatterbox? I am quite intrigued to hear the tale from a lady so renowned for her silence!'

He is teasing me, Clemency thought despairingly, and I will not be provoked. Nor would she stand watching idly while Deveril sat with his arms so possessively wrapped about his son – *her* son.

'It is time for you to go and wash your hands before tea,' she told the boy abruptly. 'Run along now, Adam!'

For once the child did not obey her command instantly.

'When my Uncle 'Vril is home, he and Aunt Meg have grown-up dinner, and I have high tea in the nursery,' he said, uncertainly.

'Then I will join you in the nursery,' Clemency replied firmly.

Deveril rose slowly to his feet.

'I shall be pleased if you will join us downstairs, Ma'am,' he commented. 'It is obvious that I should become better acquainted with you, since it appears that you are as much Adam's companion as my great-aunt's.'

Clemency's thoughts whirled in confusion. Deveril had every justification for desiring to know more about her, yet she sensed that this was only an excuse, and that he was really flirting with her in much the same manner as he had done the evening they had last met at the theatre in Brighton. But her feeling of bitterness was paramount.

'I am sure Lady McDoone would prefer to dine with you

alone,' she said stiffly. 'Doubtless we shall have occasion to meet on the morrow.'

'Stuff and nonsense!' Deveril replied airily. 'My great-aunt will be as delighted as I to have you grace our table.'

As he left the room, his face was slightly puzzled. He had been perfectly agreeable towards the young woman and could see no reason whatever for her churlishness. Nor was he accustomed to having his invitations refused. However well-bred the lady might be, he thought, she was only an employee and should have been honoured by his invitation.

Suddenly memory stirred and he recalled that he had suspected the pretty Mrs Forest of being Brook's mistress. If that were so, then she must have found his detrimental comment about the physician offensive when he had intended only to be flippant. The *faux pas* irritated him.

But as he descended the stairs to go to his great-aunt's sitting-room, his good humour returned. He had escaped from London and Muriel for four whole weeks, and there was plenty of time to win the pretty Mrs Forest's interest, if that was what he wanted. He would enjoy the challenge, just as he had once enjoyed the challenge Anthea presented. He thought now of his former mistress with affection and a faint regret that their affair had ended when he and Muriel left the Middle East to return to London and Anthea had departed to New York.

Anthea had been right, of course. They had parted before either could become bored with the other. Moreover Muriel had begun to suspect that he had more than a casual interest in their American friend and turned tiresomely jealous. It was typical of his wife, Deveril thought, as he stopped to pat one of the deerhounds wandering along the passage, that Muriel did not openly accuse him of being unfaithful. It had been always with a parody of a smile that she insinuated her suspicions.

His marriage might be considerably more tolerable, Deveril thought with a sigh, if Muriel were to accept as he did that it was no more than a convenience, lacking any degree of personal warmth. It was several years since he had shared her bed, and unless she were totally ignorant of a man's needs, she must suppose he found his pleasures elsewhere. But Muriel had become more and more possessive, and Anthea had several times cautioned him that his wife was obsessively in love with him, even if her way of demonstrating affection was not his own.

Bitterly he reflected that his wife's 'love' for him did not include any consideration for his happiness. When word had reached her that Adam was at Castle Clunes, she had made clear her determination that the boy should remain there, out of sight and supposedly out of mind. He had been somewhat surprised that she had not learnt sooner of the boy's presence in Scotland, although while Adam was still an infant, he had been confined to the nursery quarters and therefore unremarked by visitors. But on Adam's fourth birthday, Deveril had decided that the little boy was quite old enough to make his appearance in the drawing-room and, in any event, it pleased him to show off the child to his friends.

But Muriel refused to listen to his praise of the boy's appearance and charm, obsessed as she was by the idea that Percy's child carried strains of his father's imbecility, even although they might not yet be obvious.

Several times Deveril had been tempted to declare his paternity, but instinct forbade such a confession. He was not ready to give Muriel this piece of ammunition with which to upbraid him. For the time being, he was content to enjoy his visits to his son whilst preserving peace in his household. Muriel's knowledge of Adam's presence at Castle Clunes served to reinforce her refusal ever to go to Scotland – a state of affairs which served him very well.

As he did so often nowadays, Deveril pushed the unwelcome thought of Muriel to the back of his mind and went into his great-aunt's room with a cheerful smile upon his handsome young face. The old lady pushed the Manx cat off her lap, removed a cockatoo from his perch on the end of her invalid chair, and held out her arms to receive Deveril's hug.

'How well you are looking, dearest boy!' she said, as Deveril sat down beside her, retaining her hand in his. 'How was your journey? The servants know of your arrival, I trust? Cook has been preparing food all this week for you and your shooting party, and is sure to have some tasty dishes for your dinner. Have you seen young Adam?'

Deveril laughed.

'Which question shall I answer first? Yes, the servants know I am here and yes, I have seen young Adam. He was singing songs with the charming Mrs Forest, who, I might add, I have invited to dine with us tonight. I hope that meets with your approval, Aunt Meg?'

The old lady tapped his hand in a playful slap.

'Now young man, I will not have you breaking any hearts up here. You can confine your flirtations to London. Clemency, that is to say Mrs Forest, is a perfect treasure, and not at all the kind of girl with whom it would be proper for you to do any philandering.'

Deveril gave a full-throated laugh.

'What have I ever done, dearest Aunt, to earn such an evil reputation?' he asked. 'And who said I had any intention of "philandering" with the pretty Mrs Forest?'

'You would not have invited her to dine with us if you had not found her attractive,' Lady McDoone said shrewdly. 'And she *is* a pretty girl as well as being a delightful and charming companion. But what is proving of even greater worth than her attentions to me, Deveril, is her rapport with young Adam.' Her face took on a more serious expression as she added: 'You know, my dear boy, we have been remiss in not realizing that the child has been lacking a feminine influence in his life. Oh, I know I am a female, but that is not at all the same as providing him with maternal companionship. I ensure that he is happy and well looked after, but I am an old woman, and even when I was young, I did not enjoy such feminine accomplishments as playing the spinet and singing. Moreover, Mrs Forest is beautifully mannered and the boy is at last absorbing some of the social graces as well as copying her diction.'

'So long as Mrs Forest does not namby-pamby the child, I have no objection to her taking on the rôle of governess,' Deveril said. He rose without haste from his chair. 'There will be a dozen of my friends arriving tomorrow,' he said, 'most of whom you already know. I wrote to Hutchins last week telling him we would begin shooting on Thursday. Excellent gamekeeper that he is, he will have everything prepared as usual. Hopkins has the guest list for Mrs Dewar, so you have no need to trouble yourself.'

'Dewar is getting a little too old these days to be relied upon,' Lady McDoone informed him. 'Hopkins had best check with her that all is in order.'

It was with a feeling of well-being that Deveril settled into his familiar suite of rooms in the east wing and allowed his valet Hopkins to dress him for dinner. Here at Castle Clunes they adopted a less formal way of life than was customary in London, and in place of his travelling costume, he donned a dark green frock-coat and a comfortable pair of nankeen trousers. As his valet straightened his cravat, his feeling of contentment increased.

'Just think, Hopkins, for the next few weeks there will be no soirées, no long-drawn-out luncheon parties or musical evenings!' he said, grinning. He would be shooting over the moors all day with a band of young men who favoured the sport as greatly as he. When he returned to the house at dusk, he could look forward to an hour or two in company with his little son, and later there would be a jolly party gathered around the dining-table with dear Aunt Meg a benign hostess. When the meal was over and she had retired, he and his friends would play cards and carouse the night away. What more could a man want? he asked himself as he dismissed his valet and went downstairs to dinner.

Clemency was already in the anteroom with Lady McDoone. She, too, had changed, and was wearing an indigo blue merino dress with a deep rounded neckline, the edge of which was softened by a pleated lace frill. The blue bouffant sleeves were also edged at the wrists by tiny lace frills, and the bodice was tightly waisted, flaring into a full gathered skirt. Her fair hair was caught in a classical knot at the back of her head, and her forehead was crowned by a narrow gold *ferronière*, a treasured parting gift from Caroline Norton which she had had no previous opportunity to wear.

Lady McDoone was in a plain black velvet gown, a frilled lace cap covering her wispy white hair. She was listening intently as Clemency read aloud to her from the latest copy of the *London Gazette* which Deveril had remembered to bring her.

She welcomed her nephew with a fond smile.

'Deveril, you are just the person to enlighten us. It says here that the Duchess of Sutherland has been seen driving in Hyde Park with Mrs Norton. Can this mean that Mrs Norton is regaining her place in Society?'

Deveril laughed.

'Not as far as my wife is concerned,' he said bluntly. 'The famous Mrs Norton is certainly not on Muriel's calling list these days. If you want my view, Aunt Meg, I think Society has treated that poor woman quite abominably. All praise to the Duchess of Sutherland, and come to that, to Mrs Leicester Stanhope and Lord Lansdown for rallying to Mrs Norton's side.'

Lady McDoone nodded.

'I am personally indebted to her,' she said, placing an arm affectionately around Clemency's shoulders. 'It was on Mrs Norton's recommendation that I engaged Mrs Forest, you know. Clemency worked for her for several months last year and became a personal friend, did you not, my dear?'

Clemency's eyes met Deveril's curious gaze.

'I became very attached to Mrs Norton,' she said bluntly,

'and I feel she has been grossly misrepresented and most unfairly punished for an offence she did not commit.'

Deveril's expression changed to one of amusement.

'Come now, Ma'am, you cannot really believe that the beautiful Caroline's relationship with Lord Melbourne was purely platonic. Why, it is a known fact that he spent as much time at her house as in his own!'

Clemency's cheeks flushed with indignation.

'It was clearly and definitely stated at Lord Melbourne's trial that they were innocent of any impropriety,' she said. 'Yet poor Caroline has been ostracized as if the very opposite were true.'

Deveril shrugged indifferently.

'Since George Norton thought fit to accuse the Prime Minister of adultery with his wife, what is more natural than that the world should assume there was far more to the relationship than came out at the trial!' he commented.

'I am inclined to agree with Clemency,' Lady McDoone interposed. 'We all know that George Norton was politically motivated. The Tories wanted to discredit the Whigs, and persuaded him to take action against his better judgment – or such is my opinion. After all, Melbourne and Mrs Norton had been close friends for years, and Norton encouraged the association. He even managed to obtain employment through his wife's influence with the Viscount.'

'Yet he has repaid her for her efforts by taking her sons from her!' Clemency protested impulsively.

'As I understand the situation,' Deveril replied, 'Norton has kept his sons because his wife left the matrimonial home, and so long as Caroline continues with the separation, he will not permit her to see them. It is the only hold he now has over her since, according to my wife, Caroline has made herself financially independent by her literary earnings.'

Clemency could not withhold a gasp of indignation.

'I consider that is quite outrageous!' she said.

Both Deveril and Lady McDoone looked surprised at the

vehemence of her tone. Deveril noted the bright spots of colour in her cheeks and his interest in her deepened as he said:

'My dear young lady, the courts may have declared Mrs Norton innocent of any misconduct with Lord Melbourne, but that is not to say that she has been a good wife to her husband. One must appreciate, for example, that it was hardly supportive of her to use her not-inconsiderable influence in favour of the Whig party when her husband is such a staunch Tory.'

'Politics!' Clemency said bitterly. 'What have they to do with a mother's love for her children? What kind of husband would deny his wife the right to be with them?' She broke off, realizing that if she allowed herself to be carried away on this theme, she could all too easily betray her own feelings regarding Adam.

'Forgive me,' she said quietly to Lady McDoone. 'It is not my place to air my opinions. I am afraid I feel so strongly about the subject that I quite forgot myself!'

'Nonsense, my dear child,' Lady McDoone said, smiling. 'It always interests me to hear a modern point of view. Besides, I admire your loyalty to Mrs Norton. It proves you are no fair-weather friend!'

The conversation ended there, as a footman announced that dinner was served. While the servant took charge of Lady McDoone's chair, Deveril offered his arm to Clemency. She had no alternative but to take it. As they walked into the dining-room, he was smiling in the most irritating manner.

'I confess myself quite delighted,' he was saying in that teasing voice she now knew well. 'My silent lady of the past has found her voice in no uncertain terms – and, if I may say so, a most expressive one it proves to be. I find myself intrigued to know more about you, Ma'am. You obviously have many accomplishments besides that of looking quite remarkably beautiful, and I am curious to know what has brought you to this remote corner of the British Isles when you should clearly be adorning the salons and drawing-rooms of London.'

Clemency withdrew her hand from his arm and said stiffly:

'I hardly think my affairs will prove of interest to you, Sir, and since Lady McDoone has employed me, I assume she has already taken up my references and is quite satisfied with them.'

To her annoyance, Deveril laughed.

'You know quite well that I am not interested in your references,' he said, in a tone too low for Lady McDoone to hear. 'My interest is in *you*, dear lady!'

Clemency made no reply, although her heart was beating with a fierce resentment at the chains of silence which bound her. The truth as to her past would wipe that flirtatious smile from Deveril's face, she thought angrily. He would be shocked – perhaps even afraid of what she might do. Now that she had found Adam, he had good cause to fear her. These past two weeks, she had kept uppermost in her mind her plans to remove Adam to North America to live with her father. Only the previous night she had written to her papa, promising that he would not have to wait much longer.

'But I realize that it would be remiss of me to act too precipitately,' she had said. 'I am almost a stranger to Adam, although thankfully he grows more affectionate each day and Lady McDoone encourages me to spend a great deal of time with him . . .'

She had paused as she wrote that last sentence, suddenly disturbed by the knowledge that the old lady clearly doted on Adam, and that it would cause her untold heartache the day Clemency spirited him out of the house for ever.

But she refused to allow sentiment to deflect her from her purpose. No member of the Grayshott family had cared when *her* heart had been broken the day they took Adam away, she reminded herself. Her letter to her father had ended with another assurance that it would not be long before he could expect to see them. But first, she told him, she must make foolproof plans for their escape, covering her movements so thoroughly that she and Adam could not be followed to the seaport where they could embark for the colonies.

Deveril's voice as he seated himself at the head of the oak refectory dining-table brought her mind back to the present.

'You must give me news of our mutual friend, Doctor Brook,' he was saying. 'I have not been down to Dorset for some months. A most worthy fellow! It surprises me that he has not yet found himself a wife. Would I be wrong in hazarding a guess that he has a certain fondness for you, Mrs Forest?'

'Deveril!' Lady McDoone protested sharply from across the table. 'That is most impertinent. Mrs Forest's private affairs are no business of yours.'

Stealing a glance at Deveril's face, Clemency's emotions whirled into confusion. He had earned his rebuke and she was grateful to Lady McDoone for making it, but he looked so absurdly like Adam when she herself had had cause to rebuke the boy for some minor offence, that despite everything, she could no longer feel anger towards him. It was even harder to maintain that anger when he smiled at her disarmingly and begged her forgiveness.

'I assure you it was not my intention to pry!' he said in a low gentle voice. 'Pray do not be cross with me.' Unable to play the penitent for long, his dark eyes turned suddenly mischievous as he added in a voice too low for his great-aunt to hear: 'You do not look half so pretty when you frown. What can I say to make you smile again?'

To Clemency's intense relief, he suddenly changed the topic of conversation. Looking towards Lady McDoone, he said:

'Muriel was greatly disappointed that the King and Queen did not after all attend her parents' golden wedding party last week. I fear our worthy monarch has not been too well of late. If aught were to happen to His Majesty, it would mean yet another Regent for the country.'

'Is that niece of his, Victoria, still a minor?' Lady McDoone enquired.

'Seventeen, I believe. One thing is certain: such is the Duke of Cumberland's reputation, no one would consider him a proper counsellor to an innocent young girl. In any event, that pushing female, her mother, the Duchess of Kent, has been scheming for years to adopt the role of Regent should ever it become necessary. She insists that her daughter is kept from attending the Royal drawing-rooms and that the girl goes only to Windsor on the fewest possible occasions. Of course, the Duchess is a dreadful prude and fears her daughter's innocence will be corrupted.'

'But I had thought that the King and Queen were a most proper and conventional couple,' Clemency remarked, recalling one of the Professor's treatises on their Majesties.

Deveril laughed.

'That is quite true, if you can call a man conventional who has had ten children by his former mistress, the faithful Mrs Jordan, or a Queen prudish who enthusiastically welcomes the entire brood as if they were her own.'

'Deveril, we should perhaps explain to Clemency that the King might never have discontinued his association with Mrs Jordan but for the unexpected requirement for him to marry when the late King's only daughter Charlotte died. Not that our poor Queen has been able to provide the throne with a legitimate heir; she suffered three miscarriages, and the premature birth of a little girl ended tragically with the infant's death four months later. The King's natural children, therefore, and his grandchildren, have proved a great joy to him, and Queen Adelaide's maternal instincts have been wisely channelled.'

Deveril remained silent, his flippancy disappearing as the thought occurred to him that the Queen's attitude to her husband's bastards could be an object lesson to Muriel. Perhaps the time had now come when he should inform his wife that Adam was *his* child and not Percy's, as she supposed. Would the true facts make her more tolerant of his desire to have the boy to live with him? Or less so? he wondered. Maybe now that Adam had grown from babyhood into a handsome five-year-old, Muriel would be as charmed by the child as he. He had made no attempt to reconcile her to his plans during the past three years. The occasional desire to do so had only pressed itself upon him subsequent to his visits to Scotland. Those moments of farewell to the boy, when Adam begged to be allowed to accompany him to London, always caught at his heartstrings, and he longed to be able to take him in the carriage with him. Once back at Grayshott House, other thoughts had occupied his mind.

How much easier life would be if his relationship with his wife allowed frank and honest discussion between them as between friends. Muriel, however, skilfully avoided any controversy, more often than not only hinting at her displeasure. The subject of Adam was the only one on which he had heard her express her views with any degree of veracity, which led him to believe that Muriel was not as naïve as she often chose to appear.

There was very little, he had discovered in the four years of his marriage, that she said or undertook without some ulterior motive. The mainspring of Muriel's life was centred around her social engagements, and true friendships were unimportant to her. Deveril was forced to admit that as a consequence of her time and effort, his wife was recognized nowadays as one of London's leading hostesses, a tribute which brought a glow of genuine delight to her sallow cheeks. To read a complimentary comment about herself in the *Gazette* or the *Morning Post* was to transform Muriel from a cold, practical, determined, self-centred woman into someone more nearly human. A sparkle would light up her eyes, her mouth would soften into a contented smile, her voice become less shrill, as she read these accounts aloud to Deveril over the breakfast table.

For Muriel's sake, he tried to conceal his boredom and lack of interest; but her aspirations were not his. He wanted a purpose in his life and he had two now – Chiswell Hill House estate and his son, Adam. The two were interlinked, for it was

Adam who would one day inherit the Dorsetshire estate and he was determined that the boy would find it in better shape than he had done. Two years ago, he had set in hand the improvement of the farms and cottages. He had had planted many thousands of fir trees on ground to the north which had been allowed to grow into neglect. He had also had land drains put into a large area of swampy ground bordering Bourne Brook.

'Will you carve the venison, Milord?'

The servant's question broke in on Deveril's thoughts. He stood up, smiling at Lady McDoone.

'How thoughtful of you to remember that venison is my favourite dish, dearest Aunt,' he said, inclining his head as if in tribute.

'You know very well it is my pleasure to spoil you!' she replied happily.

The brief exchange of words, simple though they were, betrayed an underlying depth of affection which moved Clemency strangely. Sensitive as she was, she recognized the love between this young man and the great-aunt over fifty years his senior. It held possible dangers for her, she thought. She must never count on Lady McDoone's support. The old lady would almost certainly align herself with her nephew, whatever the rights and wrongs of Clemency's cause.

As if to compound her unease, Deveril was saying to his aunt:

'I'll wager you spoil young Adam as much, if not more than you spoil me!'

Lady McDoone laughed.

'And why not, pray? The pair of you are as alike as two peas in a pod, and I am not in the least ashamed to admit that I would do anything for either of you. But you know that very well, young man, do you not?'

Deveril nodded, his voice quiet as he said:

'Had I not been convinced of it, dearest Aunt, I would never have entrusted Adam to you. I have always known he would be safe in your hands.'

Clemency's head dipped lower over her plate as she sought to conceal her expression. Deveril had used the word 'safe', by which he must have meant that Adam was safe from *her* intervention.

She drew a long deep breath to steady herself. Then in a clear voice, she said lightly:

'But in this life we lead nowadays, Lord Burnbury, surely nobody can be entirely safe all the time? However carefully we may plan, there is always Fate in the wings threatening to intervene.'

Deveril paused in the act of carving, and holding the knife aloft, he smiled at Clemency.

'Your very profound remark leads me to suppose that the Fates have not always treated you very kindly, Mrs Forest. I myself have been fortunate. They have so far served me well, and I have reason to believe those fair goddesses favour me.'

Clemency made no reply, although she longed to tell him that Fortune would not favour him much longer. Soon it would be *he* who must plead with *her*; *his* letters *she* would ignore as he had ignored hers; *he* and not *she* who would beg for the right to see their Adam.

Seeing his gaze still centred upon her, Clemency could afford to return his smile; for she knew now, as he did not, that it was only a matter of time before his luck ran out, and it would be her turn to abduct their son.

CHAPTER TWENTY-ONE

October 1836

The door of Clemency's sitting-room burst open and Adam came hurrying in, his cheeks pink with excitement, his eyes sparkling.

'Forrie, you are to come downstairs at once,' he cried, tugging at her hand. 'Aunt Meg wants to talk to you. It is about the masquerade, and Uncle 'Vril says I may help you to choose a costume and . . .'

For once Clemency could not bring herself to send him back into the corridor with the admonition to knock first before entering a lady's apartments. The small boy had only this past week adopted his own pet name for her, and its implication of intimacy between them touched her too deeply for a remonstration. She put her arms around him and hugged him. There was a large pheasant's tail feather stuck in his hair which, she now told him, gave him the ferocious appearance of a Red Indian.

Adam laughed happily.

'Uncle 'Vril gave it to me. Do you know, Forrie, they brought back two hundred brace; that is why we are to have a party – to eat them all up. Uncle 'Vril said it was a far better day's sport than they enjoyed last week shooting grouse on the moors. Uncle 'Vril said . . .'

Clemency released her hold upon the boy and stood up, her happiness suddenly dispelled. She had now been a whole month at Castle Clunes, and although there was no doubt whatever that Adam was developing a genuine affection for her, nevertheless his conversation invariably was punctuated

with 'Uncle 'Vril said' or 'Uncle 'Vril did'. Her son's adoration for his father was paramount, and no matter how great
she wished it otherwise, she could not ignore it. Deveril was
the idol, the hero of Adam's small world, and consciously or
otherwise, he copied his Uncle 'Vril in everything he did
or said.

He was still too young to be permitted to go out with the
guns, and so while his father and friends were gone from the
house, he had perforce to spend his days either at his studies
with his tutor or with her. The weather was cold and a bitter
wind blew from the north, precluding more than the shortest
of walks in the garden surrounding the castle. The boy, therefore, was often to be seen kneeling on the window-seat in his
great-aunt's sitting-room, staring wistfully out towards the
moor in the hope of catching a glimpse in the distance of the
dogs or guns.

Clemency had been present each evening when Deveril and
his friends returned to the castle, muddied, windswept but
happily triumphant as they drank Lady McDoone's special
hot toddy from silver goblets. It was a highly potent beverage
called Athole Brose, made of whisky, eggs and honey, which
seemed very quickly to dispel the young men's fatigue and
chills. As they toasted one another's triumphs and boasted of
the size of the day's kill, Adam stood by his father's side,
holding on to the tails of Deveril's broadcloth frock-coat and
wearing his Tilbury which, being sizes too big, fell over the
child's forehead.

Yesterday, Lady McDoone had smiled at Clemency and
said:

'The men boast the more because *you* are there, my dear!'
Noting Clemency's blushes, she had patted her hand, adding:
'You are very pretty, child, and you should make the most of
that asset. You are only twenty-two years old, and you do not
want to remain a widow for the rest of your life. That young
man with the chestnut-coloured hair – Mr Dominic Wade –
now he would make an excellent match. His family are quite

well connected, I believe, and he is a bachelor. Moreover, he cannot keep his eyes from you, my dear. You should encourage him. I trust I do not offend you by speaking so bluntly?'

'There is no offence taken, Lady McDoone,' Clemency had said quickly, 'but I am not in search of a husband. I am content here at Castle Clunes with you and Adam.'

Fortunately, Clemency thought, as she took Adam's hand to go downstairs, the old lady did not pursue the subject, for there was no possible way that she could have given the true reason why she was not interested in finding a husband – that she hoped by the following spring to be on her way with Adam to her father's house in Fort William. And even that would not have been the entire truth, she thought. The pleasant-looking Mr Wade, despite his charm and good manners, did not arouse in her even the slightest desire for flirtation, let alone romancing. It would have been difficult not to like him; indeed, she liked all the young men Deveril had invited to shoot with him. Not one of them treated her as an employee, but teased her gently as they might have done Deveril's sister. It was only Deveril who did not treat her as such. He flirted in the most outrageous fashion when they were in company, and on the few occasions they were alone, he paid her compliments in a low, intense voice that did far more to disturb her than his flippant gallantry. She openly ignored him, but inwardly she knew herself affected; and now as always, she steeled herself to go into the same room with him with a carefully assumed indifference.

Nevertheless, her heart jolted when she saw him standing, legs astride, his back to Lady McDoone's blazing fire. Adam left her side and ran to his father.

'It is true, is it not, Uncle 'Vril, that we are to have a masquerade?'

Deveril ruffled the boy's hair, his eyes laughing as he looked over Adam's head at Clemency.

'Indeed it is, and we shall require your help, Ma'am, since we intend to invite all our neighbours. Invitations will have to be written, and I understand from my aunt that you pen a very neat hand.'

Clemency obeyed Lady McDoone's indication to go and sit beside her.

'I will prepare a list of guests with my nephew this evening, my dear,' she said, 'and you may begin your task tomorrow. It will take a little time, I fear. We will be inviting some forty families, although I doubt very much if all of them will be able to come at such short notice. The ball is to take place on Friday week, before my nephew and his friends return to London.'

Adam left his father's side to go to Clemency.

'You will need time to make a costume, Forrie,' he said, his face solemn. 'Uncle 'Vril says lots of people will come disguised as well as masked. You could be the Lady of Shalott in Aunt Meg's new book Uncle 'Vril gave her, 'cos you live in a sort of tower, do you not, Forrie?'

Lady McDoone laughed.

'I was telling Adam the story of Mr Tennyson's new poem this morning,' she said. 'It has a very easy rhythm to it, and I am not surprised that the boy has remembered it, although it ends so sadly. I consider Mr Tennyson to be a very talented young man, and 'tis my opinion that we have not had so promising an English poet since that tragic boy Lord Byron died.'

Clearly amused by his son's suggestion to Clemency, Deveril said:

'While it is true that Mrs Forest has one of the turret rooms, Adam, it is to be hoped that there is no curse upon her as there was upon the poor Lady of Shalott. You would not wish her to drown by her own folly as did the lovely damsel in the story?'

Adam regarded his father uneasily, but seeing that Deveril was only teasing him, he turned back to Clemency.

'It was her own fault that she drowned,' he said solemnly, 'because she looked out of her casement window when she had been told not to, because she wanted to see Sir Lancelot, but *I* think . . .'

Clemency laid a restraining hand on his shoulder.

'You are being a chatterbox again, Adam,' she said. 'In any case, I shall not be attending the ball since I . . .'

'Indeed you will, my dear,' Lady McDoone broke in. 'I shall need you with me for one thing, tied as I am to this miserable chair; besides which, my nephew tells me there may be a dearth of unattached young ladies and later in the evening, he and all his friends will be requiring dancing partners for the reels.'

Clemency's cheeks reddened.

'I fear I am not familiar with any of the Scottish dances . . .' she began, but this time it was Deveril who interrupted her.

'Forgive me, Ma'am, but that is insufficient excuse. We shall all practise the reels this week and you will very soon become accomplished. We shall have dancing lessons of an evening instead of cards and Adam shall be present, too.'

Adam ran back to his father, his small face bright with excitement.

'I will be very good and do everything I am told, I promise!' he cried.

Lady McDoone laughed.

'"Promises are like pie-crust, lightly made and easily broken",' she quoted. 'Away with you now, young man, for it is long past your bedtime and your nurse will be searching for you.'

Dutifully, Adam kissed his great-aunt's hand and then Clemency's, as she had taught him to do. As he left the room, Deveril looked after him delightedly.

'At last the boy is learning to comport himself in a drawing-room,' he commented; 'thanks, no doubt, to your efforts, Ma'am,' he added with a grateful look at Clemency.

It was on the tip of Clemency's tongue to retort sharply that it was the least she, his mother, could do; but she managed somehow to withhold the words. It always irritated her profoundly when she felt that Deveril was patronizing her, although even she herself doubted if this was really his intent. But he should save his pretty compliments, if such they were, for other ears, she thought bitterly. He might not know it, but his attentions to her were unwelcome and deeply resented . . . the more so because against her will, she felt herself responding to them. It was unfair, she thought, that he should have been blessed with such exceptional good looks. With his dark hair tousled and curling from his day's outing, his tall figure manly and yet distinguished in his shooting attire, he drew the eye as if by some magnetic force. Nor could she ignore that look of provocative amusement in his dark eyes, which always seemed to linger over-long on her.

While Lady McDoone engaged him in conversation, she tried to turn her thoughts to Benjamin. His letters arrived with punctual regularity every week, each one only thinly disguising his affection for her and his loneliness, but reflecting her own joy in her reunion with Adam.

His unselfishness made her feel guilty, since she so rarely thought of Benjamin now that she was living at Castle Clunes with her son. It was only when one of his letters arrived that she remembered him. Indeed, she thought far more often of his father, the Professor, since Lady McDoone referred frequently to his beautiful book. Clemency wished very much that she was not growing so fond of the old lady, whose kindness and consideration towards her were in daily evidence. She seemed to respect Clemency's reticence and never pursued questions about her childhood, which she sensed Clemency wanted to avoid. But frequently they discussed Clemency's short employment with Caroline Norton. Lady McDoone seemed intrigued by the irrelevancies of the trial of Lord Melbourne, and although she sympathized with the novelist, she insisted that Caroline had behaved unwisely and indiscreetly to say the least, thus bringing upon her own head her subsequent rejection by Society. The old lady approved Clemency's defence of her friend, but could not share in her bitter outcry regarding her three young boys.

'If they mean as much to her as you imply, my dear, Mrs Norton would go back to her husband on whatever terms he demands.'

'Even although he was physically violent towards her on occasions?' Clemency had argued, 'or that it was Caroline who supported her husband with money *she* had earned? What right has he to prior claim upon their children?'

'The right of the law!' Lady McDoone had replied. 'One cannot disregard the law of the land, child.'

But it was *her* intention to do so, Clemency reflected. As soon as she had fully gained Adam's confidence and love, she would remove him for ever from England and his father. But her own father's last letter had made it clear that the winters in the North Americas were so cruelly cold and of such severity that even the most hardened trapper could not travel far in safety. She must not think of leaving before the early spring.

Perhaps that would be soon enough, Clemency thought now, as she watched Deveril seat himself beside the fire and pull his son on to his lap. The boy had begged to be allowed a further five minutes before going to bed and Deveril had relented. Adam's dark head now nestled against his father's shoulder and his young face had an expression of relaxed contentment and happiness. There had been several occasions before Deveril had come to Castle Clunes when Adam had sat just so on *her* lap, his head on *her* shoulder, Clemency thought jealously. But soon, she comforted herself, Deveril would be gone back to London and the boy would be wholly hers again.

For the following two days, Clemency was kept fully occupied writing out the invitations to the Castle Clunes Masquerade. It was the first big party to be held there since Deveril's seventeenth birthday, Lady McDoone informed her, and it would do the staff a world of good, for she was too lax with them as a rule and they did not have nearly enough to do. Extra girls were brought up from the village to help scrub the big reception rooms and bedrooms. Curtains were taken down and cleaned along with the portraits, pictures and ornaments. In the kitchen, Cook and her minions roasted, baked, boiled and jellied from dawn to dusk. Footmen were despatched to buy extra provisions and gardeners were brought in to move the heavy furniture for the cleaning maids. Fresh candles were put in all the candelabra, and the oak floor of the ballroom was polished until Lady McDoone warned that the dancers would never keep their feet if it was made to shine much brighter.

As the heap of invitations grew, footmen delivered them to the recipients, some of whom lived several hours distant. Despite the short notice given, the number of acceptances surprised Lady McDoone, if not Deveril.

'It is so long since we last entertained on so large a scale, dearest Aunt,' he said with wry humour, 'that I daresay most of our guests are coming simply to assure themselves we are still alive. How many can we expect so far?'

'At least a hundred,' Lady McDoone replied, 'and thirty of those will require accommodation for the night. I suppose we do have sufficient number of beds!'

'With seventy bedrooms, I would imagine so,' Deveril laughed good-naturedly.

It was Clemency's next task to apportion the rooms, Lady McDoone providing her with the degrees of rank of their expected guests so that the best rooms were provided for those who would expect them. Their personal servants, too, must be accommodated near at hand to see to their masters' and mistresses' requirements.

Gradually, the bustle and excitement reached Clemency herself, and despite her earlier reluctance to be present at the masquerade, she sat up late into the night stitching the white muslin gown that she had agreed to wear to please Adam. The little boy was exhilarated and ran from room to room chattering ceaselessly. It seemed he knew what costume his Uncle 'Vril intended to wear but had been sworn to secrecy.

Clemency tried very hard to remain withdrawn from the jollity which pervaded the whole household, but gradually, day by day, it became impossible to do so. For a start there were the nightly dancing classes with a piper playing the reels while Dominic Wade took on the guise of dancing master and gave instruction. Clemency was the only one who was unfamiliar with the steps, but to put her at ease, several of the young men made deliberate turns in the wrong direction and there was a great deal of tomfoolery and laughter as Mr Wade tried to restore order. As Clemency was the only female present at these 'classes', two of Deveril's friends adopted the roles of ladies, exaggerating their toe point, mincing about the room fanning themselves, and dipping into ungainly curtseys whenever a dance ended.

'I shall never master the steps,' Clemency cried breathlessly at the end of a reel, 'and it would save a great deal of bother were I to sit out the Scottish dances.'

'You will do no such thing!' Deveril said firmly at her elbow. 'I for one require you to partner me at least for the Strathspey and the supper dance; nor do I doubt for one minute that you will be greatly in demand, since it is most unlikely that any Scots lass will match your beauty even if her dancing *is* more practised than yours.'

It was so difficult to reply to a remark such as that, Clemency thought, as she deliberately moved away from Deveril's side. It had been made in that light teasing tone he so often employed when addressing her, and for her to take offence or protest would seem slightly ridiculous.

Was she really pretty, she wondered, as she undressed later that night to go to bed. Despite the warmth of the fire that still burned cheerfully, the big room was filled with draughts, and she shivered as she stood in her long white nightgown surveying her reflection in the cheval mirror. She reached up and felt the soft swell of her breasts. They were more shapely now since Adam's birth, more womanly. Her hips were rounder, too.

She leant forward and studied her face. She looked pale and tired, and rubbing her cheeks with her fingertips brought only the faintest colour to them. But her mouth was full and red, she consoled herself, and her eyes shone a bright deep blue. She was fortunate that despite the pale gold of her hair, her lashes were dark and curled upwards in a way Caroline had described as 'beguiling'.

With a sigh, she turned away from the mirror and jumped into bed, searching for the welcome warming pan she knew would be there. She must not allow anything to deflect her from her true purpose here, she thought – to win her little boy's love and to escape with him out of the country. Nothing else mattered, least of all her own appearance. To please Adam – and only him – she would appear as pretty a Lady of Shalott as she could make herself. By Saturday, the ball would be over, and by next week, Deveril and his friends would be gone. Soon there would be only Lady McDoone and Adam at Castle Clunes, and life would return to its former peace and serenity.

Clemency's costume, by virtue of its simplicity, was far more striking than she realized, as three days later she made her way along the corridor towards the nursery wing. Those guests who were staying the night had arrived two hours earlier and were now in their bedrooms donning their evening attire. Maids and valets scurried about the corridors carrying jugs of water or armfuls of clothes that had been smoothed with flat-irons below-stairs.

The servants stared at Clemency as she went past, bobbing curtseys or inclining heads as they looked curiously at her unfamiliar face. Her long flowing muslin dress was fastened at the waist with a plait of undyed yarn which one of the footmen had purchased for her in the village. A thinner plait was coiled in her hair, and in one hand she carried a weaver's reed which she and Adam had discovered in the attic beside an old hand loom. Across the bosom of the dress she had embroidered the word CAMELOT, by which she hoped to be recognized by those less familiar than were Adam and Lady McDoone with Mr Tennyson's poem. Her eyes and part of her forehead were concealed behind a white domino.

She had promised to visit Adam before going downstairs and she now discovered him sitting up in his bed, far too excited to be close to sleep despite the lateness of the hour. As Clemency sat down beside him, he gazed at her round-eyed.

'You look so real!' he commented enigmatically. 'Tell me the poem again, Forrie. I can only remember the beginning: "*On either side the river lie, Long fields of barley and of rye, That clothe the wold and meet the sky . . .*"'

'"*And thro' the field the road runs by, To many-towered Camelot,*" Clemency finished for him as she bent down to kiss him. His small arms tightened about her as he returned her embrace.

'You smell all nice and flowery!' he murmured. 'I wish you could stay here with me. I do not want you to go downstairs, Forrie.'

'Whist the noo!' his nurse said sharply from her seat by the fire. 'If that's nae a gae selfish wish ye're mekking, Maister Adam. Puir wee Mrs Forest would be missing a' the plaisure, would she no?'

Adam scowled.

'I suppose so,' he said grudgingly, hugging Clemency closer to him. 'But you like being with me, do you not, Forrie, better'n you like being with anyone else? You love me best in the whole world, do you not?'

'Yes, my darling, I do!' Clemency whispered. 'But I shall have to leave you now because the carriages will be arriving at any minute and it is my duty to help your great-aunt receive the guests.'

The boy sighed and lay back against his pillow, only partly mollified.

'I do not like "duty",' he commented. 'It is always doing

what you do not want to do, instead of what you would like to do!'

Clemency smiled.

'Well, not always. Sometimes it is my duty to read to you, but I very much enjoy doing so. And it is your duty to take care of me when we go out walking together, and you enjoy that. So you see, duties are not always nasty!'

The small face broke without warning into a mischievous smile so reminiscent of his father's that, for a moment, Clemency's heart jolted.

'I will always take care of you when we go walking if you will always read me stories when I want,' he said.

Clemency laughed.

'I am not quite sure if that is a promise or blackmail,' she said, as she rose from the bed. 'And do not ask me what blackmail means, for I have not the time to tell you. Now be a good boy and if I can, I shall bring you up a sweetmeat from the dinner table and put it by your pillow for the morning.'

The child was uppermost in her thoughts as she went slowly down the stairs. The big hall below was ablaze with the hundreds of candles the footmen had lit some time ago. A huge log burned in the big stone grate, and the servants stood at their posts like colourful statues in their green and silver livery-white wigs and gloves, and silver-buckled shoes.

Lady McDoone smiled approvingly at Clemency as one of the footmen pushed her chair into the hall. She was not wearing costume but held a black mask in her hands.

'You look charming, my dear,' she said, just as Deveril appeared at the top of the staircase in company with Dominic Wade. Both were in costume, and there was no mistaking Deveril's identity, for he wore a large red cross on his chest and carried a silver bugle hung from his baldric. Clemency felt her cheeks burn as, remembering Mr Tennyson's poem, she recognized Sir Lancelot, the bold knight in the story who tempted the Lady of Shalott to abandon the safety of her tower to follow him to Camelot. It was outrageous of Deveril to have so disguised himself, she thought, refusing to meet his laughing eyes.

But now the great front door had been opened to receive the first arrivals, and Clemency could see a steady stream of carriages, their lanterns lighting the driveway as they waited their turn to disgorge their occupants.

For over half an hour, she stood beside Lady McDoone's chair as she and Deveril received their guests – local landowners or dignitaries from towns such as Perth, Dunkeld and Crieff. They were accompanied by their sons and daughters and any other relatives who were living or staying with them. For the most part, the young people were costumed, but the older guests, like Lady McDoone, were only masked. When it seemed that nearly all the visitors had arrived, Deveril said to his great-aunt:

'I think we should begin the dancing. I will take our lovely Lady of Shalott into the Great Hall and start the ball with the Reel of Tulloch . . .' He turned to smile down at Clemency. 'We practised it last night, you will recall, so you have no need to be nervous.'

Before she could protest, he put his hand beneath her arm and ushered her upstairs to the Great Hall, which stretched almost the entire length of the first floor. Curtains were now drawn across the many tall windows overlooking the garden. Huge logs burned in the Carrara marble fireplaces at each end of the big room, and the beautiful Waterford chandeliers hanging from the coloured stucco ceiling were ablaze with light. The candle flames were reflected in the gilt-framed pier-glass mirrors lining the walls.

At one end of the ballroom was the gallery where the musicians – pipers and fiddlers – were concealed behind screens, awaiting Deveril's signal to begin playing. As he raised his hand in their direction, the bagpipes struggled into life and suddenly the Reel of Tulloch filled the room. In a matter of minutes, the floor was crowded with men and their partners as they made up their sets.

It was the first ball Clemency had ever attended, and in the light of the circumstances which had brought her to Castle Clunes, she had not expected to enjoy it. But as the evening wore on, she found it impossible not to react as would any young girl in her early twenties who was discovering herself, if not the Belle of the Ball, then one of the most sought-after dancing partners. There was not only Dominic Wade at her side paying her compliments, but a host of other young men, too; and Deveril was never far away. It was he who took her into the dining-room where a table running the length of one entire wall was covered with the most delicious dishes of food.

Deveril was obviously enjoying himself, and Clemency noticed that wherever he went a circle of admiring females soon gathered around him. But he was never inattentive to her, and she did not know whether to feel flattered or embarrassed by his compliments and his undisguised possessiveness.

Patently displeasing to her were the attentions of a certain Mr Robert McUist – a big red-headed Scot in full Highland dress. He had massive shoulders and hands which, when they clasped Clemency's back, seemed unpleasantly hot and sticky. His voice was loud, his florid complexion reddened still further by the excessive number of goblets of whisky punch he drained whenever a footman proffered a tray of liquid refreshments. He was, he informed Clemency, from the very north of Scotland and his parents were friends of Lord and Lady Lawrence. He and a party of friends had been lent a shooting lodge not far from Strath Clunes for the season.

'If I had known you were heer, I would have paid ma respects tae Lady McDoone weeks past,' he told Clemency with a look which struck her as being more of a leer than a friendly smile. His eyes roved constantly and with far too much familiarity over her body. Unwittingly, she was reminded of those distressing afternoons in Miss Fothergill's parlour with her late uncle.

In a most ungentlemanly way, Mr McUist ignored her refusal to dance with him a third time and by sheer physical force, dragged her onto the floor for an eightsome reel. Ten minutes later, he claimed her yet again for a quadrille at the end of which she firmly excused herself, saying that it was high time she went to see if her employer needed her services.

By now, it was past midnight but Lady McDoone had not retired to bed. She was happily playing whist in the card room with two other ladies and a General. With a smile at Clemency, she told her to 'away and enjoy yourself, child. There is nothing I require!'

Loath to be claimed yet again by the odious Mr McUist, Clemency paused in the hall, uncertain whether to retire to bed herself. But the strains of a beautiful waltz reached her ears at the same time as Deveril appeared from the Great Hall, his face lighting up as he espied her.

'There you are,' he said. 'I was searching for you as I particularly want you to partner me in this waltz.' His tone was low and persuasive. 'I think I mentioned that I had engaged an orchestra from Perth to play the modern dances.'

He put his hand beneath her arm, taking it for granted that she would go with him, Clemency thought resentfully, but knowing herself without the strength of will to refuse him.

'This is one of Mr Johann Strauss's compositions called "Tauberil-Waltzer",' Deveril informed her. 'I heard it in Vienna when I was there a year or so ago, and I believe Mr Strauss is becoming very popular throughout Europe. Are you not pleased that I insisted you learn the steps?'

He was laughing, and yet there was a different look in his eyes that she could not define as they entered the Great Hall and he put his arm around her waist.

Clemency had always loved music, and now the haunting lilt of the Viennese composer's beautiful melody relaxed the tension in her body, which seemed of its own accord to melt into Deveril's embrace. Her heart thudded and her breathing quickened as the room swirled around her. Deveril was looking down into her eyes, and much as she longed to do so, she could not withdraw her own from the questioning gaze. There must have been at least thirty couples dancing, and yet it seemed as if they were alone on the floor.

Involuntarily, Clemency's eyes closed. She felt her thoughts winging back over the years to a summer's night in the cornfield; to the half-forgotten sweetness of Deveril's kisses, his touch on her body, her own breathless expectation and excitement. No matter what had been told her afterwards, at the time it had seemed right, beautiful, inevitable; and the same feeling was with her now. It was useless to tell herself that she hated this man; that he had wronged her most cruelly, not once but a second time when he had stolen her child from her. But those feelings were in her mind, whereas her heart and her body were telling her that she wanted this dance to go on for ever; that she could stay for the rest of her life here in this room in Deveril's arms.

He continued to hold her for a moment or two after the music stopped.

'I have the strangest feeling that you and I have danced together before,' he murmured. 'Yet it cannot have been so, since my aunt tells me you have never been in Society.'

Clemency had by now recovered her senses. In as curt a tone as she could command, she said:

'We have met but twice before, Lord Burnbury; at Poole when your yacht was beached, and at the New Theatre in Brighton during the period of my employment by Professor Brook!'

The serious expression left Deveril's eyes and he laughed.

'Ah yes, you helped the redoubtable Doctor Brook's father with his book. Tell me, Ma'am, you are not really going to marry that worthy physician, are you?'

Clemency's cheeks flamed.

'I do not consider that is any of your business,' she said sharply.

Unabashed, Deveril replied calmly:

'In a way it is, for I do not think you are in the least aware how very much better you could do for yourself. You are a

very beautiful and fascinating young woman and, if it should
interest you to know it, my friend Wade is much taken with
you. So too . . .' he added with a frown, 'is that rather objec-
tionable Highlander who has been pursuing you all evening.
A most uncouth gentleman, if indeed he can be called a
gentleman at all.'

'You seem to have been taking a great deal of interest in
my affairs this evening,' Clemency remarked coldly. 'I am quite
capable of conducting my own life without your help, Sir. I
have done so for many years, and do not require your advice.'

Deveril laughed.

'I really do not know why you should always feel the need
to rebuff me,' he said. 'More especially as my concern for you
is quite genuine. My aunt has told me that life has not treated
you kindly, and I would like to see the future happier for you.'

Clemency looked away from his searching gaze and said
harshly:

'Then if you are genuine in your concern, Sir, you will
respect my wishes and leave me alone.'

Deveril looked upon the point of a reply, but the music had
begun once more and, with a sigh, he bowed over her hand.

'I fear I have promised this dance to Lady Cynthia Menzies.
If you will excuse me . . . And here is Wade to claim this
dance with you – lucky young devil you are, too, Wade!' he
added with a grin, as he disappeared into the crowd.

Throughout the dance Clemency's thoughts remained with
Deveril. Her eyes searched for him and noted the dark beauty
of the girl in his arms. He was smiling down at her as if *she*
were now the most important woman in his life. Well, I do
not care, Clemency thought. He is nothing to me, and I must
never forget that he is my enemy – and always will be.

Nevertheless as he disappeared amongst the dancers she
wished him back, for the big Highlander Robert McUist was
suddenly once more at her side, and she could feel his hot
damp hand through the thin muslin of her dress as he tried
to urge her onto the floor.

'Please forgive me, but I am tired and do not wish to dance, Sir,' she said. At first he ignored her protests, but then he laughed.

'Verra wull, Mistress Forest. We will sit the dance oot taegither!'

Without manners enough to wait for her acquiescence, he took her arm and pulled her after him out of the ballroom, down the stairs and into the deserted gunroom, kicking the door shut behind them with his black buckled shoe. It was immediately obvious to Clemency that he was now very drunk. She could smell the whisky on his breath as, without warning, he pulled her roughly into his arms.

'Dinna refuse me a kiss!' he muttered. As she struggled to release herself, turning her head aside, he added: 'Be done with those airs and graces ma fine lady. I know verra wull ye're nae mair than a servant in this hoose for a' they've let ye attend the ball the nicht.'

'Let me go this instant!' Clemency cried, 'or I will ring for the footman. Let me go . . .'

But his loud laughter drowned her words, and powerless to release herself from his massive arms, Clemency felt his mouth hard against her own. At the same moment, the man began to fumble with the bodice of her gown, pushing his hand roughly beneath the soft fabric until he could feel her breast. The material tore open and she tried ineffectually to twist her head away. The man's breathing quickened as he forced one knee between her legs, only his kilt and the thin muslin of her skirt protecting her from this further contact.

Clemency's anger gave way to fear. She still could not believe that this huge drunken Scot was about to rape her, here under the roof of Lady McDoone's house where he was a guest. Even if it were true that her status was that of a servant, he surely could not believe that gave him the right to behave like an animal. But he seemed quite impervious to her struggles as her arms flailed in a useless attempt to fight him off. When finally he drew his head away and she cried out, he merely laughed, muttering that he liked a girl with spirit, but that she might as well submit since he fully intended to have his way with her.

Without warning, the door opened and a voice like a gunshot echoed round the room.

'Let her go! Do you hear me, McUist. *Let her go!*'

There was no slackening of the man's hold upon her, and the momentary relief Clemency had felt when she heard Deveril's voice quickly evaporated.

'If you do not let her go this instant, McUist, I shall kill you!'

She could feel the man's laughter, or was it anger, as his hold upon her tightened.

'So the girl's your doxy, is she, Burnbury? Wull man, ye'll hae tae fight me fur her. I'll not let her go on *ye're* command!'

'Indeed you will!' Deveril's voice was ice cold as he took a step towards the Highlander. 'Were it not for the fact that you are obviously too drunk to know what you are doing, I would call you out. Instead I shall have you thrown out – if you have not the decency to remove your unwelcome presence immediately. Do I make myself clear?'

To Clemency's intense relief, the man's hold upon her slackened, and slowly he dropped his hands to his sides and shrugged his shoulders.

'Hae it ye're ain way, Burnbury. I didna think the wee lass was a' that important tae ye. I'll nae fight ye for a hussy for a' she's a pretty one.'

He wiped the sweat from his forehead with the back of his hand, and with a fatuous smile on his reddened face, he pushed past Deveril and staggered out into the hall.

Deveril hurried to Clemency's side.

'Are you all right, Ma'am? I cannot apologize adequately for such a disgraceful exhibition of bad manners beneath my roof. Perhaps I *should* have called him to account . . . fellow deserved no less . . .'

His dark eyes were flashing so angrily that Clemency forgot

her own embarrassment and, fearing lest he should hurry after the Highlander and force him to a duel, she murmured:

'As you say, he was very far from sober, and I doubt if he intended to insult me . . .' Without warning, her voice broke as the full horror of the past ten minutes finally overcame her. Seeing the pallor of her face and believing she might faint, Deveril put his arms around her, his fury with McUist forgotten as all that was most protective and chivalrous in his nature rose to the fore.

'I should have killed him!' he muttered darkly. 'I dare not think what worse harm might have befallen had I not come in search of you. Fortunately, one of the footmen saw McUist drag you into this room.'

Clemency tried to smile.

'You have proved yourself a veritable Sir Lancelot!' she said shakily. 'I am grateful for your timely rescue, Sir!'

At almost the same instant as Deveril, Clemency realized that his arms were still around her. Instinctively she stiffened and made as if to move away, but he retained his hold on her. Putting one hand beneath her chin, he tilted her face upward so that she was forced to meet his eyes. They were gentle, without threat, and yet at the same time they seemed to burn into her very soul.

'McUist was right in one thing, you are *very* pretty. I cannot in all faith entirely blame him for succumbing to temptation. No man could hold you in his arms and remain unmoved. Mrs Forest . . . no, I cannot call you that . . . I shall call you by your true name, Clemency. *Clemency* . . . all evening long I have wondered if I might claim a kiss. I do so now, not as the right of your rescuer but given of your own free will?'

Clemency's eyes closed as she tried despairingly to ignore the demand in that dark, compelling gaze; to slow the tumultuous beat of her heart; to deny the terrible urgency of her own desire to lift her mouth to his. With a sense bordering on panic, she reminded herself that this man was married; that there could never be any love between them; that above all, he was her enemy, the man who had stolen her child and hidden him from her.

'No, no!' she whispered, but her denial came too late. Deveril's lips were on hers, and against her will, her body melted into his until it seemed they were a single being.

For one long moment, Clemency allowed herself to drown in the turbulence of senses and emotions which enveloped her. For one long moment, she permitted herself to return his kisses, her own as desperate and demanding as his.

We belong, he and I! she thought, and then sanity returned. Feverishly, frantically, she pushed him away.

'Never, never!' she cried violently as he stared at her uncomprehendingly. Her voice rose. 'Do you understand? I do not want you to touch me – kiss me – *ever again!*'

Unaware of the tears that were spilling down her cheeks, she gathered the torn edges of her dress together, and without daring to look at Deveril's disbelieving face, she ran past him out of the room.

CHAPTER TWENTY-TWO

October–November 1836

'It is not bad news, Madame?'

Muriel regarded her maid's sympathetic face and decided that there could be no harm in confiding her true feelings to Celeste. It was becoming her habit these days to treat her French maid as a confidante. The woman's unerring ability to soothe her mistress's ruffled feelings invited this intimacy.

Muriel had first met the maid in Paris almost three years ago, when her own girl had suddenly and most inopportunely contracted the smallpox. The Comtesse de Maurois had gracefully rescued Muriel from her predicament, offering to let her have Celeste for the remainder of the Grand Tour. The Frenchwoman had proved such an excellent worker, and personal support to her new mistress, that Muriel had decided to risk the consequences as far as the Comtesse was concerned and bring Celeste back to England.

Deveril had been furious – far more angry, in fact, than Muriel had anticipated, asking how could she repay the Comtesse's kindness in such an immoral manner and going on for hours about the ethics of the matter. Her reply, that Celeste had begged to be permitted to accompany her to England, had done little to mollify him. Now, nearly three years later, it was a *fait accompli* and even Deveril accepted Celeste as part of his wife's personal entourage. Not that he liked the Frenchwoman any the better, complaining that she fawned upon Muriel in a quite unnatural way, and that the only time Celeste's ugly countenance bore any relation to humanity was when she was brushing Muriel's hair or smoothing unguents into her skin.

'Why, I do believe you are jealous – of my maid!' Muriel had once accused him, but she had quickly regretted the taunt, for Deveril had looked quite disgusted and walked out of the room in a huff.

'Yes, I am afraid it *is* bad news, Celeste,' she said now, as the maid fastened an emerald necklace around her throat and proffered her gloves and fan. 'Lord Burnbury has sent word to say he is detained in Scotland for a further two weeks. I am *most* put out.'

'But Madame, it means that Monsieur le Vicomte will not be with you on your birthday!' Celeste's voice held just the right amounts of criticism, reproach and sympathy.

Muriel picked up her reticule and allowed Celeste to place her chinchilla boa lovingly around her white neck.

'That is exactly my point,' she said petulantly. 'I suppose as usual he has forgotten, just as he forgets every occasion of importance to me.'

'*Les hommes!*' Celeste murmured. '*Ma pauvre Madame.*'

Muriel did not need reminding that Celeste's opinion of men was very far from complimentary.

'He writes that the shooting has never been better and begs me not to begrudge him this extra two weeks in Scotland,' she said. 'It is really too bad. I had booked seats for Rossini's *William Tell* and now I suppose I must cancel them.'

Celeste began picking up Muriel's discarded garments as she said:

'Perhaps Madame would consider offering Signor Fonelli the chance to escort her? It would not be the same pleasure, of course, but at least Madame need not miss the enjoyment of the evening.'

Muriel looked doubtful. Her singing master was sixty, balding, and boring with his ceaseless chatter about all the famous singers he had taught in his younger days. Nevertheless, he was one of the few men with whom she could be seen *à deux* at the opera without causing comment.

Her face softened almost to a smile as she patted Celeste's hand.

'That is not a bad suggestion, my dear Celeste,' she said, knowing that the endearment would bring a flush of pleasure to the woman's sallow cheeks. 'Now I must hurry, or Mama will be fussing that I have come to some harm. I shall not be late back.'

There was no necessity for Muriel to instruct the maid to wait up for her, as Celeste would do so whether Muriel requested it or offered her the evening off. Nothing would prevent her nightly ritual of tucking Muriel safely between the warm sheets, she often declared, for she could not sleep without first reassuring herself that her beloved mistress was no longer in need of any little service.

There were moments, however few, when Celeste's devotion could be irritating, Muriel thought, as the coachman drove her to her parents' house in Grosvenor Square. At such times, she would snap at Celeste or dismiss her, and not give a fig for the fact that the maid would be weeping until such time as Muriel sent for her once more. It needed only one kind word or a smile to restore Celeste's uncomplaining attentions to her requirements.

'I am your faithful shadow, am I not, Madame?' Celeste quite often remarked, and it was true that she was never far from call, hovering in the background ready even to lift Muriel's handkerchief if it fell to the floor.

She was present, therefore, when Mrs Jacobs, the house-keeper, requested an interview on the morning following the arrival of Deveril's letter. Muriel sighed as she told the butler he could send Mrs Jacobs to the morning-room to see her. The housekeeper only asked for an interview when she had had trouble with one of the servants and wished to dismiss them.

'Well, what is it this time, Mrs Jacobs?' she asked as the woman bobbed a curtsey and stood red-faced, fumbling with her bunch of keys with one hand while she held tightly to a terrified servant girl standing behind her.

'It's Olive, Milady,' the housekeeper said. She looked flustered and more out of countenance than was customary in such circumstances. 'She'll have to go, Milady, and this very morning. I'll not have her a minute longer under this roof. Disgraceful! Shameful! I doant know as how ever I can tell you about it, Milady!'

Muriel's curiosity was momentarily aroused. Whatever the wretched scullery-maid had done, it was more than a failure to please Cook in her duties. Mrs Jacobs would intervene only in a matter of morals. The girl, who looked to be about sixteen years of age, was holding her none-too-clean apron to her eyes and her shoulders were shaking with half-muffled sobs.

'You had best speak frankly, Mrs Jacobs,' she said. 'I have not much time to spare. What has the girl done?'

Olive's sobs now intensified as the housekeeper replied:

'It is not a matter of what she has done exactly, Milady. It's what I found in her bedroom.' She reached in her apron pocket and drew out a dog-eared piece of newsprint which she handed reluctantly to Muriel.

Muriel regarded the dirty piece of paper with distaste.

'And what is it about?' she queried.

Mrs Jacobs' mouth tightened.

'I cannot speak about it, Milady, it's that scurrilous! First I thought it my duty to burn it, but . . . well, Milady, it occurred to me as how you might want to call a constable . . .'

Muriel's curiosity was now fully aroused. She walked away from Mrs Jacobs' excited eyes, and in the comparative privacy of the bay window, she studied the offending paper. It was a cutting from an article by a journalist called Richard Carlile, published in his periodical *The Republican*. The name was familiar to Muriel, for she recalled that the man had recently served a term in prison (by no means his first) for publishing material considered to be obscene.

Naturally, neither Muriel nor any of her woman friends had read these publications, but she had heard a rumour that the subject matter concerned the moral depravity of the women and girls working in factories. The much-read piece of paper she now held would appear to be one of the hand-bills distributed by those who supported Mr Carlile's opinions, she thought, as she read that it was intended for '*the Married of Both Sexes of the Working People*'.

Muriel's interest quickened, and a faint colour stained her cheeks as with a faint feeling of guilt, she allowed her eyes to scan the context.

'. . . It is not intended to produce vice and debauchery, but to destroy vice and put an end to debauchery . . . working people on low wages cannot maintain their children . . . How are we to avoid the miseries . . . premature deaths . . . privations . . . avoid having more children than they wish to have and can easily maintain . . .'

Muriel's gasp was only just subdued enough not to reach the ears of the servants. Was it possible, she wondered, that this document was about to inform her that there was a method by which the advent of unwanted children could be avoided? If so . . .

Her eyes returned to the print as she read on eagerly:

'What is done by other people is this. A piece of soft sponge is tied by a bobbin or penny ribbon, and inserted before sexual intercourse takes place, and is withdrawn again as soon as it has taken place.

'. . . they take care not to use the same sponge again until it has been washed. If the sponge be large enough, that is, as large as a green walnut, or a small apple, it will prevent conception without diminishing the pleasures of married life, or doing the least injury to the health of the most delicate woman . . .'

Muriel read no further. Although deeply shocked, her heart was nevertheless thudding with an excitement which she knew she must somehow conceal from the servants. With a proper display of indignation, she turned to Mrs Jacobs.

'The girl must be dismissed immediately and without a character. I am shocked almost beyond words by this . . . this revolting document . . . and to think that it has been brought into this respectable household . . . get the girl out of my presence, Mrs Jacobs. I shall not call the constabulary, for how could I possibly bring myself to show this . . . this horrible, improper, disgraceful piece of evidence to the police. You may consider yourself fortunate, Olive, that you have got off so lightly . . .'

It did not concern Muriel that without a character, there was little likelihood that the scullery-maid would ever again find work in domestic service; that if she was to survive, she would now have to go into a factory where slave labour virtually prevailed; or even end up on the streets as a common prostitute. Eight out of every fifty factory girls ended up as streetwalkers, very often as a means of survival. But Muriel neither knew nor cared about such matters and still less about the ultimate fate of her scullery-maid.

As Mrs Jacobs hurried the sobbing girl out of the room, Celeste stepped forward from the shadows.

'Can I fetch a shawl for you, Madame?' she enquired solicitously. 'You are shivering!'

'I am not cold!' Muriel retorted, as she allowed Celeste to lead her to a chair. 'I am just a little *bouleversée* as you would say in France.'

'Madame is shocked?' Celeste enquired curiously. She had seen Muriel in most of her moods and knew how to cope with them, but she had seldom seen her so visibly perturbed . . . or was it excited?

Muriel hesitated. Although she enjoyed gossiping with her friends about the trivial affairs of Society, she was reticent about herself, and most particularly about her relationship with Deveril. Other married women might talk at length about their husbands' shortcomings and even, upon occasion, their behaviour in bed, but Muriel preferred to keep to herself the knowledge that she and Deveril had not shared the marriage bed for many years – not, in fact, since the stillbirth of her child, when the physician had pronounced it dangerous to her health ever to have another. It was not that she had any desire for a more intimate relationship with Deveril. Other women might envy her so physically fascinating a husband, but Muriel felt no such attraction. The very intimacy of marital union offended her fastidious nature, and she had been glad to have the physician's warning to keep Deveril away.

But more and more frequently these past few years, Muriel had questioned the advisability of maintaining this gulf between them. She had never forgotten her mother's dictum – that to deny a husband his rights was to throw him into the arms of a mistress. She suspected he enjoyed the occasional discreet affair to which she was prepared to turn a blind eye, but of late she was growing very concerned about his behaviour in Scotland. Despite the length of the journey, he went more and more frequently and stayed for longer and longer periods, and she could not ignore the possibility that he kept a mistress up there. She feared that people could be talking behind her back, and she did not believe Deveril's assurances that it was his nephew and not a woman tempting him over the border.

There had been several occasions when she had made up her mind to travel with him on his next visit, to see for herself if she had need to be worried. But Deveril had an infuriating habit of deciding at the last minute that he would leave the next day when her diary was full and it was too late for her to cancel her engagements. Or else he would choose to go when the weather was so appalling that only a madman would consider travelling for six days in such conditions.

Muriel's hands tightened about the paper she was still grasping. Here, perhaps, lay the answer to her problem. If the facts were true, she could explain them to Deveril and pretend an eagerness to resume their married relationship. He need be in no fear that her life would be at risk, and once satisfied beneath his own roof, he would have no need of a mistress. But could she be sure the method described in the handbill was effective? There was no female with whom she was on such terms of intimacy that she could ask advice on so delicate a matter. But she could ask Celeste . . . in an indirect way . . . as if it were mere curiosity that prompted the question. Celeste was no silly young girl, but a woman approaching forty who had lived most of her life in Paris, a city surely embracing as many vices as London! Celeste had proved herself a fount of extraordinary pieces of information relating to females, such as the dusting of a dark powder between the breasts to make them appear larger by deepening the cleft; or a remedy for Muriel's monthly pains consisting of thirty drops of laudanum with five drops of tincture of belladonna.

She looked now at her maid's attentive face and said:

'It would do no harm for you to see this, Celeste. It is indeed a shocking article for a young unmarried servant girl to have in her possession. However, it seems to be worded most authoritatively and I wondered if you yourself have ever heard the subject discussed.'

Celeste's expression retained its inscrutability as she carefully perused the information. It was not the first time she had heard of the subject of controlling the births of children, but she had not hitherto seen it in print. She returned the paper to her mistress without embarrassment.

'I do not question its authenticity,' she said, 'for I have heard it remarked that women of the streets seldom burden themselves with unwanted offspring. One must assume, do you not agree, Madame, that a method of avoiding conception is well known to them.'

Muriel nodded.

'Who did you hear speak of it, Celeste?' she enquired with pretended casualness.

'I cannot recall who exactly, Madame. But I do know that there are eminent physicians in Paris who are aware it is common practice amongst Frenchwomen to employ the protection of sponges. As a personal maid to several ladies, I could not help but overhear their exchange of intimacies upon subjects such as this.'

Muriel permitted herself a wry smile.

'I can well believe it, Celeste. You stand so quietly in the background that even I forget at times you are there.'

'Which is as it should be, Madame, no?' Celeste enquired. 'But Madame can rely upon me never to discuss her affairs with others.'

Muriel stood up.

'I do not doubt you are the soul of discretion, Celeste. That is why I give you more privileges than the other servants. Now be off and get my reticule. I am already quite shamefully late for my meeting at Fortnum and Mason with the Duchess of Sutherland.'

When Muriel returned home that afternoon, she went straight to her bedroom and removed the handbill from her reticule, where it had been burning a hole in her lap throughout luncheon. Dismissing Celeste, she read it through more carefully. On this second reading, the facts did not have the same shocking effect upon her as they had when first she saw them. The phrasing was educated, and the meaning clearly not intended to give offence so much as information. Dared she, therefore, question her physician on so delicate a subject? Sir John had attended her both during her miscarriage and at the horrible birth of her child, and she could imagine no greater exchange of intimacies when she recalled how shamelessly she had been forced to expose her body to his view and, subsequently, his handling. He had actually had his hands inside her, searching for the unfortunate baby's head. Nor, since she had the handbill, need she be obliged actually to mention the indelicacies referred to, but merely present the paper and ask Sir John's professional opinion.

Her mind made up, Muriel recalled Celeste and told her to

summon her coachman. She was going to call upon Sir John, she said, and Celeste could accompany her.

Although Muriel was obliged to wait for almost half an hour before the physician was free to receive her, her eventual interview with him proved entirely satisfactory. He had, he told her, seen many of these handbills before.

'It may interest you to know, Lady Burnbury, that I have actually met Mr Richard Carlile,' he said, 'and I agree entirely that the practice recommended by him is – I think I quote him correctly – *"a real blessing to weak and sickly females and to those to whom pregnancy and parturition are dangerous"*.'

Seeing that he had Muriel's close attention, he added:

'There are many men of first-rate character and learning who do not consider this practice "indecent". Their numbers include politicians and philosophers. Although initially these benefits were intended to assist the poor and the labouring classes, it is my opinion that they could apply *without disgrace* to other echelons of Society.'

Muriel made her way back to Grayshott House secretly elated. While she did not look forward to putting her new knowledge into practice, she never doubted the rightness of her decision to do so. Deveril would return home to discover a new wife, able and willing to perform her duties. An agreeable surprise awaited him, and her straying husband would be transformed at last into an attentive slave.

Muriel's welcome was certainly a surprise to Deveril. It was late in the evening when he reached London, and he was tired and dispirited. His last few days at Castle Clunes had proved frustrating, to say the least. The beautiful Mrs Forest – Clemency, as he now preferred to think of her – had retired to bed indisposed after the night of the masquerade. He had sent a note via one of the maids to wish her a quick recovery and to tell her he desired to talk to her. But either by deliberation or by virtue of true indisposition, she clearly had no wish to talk to him. He was at a loss to understand her. Not even the questions posed to his great-aunt had enlightened him as to the reason for the girl's hostile attitude towards him. Aunt Meg knew surprisingly little about her. It seemed she had married very young and been widowed almost immediately; but his aunt was not of the opinion that it had been a love-match, since the girl never spoke of her late husband. If her heart was anywhere at all, Aunt Meg told him, it was in the keeping of the physician Doctor Brook, from whom she received weekly letters and to whom she replied as often.

Deveril had been none too happy to hear that Brook held any real importance in Clemency's life. If she truly loved the physician, he told himself, she would not have removed herself to the opposite end of the British Isles where distance would prevent them seeing one another. Moreover, she could not have responded to his kisses with such total abandon, even if within minutes she regretted it. His instinct told him that she was hiding herself away from him not so much because she did not like him but because she did! Was it therefore a matter of morals, he being a married man, that frightened her? he had asked himself repeatedly. It was true that there could never be any question of marriage, but there were many young women in her circumstances who would settle for becoming the mistress of a man of wealth and title.

The history books were full of royal mistresses and Society abounded with them. Was the girl looking for a *respectable* marriage? If so, in kindness he should cease his pursuit of her. But he did not wish to do so. No female had affected him since Anthea Wilcox as this strange, quiet girl had done. Without one word spoken, she succeeded in arresting his attention, disturbing his dreams, occupying his waking thoughts. And not least, he had discovered himself furiously jealous of young Wade, who was free to marry the girl if she cared to have him. As for McUist, he had been close to running a sword through him – as much from jealousy, he knew, as from a duty to protect Clemency's honour.

Although Deveril had delayed his return to London, he had

glimpsed Clemency only on the day of his departure, and then she had spoken no word to him but stood with her arm about Adam's shoulders, comforting the boy, who was weeping at the impending parting with his beloved Uncle 'Vril. On this occasion, Deveril reflected as he drove away from Castle Clunes, it was not just his son he regretted having to leave behind him, but the girl, too!

Nevertheless it was Muriel who occupied his thoughts as his valet undressed him and he climbed into bed. Dismissing the servant, he put out the light and lay back against his pillow, trying not to think of the reproachful glances that his wife would cast at him across the breakfast table in the morning. At first he could not believe his ears when the door opened and he heard Muriel's voice softly calling his name.

He sat up, staring in surprise at the dark-haired woman standing beside his bed, her candle revealing the white frills of her negligée, a questioning smile on her face.

'Muriel, my dear, is something amiss?' he enquired. Surely she had not come to his room at this late hour to berate him?

'No, my dearest, on the contrary. I came to tell you how delighted I was to hear your arrival. I had been lying awake, hoping that you might yet return this night.' She glanced across at the dying embers of the fire Hopkins had struggled to light and which was now flaming feebly, and shivered.

'It is very cold, is it not? Did the servants put a warming pan in your bed as I ordered?'

'Why, thank you, yes!' Deveril said awkwardly. It had not yet occurred to him the true reason for Muriel's nocturnal visit, and he was uncertain how he should receive her in this unaccustomed situation.

'I have missed you – terribly . . .'

Not even Deveril could mistake her tone for reproach. It held a soft warmth he did not understand.

'I missed you, too,' he lied, knowing this much at least was expected of him. 'But Muriel, you will get cold standing there! Should we not talk in the morning?'

But Muriel was undoing the ribbons of her negligée. Beneath her thin robe her nightgown was transparent, revealing the contours of her body. In the golden glow of the single candle, the outlines of her figure appeared softer, more rounded than he recalled. Her waistline was still slender, and with her dark hair tied back with white ribbon matching her negligée she looked many years younger than her age.

She took a step closer to the bed and set the candle upon the side table.

'If I were to climb beneath the coverlets, I should not feel the cold. We have so much to talk about after so long a separation. So long . . .' she murmured in a low seductive tone, 'that I almost feel like a bride. Do you remember the nights of our honeymoon, Deveril?'

With difficulty, he concealed his utter astonishment and pulled back the covers so that Muriel could climb in beside him. This was a Muriel quite unfamiliar to him. Not even on the honeymoon nights to which she had referred could he remember her behaving in so seductive a manner. What could have changed her? He could not imagine that she had come here to his room, to his bed, in such a fashion, unless it was her intention to . . .

Muriel laid her head on his shoulder and put one arm around his waist. Somehow the ribbons of her nightgown had come undone and her naked breasts touched his chest. He could feel their warmth through his nightshirt and his body responded. He had had no woman during his sojourn in Scotland and his need was basic, the more so after the inner conflict aroused in him when he had held Clemency's sweet young body so close to his and felt the fire of her mouth. He had thought of little else since, and his dreams had been tormented with longing for her. Now Muriel was offering herself to him with the promise of release from his desires.

'We have no need to worry!' she was saying. 'I have been to see Sir John whilst you were away, and he has recommended a method by which we may pleasure ourselves without fear that I shall have another child. Does that please you, dearest? You may take me if you wish.'

It was clearly a night of inexplicables, Deveril thought. He was not at all sure to what Muriel was referring, but he presumed she knew exactly what she was about. One thing he could be certain of was that Muriel would not risk having another child.

If Muriel's kisses were ardent, her response otherwise could not be called so. Somewhere in the back of Deveril's mind, as he gave way to his own desire, was an awareness that Muriel's attitude to the intimacies of lovemaking had remained unchanged in the four years since they had last shared a bed. But she was unresisting, and when finally he lay quietly beside her, she sounded well satisfied.

'You are happy to be home now, are you not?' she enquired. 'I want you to be happy, Deveril. I want us to be happy – together!'

More conundrums, Deveril thought, as dutifully he kissed her hand. Had one of her women friends been preaching to her on the subject of keeping her husband satisfied? Or was this some devilish ruse of that furtive French maid of hers? He had never liked or trusted the woman, and although Muriel denied it, Deveril was convinced that Celeste's ill-concealed adoration of her mistress was unhealthy, unnatural. He would have dismissed her were not Muriel so furiously opposed to any such idea. But he was too tired to ponder the matter now, and he was relieved when of her own accord Muriel left the bed and bade him goodnight.

Awakened by Hopkins with his breakfast next morning, he found that his bewilderment had not lessened, and he almost wondered if he had dreamt the entire interlude. But when finally he was dressed and had descended to the morning-room, Muriel was waiting for him with a coy smile. He kissed her proffered cheek and wished irrelevantly that she would not wear purple. The colour did not flatter her sallow cheeks. Nevertheless he managed the compliment expected of him, informing her that she looked charming.

Muriel beamed.

'I have sent word to your dear sister Selina that we shall expect her to luncheon,' she told him. 'And this evening, I have seats for the play at Covent Garden. Helen Faucit is taking the part of Lady Teazle, and I know you admire her talent.'

So life was back to normal, Deveril thought, as he picked up the morning paper and glanced at the headlines. Nothing had happened of any import, he thought, as he turned the pages. Snow was already falling in the north of Scotland and severe weather was expected. At Castle Clunes, they would be preparing for it, he thought despondently. Adam would enjoy the snow. There would be sleigh rides and doubtless the attentive Mrs Forest would teach him to skate when the loch froze – Adam had told him it was her intention. But he would not be there to share their enjoyment. He would perforce be squiring Muriel to drawing-rooms and theatres. It was a dismal and far from happy thought.

His sense of deprivation increased steadily as it neared Christmas. Selina's house was a positive bedlam of excitement as her large family prepared for the festivities. It was a time of year expressly given to children, he told himself, and but for his wife's objections, Adam would have been here with him, enjoying the good times he might have provided.

Not two weeks after her first visit to his room, Muriel invited him to share her bed. She was obviously seeking to please him, he thought, not unmindful of her ingratiating manner towards him since his return. If it was a fact that she wished to put their marriage on a better footing, he welcomed it, and if Muriel was willing to make further efforts to please him, perhaps they might yet find contentment in their married life.

Muriel gave him the opportunity to express his feelings.

'You know, Dearest, that I would do anything in the world to please you,' she said, when they awoke one morning in the same bed.

Deveril decided to take the bull by the horns.

'I believe you mean that, Muriel, and I too, will seek to please you in every way I can, but first I need proof of your declaration, my dear. I am sure you are aware that I spend a great deal of my time in Scotland these days and know the reason for it . . .'

The colour rushed into Muriel's cheeks. Was Deveril about to confess to his mistress, if such there was? In quiet, level tones, he raised the subject of the child at Castle Clunes – Percy's child.

'He has grown into the most agreeable small boy, Muriel,' Deveril said, encouraged by her silence. 'I do assure you that Aunt Meg has raised him excellently and he would be very little trouble to you were he to come here to live with us. It has been my intention for some time to talk to you again about Adam, but I did not feel I could count upon your understanding. Now, perhaps . . .'

At last Muriel found her voice.

'You know I have never cared for children, Deveril!' she said flatly.

Deveril nodded.

'I understood your objections to a squalling infant, Muriel, but Adam is no longer so. He is a handsome little boy who will do us credit, and were you to see him, you would realize your refusal to accept him is quite unjustified.'

Muriel's mind was working furiously. If the child would keep Deveril at home . . . but Percy Grayshott had been an imbecile, and she still recoiled from the thought of his son beneath her roof . . .

'Perhaps I would not object to having a child here in the house had it been *your* son, Deveril,' she said with rare honesty. 'But your brother's child . . . sickly . . . retarded . . . you cannot really expect me to . . .'

It was Deveril's turn to think carefully before he spoke. Muriel's meaning was clear enough. She feared Adam might have inherited poor Percy's illness. But had she really meant she would have no objection to *his* son? Or had she meant to their own child? Knowing his wife's strictly moral attitudes, he could not envisage her acceptance of his bastard. He sighed, aware that this was no time for a confession of the truth. Nevertheless, he was determined to have Adam here with him.

'Muriel, *the boy is as normal as you or I*. I would not otherwise ask you to comply with my wishes. If you will agree at least to seeing him, I know your objections will vanish. Come with me to Castle Clunes next spring, and if you find yourself drawn to him as I am, we will bring him home together.'

'But Deveril, have you forgotten? It was our intention to go to America next spring. Why, you yourself instructed me to accept Anthea Wilcox's invitation . . .'

'So we will find an excuse to postpone our visit until later in the year,' Deveril broke in. He had quite forgotten Anthea, and now that Muriel had reminded him, he knew that he no longer felt the same desire to see her again. It was not Anthea who occupied his thoughts these days – it was the fair-haired girl in Scotland.

Suddenly his heart jumped. Only yesterday he had had a letter from Aunt Meg telling him she had discarded her invalid chair and was now able to walk with sticks. By the spring, she would no longer need the services of a companion, and that would mean Mrs Forest's duties would be at an end. Seeing that the girl's circumstances necessitated employment of some kind, Deveril thought, and that she was already devoted to Adam, what better plan than that she should come to London with the boy, as his governess. She would be here, in this house, where he could see her, talk to her . . .

'I am waiting for your answer, Muriel,' he said.

But he knew already that he would override any objections his wife might have. Nothing now would stop him bringing his son and the girl to live with him. He wanted it more than he had ever wanted anything in his whole life.

CHAPTER TWENTY-THREE

December 1836–March 1837

Once Deveril and his friends had returned to London, life at Castle Clunes settled back to normal for Clemency. Adam seldom spoke of his Uncle 'Vril, and with only Lady McDoone, Adam and herself in the big house, they were happily content with one another's company.

Sometimes she read aloud from Lady McDoone's extensive collection of books; sometimes she played the spinet and sang songs or composed simple tunes to nursery rhymes so that Adam, too, could play the instrument. Sometimes they played cards or made paper and cardboard toys. They started several scrapbooks, Clemency sewing linen covers so that they would not become dog-eared with time. They made snakes from cotton reels, paper hats and boats and boxes, skipjacks, suckers and water-cutters.

Time never hung heavily on their hands. At Christmas there were holly-berry decorations to make and presents to wrap, and if it stopped snowing long enough, they would dress warmly and skate on the frozen loch or go out in a sleigh pulled by one of the dogcart ponies.

There were, too, Clemency's weekly letters to Benjamin to be penned. One of the last letters she received from him before the weather deteriorated concerned Mary, the loyal little rectory maid who had once befriended her. Now happily married to her Jack with five young ones to feed and clothe, Mary had returned to the rectory as a maid. The new parson, engaged by Deveril, was a bachelor who shared his home with his spinster sister, a former schoolteacher by the name of

Dorothy Fields. Miss Fields, so Benjamin wrote, was a kindly soul who, on learning that Mary's abiding desire was to learn to read and write so that she could communicate directly with Clemency, had set about the none-too-easy task of teaching her. Now, after two years, Mary had written her first letter, which Benjamin had posted for her.

The simple misspelt sentences brought tears to Clemency's eyes, reminding her as they did so vividly of the little red-haired maid's loving kindness and care of her when she had so badly needed a friend.

'I've not never forgot you, Miss Clemtine. I corld my eldst arter you. Dokter allus tells me how you is and Jack and me prays you finds your prechus baby. Plees rite big letters wot I can reed my ownself. Rektrys not like it used to be and I be rite happy working for parsons sister. Candles guttering so I wont rite no more but close now respectably, Mary, as wot remebrs orl our good and bad times wot we shared . . .

'P.S. Jack and me wishes you a Happy Crismus.'

With great care, Clemency printed a reply in short uncomplicated words which she hoped Mary could decipher. Adam, leaning against her shoulder, looked puzzled, until she informed him that the letter was for someone who like himself, had only just learned to read and write . . . someone very special and dear to her, she added, causing Adam to scowl and say anxiously:

'But you do not love her more'n me, Forrie?'

'No, my darling!' she said, laying down her quill and hugging him. 'Nevertheless, I am very very fond of her, and one day I shall take you to visit her.' With which promise he was more than content.

It was the last letter to reach Castle Clunes before the worst coaching winter the country had ever known closed all the roads and prevented the running of the mails. Clemency welcomed their total isolation. It was an idyllic life for her with Adam, and she settled so happily into it that thoughts of taking him abroad receded to the back of her mind. Even the longing to see her father could not persuade her to bring to an end this most perfect time in her life.

But by February the first threat to that dream-world arrived in the form of a letter delivered by one of Deveril's servants who had managed to make a way through the heavy drifts. It informed Lady McDoone that his wife had at long last consented to have Adam to live with them in London.

'I have always known the day would come when I must lose Adam,' Lady McDoone said unhappily, as she passed on this information to a shocked Clemency. 'But I shall miss the child sorely. Of course, it is best for him to be with his uncle. I do not doubt you and I spoil the boy, and some masculine company will do him the world of good.'

Horrified, Clemency enquired when this removal was likely to take place.

'Not yet awhile, as far as I can read between the lines,' Lady McDoone informed her. 'We shall have Adam with us a little longer, I imagine.'

Clemency sent a letter back to London by Deveril's servant, addressed to Benjamin, which she hoped would reach him despite the weather. She was desperately in need of his advice. But it was a further few days before the last of the snow had vanished and the mail services were finally restored. At long last, letters began once more to reach Castle Clunes. Benjamin's reply was one of the first to be delivered.

'How can I advise you, Dearest Girl,' he wrote, 'when I must by virtue of my feeling towards you, be so heavily biased in favour of your remaining in this country. At the same time, I understand how you feel at the prospect of being separated from Adam yet again. It is a decision only you can make.

'In anticipation of your sudden need for information

upon the matter, I have ascertained that you can, should you so desire, sail to the Americas from the Port of Glasgow. You would have therefore only to conduct yourself and the boy to Stirling and from thence on a steam packet by canal to Glasgow where I myself would meet you to see you safely aboard.

'But I beg you, Dearest Clemency, to give me good advice of your planned date of leaving, if it comes to this, as I could not bear it were you to depart, perhaps for evermore, without my seeing you again . . .'

On the following day she received a letter from her father in which he used every persuasion to encourage her to take Adam with her to live with him. It was a wonderful country for a boy to grow up in, he enthused. There in Fort William was a new world which he could build to his own liking – a man's world, hard, rugged but full of adventure.

Clemency realized that she dared not wait for Deveril to carry out his intention to take Adam to London. But for the feelings of Lady McDoone, she would have hesitated no longer and made the final decision to do as her father wished and take Adam to the colonies immediately. But she dreaded the thought of betraying the old lady's trust; and try as she might, she could not stop herself imagining how great would be Lady McDoone's grief when she realized she would never see Adam again. Nevertheless Clemency knew that she could not afford to let sentiment deter her from her purpose. If she did not soon remove Adam, it might be too late to effect their escape undetected. Deveril's warning of his intent obliged her to make the final decision to go.

It was a decision she would have made in any event, Clemency thought, as she read with dismay a letter but newly arrived from her good friend Caroline Norton. Penned by Caroline a week previously, it was a desperate cry from the heart, for now her husband had not only denied her access to her children but had hidden the boys where she was unable to find them. Caroline was ill with worry, she wrote, but she was not entirely without hope. She had lawyers fighting for her; and as a last resort, she was appealing to a Member of Parliament, Serjeant Talfourd, to put forward a Bill entitling married women to custody of their children in the case of marital disputes. The Bill was to be read in May, and since Caroline was an innocent party with regard to her own marriage breakdown, she believed the new law must entitle her to see and be with her three sons.

'I have been engaged in the writing of a pamphlet which I have called: "Separation of Mother and Child by the Custody of Infants Considered",' she wrote. 'Could you have foreseen the future, Clemency, you would never have contracted that marriage with Percy Grayshott. I tell you this because, unbelievably, had your son remained Lord B's illegitimate child, you could by law have claimed access. Yet I, as a married woman, have no legal existence and therefore no recourse to law.

'I had hoped that if my pamphlet were widely circulated, it would influence the voting for Mr Talfourd's Bill, but my family are greatly opposed to my making a public appeal of this nature and I am currently engaged in editing it, although it goes against my inclination to do so. How can the law justify a situation where a husband can put his children in the care of his mistress even although his wife is innocent of any wrong-doing?

'I believe my sons to be at Rannoch Lodge in Scotland in the doubtful care of my sister-in-law Lady Menzies, and I am not permitted to communicate with them, nor they to receive letters from me. That odious woman has never liked me or approved of me, and I remain dependent upon George's goodwill for any hope of being reunited with my boys.

'How I envy you your proximity to your child and the reassurance it must give you to know he is loved and cherished . . .'

Clemency's concern for Caroline's predicament compounded her concern for herself, she thought, as hastily she sat down to write to Caroline.

'. . . I could not bear another separation from Adam and my mind is made up – I shall take him with me to my papa. I do not think Lord B will ever think to search for Adam there . . .'

But before this letter could reach Caroline, further communications arrived from Deveril. Lady McDoone sent for Clemency after breakfast.

'Well, my dear, I have news for you – and I think you will consider it good news,' she said, removing the fantailed dove perched on her shoulder. 'My nephew has finalized his plans for Adam to go to London and is offering you the post of governess – provided I have no further need of your services, of course.'

She smiled at Clemency in her usual kindly way.

'Now that I am no longer confined to that horrible invalid chair, I can manage quite well by myself.' She gave a soft chuckle. 'I may appear quite stupid at times, but it has not escaped my attention that you, child, have become increasingly restless these past few weeks. Moreover, I realize that Castle Clunes has little to offer a young woman of your age, and that it would be selfish of me to wish to keep you here any longer.'

She broke off, puzzled by the look of dismay on Clemency's face.

'You do not want to go to London?' she asked in a surprised tone. 'I personally think it is an excellent idea both for you and the boy. Adam may find life a little strange at first, and your presence at Grayshott House would mean he could turn to you for comfort and understanding. He is devoted to you.'

Clemency barely heard the conclusion of Lady McDoone's statement, for the old lady's reference to her restlessness both embarrassed and frightened her. Yet there was no possible way, she thought, by which her employer could have discovered her plan to take Adam with her to North America.

She felt the colour rush to her cheeks as she realized that Deveril wanted *her to go with Adam* to live in his house, under the same roof as his wife!

'No!' she whispered. 'No, I would not want to go . . .'

Lady McDoone looked even more surprised.

'Not want to accompany Adam?' she questioned. 'But I thought you so attached to the child.'

Clemency did not reply. How could she give a satisfactory explanation without revealing that she had no intention of being separated from Adam – that he would be going to the colonies with her and not to London, as Deveril was demanding. Not even if she wanted to accompany Adam to Grayshott House could she do so, since Lady Burnbury would recognize her as Adam's mother. But for Caroline's insistence that Muriel *never* went to Scotland, Clemency would not have dared to take the post as Lady McDoone's companion. One word now from Lady Burnbury to Deveril, and he might bar her from seeing her child again. Only if Mr Talfourd's Bill was passed in May might she be able to claim legal access to Adam, and there was no certainty the Bill would go through. According to Caroline, there were those – the ex-Chancellor, Lord Brougham, in particular – who were bitterly opposed to it. To reveal her carefully preserved incognito at this stage was to take too great a risk that she might lose Adam for ever

Momentarily bitterness overwhelmed her, leaving her speechless and unable to reply to Lady McDoone. Had some sixth sense warned Deveril at the eleventh hour that she had made up her mind to take Adam away?

'Does Adam know of his uncle's plan to take him to London?' she enquired.

Lady McDoone nodded.

'There was a letter for him which he has taken to the school-room to read. Do you doubt his enthusiasm for the prospect? I do not, for he worships his Uncle 'Vril, as you well know.'

Clemency bit her lip.

'Perhaps it is not my place to say this, Lady McDoone, but I have assumed, wrongly maybe, that Lady Burnbury was averse to receiving the boy, else surely she would have done so long before this. He is nearly six years old!'

Lady McDoone's eyebrows rose imperceptibly.

'You are very astute, my dear, but whatever the objections Muriel held in the past, we must presume they no longer exist. Deveril tells me that his wife is now prepared to welcome Adam as soon as his removal can be arranged.'

Once again Clemency made no reply. Her mind was filled with the memory of the tall, dark-haired woman whom she had seen but once in the drawing-room of Grayshott House. Lady Burnbury's bitter, harsh tones still rang in Clemency's ears, and she felt again that same determination never to allow her to have Adam.

I shall not change my plan to take him to Papa! she thought, and in the circumstances, it would have to be soon. She must write and advise Benjamin at once, she decided.

But Clemency had not taken into account her small son's reactions to Deveril's proposal. He came running into the room, his face scarlet with excitement.

'I am to go to live with Uncle 'Vril in London!' he cried. 'He has everything arranged and Forrie, you are to come with me, and Uncle 'Vril says he has already bought me a pony so that I can go riding with him in Hyde Park in a place called Rotten Row. Is it not wonderful? We are to go as soon as possible.'

He ran to Lady McDoone's side, the pleasure leaving his face as he said anxiously:

'You will not miss me too much, will you, Aunt Meg? I will write to you often, and if Uncle 'Vril allows me, I will come and visit you.' He regarded her doubtfully. 'Are you too old, Ma'am, to travel to London to visit us? I would like it best if you were coming with Forrie and me.'

Lady McDoone's voice was husky as with an attempted smile she said:

'I am far too old to travel to London, my darling boy, but we will do as you say and write to one another often, and Uncle 'Vril will bring you to stay with me I have no doubt.'

The child looked radiant again as he turned to Clemency.

'Is it not exciting, Forrie? You and Uncle 'Vril and me can see all those places you told me about – the Tower of London where the little Princes were murdered, and the Maze at Hampton Court, and St James's Palace where the King and Queen live.'

Clemency bit her lip in an effort to withhold a cry of dismay.

'Adam, I do not know if I *can* come to London . . . I have not yet had time to consider the matter and . . . and I will have to think about it.'

Adam's dark eyes were wide with disbelief.

'But Forrie, you said you would stay with me. You said . . .'

Clemency was all too well aware of what she had said – that she would never leave him for as long as he needed her. The promise had followed a conversation between them when he had remarked upon her cleverness in finding games for him to play and books for him to read. 'You always seem to know just what I am needing!' he had said, 'even when I cannot think of it myself! I do not know how I should manage without you.'

She was now painfully aware of Lady McDoone's puzzled stare. There was no explanation she could make to her or to Adam without revealing her plans; but now the boy's unqualified enthusiasm for going to London to live with his Uncle 'Vril had undermined that decision in the most frightening way. She now realized that she had seriously underestimated the extent of his love for his father.

'Uncle 'Vril will take me to see his house in Dorset,' he was telling his great-aunt, his dark eyes bright with pleasure. 'He has told me all about Chiswell Hill House and I shall love it there. And in England there are big engines with carriages called "trains" which travel much faster than the fastest mail coach, and you can sit in a carriage pulled by the engine, which goes all by itself without horses to pull it . . .'

Lady McDoone put aside Deveril's letter and reached for the two sticks she now used to aid her walking. Her eyes regarded Clemency over the top of the boy's head.

'You will need time to consider your future, my dear,' she said gently. 'I see no reason why any hasty decision has to be made. It has taken my nephew years to make up his mind to have Adam to live with him in London, and he cannot expect us all to turn our ordered lives topsy-turvy in a matter of minutes. I shall delay any reply until the end of the week. As far as I am concerned, you must consider yourself perfectly free to do exactly as you wish. I am well used to being alone, but on the other hand, if you would like to make your home here with me, I have grown very fond of you, child, and would be more than happy to have you remain here with me for as long as you need a home. However, I have never thought Castle Clunes a proper place for a young woman of your age, and my advice would be for you to seek a new life – if not in London, then at least nearer to civilization.'

She turned to Adam and said: 'Come now, Milord Chatterbox, I shall need you to help me feed my birds. Your precious Forrie shall join us later.'

Clemency was unhappily aware of the backward glance Adam gave her as he followed his great-aunt obediently from the room. It was almost, she thought, as if he sensed that she might be about to abandon him. That he loved her she was in no doubt. But whether this affection was as great as the love he had for his father was now the all-important question. How was it possible, she thought wretchedly, that she had so underrated it when she had seen with her own eyes how father and son had greeted each other on Deveril's last visit; how Adam had always to be prised from his father's side! But then Deveril's visits were infrequent, and Adam quickly forgot him once he had returned to London.

Must she now find the courage to bear yet another separation from her son, she asked herself? Were Adam's chances of happiness really greater living with his father in London? If she could only have accompanied him as Deveril suggested! But it was useless to pretend to herself that Deveril's wife could fail to recognize her as Adam's mother; and even if by some miracle she did not, there was always the fear that the horrible little lawyer Mr Grimshaw would do so were they to meet.

As Clemency made her way up to her room, she was reminded suddenly of that night of the masquerade when Deveril had kissed her and she had returned those kisses. In this moment of honesty, she acknowledged that there had been a fire between them needing only a breath of wind to fan it into an inferno. Were she to live beneath Deveril's roof, how long would it be before her heart and body betrayed themselves once more? Had Deveril been thinking only of Adam when he proposed her going with the boy as his governess? Or had he wanted her, Clemency, nearer at hand? Knowing his nature, she did not think it in the least surprising that he might choose to pursue his flirtation with her beneath his wife's gaze. It was the kind of daredevil risk that would amuse him, she told herself bitterly.

But she herself would not be a party to it, if such was his plan. Her options were very clear now. Either she must disregard Adam's clear desire to go with his father, and set sail with the boy at the very earliest opportunity; or she must quietly allow Deveril to take him away from her without further fight.

Memories of the long winter hours she had spent with her son filled her mind. They had laughed and played and sung together; skated, walked, thrown snowballs at each other, even built a snowman effigy of Deveril, complete with tall hat, old coat and a stick for his gun. When the snow was gone, they had wrapped themselves in warm coats and gone down to the lake with stone jars to see if the first tadpoles were to be caught. They had driven in the dogcart to the farms to see the first spring lambs and Robbie had stalked a hind with them, enabling them to discover where she had concealed her tiny calf in the undergrowth.

Tears filled Clemency's eyes and spilled down her cheeks as her heart ached with renewed bitterness towards Deveril. Had he not determined for another two months to remove Adam to London, by then it would have been too late – she and Adam would have been on the high seas beyond his reach. Were the Fates always going to play into *his* hands and never into hers? Must she allow Adam's love for his father to supersede her need to have her son with *her*? At the tender age of six, would he not quickly forget his father and settle happily with her and his grandfather? He did truly love her – of that she was in no doubt.

But despite the cry of her heart, Clemency knew the decision had already been made – by Adam himself. From that morning on, he talked of little else but going to live with his Uncle 'Vril. A week passed before Clemency found sufficient courage to break the news to him that she herself would not be accompanying him.

As soon as luncheon was over and Adam had followed her into Lady McDoone's suite, she took him onto her lap and, in as casual a voice as she could assume, she said:

'I know you will be disappointed, Adam, but I must tell you that I shall not be coming to London with you. You are quite grown-up enough now not to need me to fuss over you. You must try to remember everything I have told you and be a very good boy.'

Tears welled into Adam's eyes as he regarded her reproachfully.

'But why can you not come with me, Forrie?' he sobbed. 'Do you not love me more than you love Aunt Meg? You promised we would always be together – for ever and ever! I want you to come with me . . . you *promised* . . .'

Clemency could not meet Lady McDoone's eyes as the child buried his head in her lap. When she had given that promise so readily at Christmas, she had believed implicitly that they would never again be separated; that his future lay with her and her father in the colonies.

Although until now she had given little thought to her own future without him, her longing to comfort him prompted her to say impulsively:

'But we shall still see each other, dearest boy. I shall not be far away in Brighton – for that is where I shall almost certainly be living. It is but a few hours journey from London, and quite possibly your Uncle 'Vril will allow you to visit me there. It is very jolly in the summer and I shall take you sea bathing. You would like to learn to swim, would you not? And I dare say Professor Brook will take you walking on the Chain Pier. Remember how much you wanted to go on a pier?'

Slowly he raised his head, and although his eyes were still full of tears and his face had not lost its expression of reproach, he said shakily:

'But who will read me a story at bedtime? And who will mind my manners? And who will kiss me goodnight?'

'Why, your Aunt Muriel will be there to spoil you,' Lady McDoone broke in firmly. 'She is your Uncle 'Vril's wife, as you know, and she is looking forward to having you to live with her in London. She has no little boys of her own, you see.'

Somehow, Clemency managed to release herself from Adam's hold upon her and escape from the room. She was no longer sure that she could endure this parting. In the privacy of her room, she lay on her bed, remembering suddenly the warning she had been given – was it by the Professor? – that were Deveril to have permitted Adam to remain with her while he was a baby but had later taken him from her, her suffering would be even greater than it then was on losing her child in babyhood. How true that warning was proving to be – for it was not just her own pain she must now endure, but Adam's too.

The day of their departure from Castle Clunes seemed to Clemency to come with surprising rapidity. Only Adam talked cheerfully at their last breakfast together, Clemency and Lady McDoone too aware of the impending separation to find appetite or words.

While the servants carried the luggage out to the waiting carriage, they stood silently side by side in the hall, their eyes focused on the excited child.

'I know you are trying not to let the boy see what this separation means to you, my dear, as indeed am I,' Lady McDoone said gently when the moment came for them to leave. 'He is coming to terms with the knowledge that you will not be at Grayshott House with him, and these past few days he has even shown curiosity about his Aunt Muriel. It would make the future more difficult for him were his affections to be divided between her and you, and I think you may have had this in mind when you made your decision not to go with him as his governess.'

The old lady put an arm around Clemency's shoulders.

'Perhaps . . .' she said softly, 'I understand more than you realize. Old I may be but silly I am not, and my heart goes out to you because I have seen with my own eyes how dearly you love the boy. I shall feel his loss almost as deeply as you, so I understand your suffering . . .'

Then she took Clemency's hands in hers and said softly:

'You should get married, child – have a family of your own. But in the meanwhile, we will write to one another and exchange such news as we both have of our young scallywag, eh?'

She brushed aside Clemency's attempts to thank her for all her kindness these past six months.

'I shall miss you too, Clemency – almost as much as I shall miss Adam. I have grown very fond of you, my child, very fond indeed.'

Mercifully, Adam was too excited at the prospect of the journey ahead of them to shed any tears at the parting from Lady McDoone. He waved cheerfully from the phaeton to the old lady standing at the top of the stone stairway to see them upon their way. Robbie had been permitted to ride with them as far as Perth, and he chattered happily to his friend as they drove eastward over the moors.

Adam's preoccupation gave Clemency the chance to recover most of her composure and she succeeded in controlling the threatening tears before they drove through Strath Clunes. But for the whole of the two-hour drive to Perth, she was tormented by uncertainty. What exactly had Lady McDoone meant when she had said that she 'understood more than Clemency realized'. Did the old lady mean that she had guessed who she really was? Had she, Clemency, betrayed her relationship to Adam by showing too obviously her love for him? Caroline Norton would not have betrayed her confidence – of that Clemency was certain – and the odious Mr Grimshaw knew her only as Clementine Foster, the Rev Foster's niece.

Clemency's inner turmoil continued even after she and Adam had boarded the mail at Perth. Did it matter if Lady McDoone had guessed the truth, now that she was surrendering Adam to his father? she asked herself with a feeling of hopelessness. Perhaps, once she had ascertained that the boy was settling happily into his new life, she should take Lady McDoone's advice and marry Benjamin – have a family of her own. Poor Benjamin had waited so long and so patiently; at least *he* would be overjoyed to learn she was not leaving England.

Her thoughts returned to Lady Burnbury. When Clemency had last met her, both of them had been in a highly emotional state. It was possible therefore that she had misjudged Deveril's wife during that brief encounter, although in her heart she did not think so. Did she *really* intend to make Adam welcome?

Such doubts tormented her continuously throughout the long journey south. At one moment, she felt relief that the boy's attitude towards his new life was one of intense excitement and pleasure. At the next, she was overcome once more by fears that Lady Burnbury would not love him as she should, and that he would grieve for her, Clemency.

Deveril had taken it for granted that she would deliver Adam direct to Grayshott House; but she could not comply with this order lest she encountered his wife. On their arrival therefore at the final staging post in London, she took Adam into the Travellers' Room of the inn and while they sat down to eat, she despatched a messenger to Grayshott House, asking that a carriage be sent to collect the boy and his luggage. She did not anticipate that Deveril would come himself to fetch the child, supposing it unlikely he would be at home when her messenger called. She expected that the new tutor Deveril had engaged or a servant would collect him. It came as a considerable shock when less than an hour later, she saw Deveril's tall figure striding purposefully into the room. Beside her, Adam gave an excited cry of welcome and ran to meet him.

Clemency watched as Deveril gathered the boy into his arms and swung him high in the air, unmindful of the other travellers regarding them with idle curiosity. Tears stung her eyes and she longed to slip away quickly, unnoticed. But Deveril was already seating himself at their table, Adam at his elbow clinging to his arm.

'You have had a good journey, Ma'am? You have made excellent time!' he commented, smiling and quite at ease. 'But why did you not bring this young rascal to the house? If you were short of money, the hackney could have been paid at the door . . .'

Clemency found her voice.

'I am short of time, not money!' she interrupted quietly. 'I wish to reach Brighton before nightfall, and if you will excuse me, I should like now to be on my way.'

The smile left Deveril's face and his eyes narrowed.

'I do not understand your haste, Mrs Foster. Could you not stay at least one night with Adam to see him settled in? I had hoped that I might even at this late stage persuade you to change your mind and remain with us as Adam's governess. My wife has engaged a nurse but . . .'

'No, I am sorry, but Professor Brook is expecting me, and I have other plans for my future,' Clemency improvised hurriedly.

Deveril's eyes revealed both disappointment and irritation.

'My great-aunt went to considerable pains to point out to me your affection for Adam,' he said, 'and on the occasion of my last visit to Castle Clunes, I saw it for myself. Can you therefore not set aside your plans for the time being? I had counted upon your willingness to do so for Adam's sake.'

'Oh, Forrie, do *please* stay with us!' Adam cried, detaching himself from Deveril's embrace and hurrying to Clemency's side. Deveril's words had made him aware once more of the impending parting, and he looked as unhappy as Clemency herself was feeling. Deveril had no right to allow Adam to believe she was open to persuasion, thus raising the child's hopes unfairly, she thought angrily. She regarded Deveril coldly.

'Your great-aunt is in agreement with me that since I cannot take the position you offered me as Adam's governess, then a clean break now is best for him,' she said. 'Doubtless Lady Burnbury will adequately provide all the maternal affection he needs.'

Deveril bit back the retort that rose to his lips. Despite all Muriel's promises of devotion to Adam, he doubted very much that she possessed the maternal instincts this girl had shown towards his son. Moreover, the nurse Muriel had engaged was elderly, plump and singularly ugly, and he himself did not enjoy the thought that the woman would perforce accompany him and Adam upon many different occasions. How much more enjoyable it might all be if the delectable Mrs Forest decided to remain in his employ, he thought, with a surge of fresh hope.

He leant forward and before Clemency could withdraw her hand from the table, he covered it with his own.

'It is not just Adam who would like you to be with us,' he said in a low vibrant voice. 'I would, too. I promise that you will have no cause to regret it if you will but change your mind.'

Clemency's cheeks burned as she tried to look away from Deveril's dark, intense gaze. The touch of his hand on hers had set her heart racing and her legs trembling. Her own weakness appalled her. Once again her body was betraying her, forcing her against her will to respond to this man's charm. The strange hold he had upon her added to her bitterness towards him. With his casual uncaring beauty, he had flawed her whole life. She would not allow him to go unscathed.

'I should most certainly regret it if I changed my mind, Lord Burnbury,' she said stiffly. 'You see, I am about to become betrothed to Doctor Benjamin Brook. As his wife, I shall have no need of employment – indeed, I hope to be fully employed assisting him in his work.'

The look of dismay on Deveril's face gave her a moment of intense satisfaction.

'But you cannot marry Brook!' The words were out before he could stop them. 'You would be wasting your life married to a penniless country physician!'

Clemency's chin rose defiantly.

'Since I am not in your employ, Lord Burnbury, I am free to speak my mind – which allows me to say that I consider your remarks most impertinent and my affairs none of your business.'

Disconcertingly, Deveril ignored the rebuff and suddenly grinned.

'I accept both rebukes, Ma'am, but I spoke only the truth. I cannot believe that you love the fellow sufficiently well to renounce the whole world for him. Why, I will wager you could have any man you pleased if you chose to charm him. Can you really be so ignorant as to your own beauty? Have you forgotten how young Wade was your slave without one sign of encouragement from you? Or how you innocently inflamed McUist? Or *me*?'

Clemency jumped to her feet.

'You would not speak in such terms if Benjamin were here!' she cried in a low fierce tone. 'But since you show an interest in my affairs, I can assure you that he and I are perfectly suited and we shall be entirely happy together. Now I must be on my way. Adam has Professor Brook's address in his pocket. It is my hope that you will permit Adam to visit me from time to time, as it is unlikely that I shall come to London. Now I will bid you goodbye, Lord Burnbury. I do not think we shall meet again.'

Deveril rose slowly from his chair. He was no longer smiling.

'*You* may think it unlikely, Ma'am, but *I* do not,' he said in a quiet tense voice. He glanced at the boy, who was clinging now to Clemency's skirt. 'Come, Adam,' he said, his tone gentle, 'you will see your precious Forrie 'ere long, I promise.'

Adam allowed himself to be drawn to his father's side, but his eyes searched Clemency's as he said urgently:

'You will write to me, Forrie. You *promised* . . .' His voice broke, and Clemency forgot Deveril as she bent to hug Adam for the last time.

'Of course, I will, my darling,' she said huskily, 'and we shall see each other very soon. Now off you go and show your Uncle 'Vril what a big boy you are; and do not forget your bow to Lady Burnbury and be sure not to chatter too much when you are in the drawing-room with your elders.'

Too close to tears for further conversation, she looked up at Deveril appealingly. For a moment, there was a puzzled expression on his face as he stared first at Clemency, then at the boy. He sensed the current of love between them and felt the sadness of their parting as if it were his own. He could well understand Adam's feelings. *He* did not want the girl to go out of his life, either! And it was not only because she was pretty and might have afforded him some considerable pleasure and amusement in the background of his home life. He wanted more than that. He wanted . . . he wanted to be where Adam now was, held tightly in her arms, her cheek against his, her tears of loss for him, not his son.

The absurdity of his emotions both confused and upset him.

It was not in his nature to delve deeply into his relationships with others – and certainly not with women. He had been excited by and attracted to Anthea and frequently piqued by that independent spirit of hers, but it had been only his pride that had been hurt when she ended the affair.

'I wish you well in your marriage,' he said stiffly but without conviction. 'We must be on our way, Adam. Now dry those tears, I have a surprise awaiting you at home. Shall I tell you what it is?'

To Clemency's intense relief, Adam released his hold upon her and, the tears still wet on his cheeks, he regarded Deveril with a half-hearted curiosity.

'I will tell you the secret when we are in the carriage,' Deveril said, taking Adam's hand. He bowed to Clemency, his eyes lingering on hers until she looked down. But as father and son moved away towards the door, her gaze quickly returned to them. Adam looked so small beside Deveril, and yet there was so obviously a resemblance between them that few could have doubted their relationship. She watched them until the closing of the door hid them both from her view.

As she gathered up her gloves and reticule, a sudden cold chill of fear swept over her, stronger even than her sense of loneliness and despair. Had Deveril considered that his wife might see the resemblance between himself and his son? Lady Burnbury must know that Percy Grayshott had been fair-haired, blue-eyed. How adversely might it affect Adam if she ever suspected the truth?

Clemency chided herself for her misgivings. It was too late to worry about it. Whatever Muriel Burnbury felt, she, Clemency, had no doubt that Deveril loved his son. Nor could she doubt that Adam loved his father. She must not waver at this stage, for no good could come of it. She was renouncing Adam for the sake of his happiness; denying her own need for him. He had begun a new stage of his life without her and she had no choice now but to wait and see how he would settle down. As for herself, she was assured of the Professor's welcome, and her future would not seem entirely pointless if she carried out her impulsive statement to Deveril and told the patient, loving Benjamin that she was at long last willing to marry him.

At least *he* will be happy, she told herself, as she took a hackney to Blossoms Inn to board the mail to Brighton. For she knew that despite her angry protests to Deveril, the thought of marriage to Benjamin gave her both solace and comfort – but very little joy.

CHAPTER TWENTY-FOUR

April–August 1837

Insofar as it was possible for Clemency ever to be really happy without her son, by the beginning of April she was almost resigned to her future. On Easter Day she and Benjamin were formally betrothed, and a date for their marriage was fixed for the fifteenth of September, her twenty-third birthday. Benjamin's quiet delight had its effect upon her, and she was able to conceal her misgivings from him. He returned to Poole after the Easter vacation with the intention of finding a practitioner to replace him.

Shortly after his departure, his brother Frederick wrote to announce that he had been recently married and would shortly be returning to England as they were expecting their first child. Having very little money to support themselves, Frederick was hoping that he and his bride could make a home with the Professor.

'So you and Ben can have your own house,' the old man said, 'since I will have Frederick's wife to look after me here.'

But although the prospect contributed to Clemency's growing peace of mind, what really brought her happiness were the regular weekly letters she received from Adam. The letters were short, written under the guidance of his new tutor, but nevertheless they reflected his enjoyment of his life with his beloved Uncle 'Vril. Adam's brief sentences began always with '*Uncle 'Vril and me*' did this or that together. Deveril, it seemed, was devoting himself to entertaining the boy.

'So you see, my dear, you made the right decision,' the Professor said, smiling, as Clemency penned her replies to

the child. 'The boy's place is with his father after all. Nor
need you feel yourself forgotten, since Adam never fails to
end his letters with the words: "*I wish you were here,
Forrie!*"'

Clemency smiled, remembering the row of kisses which
always followed his signature.

A great deal of the bitterness Clemency had felt towards
Deveril vanished as April gave way to May and thence to
June.

'His father has taken Adam down to Chiswell Hill House,'
she told the Professor as they walked together along the
Esplanade. 'It seems they are spending an idyllic three weeks
together and Deveril has given him a real telescope for his
birthday.' She watched without heartache as a small boy of
Adam's age ran past them bowling his wooden hoop. 'He
makes no mention of Lady Burnbury,' she added, 'so I assume
she has not accompanied them to Dorset.'

At the end of June, Adam wrote once more from London
saying that his Uncle 'Vril was going to a country called
Switzerland with nice Mr Wade. The two intended to climb
a mountain called Mont Blanc, which they had read about in
a book called *Impressions de Voyage*, by Monsieur Alexander
Dumas. Adam's tutor, a Mr Crowley, was going to read it to
him when his French improved. Uncle 'Vril would be away
for two whole months, during which time Adam was to go
to the seaside with his Aunt Selina, he wrote. His next letter
spoke of his excitement at the prospect of his holiday in
Worthing with his many cousins. Uncle 'Vril said that his Aunt
Selina could take him to visit Forrie – was that not indeed
wonderful news?

But during the first week of July, there was no letter.

'I expect he has been busy preparing for his holiday,' the
Professor said, as the letter-carrier passed by without stopping
at the house. Fortunately Clemency's attentions were diverted
by the arrival of Benjamin's brother. Older by five years,
Frederick Brook turned out to be a forty-year-old replica of

his father. His blue eyes were spectacled and he peered short-sightedly at Clemency with the same kindly smile. His wife was several years younger, a mouse-like little woman obviously devoted to her tall husband and touchingly pleased to find herself not only married but pregnant at this late stage of her life. She, too, had been a missionary, she told Clemency shyly.

They quickly settled into the simple routine of the household, and by the middle of July, it seemed as if they had always been there. The Professor and his son became engrossed in the writing of a book about African tribal laws whilst Clemency and Edith Brook managed the household. When she was not thus engaged, Clemency busied herself sewing her trousseau. She had completed the task of embroidering monograms on several sets of linen sheets and pillowcases and had now begun to trim, with Hannington's best lace, the three chemises and long-cloth petticoats which she had already made. She had yet to cut out and stitch camisoles, drawers and aprons, and three nightdresses which she intended to adorn with pretty French ribbons after she had stitched the tiny tucks and insets.

She pushed to the back of her mind the thought that in eight weeks' time, she might be wearing one of the prettiest of her nightdresses on her honeymoon. The thought of the intimate side of her marriage to Benjamin filled her with trepidation. Although now they were betrothed he had many times kissed her cheek or brow, their relationship had not passed beyond the point of companionship. He was very dear to her – but as a friend rather than as a lover. She could but pray now that she would not disappoint him when the moment came for her to surrender her body to him. It was beyond her understanding that she could feel hatred for Deveril and yet feel her body thrill to *his* touch or *his* kisses, but shrink from Benjamin whom she loved so dearly.

But this private worry was put to the back of her mind with the passing of yet another week without a letter from Adam. It was now nearing the end of July, and she supposed that Deveril must long since have departed to Switzerland. If

Adam was in Worthing with Lady Allendale, why had he not yet visited her, she wondered. The resort was but fourteen miles distant.

But Adam was not in Worthing, and when at the end of July Clemency finally received a letter from him, it caused her the deepest distress.

'Dearest Forrie,' he wrote, the childishly formed letters all too obviously blotched by tears, 'Uncle 'Vril is gon. She beets me wen I am norty. I cry a lot. I love you.

Adam.'

Clemency ran with the letter to the Professor.

'Now calm yourself, my dear,' he said quietly. 'I dare say the boy has misbehaved and is resenting the punishment he has received. You will get another letter before long and find this is but a storm in a tea-cup and long since forgotten.'

'But Professor, why is he not with his cousins in Worthing?' Clemency persisted. 'I feel something is wrong. I just know it here.' She placed her hand over her heart. 'If only I could go to London and find out for myself if all is well. But I cannot go to Grayshott House with Lady Burnbury there.'

'It would be far too great a risk,' the Professor agreed. 'Be patient, my dear girl. You will receive a happier letter before long.'

All day long, her eyes scanned the street for a glimpse of the letter-carrier. But although he brought mail for the Professor, none came for her from Grayshott House.

It was as well Clemency was ignorant of the true state of affairs at Grayshott House, for despite the pleasant July weather which might otherwise have tempted Muriel to go out for a drive in her carriage, she now lay on her bed with closed eyes, her maid hovering attentively over her.

'Madame has a migraine, *la pauvre!*' Celeste was saying, her voice husky with sympathy as she smoothed Muriel's pillows and bathed her forehead with eau de Cologne. The curtains of her mistress's bedroom were almost fully drawn, blocking out the bright sunshine. The dim twilight gloom did little to brighten Muriel's bitter mood.

Despite every attempt she had made the previous week, the pleading, the cajoling, and even a night of pretended passion in her husband's arms, Deveril had refused adamantly to cancel his plans to go mountaineering in Switzerland. Finally her control had snapped and she had remarked bitterly:

'I might have known that you would not stay home at *my* request since you refuse to do so at the boy's!'

But Deveril would not be provoked into an argument and had merely shrugged his shoulders and told her she was being unreasonable.

Unreasonable! The word tormented Muriel. When she had first agreed to have Adam at Grayshott House, Deveril was grateful enough to be genuinely affectionate towards her. He had given way to her demands upon his time and even acquiesced to her request that he should spend a week with her at her parents' country house in Buckinghamshire before the boy arrived. At first it did seem as if their marriage were taking a turn for the better. The boy, when he arrived, was little trouble to Muriel, and his presence in the house served to keep Deveril at home far more often than had been his wont.

'I have never before seen so devoted an uncle,' Celeste commented, voicing Muriel's own reactions to her husband's undisguised interest in the child. Muriel, however, was less happy with the situation when Deveril took Adam off to Chiswell Hill House for practically the whole of the month of June. Fortunately, the sudden death of the King on the twentieth of June obliged an unwilling Deveril to hasten home with Adam to attend His late Majesty's funeral. It was the kind of formal occasion Deveril disliked, and he complained bitterly when he had to be fitted with his mourning robes. Muriel, however, was happy enough as she took her place in St George's Chapel, sitting proudly beside him.

She was convinced that Deveril would not leave the country now that such momentous changes would be taking place. But he was interested neither in politics nor in the new girl queen, Victoria, and talked only of Monsieur Dumas' book and the places he and Dominic Wade intended to explore in like manner to the French novelist.

On the afternoon before his planned departure, he sent for his lawyer. Muriel was not present at the interview, but her maid Celeste, with that unerring instinct of hers for gossip, was hovering in the hall. The door of the library was ajar, and Celeste overheard part of a conversation that was now largely responsible for Muriel's headache.

'I did not mean to eavesdrop, Madame,' Celeste said but a quarter of an hour after Deveril's carriage had departed to Dover and her mistress had retired to her room with a migraine. 'But the two gentlemen's voices were raised and I could not help but overhear . . .'

Celeste knew of course that she had said enough to arouse her mistress's curiosity, Muriel thought, as she pushed the maid's hand away from her forehead and told her to sit down by the bed. As was customary when the Frenchwoman was relating gossip, usually picked up from belowstairs, Muriel upbraided her for being a tittle-tattle, telling her that she was little better than a kitchenmaid!

But now, as on past occasions, she requested Celeste to repeat what had so startled her.

'It concerns the boy, Madame,' the maid said, watching Muriel's face from half-closed eyes. 'I do not know if I should repeat what I heard. It will not make my poor Madame happy.'

'Oh, for heaven's sake, say what you have to say, Celeste,' Muriel replied sharply. 'You can save your sympathy for later!'

But as always, Celeste imparted her information by insinuation.

'Madame has always remarked to me upon the likeness of the boy to Milord Burnbury. Madame has told me that the child's father was golden-haired and had blue eyes. Madame once said . . .'

'If you do not tell me now what you overheard, I shall dismiss you!' Muriel interrupted fiercely. She could no longer bear to wait for the facts that she herself had suspected ever since the boy's arrival.

Celeste dropped her eyes as if to cover her confusion.

'Madame, the lawyer was discussing Milord's heir should any mishap befall Milord Burnbury whilst he was on his travels. He referred to Master Adam as *Milord's son*. At first, I was certain I must have been mistaken, but then Milord said quite clearly: "No, Grimshaw, *my son* will inherit as is his legal right. Provision must of course be made for my wife until her death . . ." And that was all I heard, Madame, for the footman returned with refreshments and I was obliged to move away.'

It was opportune, Muriel thought, that she had developed one of her frequent migraines. Lying in the darkened room, she had time to think, to recover her composure. There was little point, she decided, in trying to pretend to Celeste that she had not heard Deveril and the lawyer correctly. If the facts were true and Adam *was* Deveril's child, it made sense of everything that had led up to this moment – Deveril's determination to remove the boy from his mother; his sending him to Scotland, where he could visit him as often as he wished without causing comment; his intention to have the child eventually at Grayshott House. It explained Deveril's extraordinary interest in a mere five-year-old; and, most of all, it explained why the two were as alike in looks as two peas in a pod. The boy was a walking replica of his father and she had noticed it instantly. So, too, had Selina, but fortunately she remarked only that Adam was a true Grayshott with his dark curly hair and dark eyes; that Percy was the only member of the family who had taken after his mother.

While Celeste rubbed eau de Cologne onto her mistress's wrists, Muriel's hands clenched in sudden anger as she remembered the young girl who had once come to the house claiming to be Percy's wife and accusing Deveril of abducting *her* child. She had been pretty and very young, but despite her shabby appearance, Muriel recalled her as being of genteel birth. *Who was she?* she now asked herself. Did Deveril still see her? Was the girl his mistress? How many people other than herself and Celeste knew the truth? Obviously that odious little lawyer was aware that the boy was Deveril's bastard. And Deveril had had no thought for the humiliation it must cause her, his wife, bringing his by-blow to live under her roof!

She gave a short, bitter laugh, recalling how she had once feared that the boy had inherited Percy Grayshott's mental weakness. How Deveril must have longed then to confess the truth! But he had not dared – and she could well understand why not, for she would never, as long as she lived, acknowledge the boy. When Deveril returned to England, she would make it clear that either he got rid of the child or she would cease to live with him as his wife. No one could blame her for leaving her husband in these circumstances. Her parents, her friends, would all support her. The boy was a living insult, witness to her husband's profligacy – even if the brat had been conceived before Deveril's marriage to her.

Muriel looked at her maid's impassive face and said:

'You do not look surprised, Celeste. How is it that you are not a great deal more shocked if you believe what you have told me?'

Celeste's ugly face slackened into the hint of a smile.

'No one could understand better than I how terrible this is for you, Madame, but at the same time I must confess that it does not come as a surprise to me. It is not my place to say so, but I have always felt milord has never shown quite the degree of respect due to a wife. It has grieved me to see how insensitive he is to poor Madame's feelings.'

'I may have put up with a great deal from him in the past,' Muriel agreed, 'but I can assure you, Celeste, *this time my husband has gone too far*. Go and find the nurse. Tell her I want the boy brought here to me immediately.'

It was not Muriel's nature to be self-analytical. Her manner was both positive and self-righteous. She did not question, therefore, why she should feel such a great antipathy to the small boy who, she openly admitted, was a handsome and well-mannered child. It was not even his newly-discovered bastardy that caused her to feel so violently opposed to him, although she was more shocked than she had allowed Celeste to see. It was Adam's extraordinary similarity to his father – and not just in appearance – which bit into her soul. When he stood by the bedroom door where his nurse left him on Muriel's orders, his small face looked as innocent and, she thought bitterly, as unconcerned as Deveril's when she called *him* to account for some oversight or aggravation. Like Deveril, he even had the audacity to smile as he bowed and said cheerfully:

'Good afternoon, Aunt Muriel!'

Muriel surveyed him critically. He was prettily dressed in bright blue pantaloons, buttoned to a short, frogged jacket beneath which was a clean white frilled shirt. She could find no fault in his appearance. His hair was neatly brushed, his face clean. A wave of pure hatred swept over her, robbing her momentarily of speech.

Adam was unaccustomed to silence. All his life, he had been permitted by his indulgent Aunt Meg to chatter freely when he was with her. Even his darling Forrie only forbade him talking when grown-ups wished to hear themselves converse. He looked now at his aunt and said happily:

'Nurse has been packing my trunk all ready for Worthing, Aunt Muriel, and I have packed my toys.' His dark eyes were glowing with excitement.

Unknowingly, the child had placed in Muriel's hands the weapon she needed. She drew in her breath sharply.

'You will not be going to Worthing, Adam. I am sending a note to your Aunt Selina this afternoon to tell her so.'

Adam's face was a mask of disbelief.

'Not going?' he echoed. 'But why not, Ma'am? Is my Uncle 'Vril coming back?'

'No, he is not!' Muriel retorted viciously, her resentment deepened by the boy's reference to *his* Uncle 'Vril. 'The reason you will not be going to Worthing is because I consider your educational progress is way below standard for a child of your age. Your tutor, Mr Crowley, has tried to excuse your quite atrocious spelling with the explanation that you have been too long accustomed to the Scottish accent of Lady McDoone's servants. Therefore it is my duty to curtail your holiday and arrange for Mr Crowley to give you extra tuition. You have not earned a holiday.'

'But Ma'am, Uncle 'Vril said it was all arranged and . . .'

'I will not permit you to stand there arguing with me,' Muriel cut him short, her voice rising. 'And do not think I shall be moved by tears. My mind is made up. It is quite clear to me that you have been thoroughly spoiled. You have had but to plead with your uncle to gain your own way, and I suspect that the same was the case with Lady McDoone and that young governess you are always talking about.'

His brown eyes luminous with tears of disappointment, Adam nevertheless said defiantly:

'Forrie did not spoil me, Ma'am. If I was naughty, she punished me. But I have not been naughty, and I do all my lessons Mr Crowley gives me.'

Muriel swung her feet over the edge of the bed and stood up. From the side table she took the ivory fan Celeste kept there to use if the summer nights were too hot for sleep.

'Hold out your hand, boy!' she ordered.

Frightened now as much by the undertones of her voice as by the look in her eyes, Adam stretched his arm reluctantly towards her. The blow she struck him across the knuckles was the more painful by virtue of the fact that his small fist had been clenched. Tears rolled down his cheeks and his head drooped. Muriel could now see the small tuft of hair springing from the crown – a wayward curl exactly similar to the one that she had so often seen Deveril smooth on *his* head.

'Now remove yourself this instant!' She spat the words at

him with a bitterness the child had no way of understanding. 'And tell Mr Crowley you are to write out twenty times: "*I must not argue with my elders and betters*". I shall want to see your lines before you are permitted to leave the schoolroom again today.'

It was several minutes before Adam's tutor could make sense of the boy's words, garbled as they were between gasping sobs. A thin, pale man in his late fifties, Joseph Crowley suffered occasional crippling bouts of asthma which prevented him from securing a permanent post as a schoolmaster. He was entirely dependent upon his intermittent employment by rich gentlemen who paid him a meagre salary to teach their sons until they were of boarding school age. His intellectual qualifications were far in advance of the tasks required of him, and his sharp mind quickly detected in Lord Burnbury's small nephew a lively and quite exceptional intelligence. The boy responded easily to any new concept, and he was as eager to learn as Joseph Crowley was to teach. The man was at a complete loss therefore to understand Lady Burnbury's complaint that the child was falling behind with his work. So deeply did he feel the injustice, he decided to question the austere lady of the house.

Muriel received him in the library, her face expressionless as she heard the thin, gaunt tutor plead for leniency for his pupil. Adam, he told her earnestly, had been looking forward with the greatest enthusiasm to the seaside holiday. Not only would it be beneficial to his health but educationally too, since the boy had never yet seen an ocean. Moreover, he pointed out, it would be good for him to be with his young cousins. He spent too much time with adults.

'Have you quite finished, Mr Crowley?' she asked coldly. 'I really do not think it is your place to question my orders. But since you have seen fit to do so, I will inform you that I do not consider the boy's work *is* up to the standard of his age – in any respect. He has been permitted to run wild whilst in Scotland, and it is my intention that this state of affairs shall be rectified.'

She stared pointedly at the tall thin man.

'Of course, if you do not care to carry out my orders, you are at liberty to tender your resignation, Mr Crowley. I do not doubt I shall have little difficulty in obtaining the services of someone quite as well qualified as your good self to tutor the boy. He needs discipline, and I shall see that he receives it.'

For a brief moment, Joseph Crowley allowed himself the luxury of anger and an acute dislike for the aristocratic female now challenging him to risk his livelihood. Were he to resign his post, she would not, of course, give him a recommendation. Looking at her cold, austere face, he imagined she might well go out of her way to speak against him.

'The boy is still very young, Milady,' he said quietly. 'There is a limit to how much his brain can absorb in a day.'

'That is a matter of opinion,' Muriel said sharply. 'You may take him for an hour's walk after his rest in the afternoon. For the remainder of the day, I wish him to be gainfully employed in the schoolroom. It would do him no harm to memorize some passages from Shakespeare. See that he learns some of the better known soliloquies. I shall hear him repeat them before his bedtime each evening.'

So began a systematic form of physical restriction and mental torture for Adam which his kindly tutor was unable to prevent. Within a week, the boy was so fearful of his evening appointment with Muriel that the long stanzas he had memorized remained blurs in his mind, and although he could repeat them perfectly to Mr Crowley, he faltered before he was halfway through them when he stood facing his aunt that same evening.

Muriel's face never lost its curious half-smile as she regarded the shaking child. Impassively, at the first mistake, she reached for the small leather strap she kept for the purpose and rapped the boy's outstretched palms. If he did not hold them out at her command, he received an extra stroke. He grew pale and listless, and his sleep was fitful, punctured by nightmares. Letters to his Aunt Meg and to Forrie were forbidden and he received none. Despite Mr Crowley's unspoken sympathy, he felt abandoned and totally bewildered. By the end of July, he had changed from a laughing, happy, trusting child into a pale, silent little ghost.

At first, Mr Crowley was puzzled by Lady Burnbury's extraordinary antipathy to his charge. It was not his habit to listen to servants' gossip, but gradually a few facts emerged as the majority of the staff began to realize what was happening. It reached his ears that Lady Burnbury's French maid, who was mistrusted and disliked by everyone belowstairs, had actually dared to refer to Adam as Lord Burnbury's *bâtard*. The French word was similar enough to its English counterpart for no one to doubt its meaning. At once, Mr Crowley understood the reasons for Lady Burnbury's hatred of the child. He himself had seen the extraordinary similarities between father and son and he did not doubt the truth of the matter.

After a sleepless night worrying over the dangers of his own involvement, Mr Crowley hinted to Adam that while he, his tutor, was forbidden to give letters to the bellman for postage, perhaps one of the footmen or Mr Dawkins, the butler, might be persuaded to perform the task. He absented himself from the schoolroom long enough for Adam to pen a letter to his beloved Forrie. When the time came for their afternoon walk, he deliberately looked away when the child stopped to give Dawkins his letter as the butler opened the front door for them.

Whether or not the letter ever reached Mrs Forest, Mr Crowley could not know, for Lady Burnbury received all the incoming mail, and if there had been a reply for Adam, it was confiscated along with the letters which arrived at irregular intervals from his uncle.

As Adam grew daily thinner, paler and more listless, Mr Crowley decided to take matters into his own hands. According to the servants, Lord Burnbury had postponed his return to England and was not now expected home before the middle of September. Fearing that his small charge would not survive another month without serious consequences to his health and character, he took it upon himself to write to the woman he supposed had been Adam's former governess. As far as he had been able to ascertain from the boy, Mrs Forest had been employed by Lady McDoone and was not bound by loyalties to Lady Burnbury. He could but hope, therefore, that the woman might find some way, which he could not, of appealing to Lord Burnbury's sister, Lady Allendale, to speak up for Adam.

When Clemency received the tutor's letter, all the colour left her cheeks as her eyes scanned the neatly formed lines with anxious haste. He was, Mr Crowley informed her, putting himself at great risk by revealing to her the present state of affairs appertaining at Grayshott House.

'Milord Burnbury is abroad as you may know,' he wrote, 'otherwise I could have turned to him for guidance in *the most delicate matter of his nephew's welfare.* I have to confess that I fear for the boy's sanity as much as for his health. He is unwell and the greater distressed by virtue of the fact that he is no longer permitted to receive your letters or even those of his uncle, Lord Burnbury.

'I understand from past conversations with my pupil that he is devoted to you. As Lord Burnbury is not due back from abroad for some weeks yet, perhaps you could pay a 'casual' visit to the boy and ascertain from him the true facts of the matter which I do not feel it advisable to relate in this letter.

'I remain your humble servant,
Joseph Crowley Esq.'

'I shall go to London immediately,' Clemency said to the Professor. 'Mr Crowley would never have written such a letter unless Adam was in great trouble. If that horrible woman has been cruel to him . . .' Her voice broke as the Professor forced her to be seated, urging her to calm herself.

'Until you know what has happened, Clemency, you cannot present yourself to Lady Burnbury,' he said forcibly. 'This may be only a temporary setback in Adam's young life, and by revealing your identity now, you would put the whole of your future relationship with him in jeopardy. I suggest that you write a letter immediately to this tutor, who sounds a sympathetic fellow. Ask him to meet you the day after tomorrow at a rendezvous away from Grayshott House. You can question him more closely as to Adam's condition. I do not think the man will refuse you an interview since he felt it necessary to write to you inviting your intervention.'

Slowly, the fierce beating of Clemency's heart steadied to a more normal pace as she realized that the Professor's counsel was a wise one. At his suggestion, she selected the Poultenay Hotel in Piccadilly as a suitable place to rendezvous, being not too far distant from Hanover Square. She told Adam's tutor that she would wait in the foyer for him between the hours of two and six o'clock.

'If it should be possible,' she ended her brief letter, 'I beg you to bring Adam with you . . .'

Clemency's anxiety and impatience would have been far greater had she known that there would not be the slightest hope of her seeing her child. Adam was allowed out of the house each day for no more than an hour's exercise in Hanover Square Gardens. Otherwise he was confined to the schoolroom, where he also took his meals. It was only after tea that he was permitted to leave the schoolroom again for his evening visit to his aunt – an ordeal he now dreaded to such a degree that invariably he vomited his meal when the time came for him to present himself to Lady Burnbury.

Frederick offered to accompany Clemency to London, and she accepted the suggestion. He might be better able to assess the situation than she herself in her present state of anxiety, she agreed.

She was glad of his presence when finally Mr Crowley joined them two days later in the foyer of the hotel. He was without coat or hat and greeted them with the announcement that he had slipped out of the house unnoticed and could spare only a few minutes, lest his absence were to be remarked.

Clemency's heart was torn with anguish as he described the conditions under which Adam was now living. Unaware of her true relationship to the boy, Mr Crowley referred quite openly to the suspicions he held that Lady Burnbury's dislike of the child was as a result of her discovering him to be her husband's by-blow.

'Perhaps you could pay a formal call on Lady Burnbury,' he suggested, 'and request to see the boy . . .'

Before Clemency could speak, Frederick Brook intervened.

'I do not think that would be the best step to take at this stage,' he said. 'But be assured, Mr Crowley, we shall not leave matters as they are. Mrs Forest is devoted to Adam, and we are both very grateful indeed to you for your intervention. Naturally, you may count upon our discretion with regard to your part in informing us of this unfortunate state of affairs.'

'Then I shall be on my way,' the tutor said, bowing politely before he hurried off.

Clemency's face was pale with distress as she watched the tall thin figure leave the hotel.

'I should have relied more upon my instinct,' she said, as much to herself as to her companion. 'I never in my heart believed Lady Burnbury would welcome Adam, but I allowed Deveril to influence my judgement. I never anticipated that he would go abroad and leave Adam alone with that cruel, heartless woman.'

She regarded Frederick unhappily.

'Mr Crowley said that it might be a further month before Deveril returned home, and the only respite Adam can hope for would be next week when Lady Burnbury is leaving on the Friday to stay for a few days with her parents in Hertfordshire.'

'And that might be only a temporary respite,' Frederick

agreed, 'for even when Lord Burnbury returns home, what guarantee is there that he can prevent his wife's further torture of the child? Lady Burnbury might pretend kindness in her husband's presence, but the moment his back is turned . . .'

I should have taken Adam to North America in the spring, Clemency thought, as her own longing to be reunited with him swept over her. These past two months when she should have been concentrating upon her approaching marriage to Benjamin and upon the search for the little house they had planned to live in together, she had behaved as if their wedding was years and not weeks away. It was as if she had known deep within her that the future she and Benjamin had planned would never evolve; that Fate had never intended it should take place. Only yesterday, Benjamin had written to say that he had not yet been successful in finding a replacement for himself.

Now it seemed as if the Fates were warning her that she must not tie herself irrevocably to a future that might prevent her acting as she pleased with regard to her son. She was mercifully still free to do as she wished. She could, she realized, *still take Adam to North America*, far away from Lady Burnbury's interference. She was no longer disturbed by thoughts of Deveril's anguish at the loss of his son, for it had taken only three months for him to become bored with the novelty of Adam's company.

Her heart raced with nervous excitement as she contemplated the prospect of removing Adam once and for all from his father's custody. Mr Talfourd's Bill had been withdrawn from the Parliamentary list, and any hope of her obtaining legal custody of her son in the near future was gone.

'My situation is worse even than Mrs Norton's,' Clemency explained to Frederick, as they took a hackney to Blossoms Inn. 'She at least has some hope of being legally reunited with her sons. Her husband brought them back from Scotland in June with the promise to let her see them and she was permitted a brief glimpse of them. But Mr Norton did not fulfil his promise to permit her regular access, and the boys are now in Wonersh in Surrey. Understandably, she has put in abeyance the legal and political pressure she had been exerting on her husband, in the hope of obtaining his goodwill. I understand her bitterness, Frederick. Why should it be necessary for a mother to humble herself and be forced to beg for the right to see her own children!'

Such could all too easily be her own position, Clemency thought, as she and Frederick rode back to Brighton on the evening coach. Were she to approach Deveril and confess her maternal interest in Adam, he might well prove as harsh and unrelenting in his attitude as George Norton. She dared not take the risk, and however sadly it would affect poor Benjamin, she could do no other than put Adam's welfare and happiness first. Benjamin had always known her son was her first priority.

But she could not confide such thoughts to Frederick, who was still something of a stranger. She feared, too, that he might try to dissuade her from taking such a drastic step. Benjamin must be told immediately, and she would talk to the Professor as soon as they arrived home. But not even *he* could change her mind, she decided, as they crossed the South Downs and the first lights of the town could be seen from the coach window. Mr Crowley's graphic description of Adam's white, frightened face was imprinted too deeply on her mind for doubts to assail her. The thought of him vomiting after his tea as his coming ordeal approached was more than she could bear to contemplate.

Clemency realized that it was going to require courage as well as resourcefulness to carry out her plan to leave England within the week. But the courage she must find was not merely for practical necessities. She would need it even more when she faced Benjamin, knowing how deep would be his sorrow and disappointment when she told him she could not after all become his wife.

CHAPTER TWENTY-FIVE

September 1837

On the following Friday Clemency was back in London, waiting at the corner of Hanover Square in a hackney. She had spent the night at the Porchester Hotel where her luggage was now deposited. After a very early breakfast, she had hired the hackney to take her within sight of Grayshott House and here she intended to remain until Lady Burnbury left for Hertfordshire. She was praying that there had been no change in the woman's plans.

Clemency felt strangely calm. Her own plans were carefully formulated and barring some unforeseen event, by evening at the latest she would be on her way with Adam to Bristol. Benjamin would be awaiting her there at the Talbot Inn. But for the moment, she did not want to think about their impending farewell. Her thoughts were revolving round the letter in her reticule. Addressed to Adam's tutor, it purported to be from Lady McDoone.

'As I find myself unexpectedly in London, I wish to take the opportunity to see Adam. Would you please arrange for the boy's nurse to bring him to the Porchester Hotel to take tea with me today . . .'

With the greatest of care, Clemency had forged the signature: *Margaret McDoone.*

She sighed, her inner excitement momentarily tempered by memories of the assistance the old Professor had afforded her once he realized her mind was made up to take Adam to live with her father. It was he who had suggested that Clemency in person ensured that the letter was delivered after Lady Burnbury's departure. Clemency herself had planned it as a means of protecting the well-intentioned Mr Crowley. She did not wish him to be held responsible were she to abduct Adam while he was in his tutor's care. Lady Burnbury could not expect him to guess that the letter was forged, and no blame would attach to him for assuming its authenticity and for acting upon Lady McDoone's orders.

Also in Clemency's reticule was a letter from Benjamin. It compounded her feelings of guilt towards him by its marked absence of any criticism and its complete understanding of her sentiments. As for her suggestion that they must now break their engagement, he would not hear of it, he wrote. Now that Frederick and Edith were in England and could keep an eye on his father, he could happily contemplate forging a new life for himself with Clemency and Adam in the colonies – unless, of course, she no longer wished to marry him, which matter could be discussed in Bristol. If, as he hoped with all his heart, she was still prepared to become his wife, then he would follow her to North America at the earliest opportunity and they could be married soon after his arrival.

If her plan succeeded, Clemency thought, and Adam was brought by his nurse to the hotel, her worries were at an end, for no matter how the quality of the sailing ship, she intended to embark upon the first one due to sail across the Atlantic. Once at sea, she would be safe from discovery. Let the nasty Grimshaw try to find her whereabouts in Poole – or even in Brighton! As far as Clemency knew, he had no knowledge of her father's address in the colonies, even if he guessed that was where she was taking Adam.

One after another the minutes ticked by. Tradesmen called at the house and a footman departed carrying a parcel, but there was no sign of Lady Burnbury. The clock of St George's church on the far side of the square struck ten. Clemency's driver got down from his cab to put a nosebag on his horse.

He suspected a marital tiff, and that the pretty young woman in his cab was keeping watch on a nearby house to see if her husband or lover emerged. He was surprised therefore when he saw the Burnbury carriage come to the front door and shortly after, the Viscountess leave the Square by Brook Street.

'You are to deliver this to the front door of Grayshott House,' Clemency called to him, as she handed him a note. 'There will be an extra shilling for you if you tell the butler that you have come from the Porchester Hotel. Under *no* circumstances are you to reveal my presence. Do you understand?'

Grinning broadly, the man nodded and went across the street. As Clemency anticipated, the butler opened the door and she saw the two men in conversation. Then the driver returned and said amiably:

'Like you thourt, M'um,'e did ask'oo I was, and I told'im I'd been sent by a lady at the 'otel. Where to now, M'um?'

'Back to the Porchester,' Clemency said with a deep sigh of relief. It was now nearly half past eleven. There was no point in waiting for Adam and his nurse to come out, since she could not expect their arrival at the hotel much before three.

Returning there, she paid her bill and had her luggage brought downstairs. From then on, she sat in a chair near the front door so that she would be certain to see Adam the instant he arrived. At a quarter past three o'clock, Adam and a woman Clemency assumed was his nurse walked in through the door of the hotel.

With a sharp pang of distress, Clemency stared at the thin, pale little boy who was her son. His head was turned towards her, and she could see great hollows in his cheeks and dark shadows beneath his eyes. He seemed visibly to have shrunk, and when finally she caught him in her arms, she realized with horror that he had lost an excessive amount of weight.

Instead of the smile of pleasure she had anticipated when he recognized her, Adam burst into tears. With a muffled cry of 'Forrie, oh Forrie!' he flung himself into her arms and clung

to her as if he were clinging to a lifeline. With an effort to
restrain her own tears, she looked over the boy's head to the
nurse.

'I am Lady McDoone's former companion,' she said in an
authoritative tone. 'Milady will be down directly. You may
leave Adam in my charge meanwhile. Perhaps you would like
to take the opportunity of a walk in the fresh air? Or you
may have shopping to do? In any event, Lady McDoone asked
me to tell you that there is no need for you to return before
six o'clock. And please tell the coachman he need not wait.'

Reassured by the fact that her young charge was obviously
quite content to be left with a familiar adult, the woman made
no demur. She had a sister living in Fulham, and if she made
haste, there might be time to visit her, she thought, delighted
to be free of her charge for an hour or two.

Clemency took Adam by the hand and led him to a sofa
in a quiet corner of the foyer. He still made no attempt to
speak, but grasped her skirt in both hands as if to assure
himself that there was no chance of her suddenly
disappearing.

'Now, my darling, as there is not a great deal of time,' she
said softly, 'we must talk together about the future. I know
you have not been happy these past two months, and another
time you shall tell me about it. But first of all, I want to know
if you would like to come and live with me?'

The boy's eyes were still full of tears as he raised his head
and regarded her with a combination of hope and disbelief.

'Oh, Forrie, could I?' he whispered. 'I do not want to live
with *her* – not ever. She hates me. I know she does . . .'

There was a note of rising hysteria in his voice and Clemency
broke in quickly:

'You shall not return there, Adam. If you would like it, you
and I will live together.'

'You mean we can go back to Aunt Meg?'

Clemency bit her lip.

'I am afraid it would not be safe for us to go to Castle

Clunes,' she said softly. 'Your Uncle 'Vril would look for us there and bring you back to London.'

'Then where will we go?' Adam asked doubtfully.

Clemency drew a deep breath.

'I thought you might like to come to North America with me, Adam. I am going there to live with my papa. You would like him, my darling.'

'Would he beat me if I was naughty?' Adam asked anxiously.

Clemency's heart twisted with pity.

'No, Adam, I should not permit it; besides, my papa is one of the kindest men you could ever hope to meet. He is very jolly, too.'

'Is he as jolly as Uncle 'Vril? Will Uncle 'Vril come and live with us when he returns from Europe?'

Clemency regarded her son's face anxiously as she replied:

'No, darling, he would not. But you might have a new "uncle" who you would like every bit as much as your Uncle 'Vril. He is a physician, and he and I will probably get married and you would become our little boy.'

For what seemed an interminable minute, Adam did not speak, and Clemency feared that he might be about to inform her that he could not bear to leave his Uncle 'Vril for ever. But when he spoke, it was only to ask:

'Will we go on a sailing ship, Forrie? I have never seen the ocean. *She* would not allow me to go to the seaside with Aunt Selina. Why does she hate me, Forrie?'

'Do not worry about her any more, Adam,' Clemency said quickly. 'You will never see her again. We shall go together now in a coach to Bristol and there we will meet your new uncle. His name is Benjamin. He will find a sailing ship for us in which we will travel to America. It will be quite an adventure, will it not? And we shall be together – just as I promised.'

As she hired a hackney to take them to the staging post at Hounslow, Clemency felt a moment of unease. She knew that the small boy sitting so trustingly beside her was not yet fully aware of the vastness of the distance – over four thousand miles – that she was about to put between him and his father. But it was never her intention to leave such a momentous decision to so young a child. It was her hope and belief that he would forget Deveril with so much that was new and exciting to distract him. One day, perhaps, when he was a grown man, he could return to England and renew his association with his father. But for the next fifteen years she intended his childhood should be happy and without the kind of fear that had so debilitated him these past two months. It horrified her that Adam, who had always been such a chatterbox, was now for the most part silent, only occasionally asking a question as they boarded the mail for Bristol at the George Inn.

By six o'clock, when his nurse would be returning to the hotel to collect him, they were already beyond Slough and were crossing the Thames at Maidenhead. Not without anxiety, Clemency imagined the uproar when Muriel Burnbury learned that Adam had disappeared and that Lady McDoone had not been staying at the Porchester. If the nurse gave Lady Burnbury Clemency's description, or if she had overheard Adam's sad welcome to 'Forrie', then Lady Burnbury would most likely send Mr Crowley to look for her in Brighton. The Professor, Frederick Brook and his wife would truthfully deny any knowledge of her whereabouts, for Clemency had refused to advise them of her immediate plans. She was well aware that she was contravening the law, and did not wish them to risk accusation at a later date of being accessories to her 'crime'.

She smiled grimly to herself as she glanced at the small boy leaning drowsily against her side. How could anyone consider it a crime for her, his mother, to take him away from the woman who hated him enough to torture him physically and mentally! It would be Muriel Burnbury's turn to suffer, she thought, if not now, then when Deveril returned home. He would suffer too, but she would not permit herself to feel pity for him. She turned her thoughts quickly away from the memory of his face as he swung Adam onto his shoulders or sat him on his lap, ruffling his hair affectionately. She would not feel sorry for him. Had he not abandoned his son to the uncertain care of a woman he knew had no love for him?

She turned her thoughts instead to Benjamin, who would even now be on his way to await their arrival. By the time she and Adam reached the Talbot in the early hours of the morning, he would have had a room prepared for them. It was even possible that he might already have paid a visit to the shipping office to list the dates of sailing so that she and the child could leave England as swiftly as possible. She would not feel safe until they had left the shores of England behind them.

The boy slept fitfully, moaning sometimes in his sleep, as the coach rattled on through Berkshire and Wiltshire. The open countryside of the Wiltshire Downs reminded her suddenly of the Purbeck Hills, and she felt a moment's sadness that there would be no opportunity now to visit Mary. In her last letter to the little maid, posted two weeks ago, she had promised to make the journey from Brighton to see her, never imagining when she wrote it that Adam was not happily settled at Grayshott House with his father. Mary would be no less disappointed than she was herself that their reunion after six years could not now take place.

Darkness fell and the night sky was filled with stars. Wide awake, Clemency found herself recalling the journey she had taken to Bristol with Benjamin all those years ago. Adam had been only eight weeks old, and but for the letter revealing the death of her parents, she might so easily have departed then to the colonies.

Her arms tightened around the sleeping child. She would never let Adam go again. If in years to come, he wished to claim his heritage, she would not stand in his way. Meanwhile, she need not concern herself with so far distant a future. Her plan to take Adam away from Grayshott House had worked without a hitch, and it was the immediate future which mattered.

It lacked but a few hours to dawn by the time the coach drew into the familiar yard of the Talbot, but Benjamin was waiting up for her. His smile of welcome faded as with professional concern he viewed Adam's pale little face and drooping figure.

'The boy is too thin!' he commented, but noting Clemency's anxiety, he added with a smile: 'But he will soon put on weight. Now I can see that he is quite exhausted. You too, my dear. As your physician, I therefore order you both to bed. But I think you will sleep the better if I tell you that there is a ship leaving tomorrow on the afternoon tide and I have booked your passages.'

As Clemency opened her mouth to thank him, he bent and kissed her cheek.

'No talking now,' he said firmly. 'We will have plenty of time to discuss everything after breakfast. Now off to bed – both of you!' he added, with a smile at Adam's solemn little face.

It was as if a great burden had been lifted from her shoulders, Clemency thought, as she led Adam up the winding staircase to a big bedroom at the far side of the inn where they would not be disturbed by the coaches clattering into the cobbled yard. Benjamin was taking care of everything, and she could safely leave matters in his capable hands.

I owe him so much! was her last thought before she fell asleep, Adam safely tucked up in a little truckle bed beside her. How could I ever have doubted that I would be other than the most fortunate of women to become his wife!

The following morning, Benjamin made light both of her thanks and her apologies for disrupting their wedding plans so abruptly. He glanced at Adam, who was tucking into a big breakfast as if he had not a care in the world, and said softly:

'You have never pretended that this young man did not hold first place in your heart, my dear. Believe me, I am quite content to come second. As for my following you to North America, I profess myself excited at the prospect.' He gazed deeply into her eyes as if attempting to read the truth in her heart. 'You do want me to join you there, Clemency? You have not changed your mind about our marriage?'

Clemency could not bring herself to lie to him.

'I have questioned the rightness of it,' she said truthfully. 'When I learned that Adam was so unhappy, it frightened me that I could so easily disregard *our* plans as if they were unimportant. It does not seem fair to you, Benjamin, that I should put his needs before yours.'

He smiled at her disarmingly.

'My dearest Clemency, I might have felt disturbed had you placed another *man* higher in your regard. But I am not – nor ever would be – jealous of your son,' he added in an undertone.

Clemency was close to tears as she smiled tremulously.

'You have been steadfast in your love for so long now,' she said. 'Perhaps it is just the idea of marriage to me that has become a habit, Benjamin, and one day you will come to your senses and discover you do not love me at all.'

Benjamin took her hand in his.

'Whatever the future holds for us, my dear, *I will never stop loving you*. Of that you can be assured. Now let us put sentiment aside and consider this young man. What do you say to a quick visit to the harbour to look at the sailing ships?'

'Will Forrie come with us, sir?' Adam enquired anxiously.

'But of course!' Benjamin reassured him. As Adam put his hand trustingly in Benjamin's, Clemency was filled with new joy and certainty in the rightness of her decision. It seemed now on this sunny morning as if this had always been her destiny – Adam's too. She accompanied her two menfolk out on to the busy street.

On the same day three weeks later that Deveril reached the shores of England, Clemency and Adam arrived safely in New York; Benjamin was finalizing his plans to depart from Southampton and Muriel retired to bed with a migraine. She

developed this attack as she heard Hopkins' voice in the
entrance hall announcing Deveril's imminent arrival.

'Draw the curtains – quickly, Celeste!' she said, as she lay
down upon her bed. 'And then go down and tell Lord Burnbury
that I am prostrate!'

For two whole weeks she had been dreading Deveril's home-
coming with increasing trepidation. When first she learned
that Adam had vanished, her immediate reaction had been
one of 'good riddance'; but a moment later, she felt the early
stirrings of fear. 'Whatever fate has befallen the wretched boy,
Lord Burnbury will of a certainty blame me!' she said bitterly
to Celeste. She had dismissed the nurse upon the spot and
would have dismissed the tutor too, but that she feared what
he might tell Deveril when he returned home. It was better,
she decided, to keep Mr Crowley as an ally, leaving Deveril
to dismiss him – which he surely would. It was not Mr
Crowley's fault, she told the tutor, that he had failed to recognize that Lady McDoone's handwriting was forged.

Since Adam's disappearance, Muriel had had the lawyer Mr
Grimshaw searching for the child. He, like herself, suspected
Mrs Forest of having abducted Adam, the frightened nurse
having insisted so vehemently that the boy had addressed the
young lady at the hotel as 'Forrie'. He said nothing to Lady
Burnbury, however, regarding his growing fear that the
so-called Mrs Forest might be one and the same person as
Clementine Foster, the boy's mother. If it proved to be the
case, he dared not imagine the accusations of incompetence
he must expect from Lord Burnbury. With growing unease,
he had told Lady Burnbury that Mrs Forest was not in
Brighton.

'It is my belief that the woman has taken Adam back to
Scotland,' Muriel replied. 'But since Lord Burnbury should be
home any day now, I prefer to leave the decision to him as
to whether he wishes his great-aunt advised of the boy's
disappearance.'

Lady McDoone would be greatly concerned – as much as

Deveril, Muriel thought, remembering how he had reiterated on many occasions that his great-aunt doted on the child. If she herself was not to be held responsible for this débâcle, she must handle the matter with the utmost care. Her attitude to Deveril, she decided, would be one of remorse and anxiety. For the time being, she would make no mention of her awareness that the boy was *his* child. She had been very careful not to admit to any such knowledge when she was speaking to the lawyer.

Now her heart jolted as she heard Deveril's voice on the landing outside her bedroom. It cut across Celeste's ineffectual attempts to bar his way.

'Migraine or no, I shall speak to Lady Burnbury! Now stand aside, woman!'

Deveril strode into the room, his Petersham still slung round his shoulders, his ebony cane and pink kid gloves still in his hands. His hair was in disarray and his eyes were flashing.

'I left the boy in your care, Muriel. Where is he?' he stormed at her without preliminary greeting or enquiries as to her health.

She passed a hand wearily over her forehead and gave a slight moan.

'I cannot answer you, Deveril,' she said in a frail, sad voice. 'I have, as you can see, been ill with worry. Celeste will tell you that I have not slept a wink at nights and I am as distraught as you.'

Deveril was momentarily silenced. Muriel did not look well, insofar as he could see in the dim light of the bedroom. Moreover, she sounded genuinely distressed. He drew a deep breath, and trying to curb his anger – and fear – he sat down heavily in the chair usually occupied by Celeste. In as quiet a tone as he could assume, he demanded that Muriel told him the whole story – from the moment when Adam had been taken by his nurse to see Lady McDoone.

Haltingly, with many sighs and occasionally dabbing her eyes with a handkerchief, Muriel related the events. She was aware of the impatient tapping of Deveril's cane against the side of the chair as he listened, but he did not interrupt. Finally, she said:

'I did not permit Grimshaw to go to Scotland, fearing it might cause the poor old lady unnecessary distress if the boy was not with her. I hope I did right Deveril, and that you are not angry with me?'

'I am sure you acted as you thought best,' Deveril said grudgingly. 'But I have not yet understood, Muriel, why Adam did not go with Selina and his cousins to Worthing as I had arranged. For what reasons were my orders countermanded?'

Muriel had anticipated the question. She said gently:

'The boy was far from well, Deveril. He had been sleeping badly and vomiting his meals, and I feared he was sickening for some childish complaint. I did not think your sister would welcome it were I to send an infectious child to mix with her own young ones.'

Deveril shrugged.

'I suppose that was good reason, although if the boy was ill, the sea air would have benefited him. But it is done now, and the unacceptable truth remains that Adam has gone and we do not know where. It is intolerable!'

Deveril had not known such an ache in his heart since the night his grandfather died. Exhausted by the long journey, he had been devastated by the news awaiting him on his arrival, the more so as he had been greatly looking forward to the welcome he expected to receive from his little son.

Dejectedly, he ran his hands through his hair and suddenly an unwelcome thought froze him into complete stillness. Was it possible that after all these years, the boy's *mother* had discovered his whereabouts and spirited him away?

No sooner had the thought entered his mind than at once he rejected it. Whoever she was, the mother had surrendered the boy without great fuss and, according to Grimshaw, had been happy to accept financial recompense for her loss. There could be no reason why she should suddenly change her mind

– unless she wanted more money. If that were so, she would sooner or later approach Grimshaw and he, Deveril, would willingly meet her demands. But he did not believe she had stolen the boy! He thought the most probable solution was that Adam had pleaded with the soft-hearted Mrs Forest to take him back to his great-aunt in Scotland. He had probably been homesick – the more likely with Deveril himself away in Europe.

Muriel was watching his changing expressions as she tried to assess his mood. She knew it might not be long before he discovered from that stiff-necked old butler Dawkins that she had not treated the boy very kindly. There were too many of the old Grayshott servants who did not like her and might tittle-tattle to their master. If Deveril discovered she had chastized the boy – kept him a virtual prisoner in the school-room . . .

'I beg you to try to forgive me,' she said in a self-deprecatory tone. 'I know I was not as affectionate towards the boy as you would have liked. But believe me, my dear, I did my very best. As you know, I do not have a natural love for children and it has not been easy for me.'

Deveril was not really listening. Tired as he was, he was assessing the length of the journey to Scotland. If he left immediately in his fastest carriage and made no overnight stops, he could be at Castle Clunes within three days. He would take the chaise and two coachmen to drive alternately. If he did not take his valet Hopkins with him, he would make even better time.

When he announced his intention, Muriel looked at him aghast.

'But Deveril, you have only just reached home! There is no need for such haste. After all, a day or two longer cannot count for much, and if Adam is with your great-aunt, he will be perfectly safe.'

Deveril stood up and looked down at his wife, his voice edged with scorn.

'And if Adam is *not* at Castle Clunes?' he asked pointedly. 'I would have wasted even more time than has already been dissipated. Be so good as to send a note at once to Grimshaw advising him of my movements. And do not bother me with questions – Grimshaw will understand why I must find Adam immediately.'

He took Muriel's hand and kissed it with informal haste before he bowed and left the room. His feelings of anger and frustration had renewed his energy and he swept through the house like a whirlwind, giving orders right and left as he snatched a cold meal sent up by Cook. She was even now packing a hamper of food for him to take on the journey, avoiding the necessity for prolonged stops en route.

The belief that he would find Adam at Castle Clunes sustained him on the long journey north. He slept a great deal of the way, and for several hours each day he rode up beside the coachman, allowing the second driver to doze inside the chaise. His spirits lifted as they crossed the border into Scotland. He could even bring himself to grin inwardly at the audacity of the pretty little Mrs Forest in whisking Adam away from under Muriel's wing – if indeed she had done so. She would have to be reprimanded, of course, for it had undoubtedly caused an unholy commotion these past two weeks. Not that he was displeased at the thought of Grimshaw running around like a scalded cat; nor indeed of Muriel's apprehension knowing the fuss he would raise when he arrived home. She could not have put herself out to keep the boy content, else Adam would not have wanted to go back to Castle Clunes.

Although Adam had seemed happy enough at Grayshott House, doubtless his life had been somewhat devoid of excitement after he, Deveril, had left, he thought; but it would not have been so if Muriel had left matters well alone and the boy had been permitted to go to Worthing with Selina. Perhaps he would do well to leave Adam with his Aunt Meg for a year or two longer, he speculated.

His thoughts returned with relief to Clemency Forest. He and Dominic Wade had discussed her on several occasions whilst they had walked or climbed in the mountains of Switzerland. Wade had remarked upon that strange haunting effect the girl unconsciously evoked in a man.

Deveril knew very well what Wade meant. There was a sweetness and an essential femininity about her, yet he had seen strength too – and passion. He had not forgotten her kisses, nor indeed his own overwhelming desire for her. It had been a bitter disappointment when she had refused to go to Grayshott House with Adam as his governess. But then, he reminded himself, she had stated her intention to marry Brook, and he must assume it was respectability that she craved.

By now they had reached Castle Clunes, and as the front door swung open, Lady McDoone's large deerhounds came bounding down the stairway to greet him, barking their welcome. There was no sign of Adam or his great-aunt as two of the footmen hurried to assist his coachmen with the luggage.

'I am afraid her Ladyship is indisposed, Milord,' one of them told him as he entered the house. 'She has been unwell this past fortnight and the physician we summoned from Perth fears she may be suffering from pleurisy. He has ordered hot linseed-oil poultices which Campbell is applying every hour, and we believe her Ladyship is a little better. I will instruct Campbell to inform Milady that you are here, Milord.'

Deveril heard this news with dismay. His great-aunt was only four years short of eighty, and he felt a sudden chill of alarm that he might lose her. Like his grandfather, he thought uneasily, old people who had always been old for as long as he could remember gave an illusion of indestructibility. It was only when one was on the point of losing them that their mortality was suddenly apparent.

'I will visit my great-aunt immediately if she is well enough to receive me,' he told the waiting servant. 'But first tell me, are Mrs Forest and the boy here?'

The butler looked puzzled.

'No, Milord. They have not yet arrived. As far as I know, we have not been advised to prepare rooms for them – or for yourself, Milord.'

Deveril's shoulders drooped. To have come so far only to receive two such items of bad news! For the first time since he had learned of Adam's disappearance, he felt a real anxiety. For some reason he could not now justify, he had been more or less convinced that he would find the boy in Scotland. And since Adam was neither here nor in Brighton, then where was he? And with whom?

His reverie was interrupted by his great-aunt's elderly servant Campbell.

'Milady will be pleased to see you the noo!' she declared, her eyes glancing disapprovingly at Deveril's muddy boots. 'She's aye happy ye're heer!'

For once, there were no animals or birds to be seen in Lady McDoone's room. The physician had ordered them removed, the old lady told Deveril with a smile. As he bent to kiss her shrunken, wrinkled cheek, Deveril could hear the harsh rasp of her breath, and he guessed that she must be in pain. But indomitable as ever, she waved him to a chair by the bedside and asked him tartly what reasons brought him to Scotland now that his precious Adam was not there to tempt him to Castle Clunes.

'If I had known you were ill, dearest Aunt, I would have come much sooner – and just to see *you*,' he declared honestly. 'But I was unaware of your indisposition, having only three days ago returned from a climbing tour in Switzerland.' He looked anxiously at her white, drawn face and added: 'Are you in pain? Is there anything at all I can do for you?'

She shook her head.

'There is no need to fuss. I shall recover in my own good time, and I could have no better nurse than old Campbell. She is making me take that perfectly revolting tonic of hers – iodine of iron!'

Deveril smiled in spite of his concern, remembering from his boyhood the old servant's panacea for all ills.

'Now, my dear, we will cease discussing my health, which topic I find exceedingly tiresome, and you shall tell me what has brought you to Scotland. I suppose it is too much to hope that you have Adam with you? I have had no letter from him for several weeks.'

She listened in silence while Deveril recounted as briefly as he could all that he knew of Adam's disappearance. Watching the old lady's face, he was surprised to see no expression of astonishment in her eyes, and when finally he came to the end of his story, she said quietly:

'It is my belief that our Mrs Forest is Adam's mother.'

She saw the look of incredulity on Deveril's face and said carefully:

'Is it so unlikely? At first I thought so too, and I decided that it could serve no purpose to mention my suspicion to you. But now I believe it to be well founded. Consider all the facts, Deveril. You yourself admitted when you first brought Adam to live with me that you could not remember the unfortunate girl you seduced! When Clemency came here last year as my companion, *she* knew you would not recognize her. I believe Mrs Norton had her confidence, and having ascertained that Adam was living here with me, applied for the position for her. Mrs Norton's recommendation was a little too perfectly timed, was it not? Moreover, it gave little information as to Mrs Forest's past, referring to her in the vaguest terms as "a young widow of genteel birth". I was perfectly satisfied with her reference at the time, and with that of the eminent Professor Brook, and I did not consider it necessary to look further into her past. How do we know that Clemency did not live in Dorset before taking employment with the Professor?'

The long speech had left her breathless, but there was little need for her to elaborate her theories. Deveril's mind had raced back to the day he had encountered Clemency on the beach at Poole. He had paid no attention to the fact at the time, but now he recalled there had been an infant there too, in the arms of the elderly female accompanying Brook and

the girl. And Grimshaw had first discovered Adam's whereabouts in Poole!

Slowly, as he searched his memory, he found that every
piece of the jigsaw fitted perfectly: Clemency's age; her
devotion to the boy; her antipathy to him, Deveril! But why,
he asked himself, having been reunited with her child, had
she refused to go with Adam to Grayshott House?

This puzzle too, he could solve, remembering that Muriel
had actually met Clemency on one occasion. Muriel would at
once have recognized Mrs Forest as the boy's mother and
informed him! No wonder Adam's 'Forrie' had not dared take
the position he had offered as governess!

Lady McDoone had remained silent whilst Deveril was
speculating, but now she said:

'There is only one thing which puzzles me, Deveril. You went
to great lengths to assure me that Adam's mother had surrendered the boy to your lawyer without fuss; that she had been
tempted by the large sums of money you offered, and that you
had no conscience regarding her feelings on that account. Having
lived at the closest possible quarters with Clemency for over
half a year, I cannot reconcile her gentle, loving disposition with
that avaricious girl you described to me.'

Deveril nodded, his eyes thoughtful. He could not but agree
with his great-aunt. Yet, Grimshaw had assured him . . .

'Grimshaw!' he said aloud. 'I never trusted him, but because
it suited me, I believed him without question. *I wanted the
boy . . .*'

Lady McDoone sighed.

'So too, did his mother – if, as I am now convinced,
Clemency Forest is his mother. And you, Deveril, have only
your wife's account of what happened at Grayshott House
in your absence. I believe Clemency would have left Adam
there so long as she was convinced he was happy. But if he
was not . . .'

Deveril stood up and began to pace the room in restless
anxiety.

'But if Mrs Forest – Clemency – *has* taken Adam, where is she hiding him? Muriel told me that Grimshaw could get no information from Professor Brook, and Doctor Brook was away . . .' He broke off, frowning. 'Clemency intends to marry Brook. If they are together . . .'

He was unable to explain to Lady McDoone – or even to himself – why the thought of Clemency with Benjamin Brook should rouse him to such anger, but he could feel the tension within him as he visualized the girl in Brook's arms; see the man kissing her upturned mouth as he, Deveril, had done. Momentarily, Adam was forgotten as he tried desperately to recall that night in the cornfield when, so Grimshaw had told him, he had seduced the girl. The colour burned in his cheeks as he thought of holding Clemency Forest in so intimate an embrace. Was that long-ago seduction the reason why he had subsequently found himself so attracted to her? Why she had always seemed to linger in his mind – a half-forgotten memory? If his Aunt Meg's deductions were true, then Clemency herself must have known all along that it was he who had lain with her that hot summer's night. How she must hate him! How she must have suffered at his hands! And now she was having her revenge, depriving him of his son as once, unwittingly, he had deprived her. But would he have acted differently all those years ago if Grimshaw had told him the boy's mother was *not* willing to relinquish the boy to him?

In this moment of truth, Deveril was obliged to admit that he had wanted Adam at all costs. He had understood nothing then of the immensity of love a parent could feel towards a child. His own love for Adam had grown with the years, and now the boy was so much a part of his life, he could not envisage the future without him.

He turned to Lady McDoone with a look of helplessness in his eyes.

'I want Adam back,' he said simply. 'As you know, my marriage is not exactly a happy one. Adam made up for it. I will not let him go.'

Lady McDoone regarded him thoughtfully.

'I know you love him, Deveril. But Clemency loves him, too . . . enough to have surrendered him to you without a fight when she believed Adam would be happy with you in London. Moreover, I have seen with my own eyes Adam's adoration of her. There is a bond between them and I believe you saw it too.'

Deveril nodded.

'I do not deny it. But a solution can be found. Muriel never wanted the boy to live with us. I could reopen Burnbury House. Clemency could live there with Adam and I could see the boy whenever I wished.' He warmed to this sudden idea and elaborated: 'It would solve everything, Aunt Meg, don't you see? Clemency is Percy's widow. Why should I not offer her one of the family homes for herself and her child? We can share the boy . . .'

He broke off, aware that his aunt was not sympathetic to the proposal.

'What kind of future would that afford Clemency?' she asked pointedly. 'It would put an end to her plan to marry her physician; debar her from having further children; and not least, Deveril, it would put her at your mercy.'

She smiled at the look of bewilderment on Deveril's face.

'Do not deny that you find the girl attractive! As I have told you before, I may be old, but I am not yet in my mental dotage. You seduced her once before and you would try to do so again. As for the girl, how long before her resistance weakened? You are a very handsome man, attractive to women, and Clemency would be hopelessly vulnerable. You would be relegating her to the position of a mistress, Deveril, *your* mistress.'

Deveril's eyes narrowed.

'Would that be such a terrible fate, Aunt Meg? Mrs Jordan was content enough to be the late King's mistress for twenty years. I could name a dozen others.'

Lady McDoone sighed.

'I see the advantages – for you!' she said caustically. 'Perhaps for Adam, too. But I do not think you have the right to come between Clemency and the man she intends to marry. Moreover, you have your wife to consider. I never liked Muriel even as a girl, but I cannot agree you have the right to humiliate her so openly, so publicly. To have a mistress hidden away discreetly may seem hypocritical, but it is kinder, Deveril, especially for someone like Muriel whose place in Society is of such importance to her.'

The effort of talking was taking its toll and the old lady began suddenly to cough so violently that Deveril hurriedly summoned Campbell.

'Forgive me for worrying you when you are ill!' he said, as the faithful old servant hurried to his great-aunt's bedside. 'And please do not worry on my account. We are not even certain that the girl *is* Adam's mother – or that she has taken him. But I shall find him, I promise, and bring him to visit you!'

But despite the convincing tone of his voice, there was a look of deep concern on Deveril's handsome face as he went downstairs. There were too many questions awaiting answers. Not least of his worries was that this time, Grimshaw might not be able to find Adam; that he, Deveril, might never see his son again. As for Clemency Forest, he could not reconcile himself to the thought of her as Brook's wife. He, Deveril, wanted her for himself – as much as, if not more than, he wanted his son.

CHAPTER TWENTY-SIX

September 1837–May 1838

They had been but three days out to sea before Adam was once again the happy, healthy little boy Clemency had known when he lived with his great-aunt in Scotland. The colour had returned to his cheeks and the bright sparkle to his eyes. Gone was the downcast look of fear that was so painfully apparent the day she had been reunited with him in London.

The dangers and discomforts of the long journey ahead of her paled into insignificance as Clemency watched her son consume his breakfast with a voracious appetite. A large helping of pickled fish preceded a plateful of hot meat, and she was obliged to restrain him from eating too many biscuits, fearful lest he should become seasick as their packet ship forged westward across the Atlantic.

There was little problem in keeping him happily entertained. His curiosity embraced every new sight and smell, diverting his thoughts from memories of his ordeal at Lady Burnbury's hands. The packet – only eight hundred tons – carried a full complement of passengers and everywhere there was noise, confusion and merriment. Meals were taken at long tables, sitting on benches, and Adam began once more to chatter to strangers, making friends with passengers and crew alike.

For most of the day, he watched the sailors furling or reefing the sails, excited by the dangerous heights to which they climbed high up in the rigging. As the days passed, the captain befriended him and permitted him to go up to the deckhouse and talk to the sailors or to stand at the wheel, supposedly helping to steer the vessel.

Only at night, when they settled to sleep on the hard wooden bunks in the communal cabin, did Adam's interest in his surroundings give way to halting questions about the life he had left behind him.

'Will we go back to England one day, Forrie? Do you think Uncle 'Vril will be sad that I have gone away? When will Doctor Brook come to America? Will he travel on a boat like ours? Can I write to Aunt Meg when we get to America?'

He never mentioned Lady Burnbury's name although he did from time to time speak of Mr Crowley, not without a degree of affection.

'He will have to teach some other little boy now, won't he?'

But the distractions were too many to permit him to think often of the past.

Not unnaturally, many of their fellow passengers assumed that Clemency was Adam's mother and spoke of her to Adam as 'your mama'.

'Why do you not tell them, Forrie, that my mama is dead?' he enquired one evening as they walked together on deck before bedtime.

She longed then to be able to tell the truth, but to do so, she realized, would involve her in explanations that would be beyond the comprehension of so young a child. The truth would have to wait a year or two at least, she thought anxiously. In the meanwhile, perhaps a half-truth could serve the same purpose.

'As you do not have a mama, and I do not have a little boy,' she suggested tentatively as she tucked him up for the night, 'would it not be nice if we pretended that we really do belong to each other? You shall call me "Mama", I shall stop being Mrs Forest and become Mrs Grayshott when we reach America, and I shall tell everyone that you are my son, Adam Grayshott.'

Adam beamed happily.

'But that is a splendid idea, Forrie . . . I mean Mama!' he

said sleepily, as he put his arms round her neck awaiting her goodnight kiss.

'And when we reach Fort William,' Clemency added as she hugged him, 'you will meet your new grandpapa. You will like him very much.'

But Adam was not greatly concerned with the acquisition of a grandfather. He wanted to know if there were soldiers at Fort William, and whether he might see Red Indians there. Clemency's last misgivings vanished as she saw the child's eyelids close, and she knew she had been right not to fill his young mind with complicated relationships.

By the time they were nearing New York harbour, he was calling her 'Mama' as naturally as if he had always done so. By then they had been almost three whole weeks at sea and travelled over three thousand miles, but almost as many miles remained to be covered before they reached Lake Superior. Journeying as she was alone with a young child, Clemency was at times overcome by the enormity of her undertaking. There were moments when she wished she had waited until Benjamin could have accompanied her, but he too had appreciated the necessity of her leaving England quickly.

Ironically, she thought, she had the Grayshott money to ease their way, and she could well afford the comfort of staying in New York at the Mansion House. The ship's captain had advised her that it would take a whole day for the lengthy procedure required by officials to examine their baggage. It was a tedious and fatiguing formality, and Clemency was glad to spend a second night at the Mansion House to recover from it. On the following day – the twenty-fifth since they had left Bristol – she went with Adam to book their passage by steam packet to Albany, a town situated on the Hudson River some hundred and forty miles north of New York.

Adam was engrossed by so much that was novel, and gave Clemency little cause for anxiety. Only occasionally did he speak of his Uncle 'Vril and Aunt Meg, a doubtful expression in his eyes, and she felt obliged to permit him to send letters to them care of Professor Brook. A covering one from herself asked if Frederick would oblige her by posting them from London on the occasion of his next visit there. She dared not risk that Deveril would guess by the Brighton frank mark where they had come from.

But England was quickly forgotten by the small boy as the packet wound its way through beautiful scenery to their first night's halt halfway to Albany, at a town called West Point. The hotel where they stayed the night was full and very noisy, but from every window Clemency and Adam could look out on lovely views of the river bounded by great rocks and palisades.

Despite the fact that it was now mid-September, it was very hot as they set off once more on the following day. They sat on the upper deck of the packet in order to get as much air as possible and to avoid the noise of the crowded lower deck. Eight hours after leaving West Point, they were in Albany, where they spent the night at the Eagle. The countryside was thickly wooded, and the view from the room enabled Adam to stand and watch the vessels of all shapes and sizes traversing the busy shipping route.

He was too excited to sleep well, having been told by Clemency that in the morning, at half past nine, they would be travelling on a six-hour railway journey to Utica.

'Uncle 'Vril promised to take me on a railway when we were in London,' he said. 'But we went to Dorset instead, and Uncle 'Vril said I would have to wait until he came back from Switzerland. I did not want him to go to Switzerland, Mama, but he wanted to climb a mountain. I do not think I would like to climb a mountain. I shall much prefer to go on a train.'

Clemency found the experience more frightening than she permitted the boy to realize. It was too hot to have the windows of the carriage closed, but when they were open, sparks from the engine blew in and set her dress alight. She was frightened, too, by the immense speed of the train, and a fellow passenger added to her anxiety by professing that at times they were travelling at no less than twenty miles an hour. She was thankful when at last they arrived safely at Utica and could spend a restful afternoon in Inn Bagges, Adam talking happily of the journey and of the fresh strawberries and ices he was given for luncheon in the public dining-room.

In company with a young American couple whose acquaintance they made at luncheon, they set out for a short walk along the tree-lined street to look at the shops and, more interestingly for Adam, to see the boat that was to take them next morning up the Erie Canal to Rochester. He was once again excited to be told that this part of their journey would continue for thirty-six hours and that they would sleep on mattresses put down on the cabin floor for the purpose.

Despite her growing fatigue, Clemency enjoyed the trip up the canal, past Syracuse and through magnificent forest scenery to Rochester, where they disembarked. She was dreading the next leg of the journey, which necessitated a ride in another train to join the packet to Lake Ontario. But she suffered her misgivings in private, aware of the pleasure the novelty afforded Adam. Content once more as they sat on the deck of the packet taking them to Lewiston, Clemency allowed herself to relax in the cool breeze blowing off the lake and to think of her parents making this same journey seven years previously. How frightened her gentle mama must have been, she mused, although with Papa there to comfort and support her, she would have been happy enough. But as they must have done all those years ago, Clemency felt a sense of awe at the immensity of the distances she and Adam had travelled since they left New York. It had been impossible to imagine such a vast country. At least, she told herself, Deveril would never find them here!

They had been travelling for exactly thirty-two days when finally their boat docked at Hamilton on the most westerly shores of Lake Ontario. Clemency's excitement now matched Adam's as she hired a buggy to take them to the house of Mr and Mrs Matheson. Remembering her parents' account of the couple who had befriended them and offered them the hospitality of their home for the winter of 1830, she was hopeful that she and Adam would be made as welcome. She hoped, too, that they would have recent news of her father, although she realized that Fort William was almost a thousand miles northwest of Hamilton.

The Mathesons had settled in the town over twenty years ago. Their cottage, built of wood, was situated down a little lane in a clearing in the forest. There were several other small houses in the road, all with white wood fencing and front verandas. As the buggy stopped outside the Mathesons' house, a manservant came out to enquire their business.

'If Mrs Matheson is at home, would you please inform her that Mr Clement Foster's daughter has come to visit her,' Clemency instructed him.

But before he could so do, a middle-aged woman came down the path. She was wearing a simple batiste dress and a straw bonnet and was carrying a parasol to shade her from the sun. Her pleasant homely face was lit with a smile, and she greeted Clemency with the same words as those of Lady Whytakker:

'You have no need to introduce yourself, my dear. You bear such a marked resemblance to your dear mother, I have no doubt whatever that you are Enid Foster's daughter – Clementine, is it not?'

Giving Clemency no time to reply, she instructed her servant to take the luggage into the house and pay off the driver. Then she linked her arm in Clemency's, and taking Adam's hand as if she had been expecting the arrival of old friends, she conducted them into the house.

When they were seated, she looked from one to the other.

'And who is this handsome young man?' she enquired, with a smile at Adam's solemn little face.

'My name is Adam Grayshott, Ma'am,' he said with a courtly bow. 'We have come all the way from England,' he added, 'and we rode on two railway trains!'

Mrs Matheson looked questioningly at Clemency.

'We are on our way to Fort William to live with my father,' she explained. 'But he and Mama wrote so gratefully of your many kindnesses to them in the past that I wanted to meet you and your husband before we proceed on our journey.'

The smile had left Mrs Matheson's face as she listened to Clemency. It was obvious from what the girl had said that she was quite unaware that her poor father was no longer living. She herself had written to England some three weeks ago, when first she learned of the mining disaster which had been responsible for Clement Foster's death. Obviously his daughter had not received the letter before leaving the country. Mrs Matheson was saved the immediate necessity of imparting the distressing news by the entrance of a young woman whom she introduced to her guests.

'This is Jane, my youngest daughter,' she said. 'I believe she is quite close in age to you, Clementine – if I may call you that. Your dear mother talked of little else but you, you know. I have another daughter Katherine, who is married and lives only a mile away. You shall meet her later. She has two little boys about your age, Adam, with whom you shall go to play. Jane, my dear, it might be more entertaining for Adam to meet my grandsons now, while Clementine and I have a little talk.'

Clemency half-expected Adam to cling to her side, but after staring speculatively at Jane Matheson's face, he placed his hand trustingly in hers and allowed her to lead him out of the room.

Seeing Clemency's look of surprise, Mrs Matheson smiled.

'My Jane is a school-teacher and she dotes upon the little ones.' She gave a sigh. 'I wish she could have married and had children of her own. Not that she lacked suitors, I can assure you, but our Jane is unusually intelligent for a female, and she has always maintained that if she cannot share her life with "Mr Right", then she prefers to live at home with her father and me. Her father, you see, values her intelligence as younger men do not.'

She glanced at Clemency's ungloved hand and said:

'Am I right in recalling that you are married, my dear? Your father wrote to say so – if my memory is not failing.'

Clemency nodded.

'I was married, Ma'am, but my husband, Mr Percy Grayshott, died three years ago. I am now affianced to a physician who will shortly be coming to this country. He and I hope to marry and he plans to obtain work at Fort William.'

Mrs Matheson knew that she could no longer put off the moment when she must reveal the truth to Clemency about her father. With the boy out of the house, this poor girl could give way to her grief.

But although Clemency was deeply shocked and indescribably saddened by the news of her father's death, she could not weep. It was as if she had already suffered so much in her short life that the fount of tears had dried.

'At least I have Adam to comfort me,' she told Mrs Matheson, 'and soon Benjamin will be joining us.' Fate might still be dealing her adverse blows, she thought, but could not eradicate all joy, all hope. 'It would seem there is no point now in pursuing the long and arduous journey to Fort William,' she added sadly.

'I would not hear of it!' Mrs Matheson cried as she put a comforting arm around Clemency's shoulders. 'It is no fit place for a young woman – at least not until your fiancé arrives. You and the little boy shall stay here with us. It is all too rare that we have visitors from England, and we thirst for information about our motherland. Moreover,' she added, 'it will be very pleasing for Jane to have a companion of her own age. Most of the childhood friends are married, and she has few young women to talk to who are not wrapped up in their domestic pursuits.'

A friend of her own age was something she too, had lacked, Clemency thought, as she allowed Mrs Matheson to show her to one of the guest rooms. She was to consider it her own for as long as she wished, the kindly woman told her, adding: 'I will leave you to unpack your belongings, and when you are rested, you shall meet my husband.'

She patted Clemency's hand maternally.

'I became very fond of your dear mother while she lived with us that winter of 1830,' she said. 'For someone so delicately reared, she showed astonishing courage. I have a feeling that you have inherited her inner strength, child. If it is of any comfort to you, Clementine, I don't think your father would ever have found true happiness again after her death. Sad though it is that his life came to an end both violently and prematurely, I truly believe he is well content now that he is reunited with your mother.'

So began a new friendship that was to deepen and flourish each week that passed. In Jane, Clemency found the sister she had often longed to possess. They talked endlessly into the night, exchanging opinions as if they had known each other all their lives. For the moment, Clemency preferred not to think of Deveril or speak of his true relationship to Adam. It was far easier to talk to Jane of Benjamin and his father. The Mathesons were naturally filled with curiosity to meet him and were trying to persuade her to use her influence with him when he arrived, to remain in Hamilton.

'We have great need of hard-working physicians here,' Jane said earnestly, 'and he sounds such a good person, our whole community would welcome him. Had I been a man, it is the profession I would have liked to follow. But I do enjoy teaching nonetheless.'

Perhaps, Clemency thought, she herself would in time join Jane at the school where Adam had already settled happily to lessons. He made friends with children of his age quickly and easily, and Clemency had no worries about him. Such worries as she had revolved around the possibility – however remote – that Deveril would eventually discover Adam's whereabouts; and as the weeks passed with no sign of Benjamin, that he had been apprehended for assisting her to escape with Adam.

It was mid-November before at long last Benjamin arrived.

It had been agreed between them before her departure that he would call at the Mathesons to ascertain that she had passed through on her way to Fort William; and to discover the easiest route to travel. The main reason why Clemency had had to wait so long for him was that he had been forced to postpone his departure from England, he informed her.

As soon as Clemency had introduced him to her new friends, the Mathesons tactfully left the young couple alone together. Clemency sat down beside him on the sofa and tried not to feel shy when he took her hands in his.

'Do not look so anxious, dearest girl,' he said tenderly. 'I am here now and very happy indeed to be so. But before we exchange news about ourselves, I know you will want to hear the reason why I could not leave England sooner.'

Deveril, he told her, had had him followed. When he had been packing up his belongings in readiness to leave Lower Chiswell, he had noticed the surveillance of a stranger he took to be an investigator. The same man had pursued him to Brighton.

'I do not know how it has come about,' he said quietly. 'But it is clear that you are implicated in Adam's disappearance, and because it is known we are betrothed, someone appreciated that eventually I might lead them to you – and presumably to Adam.'

'You were questioned as to my whereabouts?' Clemency asked anxiously.

'Not by the constabulary, but by Burnbury's lawyer, Grimshaw. He called at Adelaide Crescent and demanded that I told him where you were. I said you had broken off our engagement without giving me any reason for your change of heart and that you had left my father's house that same day; that neither of us knew where or to whom you had gone. I suggested that his investigator was wasting his time keeping watch upon me as I did not expect ever to see you again since we had parted in anger.'

'And he believed you?'

Benjamin shook his head.

'I do not think so, Clemency – not for one minute. His men still kept watch on the house day and night. Finally I realized that there was only one way I could remove myself from Adelaide Crescent undetected – and that was in disguise. Dear Edith purchased a wig for me and lent me her cloak. I left the house one evening in the company of my brother, he instructing the coachman in a loud voice to conduct us to the New Theatre as we were already late for the performance. We went to the theatre – I pretending to be Frederick's wife – and in the interval I managed to slip out by the stage door. It was quite an adventure. I immediately took the next mail coach to Southampton and embarked on a ship two days later. And do not look so worried, my dear. I am confident I wasn't followed.'

As Clemency breathed a long sigh of relief, Benjamin looked deep into her eyes and said huskily:

'Have you missed me, dearest girl? The weeks have dragged quite unbearably. There has been hardly a moment in every day when I have not thought of you and the new life we shall be sharing together.'

Instinctively, Clemency closed her eyes. After all Benjamin had endured to be with her, she could not now disappoint him by telling the truth – that she had only occasionally thought of him, mostly when Jane had been questioning her about her fiancé. She had prayed that he and the Professor had not been harassed because of their assistance to her. But she knew very well that Benjamin wanted more than her concern when he asked if she had felt the same longing for their reunion as he. She could not lie to him, and yet she could not hurt him. Prevaricating, she said softly:

'So much has happened since I arrived here, Benjamin . . . my father's death has preoccupied my thoughts . . . and, of course, Adam; truly I have not had a great deal of time to speculate often on our future. But now you are here at last, we shall talk about our future at length, shall we not?'

Before he could speak, she hurried on to explain that Hamilton was a delightful place to live and that there was work aplenty for him; that Adam had settled happily into school, and that there was a plot of land at the end of the lane where they might build a little house to live in.

'Then, once the house is built, we can make plans for our wedding – in the spring, perhaps. Would that not be agreeable, Benjamin?'

This time it was he who dropped his gaze, unwilling for Clemency to see the disappointment he was sure must be revealed in his eyes. He had hoped they might be married at once – as soon as the banns were read. Spring was a long way off yet, with the whole of the winter to pass before he could make the girl he loved so much his wife.

But the habit of patience was too strong in him for impulse to gain the upper hand. If it was what Clemency wanted, he would wait a little longer. She looked so well, so pretty, with the bright colour back in her cheeks and the sparkle in her eyes. It was as if five years had dropped from her. Only when she talked of her father's death did the familiar look of sadness return.

'I have no plans other than to make you and Adam happy,' he said simply. 'And if Hamilton is as agreeable as you say, then we will build our little house as you suggest – and get married in the spring.'

He thought Clemency was about to throw her arms about his neck and kiss him, but at that moment Mr and Mrs Matheson came back into the room accompanied by their daughter Jane.

'You are an incompetent dunderhead, Grimshaw!' Deveril said angrily as he paced the floor of the library at Grayshott House. 'Not only have my son and that girl been gone for three whole months, but you let Brook vanish too. You should have done as I suggested weeks ago and set the police searching for them.'

Grimshaw regarded the furious face of his client uneasily.

He was painfully aware that his investigator in Brighton had slipped up – and badly. He himself was reasonably certain that Brook had left the country, but all his enquiries had proved fruitless, as had his personal questioning of Professor Brook and his son and daughter-in-law. He knew they could not be bribed or threatened, and unless he could prove they had assisted in the boy's disappearance, there was no crime with which they could be charged.

He now accepted Deveril's opinion that Clemency Forest and Clementine Foster were one and the same female. The physical descriptions tallied. Only the fact that no one had thought fit to inform him of Mrs Forest's employment by Lady McDoone exonerated him from any blame for not suspecting the truth a year ago. He now realized that the girl had proved far more clever than he had supposed her to be. The long years of silence after she had given up writing those interminable letters of appeal had misled him into believing that she had finally accepted the *status quo*. Now he knew that she had only been biding her time.

He had been summoned this cold December morning to Grayshott House to make a report to Lord Burnbury. Reluctantly, he was forced to admit that his man had returned from Fort William in Upper Canada but with no good news to offer him. It appeared that Mr Clement Foster had died recently in a mining accident and that no one in the settlement had seen or heard from his daughter.

'Which is scarcely surprising, is it!' Deveril now remarked scornfully. 'There would be little point in her travelling to Fort William unless her father was alive!' He paced the room with angry impatience, his anger in part caused by his bitter disappointment at Grimshaw's news. Ever since the boy's disappearance, he had found it impossible to settle to a normal way of life. The house seemed a quiet and dismal place without Adam's chatter. He and Muriel were barely on speaking terms now that he had learned from the servants how harshly she had treated his son. In an attempt to soften his anger, she had finally confessed that she knew Adam was his child.

'Can you not understand what a shock it was to me, Deveril?' she had pleaded, 'more especially when I realized that from the beginning you had lied to me.'

Deveril was by nature honest and forthright, and her well-deserved accusation tempered his anger towards her. He had, he knew, taken the easy way out of his difficulties, when a great deal of trouble might have been avoided if he had declared from the first that Adam was his son. Nevertheless, he did not believe her repentance to be genuine, and he no longer discussed Adam with her.

He looked now at Grimshaw's sallow face with acute dislike. It irked him beyond measure that he was dependent upon this man for advice. He himself could think of no further action that could be taken; and to add to his malaise, his beloved Aunt Meg was little better and he was by no means certain that she would survive the winter. *Her* advice to him had been to allow Adam's mother to keep him for the next decade.

'She loves him, Deveril. She will not lie to him about his heritage. When he is old enough, she will tell him . . . and then you will have him back.'

But he could not accept her advice. It was no longer simply that the family needed an heir to carry on the name. He loved the boy. He missed the simple warmth of the child's love; his adoration. He would have given half his worldly goods just to hear that excited little voice saying 'Uncle 'Vril, Uncle 'Vril'; to feel those chubby little arms clasped around his neck.

Bitterly, he wondered whether to dismiss the lawyer for incompetence, but he knew he would not. Grimshaw was still convinced that sooner or later a clue would emerge; a letter perhaps, like the two already received by Deveril and Lady McDoone. But the letters had a London franking and were of no assistance.

'I realize that it is but a straw in the wind, Milord,' Grimshaw said tentatively, 'but you informed me that Mrs

Norton had once befriended Mrs Forest. If you were to go and see her . . .?'

'If you had done your job properly, it would not now be necessary for me to do it for you,' Deveril snapped, as he indicated to Grimshaw that the discussion was at an end. He had not the slightest wish to air his personal misfortune to a comparative stranger, he thought unhappily, as Grimshaw hurried out of the room.

But having endured an exceedingly tiresome week celebrating the festivities of the season with Muriel's parents, his restlessness caused him seriously to consider Grimshaw's suggestion that he should question Caroline Norton.

He feared that she was probably as ignorant as he of Adam's or Clemency's whereabouts, but nevertheless he travelled down to Dorset, to Frampton Court, having ascertained that Mrs Norton was staying there at the house of her brother, Brinsley. Caroline received Deveril readily enough, but the warmth of her greeting quickly chilled when she realized the purpose of his visit.

'If I *did* know where the poor girl was, I would not tell you,' she said, her dark eyes flashing as she regarded Deveril. 'Clearly, Lord Burnbury, you are unaware of my circumstances or you would know better than to expect any sympathy from me!'

She crossed the room and went to the bureau from which she extracted a letter.

'You shall read it for yourself,' she said, handing it to him. 'It is from my husband's legal adviser, Mr John Bayley.'

But for Caroline's passionate insistence that he should read her correspondence, Deveril would have avoided doing so. He knew, as did everyone else, that the bitter quarrel between George Norton and his wife had been continuing for over a year and a half. Caroline had made herself notorious by losing no opportunity to publicize the fact that she believed herself grossly mistreated. Her affairs were of no concern to Deveril, but he now found himself astonished to read that Norton's legal adviser had actually written to say he considered Caroline to have been 'cruelly treated' and that Norton's conduct was 'disgraceful'.

He had heard Muriel speak of Caroline as both tiresome and hysterical and fully deserving of the treatment her husband had meted out to her. But now he readily accepted the more balanced judgement of a man of Bayley's stature. Norton, it appeared, had refused his wife any access to their children. He had offered an allowance to Caroline of £400 a year, but intended to give tradesmen notice not to trust her – an indignity that surely even Muriel could not condone!

He handed Bayley's letter back to Caroline, who was regarding him with a look of bitterness in her eyes.

'I cannot begin to tell you what I have endured at my husband's hands with regard to my children – and they alone concern me,' she said forcibly. 'For five days in June, I was allowed to take my boys out each day in my carriage but what should have been a joy was heartbreak, for all three were unkempt and my youngest, Brinsley, was far from well. Their father was away at Wonersh and his sister, Augusta Norton, had charge of the boys. Brinsley begged to be allowed to spend the night with me . . .'

Her voice broke and tears filled her eyes as she continued:

'He is but five years old, Lord Burnbury – a little boy who was ill. That vile woman lost her temper with him and upbraided him. What could I, his mother do, but speak in his defence? The following morning when I called in my carriage, Miss Norton barred the door against me, saying I could not see my sons again. They were sent to Wonersh, where all three became ill with the measles. I went there immediately, and my brother-in-law Lord Grantly being out, I was able to get up to the nursery. I was nursing my sick babies when he returned, but despite the screams of the children, they were dragged away by the servants he summoned for the purpose. The children tried to escape, but milord Grantly ordered them pursued and locked up. Following upon this terrible scene, I myself became ill – and I have not seen my boys since.'

Her eyes still full of tears, she looked pointedly at Deveril.

'I am aware that the law is entirely to the advantage of men like my husband – and you, and I am doing all I can to rectify this shocking injustice to women. I do not expect a man to feel the same bond that exists between a mother and the child she has borne, but I do expect understanding from the more intelligent members of the male sex. Yet you, whom I would rate a kindlier man than the heartless brute I married, have acted no better than he! My heart ached for poor little Clemency when you refused her access to her son. Therefore I tell you now in all honesty that if she *has* recovered him, I applaud her courage and *I hope you never find her.*'

Deveril was effectively silenced. Caroline Norton's words were but a confirmation of his own growing certainty that Grimshaw had lied to him; that the baby had been forcibly removed from his mother; that she had certainly not relinquished Adam voluntarily. Clearly if this tormented woman Caroline Norton was to be believed, Clemency had made desperate appeals to him for access to her child. *But Grimshaw had not shown him those letters.* How easy it was to understand now why Clemency held him, her child's father, in such contempt!

He apologized to Caroline for taking up her time to no purpose and, bowing, made his departure as quickly as he could. He wanted to get back to London without delay and ask Grimshaw a few pertinent questions.

But long before he reached London, he knew that Grimshaw would lie if it suited him; deny there had ever been any letters of appeal. Or if he did not, he would excuse his withholding of them by stating that he believed it to be in his, Deveril's, best interest to do so. Once he had found Adam, Deveril told himself sharply, he would rid himself of the man's services. Let Grimshaw threaten to expose the truth about that un-savoury contract made between his grandfather and the Rev

Foster – if he dared. The man could not harm Adam or Clemency, still less his poor dead brother Percy. The lawyer would have to manage as best he could without the Burnburys' patronage.

Walter Grimshaw was left in no doubt as to his client's displeasure, and he was painfully aware that if Lord Burnbury disposed of his professional services, it might not be long before other illustrious clients who were friends of the young Viscount did likewise. Grimshaw was not a little frightened.

He had a man permanently on surveillance at Adelaide Crescent; one of his most able fellows, who had managed to strike up a friendship with the young maid, Susan. The fellow had ascertained from her that the Professor received regular letters from his son; and she had overheard the family speaking of the colonies – but she was not sure where. As a consequence, Grimshaw's man was trying to intercept both incoming letters and those given to the bellman for postage whenever he passed by the house ringing his bell to notify the occupants of his presence. But these attempts had so far proved useless.

Although at times Grimshaw believed the watch being kept upon the Brooks was a great waste of time and money, he knew from past experience that patience and persistence frequently paid dividends, and he informed Deveril with a lot more confidence than he felt that sooner or later they would obtain a new lead.

He was unaware that before leaving England, Benjamin had arranged with his father that all correspondence between them should pass through the hands of the Professor's lifelong friend, the botanist Henry Phillips. Once a fortnight, the Professor called upon this good friend in Western Terrace to receive any incoming letters from Benjamin and to hand his own to Phillips for postage. The poor fellow, now blind, was only too happy to act as a go-between, and Clemency's letters to Miss Fothergill and to Lady McDoone, reassuring her as to Adam's welfare, were likewise handled in complete safety. There was one, too, for Deveril from Adam, which did little to comfort him, only serving to highlight his longing to see the boy. Deveril spent many hours alone in the library reading the brief epistle, but it gave no single clue as to his son's whereabouts. Clemency, he thought bitterly, had made certain of that!

But on New Year's Day, he received an unexpected letter from Caroline Norton which greatly tempered his bitterness and gave him cause for thought.

She apologized for receiving him so coldly but not for the views she had expressed. There were many, she wrote, who were only too ready to misrepresent her, and she expressed her hope that Deveril would not be one of them.

'The wild and stupid theories advanced by a few women, of 'equal rights' and 'equal intelligence' are not the opinions of their sex,' she wrote. 'I, for one, (I, with millions more), believe in the natural superiority of men, as I do in the existence of God.

'The natural position of woman is inferiority to man. Amen! That is a thing of God's appointing, not of man's devising. I believe it sincerely, as a part of my religion. I never pretended to the wild and ridiculous doctrine of equality.'

Women had only one right, Caroline declared, and that was to protection from those wiser and stronger than themselves. If men failed them, then they needed protection from the law.

So logical and honest a view could not fail to make a deep impression on Deveril – the more so when he considered that Clemency had had no protection from those 'wiser and stronger' than herself and, least of all, from him. In spiriting their child away, she had taken the only step she could to safeguard Adam. He too, would have removed Adam instantly from Muriel's custody had he known of her persecution of the boy.

Ignoring Muriel's complaints, he went up to Scotland in late January to visit Lady McDoone. She seemed a little better, but he had the impression that she was no longer trying to put up a fight for life, although she told him wistfully that she would do her best to make a full recovery as she would dearly love to see Adam again before she died. It was not a happy sojourn, Castle Clunes being too full of memories of Clemency and the boy.

On his return to London, Muriel made obvious attempts at reconciliation.

'If you wish to go down to Dorset for some hunting, I will gladly accompany you,' she said. 'We will open Chiswell Hill House and invite a number of our friends.'

Lacking the will for anything else, Deveril agreed, and it was April before they were once more back at Grayshott House. By then, plans were afoot for the coronation of the young Queen Victoria in June, and loath as he was to be bothered by such ceremonial formalities, Deveril was obliged to be measured for his coronation robes. He felt little heart for the proposed celebrations, for in the month of June he should have been preparing to celebrate Adam's seventh birthday, he thought bitterly.

Sensing Deveril's restlessness, Muriel suspected it might not be long before he went in search of consolation elsewhere, and ever-mindful of her mother's advice, she resolved to make new attempts to entice her husband back to her bed. She had managed with some success to divert Deveril's furious anger towards her to her maid Celeste. In a desperate attempt to exonerate herself, she insisted that she had acted against her own better judgement.

'Celeste kept telling me that I was too weak with the boy,' she said, 'and finally I allowed myself to be influenced by her. I should have listened to your opinion years ago, Deveril. You always said she was an evil and unnatural female.'

She was uncertain if Deveril was entirely convinced by the lie but, inevitably, he demanded that the unfortunate Frenchwoman be instantly dismissed.

'I have long been convinced the woman was a pervert,' he

said, shocking Muriel by his bluntness. 'She was unnaturally jealous and possessive of you and you should have suspected that she would resent any kindly interests you showed towards Adam.'

Grateful to have found a scapegoat, Muriel made no protest about her maid's dismissal. Since then, Deveril had upon occasion wandered into her bedroom, not because he needed her but because he needed a sympathetic listener as he talked of his desperate concern to discover his son's whereabouts. Muriel managed to conceal her disinterest, and took care not to make it obvious that she hoped he would never find the child.

After she had discovered the means of preventing an unwanted pregnancy, she had from time to time encouraged him to share her bed. These visits had ceased when the boy disappeared, and she had not dared risk Deveril's rebuff by putting his feelings for her to the test. Now, reassured by the comparative success of their stay in Dorset, she decided that the time had come to establish a more complete reconciliation.

Bored, frustrated and still missing Adam's presence at Grayshott House quite unbearably, Deveril allowed himself to be seduced. There was no love in his heart for Muriel, but he believed that she was making a genuine attempt to console him. At least, he told himself, making his peace with Muriel provided a pleasanter atmosphere in his home. With as good a grace as he could muster, he fitted in with Muriel's personal invitations and those of her social calendar.

At the beginning of May, he received an unexpected but for once totally welcome visit from Grimshaw.

'Our patience has finally been rewarded,' the lawyer told Deveril, a bright gleam of satisfaction in his eyes as he handed his client a letter. 'This is from Professor Brook to his son and it includes messages of goodwill to both Miss Foster and the boy,' he added smugly. 'It seems there has been a go-between, a Mr Phillips, through whom letters were exchanged, but the Professor – whose practice it was to take and receive these letters in person – fell ill a few days ago and his young maid was asked to deliver this latest missive for him.' Seeing that he had Deveril's full attention, he continued boastfully:

'I had my most able man on the job and he intervened, Milord, offering to deliver the letter to Mr Phillips himself. The girl was flattered by his attentions and did not suspect his motives . . .'

But Deveril was no longer listening. He was staring at the address.

'*Hamilton, Upper Canada!*' he muttered, as he realized with dismay that this was halfway across the world. But a moment later, he was on his feet, his dark eyes alive with excitement as he looked at Grimshaw. 'However distant, it is not too far for me to retrieve them, Grimshaw,' he declared. 'I shall leave at once.'

Grimshaw's mouth fell open.

'You intend to travel so far *yourself*, Milord?' he stammered. 'There is no need, I assure you. I can despatch one of my men immediately or, if you wish, I will go myself. It is over three thousand miles, Milord . . .'

Deveril scowled.

'I do not recall asking your advice, Grimshaw,' he said coldly. 'In any event, do you really think I would trust you – or anyone else – to deal with this matter now?'

'You have the law on your side, Milord,' Grimshaw faltered. 'You are the boy's legal guardian and . . .'

'And you are a fool!' Deveril interrupted. 'I am not ignorant of the fact that you kidnapped the boy from his mother against her wishes. That will not happen again. This time she will let me have my son *of her own free will* because I shall make it clear that she shall share him with me. I will not be duped a second time by your lies.'

He saw the astonishment and fear on Grimshaw's face, but there was no pity on his own. Clever though the fellow might be, he thought, Grimshaw was not honest in his dealings.

'I will pay you what is due,' he said coldly as the lawyer

turned to go, 'but it will be for the last time, Grimshaw. And as I see you are on the point of protesting, let me remind you that Miss Foster's letters appealing for my compassion were, I now know, *addressed to me*. It was my prerogative and not yours to decide upon my actions. If for no other reason, that alone suffices for your dismissal.'

He did not look at the lawyer's despairing face as he backed out of the room. The man was not deserving of his pity, he thought, as the door closed behind Grimshaw. Now that he knew he would never again have to deal with the fellow, he felt as if a heavy burden had been lifted from his shoulders. His mood was one of elation matching the brightness of the autumn sunshine pouring through the library windows. Now, with a clear conscience, he told himself, he could set off for Hamilton, Lake Ontario, to find Clemency and his beloved little son.

CHAPTER TWENTY-SEVEN

July–August 1838

On the twentieth of July, exactly one month after Queen Victoria's coronation, Deveril and his valet Hopkins booked into the largest of the inns in Hamilton. The landlord and his wife were in a fluster of excitement at having a real English milord as a guest and turned out of their rooms two Hudson's Bay officials in order to give Deveril the most comfortable and airy suite at their disposal.

Despite his fatigue, Deveril was in excellent spirits. On the packet bringing him into the harbour, he had encountered two residents of Hamilton who were acquainted with the Mathesons. Thus he had been able to confirm that a young Englishwoman and her son were residing with them. He therefore now knew himself within a mile of two of seeing his son – and the girl who had dominated his thoughts for almost a year.

Deveril ordered a bath to be prepared for him, then despatched Hopkins to hire a private buggy for his use. He was not anticipating that it would be an easy task to persuade Clemency to return to England, and he fully expected it might take him several weeks to do so. His only anxiety lay in the possibility that she had already married Brook . . . and this very real likelihood disturbed him a great deal more than he cared to contemplate. It was reassuring, he told himself, to know that Clemency was still residing with the Mathesons. The fact that she and Brook had not set up house together indicated that they were not yet wed.

It was late in the afternoon before he set off in his carriage to the Mathesons' house. As fashionably attired as if he intended paying an afternoon call upon friends in London, his appearance invited many curious glances. He sat perched up on the buggy seat beside Hopkins, who was in Grayshott livery.

It was very hot, the temperature in the nineties. To obtain what benefit there was from the slight breeze, the entire Matheson family were taking tea in their garden beneath the shade of a big maple tree. Adam was playing with Katherine's three small children, but there was no sign of Clemency.

As the servant conducted Deveril towards the family group, Adam was the first to espy him. With a wild cry of delight, he flung himself into Deveril's arms.

'Uncle 'Vril! Oh, I hoped you would come. I prayed every night that you would. Did you ride in the train? Did you see any Red Indians?'

The questions might have continued endlessly had Deveril not set him down as the servant announced him. He bowed to his surprised host and hostess.

'Burnbury – at your service Sir, Ma'am! I hope you will forgive this intrusion. I would have sent my card ahead of me had I not been so impatient to see this young rascal!'

'You are most welcome, Milord. Please be seated and take tea with us,' Mrs Matheson said with her customary hospitality.

In the confusion that followed, Deveril gathered that Clemency was with the architect at the site a half-mile further up the lane where a house was being built for her and Benjamin. Jane offered to go at once and advise her of his arrival, and Deveril took Adam into his arms.

'Now let me take a good look at you!' he said with a smile. 'You have grown since last I saw you. Have you also grown wiser?' he teased gently.

Adam grinned shyly, suddenly overcome by the underlying emotion of their reunion.

'I go to school now, Uncle 'Vril. Miss Jane teaches me, and I have been learning American history as well as English; and I can do multiplication and division and . . .'

'But you have still not learned to cease being a chatterbox,' Deveril interrupted, drawing the child close against him in a gesture of undisguised affection. Adam had long ago pushed to the back of his young mind those terrible weeks spent alone with his Aunt Muriel. He did not wish to be reminded of them, and he was suddenly deeply afraid.

'You have not come to take me back to *her*, have you, Uncle 'Vril?' he asked.

Mr Matheson saved Deveril the necessity of a reply as he enquired politely what route Deveril had travelled from England. The conversation turned to politics as Deveril explained that he had travelled the same route as Lord Durham, the new Governor General sent out to Quebec by Lord Melbourne after the rebellion of the colonists the previous autumn. There had been no fighting in their neighbourhood, Mr Matheson said in answer to Deveril's question. But so far as he could assess the situation, he believed that no permanent peace could be achieved until the colonists were permitted to govern themselves.

'We are all loyal to our Mother Country,' he said, 'and quite responsible enough to be permitted home rule. How can we be governed from so far distant a country? Let us hope Lord Durham can explain this in his report to those in Parliament.'

But Mrs Matheson would not permit the conversation to continue on such serious topics.

'I wish to be regaled with every detail of our young Queen's coronation, Lord Burnbury,' she said with her friendly smile. 'I am sure you must have seen everything at first hand from your place in the Abbey. How I envy you such an opportunity! Did Her Majesty look as enchanting as the newspapers recounted?'

Deveril attempted to satisfy her curiosity, while half a mile away Jane was announcing to Clemency that an uncle of Adam's had arrived upon their doorstep without prior notification. Despite the heat of the afternoon, Clemency looked pale and deeply concerned. Her heart was racing and her legs trembling for she did not doubt that the visitor must be Deveril. Knowing her worst fears finally realized, she could not hide her dismay. Watching her curiously, Jane said:

'Are you not pleased, Clemency? Lord Burnbury struck me as a charming man – and quite exceptionally handsome! Mama and Papa will be most flattered to have a viscount call upon them. We are not accustomed to entertaining nobility in our house. Not that young Adam paid his lordship much respect, for he was climbing all over him when I left.'

Adam! Clemency caught her breath, realizing that she must return at once to the house lest it was Deveril's intention to steal the child before she had the opportunity to prevent it. *He shall not have him* – not while there is breath in my body, she vowed silently.

But ten minutes later, seeing Deveril rise gracefully from his chair and make his bow on her arrival, a new emotion assailed her. He had no right to be so handsome; no right to be smiling at her as if he expected her to be pleased to see him, she thought indignantly. He was behaving as if this was the most casual of encounters and had no underlying import.

'May I enquire the purpose of your visit, Sir?' she asked coldly. 'You are a very long way from home, are you not?'

'No more than you, Ma'am!' Deveril replied, grinning as he pulled a chair forward for her to be seated. As if he were a long-standing friend, he spread himself casually on the grass at her feet. Adam squatted on his heels beside him, his arm affectionately around Deveril's neck. Clemency felt her heart twist. Adam had not forgotten his father, and she had been very much mistaken in supposing that because he so seldom spoke of him, the memory of Deveril was fading from the boy's mind.

Her silence during tea was noted by Mrs Matheson, who tactfully suggested to her husband that it was now cool enough for them to enjoy the ride back in the carriage to Katherine's house with Jane and the children.

'We will take the wagonette,' she said, 'and Adam shall

come with us, since there will be plenty of time later, I have no doubt, for you to enjoy your uncle's company, young man.'

Powerless to prevent this obvious ploy to leave her alone with Deveril, Clemency remained seated in her chair as the family prepared to leave. She glanced at the timepiece attached to the bodice of her yellow muslin dress and saw that it was nearing six o'clock. Benjamin would be busy in his surgery for at least another hour, she thought. More than anything in the world, she wanted him here beside her, to lend her strength and support. She knew very well that Deveril would never have come so far – and in person – if he did not intend to take Adam away from her.

Deveril, who had risen politely when the family departed, now reseated himself at her feet. She could see the crown of dark curls on top of his head. His shoulder was almost touching her knees and instinctively she drew away. Adam, she thought, had just the same little twist of hair on the crown of his head. Deveril looked up into her panic-stricken face and in a voice which surprised her by its gentleness, he said:

'I beg you, Clemency, do not be frightened of me. I assure you I have not come as your enemy but as your friend.'

The colour flared in Clemency's cheeks and her fists clenched.

'You have come to take Adam away, have you not?' she accused him.

Deveril's eyes bored into hers.

'I do not blame you for speaking so harshly,' he said. 'I have discovered many things since you removed Adam from Grayshott House. Nor do I blame you for causing me such anxiety and despair when I discovered Adam gone and was unable to find him. You see, Clemency, *I now know that you are Adam's mother.*'

Clemency caught her breath. She was not surprised to hear that he had finally uncovered the truth. What did cause her surprise, however, was the gentleness and understanding in his tone. She had often in her tormented dreams imagined Adam's outraged, wrathful father arriving on her doorstep to reclaim his child, demanding his rights according to the law of England. Yes, she had expected an enemy; but could she even now be certain he was her friend?

'Do not judge me until you have heard the truth,' Deveril said, his hand reaching out to cover hers, 'the whole truth, Clemency, from the beginning. For a start, I was not told of it when Adam was conceived. I do not know why I was kept in ignorance, unless it was to make certain that I did not marry you to legitimize my son. Grimshaw, the lawyer, told me that my grandfather devised the plan to wed you to my brother – but I have long doubted that it was my grandfather's scheming. Nevertheless, he did countenance that first wrong done to you. I myself had no knowledge of it or any part in it.'

Clemency bit her lip.

'Even so, you did not hesitate to take my child by force when you learned of his existence and decided that *you* wanted him,' she said bitterly. 'I saw *your* need, but you did not see mine. Adam was but two years old when he was snatched from me, and it was three long, agonizing years before I saw him again – and then only by subterfuge. You ignored my every letter appealing to be allowed to see him. I shall never forgive you for that – *never!*'

Deveril's grip upon her hand tightened, imprisoning it so securely that despite her efforts, she could not draw it away.

'You *will* listen to me, Clemency, because I have come a very long way in order to explain the truth . . . no less. *I did not receive one single letter from you*. Grimshaw kept them all from me, fearing, no doubt, that I would weaken and permit you access to the boy and possibly thereby lay myself open to claims by you, his mother, for his custody. Legally, I am only Adam's uncle, although Grimshaw made certain I was declared his legal guardian! On my solemn oath, Clemency, I believed you had surrendered the child willingly – in return for a large sum of money.'

Seeing the look of horror on her face, he said quickly:

'Knowing you as I do now, I realize that you would never have behaved in such a way. *But I did not know then.* It causes me the most bitter shame to admit that I did not remember you that night when . . .' He broke off, momentarily averting his eyes. But suddenly he smiled. 'Maybe my heart never quite forgot you,' he said softly. 'Each time I encountered you – at Poole when I mistook you for Brook's wife – at the theatre and later at Castle Clunes, I felt drawn to you in a way I could never explain. I think it was when I kissed you the night of Aunt Meg's masquerade that I first realized I loved you. Does that shock you, Clemency?'

At last Clemency managed to free her hand. She put it to her forehead in an unconscious gesture of dismay. Whatever she had expected from Deveril, it was not this last declaration. For so many years she had believed Deveril to be heartless, cruel, unrelenting in his attitude to the mother of his child. Now she realized that he had been almost as much a victim of Grimshaw's duplicity as herself. He was not uncaring – and never had been. Nor was it only Adam he cared about but her too! Deeply perturbed, she said awkwardly:

'I am engaged to be married to Doctor Benjamin Brook. We would be married already but for the fact that the severe winter months have curtailed the building of our house. Our wedding date is now fixed for September. I can have no interest therefore in your feelings towards me.'

Deveril jumped to his feet and pulled her up beside him.

'I have told you before, Clemency, *you cannot marry Brook.* I want to take you back to England with me. I want to put right the wrong done to you and to have you openly acknowledged as Adam's mother. I will never again allow my wife to have charge of Adam. You shall have Burnbury House and the boy can live with you. You shall have everything in the world you want. That is what I have come so far to tell you!'

Clemency's mouth fell open and she stared into Deveril's

face in disbelief. Her mind was racing and as the full import of his words hit her, the hot colour rushed into her cheeks.

'You want me to live at Burnbury House where you can be with Adam,' she murmured. 'You would expect me to welcome *you* there . . . to be . . .'

Deveril reached out and caught her shoulders, holding her so close that their bodies were almost touching.

'Yes, that is what I would like,' he said simply. 'I cannot marry you, Clemency – which I would do were I free. But although I am unable to make you my wife, I would do everything else possible to ensure your comfort and happiness. You would have the respect of my friends and my protection. I beg you, Clemency, agree to my proposal. I could make you happy. I could make you love me!'

'I am going to marry Benjamin!' The words sounded faint and ineffectual. She tried to avert her eyes from his searching gaze; tried to still the fierce beating of her heart. Why, oh why, she thought despairingly, must her legs tremble so at his proximity! It would be so easy to stop fighting him; to let herself melt into his embrace; so easy . . . and so wrong.

'You are asking me to become your mistress,' she said in a cold hard voice. 'And that I will never do. You speak of assuring me of your friends' respect, but what of my son's? Adam will not always be seven years old and too young to understand what his mother is about. I appreciate your offer to share him with me, Deveril, but not on those terms; *never* on those terms.'

Deveril's eyes darkened. He ignored her struggle to break free of his grasp and pulled her closer. He could feel the trembling of her body and the rapid thud of her heart against his chest.

'You are not indifferent to me,' he said in a low fierce tone. 'You would not fear me touching you if you were. But it is your feelings you should fear, Clemency, not mine. I will never force you to act against your heart – but your heart is betraying you, it is not? You can no more deny that you and I belong together than can I.'

He was too close to the truth for Clemency not to cry out in dismay.

'You are wrong, wrong, wrong!' she stormed. 'I do not care if you live or die. I wish I had never met you, never seen you. I wish you had never come here. All you really want is my son . . . and you shall not have him. You shall not!'

Unaware of it, tears were streaming down her cheeks. Deveril reached out and wiped them gently with his fingertip.

'I will not hurt you – ever again,' he said, his voice soft but intense as he added: 'I did mean what I said, Clemency, I love you. Were I free, I would ask you to be my wife.'

She twisted her head away from the touch of his hand.

'Would you?' The question rose to her lips unbidden. 'Are you aware that my father was a slave-trader? That he was once imprisoned for debt? I do not think you would wish to make me your wife, the Viscountess Burnbury! Your grandfather understood that very well!'

Deveril's eyes flashed.

'Can you believe that I would let such paltry matters from the past influence me?' he asked. 'I do not care who your parents were, Clemency. It is you I want – the mother of my son. And I will not lie to you. I have come to take Adam home if you will allow it. I want him very much. But I want you, too. I want to share him with you. I understand how much you love him. I know how much he loves you. But I love him too, Clemency, as indeed I love you.'

Perhaps, Clemency thought afterwards, she might have weakened, allowed Deveril to kiss her. He was about to do so when her ears caught the sound of carriage wheels in the lane and she realized that Benjamin was arriving home. Benjamin, she thought! She had almost forgotten his existence. Hurriedly, guiltily, she dragged herself from Deveril's arms.

'I cannot go back to England with you,' she said. 'Even if I wanted to, I cannot. I am going to marry Benjamin. He has waited seven years for me, followed me half across the world.

He has started a new practice here and our home is nearly built. I *cannot* disappoint him.'

She turned and ran across the garden towards the man now approaching them. Linking her arm in his, she reached up and kissed his cheek.

'Benjamin,' she said quietly, 'Lord Burnbury is here. He is seeking a compromise with me regarding Adam. I would be pleased if you would be present at our discussion.'

Benjamin viewed Deveril's elegant figure with narrowed eyes. He could well imagine the shock the man's unexpected appearance must have caused Clemency. He could feel the trembling of her hand on his arm and his own covered hers protectively.

As he and Deveril bowed formally to one another, Benjamin said coldly:

'I would be a liar were I to say you were welcome, Lord Burnbury. Your presence here can only cause my fiancée further heartbreak.'

The angry reply Clemency expected from Deveril was not forthcoming. In a quiet voice, he said:

'On the contrary, Brook, I have no desire to cause Clemency further distress. Unwittingly, I have wronged her greatly in the past and I freely admit it. I shall not make any attempt to take Adam from her. My purpose is quite otherwise. If she will return to England with me and the boy, I am more than willing to allow her such access as she wishes.' He glanced at Clemency meaningfully. 'And I make no conditions. If she prefers, Adam can live with her – at least until he is a great deal older. But I want him to grow up in his own country, Brook. One day, he will take my place as a peer of the realm; as guardian of our estate. He will sit in the House of Lords and participate in the government of his country. It would not be right for him to grow up here, knowing nothing of his true home; his obligations; his heritage.'

He saw the pallor of Clemency's cheeks and added softly:

'I do not think there is much to be served by talking further on these matters at the moment. I do not intend to hurry back to England and I accept that Mrs Forest will need time to consider my proposals very seriously.' He stared into Clemency's eyes as he added: 'I give you my word I shall make no attempt to spirit the boy away whilst your back is turned. If Adam wishes to see me, you may safely permit him to visit me with complete assurance that he will be returned to you. Nor shall I try to prejudice him as regards his future. That remains for you and you alone to decide. You have my oath upon it, Ma'am.'

He bowed formally to Benjamin and kissed Clemency's hand.

Long after he had departed in his carriage, she could feel the warmth of his lips burning into her skin. Beside her Benjamin said happily:

'It seems, my dearest, as if you have nothing to fear after all. I must confess myself most agreeably surprised by the fellow's attitude. So wipe away that look of woe, my darling. Unless I misheard his lordship, Adam is yours for as long as you wish to keep him. That must take a great load from your shoulders!'

But it did not, Clemency thought despairingly, as she followed Benjamin into the house. Deveril had removed one fear, but only to leave another in its place – a fear that she might never again be able to ignore the fact that she loved him . . . loved him with all her heart.

She was aware that Benjamin was regarding her with a look of concern as she attempted to smile. But he was not deceived. With a display of emotion quite at variance with his normal quiet manner, he caught hold of her hand and said urgently:

'Clemency, you cannot be contemplating returning to England with . . . with Burnbury? Tell me that is not in your thoughts!'

'No, no, I swear it!' Clemency cried quickly. She looked away from Benjamin's penetrating gaze and murmured:

'Deveril did suggest that if I returned to England, we could share Adam. But . . . but I told him I would not consider it . . . that you and I were shortly to be married and that my life was here with you.'

She could see that Benjamin was not entirely reassured. He knew her too well, she thought; knew every nuance of her voice.

'I do not think I could bear it were I to lose you now,' he said quietly. 'And yet if I believed in my heart that it would make you happy, I would even now stand aside. But there can be no future for you with Burnbury . . . you know that yourself.'

Clemency nodded. She could not endure the look of pain in Benjamin's eyes, and she said quickly:

'You need not worry, dearest Benjamin. Nothing has been said or could be said to make me change my mind regarding our marriage. If I appear worried, it is because I believe that I shall even now lose Adam.'

'But Burnbury said . . .'

'I know he has promised not to take Adam from me without my agreement, Benjamin. But how can I justify withholding it? You yourself heard Deveril's point of view regarding his son. I want to ignore what he said, but I cannot. Adam will one day be Viscount Burnbury. I have no right to deny him that heritage, and deep in my heart, I suppose I have always known it. Your dear father said so; so too, did Lady McDoone. Even Caroline Norton advised me to consider it.'

Benjamin's eyes reflected his unease as he said:

'But it could be twenty, thirty, even forty years before the boy inherits. There is no reason I can see why he cannot grow up here with us and then, when he is a man, he can return to England and . . .'

'Benjamin, Adam is the only son Deveril will ever have. If illness or an accident were to befall Deveril, Adam's life would be disrupted whatever his age. I do not think I can justify keeping him here with me. I do not know if I am strong enough to set aside my love for my son in his interests, but I feel I should do so.'

'And return him to that household where he was so ill and unhappy?' Benjamin asked pointedly.

Clemency sighed.

'I do not think Deveril will permit Lady Burnbury to have any part in Adam's life ever again,' she said quietly. 'Before you returned home this afternoon, he admitted he had been at fault leaving Adam in her care.'

'The boy would not be happy now at Castle Clunes,' Benjamin commented quickly. 'He is accustomed to the companionship of other children; and you would not be there to mother him.'

'It is possible Deveril might suggest his sister, Lady Allendale, should raise Adam with her children. Caroline told me that she is a charming, motherly woman. That might be for the best, Benjamin. I am sure only of two things – one is that Deveril and I cannot both have Adam and that it is not right for the boy to be torn between us; the other that Deveril is not the cruel, heartless, irresponsible rakehell we had supposed him.'

Cruel possibly, but not irresponsible, Benjamin thought, trying to clear his mind of prejudice. No one could deny the magnitude of the reforms Burnbury had instigated on his estate since his grandfather's death. Every tenant was now decently housed and received a fair wage for his labours. But perhaps most important to Benjamin himself was the health of the community. It had improved immeasurably since Burnbury had ordered that no man was to lack adequate medical care and that he, Benjamin, had but to proffer names of the needy for his fees to be met. There had been no quibble from the bailiff when Benjamin had requested this same arrangement should continue with his successor. No, Burnbury could not be without heart, he admitted to himself, but it was for Clemency to judge what was best for her son.

Very gently, he raised her hand to his lips and kissed it.

'I shall abide by whatever decision you reach,' he said softly, 'and I shall support you in that decision with all my heart. I love you very much, Clemency, and if you were to let Adam go, I should do everything within my power to make up to you for his loss. If God is willing, you and I will have children, and they will occupy your thoughts and your heart more completely than I myself can do.'

Clemency's eyes filled with tears as she regarded him.

'You must not consider yourself so unimportant to me!' she said with an attempted smile. 'You speak as if I do not truly love you. I have needed you beside me for as long as I can remember – and you have always been there, Benjamin, a rock of strength and devotion upon which I could lean. I wonder sometimes that you are not thoroughly tired of the responsibility!'

He looked at her with the deepest tenderness.

'It is my self-appointed task to protect you insofar as I can,' he said.

Clemency rested her head against his shoulder, a feeling of great weariness stealing over her. It seemed she had been fighting all her life, and now that victory was within her grasp and she knew that she could keep Adam if she so wished, her triumph was to be denied her – and by her own choice. If Deveril could satisfy her as to Adam's well-being, and if Adam wanted to go, she would give him up. The fight was over and her future lay with this dear, kind, faithful man. And she did love Benjamin. How could she not when she owed him so much? When she needed him so much? The Mathesons thought the world of him, and he had already succeeded in building up a fine reputation in Hamilton as a physician.

'Whether our house is completed or not by September,' she said with sudden urgency, 'let us not postpone our wedding again, Benjamin. I want to marry you as soon as it can be arranged. I wish I was already your wife!'

Delighted by this rare show of emotion, Benjamin bent his head and kissed her. It did not cross his mind that behind

Clemency's declaration was a cry for help, for he was unaware of her innermost longing to give in to the demands of her heart and submit to Deveril's proposal. She wanted to return to England . . . never to be parted from Adam or Deveril again. Deveril had been painfully near the truth when he had said that they belonged together. She wanted to belong to him . . . even to become his mistress if she could not be his wife. She wanted him to kiss her, to touch her. She wanted to surrender herself to him totally.

But stronger even than that longing was her will. Adam came first in her heart. He always had and he always would. She did not want a future where one day he would look at her with contempt; or at least feel her unworthy of his respect. She did not want him to know her as his father's mistress. If she was to lose Adam now – his physical presence – at least he would always remember her with love . . . with the kind of love a child should feel towards his mother.

She felt a bitter-sweet pain as the door opened and Adam came running into the room to fling himself into her open arms. His cheeks were pink with excitement and, with Deveril's eyes, he regarded her warmly.

'Has Uncle 'Vril gone, Mama? He will be coming back, will he not? I want to show him my tomahawk. Aunt Katherine said I might keep it for my own. It belonged to a real Red Indian chieftain. Mama, where *is* Uncle 'Vril?'

That night when she tucked him into bed and kissed him goodnight, he wound his arms around her neck and said thoughtfully:

'Mama, do you think Uncle 'Vril was lonely in London without me? Do you think he wants me to go and live with him again?'

Clemency bit her lip. She could not lie to him.

'I expect he does, Adam. I know he loves you very much. It made him very sad when he heard how harshly your Aunt Muriel had treated you.'

'I hate her!' Adam announced. 'She beat me and I hate her.'

'Yes, well he would not want you to go back and live with her,' Clemency said with conviction. 'But suppose your Uncle 'Vril sent you to live with Aunt Selina? You told me you liked her very much, and all your cousins, too.'

Adam's face brightened.

'She is very nice, and Cousin Jack, who is only a little bit older than me, was going to teach me to play cricket when we went to the seaside. But *she* would not let me go.'

'I know, darling, but that was all a long time ago. Would you like to live with Aunt Selina? You would see your Uncle 'Vril every day, I expect.'

Adam looked interested.

'Would you be there too, Mama?' he asked.

Unable to speak, Clemency shook her head. Adam's hold upon her tightened.

'But I would want you to be there,' he said. 'I love you better'n anybody in the whole world . . . except Uncle 'Vril,' he added. 'I love him very much, too.'

'Well, it is far too late to worry about it all now,' Clemency said with difficulty, as she detached his arms from around her neck. 'We can talk about it tomorrow with your Uncle 'Vril and decide what is best. Now off you go to sleep – and do not forget your prayers!'

Adam smiled disarmingly.

'Sometimes I have forgotten them, but God was not cross with me or He would not have answered my prayers, would he, Mama? I prayed and prayed Uncle 'Vril would come and see me and he is here. Will we see him tomorrow?'

Clemency nodded, her heart aching. She had known nothing of Adam's secret longing to see his father. It only highlighted her growing awareness that at whatever the cost to herself, she was going to have to let her son go.

Much later that evening, Jane knocked on her bedroom door as she was preparing for the night. As she had done so many times these past ten months, she curled up on the end of Clemency's bed. Normally, the girlish confidences they exchanged were pleasurable for them both. But tonight, Jane could talk of little but their visitor. She thought Deveril one of the most handsome men she had ever met, and was curious to know why Clemency had married his younger brother. Or had *he* been even more handsome, she enquired, smiling.

To avoid further explanations, Clemency told the girl that Deveril was already betrothed when she had first met him – to a young woman who was far more suited to become a viscountess than herself.

Jane laughed.

'But that cannot be true, Clemency dear. Even Mama has remarked upon your grace and refinement, and only the other day, bid me try and emulate your bearing and manners.' She sighed. 'It does not surprise me that Benjamin dotes upon you. You are quite perfect in his eyes. When you are not there, he talks endlessly of your virtues.'

Clemency laid down her hairbrush, conscious of the guilty blush that had coloured her cheeks.

'Then he is wrong to do so,' she said almost angrily. 'In many ways, I am less deserving than most of adulation. It is Benjamin who should receive the accolades.'

It was Jane's turn to blush.

'I did not mean to infer he was not good enough – in *every* way – to be your husband,' she faltered. 'On the contrary, Clemency, I . . . I admire him very much. Were I in your shoes, I should consider myself the most fortunate of women . . .'

She broke off, looking quite unnaturally flustered as she stood up and went to kiss Clemency goodnight.

'Please forgive me,' she said abruptly. 'I did not mean to pry. Until you told me just now that Lord Burnbury was married, I had been wondering whether he was a former suitor who had come to Upper Canada to find you. I do not know why I should have entertained such a notion but . . . well, I found myself imagining how heartbroken Benjamin would be if . . . but I should not be saying all this. It is not my place and you have every right to tell me so.'

She looked so agitated that Clemency smiled and kissed her cheek.

'I know that you speak as a friend, and as such, you are privileged to speak as you please,' she said simply. 'But you have no cause for concern, dearest Jane. I told Benjamin earlier this evening that I wanted no more postponements of our wedding. We shall be married this autumn. Does that relieve your mind?'

Jane nodded, although there was no answering smile as she returned Clemency's goodnight kiss.

'You and Benjamin have become very dear to me,' she said as she went to the door. 'You have become like a sister to me, Clemency, and although you never speak of it, Benjamin told me your life until now had been a sad one. All I want is for you both to be happy together.'

But Clemency knew there could never be true happiness for her were she to follow the dictates of her mind rather than her heart – and let her son go.

During breakfast next morning, Hopkins arrived with a note from Deveril for Clemency.

'We have much to discuss,' it said, 'and I propose calling for you in my carriage at midday. With your fiancé's permission, we will go for a drive when hopefully we can reach a decision regarding Adam's future . . .'

Clemency handed the note to Benjamin.
'You will come with me, of course?' she enquired.
Benjamin regarded her with surprise.
'But there is surely no need for my presence, dearest girl,' he said gently. 'Lord Burnbury is quite right in wishing to speak to you in private about matters that concern only the two of you. Besides, my dear, I have a great deal of work to do. I did not tell you yesterday, but I fear our little town may be on the brink of an epidemic. There were twelve cases of

fever two days ago and by last night there were twenty-seven.'
He looked across the breakfast table at Jane. 'I was wondering,
Jane, if you are not too busy . . . it would be most helpful if
I had some statistics to . . .'

Jane was already on her feet, her napkin put down upon
the table as she said:

'I will be glad to help, Benjamin. Time always hangs heavy
for me when there is no school to teach, and the summer
holidays are so long! May I take the buggy, Father, if you have
no requirement for it? You may come with me, Adam, if you
promise to be very good. I do not imagine your mama will
want to be bothered with your chatter if she has serious
matters to discuss.'

Clemency nodded, and with an effort, she smiled at Adam.

'Have no fear, my darling, you shall see your Uncle 'Vril
later in the day,' she said, understanding his disappointment
at being left out of her plans. Since Benjamin could not go
with her, she would have been pleased to take the boy – in
order not to be alone with Deveril. She was far from certain
if she could remain at least outwardly indifferent were he
once more to declare his love; or try to force her to admit
hers! But she did not love him – she loved Benjamin, she
told herself, as she left the breakfast room. Such feelings as
she had for Deveril bore no resemblance to the pure, whole-
some, virtuous devotion she felt towards Benjamin. As it
had in the past, her body was once more betraying her,
demanding satisfaction for her most primitive instincts. The
strange bond between her and Deveril was born of lust, not
love, and his passionate words did not deceive her. True
love, as Benjamin had taught her, meant self-sacrifice, and
yet Deveril, desiring her, was prepared to make her his
mistress were she willing, despite the shame this must bring
upon her.

Clemency went up to her bedroom where she donned a simple
gingham day dress. Not even to please Mrs Matheson would she
take her best Sunday bonnet or wear her grandmother's emerald

brooch – the only piece of jewellery she possessed other than Benjamin's sapphire engagement ring.

'It may not matter to us ordinary folk,' the flustered matron said anxiously as she viewed Clemency's simple attire, 'but surely, my dear, in the company of a viscount . . .'

'I am not seeking to impress Lord Burnbury, dear Mrs Matheson,' Clemency replied truthfully. 'He must take me as I am or not at all!'

But she could not subdue the bright spots of colours in her cheeks nor the golden glints in her fair hair, and when on the exact moment of midday Deveril called for her, she was immediately aware of the look of admiration in his eyes. He smiled disarmingly at Mrs Matheson and politely refused an invitation to return for luncheon, stating openly that he had had his landlord pack a picnic luncheon for Clemency and himself to enjoy as they drove along the shores of the lake.

'We shall endeavour to keep within the shade of the trees,' he promised, the day being already almost too hot for comfort.

Going out to the carriage, Clemency was dismayed to see that he had not brought Hopkins with him. Awaiting her was a two-wheeled buggy in which she had no alternative but to sit beside him. No sooner were they out of sight of the house than Deveril turned the horse's head away from the harbour.

'Since you told me yesterday that you are determined upon marrying your physician, it will raise fewer eyebrows amongst the local inhabitants if we are not seen alone together by too many,' he stated calmly, as he turned along a rough lane leading upwards into the escarpment overlooking the town. 'I have no wish to compromise you, Clemency.'

Was he teasing her? Mocking her? she asked herself, as the spirited young horse tackled the steep incline with ease. Or was he truly concerned with her reputation? He was chatting easily about the topography, the beautiful view, and his desire to make a diversion to Niagara Falls on his way back to England. He seemed unaware of her silence until after ten minutes, he said suddenly:

'I am reminded of the past, Clemency. Do you recall that when I first knew you, you were so silent I was almost persuaded you were mute?'

Despite herself, she smiled.

'It would seem that our son takes more after his father than his mother,' she retorted, her eyes clouding as she considered the real purpose of this drive with Deveril. 'It is time we spoke of Adam and the future. I slept very little last night, kept awake by my uncertainties.'

'I too, slept badly,' Deveril said. 'I can see no solution, Clemency, unless you change your mind and agree to come back to England with me. I do not want to separate you from the boy, but I am sincere in my belief that his rightful place is with me.'

'I do not disagree with your point of view,' Clemency said quietly. 'But how can I be certain he will be happy, Deveril? On the last occasion you took him with you, you allowed his life to be made intolerable at Grayshott House.'

Deveril turned his head to look at her.

'I am sure I do not have to tell you that I would never have allowed it had I been there,' he said in a fierce angry voice. 'I believed that Adam would be spending the summer holidays with my sister Selina. I could not guess Muriel would countermand my arrangements, any more than I could guess that in my absence, she would discover the boy was my son. I know now that she can never take him to her heart. But Selina is everything a mother should be. I know Adam. He will be happy with my sister and I should see him every day.'

'Whereas I should never see him again,' Clemency spoke her thoughts aloud. She heard Deveril's sudden intake of breath.

'Does that mean you will not return to England? That I shall never see you again?' Before she could reply, he added swiftly: 'But I would make the journey to Canada with Adam – in a year or two's time. And in the meanwhile, I would write letters telling you of his progress. He too, could write and reassure you that he is happy. If he were not . . . then I would return him to you.'

'No!' Clemency said sharply. 'If I let you take him, Deveril, then I must resign myself to the idea that it is for ever. I have wasted too many years waiting, hoping, longing for the day to come when I could see my son again. Nor would it be fair to Benjamin. I must make my life here with him . . . a new life.'

Without warning, Deveril pulled the horse to a standstill and jumped down from the buggy. He held out his arms to help Clemency alight. The track was deserted and the giant redwoods bordering it on either side were casting a welcome shade.

'We will sit beneath one of those trees,' he said, as he hitched the horse's reins over a fallen log. 'And do, I beg you most earnestly, wipe that look of fear from your face. Can you really believe that I will try to take advantage of you, Clemency? I am no longer the same irresponsible rake you think me.'

He spread his coat beneath one of the big tree trunks and invited her to be seated. A half-smile played at the corner of his mouth as he sat down beside her.

'I do declare you look as though you are in the schoolroom, sitting there so primly with your hands folded. Clemency, do you have any idea at all how much I love you?'

He watched the colour flare in her cheeks and said gently:

'Does it frighten you so much to know it? Or can it be that you feel more for me than you care to admit? I know that you do not love Brook.'

'How can you know it!' Clemency cried. 'It is because I love Benjamin that I cannot return to England with Adam. Oh, yes, I will admit I have considered it – not to live as your mistress at Burnbury House, but in Brighton, perhaps, where I could have Adam to stay with me during his holidays. Yes, that is what I would want if I did not love Benjamin. But I could not ask him to leave the new life he has made for himself here in Hamilton. He is happy here. And he loves me. I cannot take my happiness at the expense of his!'

Deveril had been watching her face as she spoke. His dark eyes were serious as he suddenly reached out and imprisoned her hand.

'Clemency, try to forget for one moment who I am and all that has passed between us. Forget even Adam's existence and think only of yourself. I have never believed you truly loved Brook, and now I am even more convinced of it. You have told me that you cannot take your happiness at *the expense of his*. That can only mean that your true happiness does not lie *with* him. I beg you, do not marry a man you do not love.' He put one hand gently beneath her chin and lifted her face so that she was forced to look into his eyes. The intensity of his feelings was reflected in their depths as he said in a low, vibrant voice:

'Clemency, you must believe me when I tell you that I know only too well the bitter rewards of a loveless marriage. I do not seek to compare Brook's nature with Muriel's; I believe he is a good man, kind, considerate, with all the attributes that make a good husband; but there is more to marriage than you might imagine. Muriel never wanted me in her bed, and although she has tried to hide the fact from me, I was always aware of it. I am sure she could not help her feelings. But they were hurtful and destructive to our marriage. And you, Clemency, will *you* be able to welcome Brook to *your* bed? Or will you hurt him with the knowledge that you will never belong to him totally?'

Clemency tried to draw her hand away, but Deveril would not let her go. Her cheeks were aflame and her voice bitter as she cried out:

'What right have you to ask such questions? How can you know what feelings I entertain towards the man I mean to marry? I am sorry your wife rejected you, but I shall not reject my husband in like manner. I shall . . . I shall . . .'

'What will you do, Clemency?' Deveril broke in softly, his face nearing hers as he said: 'Will you kiss him as you kissed me that night of the masquerade? Will your heart pound with excitement as it is now? You are trembling, but it is not with fear, for you know I will not force you against your will. You may lie to me, Clemency, but you cannot lie to yourself. Your heart does not lie. Your eyes, your mouth tell me the truth. You do not love him.'

For one long moment, Clemency continued to gaze into those dark compelling eyes and then, without warning, the rigidity of her body slackened and she allowed her weakness to overcome her. Deveril was only voicing what her heart already knew. She did not love Benjamin, no matter how hard she had tried to do so. The great affection she felt, the respect, the gratitude were genuine and deeply ingrained, but they were not love, however close they came to being so. Her feelings towards him bore no resemblance to the tumult of emotion this man, Deveril Grayshott, evoked with no more than a look, a touch, an inflection of his voice.

She was filled with a terrible sense of despair as she realized that the only man she ever had or could love would, in a day or two at most, be gone from her life for ever. She would marry Benjamin, raise a family, find happiness of a kind – but never again would she feel this terrible desire to become one with another human being. Every part of her body ached for his touch. She wanted to bury her hands in those dark, unruly curls; she wanted to kiss his mouth, his eyes; the dark straight column of his throat. She wanted to take him into herself and make him as one with herself. It no longer mattered whether he was her friend or her enemy; her true love or her false. Good or evil, he was beautiful and desirable, and the only one who could make her feel complete. He was her destiny.

As his arms encircled her, they fell backwards onto the soft warm earth. Then his mouth came down on hers and Clemency closed her eyes. Her hands reached up and, involuntarily, her fingers dug into his back, drawing him closer and closer against her. She could feel the thudding of his heart against her breasts and as he released her mouth, she heard his voice saying over and over again:

'I love you, Clemency. I love you. I love you . . .'

But suddenly, without warning, he drew away and his hands clenched at his sides as he sat up. His eyes as he looked down at her were dark pools of pain. As his breathing steadied, he said in a low, quiet voice:

'I cannot take you, my love – not like this; not when I know you intend to marry another man. God knows I want you – more than I ever wanted a woman in my whole life. I love you. But it would be wrong . . .'

'Wrong?' The word echoed from her lips without thought.

'Yes, wrong!' Deveril cried as he jumped to his feet. 'Perhaps I understand more of such things than you. But this much I know, Clemency. We were fated to love one another; made for that purpose. Were I to prove that to you now, you would never forget me; never find true contentment in another man's arms. You have told me you must marry your physician. Well, marry him if you feel that is the right thing for you to do. I cannot offer you marriage, though I would give everything in the world to find myself free to do so.'

He brushed the hair from his forehead, his eyes deeply unhappy as he said bitterly:

'But I am not free, and I know now I was wrong to think it would make me happy if you became my mistress. It would never satisfy me! I should want to be with you all the time – every minute of the day and night. I should want more children by you, Clemency. I would want everything a man needs from *his wife*, not just those few rewards he would receive from his mistress.'

Clemency drew a long shuddering breath as she sat up, passing a hand hopelessly over her burning forehead. She could never again doubt that Deveril loved her, she thought. But that assurance brought only pain, for now she must surrender not only her son but also the man she loved. She and Deveril must never live within reach of one another, for sooner or later, they would weaken and give way to the burning need within themselves. If she could only have continued to hate him; to feel bitter and resentful; to remember him as a thoughtless, unfeeling profligate. She did not want to have to think of him with gentleness, with tenderness, with pity for his marriage to a cold, uncaring wife. She did not want to remember him with love.

Tears ran unheeded down her cheeks as she rose to her feet and confronted him.

'I cannot come with you to England,' she said, her hand reaching out involuntarily to touch his cheek. 'It is not only because of what my desertion would do to Benjamin. It is also because you were right – I do love you. I think I always did from that first moment I saw you from the rectory window! I think I love Adam so much because he looks just like you. But for his sake as much as for yours and Benjamin's, we cannot ever be together. I want you to have our son, Deveril. I know you love him. He will be a comfort to you and I shall think of him as such.'

Deveril's face looked tormented as he tried to kiss away her tears.

'I am no longer sure if I can take him from you,' he said huskily. 'What will become of you, my darling, my love, my only true love?'

With a great effort, Clemency managed a smile.

'I shall settle down to marriage – have another child,' she said. 'One day, perhaps, I shall come and see Adam – or when he is older, he shall come and see me. I shall find contentment of a kind, Deveril. You must not worry about my happiness. I learned once before how to live without Adam, and I shall do so again – this time more easily, knowing he is with you. I am in no doubt that he loves you.'

Despite his intention not to touch her again, Deveril caught Clemency in his arms and kissed her with a violence born of despair.

'Oh, my darling!' he said huskily. 'I cannot bear to think

of the unhappiness I have already caused you, still less the thought that I shall cause you further suffering. How you must have hated me that night when unwittingly I despoiled you! I feel so ashamed, so appalled at the memory.'

Her voice choked with tears, Clemency tried to smile.

'We were both little more than children, Deveril, and never forget I was a willing partner. I wanted you to love me . . .'

He covered her face with kisses that were both tender and yet possessive as he whispered:

'I made you mine, Clemency. You belong to me.' He drew a long, shuddering sigh. 'How can you forgive me?' he asked. 'I have caused you so much pain. I know now what you suffered when I took Adam from you, but I swear I did not know it at the time. Grimshaw insisted you had surrendered him willingly . . .'

'Hush!' Clemency said, covering his mouth with her hand. 'We must try to believe that your lawyer was right to fear the consequences if ever we discovered the truth about each other. You were married to Muriel and I to Percy . . . there was no future for us.'

Deveril rocked her gently in his arms.

'And still there is to be no future, Clemency, if you will not return to England. Perhaps I should stay here with you – write to poor Muriel and tell her I am never going back. We could take Adam and go to this place your father discovered – the three of us. No one would care that we were not legally married, or ever know we were not. We could build a life together . . .'

'Deveril!' Her cry interrupted him, for she could not allow him to pursue this dream – one she was so very tempted to believe in. 'Deveril, I cannot run away from Benjamin. It is now over four years since I was widowed, and Benjamin has waited all that time for me, travelled half across the world to marry me. And you, you are no ordinary man who can disregard conventions. You are the Viscount Burnbury, and you have responsibilities to your family, your ancestors. Have you forgotten why you wanted Adam so much? You knew you must have an heir. Even if you had no wife to consider, you are not free to live as another man might.'

She knew by the expression on Deveril's face that her words had touched upon the truth. He looked suddenly older – much as he might one day look when he was middle-aged. With a cry, he gathered her back into his embrace.

'But I love you!' he said. 'I do not know if I want a life without you.'

'You will have Adam to comfort you,' she said quickly. 'I am giving him to you, Deveril, because I know you will be able to make a man of him. That will be sufficient purpose for your life.'

'It is you I love!' he cried. 'You I want!'

As his arms drew her against him and his mouth came down on hers, Clemency clung to him, the tears once again falling unheeded as she permitted herself this one last embrace. She would not see him again once they returned to the Mathesons' house, she told herself. Jane or Benjamin could take Adam to him when she had prepared the boy for his departure. She hoped desperately that her son would not be too unhappy at the thought of leaving her; and somehow she must not let him see the pain the parting would cause her. Children lived very much for the moment, and if Deveril suggested visiting the Niagara Falls – and perhaps the nearby encampment of Red Indians – Adam would accompany his father happily enough.

But for this last precious minute, she could not be brave. For a little while longer, Deveril must share her pain. She clung to him, weeping unashamedly for the love she was about to lose for the glimpse of happiness she knew would never be hers again.

CHAPTER TWENTY-EIGHT

September–October 1838

When Clemency awoke, it was to find Jane seated at her bedside. The curtains were drawn and the room was filled with the aroma of camphor.

She felt very weak – her arms and head too heavy to lift from their resting places. Her thoughts were so confused that she wondered at first if she was still dreaming. Hazy memories of people leaning over her, spooning physic into her mouth, wiping her face and hands, crowded into her mind without form or substance. She could remember Benjamin's voice insisting that she make the effort to get well . . . to live . . .

'Clemency, you are awake!' Jane's voice . . . her smiling face as she leant over her, holding a glass of lemonade to her lips.

She drank thirstily, the effort momentarily exhausting her.

'Benjamin will be so pleased!' Jane said, smiling down once more and taking Clemency's hand in hers. 'You have been very seriously ill, you know. We even feared at one point that you might die!'

Clemency was surprised. She could remember so little after Adam had gone . . . only a terrible pain in her head and an aching in her limbs . . . and the searing heat of her body. But her bodily suffering had been as nothing beside her grief at the parting with her child, and although she had allowed herself to be put to bed, she had not supposed she was ill.

'You have had the ague,' Jane was saying. 'There have been many hundreds ill with the infection.' She forbore from adding that there were many, too, who had died of it. Fortunately Benjamin still had a supply of quinine although this was now running short, and those poor people who were not strong enough to make their way into town had no choice but to let the fever take its course.

'Benjamin says that reports have come in of epidemics from all around the lake,' Jane said. 'He believes the miasma is brought about by the sunlight reaching the decaying vegetation of our forest clearings . . .'

She broke off, aware that Clemency's eyes were closed and that she was too weak yet to concentrate upon the project currently occupying her own thoughts.

'I will leave you to go to sleep for a little while,' she said, but Clemency laid a hand on her arm.

'Don't leave me,' she pleaded. 'I want to know . . . is Adam ill with this fever?'

Jane regarded her patient anxiously. Benjamin had warned her that when Clemency regained consciousness, she might be confused. Gently, she explained that Adam was by now safely in England with Lord Burnbury and, hopefully, in the best of health.

'In England? Already?' Clemency repeated as she struggled to come to terms with time. 'How long then have I been ill?'

'For almost a month,' Jane told her. 'You caught the fever mid-August and it is now the twenty-second of September.'

'The twenty-second? But Benjamin and I were to have been married on the twentieth . . .'

'You are not to worry about anything,' Jane broke in. 'Mama has postponed all the arrangements for the time being. The only thing that matters now is that you concentrate your efforts upon getting well again.' She smiled. 'If you do not, it is I who will suffer the consequences, since Benjamin has put you in my charge. He is so busy he can barely find time to see you more than once a day, when he comes home for his evening meal. I fear if he does not soon take a rest, he too will fall ill! Mama says she cannot think how our township would ever have managed without him for he does the work of ten physicians. Once you are a little better, Clemency, I shall be able to assist him more often. But it would have been too much for Mama to manage alone . . .'

'I am causing everyone a great deal of trouble,' Clemency said weakly.

'You could not help it,' Jane said firmly. 'But now you must do as I say and sleep. I will come back in a little while with some beef tea to build up your strength. We shall talk then if you wish.'

When she left the room, Clemency lay for a moment trying to muster her thoughts. She wanted to think of poor Benjamin struggling so hard to take care of all the sick people like herself. But she could think only of Adam's face as she had helped him into the buggy beside Jane who was taking him to Deveril. Tears had been streaming down his cheeks and until the very last moment, he had pleaded with her to go with him. She could remember with sharp clarity how desperately close she had come to running after the carriage as it disappeared from view. She could remember the terrible pain in her head . . . Mrs Matheson's arms catching her as her legs gave way beneath her . . . then nothing more.

But the desire for sleep was suddenly overwhelming and her eyes closed. When next she woke, it was dark and a single candle lit the room. Jane was once more seated by the bedside. Clemency managed a smile.

'I think I am feeling much better,' she said. 'I do believe I am hungry!'

She managed to drink a little of the beef tea Jane brought her, and after she had been washed and changed into a clean nightdress, she lay back against her pillows, tired but without any signs of fever.

'There are two letters awaiting you, Clemency. Do you feel well enough to read them?'

Clemency felt her heart lurch. Was it possible Adam had written so soon? Perhaps Deveril, too . . . But she had forgotten she had been ill for so long.

'Please . . .' she said weakly. 'I would like to read them.'

Jane pulled open the little drawer of the bedside table and gave Clemency the letters. Both had been franked HALIFAX – NOVA SCOTIA. Adam's was brief, clearly not dictated by Deveril, mentioning their diversion to Niagara Falls and the visit to the Red Indian settlement nearby. Only at the end of his account did he add:

'I wish you were here, Mama. I miss you *very much* . . .'

Tears filled her eyes, momentarily blurring Deveril's bold hand as she opened his letter.

'The boy is in good health and for most of the time, in good spirits. He talks of you often and I do not discourage him. Understandably, he misses you, but there are many diversions and he speaks happily enough of going to live with his cousins. You may rest assured that his Happiness will at all times be my first responsibility. I have it in mind to request my sister to keep you posted with regard to Adam's progress and well-being as I believe it to be in our joint interest that *our* parting is absolute.

'I now wish you and Brook every happiness in your future life together – and I write with the utmost Sincerity.

'Thank you for giving me my son. I shall be forever indebted to you.

'Your most Obedient Servant,
Deveril Burnbury.'

And then, as if he regretted the formality of the letter, he added a postscript which could only have been prompted by the outpourings of his heart.

'Oh, my dearest, beloved Clemency, believe me when I tell you that your little son does not grieve for you as I do. He talks of you with great love and longing and his childish words echo in my heart. Not even the boy can fill that loneliness of the spirit which will always be mine without you. You will not believe me but I shall say it nonetheless – I shall love you until the day I die. If you should ever hear my name linked with some other woman, do not judge me too readily, for whoever I hold in my arms, whoever I may kiss, however pretty the eyes I gaze into, it is your face, your eyes, your dear, dear self I shall be seeing. Remember me sometimes in your dreams. I shall have no need of reminders of you since I have Adam, your son, Clemency, and mine. In him we are united forever. I beg you, be happy, my darling, and should you find your separation from the boy too painful, you have but to notify me and I shall return him to you at once.

'I will love you always.

D'

Unmindful of Jane's presence, Clemency gave way to the overwhelming sadness which filled her heart and mind and she wept uncontrollably. Jane rose swiftly from her chair and took Clemency in her arms. After a few moments, she said softly:

'Although I may be older than you, Clemency, I realize that in comparison, I have had very little experience of life. Nevertheless, I do know that it places a great strain upon a person if they are obliged to pretend to emotions they do not feel or, perhaps even worse, to pretend not to feel emotions that torture them. For this reason, I shall confess that I am aware of your love for Lord Burnbury.'

She saw the colour rush to Clemency's cheeks and said quickly:

'You were often delirious, my dear, and unable to conceal the truth. But do not let this distress you, for only I heard you and I promise that I shall never reveal anything that you said to another human being – least of all to Benjamin. Do you wish me to continue?'

'You may as well tell me, Jane, how many more of my unhappy secrets are now revealed to you.'

The older girl's eyes were filled with compassion as she stared at Clemency's pale, thin face.

'I know that Lord Burnbury is Adam's father; that you gave Adam back to him because you love him, and because the child is his heir. Oh, Clemency, how could you ever find the courage, for I am certain that had I been in your place, I could not. I admire you so much!'

'Admire me!' Clemency echoed, her eyes wide with surprise. 'Despite what you now know about . . . about my past?'

Jane's cheeks were bright with indignation.

'I know that you could never do anything unkind or evil,' she said hotly. 'That is why Benjamin loves you so much. But what I do not understand, Clemency, and greatly wish to do so, is why you are going to marry Benjamin when your heart is in the keeping of another man. Can you truly believe you will be happy in such a marriage?'

Clemency gave a long sigh.

'I cannot answer for myself, Jane,' she said quietly, 'but I do believe I can make Benjamin happy – and that is what matters to me now. I intend to dedicate my life to that purpose.'

Jane stood up suddenly and walked across the room to the window. She seemed deep in thought. When she turned to face Clemency, her expression was one of bewilderment.

'Then you must love Benjamin too, since you are putting his happiness before your own.'

Clemency gave another sigh.

'Try to understand, Jane. For eight long difficult years, Benjamin has looked after me; put my happiness before his. We were to have been married in England last year, but two months before our wedding date, I suddenly decided to leave England . . . to bring Adam here. I had discovered, you see, that he was unhappy and far from well with Lord Burnbury's wife in London. Benjamin had every right to feel aggrieved; to expect me to put our wedding plans first; *but he did not.* As if his wishes were of no consequence, he helped me escape with Adam. I cannot now ask him to make the same sacrifices again – and most of all because I know he *would* make them if he thought it was for my happiness. He has waited long enough for me to marry him.'

The long speech exhausted her, and she closed her eyes as her head fell back weakly against the pillows. For a long time, Jane stood looking down at her, an enigmatic expression in her eyes. Then with a sigh she left the room and went downstairs, knowing that at any moment now, Benjamin would be home and she could impart to him the good news that Clemency was better. Between the long gruelling hours of work he had been putting in and his fear that Clemency would die, he had aged five years in as many weeks.

They had all aged, Jane thought, for even her mother and father had been occupied from dawn to dusk, taking baskets of food to the sick and needy in the town. She herself assisted Benjamin whenever her mother relieved her in Clemency's sick-room. She had become quite adept at measuring doses of quinine for the long queues of patients attending Benjamin's surgery – half to one grain for the convalescents; three to four grains three times a day as a preventative; ten grains for the severely affected. She also prepared bottles of tincture for Benjamin to take on his rounds, the mixture containing aloes, opium, rhubarb, camphor and aromatics as well as the precious quinine, to be administered to the sufferer in doses of from one to four teaspoons. Benjamin had great faith in this conglomerate, and Jane could not prepare sufficient for his needs quickly enough.

At night when he arrived home, he was almost too weary to climb the stairs to Clemency's bedroom. Several times he had fallen asleep in his chair whilst eating his supper, and twice he admitted that he had been too tired to undress himself before going to bed. By dawn, he was breakfasting and on his way back into town.

At least, Jane thought now, he would have one less worry. His beloved Clemency was not after all going to die . . .

'And that is in very large part due to your nursing, Jane,'

he said gratefully when he heard the news. His lined, tired face relaxed into a smile. 'Now I shall be able to claim more of your time,' he said. 'Your kind mama will doubtless attend to Clemency's convalescence and free you for more urgent tasks.'

Thus a further two weeks passed before Clemency was permitted to go downstairs for a short while every day. Only then did she fully appreciate how the epidemic had affected not just the Mathesons' household but the whole town and surrounding areas. It was not only the clearing of the trees by the settlers that was causing the trouble, Benjamin told her. The construction of dams and locks had raised the level of the lake, but as the level fell in the dry summer season, an immense amount of decaying vegetation was exposed to the sun.

'When this epidemic is over,' he said, 'I intend to study the subject in detail, and Jane has written on my behalf to Toronto and New York requesting such information as may have been written about it.'

Clemency was determined that as soon as she had regained her strength, she would offer her services to Benjamin as Jane was doing.

'I feel so guilty,' she said, 'lying in this chair whilst you two are working nearly twenty hours a day.'

But Benjamin would not entertain even the idea that she might lend assistance.

'It will take far longer than you think, my dear, to regain your health,' he said. But seeing Clemency's agitation, he finally relented sufficiently to agree that she might write the labels for the medicine bottles. Thereafter Clemency spent her mornings and afternoons thus employed.

As September gave way to October, she had little opportunity to appreciate the beauties of the Fall – the autumn colouring of the trees surrounding the town. The first chill winds of winter had not yet touched them, and Mrs Matheson agreed that a short ride into town in the buggy would not harm Clemency.

'Then I shall take these labels down to the surgery,' Clemency said, 'for Benjamin may be in need of them. I can take my letters to the Post Office at the same time.'

She had written at length to Adam, now in the care of Lady Allendale; and also to the Professor and Miss Fothergill. But the letter she was most anxious to see upon its way was one to Lady McDoone who, Deveril had told her, had been quite seriously ill but was now at long last making a recovery. Deveril had also told her that it was his great-aunt who had first suggested to him that she, Clemency, was Adam's mother. Now it was Clemency's wish to request the kind old lady's forgiveness for the deception she had been obliged to employ in order to be near her son.

But although she had longed with all her heart to reply to Deveril's letter to her, she had forced herself to resist the temptation. She was determined to put him from her mind, if not from her heart, and devote herself to Benjamin, whose undisguised joy in her recovery was yet another proof of his devotion to her.

Glad to have at least one small task that would assist him in his work, Clemency set off to town, a fresh supply of labels in her shopping basket. With one of the Mathesons' servants driving her, she called first at the Post Office and despatched her letters. It was quite late in the afternoon when the buggy drew up outside Benjamin's little surgery, but there was not one vacant chair in the waiting room.

Clemency paused, wondering whether she should simply leave the labels on the table for Benjamin to discover rather than interrupt him when he was clearly so busy. But at that moment, a woman came out of the surgery, her eyes red-rimmed, her face drawn. In a quiet shocked voice, she announced that her baby girl had just died.

'Last week, I lost my husband and my son,' she told Clemency. 'Now there is no one but me . . .'

She passed Clemency like a sleepwalker and disappeared out of the door. Clemency's heart ached with pity and she longed to help in some way. Perhaps Benjamin could tell her who the woman was, so that she could call at her home and try to comfort her. Without thinking to knock first upon the surgery door, she opened it and went in.

Benjamin was standing with his back half-turned towards her. Jane was in his arms, her face pressed against his chest as she sobbed uncontrollably. In a low comforting tone, Benjamin was trying to soothe her.

'You must not give way now, Jane. You have been so very brave, so magnificently courageous. Come now, my dear girl, lest I start blaming myself for subjecting you to such ordeals. You are my assistant, had you forgotten? My right hand? I do not know how I could have survived these past months without your help and support. Dry those tears, I beg you, and let me see your pretty smile!'

Neither was aware of Clemency, and Benjamin's tall figure hid her from Jane's view as the girl said in a small, desolate voice:

'Forgive me, Benjamin. I know I should not let a baby's death affect me so deeply. But you were so gentle, so kind to the mother, and suddenly I could not bear the emotion I felt. Perhaps self-pity was uppermost, for I realized how helpless I was; how unimportant and pointless my life. I had no comfort to offer her and I could not help *you*; and you looked so tired, so dejected. But you think only of others, never of yourself. If only Clemency . . . *if only I had the right to take care of you* . . .' She broke off and gave a horrified gasp. 'No, I did not mean . . . I . . . I know how deeply you love Clemency and she loves you too, but . . .'

As Benjamin's hand reached out to stroke Jane's hair, Clemency knew that she could not allow another second to pass without making the couple aware of her presence. But she was momentarily paralysed by what she had just heard. In all the months she had spent at the Mathesons' house, sometimes in intimate conversation with Jane, she had never once suspected that Jane might be falling in love with Benjamin.

It seemed quite impossible now that she could have overlooked such a possibility.

'You have been under a great strain, my dear,' Benjamin was saying gently. 'At such times, it is very easy to allow emotions and judgements to become confused. You and I are the very best of friends . . . and colleagues too, and I hope we shall always remain so. You are a good, sweet, kindly person and I have you to thank, since dear Clemency's recovery is almost entirely due to your good nursing.'

Clemency's feet were drawing her backwards through the doorway behind her. She realized that she must somehow convince Benjamin and Jane that she had only just arrived. To let either of them know she had overheard their conversation would cause too much embarrassment to all of them.

Her fingers grasped the door handle and she rattled it noisily.

'I came to see if there was anything I could do for that poor woman,' she said in a bright unnatural voice, moving across the room to Jane as if she was not in the least surprised to find her in Benjamin's arms. 'No wonder you are so distressed, my dear. I too, was nearly in tears although I was not, like your poor self, present when the baby died.' She turned to Benjamin, whose arms had dropped to his sides. 'Now that I am better, you must tell me if there are others like that unhappy mother whom I might visit, Benjamin, and advise me if I can lend my assistance in any other way.'

Benjamin bent to kiss Clemency's cheek.

'I have one task for you already,' he said, 'and that is to take Jane home with you. I had not realized it before, but I have been asking far too much of her and she is in need of a good rest.' He put a restraining hand on Jane's arm as she opened her mouth to protest. 'It is not a suggestion, young lady, but an order from your physician,' he said firmly. 'Now off you go, both of you. I have patients awaiting me.'

Jane's unusual silence as they drove home compounded Clemency's suspicions that her nerves were at breaking point. It was small wonder, she thought, realizing the strain under which her friend must have been living for these past weeks. It could not have been easy for Jane watching Benjamin – the man she loved – agonizing over her, Clemency. It must have been all the more difficult for Jane, knowing as she did that Benjamin's love was not returned. She said nothing of her thoughts until she had put Jane to bed, drawing the window drapes so that the room was only dimly lit. Then she seated herself by the bedside and said:

'Our rôles are reversed, dearest Jane. Now *you* are the patient and I am the nurse!'

Jane attempted a smile, but her lips were trembling.

'Oh, Clemency!' she whispered. 'If you only knew! I have made such a fool of myself! I could almost wish myself dead.' Her voice rose on the edge of hysteria. 'You would wish me dead too, if you knew . . . if . . .' She burst into a storm of tears.

Clemency took both her hands and held them tightly between her own.

'You once told me, Jane, that nothing was more destroying than the need to pretend or conceal a truth. I opened my heart to you then because you are my closest friend and I trust you. Now you must open your heart to me with the same trust.'

Jane's head twisted from side to side.

'I cannot do so! You do not understand, Clemency. You spoke of your love for Lord Burnbury in your delirium. But if I were to tell you . . . to confess . . . you would hate me. *You would have every right to hate me.*'

She broke into tears once more, sobbing quietly as Clemency said:

'No, Jane, I would never blame you for something that is outside your control. And you have no need to confess, since I am certain I know the truth already. You love Benjamin, do you not? And you are afraid that he may now know it? Or that I should know it?'

The colour flooded Jane's cheeks as her tears ceased and she stared at Clemency in shocked dismay.

'You know? You guessed? Clemency, for pity's sake, tell me that I have not let it be so obvious to all. Oh, I am so ashamed!' she cried piteously.

'But of course you have not betrayed yourself,' Clemency said quickly, reassuringly. 'And truly, Jane, I can see no reason for shame. Everyone who knows Benjamin loves him. You who have worked so closely beside him and perhaps know him even better than I . . . what more natural outcome than that you should have grown to value him, respect him, care for him. I can understand why you love him.'

'Then you are not angry? Shocked?' Jane asked disbelievingly. 'He is your fiancé, Clemency, the man you are going to marry!'

Clemency gave a wry smile.

'Ask yourself, Jane, how could I lay blame at your door for loving a man who is betrothed to another, when I myself love a man who is *married* to another,' she said simply.

Jane drew a long, shuddering sigh and a little colour returned to her cheeks.

'If you could only know how I have struggled against my feeling,' she whispered. 'It has been so terribly difficult, Clemency, seeing Benjamin every day, working with him, sharing his life.'

'You did not seek that proximity,' Clemency said reassuringly. 'My illness and the fact that Benjamin needed your help were circumstances beyond your control. Now do as Benjamin asks and try to get some rest. This is far from being the tragedy you suppose. We will talk further when you are calmer.'

Leaving Jane alone, she went to her own bedroom where she sat for a long time at her bureau, deep in thought. When finally she went downstairs, it was to inform Mrs Matheson that she intended paying her elder daughter a visit as soon as Jane had recovered.

'I have not seen Katherine since I became ill,' she said. 'And her dear children will comfort me a little for the absence of my Adam.'

Katherine was delighted to receive her when she called two days later. Two of her servants were ill with the fever and she was trying, with the help of only one young girl, to cook, milk the cows, do the baking, washing, ironing and attend to the needs of her husband and children. Clemency's visit therefore was most fortuitous.

Once or twice in the ensuing fortnight, Clemency stayed overnight at Katherine's house, glad to be able to lend assistance while at the same time laying the foundations for the plan she intended for herself as soon as she felt strong enough to carry it out. She was going back to England.

It was the end of October before she felt fully restored to health. She invited Jane into her room one night as they prepared for bed. Although Jane still looked pale and drawn, she had refused to remain an invalid for longer than a day and was fully occupied once more in assisting Benjamin. She seemed inordinately pleased by Clemency's invitation.

'I was beginning to fear that you were seeking excuses to avoid my company, Clemency,' she said awkwardly, as she sat down on the edge of the bed. 'We seem to have seen so little of each other since . . . since . . .'

Clemency continued to brush her hair with long, steady strokes.

'My purpose was not to avoid you, dearest Jane,' she said quietly. 'I have been establishing an alibi!' She gave a brief smile. 'You see, my dear, I am leaving tomorrow for England. I am returning to be near Adam. I have not yet told Benjamin and I do not intend to do so in person. I shall leave a letter for him, but which I do not wish him to receive at least until I have had time to reach the high seas.' She heard Jane's gasp and turned to look at her. Jane's face was a mask of astonishment.

'I shall announce to your mama at breakfast that I shall be spending at least a week with your sister Katherine. No one, not even Benjamin, will be particularly surprised,' Clemency continued calmly. 'This will afford me the time to be far away before Benjamin learns the truth of my absence. I do not want him to come hurrying after me, which he might feel obliged to do. I shall be counting upon you, Jane, to make him see the folly of such a course of action and, above all, *to comfort him.*'

A deep blush spread into the older girl's cheeks.

'You are not leaving because of me . . . because of what I told you . . .' she whispered. 'I give you my word, Benjamin has never shown me anything but friendship. He would be horrified if he knew . . . if he thought . . .'

Clemency smiled.

'No, Jane, I assure you I do not suspect a secret bond between you. But when you confessed that you loved Benjamin, it gave me a new insight into the situation . . . one upon which I have thought long and very carefully. I believe you love him as I have never done. I had thought it my duty to Benjamin to remain here and marry him when Deveril took Adam back to England, but suddenly I realized that far from ensuring what was best for Benjamin, I was making it impossible for him ever to realize the joys of being truly loved – as he would be loved by you, Jane.'

She stood up and went to put her arm around the older girl's shoulders. Quickly she continued:

'I thought how nearly I had died of the ague, Jane, and that if I *had* died, Benjamin would almost certainly have turned to you for solace. So long as I am here, he will continue to believe he loves and needs me because to do so has become a habit for him. But I have never been able to feel as passionately devoted to him as I know a wife should. There is a part of me that can never belong to him, no matter how hard I try or what vows I make. Do you understand now why I am going?'

Jane was staring at her wide-eyed.

'But Benjamin loves you, Clemency. He always has. I think he always will!'

Clemency nodded.

'I think that is true in a way. I know Benjamin believes it. But I have never been able to give him much happiness, Jane. I was always running away from him and in his heart, he must know it. Can you not see, as I do, how much better suited to him you are than I? You have so much you can share with him. I have nothing but my unhappy past. I sincerely believe that in a little while, he will turn to you, Jane – at first for consolation and then for love. He needs you. He needs a home, a family. Above all he needs someone to love and care for him as you do. One day he will be grateful that I left him, and you will have to be patient until that day comes.'

She went over to her bureau and opened one of the drawers.

'I shall leave a letter in here for Benjamin. I want you to promise me you will withhold it until my disappearance is discovered. I do not want him to be angry with you for not presenting it sooner, so I have planned that you shall "discover" it after it is known that I have gone not to Katherine but to England. It will be supposed the maid placed it there when she cleaned my room. Jane, you will help me, will you not? I must have your promise.'

At first, Jane would not give it.

'You speak with such conviction, Clemency, but how can you be sure that you are right? You say Benjamin's love for you is habit, but suppose it is that once-in-a-lifetime love that can never be denied? Suppose it is no different from the kind of love you have for Adam's father?'

Clemency shook her head gently.

'It cannot be, Jane. That kind of love is too urgent, too demanding, too full of passion to be set aside for so long and for such easily surmountable obstacles as those which prompted Benjamin to wait for me so patiently. I realize now that there were many times I came close to wanting marriage. Had he shown his need of me, an urgent, passionate need, I might have allowed him to claim me – to make me his wife. I was alone, unhappy, in great need of love, but a different kind of love from the quiet, selfless devotion Benjamin offered me.'

Jane's doubts were only partially dispelled.

'You cannot be sure that Benjamin would look to me to console him,' she said. 'This could break his heart, Clemency. Have you considered it?'

Clemency nodded, a strange little smile playing about the corners of her mouth.

'Hearts may sometimes break through unrequited love,' she said. 'But never, I think, from a surfeit of it. You must not hide your feelings for him, Jane. That would be false modesty – and unwise in the circumstances. Encourage him to weep upon your shoulder if he will. But he is strong as well as good, and I am trusting that when he has read my letter he will know that I am right to leave.'

'And what will become of *you*, Clemency?' Jane cried, jumping up and running to put her arms around her. 'What hope is there for *your* future? At least if you were to stay and marry Benjamin, you would have a future . . .'

'No, dearest!' Clemency broke in. 'My mind is made up. I shall return to England where I shall be reunited from time to time with my son. That will be my happiness, my future. I have missed Adam quite unbearably these last months and long with all my heart to see him. I thought . . . I hoped that I would become accustomed to his absence, but I am not, nor ever will be. Now kiss me goodbye, dear Jane, for we are unlikely to see one another in the morning.'

When Jane was gone, Clemency unhurriedly packed such clothes as she felt she needed for the journey. When all was done, she sat down at her bureau to write to Benjamin. She had thought the task would be a hard one, but as she reached for her quill, she found the words filling her mind, tumbling over one another as they waited to be put on paper.

'It is almost eight years to the day since first you came into my life as a friend,' she wrote. 'Since that day when you told me I was going to have a child, you have never once failed to give me your help, advice, support and above all, your selfless devotion to my happiness. In all that time, Dearest Benjamin, there has never been anything worthwhile that I could give you in return. Now at long last there is something I can do – I can give you your freedom!

'Do not imagine, my dear, that I fail to understand how bitter you are feeling as you read those words. But you are not only a kind, good man, Benjamin, you are a wise one. You have always known that Adam has come first in my heart. I think you know, too, that I have never been able entirely to eradicate Deveril from my thoughts. But I am not considering either of them at this moment of decision to break our engagement. I am thinking of you. You deserve all that is best and never a half measure of love, which is all I could ever give you. You will always have my deepest respect and my deepest affection. But Dearest Benjamin, I cannot give you the kind of love Jane feels for you. I have watched her love for you grow and believe it will go on growing, more especially if she is no longer forced to conceal it. It is a true love, Benjamin, without qualifications and one you should not ignore for I believe she could make you very happy . . .'

Clemency paused to draw out a second sheet of writing paper, for she still had much she wished to say.

'I can envisage the scowl upon your face as you read those last words. Who am I, you will be asking, to presume to make such a prediction? Well, I am your friend, Benjamin – someone who knows you well and who has never been in doubt as to your aims in life . . . a home, a family, a loving wife who is also your helpmeet. I know that had you met Jane years ago before you met me, you would happily have married her. I think that even now you love her a little but you are too steeped in the habit of caring for me to know it.

'I do not want you to consider coming to England to

ask me to change my mind. I am going back where my heart is – to live near Adam. I do not expect to see or speak to Deveril ever again and you need therefore not worry that I shall come to harm at his hands! See how I know your mind, Benjamin!

'My Dear Friend, I believe that I love you – not as a lover but as someone who will remain always in my thoughts and heart and always with the deepest gratitude. Allow me to give you the chance of happiness and you will make me happy, too. I could not now leave you were I not convinced that it is Jane and not I you should take to wife. Despite her feelings for you, I believe she would try to prevent my going if she could, wanting your contentment before her own. I hope I am showing now a measure of her selflessness by removing myself from your life.

'Try not to reproach me in your heart, Benjamin, and try, as I know you will, to forgive me for taking so much of your life so thoughtlessly. I am returning to you your ring, not because I do not value and treasure it but because I know now that it should never have been mine.'

She read the letter through once and then sealed it. Despite the poignant sadness she knew Benjamin would feel when he read it, in her heart there were no doubts. Jane was no empty-headed girl who would toy with Benjamin's affections. She was a young woman, twenty-six years old and, for the first time in her life, deeply in love. Pretty, charming, intelligent, she would soon channel Benjamin's affections to herself, and he would be rewarded as he so well deserved.

With the same calm certainty that had prompted all her actions since her decision was made, Clemency slowly drew the sapphire ring from her finger and laid it on top of the letter. As she closed the drawer, she realized that symbolically she was also closing for ever an episode of her life.

CHAPTER TWENTY-NINE

January–February 1839

'You promise, Mama?' Adam persisted, as he gave her a last farewell hug.

Clemency smiled as she ruffled his dark curls.

'Yes, of course, my darling, I shall come every week unless your Aunt Selina has other plans for you.'

The uncertainty left the boy's face as he ran off happily to join his cousins in the big schoolroom at the top of Lady Allendale's London house.

Selina drew Clemency down beside her on the sofa. The drawing-room fire was throwing out a welcome heat on this cold January afternoon and the atmosphere in the gracious room was warm and friendly.

'As you can see for yourself, my dear,' Selina said, linking her arm affectionately through Clemency's, 'you have no cause for concern about your delightful little boy. In the five months he has been with us, George and I have come to love him as one of our own.' Her eyes searched Clemency's face, her own bright with esteem as she added: 'I cannot express how deeply I admire your unselfishness in returning Adam to my brother. I do not think that I myself could have acted so courageously, and I want you to know that it is not just for Adam's sake that you will be welcome here whenever you can make the journey from Brighton. I too, shall be more than happy to see you. We are going to become great friends, Clemency, and I only wish we had known each other years ago.'

'You are very kind, Lady Allendale – Selina,' Clemency corrected herself. 'You must believe me when I say that having heard from Adam this afternoon how happy he is living here with you, I know I have done the right thing.'

Which was no idle comment, she decided, recalling this kindly woman's greeting. 'I shall not call you Mrs Forest,' she had announced. 'You are Mrs Grayshott and my sister-in-law, and I insist that everyone in the family shall now refer to you as such.'

There was no doubting her genuine desire to be friends, Clemency thought, as Selina said now:

'Deveril told me that you are very fond of the old Professor with whom you are living, but would it not be far easier for you to live in London? You could then see Adam much more frequently, and without so long a journey to make.'

Clemency's hesitation was only momentary. Realizing that she had no need for reticence with this new friend, she said simply:

'I do not think it advisable that Deveril and I should meet.'

Selina nodded, understanding very well the reasons why this pretty young woman wanted to avoid her brother. Deveril had poured out his heart to her on his return from Upper Canada, and having now met Clemency, she could well appreciate how hard it must be for them to deny the love that clearly existed between them. She drew a deep sigh, knowing that she must now impart some news to Clemency that could only cause her distress.

'Perhaps you are right!' she said quietly. 'I know that Deveril is trying very hard to indulge his wife at this present time. Muriel is with child, you see.'

Involuntarily Clemency covered her mouth as she tried to withhold a gasp of surprise. Across her mind flashed Deveril's declaration that his wife rejected the intimacies of their married life.

As if aware of her thoughts, Selina said quietly:

'Of course Muriel did not want this to happen, and she made no secret of the fact when she told me of her condition, which she discovered whilst Deveril was in Upper Canada.

Her physician had forbidden her to have more children after the stillbirth of the last, but Muriel believed herself safe from misfortune since she had been taking measures to ensure against such an eventuality. It does not surprise me that those measures failed. It is, after all, tampering with the laws of nature, is it not?'

In shocked silence Clemency listened to these confidences which she would have preferred not to hear. But as if she were truly a member of the family, Selina continued: 'Muriel's physician, somewhat surprisingly, is hopeful she will survive the birth of this child. Personally, I am of the opinion that my sister-in-law is a great deal hardier than she pretends. I think that horrible French maid, who Muriel used to employ, encouraged her in playing the invalid. We could all develop *la migraine* when it suited, could we not? It would seem that Muriel is only indisposed for an occasion which my poor brother desires to attend and she does not. However, for the present he is avoiding any controversy, as naturally he is most anxious that this time the infant should survive. He has always wanted a large family, although I know he is concerned that the birth of a son will automatically disinherit Adam.'

At last Clemency found her voice.

'I cannot think that Adam would be bothered if he were disinherited. I am not, for I know that a title carries with it many responsibilities, and those not always pleasurable. In a way he would be free, as Deveril is not.'

Selina nodded.

'I see that you are wise as well as pretty, my dear,' she remarked, as Clemency rose to leave.

But wisdom had been sadly lacking so far in her young life, and it was only now as she grew older that she was beginning to make the right decisions, Clemency thought, as later that evening she joined the family group in the little house in Adelaide Crescent. They were seated side by side on the sofa in the Professor's little drawing-room. Edith was stitching clothes for her second baby, which was due in June.

'Well, my dears!' the Professor said, as he laid down his *Times*. 'New Year's Day, and I hope you have all made Good Resolutions. I have made but one – and that is not to try to predict what the next twelve months will bring.'

Clemency and Edith caught one another's eyes and smiled. Frederick was preparing a paper to read at a lecture he was to give to raise funds for one of his missionary charities. Edith's little girl, born while Clemency had been in Upper Canada, was already tucked up in bed. Outside the cold January rain had turned to sleet, and hearing its sharp lashing against the window pane, the Professor said:

'I predict we shall have snow before long!'

They all laughed as Clemency chided the old man gently for being so quick to break his resolution. He smiled at her over his spectacles.

'One can but do one's best,' he muttered, 'and since I have transgressed once, I may as well do so again. I predict we have not done yet with the Chartists – no, not by any manner of means. My own opinion is that there is a great deal to be said as to the justice of Mr Feargus O'Connor's demands – vote by ballot and equal electoral districts, to name but two. The workers are behind him, of course, which is scarcely surprising after last year's disastrous harvest and the general commercial recession we have been suffering as a consequence.'

Frederick turned to look at his father.

'I see no reason why the workers should concern themselves with parliamentary reform,' he said.

The Professor took off his spectacles and waved them in Frederick's direction.

'It is precisely because the workers have no influence upon the government that they now seek it,' he explained. 'They blame the government for falling wages, the closing of factories and scarcity of work. Most of all, they blame those ruling them for the rise in the price of food. It is fortunate that among those now agitating, there is a nucleus who demand violent action – and I think it will take place. But enough of politics . . .' he said, replacing his spectacles and smiling at Clemency. 'You have not yet told me your Resolutions, child.'

She laughed.

'The most important one, Professor, is to try to prevent myself from indulging Adam quite so much. Lady Allendale reproved me – in the kindest possible way – for giving him so many toys, and she is, of course, perfectly right. She tells me his Uncle 'Vril spoils him too.'

'It is only natural, I daresay,' the Professor said, as he smiled at Clemency over the top of his spectacles. Her heart warmed towards this kindly old man who had made her so immediately welcome on her return to England. Far from criticizing her for leaving Benjamin, he, like Selina, had applauded her courage.

'You might so easily have married my son for no more than the security it guaranteed you,' he had said. 'But that would not have been a true basis for marriage. You shall make your home here with us, child. I have always enjoyed your company'. His blue eyes had twinkled as he whispered conspiratorially: 'To tell the truth, my dear, I am frequently bored to tears with poor Edith's domestic chit-chat and sometimes may the Good Lord forgive me with dear Frederick's religious zeal. I shall be pleased to have a pretty girl to fuss over me again.'

'I am delighted to hear that Lady Allendale made you so welcome,' he said now, as he poked the fire into a cheerful blaze, 'and even more delighted to hear that we shall have young Adam to visit us at Easter.' Had it not been for the presence of Edith and Frederick, Clemency might have informed him then about Muriel's coming child. Instead, she spoke of the news Selina had given her over luncheon that day regarding Caroline Norton.

'I know you are interested in her problems, Professor, and you will be as sorry as I to hear that she has still not gained access to her boys.'

He nodded. 'I noted that the Infant Custody Bill, for which

the poor woman fought so hard, was thrown out by the House of Lords.'

'Lady Allendale told me that since that event, Caroline's name has been linked in the most scandalous manner with Mr Talfourd's; and Caroline is very bitter about the article in the *British and Foreign Review* in which she was referred to as "a she devil". Ironically the editor, John Kemble, is the brother of her great friends Fanny and Adelaide.'

'It would seem that poor Mrs Norton is fated for trouble,' the Professor said, sighing. 'That erstwhile friend of hers, Lord Melbourne, is now chief adviser to our young Queen – and much taken with Her Majesty, so I hear. Your Caroline, therefore, can no longer be of great concern to him – in fact, more of a liability I would suspect.'

The passing of the Infant Custody Act would have made no difference now to her, Clemency thought. But her heart could still ache for Caroline and all those mothers whose children were denied them without just cause.

'Lady Allendale told me she has promised to assist Caroline's efforts to raise support for the Bill,' she said. 'But I, alas, can do little other than write to her and offer my sympathies.'

In contrast to Caroline Norton's life without her boys, her own was not unhappy, Clemency thought. Soon after her arrival in England, she had received a delightful letter from Lady McDoone formally welcoming her into the family and professing herself anxious to see Clemency if ever the opportunity arose for her to go to Scotland. She had, too, received an even more profusely worded letter from dear Miss Fothergill. Not only would Clemency be visiting her with Adam at Easter, but at long last she would be able to go and see Mary and her family.

Not the least of her reasons for satisfaction with her life was the letter that had arrived on Christmas Day from Benjamin. Typical of him, he understood her reasons for leaving him, although naturally enough he expressed his deep regret at his loss. While he did not admit the possibility that he could ever love Jane as he had once loved her, it was clear to Clemency that he was already turning to Jane for comfort, so often did he mention her name in the rest of his letter.

Why then did she not feel as content as she should with her life? Clemency wondered. Was it the news of Deveril's coming child that so disturbed her? Clearly, he was reconciled to his marriage – a fact which forced her to realize that the love he had declared for her had been of a transitory nature. She did not doubt that he had been sincere when he had told her he loved her. But his marriage must have been at its lowest ebb, ignorant as he was at the time that Muriel was with child. Perhaps, had he known of it before leaving England, he would never have embarked on the journey! It was all too easy to believe now that it was his need for Adam, not for her, which had prompted it.

Glancing round the Professor's small room with thoughtful eyes, Clemency felt a sudden overwhelming sadness. Here, within these walls, was a small family – father, mother, grandfather – complete and content. Upstairs asleep was the first child of the next generation, and Edith would soon produce the second. For her, Clemency, there would never be the comfort of a loving husband; there could be no more children; no family circle to which she truly belonged. She was twenty-four years old, and yet life had already destined her to spinsterhood. She had voluntarily thrown away her only chance of marriage when she had returned Benjamin's ring, for no other man would consider taking to wife a woman with her past.

Clemency did not regret that act of self-sacrifice, but its implications were only now becoming fully apparent. Between the days when she could be with Adam, there were far many more when she must be alone – days and nights. At twenty-four, she thought bitterly, she was not too old to long to have a man's arms around her; to want the beauties and passions of love. Yet she had had no more than a brief glimpse of such joys.

Despite the heat of the glowing fire, Clemency shivered.

It was best not to think about the future, she told herself sharply as she folded away her sewing and rose to bid the Professor goodnight. She would not think beyond Easter, when she would have Adam with her for three whole weeks. She would not think of Benjamin and Jane; of Deveril and Muriel, or even of Frederick and Edith. She would not think of love – that fire at which other human beings warmed their hands and hearts. There were other kinds of love; other reasons for living.

At least, she comforted herself, she would never again be without the love of her son.

Although the Professor's predictions proved right and a little snow fell in the early weeks of January, it was soon gone, and for the rest of the month the south coast was buffeted by gale force winds and torrential rain. There were stories of carriages bowled over by the gales; of a foolhardy pedestrian walking on the Promenade being swept out to sea and drowned; of chimney pots being hurled to the ground and the Chain Pier once again in danger of collapsing.

Clemency fretted at her enforced confinement to the house. The Professor had been laid low with a bout of influenza and had temporarily abandoned the writing of his book on African tribal laws. He would not hear of Clemency travelling to London to visit Adam in such appalling weather, and time hung heavy on her hands.

By the first day of February, there was a slight improvement in the weather. Hastily, Clemency donned her heaviest cloak and set out for a walk along the sea-front. The sight of the white-capped waves pounding against the breakwaters suited her mood. The grey sky was dark with heavy clouds which threatened a further downpour, but she refused to allow the prospect to deter her. The sea-front was almost deserted, and as a gust of wind ripped her bonnet from her head, she suddenly laughed aloud, determined not to replace it. The wind tore at her hair, loosening the fine gold strands from their pins, and as she began to run, she felt it streaming out behind her, like the wake of a sailing ship, she thought.

A phaeton went bowling past her along the wet road, the driver huddled in his collared cloak against the cold wind. She heard him call out to her but ignored his shouted words, laughing at the thought of his astonishment. It was not often he might see a young woman, bonnetless, hair and cloak flying, running in so unladylike a fashion along the sea wall. Perhaps he thought her fleeing from an angry husband, she told herself, as a dozen gulls swooped screaming towards her and passed harmlessly over her head. Perhaps he thought the Devil was after her! She was running to . . . to what? she asked herself. To rediscover her youth? To find . . . to find freedom from the thoughts that tormented her?

I *am* running away! she told herself, as she slowed her pace to a walk. I am trying to escape from my loneliness – and I shall not do so in this madcap manner!

Turning to retrace her steps homewards, she felt calmer. What she must do, she thought, was find an occupation which would give her less time to think about herself. Perhaps, like Caroline Norton, she could write a book? She could write about Upper Canada and the life she had discovered there. The Professor had mentioned only a few days ago that people had begun to go in great numbers to the colonies to make better lives for themselves. Once it had been only criminals and debtors who were forced to go. Now there might be many gentlewomen interested to learn what kind of life they could expect in Upper Canada. She would write to Caroline, Clemency thought, and ask her advice upon the project. But first she would speak to the Professor, who could be counted upon to give his truthful opinion as to whether he thought she could do it.

So preoccupied was Clemency by this new idea that she was almost upon the doorstep of Adelaide Crescent before she recognized the Burnbury crest on the carriage halted in front of the house. Her heart jolted, her thoughts flying first, as they always did, to Adam. Had any ill befallen him? Had he run away from London? Was he unhappy?

She hurried into the house, forgetting in her anxiety any thought of her appearance. She could hear voices in the parlour and recognized immediately that of Adam. Her face breaking into a smile of joy, she opened the door and went in.

For the smallest part of a second, she did not recognize the man seated by the fireside. Dressed in sombre black, face white beneath the dark hair, she thought fleetingly that this was one of Frederick's missionaries. Then Adam flung himself into her arms and as the man stood up, she saw it was Deveril.

Across the top of the boy's head, her eyes met Deveril's solemn gaze. Thoughts raced through her mind like tiny whirl-winds. He had broken his promise never to try to see her! She was pleased . . . yes, wonderfully pleased, to see him. But why was he here? Where was the Professor? Frederick? Edith?

Suddenly, without warning, Deveril smiled.

'The Professor told me you were out walking, Clemency, but I must confess I was not expecting such a windswept sprite to come through the door.'

The colour rushed into her cheeks at his gentle teasing and her gloved hand flew to her hair. Adam was tugging at her skirt.

'Mama!' he burst out, no longer able to contain his excite-ment. 'I have a new cousin, and Uncle 'Vril says he can be a sort of brother for me 'cos I haven't any brothers and sisters of my own. He is very very little, and I haven't seen him yet, but Aunt Selina says I may see him tomorrow.'

Once again, Clemency's eyes met Deveril's.

'You have a son, Deveril?' she asked with difficulty. 'May I offer my congratulations.'

Somewhat to her surprise, Deveril turned away and walked over to the window. There was a droop to his shoulders that she had never seen before, and she sensed that something was wrong. Adam slipped his hand into hers and she could feel his warm body leaning against her, as if for reassurance.

'What is it, Deveril?' she asked. 'What is it you have come to tell me?'

Deveril turned, and she could see now that his face looked drawn, weary with lack of sleep – and sad.

'Muriel died last night,' he said quietly. 'There were three physicians and a surgeon in attendance. They did all they could. They told me they did not think they could save both the mother and child, and I instructed them they must save Muriel's life at any cost. But it made no difference. The child was strong and healthy and survived anyway.'

Clemency's hand tightened involuntarily around Adam's.

'I am so very sorry,' she whispered, for there was no doubting that Deveril was deeply shocked.

He drew a long sigh.

'At least Muriel did not suffer; did not know what was happening. Selina was with her and told me she died very peacefully, without pain. Selina has taken the infant home for the time being.'

Suddenly Adam released his hold on her and went to his father.

'You must not be sad, Uncle 'Vril,' he said. 'You still have me and the little baby.'

His eyes were suddenly bright with renewed excitement as he reached out once more to Clemency.

'Mama, Uncle 'Vril says that when the baby is big enough, we can take it to Burnbury House to live with us – but only if you will come to look after us. You will, Mama, will you not? Aunt Selina thought of it first, and Uncle 'Vril thinks it the most excellent idea and he said I might come with him today to see you because if I ask you, you will be certain to say "yes". He says you love me too much to say "no" to me even when you should, but I don't think anyone can love anyone *too much*, do you, Mama?'

He stood between them, his face turning eagerly from one to the other as he tugged excitedly at their hands. Clemency looked over the boy's head at Deveril, the barest question in her eyes.

'Quite often, young man, your chatter drives me to distraction,' Deveril said to Adam, 'but once in a while, Mr Chatterbox, you say something that even your elders might think to be wise. This is one such occasion.' His eyes searched Clemency's as he added: 'No one can love anyone *too much*.'

'Then you *will* come and look after us, Mama?' Adam persisted, encouraged by his mother's expression. 'You will say "yes", please, Mama?'

Gently, Clemency ruffled his dark curls, but it was Deveril she was looking at as she said softly:

'I expect so, my darling, since your Uncle 'Vril is quite right. You are one of the few people in the world to whom I cannot say "no".'

AUTHOR'S NOTE

On the 17th August 1839, the Bill for which Caroline Norton had fought so tirelessly and courageously was finally carried by the House of Lords. It was laid down that a judge might make an order allowing a mother, against whom adultery was not proved, to have custody of her children under seven years old, and, for older children, access at stated times. But despite the new law, George Norton refused to let his wife have access to her children and when Caroline threatened legal action, it was only to discover that as her boys were domiciled in Scotland, they were beyond the jurisdiction of the English Courts.

It was not until the Christmas holidays of 1841–42 that she was temporarily reunited with them. In the autumn of the following year, her eight-year-old youngest son, William, died in tragic circumstances while in his father's guardianship. But as a result of this tragedy, it was finally agreed that Caroline should have access to her remaining two boys, Fletcher and Brinsley, for half the year.

In 1854 her husband stopped her allowance, and again she took up the cudgels on behalf of the Marriage and Divorce Act, which despite great opposition was finally passed in 1857.

Caroline Norton was not a 'feminist' and she deplored the doctrine of equal rights. Her fight was for justice, and her ultimate success was of lasting benefit to her sex, although her personal sufferings and her name are now almost forgotten.

In 1877, two years after the death of her husband, Caroline married her old friend Sir William Stirling-Maxwell. She was sixty-nine years old. But the great peace and happiness she found at the end of the long struggle of her life ended tragically with her death only three months after her marriage.

The plot for *Last Year's Nightingale* evolved as a result of my reading Caroline Norton's letters, published by the Ohio State University Press, which highlight the dreadful injustices women endured one hundred and fifty years ago.

Love. Passion. War.
Family. Secrets. History.

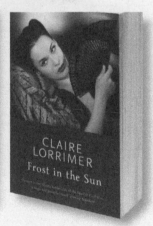

Stunning timeless classics from the bestselling
novelist Claire Lorrimer.

Available in paperback and ebook.

HODDER